PRAISE FOR THE BESTSELLING

TEA SHOP MYSTERIES

"Tea lovers, mystery lovers, [this] is for you. Just the right blend of cozy fun and clever plotting."

—Susan Wittig Albert, national bestselling author of
The Darling Dahlias and the Texas Star

"Murder suits [Laura Childs] to a Tea." —*St. Paul (MN) Pioneer Press*

"Brew yourself a nice pot of tea, and enjoy . . . It's guaranteed to delight."
—*Times Record News*

"[A] love letter to Charleston, tea, and fine living." —*Kirkus Reviews*

"Laura Childs has struck gold." —*Romantic Homes*

"Kept me hooked from opening page to ending." —*Central Oregonian*

"Childs has a great eye for local color . . . [A] delightful read."
—*Publishers Weekly*

"Delectable and delicious . . . with mouthwatering recipes."
—*Midwest Book Review*

"Tasty suspense!" —*St. Paul (MN) Sun-Sailor*

"Will leave readers feeling as if they have shared a warm cup of tea on Church Street in Charleston." —*The Mystery Reader*

TEA FOR THREE

LAURA CHILDS

BERKLEY PRIME CRIME, NEW YORK

THE BERKLEY PUBLISHING GROUP
Published by the Penguin Group
Penguin Group (USA) LLC
375 Hudson Street, New York, New York 10014

USA • Canada • UK • Ireland • Australia • New Zealand • India • South Africa • China

penguin.com

A Penguin Random House Company

TEA FOR THREE

Death by Darjeeling by Laura Childs copyright © 2001 by The Berkley Publishing Group.
Gunpowder Green by Laura Childs copyright © 2002 by The Berkley Publishing Group.
Shades of Earl Grey by Laura Childs copyright © 2003 by The Berkley Publishing Group.

Berkley Prime Crime Books are published by The Berkley Publishing Group.
BERKLEY® PRIME CRIME and the PRIME CRIME logo are trademarks of
Penguin Group (USA) LLC.

Berkley Prime Crime trade paperback ISBN: 978-0-425-26987-9

An application to register this book for cataloging has been submitted to the Library of Congress.

PUBLISHING HISTORY
Berkley Prime Crime trade paperback edition / December 2013

PRINTED IN THE UNITED STATES OF AMERICA

10 9 8 7 6 5 4 3 2 1

Cover illustration by Stephanie Henderson.
Cover design by Lesley Worrell.
Interior text design by Kristin del Rosario.

CONTENTS

FOREWORD

Dear Reader,

I'd like to share a special memory with you. Twelve years ago, on Christmas Day, my husband and I were traveling on the bullet train from Tokyo to Kyoto. I was deep into a book and hypnotized by the motion of the train, when my husband suddenly grinned and told me to look up. I lifted my head and there, directly out the window, was a spectacular, terraced tea garden with Mount Fuji in the background. The bright, verdant green of the tea plants seemed etched in neon against the white snows of Fuji, like a color photo pushed to the max. A week later, when I returned home, I learned that *Death by Darjeeling*, my very first Tea Shop Mystery, was going to be published!

I was just as thrilled, more recently, when my editor told me that the first three Tea Shop Mysteries were going to be released in an anthology. This is where it all begins, of course, with Theodosia and her tea shop dog Earl Grey, Drayton, Haley, and a cast of characters I'm dearly in love with.

So grab a steaming cup of tea and cozy up for three exciting mysteries that include tea time tips and a host of recipes as well. And, I promise, once you read about Charleston Chocolate Chip Scones, Apple Bread, and Tropical Chicken Tea Sandwiches, you're going to want to make them for yourself!

All my best,
LAURA CHILDS

DEATH BY DARJEELING

This book is dedicated to Peg Baskerville,
true friend and voracious reader.
May you rest in peace
and enjoy all the time heaven allows for reading.

ACKNOWLEDGMENTS

Thank you to Mary Higgins Clark for helping point the way; fellow writer R. D. Zimmerman for his insider's view and wise words; Jim Smith for his friendship and encouragement; and my husband, Dr. Robert Poor, for all his love and support.

Visit our website at www.laurachilds.com.

1

Theodosia Browning leaned back from the clutter of her antique wooden desk, balanced a bone china cup and saucer on one knee, and took a much-needed sip of Lung Ching tea. Savoring the emerald green color and delicate sweetness, she absently pushed back a meandering lock of the naturally curly auburn hair that swirled about her head, creating a haloed visage somewhere between a Rafael painting and a friendly Medusa.

Calmly, calmly, she told herself.

On this fine October afternoon with the temperature in Charleston hovering in the midseventies and the back door propped open to catch the languid breezes wafting off the nearby Cooper River, the Indigo Tea Shop seemed to be the epicenter of several minicrises, with all the fallout landing squarely in Theodosia's lap.

Her customs broker, usually so masterful at snipping red tape and shepherding shipments from far-flung continents, had just called with disastrous news. Three cases of silver tips from the Makaibari Tea Estate in India had been unceremoniously dumped on a dock in New Jersey and left to sit in pouring rain.

Then there was the issue of the Web site.

Theodosia directed her gaze to the colorful concept boards that lay scattered at her feet. Even with marketing and design expertise from Todd & Lambeau Design Group, one of Charleston's topflight Web design firms, launching a virtual tea shop on the Internet was proving to be a major undertaking. Selling bags, boxes, and tins of exotic teas as well as tea accoutrement required more than just being cyber savvy; it was a long-term commitment in terms of time and money.

And wouldn't you know it, Drayton Conneley, her assistant and right-hand man, had gotten a last-minute call to host a group tea tasting. Drayton was out front right now, charming and chatting up a half dozen ladies. That meant final preparations for tonight's Lamplighter Tour still weren't wrapped up.

Ordinarily, Theodosia reveled in the oasis of calm her little tea shop afforded. Tucked between Robillard Booksellers and the Antiquarian Map Store in the historic district of Charleston, South Carolina, the Indigo Tea Shop was one stitch in a romantic, pastel tapestry of Georgian, Federal, and Victorian homes, courtyard gardens, and quaint shops.

Inside this former carriage house and tiny treasure, copper teapots hissed and bubbled, fresh-baked pastries cooled on wooden racks, and patrons scrambled for a coveted seat at one of the creaking hickory tables. Leaded glass windows, a wavering scrim to temper the intense South Carolina sun, cast filtered light on pegged wooden floors, exposed beams, and brick walls.

Floor to ceiling, a warren of cubbyholes held jars brimming with black powders, crumpled leaves of nut brown and ochre, and shiny whole leaves that shimmered like Chinese celadon. And what a tantalizing spectrum of aromas! Piquant gunpowder green tea from south China, lightly fermented Ceylonese garden tea, delicate fruited Nilgiri tea from the Blue Mountains of India.

The ringing phone nudged Theodosia from her reflections.

"Delaine's on two," called Haley, popping around the corner from the kitchen to hover at Theodosia's elbow.

Haley Parker, Theodosia's young shop clerk and baker extraordinaire, worked days in the tea shop and attended college classes a few evenings a week. Although Haley currently listed her major as communications, she had, over the past three years, alternated between sociology, philosophy, and women's studies.

Theodosia looked up hopefully. "Could you help her?"

"Delaine specifically asked for you," said Haley, her brown eyes dancing with amusement.

"Lord, love us," murmured Theodosia as she reached for the phone.

"Mercury's in retrograde," Haley added in a conspiratorial stage whisper. "Going to shake things up the next couple days."

Theodosia exhaled a long breath. "Delaine, lovely you should call."

Delaine Dish owned Cotton Duck, a women's clothing boutique that featured casual yet elegant cottons, silks, and linens. Delaine was also the neighborhood gossip.

"Tell me you're not unaware of this man, Hughes Barron," came Delaine's somewhat strident voice.

"I'm unaware, Delaine." Theodosia stood and stretched a kink from her neck, preparing for a siege.

"Well, he's made an offer on the Peregrine Building."

The Peregrine Building was three buildings down from the Indigo Tea Shop on Church Street. It was an ornate, limestone edifice that had been an opera house at the turn of the century and now housed a handful of professional offices and shops on its lower two floors.

"My dear," continued Delaine, "you are an astute businesswoman. You understand complex issues such as zoning and commercial use."

"What are you really worked up about, Delaine?" asked Theodosia, unswayed by Delaine's flattery.

"Architectural integrity, of course. God knows what sins a developer with Barron's reputation might wreak on a building such as that."

The word *developer* rolled off Delaine's tongue with obvious distaste, as though she were discussing manure.

"Tell you what, Delaine . . ." Theodosia stifled a giggle. "I'll speak to Drayton. He's—"

"A muckity-muck with the Heritage Society!" interrupted Delaine. "Of course, dear Drayton. Who better to have a pipeline to all this!"

"I couldn't have said it better."

"Theo, you're a gem."

"Bye, Delaine." Theodosia hung up the phone, and carried her cup and saucer into the small kitchen. The air was delightfully fragrant from baking, the room dominated by an oversized commercial stove.

"You wouldn't have to be on the Internet if you just hired Delaine," said Haley. She yanked open the oven door, took a quick peek, and closed it again.

"Delaine's a character," admitted Theodosia, "but she does add a certain delirious passion to the neighborhood." Theodosia lifted the plastic cover on a tray of cranberry scones. "These look heavenly."

"Thanks. Hope this'll be enough for tonight. Oh . . . one more minute and you can take a fresh batch of butter cookies out to our guests."

"How's it going?" Theodosia nodded toward the front of the tea shop.

"Drayton is being his erudite self."

"Your vocabulary continues to expand at a rapid pace, Haley."

"Thank you, I'm taking a class called verbal integrity."

"Outstanding," said Theodosia. "And the credits hopefully lead one step closer to a degree?"

Haley slid the oven mitt onto her hand, and shifted her thin, lithe body from one ballet slipper to the other. "Actually, I'm thinking of taking a sabbatical from school so I can focus on more *practical* things."

"Mm-hm." Theodosia peered through a doorway hung with dark green velvet curtains that separated the front of the tea shop from the kitchen and her small office.

Six tasters were gathered around one of the large tables, listening eagerly as Drayton Conneley, professional tea blender and one of only ten master tea tasters in the United States, delivered a lively lesson in tea connoisseurship.

Formal as always in tweed jacket, starched white shirt, and bow tie, Drayton ladled four heaping teaspoons of jasmine pearl into a carefully warmed white ceramic teapot. This was followed by a gush of hot water heated to precisely 150 degrees Fahrenheit. As steaming water infused tea particles, a rich ginger color developed, followed by a sweet scent reminiscent of almonds.

"How do you know how long to allow tea to steep?" asked a white-haired woman who wrinkled her nose appreciatively.

"Green and white teas are best at between one and two minutes," said Drayton. "A Darjeeling, which we all know is delicate and fruity, shouldn't be infused longer than three minutes. And that *is* a hard and fast rule." Drayton Conneley peered over tortoiseshell half glasses that were perpetually sliding down his long, aquiline nose, giving him a slightly owlish appearance.

"Even fifteen seconds too long, and a Darjeeling will go bitter. But a Formosan oolong, especially if the leaves are tightly rolled, is an entirely different matter. Have no fear in boldly pushing the steeping time to seven minutes," advised Drayton in the carefully modulated tones his friends described as his *basso contante* voice.

Sixty-two years of age, the only child of missionary parents who originally hailed from Sullivan's Island, across the Intracoastal Waterway from Charleston, Drayton had spent the first twenty years of his life in Canton, China. It was in south China that Drayton developed his taste for tea and his passion for it, spending weeks at a time on the Panyang Tea Plantation in the high steppes of the Hangzhou region while his parents ministered to Christian Chinese in far-flung provinces. Upon returning to Charleston, Drayton attended Johnson & Wales University, the area's prestigious culinary institute, then spent several years in London working at Croft & Squire Tea Ltd. and commuting to Amsterdam where the major wholesale tea auctions of the world are conducted.

Today Drayton had arranged six different teapots on the lazy Susan that occupied center stage of the table. Each teapot was crafted in a unique motif, ranging from a colorful ceramic cabbage to a Chinese Yishing teapot of molded purple clay. Steeping inside each teapot was a different type of tea, and fanned out in front of each taster were six small cups for sampling. An ornate silver tray with a rapidly dwindling assortment of cookies seemed to be in constant rotation around the table.

"I'm never quite sure when the water is ready," a woman in a yellow twinset drawled in the slow tones of a Savannah, Georgia, native as she eagerly reached for what proved to be the last butter cookie.

"Then, dear lady, I shall teach you a famous Japanese adage that is both edifying and rippingly depictive," said Drayton. "Carp eyes coming, fish eyes going . . ."

"Soon will be the wind in the pines," finished Theodosia as she bustled out from the back room.

"The fish eyes are the first tiny bubbles," Theodosia explained as she set a fresh plate of butter cookies on the table. "The carp eyes are the large bubbles that herald a good, rolling boil. And the wind in the pines is, of course, the beginning rush of the teapot's whistle."

These charming metaphors drew a quick spatter of applause from her delighted guests as Drayton looked on, pleased by the dramatic entrance of his beloved employer.

But then, most people were charmed by Theodosia Browning the moment they met her. She was all sparkling blue eyes and barely contained energy, with a broad, intelligent face, high cheekbones, and full, perfectly formed mouth that could pull into a pucker when she was feeling perplexed.

Theodosia retrieved an apron from behind the counter, and tied it around the waist of her Laura Ashley dress. Although not overweight, neither was Theodosia thin. She was solid, had been all her life. A size ten that occasionally veered toward a twelve, especially around Christmas and New Year's when the tea shop overflowed with scones, benne wafers, cream breads, and sweet butter biscuits. And holiday parties up and down Church Street featured buffet tables groaning with she-crab soup, roast duckling, and spicy shrimp with tasso gravy.

Theodosia's mother, a confirmed romantic and history buff, had named her only daughter after Theodosia Alston, wife of former South Carolina governor Joseph Alston and daughter of former vice president Aaron Burr.

In the early 1800s, when Theodosia Alston reigned as First Lady of the state, she had cut a colorful figure. But her notoriety was short-lived. In 1812 she was a passenger on a sailing ship that sank off the coast of North Carolina. When the bodies of the unfortunate souls washed up on shore, only the remains of Theodosia Alston were missing.

As a young child, Theodosia had sat with her mother in the garden swing and speculated on what had really become of the historical Theodosia. As they whiled away afternoons, listening to the gentle drone of bees, it was exciting to imagine any number of chilling scenarios.

Had she been kidnapped by her father's enemies? Did the pirates who plied their sinister trade off the coastal waters capture poor Theodosia Alston and sell her into slavery? And years later, when the estate of an old North Carolina woman was sold, why did a portrait of the old woman, painted when she was young, look startlingly similar to the missing Theodosia?

But in Charleston, that fine city that began as Charles Town, when rice, indigo, and tobacco from the plantations were in demand throughout the world, legend and history blended into a rich patois.

And Theodosia Browning found running a tea shop to be a civilized melding of merchant and Southern hostess. Rather like throwing open one's parlor and awaiting whatever surprise guests might drop in.

But Theodosia, now at the age of thirty-six, had not always been the owner of a tea shop.

Years ago (though she'd prefer not to count them) Theodosia had been a student at the prestigious University of Charleston. As an English literature major, she'd been swept up in the poetry and prose of Jane Austen, Mary Shelley, and Charlotte Brontë. Determined to compose her own romantic, lyrical poetry, Theodosia had adapted the bohemian style of wearing a flowing purple velvet cape, walked the grounds of the old Magnolia Cemetery for inspiration, and taken a part-time job at the Charleston Rare Book Company.

But a month before graduation, Theodosia's father passed away and, with her mother long dead since she was eight, she had only a small inheritance on which to live. Knowing the life of a poet can be one precarious step down from that of starving artist, Theodosia took a job in an advertising agency.

Because she was blessed with a knack for creativity as well as a genius for business and marketing, she rose through the ranks swiftly. She began her career as a lowly media estimator, graduating to account coordinator, eventually becoming vice president of client services.

But fourteen years in a cutthroat, results-driven arena took its toll. Long hours, tight deadlines, nervous clients, and high-stakes creative decisions led to her gradual disenchantment. Theodosia searched for a way to step off the merry-go-round.

While serving on a pro bono marketing committee for Spoleto, Charleston's annual arts festival, Theodosia stumbled upon a quirky opportunity. The artistic director for a participating theater organization was trying to unload a little tea shop on Church Street that his mother had run years ago. Intrigued, Theodosia took a hard look at the dusty, unoccupied little tea shop that was up for sale and thought, *What if?*

Mulling her decision for one long, sleepless night, Theodosia made the ultimate executive decision and used her small savings to put a down payment on the property.

Convinced that the congenial atmosphere of a tea shop would be far more satisfying for the soul than helping to market credit cards, computer peripherals, and pharmaceuticals, Theodosia threw herself wholeheartedly into her new venture.

She learned how to evaluate the twist, tip, and aroma of tea leaves and acquired a spectacular shop inventory of loose and boxed teas from notable wholesalers such as Freed, Teller, and Freed's in San Francisco and Kent & Dinmore in England.

Serendipitously, America's sole surviving tea plantation, the Charleston Tea Plantation, was located just twenty-five miles south of Charleston on the subtropical island of Wadmalaw. So Theodosia was able to acquaint herself with owners Mack Fleming and Bill Hall and their 127-acre plantation that grew nearly 300 varieties of tea.

From Fleming and Hall Theodosia was able to learn about the harvest process. How to select the newest, most tender leaves. The use of withering troughs to circulate air through the leaves. Techniques on macerating leaves to break down cell walls.

She went so far as to glean special tea recipes. A wonderful orange pekoe dessert soufflé from a chef at the Four Seasons in San Francisco, a recipe for tea-smoked chicken from the Peninsula Hotel in Hong Kong.

And Theodosia hired Drayton Conneley away from his role as hospitality director at Charleston's famed Vendue Inn.

It wasn't long before the newly energized Indigo Tea Shop, as tea salon, retail tea shop, and gift shop, became a profitable enterprise and a popular stop on Charleston's many walking and carriage tours. Much to Theodosia's delight, her tea shop also came to be regarded by her neighbors as the social and spiritual hub of the historic district.

The clip-clop of hooves on the pavement outside the Indigo Tea Shop signaled that the horse-drawn coach had arrived to carry their tea-tasting visitors back to their respective inns and hotels.

"I hope you have tickets for one of tonight's Lamplighter Tours," said Theodosia as final sips were taken, mouths carefully daubed, and linen napkins refolded. "Many of the historic homes on the tour are private residences that graciously open their doors only for this one special event. It's really quite remarkable."

Sponsored by the Heritage Society, the Lamplighter Tour was an annual tradition in Charleston, held during the last two weeks of October when the long-anticipated cooler nights had returned. These evening walking tours of notable avenues such as Montagu, Queen, and Church Streets afforded visitors a leisurely stroll down cobblestone lanes and a golden opportunity to step inside many of Charleston's elegant, lofty-ceilinged grande dame homes and cloistered courtyard gardens.

"If I may impart my own personal recommendation," said Drayton, pulling back chairs and offering his arm to the ladies, "I would heartily suggest our own Church Street walk. It begins at the Ravenel Home, a stunning example of Victorian excess, and concludes in the formal garden of the elegant Avis Melbourne Home where our gracious hostess and proprietor, Miss Theodosia Browning, has been engaged to serve a repertoire of fine teas, including a special Lamplighter Blend created just for this event."

"Oh, my," said one of the ladies. "How intriguing."

"You have characterized it aptly," said Drayton. "Our Lamplighter Blend is a lovely marriage of two traditional black teas with a hint of jasmine added for high notes."

Theodosia glanced toward the counter and grinned at Haley, who had just emerged from the back room, her arms filled with gift baskets. Haley was always accusing Drayton that his role as Parliamentarian in the Charleston Heritage Society led to oratorical extravagance.

"Of course," added Theodosia in a droll voice meant to be a casual counterpoint to Drayton's, "we'll also be serving blackberry scones with clotted cream."

Pleasured groans emanated from around the table.

Catching the subtle exchange between Theodosia and Haley, Drayton snatched one of the baskets filled with small tins of tea and tied with white ribbon and held it up for all to see. "Be sure to take a quick perusal of our gift baskets before you leave. Miss Parker here has recently taken up the art of weaving traditional South Carolina sweetgrass baskets and has become quite an accomplished artisan."

Haley's face reddened at Drayton's announcement. "Thank you," she murmured.

And, of course, ladies being ladies, veteran shoppers, and enthusiastic tourists, at least three of the delightfully done gift baskets were carefully wrapped in Theodosia's signature indigo blue tissue paper and tucked safely in the carriage as they departed.

"Did you bring Earl Grey down?" asked Theodosia after the door had swung shut and the shadows lengthened enough so she knew there wouldn't be any more customers for afternoon tea.

Haley nodded.

"Earl, come on, fellow," called Theodosia as she clapped her hands together.

A furry muzzle poked through the draperies, then an angular canine emerged and padded softly across the wooden planks of the floor. When the dog reached Theodosia, he laid his head in her lap and sighed contentedly.

Earl Grey, Theodosia's adopted dog, looked a far sight better today than when she had first found him. Hungry and shivering, curled up in a cardboard box in the narrow cobblestone alley that ran behind the tea shop, Earl Grey had been an abandoned, unwanted mongrel that probably wandered the streets for weeks.

But Theodosia found his elegant head, soft, troubled eyes, and quiet temperament endearing and took to him immediately. She nursed him, groomed him, named him, and ultimately loved him.

When Drayton had objected to a stray dog being named after the popular nineteenth-century prime minister who first brought back the famed bergamot-flavored tea from China, Theodosia insisted the name was more an old English reference to the dog's mottled coloration.

"I can't see that he's particularly gray," Drayton had argued, his tone just this side of vexation.

Indeed, the dog was more salt and pepper.

"There. On the inside of his left hind leg," Theodosia had pointed out. "That area is distinctly gray."

Drayton was nonplused by the dog. "A mixed breed," he'd declared with arched eyebrows.

"Like blending a fine tea," Theodosia had said with artful cleverness. She'd placed her strong hands atop the animal's sleek head and gently massaged the dog's ears as he gazed up at her, limpid brown eyes filled with love. "Yes," she had exclaimed, "this fellow is a blend of Dalmatian and Labrador. A Dalbrador." And from that moment on, Earl Grey of the Dalbrador pedigree became the beloved, official greeter at the Indigo Tea Shop and a permanent resident of Theodosia's cozy upstairs apartment.

"How many more sweetgrass baskets can you manage?" Theodosia asked as Haley, standing on tiptoe, arranged a half dozen of the gift baskets on a shelf behind the cash register.

"How many do you need?"

"My guestimate is at least fifty between now and the holidays. If our Web site is up and running by then, double it."

"Bethany can help me finish maybe another dozen," said Haley, referring to her friend, Bethany Shepherd, who was temporarily living with her in the little garden apartment across the alley. "But we'll have to buy the majority."

"No problem," said Theodosia. "I was planning a drive out to the low country anyway. After I pop in on Aunt Libby, I'll round up some more baskets."

Sweetgrass baskets were a staple in the makeshift stalls along Highway 17 North. Handmade from bunches of sweetgrass, pine needles, and bulrush, then bound together by fiber strips from native palmetto trees, the baskets exuded both functionality and beauty, and the women of the low country took great pride in their handiwork.

"How is Bethany doing?" asked Theodosia, her face softening with concern for Haley's friend whose husband had died in a car accident just eight months earlier. In the past couple of months, the shy Bethany had helped out in the tea shop a few times, and Theodosia was hoping the young woman would soon find her rudder again.

"Good days, sad days," said Haley in measured tones. "It's not easy being a widow at twenty-seven. I think if Bethany didn't have the internship to sustain her, she'd really be at loose ends."

"So at least that part of her life is successful," said Theodosia.

"Yes, thanks to Drayton." Haley glanced gratefully toward Drayton

Conneley, who was talking on the telephone, briskly finalizing details for that evening's tea service. "If he hadn't put in a good word for Bethany at the Heritage Society, I don't know what she would have done. Bethany slaved to get her master's degree in art history, but it's still impossible to land any type of museum curator job without internship credentials. Maybe now . . ." Haley's voice quavered and her large brown eyes filled with tears.

Theodosia reached over and gently patted Haley's hand. "Time heals," reassured Theodosia in a quiet voice. "And in Charleston, time is an old friend."

❧ 2 ❧

Darkness had settled on Charleston like a soft, purple cloak. Palmettos swayed gently in the night breeze. Mourning doves that sheltered in spreading oak and pecan trees had long since tucked downy heads under fragile wings.

But up and down Church Street the atmosphere was alive and filled with magic. Candles in brass holders flickered enticingly from broad verandas. Clusters of Lamplighter Tour walkers thronged the sidewalks, gliding through dusky shadows only to emerge in pools of golden light that spilled from arched doorways of houses buzzing with activity, open this one special evening to all visitors who had a ticket in hand and a reverence for history in their hearts.

Fat, orange pumpkins squatted on the steps of the Avis Melbourne Home. On the sweeping porch where a half dozen white Ionic columns imperiously stood guard, young women in eighteenth-century garb greeted visitors with lanterns and shy smiles. Their hair was nipped into sleek top-knots, their step dainty and mannered, unaccustomed as they were to layers of petticoats and the disconcerting rustle of silk.

Inside the Avis Melbourne Home, the room proportions were enormous. This was a residence designed for living on a grand scale, with gilt chandeliers dangling overhead, rich oil paintings adorning walls, and Italianate marble fireplaces in every room. The color palette was soft and French: salmon pink, oyster white, pale blue.

More costumed guides, members of the Heritage Society, accompanied visitors through the parlor, dining room, and library. Their running patter enlightened on architecture, antiques, and beaux arts.

Down the long center hallway, footsteps barely registered on plush wool Aubusson carpets as guests found their way outside to the courtyard garden.

It was here that many of the tour guests had now congregated, sitting at tables that ringed a central three-tiered fountain. Foliage abounded, the sound of pattering water pleasantly relaxing.

Theodosia ducked out the side door from her command post in the butler's pantry. For the last hour she and Drayton had been working non-stop. He oversaw the preparation of five different teas, while she hustled silver teapots out to Haley for serving, then ran back for refills. At one point they'd been so harried she'd asked Haley to make a quick phone call to Bethany and plead for reinforcement.

Now, as Theodosia surveyed the guests in the garden, it looked as though she could finally stop to catch her breath. Haley and Bethany were moving with practiced precision among the twenty or so tables, pouring tea and offering seconds on blackberry scones, looking like French waiters with their long white aprons over black shirts and slacks. The tables themselves had been elegantly draped in white linen and held centerpieces of purple flowers nestled in pockets of greenery.

"Theodosia, darling!"

Theodosia turned as Samantha Rabathan, this year's chairperson for the Church Street walk, tottered across the brick patio wearing three-inch heels and flashing a winning smile. Ever the social butterfly and fashion maven, Samantha was fetchingly attired in a flouncy cream-colored silk skirt and pale peach cashmere sweater, generously scooped in front to reveal her matching peach skin and ample endowments.

Theodosia tucked a wayward strand of auburn hair behind one ear, and rested the large teapot she'd been holding on one of the temporary serving stations. Even in her midnight blue velvet tailored slacks and white lace top, an outfit that had received admiring glances from several of the gentlemen in the crowd, she suddenly felt like a brown wren next to Samantha's plumage.

"We've got a packed house, Samantha." Theodosia swept a hand to indicate the contented crowd enjoying tea and treats on the patio. "Your walk is a huge success."

"It is, isn't it," Samantha agreed with a giggle. "I was just calling around on my cell phone and heard that the Tradd Street walk got *half* our turnout." She nudged Theodosia with an elbow and dropped her voice to a conspiratorial purr. "Did you know we sold ninety more tickets than last year? It's a new Church Street record!"

Last year Delaine Dish had been the Church Street chair. For some reason unknown to Theodosia, Samantha and Delaine had a weird, catty rivalry going on between them, one she had no desire to explore, much less get in the middle of.

"Oh, my," Samantha cooed as she fanned herself briskly with one of the tour's printed programs. "Such a warm evening."

And off she went across the patio, the heels of her perfect cream shoes dangerously close to catching between the stones, her cell phone shrilling once again.

"I can't imagine why she's warm," whispered Drayton in Theodosia's ear. "She not exactly bundled up."

"Be nice, Drayton," said Theodosia. "Samantha worked hard on ticket sales and lining up volunteers."

"You can afford to be charitable," he said with a sniff. "Samantha's always been sweet to you. My guess is she's secretly in awe of your past life in advertising. She knows you've sold the proverbial ice to Eskimos. But in complete, unadulterated fairness, this *has* been a group effort. A lot of good people worked very hard to pull this off."

"Agreed," said Theodosia. "Now tell me what results you've gathered from our rather unscientific poll."

Drayton's face brightened. "Three to one on the Lamplighter Blend! I'd estimate we have less than half a pot left."

"Really?" said Theodosia, her cheeks flaring with color, and her usually calm, melodious voice cracking with excitement.

"The people have spoken, madam. The tea's a knockout."

"So we package more and include it on the Web site," she said.

"No, we *feature* it." Drayton favored Theodosia with an uncharacteristic grin as he picked up the silver teapot she'd set down earlier and started toward the house. "The pantry awaits. The end of the evening is blessedly in sight." He paused. "Coming?"

"Give me a minute, Drayton."

Theodosia stood half hidden under an elegant arch of vines, basking in the glow of success. It was the first tea she'd blended by herself. True, she'd started with two exquisitely mellow teas from the American Tea Plantation. And she'd had Drayton's excellent counsel. But still . . .

"Excuse me."

Theodosia whirled about and found herself staring down at two tiny women. Both were barely five feet in height, quite advanced in years, and wore identical green suits. *Twins,* she thought to herself, then peered closer. *No, just dressed alike. Probably sisters.*

"Mavis Beaumont." Birdlike, one of the ladies in green extended a gloved hand.

"Theodosia Browning," said Theodosia, taking the tiny hand in hers. She blinked. Staring at these two was like seeing double.

"You're the woman with that marvelous dog, aren't you?" said Mavis.

Theodosia nodded. This happened frequently. "You mean Earl Grey."

"That's the one!" Mavis Beaumont turned to her sister and continued. "Miss Browning has this beautifully trained dog that visits sick people. I had occasion to meet him the time Missy broke her leg."

The sister smiled and nodded.

"Early Grey is a therapy dog," explained Theodosia just in case they hadn't realized he was part of a very real program.

On Monday evenings Theodosia and Earl Grey visited the O'Doud

Senior Home and took part in pet therapy. Earl Grey would don his blue nylon vest with the embroidered patch that identified him as a certified therapy dog, and the two would roam the broad halls, stopping to interact with the aging but eager-to-talk residents, visiting the rooms of people who were bedridden.

Earl Grey had quickly become a favorite with the residents, many of whom enjoyed only occasional visits from their families. And just last month, Earl Grey had befriended a woman who'd suffered a terrible, debilitating stroke that left her entire right side paralyzed. In the woman's excitement to pet Earl Grey, she had tentatively extended her rigid right arm for the first time in months and managed a patting motion on the dog's back. That breakthrough had led to the woman going to physical therapy and finally regaining some real use of the arm.

Mavis Beaumont grasped Theodosia's arm. "Lovely party, dear."

The sister, the one who apparently didn't talk, at least not tonight, nodded and smiled.

"Good night," called Theodosia.

"What was that all about?" asked Haley as she shuffled past shouldering a huge tray.

"Fans of Earl Grey."

"That guy's got some PR agent, doesn't he?" she joked.

"Say, thanks for enlisting Bethany," said Theodosia. "I sure hope we didn't ruin her plans for tonight."

"Are you serious?" said Haley. "The poor girl was sitting home alone with her nose stuck in Gombrich's *Story of Art*. Not that there's anything wrong with curling up with an art history book, but between you and me, this was a great excuse to get her out and talking to real people. Believe me, this is the best thing for her."

From her post at the far end of the garden, Bethany glanced toward Theodosia and Haley and saw by the looks on their faces that they were talking about her. She gave a thin smile, knowing they had her best interests at heart, feeling thankful she had friends who cared so much.

With her elegant oval face, pale complexion, long dark hair, and intense brown eyes, Bethany was a true beauty. But her body language mirrored the sadness she carried inside. Where most young women her age moved with effortless grace, Bethany was sedate, contained. Where amusement and joy should have lit her face, there was melancholy.

Picking up a serving tray, Bethany walked to the nearest empty table. She cleared it, taking great pains with the bone china cups and saucers, then moved solemnly to the next table. Centerpiece candles that had glowed so brightly an hour earlier were beginning to sputter. The Lamplighter Tour visitors were taking final sips, slowly meandering back inside the house, saying their good-byes. The evening was drawing to a close.

Bethany glanced across the patio to where Theodosia and Haley had been standing just a few minutes earlier. Now they were nowhere to be seen. They must have ducked inside the butler's pantry to start their cleanup, she thought to herself.

Bethany crisscrossed the brick patio, picking up a cup here, a plate there. When she finally broke from her task and looked around, there were only two tables where people remained seated.

Correction, make that one, she told herself as the foursome sitting at the table nearest the central fountain stood up and began to amble off slowly, chatting, admiring the dark foliage, pointing up at overhanging Spanish moss.

Bethany glanced toward the far corner of the patio. Against the large, dense hedge that formed one border of the garden and ran around the perimeter of the property, she could just barely make out the figure of a man sitting quietly alone.

Bethany tucked the serving tray against one hip and started toward him, intent on asking if she could refill his teacup or perhaps clear his table.

But as she approached, goose bumps rose on her arms, and a shiver ran down her spine. The night had turned suddenly chill. A stiff breeze tumbled dry leaves underfoot, whipsawed a final brave stand of camellias, and sent petals fluttering. The candle on the table nearest her was instantly snuffed, and the candle sitting on the man's table began to sputter wildly.

Bethany was within four feet of the man when a warning bell sounded in her head. Surely her eyes were playing tricks on her! But as she squinted into the darkness, the erratic candlelight hissed and flared, illuminating the man's face.

The calm of the courtyard was shattered by Bethany's shrill scream. The silver tray crashed to the bricks. Teacups broke into shards, and a half-filled pot of tea exploded on impact.

Theodosia heard Bethany's cry from inside the butler's panty. She slammed open the door and rushed outside and through the tangle of empty tables. "Bethany!" she called, urgency in her voice, worry swelling in her breast.

Anguish written across her face, all Bethany could do was back away from the table and point to the man sitting there alone.

Heels clicking like rapid fire, Theodosia approached. She saw immediately that the man slumped in his chair, his chin heavy on his chest. One hand dangled at his knees, and the other rested on the table, still clutching a teacup. As Theodosia quickly took in this strange scene, her fleeting impression was that the tiny teacup decorated in swirling gold vines seemed dwarfed by the man's enormous hand.

"Theodosia, what are you . . ." From across the way, Samantha's voice rose sharply, then died.

Another strangled cry tore from Bethany's mouth. She pointed toward Samantha, who had crumpled in a dead faint.

Haley and Drayton had followed close on Theodosia's heels. But now they quickly bent over Samantha and ministered to her.

Theodosia's brain shifted into overdrive. "Haley, call nine-one-one. Bethany, stop crying."

"She's all right, just fainted," called Drayton as he gently lifted Samantha to a sitting position.

"Bethany, get a glass of water for Samantha," Theodosia directed. "Do it *now.* And please try to stop crying."

Theodosia turned her attention back to the man's motionless body. Gently, she laid her index and forefinger against the man's neck. Nothing. No sign of a pulse. No breath signs, either.

Theodosia inhaled sharply. This wasn't good. It wasn't good at all.

During her college days, one of Theodosia's more unorthodox professors, Professor Hammish Poore, had taken his entire biology class on a field trip to the Charleston County Morgue. There they'd witnessed two autopsies firsthand. Although it had been more than a few years since that grisly experience, Theodosia was still reasonably familiar with the body's sad signs that indicated life had ceased.

This poor man could have had a sudden heart attack, she reasoned. Or experienced an explosive brain embolism. Death from asphyxiation was a possibility as well. But if something had obstructed his airway, someone would have heard him choking.

Wouldn't they?

Theodosia was aware of hushed murmurs of concern in the background, of Drayton shaking his head slowly, speaking in solemn tones about Hughes Barron.

This was Hughes Barron?

Theodosia fixed her attention on the hand holding the teacup. In the flickering spasms of the candle she could see the man's fingernails had begun to turn blue, causing her to wonder: *What was in that cup besides tea?*

3

The magic of the night was suddenly shattered by the harsh strobe of red and blue lights. Three police cruisers roared down the street and braked to a screeching halt. Front tires bounced roughly up over curbs, sending a gaggle of curious onlookers scattering. The *whoop-whoop* of a rapidly approaching ambulance shrilled.

Klang und licht, thought Theodosia. Sound and light. So much excitement, so much kinetic energy being exerted. But as she stood under the oak tree in the dark garden, surveying the slumped body of Hughes Barron, she knew no amount of hurry or flurry on the part of police or paramedics would make a whit of difference. Hughes Barron was beyond help. He was in the Lord's hands now.

But, of course, they all came blustering into the courtyard anyway: four police officers from the precinct headquarters on Broad Street, all with polished boots and buttons; a team of EMTs dispatched from Charleston Memorial Hospital, who jounced their clattering metal gurney across the brick patio; and six firemen, who seemed to have shown up just to feed off the excitement.

The two EMTs immediately checked Hughes Barron's pulse and respiration and hung an oxygen mask on him. One knelt down and put a stethoscope to Barron's chest. When he ascertained that the man no longer had a heartbeat, activity seemed to escalate.

Two officers immediately cornered Drayton, Haley, Bethany, and Samantha for interviews and statements. Another team of officers began the business of stringing yellow police tape throughout the garden.

A tall, muscular policeman, with an impressive display of stars and bars on his uniform and a name tag that read Grady, turned his attention to Theodosia.

"You found him?" Grady had a bulldog face and a heroic amount of gear attached to his belt: gun, flashlight, radio, handcuffs, billy club. Theodosia thought he looked like a human Swiss Army knife.

For some reason—the illogic of the situation or the shock at finding someone dead—this Swiss Army knife analogy tickled Theodosia, and she had to struggle to maintain an impassive expression.

"Actually, no," she said, finally answering Grady's question. "One of the young ladies who works for me, Bethany Shepherd, noticed something was wrong." She gestured toward Bethany, who was across the courtyard, talking to one of the other officers. "She was the one who alerted us. I just checked the man's pulse."

Grady had pulled out a spiral-bound notebook and was making rapid scratches in it. "How did she alert you?"

"She screamed," said Theodosia.

One side of Grady's mouth twitched downward, passing judgment on her answer. Obviously, he didn't consider it helpful.

"And was the man breathing?" pressed Grady.

"No, unfortunately. Which is why we called nine-one-one."

More scratches in Grady's notebook.

"And your name is . . . ?"

"Theodosia Browning. I own the Indigo Tea Shop on Church Street."

"So you don't know what happened, Theodosia?" said Grady.

"Just that he died," replied Theodosia. Her eyes went to the crisscross of black and yellow tape that was now strung through the garden like giant spiderwebs. Police Line the words blared, black on yellow. Do Not Cross. Vinyl tape had been wound haphazardly around bushes of crape myrtle and cherry laurel trees, through the splattering fountain and beds of flowers transported from Charleston greenhouses and dug in for this one special night. Now plants and blossoms lay crushed.

Grady cocked one droopy eye at her. "You don't know what happened, but you knew he was dead."

"My impression was that he was cyanotic. If you look at the tips of his fingernails, there's a curious blue tinge."

"Lady . . ." Grady began.

"You seem upset," said Theodosia. "Could I offer you a cup of tea?" She looked around. "Can we get anyone a cup of tea?"

That small gesture seemed to break the tension of the moment.

Grady suddenly remembered his manners and touched his cap with a finger. "Thank you, ma'am. Maybe later. Could you wait over there with the others, please?" Grady pointed across the courtyard. "I need to confer with the medical team."

Theodosia peered toward the far corner of the garden to a round, wrought iron table, still festooned with its purple floral centerpiece. In the darkness she could just barely make out Drayton and Haley sitting there, looking rather glum. Samantha was sprawled in a wicker chair, sipping from a glass of water, fanning herself with a program. Only Bethany was illuminated by the lights from the house. She stood near the door of the butler's pantry, deep in conversation with two officers.

"Certainly," said Theodosia. She took one step back, had every intention of joining the others, when one of the EMTs, a young man with shaggy blond hair, picked up the teacup and sniffed suspiciously at the contents.

"Put that down." The voice echoed out of the darkness like the rough growl of a big cat.

Caught by surprise, the EMT sent the teacup clattering into its saucer. Luckily, it remained upright.

Grady spun on his heels. "Who are you?" he demanded.

The man with the big cat growl led with his stomach. It billowed out between the lapels of his tweed jacket like a weather balloon. Bushy brows topped slightly popped eyes, and a walrus mustache drooped around his mouth. Although his stance conveyed a certain poise and grace, his head stuck curiously forward from his shoulders.

"Tidwell," said the man.

"Show me your ID?" Grady wasn't budging an inch.

Tidwell pulled a battered leather card case out of his pocket, held it daintily between two fingers.

Grady flipped the leather case open and scanned the ID. "*Detective* Tidwell. Well, okay." Grady's voice was smooth and dripping with appeasement. "Looks like the boys downtown are already on top of this. What can I do to help, Detective?"

"Kindly stay out of my way."

"Sure," agreed Grady cheerfully. "No problem. But you need any help, just whistle."

"Count on it," said Tidwell. He swiped his stubbled chin with the back of his hand, a gesture he would repeat many times. When Grady was out of earshot, Tidwell mumbled "Asshole" under his breath. Then he focused his full attention on Hughes Barron, still sitting at the table as best he could, wearing the oxygen mask one of the EMTs had slapped on him.

"Excuse me," said Theodosia. In her crepe-soled shoes, Tidwell hadn't heard her approach.

He swung around, wary. "Who are you?"

"Theodosia Browning." She extended a hand to him.

"Browning, Browning . . ." Tidwell narrowed his eyes, ignoring her outstretched hand. "I knew a Macalester Browning once. Lawyer fellow. Fairly decent as far as lawyers go. Lived in one of the plantations out on Rutledge Road."

"My father," said Theodosia.

"Mnh," grunted Tidwell, turning back toward Hughes Barron. He

lifted the teacup, dropped his nose to it, and sniffed. He swirled the contents like a wine taster.

Or a tea taster, reflected Theodosia.

Tidwell reached into a bulging pocket and pulled out his cell phone.
His sausage-sized fingers seemed to have trouble hitting numbers on the
keypad. Finally, after several tries and more than a few expletives, his call
went through.

"Pete, get me Brandon Hart." He paused. "Yeah." Tidwell sucked on
his mustache impatiently. "Brandon?" he barked into the phone. "Me.
Burt. I need your best crime-scene techs. That skinny one's good. And
the bald guy with the tattoo. Yeah, tonight. Now. Pete'll fill you in." He
clicked off his phone.

"You're Burt Tidwell," said Theodosia.

Tidwell swiveled his bullet-shaped head, surprised to find her still
standing there. "You still here?" He frowned.

"You're the one who caught the Crow River Killer."

Something akin to pride crossed Tidwell's face, then he fought to
regain his brusque manner. "And what might you know about that?" he
demanded.

"Just what I read in the paper," said Theodosia.

Sunlight filtered through the windows of the Indigo Tea Shop. It was
8:30 a.m., and the daily bustle and chores that routinely went on had been
largely forgotten or quickly dispatched. A few customers had come and
gone, Church Street shopkeepers mostly, who'd come for take-out orders
or to try to glean information about last evening's bizarre goings-on.

Now Theodosia, Drayton, and Haley sat together at one of the tables, a pot of tea before them, rehashing those unsettling events.

"I can't believe how long the police spent talking to Bethany," declared Haley. "The poor girl was almost in tears. And then that awful, rude man came along, and, of course, she *did* burst into tears."

"You're referring to Tidwell?" said Theodosia.

"Was that his name?" asked Haley. "He had no right to push everyone around the way he did. We couldn't help it if someone had the misfortune to drop dead. I mean, it's terribly sad when anyone dies suddenly, awful for their family. But for crying out loud, *we* didn't have anything to do with it!"

"If you ask me," said Drayton, "that fellow Tidwell was far too diligent for his own good. He not only pestered everyone, but he also kept a small contingent of visitors tied up for over forty minutes. And those were people who'd been talking on the front steps, nowhere near that man, Hughes Barron! He even interviewed Samantha, and she was shrieking around *inside* the house most of the evening."

"Maybe because she fainted," said Haley. "She really did seem upset."

"Momentarily upset," said Drayton, "because she feared that a tragedy might reflect badly on the Lamplighter Tour." His voice was tinged with disapproval.

"Oh, I can't believe Samantha is that callous," said Theodosia.

"But she *was* worried about it," interjected Haley. "Over and over she kept saying, 'Why did this have to happen during the Lamplighter Tour? Whatever will people think?'"

Theodosia gazed into her cup of Assam tea. The evening *had* been nothing short of bizarre. The only lucky break was the fact that Tidwell hadn't made public his suspicion about a foreign substance in Hughes Barron's tea. Police photographers had shown up, and the evening's participants questioned, but, as far as she knew, it hadn't escalated any further.

The fact that some type of foreign substance might have been introduced into Hughes Barron's tea, and the fact that Burt Tidwell has shown up, had piqued Theodosia's curiosity, however. And she'd made it a point to nose around last night's investigation. As the last so-called civilian to leave, she hadn't arrived home at her little apartment above the tea shop until around 11:00 p.m.

But even in the familiar serenity of her living room, with its velvet sofa, kilim rug, and cozy chintz and prints decor, she'd felt disquieted and filled with questions. That had prompted her to take Earl Grey out for a late walk.

Meandering the dark pathways of the historic district, inexplicably drawn back to the Avis Melbourne House, Theodosia had seen a new arrival: a shiny black van with tinted windows. The forensic team. From her vantage point in the shadows, she had heard Tidwell's gruff voice chiding them, nagging at them.

A curious man, she had thought to herself. *Paradoxical. A genteel manner that could rapidly disintegrate into reproachful or shrewish.*

Back home again, Theodosia had fixed herself a cup of chamomile tea, ideal for jangled nerves or those times when sleep proves elusive. Then she sat down in front of her computer for a quick bit of Internet research.

On the site of the *Charleston Post and Courier,* she found what she was looking for. That venerable newspaper had loaded their archives (not all of them, just feature stories going back to 1996) on their Web site. Conveniently, they'd also added a search engine.

Within thirty seconds, Theodosia had pulled up three articles that mentioned Burt Tidwell. She learned that he had logged eleven years with the FBI and ten years as a homicide detective in Raleigh, North Carolina.

During his stint in Raleigh, Tidwell was one of the investigators responsible for apprehending the infamous Crow River Killer.

Theodosia had recalled the terrible events: four women brutally murdered, their bodies dumped in the swamps of the Crow River Game Preserve.

Even when all the leads had petered out and the trail had grown cold, Tidwell stayed on the case, poring over old files, piecing together scraps of information.

Interviews in the *Charleston Post and Courier* spoke of Tidwell's "eerie obsession" and his "uncanny knack" for creating a profile of the killer.

And Tidwell had finally nailed the Crow River Killer. His persistence had paid off big-time.

"Oh, oh," said Drayton in a low voice.

Theodosia looked up to see Burt Tidwell's big form looming in the doorway. He put a hand on the lower half of the double door and eased it open.

"Good morning!" Tidwell boomed. He seemed jovial, a far cry from his bristle and brash of the previous evening. "You open for business?"

"Come in, Mr. Tidwell," said Theodosia. "Sit with us and have a cup of tea." She remained seated while Drayton and Haley popped up from their chairs as if they'd suddenly become hot seats.

Burt Tidwell paused in the middle of Theodosia's small shop and looked around. His prominent eyes took in the more than one hundred glass jars of tea, the maple cabinet that held a formidable collection of antique teapots, the silk-screened pastel T-shirts Theodosia had designed herself with a whimsical drawing of a teacup, a curlicue of rising steam, and the words Tea Shirt.

"Sweet," he murmured as he eased himself into a chair.

"We have Assam and Sencha," Drayton announced, curiously formal.

"Assam, please," said Tidwell. His eyes shone bright on Theodosia. "If we could talk alone?"

Theodosia knew Haley had already escaped to the nether regions of the back offices, and she assumed Drayton would soon follow.

"Of course," said Drayton. "I have errands to run, anyway."

Tidwell waited until they were alone. Then he took a sip of tea, smiled, and set his teacup down. "Delicious."

"Thank you."

"Miss Browning," Tidwell began, "are you aware our hapless victim of last evening is Hughes Barron, the real estate developer?"

"So I understand."

"He was not terribly well liked," said Tidwell, smiling.

"I didn't know that."

"Miss Browning, it saddens me to be the bearer of such news, but Mr.

Barron's death was no accident." He paused, searching out Theodosia's face. "We are looking at a wrongful death. Even as we speak, a sample of the tea that Hughes Barron was drinking last night has been dispatched to the state toxicology lab."

Theodosia's heart skipped a beat, even as she willed herself to remain calm. Do not let this man rattle or intimidate you, she told herself. *You had nothing to do with Hughes Barron's death. Surely this would soon reveal itself as one big misunderstanding.*

On the heels of that came the realization that she had spent nearly a dozen years in advertising, where everything had run in panic mode. Everything a crash and burn involving millions of dollars. Could she keep her cool? Absolutely.

"Perhaps you'd better explain yourself," was all Theodosia said. *Better to play it close to the vest,* she thought. *Find out what this man has to say.*

Burt Tidwell held up a hand. "There is concern that whatever liquid was in Hughes Barron's teacup severely compromised his health. In other words, his beverage was lethal."

Now amusement lit Theodosia's face. "Surely you don't believe it was my tea that killed him."

"I understand you served a number of teas last night."

"Of course," said Theodosia lightly. "Darjeeling, jasmine, our special Lamplighter Blend. You realize, of course, everyone who stopped by the garden—and we're talking probably two hundred people—sampled our teas. No one else is dead."

She took another sip of tea, blotted her lips, and favored Tidwell with a warm yet slightly indulgent smile. "Frankly, Mr. Tidwell, if I were you, I'd be more concerned with *who* Hughes Barron was sitting with in the garden last night rather than which *tea* he drank."

"Touché, Miss Browning," Tidwell replied. He reclined in his chair, swiped the back of his hand against his quivering chin, and let fly his curve ball. "How long has Bethany Shepherd worked for you?"

So that's where this conversation was going, thought Theodosia. "Really just a handful of times over the past few months," she replied. "But surely you don't consider the girl a suspect."

"I understand she had words with Hughes Barron last week at a Heritage Society meeting."

"Bethany recently obtained an internship with the Heritage Society, so I imagine she spends considerable time there."

"Rather harsh words," said Tidwell. His eyes bored into Theodosia.

"A disagreement doesn't make her a murderer," said Theodosia lightly. "It only means she's a young woman blessed with gumption."

"We have her at the police station now."

"Indeed."

"Taking a statement. Very pro forma."

"I assume her lawyer is with her?"

"Do you think she needs one?" Tidwell arched a tufted eyebrow.

"Not the issue."

"Pray tell, what is?"

"She's *entitled* to one," replied Theodosia.

"Poison!" exclaimed Haley.

"Sshh!" Drayton held a finger to his lips. "The customers," he mouthed in an exaggerated gesture, although a couple patrons had already turned in their chairs and were staring inquisitively at the three of them clustered at the counter.

"Tidwell thinks someone *poisoned* Hughes Barron?" said Haley in a low voice, her eyes wide as saucers.

"That's his notion so far," said Theodosia. "He's already sent the contents of Hughes Barron's teacup to the state toxicology lab."

"What absolute rubbish!" declared Drayton. "We had nothing to do with the man's demise. Are you sure those paramedics checked the man's heart? Big fellow like that might've had a bad ticker."

"I'm sure they'll perform an autopsy and clear everything up eventually," said Theodosia.

"The problem is," said Drayton, "what do we do in the short term?"

Damage control, Theodosia thought to herself. *That was our PR department's job when I was still at the agency. They'd get a positive spin working before anything negative could grab hold.*

"Your point is well taken," said Theodosia. "As outrageous as the notion is that our tea killed the man, Hughes Barron's death is fertile ground for wild rumors."

"Rumors that could cast a veil of suspicion over all of us," added Haley.

"Actually," said Theodosia as she stared into the worried eyes of her two dear employees and friends, "I'm more concerned with Bethany right now. Tidwell has her down at the police station."

Haley's eyes welled with tears, and she bit her lip to keep from bursting into sobs. "Just who *is* this man, Hughes Barron? I've never even heard of him before!"

"Well," said Drayton, his dark eyes darting from side to side, "I don't mind telling you that Church Street is positively buzzing about him today." His back to the customers, Drayton edged closer to the small counter and faced Theodosia and Haley.

"I spoke earlier with Fern Barrow at the Cottage Inn. She had heard about the disturbance at last night's Lamplighter Tour and seemed to know quite a bit about our Mr. Hughes Barron."

"Really?" said Theodosia, intrigued.

"Apparently, he was born and raised in Goose Creek, just north of here, but lived in California most of his life. Santa Monica. Fern said Hughes Barron made a tidy profit out there as a real estate developer. Mostly condos and strip malls." Drayton rolled his eyes as though he were talking about organized crime.

Theodosia flashed on her conversation with Delaine yesterday afternoon. "God knows what sins a developer with Barron's reputation might wreak," she had said.

"Anyway," continued Drayton, "Hughes Barron moved back to the Charleston area about two years ago. He bought a beachfront home on the Isle of Palms. You know, Theo, near Wild Dunes?"

Theodosia nodded.

"Since he's moved back, Hughes Barron's big hot project has been developing some truly awful time-share condominiums," said Drayton. "Out on Johns Island."

Johns Island was a sleepy agricultural community known mostly for its large bird refuge.

"That couldn't have been terribly popular," said Theodosia.

"Are you kidding? He was almost *pilloried* for it!" said Drayton. "He was picketed and protested before the bulldozers scooped a single shovel of dirt. The people who opposed the development kept the pressure going all through the construction phase, too. But, of course, the condos were built anyway. They weren't able to block it." Drayton sighed. "Hughes Barron must have had powerful connections to get that land rezoned. We're talking statehouse level, of course."

"I do remember hearing about that development," said Theodosia. "And you're right. There was major opposition from environmental groups as well as the local historical society."

"Nothing they could do, though." Drayton sighed again.

"Excuse me," called a woman seated at one of the tables. "Could we please get a little more tea here?"

"Certainly, ma'am." With a quick rustle and a cordial smile, Haley flitted across the tea room. Besides refilling the teapot, she brought a fresh pitcher of milk and, much to the delight of the party of three women, also produced a plate of caramel-nut shortbread. On the house, of course.

"Drayton." Theodosia slid the cash register drawer closed. Something was bothering her, and she had to know the full story.

Drayton Conneley had pulled a little step stool out from beneath the counter. Now he was balanced on it, stacking jars of creamed honey from the local apiary, DuBose Bees. He peered down at Theodosia in mid-stretch. "What's needling you?" he asked.

"Did Bethany really have words with Hughes Barron at a Heritage Society meeting?"

Drayton's mouth opened as if he meant to speak, then he seemed to think better of it. To say anything from his lofty perch would be to broadcast trouble they didn't need right now. Drayton held up an index finger and clambered down.

"Let me put this in perspective," he said.

Theodosia looked out over the tea room, where all her customers seemed content and taken care of, and nodded.

"I'm not sure how clued in you are about this," said Drayton, "but Hughes Barron had recently become a new board member at the Heritage Society."

"So it would seem."

"I don't have exact details on who sponsored him or what the final vote was on accepting him, because, as you recall, I was up in Boston when all that took place."

Theodosia nodded. Drayton had been at Chatham Brothers Tea Wholesalers on a buying trip.

"Suffice it to say, however, that Hughes Barron was voted in by a small margin, and Timothy Neville, our board president, was *extremely* displeased. Well," continued Drayton, "last week, this past Wednesday evening to be exact, was our most recent board meeting. Because I had never met Hughes Barron before, I decided it was only fair to reserve judgment on the man. I wasn't privy to his background or what his motivations for joining the Heritage Society were. For all I knew, they could have been totally altruistic. So I maintained an open mind. Until, of course, Hughes Barron got up to speak and jumped on his own personal bandwagon concerning new development in the historic district." Drayton suddenly looked unhappy. "That's when it all started."

"When what started?" asked Theodosia.

"I'm afraid we got into a row with Hughes Barron," confessed Drayton.

"Who did?" asked Theodosia. "All of you?" She knew any kind of new development in the historic district was one of Drayton's pet peeves. He himself resided in a 160-year-old home once occupied by a Civil War surgeon.

"Timothy Neville, Joshua Brady, and me. Samantha and Bethany threw their two cents in as well. But mostly it was Timothy. He had a particularly ugly go-round with Hughes Barron." Drayton lowered his voice. "You know how cantankerous and judgmental Timothy can be."

Indeed, Theodosia was well aware of Timothy Neville's fiery temper. The crusty octogenarian president of the Heritage Society had a reputation for being bullheaded and brash. In fact, she had once seen Timothy Neville berate a waiter at the Peninsula Grill for incorrectly opening a bottle of champagne and spilling a few drops of the French bubbly. She had always felt that Timothy Neville was entirely too full of himself.

"So Timothy Neville took off on Hughes Barron?" said Theodosia.

"I'd have to say it was more of a character assassination." Drayton looked around sharply, then lowered his voice an octave. "Timothy denounced Hughes Barron as a Neanderthal carpetbagger. Because of that condo development."

"Just awful," said Theodosia.

Drayton faced Theodosia with sad eyes. "I agree. A gentleman should never resort to name-calling."

"I meant the condos," Theodosia replied.

6

Theodosia stared at the storyboards propped up against the wall in her office. Jessica Todd, president of Todd & Lambeau Design Group, had brought in three more boards. Now there were *six* different Web site designs for her to evaluate.

As her eyes roved from one to the other, she told herself that all were exciting and extremely doable. Any one . . . *eeny, meeny, miney, moe* . . . would work beautifully at launching her tea business into cyberspace.

Ordinarily, Theodosia would be head over heels, champing at the bit to make a final choice and set the wheels in motion. But today it seemed as if her brain was stuffed with cotton.

Too much had happened, she told herself. Was happening. It felt like a freight train gathering momentum. Not a runaway train quite yet, but one that was certainly rumbling down the rails.

Bethany had phoned the tea shop a half hour ago, and Haley, stretching the cord to its full length so she could talk privately in the kitchen, had a whispered conversation with her. When Haley hung up, Theodosia had grabbed a box of Kleenex and listened intently as Haley related Bethany's sad tale.

"She's finished at the police station for now," Haley had told her. "But one of the detectives, I don't know if it was that Tidwell character or not, advised her to get a lawyer." Haley had snuffled, then blown her nose loudly. "Do you know any lawyers?" she'd asked plaintively.

Theodosia had nodded. Of course she did. Her father's law firm was still in business. The senior partner, Leyland Hartwell, always a family friend, was a formidable presence in Charleston.

Jessica Todd impatiently tapped a manicured finger on her ultraslim laptop computer. Hyperthyroidal and superslim herself, wearing an elegant aubergine-colored suit, Jessica sat across the desk from Theodosia. She was anxious to get Theodosia's decision today.

As President of Todd & Lambeau, Jessica had distinguished herself as one of the top Internet marketing gurus in Charleston. And today she was fairly jumping out of her skin, eager to implement her graphic design ideas, Web architecture, and marketing strategies for the Indigo Tea Shop's new Web site.

"Would you like a cup of tea, Jessica?" Theodosia asked, stalling. Decisions weren't coming easily.

"That's the fourth time you've asked," Jessica replied somewhat peevishly. She shook her head and ran long fingernails through her sleek, short helmet of dark hair. "Again, no thank you."

"Sorry," murmured Theodosia.

Jessica reached over and plucked up a board that featured a montage of teapots and tea leaves, set against a ghosted background of green terraced slopes, one of the old Chinese tea plantations.

"If we could just revisit this concept for a moment," said Jessica, forging ahead, "I believe you'll find it meets all criteria we established. Dynamic graphics, intuitive user interface. Look at the global navigation buttons. On-line Catalog, Tea Tips, Tea Q&A, and Contact Us. Here, I'll show you how it works on the laptop."

"Jessica . . ." Theodosia began, then stopped. There was no way she could focus on this when she was so concerned about Bethany and the events of last night. She knew better than to make critical business decisions when her mind was somewhere else.

"I'm sorry," said Theodosia standing up. "We're going to have to do this another time."

"What?" sputtered Jessica.

"Your designs are perfectly lovely. Spectacular, in fact. But I need to live with them for a few days. And it's only right to share them with Drayton and Haley, get a consensus."

"Let's call them in now."

"Jessica. Please."

"All right, all right." Jessica Todd snapped her laptop closed, gathered up her attaché case. "Call me, Theodosia. But don't wait too long. We're hot into a pitch right now for a new on-line brokerage. And if it comes through, *when* it comes through, we're all going to be working twenty-four/seven on it."

"I hear you, Jessica."

Walking Jessica to the door, Theodosia thought back on her own career in advertising. *I was like that,* she told herself. *Nervous, nuts. Slaving evenings and weekends, caught in the pressure cooker. What had Jessica called it? Working twenty-four/seven. Right.*

Breathing a sigh of relief, feeling enormously grateful for her serene little world at the tea shop, Theodosia surprised Haley just as she was dusting a fresh pan of lemon bars with powdered sugar.

"I'm going to do deliveries today," Theodosia announced.

"*You* are? Why is that?" asked Haley.

"Can't sit still, don't want to sit still."

"I know the feeling," said Haley. She reached under her wooden baker's rack and pulled out a large wicker hamper. "Okay, lucky for you it's the milk run. Only two deliveries. A half-dozen canisters of jasmine and English breakfast teas for the Featherbed House and some of Drayton's special palmetto blend for Reverend Jonathan at Saint Philip's."

Once outside, Theodosia walked briskly in the direction of the Featherbed House. The sun shone down warmly. The breeze off the Cooper River was light and tasted faintly salty. White, puffy clouds scudded overhead. But what should have been a glorious day to revel in went relatively unnoticed by Theodosia, so preoccupied was she by recent events.

Why on earth were they pressing Bethany so hard? she wondered. Surely the police could see she was just a young woman with no ax to grind against anyone. Especially a man like Hughes Barron. Burt Tidwell was no fool. He, of all people, should be able to see that.

Theodosia sighed. Poor Bethany. The only thing she'd been up to lately was trying to rebuild her life. And she'd seemed to have been going about it fairly successfully.

Only last week Theodosia had overheard Bethany speaking glowingly to Drayton about her internship at the Heritage Society. How she'd been chosen over six other candidates. How she was so impressed by the many volunteers who donated countless hours and dollars. How the Heritage Society had recently staged a black-tie dinner and silent auction and raised almost $300,000 to purchase the old Chapman Mill. Abandoned and scheduled for demolition, the historic old mill would now live on in Charleston's history.

As Theodosia turned the corner at Murray Street, the rush of wind coming off Charleston Harbor hit her full on. It blew her hair out in auburn streamers, brought a rosy glow to her cheeks and, finally, a smile to her face.

The Battery, that stretch of homes and shore at the point of land where the Ashley and Cooper Rivers converged and the Atlantic poured in to meet them, was one of Theodosia's favorite places. Originally known as Oyster Point because it began as a swampy beach strewn with oyster shells, The Battery evolved into a military strong point and finally into the elegant neighborhood of harborside homes and parks it is today. With its White Point Gardens, Victorian bandstand, and no fewer than twenty-six cannons and monuments, The Battery held a special place in the hearts of every Charlestonian.

Perched on The Battery and overlooking the harbor with a bird's-eye view of Fort Sumter, the Featherbed House was one of the peninsula's premier bed-and-breakfasts. It featured elegantly furnished rooms with canopied beds, cypress paneling, and twelve-foot-high hand-molded plaster ceilings. And, of course, mounds of featherbeds just as the name promised. A second-story open-air bridge spanned the backyard garden and transported delighted visitors from the main house to a treetop dining room in the renovated hayloft of the carriage house.

In the cozy lobby, filled with every manner of ceramic goose, plush goose, and needlepoint goose, Theodosia stopped to chat with owners Angie and Mark Congdon. They were a husband and wife team who had both been commodity brokers in Chicago and fled the Windy City for a more temperate climate and slower pace.

Changes and reevaluations, mused Theodosia as she hurried back down the street toward Saint Philip's. *Lots of that going around these days.*

Saint Philip's Episcopal was the church for whom Church Street was named. It was a neoclassical edifice that had been drawing communicants for almost two hundred years. When the bells in the tall, elegant spire chimed on Sunday mornings, the entire historic district knew that the Reverend Jonathan's service was about to begin.

Theodosia stepped through a wrought iron archway into the private garden and burial ground.

"Good morning!" a voice boomed.

Theodosia halted in her tracks and looked around. She finally spotted Reverend Jonathan, a small, wiry man with short silver hair, on his hands and knees underneath a small oak tree.

"This tree didn't fare well in the last big storm," said Reverend Jonathan as he pulled a metal cable tight around a wooden stake. "I thought if I shored it up, it might have a chance to catch up with its big brothers."

The "big brothers" Reverend Jonathan referred to were the two enormous live oaks that sat to either side of the parish house.

"You've worked wonders here," said Theodosia. Under Reverend Jonathan's watchful eye, the garden and historic burial ground had evolved from a manicured lawn with a few shrubs and memorial plaques to a hidden oasis filled with a delightful profusion of seasonal plants, flowering shrubs, stepping-stones, and decorative statuary.

Reverend Jonathan straightened up and gazed about with pride. "I love getting my hands dirty. But I have to admit there's always something needs fixing. Next big project is some restoration work on our beloved church's interior arches."

Even though he had well over one thousand five hundred communicants to minister to, dozens of committees to juggle, and fund-raising to tend to, Reverend Jonathan was a tireless worker. He always seemed to find time for hands-on gardening and maintenance of the historic church.

"That's the thing about these grande dame buildings." He grinned. "Patch, patch, patch."

"Mm," said Theodosia as she handed Reverend Jonathan his canisters of tea. "I know the feeling."

On her return trip to the Indigo Tea Shop, Theodosia's thoughts turned once again to Hughes Barron's death. Although she felt saddened that a human life had ended, it prickled her that the investigators seemed to be overlooking the obvious. If someone had been sitting at that far table with Hughes Barron, wouldn't *that* person have had the perfect opportunity to slip something toxic into the man's tea?

On a hunch, Theodosia jogged over toward Meeting Street, where Samantha Rabathan lived. Samantha had been the chairperson for last night's event, she reasoned. Maybe Sam would have a list of attendees. That might be a logical place to start.

As luck would have it, Samantha was outside, bustling about on her enormous veranda, tending to the heroic abundance of plant life that flourished in her many containers and flower boxes. A divorcée for almost ten years, Samantha's only avocation seemed to be gardening. If Reverend Jonathan was the patron saint of trees and shrubs, Samantha was the guardian angel of flowers.

Samantha changed her flower boxes seasonally, so they might contain flowering bulbs, English daisies, clouds of wisteria, or miniature shrubs. Her trellises, usually hidden under mounds of perfect pink climbing roses, were legendary. Her backyard garden, with roses, star jasmine, begonias, and verbena clustered about a sparkling little pool, and tangled vines creeping up a backdrop of crumbling brick, was a must-see on the annual Garden Club Tour. And Samantha's elegant floral arrangements always garnered blue as well as purple ribbons at the annual Charleston Flower Show.

"Samantha!" Theodosia waved from the street.

"Hello," Samantha called back.

She was wearing her Mr. Green Jeans garb today, Theodosia noted. Green coveralls, green gloves, green floppy cotton hat, to go with her green thumb.

Most people in the neighborhood regarded Samantha as a bit of a hothouse plant herself. A delicate tropical flower with fine yellow hair and alabaster skin who shunned the sun. Close friends knew she was merely trying to prolong her face-lift.

"How are you feeling today?" asked Theodosia. She shaded her eyes and gazed up at the porch with its trellises of ivy and trumpet vine and window boxes with overflowing ramparts of crape myrtle and althaea.

Samantha grinned sheepishly and fanned a gloved hand in front of her face. "Fine, really fine. Just too much excitement last night. I can't believe I actually fainted over that poor man. How embarrassing. Oh, well, at least it proves I'm a true Southern lady. Got the vapors. All so very *Gone With the Wind*," she added in an exaggerated drawl.

"Samantha . . ." began Theodosia.

But Samantha gushed on. "What a gentleman Drayton was to come to my aid. I must remember to thank him." She aimed her pruning shears toward a pot of cascading plumbago, snipped decisively, and laid a riot of bright blue flowers in her wicker basket. "I know. I shall put together one of my special bouquets. Drayton is a man of culture and refinement. He will appreciate the gesture."

"I'm certain he will, Samantha," said Theodosia.

"Theodosia." Samantha peered down from her veranda. "The sun is almost overhead. Do take care."

Theodosia ignored her warning. "Samantha, is there any way to connect people's names with the Lamplighter Tour tickets that were purchased?"

Samantha considered Theodosia's question. "You're asking me if we wrote down guests' names?"

"Did you?" asked Theodosia hopefully.

Samantha shook her head slowly from side to side. "No, we just sold the tickets and collected the money. Nobody has ever bothered to keep track of who bought what or how many. Usually our biggest concern is trying to outsell the Tradd Street tour. You know, they have an awful lot of volunteers out pounding the streets. This year they even placed printed posters in some of the B and Bs!"

Theodosia put a hand to her head and smoothed back her hair. This was what she'd been afraid of. No record keeping, just volunteers selling tickets wherever they could.

"But you know," added Samantha, venturing toward the sunlight, "if we offered a drawing or door prize in conjunction with the Lamplighter Tour, that would be an extra incentive to buy a ticket! And then, of course, we'd have to record people's names and addresses and phone numbers, that sort of thing." She wrinkled her nose in delicious anticipation. "A drawing! Isn't that a marvelous idea? I can't wait to propose it for next year's Lamplighter Tour."

Samantha snipped a few more stems of plumbago, then smiled brightly at Theodosia. "Theodosia, would *you* be interested in donating one of your gift baskets?"

7

Cane Ridge Plantation was built in 1835 on Horlbeck Creek. It included a fanciful Gothic Revival cottage replete with soaring peaks and gables, steeply pitched shingled roof, and broad piazza extending around three sides. Set high on a vantage point overlooking a quiet pond and marsh-land, it had been a flourishing rice plantation in its day, with acres of flat, low fields that stretched out to meet piney forests.

Theodosia's father, Macalester Browning, and her Aunt Libby had grown up at Cane Ridge, and Theodosia had spent countless summers there. She always returned to Cane Ridge when her heart was troubled or she was in need of clearing her head.

"The cedar waxwings are here, but the marsh wrens have not yet arrived." Libby Revelle, Theodosia's aunt, scanned the distant marsh as she stood on the side piazza, a black cashmere shawl wrapped around her thin but firmly squared shoulders.

Tiny but elegant in her carriage, the silver-haired Libby Revelle was a bird-watcher of the first magnitude. With her binoculars and Peterson's *Field Guide to Eastern Birds,* she was able to identify shape of bill, tail patterns, and wing bars much the same way aviation aficionados delighted in identifying aircraft.

Theodosia hadn't intended on stopping at Aunt Libby's and staying for lunch. She had driven out to the low-country with every intention of visiting the Charleston Tea Plantation. Owners Mack Fleming and Bill Hall were good friends, and she was anxious to inspect the tea from their final harvest of the season.

But driving out the Maybank Highway in her Jeep Cherokee, Theodosia had felt a sudden longing for the old plantation, a desire to return to a place where she had always felt not only welcome, but also comfortably at home. And so, when she neared the turnoff for Rutledge Road, she pointed her red Jeep down the bumpy, gravel road that led to Cane Ridge and Aunt Libby.

Jouncing along, Theodosia had felt a certain peacefulness steal over her. The live oaks, dogwoods, and enormous hedges of azaleas closed in on the road in a comforting way. Through the forest's dense curtain were distant vine-covered humps, telltale remnants of old rice dikes. And as she bumped across a rickety bridge, black water flowed silently beneath, conjuring images of youths in flat-bottomed bateaus.

Theodosia downshifted on her final approach, thankful for four-wheel drive. She'd purchased her Jeep just a year ago, against Drayton's advice, and was totally in love with it.

Drayton, ever mindful of image, had argued that the Jeep was "not particularly ladylike."

Theodosia had countered by pointing out that the Jeep was practical. "Perfect," she'd told him, "for transporting boxes and gift baskets. And if I want to go into the woods and pick wild dandelion or wild raspberries for flavoring teas, the Jeep's ideal. I can jounce down trails and even creek beds and not worry about getting stuck."

Drayton had dramatically put a hand to his forehead and sighed. "You had to buy red?"

Haley, on the other hand, had jumped in the passenger side and pleaded that they go "four-wheeling."

"Help me put out my buffet, will you?" asked Libby. "We've eaten our soup and sandwiches, and now it's our winged friends' turn."

"You stay here and enjoy the sun while I take the seed down," said Theodosia, glad to be of help.

Aunt Libby plied her winged visitors with a mixture of thistle, cracked corn, and black oil seed. Over the coming winter, Libby would go through at least eight hundred pounds of seeds.

Theodosia carried two pails overflowing with Libby's seed mixture to a fallen log on the edge of the marsh. A fifteen-foot length of gnarled oak, the tree trunk was peppered with hollow bowls and clefts, making perfect natural basins for birdseed.

Back on the piazza, Libby's heart expanded with pride as she watched this beautiful, accomplished woman, her niece. She loved Theodosia as a mother would a child. When Theodosia's mother died when Theo was only eight, she was only too happy to fill in wherever she could. She'd enjoyed attending Theodosia's various music recitals and class plays, sewing labels on Theodosia's clothes when she went off to camp, and teaching her how to whistle with two fingers in her mouth.

Then, when Theodosia's father passed away when she was twenty, she'd become her only real family. Even though Theodosia was living in a dorm at school, she'd gladly opened her house to her on holidays, hosted parties for Theodosia's friends, and gave her advice when she graduated and began job hunting.

And when Theodosia had decided to drop out of advertising and test her entrepreneurial spirit by buying the little tea shop, Libby had backed her one hundred percent.

"I was on my way to see Mack and Bill," Theodosia said as she came up the short flight of steps. The pails clanked down on the wooden porch.

"So you said," answered Libby. She sat in a wicker chair, gazing out at a horizon of blue pond, waving golden grasses, and hazy sun.

Theodosia stared out at the old log she'd just replenished with seed, watched a striped chipmunk scamper out from a clump of dried weeds, snatch up a handful of fallen seeds, then sit back on its haunches to dine.

"We had some trouble in town last night," said Theodosia.

"I heard," said Aunt Libby.

Theodosia spun about. "What?" Libby, the sly fox, had sat through lunch with her, watched her fidget, and never said a word. Theodosia smiled wryly. Yes, that was Libby Revelle's style, the Aunt Libby she knew and loved. Don't push, let people talk in their own good time.

"What did you hear?" asked Theodosia. "And from who?"

"Oh, Bill Wexler came by, and we had ourselves a nice chat."

Bill Wexler had delivered mail in the low-country for almost twenty-five years. He also seemed to have a direct pipeline to everything that went on in Charleston, the low-country, and as far out as West Ashley.

"If people out here know, it's going to be all over town by the time I get back this afternoon," said Theodosia.

Libby nodded. "Probably."

Theodosia squinted into the sun, looking perplexed.

"Nothing you can do, dear," said Libby. "The only part you played in last night's little drama was a walk-on role. If folks are silly enough to think you're involved, that's their problem."

"You're right," agreed Theodosia. She eased herself down into the chair next to Libby, already deciding to stay the afternoon.

"But then, you're not worried about yourself, are you?" asked Libby.

"Not really," said Theodosia.

Libby reached a hand out and gently stroked Theodosia's hair. "You're my cat, always have been. Land on your feet, nine lives to spare."

"Oh, Libby." Theodosia caught her aunt's hand in hers and squeezed it gratefully. As she did, she was suddenly aware of Libby's thin, parchment-like skin, the frailness of her tiny bones. And Aunt Libby's mortality.

Teapots chirped and whistled and teacups clinked against saucers as Drayton bustled about the shop. Four tables were occupied, customers eager for morning tea and treats. Afterward, they would be picked up by one of the bright yellow jitneys that would whisk them away on their morning tour through Charleston's historic district, the open-air market, or the King Street antiques district.

"Where's Haley?" Theodosia swooped through the doorway just as Drayton measured a final tablespoon of Irish breakfast tea into a Victorian teapot.

"Hasn't shown up yet," Drayton said as he arranged teapots, pitchers of milk, bowls of sugar cubes, and small plates of lemon slices on a silver tray, then deftly hoisted it to his shoulder.

"That's not like her," said Theodosia, pitching in. She was instantly concerned about Haley's absence since she was ordinarily quite prompt, usually showing up at the Indigo Tea Shop by 7:00 a.m. That's when Haley would heat up the oven and pour out batter she'd mixed up and refrigerated the day before. It was Haley's shortcut to fresh-baked scones, croissants, and benne wafers without having to get up at four in the morning.

While Drayton poured tea, Theodosia mustered up a pan of scones from the freezer and warmed them quickly in the oven.

"It won't matter that they've been frozen," Drayton murmured under his breath. "Scones are so amazingly heavy anyway, I don't think anyone will know the difference."

And Drayton was right. Served piping hot to their guests along with plenty of Devonshire cream and strawberry jam, the scones were actually oohed and aahed over.

"Have you noticed anything odd?" asked Theodosia. She stood behind the counter surveying the collection of customers who lingered at the tables.

Drayton glanced up from the cash register. "What do you mean?"

"I'm not seeing any of our regulars," said Theodosia.

Drayton gave her a sharp look. "You're right." His eyes searched out Theodosia's. "You don't suppose . . ."

"I'm sure they'll be in later," she said.

"Of course they will."

Forty minutes later, the early customers had all departed, tables had been cleared, floors swept, and teapots readied for the next influx.

"Now that I've got a moment to breathe, I'm going to phone Haley," said Theodosia. "I'm really getting worried."

The bell over the door jingled merrily. "Here we go," said Theodosia.

"More customers." She turned toward the door with a welcoming smile, but it was Haley who burst through the door, not another throng of customers.

"Haley!" said Theodosia. "What's wrong?" Haley's ordinarily placid face projected unhappiness, her peaches-and-cream complexion blotchy. Her shoulders sagged, her eyes were puffy, and she'd been crying. Hard.

"They fired her!" cried Haley.

Theodosia flew across the room to Haley, put an arm around her shoulder. "Come, dear. Sit down." She led Haley to the closest table and got her seated. "Drayton," Theodosia called, "we're going to need some tea. Strong tea."

Tears trickled down Haley's cheeks as she turned sad eyes on Theodosia. "They fired Bethany. From the Heritage Society."

"Oh, no," said Theodosia. "Are you sure?"

"Yes, they called her a little while ago and told her not to bother coming in."

"Who called her?" asked Theodosia.

"Mr. Neville," said Haley.

"Timothy?"

"Yes, Timothy Neville," said Haley in a choked voice.

"What happened?" Drayton set a pot of tea and three mugs on the bare table.

"Timothy Neville fired Bethany," said Theodosia.

He sat down, instantly concerned. "Oh, no."

"Can he do that, Drayton?" asked Theodosia.

Drayton nodded his head slowly, as if still comprehending Haley's words. "I suppose so. He's the president. As such, Timothy Neville wields an incredible amount of power. If he were firing someone from an executive position, he'd probably have to call a formal board meeting. At least it would be polite protocol to do so. But for an intern . . . Yes, I'm afraid Timothy Neville is empowered to hire or fire at will."

"Because she's not important enough," Haley said with a sniff.

"I didn't say that," said Drayton.

"What you all don't realize," cried Haley, "is that Bethany was going to use her internship as a stepping-stone to a better job. You can't get hired by a good museum unless you have some kind of internship under your belt. And now Bethany's credibility is completely ruined!" She put her face in her hands and sobbed.

Drayton gently patted her arm. "There, there, perhaps something can still be done." He gazed sadly at Theodosia. His hangdog look implored her, *Can't you do something?*

Theodosia arched her eyebrows back at him. *What can I do?*

"Can't you at least talk to him?" Drayton finally asked out loud.

Haley's tear-streaked face tipped up toward Theodosia and brightened. "Could you? Please? You're so good at things like this. You're brave, and you know lots of important people. Please, you've just got to help!"

The pleading looks on Drayton's and Haley's faces spoke volumes.

Theodosia sat back in her chair and took a sip of tea. She had spoken with Timothy Neville once or twice over the years. He had always been clipped and formal. She recalled him the other night at the Lamplighter Tour. Sitting at one of the tables, almost holding court as he lectured about the bronze bells that hung in the tower of Saint Michael's and how they'd once been confiscated by British soldiers.

"Of course, I'll talk to him," she said with outward bravado, when what she really felt inside was *Oh, dear.*

Outrage *makes many* women belligerent and strident. With Theodosia it only served to enhance her firm, quiet manner. She strode down Church Street past Noble Dragon Books, Bouquet Garni Giftware, and the Cotton Duck clothing shop. Her thoughts were a jumble, but her resolve was clear. Firing Bethany was unconscionable. The girl was clearly not involved in anything that had to do with Hughes Barron. This had been an incredible overreaction by the Heritage Society and especially on the part of Timothy Neville. She didn't know a whit about employment law, but she did know about being an employer. Since Bethany's internship had been a paid internship, that meant she was a regular employee. So just maybe the firing could be considered illegal. Particularly since it was highly doubtful the Heritage Society could prove malicious intent or lack of ability on Bethany's part.

Her zeal carried Theodosia past the Avis Melbourne Home before she even realized it. When she suddenly became aware of just where she was, Theodosia slowed her pace, then stopped. Standing just outside a heroic hedge of magnolias, she gazed up at the lovely old home. It looked even more magnificent by day. Stately Ionic columns presented an elegant facade on this predominantly Georgian-style house with its keen attention to symmetry and grace.

But this was where the murder took place, Theodosia reminded herself. This was where Hughes Barron was—dare she say it?—poisoned.

Theodosia turned back and walked slowly up the broad front walk. The lanterns and glowing jack-o'-lanterns of the other night were gone. Now the house gleamed white in the sunlight.

It really was a wedding cake of a house, Theodosia thought to herself. The columns, second-floor balustrade, and roof ornaments looked just like daubs of white frosting.

She paused at the front steps, turned onto the winding flagstone path that led through a wrought-iron gate, and walked around the side of the house. Within moments, shade engulfed her. Ever since she'd taken a botany class, when she had first purchased the tea shop, Theodosia had made careful observation of plants. Now she noted that tall mimosa trees sheltered the house from the hot Charleston sun, and dense stands of loquat and oleander lined the pathway.

As her footsteps echoed hollowly, she wondered if anyone was home. Probably not. The Odettes, the couple who called this lovely mansion home, owned a travel agency. They were probably at their office or off somewhere leading a trip. Come to think of it, she hadn't even seen the Odettes the night of the Lamplighter Tour. Heritage Society volunteers had supervised the event, helping her get set up in the butler's pantry, and they had guided tour guests through the various downstairs rooms and parlors.

As she rounded the back corner of the house and came into full view of the garden, Theodosia was struck by how deserted it now looked. Two days ago it had been a lush and lavish outdoor space, darkly elegant with sweet-scented vines and twinkling lanterns, filled with the chatter and laughter of eager Lamplighter Tour guests. Then, of course, had come the gruff and urgent voices of the various police and rescue squads echoing off flagstones and brick walls. But now the atmosphere in the garden was so very still. The tables and chairs were still there, the fountain splattered away, but the mood was somber. *Like a cemetery,* she thought with a shiver.

Stop it, she chided herself, *don't let your imagination run wild.*

Theodosia walked to the fountain, leaned down, and trailed a hand in the cool water. Thick-leafed water plants bobbed on the surface, and below, copper pennies gleamed. *Someone threw coins in here,* she mused. *Children, perhaps. Making a wish. Or Lamplighter Tour guests.* She straightened up, looked around. It really was a beautiful garden with its abundant greenery and wrought-iron touches. Funny how it had seemed so sinister a moment ago.

Theodosia walked to the far table—the table where Hughes Barron had been found slumped over his teacup. She sat down in his chair, looked around.

The table rested snug against an enormous hedge that ran around the outside perimeter of the garden. Could someone have slipped through that hedge? Theodosia reached a hand out to touch the leaves. They were stiff, dark green, packed together densely. But down near the roots there was certainly a crawl space.

She tilted her head back and gazed at the live oak tree overhead. It was an enormous old tree that spread halfway across the garden. Lace curtains of Spanish moss hung from its upper branches. Could someone have sat quietly in the crook of that venerable tree and dropped something in Hughes Barron's tea? Yes, she thought, it was possible. Anything was possible.

10

Timothy Neville loved the Heritage Society with all his being. He possessed an almost religious fervor for the artifacts and buildings they worked to preserve. He displayed uncanny skill when it came to restoration of the society's old documents, doing most of the painstaking conservation work himself. He worked tirelessly to recruit new members.

But, most of all, Timothy Neville reveled in Heritage Society politics. Because politics was in his blood.

Descended from the original Huguenots who fled religious persecution in France during the sixteenth century, his ancestors had been fiery, spirited immigrants who'd settled in the Carolinas. Those hardy pioneers had eagerly embraced the New World and helped establish Charles Town. Fighting off the governance of the English crown, surviving the War Between the States, weathering economic downturns in rice and indigo, they were an independent, self-assured lot. Today they were regarded as the founding fathers of Charleston's aristocracy.

"Miss Browning." Timothy Neville inclined his head and pulled his lips back in a rictus grin that displayed two rows of small, sharp teeth. "Come to plead the case of the young lady?"

Standing in the doorway of Timothy Neville's Heritage Society office, peering into the dim light, amazed by the clutter of art and artifacts that surrounded him, Theodosia was taken aback. How on earth could Timothy Neville have known she wanted to talk with him about Bethany? She was certain Bethany hadn't said anything about the two of them being friends. In fact, Bethany hadn't ever really been formally employed by her.

And this morning Haley had certainly been far too upset and frightened to place any phone calls.

Timothy Neville pointedly ignored her and turned his attention back to the Civil War–era document he was working on. It was badly faded and the antique linen paper seriously degraded. *An intriguing challenge,* he thought to himself.

Instead of answering him immediately, Theodosia took this opportunity to study Timothy Neville. Watching him in the subdued light, his head bent down, Theodosia was struck by what an unusual-looking little man Timothy Neville was. High, rounded forehead, brown skin stretched tightly over prominent cheekbones, a bony nose, and small, sharp jaw.

Why, he was almost simian-looking, thought Theodosia. Timothy Neville was a little monkey of a man.

As if reading her mind, Timothy Neville swiveled his head and stared at her with dark, piercing eyes. Though small and wiry, he always dressed exceedingly well. Today he was turned out in pleated gray wool slacks, starched white shirt, and dove gray jacket.

Theodosia met his gaze unfalteringly. Timothy Neville had been president of the Heritage Society for as long as she had been aware there was a Heritage Society. She figured the man had to be at least seventy-five years old, although some folks put him at eighty. She knew that, besides being a pillar in the Heritage Society, Timothy Neville also played second violin with the Charleston Symphony Orchestra and resided in a spectacular Georgian-style mansion on Archdale Street. He was exceedingly well placed, she reminded herself. It would behoove her to proceed carefully.

He finally chose to answer his own question. "Of course that's why you're here," he said with a sly grin. And then, as though reading her mind, added, "Last week Drayton mentioned that the girl was living with one of your employees. In the little cottage across the alley from you, I believe."

"That's right," said Theodosia. Perhaps this was going to be easier than she'd initially thought. Neville was being polite, if not a trifle obtuse. And Drayton was, after all, on the board of the Heritage Society. She herself had once been invited to join. Maybe this misunderstanding could be easily straightened out. Maybe the Heritage Society had just panicked, made a mistake.

"Nothing I can do," said Timothy as he bent over his document again.

"I beg your pardon?" said Theodosia. The temperature in the room suddenly seemed to drop ten degrees. "I realize Bethany was . . . is . . . only an intern with the Heritage Society. But I'm afraid she was let go for the wrong reason. For goodness' sake, she was Hughes Barron's *waitress.* The girl had nothing to do with the man's untimely death."

"I don't give a damn about the girl or the man's death!" Timothy Neville's dark eyes glittered like hard obsidian, and a vein in his temple throbbed. "But as far as untimely goes, I'd say it was *extremely* timely. Opportunistic, in fact." He gave a dry chuckle that sounded like a rattlesnake's warning. "Not unlike the man himself."

Timothy suddenly jumped up from his chair and confronted Theodosia. Although he was four inches shorter than her, he made up for it with white-hot fervor.

"Hughes Barron was a despicable scoundrel with a callous disregard for historical preservation!" he screamed, his brown face suddenly contorting and turning beet red. "The man thought he could come to our city— *our* city, for God's sake—and run roughshod over principles and ideals we hold dear."

"Look, Mr. Neville, Timothy . . ." Theodosia began.

He pointed a finger at her, continuing his tirade. "That evil man had even been planning something for *your* neck of the woods, young lady! That's right!"

Timothy Neville bounced his head violently several times, and Theodosia felt a light spray hit her face. She took a step back.

"Property on your block!" screamed Timothy Neville. "You think you're immune? Think again!"

Theodosia stared with fascination at this little man who was clearly, almost frighteningly, out of control. She wondered if such a neurotic, brittle man could get so overwrought concerning historical buildings, could he also commit murder?

11

Wonderful smells emanated from the kitchen, a sure sign that Haley had regained her balance and slipped back into her usual routine.

"It's me," called Theodosia as she let herself into her office and pulled the back door closed behind her.

Haley popped her head around the doorway like a little gopher. "Successful meeting?" Her face glowed from the heat of the kitchen, and her mood seemed considerably improved. Theodosia thought she looked 200 percent better than she had a few hours ago.

"I'd say so."

Now Drayton appeared. "You saw Timothy," he said eagerly.

"Yes."

"Were you able to reason with him?" he asked.

Still vivid in Theodosia's mind was the sight of Timothy Neville in the throes of a hissy fit. "Not exactly," she replied.

"So you *didn't* get Bethany's job back?" asked Haley.

"No," said Theodosia. "Not yet."

Haley's smile sagged.

"I don't understand," said Drayton. "You said it was a success."

"It was, in a way. Timothy was kind enough to reveal his true character."

Drayton and Haley stared at each other. They were uncertain as to what exactly Theodosia meant by this. And Theodosia, seeing their disappointment, had no intention of giving them a blow-by-blow description of Timothy Neville's incredibly obnoxious behavior.

"Drayton, Haley," said Theodosia. "I need to make a phone call. Trust me; this isn't over. In fact, we've only just scratched the surface."

"Now, what do you suppose she meant by all that?" Haley asked Drayton as they went out into the tea room, shaking their heads.

Flipping through her hefty Rolodex, Theodosia found the number she wanted. *Step one,* she thought to herself. *Sure hope he's in.*

"Leyland Hartwell, please. Tell him it's Theodosia Browning."

As Theodosia waited for Leyland Hartwell to come on the line, her eyes searched out the pale mauve walls of her little office. Along with framed tea labels and opera programs, Theodosia had hung dozens of family photos. Her eyes fell on one now. A black-and-white photo of her dad on his sailboat. Looking suntanned, windblown, relaxed. He'd been a member of the Charleston Yacht Club and had once sailed with a crew of three others in the 771-mile Charleston-to-Bermuda Race. He had been an expert sailor, and she had loved sailing with him. Handling the tiller, throwing out the spinnaker, thrilling to the exhilarating rush of sea foam when they heeled over in the wind.

"Theodosia!" Leyland Hartwell's voice boomed in her ear. "What a pleasant surprise. Do you still have that Heinz fifty-seven dog?"

"The Dalbrador," she said.

"That's the one. Ha, ha. Very clever. What can I do for you, my dear?"

"I'm after some information, Leyland. Your firm still handles a considerable amount of real estate business, am I correct?"

"Yes, indeed. Mortgages, title examinations, deeds, foreclosures and cancellations, zoning, leases. You name it, we've got our fingers in the thick of things."

"I'm trying to gather information on a real estate developer by the name of Hughes Barron. Do you know him?"

"Heard of him," said Leyland Hartwell. There was a pause. "We're talking about the fellow who just died, right?"

"Right," said Theodosia. *And please don't ask too much more,* she silently prayed.

"Lots of rumors flying on that one," said Leyland Hartwell. "I was at Coosaw Creek yesterday afternoon playing a round with Tommy Beaumont. He told me Barron died of a heart attack. Then later on a fellow at the bar said he heard a rumor that Barron had been poisoned. Arsenic or something like it."

"I really wanted to know about his business dealings," said Theodosia.

Theodosia heard a rustle of paper, and then Leyland Hartwell spoke to her again.

"Business deals. Gotcha. Is this time-sensitive?"

"I'm afraid so."

"No problem. I'll put one of my people on it and light a fire. We'll find out what we can. Say, do you still sell that lemon mint tea with the real lemon verbena?"

"We certainly do."

"Mrs. Hartwell surely does love that stuff on ice. Awfully refreshing."

Theodosia smiled. Leyland Hartwell was devoted to his wife and always referred to her as Mrs. Hartwell. "Good, I'll send some over for her."

"Aren't you a love. One of my fellows will be back to you soon. Hopefully first thing tomorrow."

12

Click, click, click. Earl Grey took long, easy strides as his toenails hit the blue vinyl runner that ran down the center hallway of the O'Doud Senior Home. Head erect, ears pitched forward, he was spiffily outfitted in his blue nylon vest emblazoned with his therapy dog patch.

"Hello there, Earl." Suzette, one of the regular night nurses who had worked there a good fifteen years, greeted him with a big smile as he passed by. As an afterthought, Suzette also acknowledged Theodosia. "Hello, ma'am," she said.

Earl Grey and Theodosia were both officially on duty, but Theodosia had long since gotten used to playing second fiddle. Once they set foot in the door, it was strictly Earl Grey's show. And everyone, from head nurse to janitor, tended to greet Earl Grey first. It was as though *he* was the one who'd driven over for a visit and allowed Theodosia to tag along.

That was just fine with Theodosia. In fact, downplaying her role was the whole idea behind therapy dog work. You wanted the dog to approach residents first, in the hallways or recreation room, or even in a resident's private room. Let the residents themselves decide their level of interaction.

Sometimes, if a person was lying in bed, sick or infirm, they'd just smile at Earl Grey. Often he'd have a calming influence on them, or he'd be able to cheer them with his quiet presence. It was at times like those that Theodosia thought they might be remembering some lovable dog they'd once enjoyed as a pet. Earl Grey, uncanny canine that he was, seemed to understand just when a resident had gained that certain comfort level with him. When he thought the time was right, he'd rest his muzzle on the edge of their bed and give them a gentle kiss.

One elderly man who was blind and confined to a wheelchair, severely limited in his activities, enjoyed tossing a tennis ball for Earl Grey. Earl Grey would bump and bounce his way down the hallway, painting an audio picture for the man, then bring the tennis ball back to him and snuggle affectionately in the man's lap.

Then there was the foursome of fairly active women who never failed to have a plate of treats for Earl Grey. They either coaxed relatives into bringing dog biscuits in for them, or they baked "liver brownie cake," a strange concoction of beef liver and oatmeal. Theodosia thought the liver brownie cake *looked* a great deal like liver pâté but tasted like sawdust. Earl Grey, on the other hand, found it a gourmet delight.

These experiences were all enormously rewarding for Theodosia, and sometimes, driving home at night, her eyes would fill with tears as she remembered a certain incident that had touched her heart. She'd have to pull the car over to the side of the road, search for her hanky, and tell Earl Grey, once again, what a truly magnificent fellow he was.

13

Leyland Hartwell *was* as good as his word. The next morning, the phone rang bright and early.

"Miss Browning?"

"Yes?" answered Theodosia.

"Jory Davis here. I'm an associate with Ligget, Hume, Hartwell. Leyland Hartwell wanted me to call you concerning information we gathered for you. He also wanted me to assure you he would've phoned personally, but he was called into an emergency meeting." There was a slight pause. "Miss Browning?"

"Yes, Mr. Davis. Please go on."

"Anyway, that is why I am the bearer of this information."

"It was kind of you to help out on this matter."

"My pleasure." Jory Davis cleared his throat. "Hughes Barron, the *late* Hughes Barron, was a real estate developer of the worst kind. Realize, now, this is me editorializing."

Theodosia had been hunkered down in her office like a hermit crab, pondering what to do next about Bethany, about business, and now this pleasant man with the rich, deep voice was able to coax a smile out of her. She had seen the name Jory Davis mentioned several times in the business section of the newspaper and in the Charleston Yacht Club's newsletter but had never met him. Now, however, she was intrigued.

Jory Davis continued as though he were giving a final summation before a jury. "Barron's track record in California includes not paying contractors, defaulting on mortgages, and fraudulent activity regarding low-interest loans for senior housing that was never built. Obviously, there are more than a few people and government agencies in California who are . . . were . . . pursuing Hughes Barron."

Theodosia's silver pen bobbed as she jotted down notes.

"We also did a search of local city and county records and found that Hughes Barron has a silent partner, a Mr. Lleveret Dante. Not surprisingly, this Mr. Dante is currently under indictment by the state of Kentucky for a mortgage-flipping scam and, apparently, had Hughes Barron serving as front man for the pair here in Charleston. Their corporate name is Goose Creek Holdings, a nod to the area north of here where Mr. Barron grew up. Corporate offices for Goose Creek Holdings are located at 415 Harper Street. Stop me if you already know any or all of this, Miss Browning," said Jory Davis rather breathlessly.

Theodosia was impressed. Jory Davis had seemingly thrown himself headlong into researching Hughes Barron for her.

"This is enormously enlightening," said Theodosia. "And highly entertaining," she added.

"Good," said Jory Davis. "Now that I know I have such an appreciative audience, I'll continue. Goose Creek's first real estate project was a time-share condominium on nearby Johns Island known as Edgewater Estates. Edgewater Estates still has a lawsuit pending by the Shorebird Environmentalist Group, but their lawyers have been stalling on it. Early on, this Shorebird Group succeeded in obtaining a court order to stop the development but then lost when it was overturned by a higher court. Goose Creek Holdings also owns undeveloped land in West Ashley and Berkeley County. But it's just raw property, no condos or strip malls yet." There was a rustle of papers. "That's pretty much a quick overview on Hughes Barron, the Cliffs Notes version, anyway. I have a sheaf of papers that includes a little more in-depth information. On the lawsuits as well as the condos and property holdings. I'm sure you'll want to take a look at it."

"Mr. Davis," said Theodosia, "your fact-finding has been extremely helpful. I can't thank you enough."

"Please, call me Jory. Miss Browning, I understand your father used to be a senior partner at our firm."

"Yes, he and Leyland started the practice back in the midseventies."

"You're family, then, aren't you?"

Theodosia couldn't help but smile. "What a kind way to put it."

"Miss Browning, like I said, I've got some background information for you. I can drop these papers in the mail for you, or perhaps we could meet for a cup of coffee?"

"I own a tea shop."

Jory Davis never missed a beat. "Cup of tea. Better yet."

Theodosia chuckled. She liked this hotshot attorney who had started out so curiously formal and then veered toward not quite hitting on her, but darn close to it.

"The Indigo Tea Shop," said Theodosia. "On Church Street. Drop by anytime."

14

Located southwest of Charleston, Johns Island is a big boomerang-shaped piece of land. It is only technically an island in that it is surrounded by waters that include the Stono River, Intracoastal Waterway, Kiawah River, and Bohicket Creek. For many years, Johns Island was a sleepy, rural backwater. Farms dotted the landscape, and a few charming villages served as small bedroom communities for Charleston.

But all that began to change a few years before, as home prices in Charleston escalated, the economy boomed, and the entire Charleston area began to strain its boundaries.

Real estate developers eyed the still-affordable rolling farms of Johns Island as prime targets for development and began to snatch up properties. Longtime Johns Island residents suddenly saw their rural utopia and relaxed way of life about to be threatened. Tensions ran high.

In stepped Hughes Barron, thought Theodosia, as she maneuvered her Jeep Cherokee through light midmorning traffic on the Maybank Highway. Jory Davis's call this morning had made her, as they say, curiouser and curiouser. So she had jumped into her Jeep, rolled back the canvas cover, and was now enjoying the exhilaration of an open-air ride.

She knew Hughes Barron had been one of the first developers to pounce on property out there. It wasn't exactly prime oceanfront, but the Atlantic Ocean did flow in between Kiawah and James Islands and create some wonderful tidal rivers and marshes.

Exiting Maybank, Theodosia followed Rivertree Road for a good five miles, then hung a right on Old Camp Road. Those were the directions she'd gotten earlier when she'd phoned the sales office at Hughes Barron's so-called Edgewater Estates. But right now she was seeing only pastoral vistas and farmland. Just when she thought she must have gotten off course and was prepared to turn around, an enormous, colorful billboard rose up out of a field of waving, yellow tobacco.

Edgewater Estates, the sign proclaimed in painted pinks and greens. Time-Share Condominiums. Own A Piece Of History. Deluxe 1, 2, and 3 Bedrooms. Developed By Goose Creek Holdings.

Theodosia wondered just what piece of history it was that came part and parcel with your Edgewater Estates time-share condo. What had the greedy developer, Hughes Barron, been referring to?

The archaeological remains of the Cusabo Indians who had lived here four hundred years ago?

The barely visible ruins of an old Civil War fort? Constructed of crushed lime and oyster shells, an amalgam known as tabby, the old fort had begun to crumble even before the turn of the last century.

How about the nine hundred acres set aside by the Marine Resources Department?

No matter, she told herself. She wasn't here today to do a consumer confidence check on Goose Creek Holdings. She was here because, armed with information Jory Davis had provided, her curiosity was running at a fever pitch. Everything she'd heard about Hughes Barron told her the man was definitely not Mr. Popularity. He had to have made enemies. Lots of them. When land was at stake, or multimillion-dollar real estate deals, that's when people got very, very serious. And sometimes very, very nasty.

Swinging into the entrance of Edgewater Estates, a circular, white-crushed-rock drive that wound around a five-tiered fountain, Theodosia hated the place on sight. The building wasn't just the antithesis of Johns Island. Rather, it looked more like a retirement village in south Florida.

Edgewater Estates Time Share Condominiums was big, sprawling, and gaudy. Stone cherubs and doves flanked the building's main entrance, while the building itself was painted what could only be described as tropical green. Accents of white shutters and false balustrades completed the garish touches.

It's like a bad leisure suit, thought Theodosia as she slid her Jeep into the slot marked Visitor Parking. *Overly casual combined with bad design. Always a disastrous marriage.*

Hughes Barron or, more likely, his architect, had borrowed drips and drops from Charleston architecture. Unfortunately, they seemed to have thrown out what was true and good and classic and reconstituted it into something overblown and commercial.

My God, Theodosia thought to herself, *it's a good thing I didn't have to create sales materials for this real estate project! Granted, I had my fair share of turkey accounts at the ad agency. Some awful children's toys that were supposed to be educational but weren't. A shopping mall. A line of instant soup mixes that never thickened and had a chalky undertaste. But never, never anything this bad.*

"Good morning. Welcome to Edgewater Estates." A perky young woman, probably no older than twenty-six, in a bright yellow suit smiled at Theodosia from the other side of a white marble counter. "This is our sales office, such as it is." The girl spread her arms in a theatrical gesture. "We're already sixty percent sold, so the office we *were* using is now the recreation room. But you are *so* in luck. We also have several resales that have just come available, and some of them have ocean views." The young girl halted her pitch, appraised Theodosia quickly, then added, "You *are* looking for a time-share condo, aren't you?"

"Absolutely," declared Theodosia. "And I've heard wonderful things about Edgewater Estates."

The girl beamed. "We like to think we're the premier time-share property on Johns Island."

Theodosia wanted to tell the girl they were the *only* time-share property right now. And if the island's residents woke up and learned their lesson, they'd probably remain the only one. But she held her tongue. Better to play it cool, gather as much information as possible. You never knew when something interesting would pop up in conversation.

The real estate agent stuck out her hand. "I'm Melissa Chapman, sales associate."

Theodosia shook the girl's hand and smiled convincingly. "Theodosia Browning, prospective buyer." Theodosia fingered one of the oversized glossy catalogs that lay on the counter between them. "These are your sales brochures?"

"Oh, yes, help yourself." Melissa thrust one of the colorful brochures into Theodosia's hands. "There are four different floor plans available. Do you know what you're looking for?"

"Probably a two bedroom," said Theodosia.

"Our most requested model," enthused the girl. "And what about time of year? Obviously, summer is wildly popular and carries a premium charge. We only have a few blocks of time left. Late August, I believe. But what many people don't realize is that right now, October, November, is absolutely perfect out here. And the price is a good seventy percent below a summer slot." Melissa widened her eyes in mock surprise. "Interested?"

"Very," said Theodosia. "Can I take a look at some of the units?"

"I'll get my keys." Melissa smiled.

15

Tacky, tacky, tacky. Theodosia chanted her mantra as she gunned the Jeep's engine and zipped across a narrow wooden bridge. Loose boards clattered in her wake, and gravel flew as she hit the dirt road on the other side.

To her point of view, the condos had been awful. First off, they'd all had that new-apartment smell. Whatever it was, paint, carpet, adhesive, Sheetrock, every unit she'd looked at had caused her nose to tickle and twitch. On top of that, the condos felt stifling and claustrophobic. And it wasn't just their size, she told herself. Her apartment above the tea shop was small, but it was *cozy* small. Not *cramped* small. Why, the two-bedroom unit Melissa had been so proud of hadn't really been two bedrooms at all. The so-called second bedroom had been an alcove off one end of the living room with cheap vinyl accordion doors that pulled across!

Raised as she had been in homes with stone foundations and heavy wood construction that had withstood wars as well as countless hurricanes, Theodosia was exceedingly leery of these new slap-dab structures. What would happen when a September hurricane boiled up in the mid-Atlantic and came bearing down on Edgewater Estates with gale-force winds? It would go flying, that's what, *Wizard of Oz* style. And the pieces probably wouldn't land in Kansas.

She gritted her teeth, making a face. *Shabby. Truly shabby.* Oh, well, this visit had certainly given her insight into the kind of developer Hughes Barron had been. The kind of developer his partner Lleveret Dante was. The worst kind, just as Jory Davis had warned.

Cruising past a little beachfront café with a sign that read Crab

Shack, Theodosia suddenly had a distant memory of her and her dad exploring the patchwork of waterways out here, of pulling their boat up on a sand dune and sitting at one of the picnic tables to eat boiled crab and French fries. The memory flowed over her so vividly, it brought tears to her eyes.

She slowed the car, blinked at the passing scenery, and slammed on the brakes.

Five hundred yards down from the Crab Shack was a small, white-washed building with a blue and white sign that carried the image of a long-legged bird. The sign said Shorebird Environmentalist Group.

Shorebird Environmentalist Group.

She scanned her memory. Wasn't that the group that had sued Edgewater Estates? Sure it was. Jory Davis had told her about the environmentalists losing their case in court. And Drayton had confided earlier that they'd mustered nearby residents and picketed the Edgewater Estates while it was under construction. Probably their outrage still hadn't abated. Well, that was good for her. It gave her one more source to draw upon.

Tanner Joseph glanced up from his iMac computer and the new climate modeling program he was trying to teach himself and gazed at the woman who'd just stepped through his door. Lovely, was his first impression. Perhaps a few years older than he was, but really lovely. Great hair plus a real presence about her. Was she old money, perhaps?

Growing up in a steel mill town in Pennsylvania, Tanner Joseph was always painfully aware of class distinction. Even though he'd graduated from the University of Minnesota with a master's degree in ecology, most of the time he still felt like the kid from the wrong side of the tracks.

"Good afternoon," he greeted Theodosia.

Theodosia surveyed the little office. Three desks, one occupied. But all outfitted with state-of-the-art computers and mounded with reams of paper. A folding table set against the wall seemed to be the repository for the Shorebird Environmentalist Group's brochures, literature, and posters. Surprisingly well-done paintings hung on the walls, depicting grasses, birds, and local wildlife, executed in a fanciful, contemporary style, almost like updated Chinese brushstrokes.

To Theodosia, the organization appeared viable but understaffed.

Probably just a director and a couple assistants and, hopefully, a loyal core of volunteers.

She walked over to the desk where the young man who'd greeted her was sitting and stared down at him. He was good-looking. Blond hair, tan, white Chiclet teeth. Haley would have thought him "hunky."

"I'm interested in finding out about the Shorebird Environmentalist Group," she said.

Tanner Joseph clambered to his feet. It wasn't every day a classy-looking lady came knocking at his door. And classy-looking ladies, more often than not, had access to the kind of funding that could help bootstrap a struggling, little nonprofit organization like his.

"Tanner Joseph." He stuck out his hand. "Executive director."

"Theodosia Browning." She shook hands with him. "Nice to meet you."

"First let me give you one of our brochures." Tanner Joseph handed her a small, three-fold brochure printed on recycled paper.

Theodosia flipped it open and studied it. The brochure was well-written and beautifully illustrated. The same artist who had done the paintings on the wall had also illustrated the brochure. Short subheads and bulleted copy documented four different projects the Shorebird Environmentalist Group was currently involved in. The information was interesting, punchy, and easy to digest.

"Listen," Tanner Joseph said. The whites of his eyes were a distinct contrast to his deep suntan. His hands fidgeted with the front of his faded green T-shirt that proclaimed Save the Sea Turtles. "I was about to step out for a bite to eat. At the Crab Shack just down the road. If you'd like a lemonade or something and don't mind watching me eat, I could fill you in there."

"Perfect," exclaimed Theodosia.

16

Turns out, the Crab Shack *was* the exact same place where she and her dad had eaten, a quaint little roadside shack where you studied the hand-painted menu on the side of the building, then went to the window and ordered your food. All dining was outdoors, at sun-bleached wooden picnic tables with faded blue umbrellas. Because of her fond memory and the fact that it was almost noon, Theodosia ended up ordering crab cakes and a side of cole slaw. She and Tanner Joseph sat on wobbly wooden benches, enjoying the sun, salty breezes, and surprisingly tasty food.

Throughout lunch, Tanner spoke convincingly about the mission of the Shorebird Environmentalist Group, how they were dedicated to the preservation of coastlines and natural marshes, as well as nesting grounds and marine sanctuaries. He also filled her in on his credentials, his degree in ecology and his graduate work in the dynamics of ecosystem response.

"What does one actually *do* with a degree in ecology?" asked Theodosia out of curiosity. "What avenues are open?"

Tanner Joseph shrugged. "Today, you can go any number of ways. Work for the Forest Service, the EPA, or Department of Natural Resources. Go private with literally thousands of corporations to choose from, including groups like the Nature Conservancy or Wilderness Society. Or"—he spread his arms wide and grinned—"you can work for a struggling little nonprofit organization. Try to drum up public interest, writing brochures, illustrating them—"

"Those are your drawings?" Theodosia interrupted.

"One of my many talents." Tanner Joseph smiled. "And duties. Along with writing dozens of grant requests to various foundations in hopes of getting a thousand dollars here, two thousand dollars there. That is, if I'm lucky enough to touch a responsive chord with a sympathetic foundation director."

"Sounds tough," said Theodosia.

"It is." Tanner Joseph popped a French fry in his mouth. "But I wouldn't trade it for the world. After grad school, I spent a year in the Amazon studying land surface–atmosphere interaction. It was amazing how just building a one-lane dirt road through an area of jungle severely impacted the ecosystem. I was able to observe all the effects firsthand. I understand now how important it is for a community to plan and manage growth. It's okay to think big, but it's generally more prudent to take small steps."

"What about the newly expanded road out here? It makes the commute a lot easier to Johns Island from Charleston proper."

"Sure it does. But it's also probably a mistake," said Tanner Joseph, "although no one thought so at the time of construction. But think about it. There are hundreds of acres of saltwater marshes out here and almost a dozen species of wildlife on the yellow list, the nearing endangered list."

"And the Edgewater Estates?" asked Theodosia.

Tanner Joseph grimaced, set his crab salad sandwich down, and gazed intently at Theodosia. "You just touched a raw nerve. Our group was opposed to that development from the outset. Everything about it was fraudulent. The developers lied to the eighty-two-year-old farmer who sold them the land. And the shark lawyers who represented Goose Creek Holdings pressured the local town council for some fast zoning changes. We think they had two council members in their pocket."

"You fought a good fight," said Theodosia. "Got lots of press from what I hear."

Tanner Joseph snorted angrily. "Not good enough. We lost, and the damn thing got built. Right on twenty-five acres of prime snowy egret nesting ground." He shook his head with disgust. "To make matters worse, the place is a monstrosity." He peered at Theodosia sharply. "Have you seen it?"

Theodosia nodded.

Tanner Joseph picked up his sandwich again, held it in both hands like an offering. "Do you believe in karma, Miss Browning?"

Theodosia brushed back a ringlet of hair and smiled. "Some things do seem to have a way of coming full circle."

"Well," he said, staring at her intently, "Edgewater Estates turned out to generate some very *bad* karma for one of its developers. The so-called money man, Hughes Barron, died three days ago." The statement hung in the air as Tanner Joseph narrowed his eyes and smiled a tight, bitter smile. "It looks as though cosmic justice may have been at work, after all."

❧ 17 ❧

Delaine Dish was sitting at a quiet table in the corner when Theodosia returned to the tea shop. The owner of Cotton Duck Clothing, Delaine had arrived at the Indigo Tea Shop earlier, insisting to Haley and Drayton that she simply *had* to speak with Theodosia. Told that Theodosia would probably be back shortly, Delaine sat pensively, sipping a cup of tea, waving Haley off every time she advanced with a muffin or cookies.

"She's been here almost forty minutes," whispered Drayton as Theodosia brushed past him. "Didn't say what she wanted, just that she wants to talk to you."

"Delaine." Theodosia slid into the chair across the table from her shopkeeper neighbor. "What's wrong?"

Delaine Dish's heart-shaped face was set in a look of serious repose. Raven hair that normally fell almost to her waist was plaited into a single, loose braid, making her face seem all the more intense. Her violet Liz Taylor eyes flashed.

"Do you know what's being said out there on the street?" she began.

No, thought Theodosia, *but I'll bet you do.* "What's that, Delaine?" she said.

"There are rumors flying, literally *flying,* about what happened the night of the Lamplighter Tour."

"I am aware of some talk, Delaine. But I'm sure they are petty words spoken by a very few."

"Dear, dear Theo." Delaine reached across the table and grasped Theodosia's hand. "Always giving people the benefit of the doubt. Always such a positive outlook. Sometimes I think you should be put up for canonization."

"I'm no saint, Delaine. Believe me, if someone offends me or hurts someone close to me, I'll fire back. Have no fear."

Delaine's fingernails only dug deeper into Theodosia's hand. "Didn't I warn you?" she spat. "Didn't I tell you Hughes Barron was up to no good?"

"As I recall, you told me he put in an offer on the Peregrine Building next door."

"Yes. Hughes Barron and his partner, Lleveret Dante."

Theodosia stared at Delaine. She was obviously upset over something. Maybe if she gave Delaine some space, she'd spit out whatever was bothering her.

"Cordette Jordan stopped by the Cotton Duck this morning. You know, Cordette owns Griffon Antiques over on King Street?"

"Okay," said Theodosia.

"And, of course, we started chatting. Hughes Barron's mysterious death *is* a fairly hot topic of conversation right now. I mean, how many people just fall over dead in a beautiful garden while sipping tea?"

"You don't really believe he died from sipping tea, do you?" said Theodosia.

"No, of course not. And I didn't mean to imply it was *your* tea, Theodosia. It's just that . . . Oh, Theo . . . A lot of people are curious. I mean, the police are playing it very close to the vest and haven't released any information about cause of death. And the man *was* fairly dastardly in his business dealings. Who *knows* what really happened!" Delaine pulled a linen hanky from the pocket of her perfect beige smock dress and touched it to her cheek.

"What was it you and Cordette were chatting about?" asked Theodosia, trying to gain some forward momentum in the conversation.

"Oh, that," said Delaine. She swiveled her head and scanned the tea room. When she was satisfied that the few patrons who were sitting there sipping tea and munching scones were probably tourists and completely uninvolved, she leaned toward Theodosia. "This is very interesting. Cordette told me that Hughes Barron and Lleveret Dante have their office in her building. One floor above her antique shop."

"Really," said Theodosia.

"It gets better. Cordette also told me she overhead the two men in the throes of a terrible argument last week. It was when she went up to use the ladies' room. The ladies' room is on the second floor, so Cordette would have been on the same floor as their offices. Anyway, and these are Cordette's exact words: She said the two men were having a *knock-down, drag-out fight.*"

As Delaine talked, Theodosia scanned her memory. King Street was definitely *not* the address Jory Davis had given her for Goose Creek Holdings. She was sure of that. So what had Cordette really heard, if anything? Had the two men really been there that day, locked in some kind of argument? Or had Delaine heard pieces of this, fragments of that, and put it all together in one big, juicy story as she was wont to do?

"Delaine." Theodosia pried Delaine's tiny but firm paw off her own. Embroiled as she was in Hughes Barron's death, she decided to give Delaine the benefit of the doubt. "Did Cordette say what Hughes Barron and Lleveret Dante were arguing about?"

Delaine studied her ring intently, trying to recall. It was a giant, pearly moonstone that Theodosia had often admired, and now Delaine twisted it absently.

"Something about buying or selling and one of them wanting to renege or rescind," said Delaine. "Or maybe it was revenge," she added.

Not terribly enlightening, thought Theodosia. Even if Cordette Jordan's story about the loud argument *was* true, the two men could have been fighting about anything. Money, property, their long distance phone bill.

Theodosia patted Delaine's hand. "You're a dear to try to help. Thank you."

Delaine blinked back tears. "You mean the world to me, Theodosia. I mean it. When my Calvin passed on, you were the only one who really understood."

Calvin had been Delaine's fourteen-year-old calico cat. When he died last spring, Theodosia had sent a note expressing her condolences. It was what she would have done for anyone who was sad or emotionally distraught.

After Delaine had departed, Theodosia fixed herself a small pot of dragon's well tea. Technically a Chinese green tea, dragon's well yields a pale gold liquor that has a reputation for being both refreshing and stimulating. Because of the tea's natural sweetness and full-bodied flavor, milk, sugar, or even lemon is rarely taken with it.

"We need to talk about the holiday blends."

Theodosia looked up to find Drayton staring intently down at her.

"Absolutely," she replied. "Now?"

"Only if you're not too distracted," said Drayton. "I know a lot of things are weighing heavily on your shoulders right now. And haven't Haley and I helped enormously by putting added pressure on you to try to salvage Bethany's job at the Heritage Society?" Drayton rolled his eyes in a self-deprecating manner.

"Drayton, nothing would make me happier than to focus on what I love best. Which is the Indigo Tea Shop and the wonderful teas you continue to blend for us."

An enormous grin split Drayton's face as he plopped down next to Theodosia. He balanced his glasses on the tip of his nose, flipped open a leather binder, and wiggled his eyebrows expectantly.

Theodosia rejoiced inwardly at this show of unbridled enthusiasm. Drayton was in his element. Blending tea was his passion, and every autumn, Drayton blended three or four special teas in honor of the upcoming holidays.

"You realize we're starting late," said Drayton.

"I know. Somehow, with our initial work on the Web site and taking part in the Lamplighter Tour, things fell through the cracks. But if we need to jump-start things," said Theodosia, "we could repackage the Lamplighter Blend."

Drayton managed a pained expression. "We'd have to. It hasn't exactly been a top seller since . . ." His voice trailed off. "Let me put it this way. Even when we had a display of the Lamplighter Blend, nobody bought any. People seemed to view it more as a curiosity. Except for one woman who came in and bought a pound." Drayton paused dramatically. "She said she was thinking about killing her husband."

"Goodness!" exclaimed Theodosia unhappily. "Delaine might be right after all. Rumors are flying!"

Drayton nodded sagely. "They certainly are."

"Tell you what," said Theodosia. "Let's just start from scratch as usual. You've obviously put a lot of thought into the holiday blends, and I'm dying to hear your ideas."

Drayton picked up his notebook. "This year," he began, "I suggest we use an Indian black tea as our base. I'd recommend Kahlmuri Estates. It's well-balanced and rich but highly complementary to added flavors."

At the top of one of the pages in his notebook, Drayton had written Kahlmuri Estates black tea.

"I like it." Theodosia nodded.

"Okay," said Drayton, pleased. "Now for the tricky part. I've come up with four suggested holiday blends."

Theodosia inclined her head toward Drayton's notebook, following along as he read aloud his notations. For the moment, all thoughts of the disastrous events at the Lamplighter Tour were pushed from her head.

"Apple," said Drayton, tapping his notebook. "Apple pies, cider, and dried potpourris are a holiday staple, so let's add it to our black tea as well. The aroma will impart a sweet, crisp fragrance and make a delightful beverage for holiday parties. More sophisticated than apple cider, but still warming and flavorful."

"Have you got a name for it?" asked Theodosia.

"That's your province, isn't it?" Drayton grinned. "Or have you left your advertising and marketing days behind?"

"I don't think you ever stray far from that," said Theodosia. "Seems like most decisions made in business these days are marketing-related."

"Including naming these teas and creating labels." Drayton smiled slyly.

"You come up with the blends, and I'll take care of the rest."

"Deal," said Drayton. "Okay, then. Next holiday blend, black currant. This should be a big, fruity berry flavor. Great for afternoon holiday teas, pleasing with desserts."

Theodosia smiled. Dear Drayton. He had thrown himself headlong into this project and, like everything he attempted in the realm of tea, wine, or the culinary arts, it would be a rousing success.

"Next," said Drayton, "I want to do an Indian spice. Overtones of cardamom with various spices to be determined. We'll aim for a slightly heady, intoxicating fragrance."

"Sounds heavenly," said Theodosia.

"For my final tea, I pulled out all the stops. A cranberry blend. Heavy on the cranberry with an accent of dried oranges and a nip of orange flavoring. Tangy, tart, perfect for the crisp days ahead. Very complementary with holiday dinners."

"You were thinking of getting your dried cranberries from the Belvedere Plantation in the low-country?" asked Theodosia.

Drayton tapped his black Mont Blanc pen against the page. "They're the best."

Theodosia retired to her office where she brainstormed on names for Drayton's tea blends for the rest of the afternoon. By the time long shadows dappled her windows and Earl Grey rose from his rug and stretched, ready for his late afternoon walk, she had devised quite a few names.

Drawing upon her advertising background, she had come up with a list she thought might intrigue holiday shoppers. For the apple tea blend she liked the name Applejack. It was casual and fun. She had pondered the name Black Magic for the black currant tea, but finally settled on Au Currant. It sounded punchier and a little more elegant.

On the Indian spice blend, Theodosia decided to be straightforward and name it exactly that, Indian Spice. She knew from past experience that a good, descriptive name would usually outshine an overly clever one.

And for the cranberry orange tea, she went with Cooper River

Cranberry, a tribute to the nearby Cooper River that contributed to the vast, wet cranberry bogs.

Pleased with her efforts, Theodosia's thoughts turned toward the visual elements: packaging and labels. Because these were holiday teas, she decided to purchase gold-colored tea tins. They were festive looking and easily obtained from several manufacturers.

That left the labels. She would have to devise colorful labels for each of Drayton's blends.

Her first thought was to call Todd & Lambeau, the group that was working on the graphics for her Web site. They were good commercial designers, but somehow their brand of design felt a little too slick. Wouldn't it be nicer to convey a more intimate, boutique feel for these holiday tea blends?

She had a friend, Julia, who was a highly skilled calligrapher. Julia did posters for the Charleston Museum, the symphony, wedding invitations, all manner of other things. Julia's calligraphy might be well suited for this project. But, she still needed a talented illustrator to convey the essence of the holiday teas on a label.

Then she remembered the paintings she'd seen that morning at the Shorebird headquarters. The free-spirited, slightly whimsical illustrations Tanner Joseph had created also somehow embodied an Eastern spirit. Would that style work for her tea labels? The thought intrigued her and began to grow on her.

Most tea labels were what Drayton called "flowers and bowers." They were fussy and floral. But Tanner Joseph's drawings had an elegance to them. The style was slightly Asian, which would be perfect. And, if her memory served her correctly, Tanner Joseph also did lovely brushstroke calligraphy!

The notion excited Theodosia, and she vowed to call Tanner Joseph first thing the next day. She hoped he'd take on the project. Even though the tea shop didn't have a huge budget for graphics, Tanner Joseph might view this commercial assignment as a welcome windfall.

The light flickered on and off above her head.

"Time to lock up," called Haley. She stood in the doorway, a book bag slung over one shoulder. "You've been hard at it all afternoon. Did you get lots done? Drayton said you were working on the holiday teas."

Theodosia stretched both arms over her head and groaned. "I think so. You're off to class?"

"Literature in contemporary society. Tonight we're studying Cormac McCarthy."

But still Haley stood there, quietly looking at Theodosia.

"What?" said Theodosia. She knew something was brewing behind the girl's furrowed brow. She beckoned to Haley. "Come."

Haley stepped closer to Theodosia's desk. "It's Bethany," she said, her face flushed pink with embarrassment. "Without her job, with nothing to do, she's . . ." Haley left her sentence unfinished, dropped her head shyly.

"What if . . ." said Theodosia slowly, "what if Bethany came and helped out for a while? Poor Drayton's going to be awfully busy supervising the blending of the holiday teas. You'll have extra baking to do . . ." Theodosia looked at Haley as though the thought had just occurred to her. "Do you think Bethany would come back and lend a hand in the tea shop again? Of course, you'll have to give her a refresher course in brewing tea. And that old cash register is a bear to use—"

Haley's face broke into a wide grin. "It's not a problem. She can do it, I know she can. But are you sure that . . . ?"

"Am I sure we need help?" Theodosia threw her arms up in mock despair. "Thanksgiving is three weeks away, and Christmas and New Year's will be upon us in no time." She placed her palm on her chest. "I *still* haven't gone out and found those extra sweetgrass baskets. And the Web site . . . Well, the delay on that project is decidedly my fault. I haven't made the necessary decisions on graphics and Web architecture. Yes, Haley. To answer your question, I'm sure, in a matter of days, we'll be swamped!"

18

Theodosia pulled the head off the ceramic Scooby-Doo cookie jar and measured out two cups of dried kibbles for Earl Grey. She poured it into his metal dish, topped it with a tablespoon of olive oil for his coat, and set it down on the yellow rug next to his water dish.

Earl Grey responded as he always did. He gave Theodosia a look that somehow conveyed his doggy thank-you, then went facedown into his dinner.

Theodosia did not go facedown. Rather, she stood in front of the open refrigerator, pondering supper. An oatmeal and raisin cookie, eaten at four o'clock, had left her relatively satisfied. Still, if she didn't eat now, she'd be hungry later on.

She stuck her head farther inside the refrigerator, investigating. There was some leftover pasta, a couple pieces of cold chicken, fresh hamburger. Nope, nothing tripped her trigger yet. She knew the freezer compartment contained lamb chops and maybe some frozen shrimp that could be quickly steamed and put on top of rice.

No, she thought, that would be fussy, and fussy was the last thing she needed right now. Now that decisions had been made regarding holiday teas, the conversation she'd had with Delaine earlier in the afternoon came back in her mind. Delaine was a dear, gentle soul who had shockingly good taste when it came to merchandising her clothing store, Cotton Duck. But Delaine also thrived on gossip and excitement and didn't always get her facts straight.

Theodosia pulled a small carton of cottage cheese from the

refrigerator shelf. She dumped half of it onto a plate and grabbed a fork from the drawer and two bagel crisps from a glass jar on the counter.

Wandering into her living room, she eased herself down onto the couch, suddenly feeling a wave of relaxation flow over her. It was this apartment that ultimately contributed to her happiness and sense of well-being. Though small, it contained all the essential elements for a proper and genteel Charleston home. Fireplace, cove ceilings, bow windows, tiny balcony, French doors leading to a small but elegant dining room, and a cozy bedroom with a surprisingly ample closet for her many clothes.

She had decorated the place in what had become her own brand of Charleston shabby chic. The philosophy behind shabby chic appealed to her. It held that an item had to be both beautiful and functional. So that was what she strove for. Elegance married with practicality. It was a concept that worked well with the antique furniture and accessories she'd always been so passionate about, and which were easy to come by in Charleston antique shops and flea markets. Charleston was the mother lode when it came to English furniture, vintage fabrics, antique chandeliers, old prints, and silverware.

Aunt Libby had been amazingly generous, too, in helping to furnish her cozy abode, gifting her with a lawyer's bookcase, rocking chair, oriental rug, silver tea service, antique quilt, and some terrific old oil paintings. The paintings were dark, brooding seascapes in wonderfully ornate, gilded frames. Everyone who saw them tried to buy them from her.

Before she'd purchased the Indigo Tea Shop, she had lived in a sleek, modern building. Lots of squared-off angles, floor-to-ceiling windows, black countertops, white walls. Very contemporary, very boring.

This was infinitely better.

Theodosia finished her cottage cheese and offered Earl Grey the last morsel of bagel crisp. He chewed thoughtfully, gazing at her with brown, intelligent eyes.

"Want to go for a ride?" she asked him.

Earl Grey's ears pricked forward, and his tail beat a syncopated rhythm on the pegged floor boards.

King Street, between Beaufain and Queen Streets, is often referred to as Charleston's antiques district. Here antiques aficionados will discover such shops as English Patina, with their fine collection of eighteenth- and nineteenth-century furniture, Perry's Estate Jewelry, and Helen S. Martin Antique Weapons. Down a narrow walkway at 190 King Street is Gates of Charleston, an eclectic little garden shop with wrought-iron planters, statuary, and quirky sundials.

It was 208 King Street that Theodosia was searching for as she cruised the picturesque street with its palm trees, white turreted buildings, and black wrought-iron touches. Since it was early evening, traffic was light, and she was able to drive slowly, scanning the numbers above the tall, narrow doorways as Earl Grey sat serenely in the passenger seat of the Jeep Cherokee.

208 King Street was where Griffon Antiques was located. The Griffon Antiques where Cordette Jordan had supposedly overheard an argument between Hughes Barron and his partner, Lleveret Dante, of Goose Creek Holdings. Of course, Jory Davis had told her that the two partners had their office at 415 Harper Street.

Okay, Theodosia told herself, *in about two minutes we're going to find out exactly who was right.*

She saw the sign for Griffon Antiques even before she could read the street address. A large, ornate, wooden sign with a griffon, that strange mythical eagle-cum-lion, painted in gold and black, hung out over the sidewalk from what appeared to be a four-story building. Theodosia took her foot off the accelerator, let the Jeep glide over to the curb, and studied the shop.

The large front windows were filled with English and French antique furniture. All genuine pieces, no reproductions. A hand-lettered sign hanging in the glass door said Sorry We Missed You, Please Return Tomorrow.

There was no Harper Street nearby. In fact, she wasn't even familiar with Harper Street. To the best of her knowledge, the next street up was Market Street. Sure, that had to be the sign for Market Street just ahead. Without bothering to pull into traffic, Theodosia eased the Jeep along the curb, up to the corner. She gazed up at the street sign.

It read Harper Street!

What?

She checked for traffic, then took the Jeep into a slow right turn. She found Harper Street wasn't really a street at all, just a narrow lane that seemed to lead to a small garden. She could venture in with the Jeep maybe twenty feet, then she'd have to back out.

Well, wasn't this interesting. There really *was* a Harper Street. And the reason it didn't sound at all familiar was because it wasn't really a through street. Harper Street was one of the myriad little lanes that snaked through the historic district and the antiques district, lanes that often didn't have names. Sometimes they were private and therefore not on official city maps. They could have their names changed at the whim of the property owner. These streets had probably been little passages that led to carriage houses at one time. Now they appeared on tourist walking guides that gift shops and B and Bs handed out.

"Sit tight," she told Earl Grey as she hopped out of the Jeep. Rounded cobblestones poked at the soft leather soles of her Todd loafers as she ambled down the little lane toward an arched doorway flanked by a pair of stone lions. She stopped in her tracks and looked up. Over the arched doorway was a sign that read Hayward Professional Building, 415 Harper.

A tingle of excitement ignited within her. So 208 King Street and 415 Harper were one and the same! The city might not be aware of it, but, knowing the tangled bureaucracy that ministered over Charleston, chances were the postal service did. That meant that the offices of Goose Creek Holdings were here, after all. And that maybe, just maybe, Delaine's secondhand story had been correct!

19

There were two Jory Davises listed in the phone book, but one lived over in West Ashley. So Theodosia figured the one she wanted had to be the one on Halsey, near the marina. Anyway, it certainly sounded like an area where the Jory Davis she'd spoken with this morning might reside.

"Hello?"

Same voice, same Jory Davis. Theodosia breathed a quick sigh of relief. "Mr. Davis? Hello, this is Theodosia Browning. Sorry to bother you at home, but you were so helpful this morning, and I have just a quick question for you."

"Uh-huh," said the voice, sounding slightly discombobulated and not at all the calm, efficient, buttoned-up lawyer he'd come across as earlier.

"I know this is out of the blue, but does buying-selling mean anything to you?" Theodosia asked.

There was a loud clunk on the other end of the line.

"Mr. Davis? Are you all right?"

In a moment, Jory Davis was back on the line. "Sorry, I dropped the phone. I'm in the kitchen trying to whip together a vinaigrette. I know it sounds kind of dorky, but I've got this bachelor's group coming to my place tonight. Four of us, all lawyers, who get together once a month for dinner. Kind of a boy's night out. Two of the fellows are divorced, so this is probably the only decent meal they get for a while. Anyway, long story short, tonight's my turn, and I'm hysterical. I was stuck at the office writing a legal brief until almost six-thirty, and now I'm halfway through this recipe and just found out I don't have any prepared English mustard. So, my question to you is this: Can I use plain old yellow mustard? Hot dog mustard?"

"I don't see why not," said Theodosia as she thought to herself, *Bachelor's group. Interesting.*

"And chives. It doesn't look good in the chives department, either. Problem?"

"Maybe you could pinch-hit with a flavored olive oil. That would give your vinaigrette a little extra snap."

"Flavored olive oil," he muttered. "Yeah, I got some of that. Basil, I think. Awright, we're good to go."

Now there was the sound of a wire whisk swooshing against the sides of a glass bowl.

"What did you want to know about a buy-sell?" Jory Davis asked.

Theodosia inhaled sharply.

"Miss Browning?" said Jory. "You still there?"

"That's it!" exclaimed Theodosia. "A buy-sell. It's a kind of agreement, right?"

"A buy-sell agreement, correct," said Jory Davis matter-of-factly.

"Two partners would have this type of agreement?"

"They should. Although many don't plan ahead all that well."

"And one partner might want to *rescind* at some point in time?"

"Sure, it happens. But I still don't see where you're going."

"I didn't either," said Theodosia. "But I think I just arrived there anyway. Mr. Davis, thank you! Good luck with your dinner."

"That's it?" he asked.

"Oh," said Theodosia, "you're still bringing those papers by, right?"

20

"*Keeman,*" *said Haley,* her hand resting on a glass jar filled with small black leaves. "From Anhui province in central China. See the leaves? Tiny but powerful. They yield a brilliant red liquor. Slightly sweet, so you don't need sugar. Gives off a delicious aroma, reminiscent of ripe orchids."

Bethany nodded. She'd shown up bright and early, eager to learn, ready to be put to work. Now she stood behind the counter, hair wound atop her head in a casual knot, small, oval, wire-rim glasses perched on her nose, looking every inch the career-minded young woman.

Haley pointed to another jar. "This one's Dimbulla from Ceylon. Also brews into a bright reddish, amber color. But it doesn't have quite the wake-up punch of the other, so we generally recommend it for midmorning or with afternoon snacks."

"Tea shop 101?" asked Theodosia as she breezed in and smiled at the two girls who looked like elegant butterflies, dressed almost alike in colorful cotton sweaters and long, gauzy, print skirts. She was pleased to see that silver teakettles had been filled with water and were beginning to steam atop their burners, fresh linens and silverware had been laid out, and all the tables sported freshly mounded sugar bowls and pitchers of cream.

Bethany pulled off her glasses and turned to Theodosia with merriment in her eyes. "It's all so fascinating. But complicated, too. And I still can't believe how many varieties of tea there are. Assam, Darjeeling, Earl Grey, Sencha, gunpowder, the list goes on and on. It's amazing! Plus, the tea is literally from every corner of the globe. China, Ceylon, India, Nepal, Japan, even Africa."

"Don't forget Turkey, Indonesia, and Russia. And, of course, our own wonderful South Carolina tea from the Charleston Tea Plantation," added Theodosia. "Their American Classic tea is a luxurious black tea that's descended from the original tea plants brought to America after the Revolutionary War."

"You're right!" exclaimed Bethany. "But I think Chinese teas are my hands-down favorites because of their names. How quirky and creative to name a tea White Peony or Precious Eyebrows. Or even Temple of Heaven!"

"The Chinese have always had a profound and enduring passion for tea," declared Drayton as he arrived and caught the tail end of Bethany's remarks. "Good morning, good morning all." He bowed deeply to Haley and Bethany. "I hope our new apprentice is appropriately memorizing all our precious loose teas. Perhaps we shall plan a pop quiz for this afternoon."

"Don't you dare," Bethany said grinning. She turned toward Theodosia and lowered her voice slightly. "I can't thank you enough for having me here." Her brow furrowed, and her eyes suddenly glistened. "You don't know what it's been like." Bethany shook her head in confusion. "First everyone at the Heritage Society was so nice to me. It seemed like a perfect position. Then Mr. Neville . . ." Her throat constricted, and she was unable to finish for a few moments. "You just don't know," she managed to choke out.

"Perhaps I do," said Theodosia, patting her arm gently. "But keep in mind the Chinese proverb: 'There is no wave without wind.'"

"That's lovely," said Bethany. She gazed at Theodosia with something akin to hero worship. "You're not afraid of anything, are you? You're very confident about making your place in the world."

"Sometimes I think the hard part is *finding* your place," said Theodosia as the bell over the front door tinkled merrily. "Now, why don't you put an apron on. . . . That's right." She smiled encouragingly at Bethany. "That white linen is lovely against your apricot sweater. . . . Go wait on our first customers."

Enthused, Bethany fairly scampered across the room.

"It's good to see Bethany with a smile on her face," said Drayton.

"Can you keep an eye on her?" asked Theodosia. "Give her a subtle assist if she gets stuck?"

"It would be my pleasure," said Drayton. "I've got a group from the Christie Inn coming in for a tea tasting at ten, but until then, I shall kibbitz to my heart's content."

Theodosia retreated to her back office, plopped herself down in her swivel chair, and gazed at the catastrophe that was her desktop.

While she had been out and about, getting dressed down by Timothy Neville, snooping at Edgewater Estates, and cruising King Street for a fix on Goose Creek Holdings, life had gone on. Mail had arrived. Messages had piled up. The Web site story boards she was supposed to make a decision on still sat staring up at her. And, of course, there were bills to be paid, paychecks to be written, overseas orders to be untangled.

But there was something else that took precedence, that had to be done. Let's see . . . Oh, yes! She had to phone Tanner Joseph.

After greeting him on the phone, Theodosia launched directly into her proposal. "I have what could be an intriguing project," she told him.

Tanner Joseph's voice conveyed both amusement and interest. "I'm already on the edge of my chair."

"I need some labels for small canisters of holiday tea that will be for sale in my shop. Your drawings came to mind. They're very good."

There was a long pause. "You really think so?"

"Yes, I do."

"And you're serious? This isn't just a crank call?" Tanner Joseph laughed. "You're actually asking if I want to design your tea labels?"

"Yes, but only if you have time. Unfortunately, we're in kind of a hurry-up mode. I'd need to get a finished product from you relatively fast."

"What's your idea of fast?"

"First we meet," said Theodosia. "I fill you in on the project, share a few ideas. If you agree to do the illustrations, then you have maybe three or four working days to do a few pencils. You know, black-and-white sketches. We meet again to go over them. If I like what I see, you proceed to color illustrations. You'd have another few days for that."

"You're on." Tanner Joseph fairly lunged at the offer. "Hey, I'm really flattered. For a guy with a degree in ecology, which is actually a very left-brain kind of thing, this is a dream come true. But, Miss Browning, I should come to your place. Your tea shop. Get a feel for what it's all about, what your customers might expect."

"How about this afternoon, say three o'clock?"

"Perfect," agreed Tanner Joseph.

Theodosia leaned back in her chair and took stock of things. Okay. One down, about forty more to go. She gazed in disgust at her desk. Make that fifty. Hmm.

"Excuse me." There was a soft knock at the door. "I'm serving tea to a bunch of divorced lawyers and was wondering what would be most suitable."

Theodosia glanced over, pleasantly surprised to find a tall, attractive man in a three-piece suit gracing her doorway. One of her eyebrows raised imperceptibly.

"You are the distinguished colleague from Ligget, Hume, Hartwell, I presume?"

Jory Davis flashed a crooked grin. "Guilty as charged."

"In that case, I highly recommend a Chinese varietal called Iron Goddess of Mercy."

The man in the doorway threw back his head and laughed, a deep, rich, easy laugh that gave Theodosia the perfect few moments to study him.

Jory Davis wasn't quite what she'd expected. He was attractive, yes, but in a slightly rugged and reckless way. Square jaw, curly brown hair, piercing blue eyes, probably midthirties. He was well over six feet tall, with broad shoulders and a tiny maze of lines at the corners of his eyes that probably meant he spent much of his free time out of doors. He also moved as though he was completely at ease with himself and wore his three-piece Brooks Brothers suit as if it had been cut just for him. Theodosia noted that Jory Davis wasn't exactly slick, but he was certainly *downtown.* She could picture him in a dark, clubby restaurant with leather booths, clinking glasses with other lawyers, celebrating a win. What she was having trouble picturing was Jory Davis in a kitchen with a wire whisk.

"Please come in, Mr. Davis." Theodosia stood and indicated the chair across from her. "Can I get you a cup of tea?"

"Call me Jory. And, no, I can only stay a moment." He remained standing and dug into his briefcase. "I'm due in court in fifteen minutes, but I wanted to drop off the rest of the information we ferreted out on Hughes Barron." He glanced up at her. "I hope you still want it."

"Of course."

He searched intently through the massive amount of papers in his oversized leather briefcase. Finally he grabbed a sheaf of papers and plopped it on her desk. "Here you go." His smile was dazzling, and his blue eyes sparkled.

Tinted contacts? she wondered. Or were his eyes really that blue?

"Thanks," she said. "How did your vinaigrette turn out?"

"Good. Great. Thanks to you." He stood gazing at her for a moment, then said, "Hey, this is a fun office. Lots of interesting eye catchers." His hand ever so gently touched a bronze head from a Thai temple that sat atop her desk, then moved on to an antique Spode teapot.

Funny, she thought, how very gently he ran his hand over that delicate china teapot.

"I meant it about the tea," said Jory Davis. "And that Iron Goddess sounded interesting. I admire strong women." He turned to study the framed opera programs and photos on her wall. "Hey, you sail! I keep a J-24 at the marina." He glanced back at Theodosia over his shoulder. "I'm decorating her this year for the Festival of Lights. You ought to sail with us."

Every Christmas, a fleet of fifty or so boats was decked out in holiday lights and set sail from Patriots Point. From there the colorful flotilla paraded around the tip of the peninsula, much to the delight of thousands of onlookers, and ended up at the Charleston Yacht Club.

"Let me think about it," said Theodosia, oddly pleased. "I sailed in the festival four years ago on Tom and Evie Woodrow's boat. It was a lot of fun."

"Well, then, you've just *got* to sail on my boat," said Jory Davis. "Woodrow's boat is a tub, compared to my J-24." He gathered up his briefcase and stuck out his hand. "Gotta go. Great meeting you."

"Nice meeting you," called Theodosia as Jory Davis disappeared through the doorway.

"Who was *that?*" asked Haley. She stood in the doorway wearing an expectant look on her face.

"A lawyer friend," replied Theodosia.

"I know that. He told me that earlier, when I showed him back here. I meant who is he to you?"

"Haley, did you need something?"

"Oh, right. Sorry. You've got a phone call."

"It's not Delaine, is it?"

"It's Burt Tidwell," whispered Haley. She put a finger to her mouth. Since Bethany was working out front, Haley obviously wanted to keep this phone call hush-hush. "Line two. Shall I close the door?" she asked.

Theodosia nodded to Haley as she picked up the phone and vowed not to let Burt Tidwell spoil her good mood.

"Mr. Tidwell," she said brightly.

"Miss Browning," he acknowledged gruffly.

"And how is your investigation proceeding?" She tossed him a leading question in hopes of getting a little feedback.

"Extremely well," Tidwell answered.

Theodosia slipped out of her loafers and wiggled her toes in the sunlight that spilled in through the leaded panes. *He has nothing,* she thought. *Diddly-squat, to use an inelegant term.* But she would humor him. Oh, yes, she would humor him and keep going with her own investigation. And she would surely play to what seemed to be a sense of vanity on his part concerning professional prowess.

"I trust you've gotten your lab results back," said Theodosia.

"I have indeed."

Damn, she thought. *This fellow is maddening.* "And . . ." she said.

"Exactly what I suspected. A toxic substance."

"A toxic substance," repeated Theodosia. "In the teacup."

"Yes."

"But not in the teapot." She could hear him breathing loudly at the other end of the line. Short, almost wheezy breaths. "Mr. Tidwell?" she said with more force.

"After forensic investigation by the state toxicology lab, it was determined that the teapot did not contain any toxic substance. Only the teacup."

"Would you care to share with me the nature of that substance?"

"It's still being analyzed."

"I'm sure it is."

"Miss Browning," said Tidwell, "did you know that Hughes Barron was looking at a property on your block?"

"The Peregrine Building," she replied.

"So you were aware of this?"

"I heard a rumor to that effect."

"His purchase could have impacted you, don't you think?"

"In what way?"

"Oh, a commercial development could change the character of your block. Might possibly affect business."

Theodosia caught her breath. "Mr. Tidwell, are you trying to imply that *I'm* a suspect?"

Now Burt Tidwell let go a deep, hearty laugh. "Madam, until I conclude an investigation, I consider everyone a suspect."

"Surely that can't be efficient."

"It is merely the way I work, madam. Good day."

Theodosia slammed down the phone. Of all the nerve! First he let it be known that Bethany was a suspect! Then to imply she might be! A cad. The man was truly a cad. Any grudging respect she had felt earlier had just flown out the window.

She stared at her desktop angrily. Then, with both hands, she pushed everything off to the left. Files began to topple, and she let them. One of the storyboards slipped to the floor. Pink message slips that had been stacked in order of date and time were suddenly jumbled.

But she had just given herself a good expanse of wood on which to work. A place to start fresh, to think fresh. She set a piece of plain white paper in front of her. At the top of it she wrote the name, "Hughes Barron." Under that she wrote "Poison?"

Like the beginnings of a family tree, she jotted two names underneath. "Timothy Neville" and "Lleveret Dante." Because she didn't have another suspect, she put a third mark, a question mark, alongside the two names. Somehow it felt right.

She ruminated and read through the papers Jory Davis had brought her until Drayton poked his head in some forty minutes later.

"Getting a lot done?"

"Yes," she lied. Then thought better of it. "No. Sit. Please." She indicated the tufted chair across from her desk.

Drayton sat down, crossed his legs, and gazed at her expectantly.

She fixed him with an intense stare. "How well do you know Timothy Neville?"

❧ 21 ❧

Miss Dimple smiled broadly at Theodosia. "Mr. Dauphine will just be a moment," she said. "He's on the phone. Long distance."

"Thank you," murmured Theodosia as she wondered why people always tended to be more patient when the person they're waiting for is talking long distance versus a local call. Strange that distance makes us polite, and nearness makes us impatient.

After her conversation with Drayton, she had made her way up four flights of stairs in the Peregrine Building to the office of Mr. Harold Dauphine, the owner. Theodosia knew the man had to be at least seventy-five years old. His plump secretary, Miss Dimple, couldn't be that much younger. Did they scoot up and down these stairs all day? she wondered. Could that be the key to longevity? Or, once they arrived for work in the morning, did they just perch up here, recovering from the effort?

"Miss Browning?" Miss Dimple was smiling at her. "Can I offer you a cup of coffee?"

"No, thank you."

Theodosia sat and marveled at the decor of the office. The whole thing was like a throwback to the fifties. Gray metal filing cabinets, venetian blinds, an honest-to-goodness Underwood upright typewriter. You could film an old Perry Mason episode right here. She half expected to see Miss Dimple don a green eyeshade.

Theodosia thumbed through a dog-eared copy of *Reader's Digest,* skimming the "Quotable Quotes" section. She stared out the window and wondered about Hughes Barron's partner, Lleveret Dante, and she thought about Drayton's reaction to her suspicions about Timothy Neville.

As much as the look on Drayton's face had betrayed his skepticism about Timothy Neville, he'd still listened carefully to her.

"Well," Drayton had said after hearing her out, "it's interesting speculation, but it'd be another thing to prove. I certainly don't discount the fact that Timothy Neville has an abominable temper and is capable of causing harm. Most people have a dark side. And I certainly think you should find out more about this man, Lleveret Dante. Tell you what, why don't you come along with me tomorrow night? Timothy Neville is having a small concert at his home. One of the string quartets he plays in for fun. There will be people from the Heritage Society as well as people from the neighborhood that you undoubtedly know. You can listen to some good music, then have a jolly snoop in his medicine cabinet, if you like."

If Drayton had been pulling her leg, his serious demeanor hadn't betrayed the fact. So she'd agreed. She had to harness her enthusiasm, in fact, because tomorrow night would be, just as Drayton had said, the perfect opportunity to snoop. And she had a sneaking suspicion Timothy Neville wasn't the righteous pillar of the community that most people thought he was.

"Mr. Dauphine can see you now, Miss Browning."

Theodosia stood and smiled at Miss Dimple. The woman was aptly named, she thought. Even looked like a dimple. Round, sweet, slightly pink.

"Always nice to see a neighbor, Miss Browning." Mr. Dauphine struggled to his feet and shook her hand weakly.

"Nice to see you again," said Theodosia. She noted that Mr. Dauphine's office was just as antiquated as the reception area, right down to a rotary phone and an archaic dictation machine, what they used to call a *steno.*

"Of course," said Mr. Dauphine, "I don't come in every day like I used to. Been taking it a little slower." What should have been easy laughter segued into a hacking cough.

"Are you all right, Mr. Dauphine?" said Theodosia. "Can I get you something? A glass of water?"

Mr. Dauphine waved her off with one hand. "Fine, fine," he choked. Pulling a plastic inhaler from his jacket pocket, he shook it rapidly, depressed the button, and inhaled as best he could.

"Emphysema," Mr. Dauphine explained, tapping his chest. "Used to smoke." He helped himself to another puff from his inhaler. "You ever smoke?"

"No," she replied.

"Good girl. I'd advise you never to start." He looked at her and smiled. Despite his obvious frailties, Mr. Dauphine's eyes shone brightly, and his mind seemed quick. "Now," he said, "have you come to make an offer on my property as well?"

Theodosia tried not to betray her surprise. She'd come looking for information about Hughes Barron and Lleveret Dante, and Mr. Dauphine had just nicely opened up that conversational front.

"Not really," she told him lightly. "But I take it you've been under siege of late?"

Mr. Dauphine laughed. "I was, but not anymore. Fellow who wanted to buy this place died."

"Hughes Barron," she said. How interesting, she thought, that everyone she talked with lately couldn't wait to tell her that Hughes Barron had died.

"That's the one." Mr. Dauphine leaned back in his chair and crossed his arms over his thin chest. "He make an offer on your place, too?"

"Not exactly," said Theodosia slowly. "But I did want to get in touch with his lawyer."

"Sam Sestero," said Mr. Dauphine.

"Sam Sestero," Theodosia repeated, committing the name to memory. "Do you, by any chance, have Mr. Sestero's phone number?"

"Miss Dimple keeps all that straight for me. I'm sure she can give it to you." His hand reached out and depressed the button on an old-fashioned intercom system. "Oh, Miss Dimple, see if you can find Mr. Sestero's number for Miss Browning, will you?" He turned back to Theodosia. "As I recall, Mr. Sestero's office isn't far from here."

Theodosia found that it wasn't far at all. In fact, Samuel and his brother, Edward Sestero, the two managing partners of Sestero & Sestero Professional Association, turned out to have their offices just down from the stately Romanesque buildings at the intersection of Meeting and Broad Streets, known affectionately to Charlestonians as the Four Corners of Law.

22

"*You idiot! You* must have been out of your mind!" Brimming with anger, the man's voice reverberated loudly down the cavernous hallway, bouncing off marble floors with thunderous consequences.

"What was I supposed to do?" a second voice countered. This voice was also a loud male voice but pitched higher, with a tone more pleading than enraged.

Theodosia stopped in her tracks. She had been wandering down the hallway of the venerable old Endicott Building, looking for the office of Sestero & Sestero. From the angry sounds coming to her from around the corner, it would appear she might have found it.

"I expect my attorney to show a little smarts!" screamed the first voice.

"What was I supposed to do, for crying out loud?" This from the second voice now. "The man's a detective first grade. Tidwell could haul my ass before a judge and charge me with obstructing an investigation."

Tidwell? Theodosia put a hand to the corridor wall and edged forward quietly, instantly on the alert.

"What about attorney-client privilege?" the first voice countered stridently.

"Oh, please."

"You rolled, you miserable little weasel. That's all there is to it."

"Calm down, Mr. Dante. Nothing could be further from the truth. I merely answered a few innocuous questions. You're acting as if it was a subpoena from a Federal Court judge. Take it easy, awright?"

Well, well, thought Theodosia. So the infamous Mr. Lleveret Dante was paying his lawyer a little visit. And wasn't he awfully hot under the collar. Screaming and badgering and carrying on, giving the other man, obviously Sam Sestero, an earful.

On the heels of that thought came the notion that Sam Sestero might not be the sharpest tack around if he thought for a minute that Burt Tidwell had been asking what he termed "innocuous questions."

"I'm in enough hot water as it is!" yelled Lleveret Dante. "All I need is for the AG in Kentucky to make an inquiry down here!"

The AG? Surely, thought Theodosia, Lleveret Dante had to mean the attorney general. That would wash with the information Jory Davis had given her about Lleveret Dante being under indictment in Kentucky for a mortgage flipping scheme.

"Did he ask about the partnership agreement?" screamed Lleveret Dante.

There was a mumbled answer.

"You pathetic wimp, I bet you told him about the business-preservation clause."

"Mr. Dante, I revealed nothing."

"If that idiot Tidwell knows I automatically received Barron's half of the business upon his death, he'll put me under a microscope! You ought to be disbarred, you worthless sack of shit!"

Isn't it amazing what one overhears in hallways, Theodosia mused. So

Hughes Barron and Lleveret Dante *did* have a buy-sell agreement, with what Dante termed a "business-preservation clause." That meant, in this case, that should one of them die, the other automatically received the dead partner's share of the business!

But wasn't that more of a *death clause?* And couldn't it also be a motive for murder?

A door slammed shut, and Theodosia was suddenly aware of footsteps coming toward her.

My God! It had to be Lleveret Dante who was barreling down the hallway at full steam. She could hear footsteps ratcheting loudly, the man huffing and puffing like an overworked steam engine. In a matter of seconds, he would be rounding the corner, and she would be face-to-face with him.

Frantically casting about, Theodosia spied an old-fashioned wooden telephone booth next to a pedestal water fountain. She dove into the phone booth, grabbed the receiver off the hook, and held it to her face.

"Oh, did she really?" said Theodosia loudly, pantomiming a phone call. "Is that a fact. Then what happened?"

Lleveret Dante stormed past her, and Theodosia finally grabbed her first look at Hughes Barron's infamous business partner.

Lleveret Dante was a short man, maybe five foot five at best, with a shock of white hair that went off in all directions, as if he might have a giant cowlick on top of his head. Dante's face was the color of a ripe plum against the crisp white of his three-piece suit.

Dante paced back and forth impatiently as he waited for the elevator. Every time he spun on his heel, his white suit coat flared out slightly. Made him look like a top spinning on its axis.

What a bizarre vision, Theodosia thought to herself as she rose on tiptoes and peered around the corner of the telephone booth to catch a final glimpse of the man. And yes, her hunch was correct. The man was wearing white socks and shoes as well. Well, that iced the cake. Aside from his hideous temper, Lleveret Dante was obviously a strange duck, one that would bear watching.

23

In most cities and states, the position once known as the coroner has evolved into that of medical examiner. *Coroner,* at one time, meant any person in authority—a sheriff, judge, or deputy—who was empowered to make the final pronouncement that a person was deceased. But as forensic investigations became more sophisticated over the years, most jurisdictions found a pressing need for a medical examiner, one person in charge who was a doctor as well as a trained pathologist.

In Charleston, the coroner was still an elected four-year position and had been since 1868. Before that, justices of the county court selected coroners. Previous to that, they were appointed by the king of England.

Theodosia stood in the ornate marble entrance of the County Services Building. She had wandered over when she realized it was just a block down from the Endicott Building, where she'd just experienced her first sighting of Mr. Lleveret Dante.

I can't do this, she told herself. *There's no way I can waltz downstairs to the coroner's office and be convincing.*

Yes, you can, goaded a determined little voice inside her head. It was the voice that often pushed her, told her to take chances. *You're here. What have you got to lose?*

Well, she thought, *if Burt Tidwell had been snooping around Sam Sestero's office, looking for information about Hughes Barron and Lleveret Dante, then I might not be barking up the wrong tree after all.*

Theodosia gripped the metal railing and, like Alice tumbling into the rabbit hole, descended the circular staircase that led to the basement.

"County Morgue, help ya?" a receptionist with a heroic beehive hairdo was screeching loudly into her headset. She held court behind a black laminate counter where she alternately handled incoming calls, signed for deliveries, and paged through *The National Enquirer.* A second ringing phone line was currently vying for her attention.

"I'm here to check on a body," Theodosia told the receptionist. She clung to the counter for support. Even though she felt giddy and scared, she tried to sound casual, as though she'd done this a hundred times before.

The woman smiled briefly and held up an index finger. A third line had begun to ring.

Theodosia noted that the receptionist's two-inch-long acrylic nails were painted blood red. Very Vampyra.

"Delivery," announced a man in a blue uniform who suddenly appeared at Theodosia's elbow. He thumped a large cardboard box onto the counter. The office was suddenly as busy as Grand Central Station.

"Which one, honey?" the receptionist asked Theodosia as she signed for the newly arrived packaged and consulted her clipboard. "No!" the receptionist suddenly bellowed into her headset before Theodosia could reply. "We do not issue death certificates! Cremation permits, yes. Death certificates, no. That would be Records and Registration." She raised her penciled eyebrows skyward in frustration and rolled her eyes.

"Hughes Barron," Theodosia said finally.

But the receptionist was still wrangling with the caller. "Did this person die *outside* of a hospital?" the receptionist asked. "They did? Sir, you should have given me that information in the first place. That means you need a burial transit permit." She covered the mouthpiece with a chubby hand and addressed Theodosia.

"Sorry, honey. Check down the hall. Second door on the left, ask for Jeeter Clark."

The antiseptic green hallway was a traffic jam of occupied gurneys, shiny, silver conveyances all holding body bags. Full body bags, Theodosia noted. The noxious smell of formalin and formaldehyde assaulted her as she squeamishly edged past.

"Jeeter?"

Jeeter Clark jumped to his feet, startled. He'd been drinking a can of orange soda pop and munching a ham sandwich. When he saw it wasn't his boss at the door or a disgruntled bookie come to call, he seemed to relax.

"Jeez, lady, you scared me." Jeeter put the hand that held his half-eaten ham sandwich to his chest. He was wearing green scrubs, the kind doctors wear in an operating room.

"Didn't mean to," said Theodosia. "The receptionist said I'd find you in here."

"Trudy sent you?" he asked.

"Sure did," said Theodosia, falling into his folksy pattern of speech.

"Okay, sure," Jeeter replied, satisfied that she had business there. "You must be from Edenvale."

Theodosia suddenly realized that, dressed as she was in black jacket and slacks, this man had just mistaken her for one of the many funeral directors who routinely called on the County Morgue to pick up bodies!

Oh, be honest, now. Wasn't this what you had in mind all along?

"No, Indigo," said Theodosia, almost choking on her words. *Lord love a duck,* she thought. *Now I've really done it.*

"Not familiar with that one," Jeeter muttered. "And you're here to fetch . . . ?"

"Barron. Hughes Barron," said Theodosia, again trying to sound like a disinterested funeral professional who did this routinely. Whatever that was supposed to sound like.

Jeeter snatched up a clipboard and consulted it. And, wonder of wonders, Hughes Barron's name was listed.

"Yeah, I got that name," said Jeeter. " I suppose you want to know when the body's going to be released."

The ridiculousness of the situation made her bold. "That's right."

Jeeter squinted at his clipboard. "You guys are always trying to bust my hump, aren't you? Well, I guess you gotta make a buck, too." He scanned what must have been a fairly long list. "Let's see, lab work's done. They've taken tissue samples. Lung, stomach, liver, brain . . ."

"Does it say what killed him?" asked Theodosia.

"That'd be on the pathologist's report." Jeeter slid open a drawer, ran his finger down a row of file folders, and pulled one out. He flipped it open and thumbed through a dozen or so sheets. "Bradycardia," he announced.

"Bradycardia," repeated Theodosia.

But Jeeter wasn't finished. "Heart and respiratory failure induced by a toxic substance." Jeeter looked up. "Some kind of poison. Guess they haven't got a complete report from the lab yet." He smiled at Theodosia affably. "They're always backed up. But don't worry, that's no problem. You can take him anyway. Funeral's in two days, huh?"

Was it?

"That's right," said Theodosia. "The family was planning to hold services Thursday morning."

"Then you've got plenty time to get him prepped and primped. In fact, if your meat wagon's out back, I can have one of my guys haul him out right now."

"Thanks anyway," said Theodosia, fighting hard to keep a straight face, "but I'll be sending my meat wagon by this afternoon."

24

Lleveret Dante sat scrunched down in the front seat of his Range Rover. He'd been sitting there for a good ten minutes when he saw the woman with the curly auburn hair and black slacks suit emerge from the Endicott Building.

He'd caught her out of the corner of his eye as he strode past her after leaving the office of that idiot, Sam Sestero. Something about the tone of the woman's voice or the way she had appeared so decidedly blasé had raised his radar. Suspicious by nature, he had tuned her in, like a wolf with his nose to the wind. Once again, his sixth sense hadn't disappointed him. The woman had seemed to be watching him. *Spying* on him.

He'd waited for her to emerge from Sestero's building. Then what a big surprise he'd gotten as he watched her saunter down the street and disappear into the County Services Building! That had blown his mind slightly, but it had also confirmed his suspicions. He knew damn well what was housed in the basement of that innocuous building.

Such a curious coincidence that his lawyer's office was just down the street from where the body of his dead partner lay on a metal table.

But even more curious was that this strange woman was so interested in both of them.

He would follow this woman, to be sure. Find out who she was, where she lived. Tuck that information away for future use.

❧ 25 ❧

I can't believe what I just did, I can't believe it! Theodosia repeated to herself as she drove back toward the Indigo Tea Shop.

She was truly waiting for the proverbial bolt of lightning to descend from the heavens and strike her dead. She'd told so many fibs today that her head was spinning. And she figured her karma bank had to be operating at a deficit.

No, Theodosia consoled herself as she spun down Tradd Street, this is a murder investigation. You think Burt Tidwell worries about stretching the truth when he's questioning a suspect?

She braked suddenly to avoid sideswiping a horse-drawn carriage packed full of tourists.

No way, she grumbled to herself. *Burt Tidwell probably pulls out a rubber hose and threatens his suspects. And that's only after he's intimidated them into tears.*

"You're finally back!" exclaimed Drayton. "You must have had an amazingly long meeting with Mr. Dauphine. Did he regale you with tales of his days in the Merchant Marines during World War II?"

Drayton was seated at Theodosia's desk, wholesalers' catalogs spread out around him. He had gathered up the papers and files Theodosia had dumped earlier and arranged them in neat little stacks on her bookcase.

"Don't even ask," said Theodosia as she plopped her handbag on the side chair. "Oh, Brown Betty Teapots." She squinted at the colorful brochures from her upside-down view.

"We're positively down to the dregs on teapot selection," said Drayton. "I know you've been preoccupied lately, so I thought I'd make the first pass on a reorder. Besides these traditional English Brown Bettys and Blue Willow pots, Marrington Imports has some stunning contemporary ceramics. A trifle edgy, but still your taste." Drayton slid the catalog toward her. "And look at these Victorian styles with matching tea towels."

"Wonderful," agreed Theodosia. She sat down and balanced on the edge of her side chair, staring straight across at Drayton's lined countenance. "But, Drayton, don't apologize for doing my job. I should be thanking *you*. As the Indigo Tea Shop's benevolent taskmaster, you keep us all moving forward."

"Thank you, Theodosia," said Drayton. A smile lit his face, and a look of satisfaction softened the lines around his eyes. "That means a lot to me."

Theodosia jumped up and peered into the little mirror that hung on the back of the door. It was slightly pitted and wavy from age, but she gamely reapplied her lipstick and fluffed her hair.

"My goodness!" She whirled about, suddenly remembering her three o'clock meeting. "Tanner Joseph. I was supposed to meet with him. About the labels for the holiday blends!"

"No need to panic," Drayton replied mildly. "He's here." Drayton consulted his watch, an ancient Piaget that seemed to perpetually run ten minutes slow. "Has been for almost fifteen, no twenty-five, minutes. Haley took the initiative. She offered to give him the nickel tour."

"She did?" Theodosia allowed herself to relax. For all Haley's indecision about choosing a major and amassing enough credits to graduate, she could sometimes exhibit an amazing take-charge attitude.

But it was Bethany, not Haley, who was seated across the table from Tanner Joseph as Theodosia parted the green velvet curtains and stepped somewhat breathlessly into the tea room.

"Mr. Joseph," said Theodosia as she approached him, her smile warm and apologetic. "Forgive me. I am *so* sorry to have kept you waiting."

"Hello, Miss Browning." Tanner Joseph rose from his chair. Dressed in a faded chambray shirt and khaki slacks, he looked more like the executive director of a nonprofit group that he really was, and less the beach bum from two days ago. "Nice to see you again, but please don't apologize. Your very capable assistant here has been kind enough to bring me up to speed."

Bethany gazed anxiously toward Theodosia, a look that said she hoped she hadn't overstepped her bounds.

"Excellent," replied Theodosia with a reassuring smile for Bethany that conveyed *Thank you, well done.*

"I have to be honest," said Tanner Joseph with a lopsided grin. "My tea drinking has been limited to English breakfast teas and flavored ice teas that come in bottles. But all of this is fascinating. I had no idea so many varieties of tea even existed. Or that water temperature or steeping time was critical. Plus, my taste buds have just been awakened and treated to this rather amazing Japanese green tea. Gyokuro, isn't that what you called it, Bethany?"

Tanner Joseph smiled down at Bethany, and something seemed to pass between them.

Interesting, mused Theodosia as she caught the exchange. *I would have guessed Haley would be the one attracted to this likable young man.* Up until this moment, Bethany hadn't displayed a whit of interest in meeting anyone new.

"I'm delighted we had a hand in helping nurture yet another tea aficionado, Mr. Joseph," Theodosia laughed as she sat down at the table and helped herself to a cup of the flavorful green tea as well.

"Call me Tanner, please." He sat back down in his chair, picked up his cup of tea, and took a sip.

"Okay then, Tanner," said Theodosia. "You've seen our shop, enjoyed a cup of tea. By chance, has Bethany mentioned our holiday blends?"

Tanner Joseph held up an oversized artist's sketch pad. One page was covered with notes and thumbnail drawings.

"We've already been through it," he said. "She told me all about Drayton's different blends, the names you came up with, even your ideas on design. See . . ." He laughed. "I'm pumped. I've already noodled a few sketches."

"You work pretty fast," said Theodosia. This *was* a surprise.

"Oh, yeah," said Tanner Joseph with great enthusiasm. "You have no idea what a fun project this is versus the tedium of waging constant war against environmental robbers and plunderers."

Theodosia sat with Bethany and Tanner Joseph for ten more minutes, expressing her thoughts on the holiday blends and what she called the "look and feel" of the label design. Tanner Joseph, in turn, shared his few quick sketches with her, and Theodosia saw that he'd grasped the concept immediately.

They went over timing and budget for a few minutes more, then Theodosia and Bethany walked Tanner Joseph to the door and bade him good-bye.

"I had no idea you knew so much about the holiday blends," said Theodosia as Bethany closed and locked the double doors. She was pleased but a little taken aback, wondering how Bethany had gleaned so much information.

"Drayton told me all about the holiday blends this morning while we were putting together boxes of tea samplers. He really loves to share his knowledge of tea."

"To anyone who will listen," Theodosia agreed with a laugh. "But I daresay, he's taken *you* under his wing."

"It's such a rare talent to know which teas combine with different spices and fruits. And Drayton really seems to come up with some wonderful blends."

"Bethany," said Theodosia, thoroughly pleased, "you're an amazingly quick study."

Bethany blushed. "But tea is such a fun subject. And something Drayton is so obviously passionate about."

"It's been his life," agreed Theodosia.

"I didn't mean that *you're* not passionate," blushed Bethany. "It's just that . . ."

"It's just that I haven't been around much lately," finished Theodosia. "Don't worry, dear. I'm passionate about a lot of subjects."

"Like finding out what killed Hughes Barron?" Bethany asked in a quiet voice.

"Well . . . yes," said Theodosia, a little surprised by the quick change of subject. "It *is* a rather compelling mystery."

"And you love mysteries," said Bethany, her eyes twinkling. "I mean, getting *involved* in them."

"I guess I do," said Theodosia. She was somewhat taken aback by Bethany's insight. Although she loved nothing better than curling up in front of the fireplace with a good mystery, a P. D. James or a Mary Higgins Clark, she'd never consciously considered the fact that she was itching to get entangled in a real-life mystery. A *murder mystery,* no less.

She sighed. Well, like it or not, she was hip deep in one now.

26

Gateway Walk is a hidden pathway that begins on Church Street, near Saint Philip's graveyard, and meanders four blocks through quiet gardens. Visitors who venture in are led past the Gibbes Museum of Art, the Charleston Library Society, and various fountains and sculptures to Saint John's Church on Archdale Street. The picturesque Gateway Walk, named for the wrought-iron Governor Aiken Gates along the way, enchants visitors with its plaque that reads:

THROUGH HANDWROUGHT GATES, ALLURING PATHS
LEAD ON TO PLEASANT PLACES.
WHERE GHOSTS OF LONG FORGOTTEN THINGS
HAVE LEFT ELUSIVE TRACES.

Theodosia had always found the Gateway Walk a lovely, contemplative spot, conducive to deep thought and relaxation. But tonight, with darkness already fallen, she hurried along the brick path, pointedly ignoring the marble tablets and gravestones that loomed on either side of her.

She had spent the entire morning and afternoon at the Indigo Tea Shop waiting tables, focusing on tea shop business, going over the Web site designs, trying to get back in touch. She knew she hadn't really given careful attention to her business since the night of Hughes Barron's murder; she knew her priorities were slightly out of whack. The Indigo Tea Shop was her bread and butter. Her life. And nosing about the County Morgue shouldn't have taken precedence over her meeting with Tanner Joseph on label illustrations. That had been thoughtless.

Of course, sleuthing was exciting, she told herself as she passed by a marble statue of a weeping angel, a silent, solitary inhabitant of the graveyard. And trying to solve a murder did set one's blood to racing.

Feeling her guilt slightly absolved, for the time being, Theodosia's footsteps echoed softly as she moved quickly along the dark path as it wound behind the Charleston Library Society.

She realized full well that she was headed for Timothy Neville's home not just for an evening of music. Her ulterior motive was to spy.

In a patch of crape myrtle there was a whir of cicadas, the rustle of some small, nocturnal creature, claiming the darkness as its domain.

Six blocks had seemed too short to drive, so Theodosia had walked, taking this shortcut through the cemetery and various gardens. Now, ducking through a crumbling arch with trumpet vine twining at her feet, the Gateway Walk suddenly seemed too dark, too secret, too secluded.

Stepping up her pace, she emerged two minutes later into soft, dreamy light cast by the old-fashioned wrought-iron lamps that lined Archdale Street.

Drayton had said he'd meet her at eight o'clock, just outside the gates of Timothy Neville's Georgian-style mansion. And from the looks of things, she had only moments to spare.

Cars were parked bumper to bumper up and down Archdale, and lights blazed from every window of Timothy Neville's enormous, sprawling home. As Theodosia hurried up the walk, she was suddenly reminded of the Avis Melbourne Home the night of the Lamplighter Tour. Its lamps had also been lit festively. Swarms of visitors had crowded the walks and piazzas.

She fervently hoped that an evening at this grand home would yield far better consequences.

"Right on time." Drayton emerged from the shadows and offered her his arm. He was dressed in black tie and looked more at ease in formal attire than most mere mortals could ever hope for. When an invitation specified black tie, Drayton always complied with elegance and polish.

Theodosia had worn a floor-length, pale blue sleeveless dress, shimmery as moonlight. As an afterthought, she'd tossed a silver gray pashmina shawl over her shoulders. With her hair long and flowing and a dab of mascara and lipstick to highlight her expressive eyes and full lips, she looked like an elegant lady out for a night on the town.

But I'm here to spy, Theodosia reminded herself as she and Drayton climbed the stone steps.

They nodded to familiar faces standing in groups on the piazza, passed through elegant cathedral doors and were greeted inside by Henry, Timothy Neville's butler.

Henry was dressed in full liveried regalia, and rumor held that Henry had been employed by Timothy Neville for almost forty years. There weren't many people Theodosia knew who had live-in help or had help that stayed with them for so long.

"Cocktails are being served in the solarium," Henry announced solemnly. He had the sad, unblinking eyes of an old turtle and the ramrod backbone of an English Beefeater. "Or feel free to join Mr. Neville's other guests in the salon, where Mr. Calhoun is playing a piece from Scarlatti." Henry gestured slowly toward a gilded archway through which harpsichord notes flowed freely.

Theodosia noted that the venerable Henry seemed to move in slow motion. It was like watching a Japanese Noh drama.

"Wine or song?" Drayton asked good-naturedly.

"Let's get a drink first," suggested Theodosia. She knew if they repaired to the salon, courtesy required them to pay strict attention to the music, not exactly her motive for coming here tonight. But if they grabbed a cocktail first, they'd be free to move about the house and greet other guests.

And get the lay of the land, Theodosia told herself. Try to get a better fix on the very strange Mr. Timothy Neville.

Although she had passed Timothy Neville's house many times on her walks with Earl Grey, Theodosia had never before been inside this enormous mansion. She was in awe as she gazed around. This was splendor unlike anything she'd seen before. A dramatic stairway dominated the foyer and rose three floors. Double parlors flanked the main hallway, and Theodosia saw that they contained Italian black marble fireplaces, Hepplewhite furnishings, and ornate chandeliers. Gleaming oil paintings and copperplate engravings hung on the walls.

Built during the Civil War by an infamous blockade runner, this home was reputed to have sliding panels that led to secret passageways and hidden rooms. Some folks in the historic district even whispered that the house was haunted. The fact that Timothy Neville's home had once served as residence for a former governor and was a private girl's school for a short time, only added to the intrigue.

"Theodosia!" The shrill voice of Samantha Rabathan rose above the undercurrent of conversational buzz as Theodosia and Drayton entered the solarium. Then Samantha, resplendent in fuschia silk, came determinedly toward them, like the prow of a ship cutting the waves.

"I didn't expect to see you here tonight," cooed Samantha as she adjusted the front of her dress to show off just the right amount of décolletage. "Drayton, too. Hello there, dear fellow."

Drayton inclined his head slightly and allowed Samantha to peck him on the cheek.

"Our illustrious chairwoman from the Lamplighter Tour," he said in greeting. "You're looking lovely this evening."

Samantha held a finger to her matching fuchsia-colored mouth. "I think it best we downplay the Lamplighter Tour." She grasped each of them by an elbow and started to haul them toward the bar. "That is, until this nastiness blows over." She smiled broadly, seemed to really notice Theodosia for the first time, and instantly shifted her look of amusement to one of concern. "How *are* you holding up, Theodosia? So many rumors flying, it's hard to know what to believe. And how is that poor, dear child . . . What is her name again?"

"Bethany," replied Theodosia. Samantha was being incredibly overbearing tonight, and Theodosia was already searching for an excuse to escape her clutches.

Just as a waiter offered flutes of champagne from a silver tray, the perfect excuse arrived in the form of Henry, announcing that the Balfour Quartet was about to begin their evening's performance.

"Got to run," burbled Samantha. "I'm sitting with Cleo and Raymond Hovle. From Santa Barbara. You remember them, Theodosia. They also have a house on Seabrook Island."

Theodosia didn't remember Cleo and Raymond at all, but she smiled hello out of politeness when Samantha pointedly nudged a small suntanned couple as she and Drayton entered the parlor for the concert.

They found seats in the back row, not in cushioned splendor as did the guests at the front of the pack, but on somewhat uncomfortable folding chairs.

Unaccustomed as she was to wearing three-inch high-heeled sandals, Theodosia surreptitiously slipped them off her feet and waited for the music to start.

27

Timothy Neville tucked his violin under his chin and gave a nod to begin. He had done a brief introduction of the other three members of the Balfour Quartet. The two men, the one who'd played the harpsichord earlier and was now on the violin, and a red-faced man on the viola, were also members of the Charleston Symphony. The fourth member, a young woman who played the cello, was from Columbia, South Carolina's capital, located just northwest of Charleston.

As Timothy Neville played the opening notes of Beethoven's *Die Mittleren Streichquartette,* he was surprised to note that the Browning woman was sitting in the back row. He gave a quick dip of his head to position himself for a slightly better view and saw immediately that she was sitting next to Drayton Conneley.

Of course. Drayton worked at the woman's little tea shop. It was logical that she might accompany him tonight. His command-performance concerts were legendary throughout the historic district, and it wasn't unusual for his invited guests to bring along guests of their own.

He frowned. The Browning woman was staring sharply at him as though she were waiting for something to happen. Silly girl. They had just begun the allegro, and there were a good fifty minutes to go. Still, she had been bold to come see him at the Heritage Society and plead the young intern's case. Even though he may have been dismissive of Theodosia Browning, it didn't mean he didn't admire her spirit. Lots of complacency these days. Hard to find the plucky ones. All the same, he would keep a close watch on her. She had stuck her nose in matters that didn't concern her, especially her inquiry about the Peregrine Building. That just wouldn't do at all.

The Balfour Quartet was very good, far better than Theodosia had expected they'd be, and she soon found herself lost in the musical depths of Beethoven's Quartet no. 9.

It was haunting and evocative, pulling her in and holding her complete attention until it came to a crashing conclusion.

Theodosia, suddenly reminded of why she was there in the first place, applauded briefly, then dashed out the door ahead of the crowd. There would be a twenty-minute intermission, an opportunity for men to refill drinks and ladies to visit the powder room.

Theodosia headed up that grand staircase, her toes sinking deep into plush white wool, and dashed down the long, arched hallway when she hit the second floor. Peeking into several bedrooms along the way, she found that all were elegantly furnished, and yet none showed signs of being occupied. Finally, at what would be the front of the house, she found the set of double doors that led to Timothy Neville's private suite of rooms.

As she pushed one of the massive doors slowly inward on its hinges, it emitted a protesting groan. Theodosia held her breath, looking back over her shoulder to see if anyone had heard or might even be watching her. No. Nothing. She swallowed hard, stepped inside Timothy Neville's private office, and closed the door behind her.

A single desk lamp, what looked like an original Tiffany dragonfly design, cast low light in the suite. Massive furnishings were dark, shadowy lumps. Flames danced in the ornate marble fireplace.

Theodosia's sandals whispered across the Aubusson carpet. Even in the dim light she could see portraits of Timothy Neville's ancestors, various fiery Huguenots scowling down at her from their vantage point on the burgundy-colored walls.

Then she was standing at Timothy Neville's Louis XIV desk, her hand on the brass knob, about to pull open the top drawer. She hesitated as a pang of guilt shot through her. This was snooping of the first magnitude, she told herself. Not terribly above board. Then she also remembered Timothy Neville's incredible rage and Hughes Barron clutching his teacup.

She slid the drawer open.

Inside were pens, stamps, personalized stationery, eyeglasses, a sheaf of household papers, and Timothy Neville's passport. Everything in an orderly arrangement, nothing of great interest.

What were you expecting to find? she asked herself. *A little blue glass bottle of arsenic? A crackling paper packet of strychnine?*

She padded back across the room to the door opposite the desk and sneaked it open. Timothy Neville's rather splendid bedroom met her eyes. Four-poster bed draped in heavy wine- and rust-colored brocades. Small Chippendale tables flanking each side of the bed. An elegant linen press that looked as though it might have been created by the famous Charleston cabinetmaker, Robert Walker. Two armchairs in matching brocade sat next to the small fireplace. And, on the walls, more oil paintings. Not ancestral portraits but eighteenth-century portraits of women. Women in gardens, women with children, women staring out dreamily.

The paintings hinted at a softer, more humane side of Timothy Neville that Theodosia wouldn't have guessed.

In the bathroom, next to a large walk-in closet, Theodosia hit the light switch. The bathroom was restful and elegant, replete with enormous claw-foot tub, dark green wallpaper, and brass wall sconces and towel racks. Without hesitation, Theodosia pulled open the medicine cabinet and scanned the shelves.

It was as predictable as his desk drawer had been. Shaving cream, toothpaste, aspirin, a bottle of Kiehl's After Shave Balm, a bottle of prescription medicine. Theodosia reached for the brown tinted bottle and scanned the label.

Halcion. Five milligrams. *Sleeping pills.*

She pondered this for a moment. Incriminating evidence? No, not really, she decided. Timothy Neville was an old man. Older people often had difficulty sleeping.

Theodosia placed the medicine back on the shelf, swung the mirrored door shut, and turned out the bathroom light. She crossed back through the bedroom into Timothy Neville's private office. She scanned the room again and shook her head. *Nope, nothing unusual here.*

Her hand rested on the doorknob when she noticed a tall English secretary just to the right of the door. Rather than housing fine porcelains behind its glass doors, as it had been designed to do, it now appeared to hold a collection of antique pistols.

Theodosia hesitated a split second, then decided this might be worth investigating.

Yes, they were pistols, all right. She gazed at the engraved plates that identified each weapon. Here was an 1842 Augustin-Lock Austrian cavalry pistol. And here an Early American flintlock. Fascinated, she pulled open one of the glass doors, slid her hand across the smooth walnut grip, and touched the intricate silver with her fingertips. These pieces were fascinating. Some had been used in the Civil War, the American Revolution, or quite possibly in gentlemen's duels of honor. They were retired now, on display. But their history and silent power were awe inspiring.

In the stillness of the room, a slight noise, an almost imperceptible tick, caught her attention, caused her to glance toward the door. In the dim light, she could see the brass doorknob slowly turning.

In a flash, Theodosia flattened herself against the wall, praying that whoever opened the door wouldn't peer around and see her hidden here in the shadows.

The heavy door creaked slowly inward on its hinges.

Needs a shot of WD-40, Theodosia thought wildly as she pressed closer to the wall and held her breath.

Whoever had opened the door halfway was standing there now, silently surveying the room. Only two inches of wood separated her from this mysterious person who, quite possibly, had followed her!

Theodosia willed her heart to stop beating so loudly. Surely, whoever was there must be able to hear it thumping mightily in her chest! Her mind raced, recalling Edgar Allan Poe's prophetic story, "The Tell Tale Heart."

That's me, she thought. *They'll hear the wild, troubled beating of my heart!*

But whoever stood there—Timothy Neville, the butler, Henry, another curious guest—had peeked into the room for only a few seconds, then pulled the door shut behind them.

Had they been satisfied no one was there?

Theodosia hoped so as she slumped against the wall, feeling hollow and weak-kneed. *Time to get out of here,* she decided. This little adventure had suddenly gone far enough. She moved toward the door.

Then she remembered the gun collection.

Theodosia glanced quickly toward the cabinet. In the half-light, the polished guns winked enticingly. *All right,* she told herself, *one quick peek. Then I will skedaddle out of here and join the others downstairs.*

The guns were all displayed in custom-made wooden holders. Beautiful to behold. Probably quite expensive to create. A key stuck out from the drop-leaf center panel. She turned it, lowering the leaf into the writing desk position.

Tucked in the cubbyholes were polishing cloths, various gun-cleaning kits, and a bottle of clear liquid.

Theodosia squinted at the label on the bottle. Sulfuric acid.

It was a compound often used to remove rust and corrosion from antique bronze statues, metal frames, and guns. And, unless she was mistaken, sulfuric acid was also a deadly poison.

If Timothy Neville had slipped something toxic into Hughes Barron's tea, could it have been this substance? That was the 64,000-dollar question, wasn't it? And nobody was saying yet. Not the coroner. Not Burt Tidwell. Certainly not Timothy Neville.

The Balfour Quartet had resumed playing when Theodosia slipped into the room and took her seat beside Drayton. As she adjusted her shawl around her shoulders, she felt his eyes on her.

"You look guilty," Drayton finally whispered.

"I do?" Her eyes went wide as she turned toward him.

"No, not really," he answered. "But you should. Where in heaven's name have you been?" he fussed. "I've been worried sick!"

Theodosia fidgeted through the second half of the concert, unable to concentrate and really enjoy the Balfour Quartet's rendition of Beethoven's Opus 18, no. 6. When the group finished with a flourish and the crowd rose to its collective feet, cheering and applauding, she breathed a giant sigh of relief.

Jumping up with the rest of the guests, Theodosia leaned toward Drayton. "I'll tell you all about it," she finally whispered in his ear. "But first, let's go back to the shop and have a nice calming cup of tea!"

28

"*You look like* the cat who swallowed the canary," said Drayton.

Haley was bent over the counter, artfully arranging tea roses in a pink-and-white-flowered Victorian teapot.

"Who me?" asked Haley with wide-eyed innocence. She tied a lace bow to the teapot's arched handle and stood back to admire her handiwork.

Drayton had been asked to organize a bridal shower tea for that afternoon, and everyone was pitching in to help. Since a nasty squall had blown in overnight, causing the temperature to plummet and drenching Charleston with a frigid, pounding rain, it didn't appear that many customers would be dropping by the tea shop anyway.

"Come on, what gives?" prompted Drayton. He had carefully wrapped a dozen bone china teacups in tissue paper and was gently placing them in a large wicker basket atop a white lace tablecloth. With the weather so miserable, he would have to add a protective layer of plastic to keep everything tidy and dry.

"What time do you have to be at the Lady Goodwood Inn?" Haley asked with feigned indifference.

"Haley . . ." pleaded the exasperated Drayton. When Drayton thought someone was nursing a secret, he was like a curious child—impish, impatient, prodding.

"Well," said Haley, "it's a trifle premature to say anything."

"But . . ." prompted Drayton.

"But Bethany was out on a date last night," Haley chortled triumphantly.

"A date!" exclaimed Theodosia. Up until now she had stayed out of

Drayton and Haley's little go-round. Let them have their fun, she'd thought. But this was news. Big news. While she and Drayton had been attending the concert at Timothy Neville's last night, Bethany had been out with a young man. Theodosia wondered what special person had coaxed the wistful and reclusive Bethany out of her shell. This had to be the first time Bethany had ventured out since her husband passed away.

"Dare I ask who with?" inquired Drayton. He was positively dying to know all the details.

"Why, with Theodosia's friend, of course," said Haley.

A thunderclap exploded loudly overhead at the same moment a jar of lemon curd Theodosia had been holding went crashing to the floor. As lightning strobed and windows rattled, glass shards and huge yellow globs scattered.

For some reason the name Jory Davis had popped into Theodosia's head. "Which friend do you mean?" she asked quickly.

"Oh, don't move, Theo!" cried Haley. "There's a huge sliver of glass pointing right at your foot. Move one inch, and it's liable to slice through your shoe. Hang on, and I'll get the dust pan and broom." She scurried off to fetch cleaning supplies.

"Who did she mean?" Theodosia asked Drayton.

"I'm just as much in the dark as you." Drayton shrugged.

"Okay, stand still!" Haley laid the dust pan down, hooked two large shards of glass with the broom, and slid them onto the dust pan. She surveyed the smaller pieces of glass and the pools of yellow liquid. "Gosh, what a mess." She furrowed her brow, ready to go on the attack. A compulsive neatnik and organizer, Haley always relished a cleanup challenge.

"Haley." Drayton snapped his fingers, amused by her fierce concentration. "Which one of our fine lads had the honor of squiring Bethany last evening?"

Haley looked up at Drayton and blinked, trying to regain her train of thought. "Oh. Tanner Joseph. The fellow who's doing the illustrations for the holiday tea labels."

"Tanner Joseph," repeated Theodosia. Now it made perfect sense. Bethany had been so cordial and helpful the other day, explaining teas and holiday blends to him.

"Of course, that fellow," said Drayton. Now that he knew who Bethany's date had been, his interest level had waned. If it had been someone new, someone who'd just opened a clever new shop on Church Street or someone who'd just bought a home in the nearby historic district and was going to renovate in a historically accurate way, then Drayton would have demanded all the details. Who were his family? Where had he gone to school? What did he do for a living?

"Where is Bethany, by the way?" asked Theodosia.

Haley scooped up more of the splintery mess. "Doing deliveries."

"In this rain?" said Drayton.

"She said she wanted to clear her head," replied Haley. "Besides, she's a jogger. Joggers are used to being out in all sorts of weather." She gazed out a fogged window toward the deserted, rain-slick street. "At least I think they are."

His curiosity satisfied, Drayton turned his attention back to preparations for the bridal shower tea. "I wish it weren't pouring buckets," he fussed.

"They weren't planning on holding the bridal shower tea outdoors, were they?" asked Haley.

He grimaced. "Yes, they were. Obviously that's not a possibility now." Drayton reached up and took a tiny tea candle nestled in a white porcelain bowl from the shelf. "The whole thing will have to be rethought," he said mournfully as he gazed down at the little candle in his hand.

"Doesn't the Lady Goodwood have a solarium?" asked Theodosia. "Just off the dining room?"

Drayton considered her question. "I believe they do. Very much on the order of a greenhouse. Verdant, lots of plants, a few tables. I think there might even be a small fountain. Of course the space is abysmally hot when the sun is shining, but on a day like today, cool, rainy, it might be just right." His face began to brighten significantly as he weighed the merits of this new locale. "Maybe even a touch romantic, what with rain pattering down on the glass roof."

"What a nice image, Drayton," said Haley, smiling. "I like that."

"Theodosia," Drayton said as he frantically scanned the tall shelves where all manner of tea candles, jams, and jellies were displayed. "Don't we have some floating candles?"

He whirled about as Theodosia, a step ahead of him, plunked four boxes of the miniature round disks into his hands.

"That's it!" cried Drayton. "What else?"

"Tea cozies for all the pots!" exclaimed Haley, getting into the spirit. "And exchange the wrought-iron chairs that are probably there now for upholstered chairs from the dining room."

"Perfect," declared Drayton.

"What about food?" inquired Theodosia. "What's on the menu so far?"

"Chocolate-dipped strawberries, shortbread cakes, apricot chutney, and Stilton cheese tea sandwiches," said Drayton.

"Okay," said Theodosia. "Now just add some of Haley's hot crab dip with Irish soda bread."

"My God, Theo, you're a genius," declared Drayton. He whirled about. "Haley, do you have time to whip up crab dip?"

"Drayton. Please." Haley had already shifted into her search-and-rescue mode and was headed for the kitchen.

It was after eleven when Bethany finally returned to the Indigo Tea Shop, face shiny, hair wet and smelling faintly of fresh rain.

"You all look so busy," she cried. "Can I help?"

Theodosia took one look at her. "You're soaked clear through. Better pop across the alley and change first. You're liable to catch cold."

"Colds come from viruses," said Haley. "Not cold weather." She had finished the crab dip and was now tying raffia and gilded leaves around bunches of cinnamon sticks.

"Which is why you drink my hibiscus and orange spice tea in winter? To thwart any possible virus?" asked Drayton in a faintly critical tone.

"Well, not exactly," said Haley.

"You're right, Theodosia. I'd feel better if I changed into dry clothes," said Bethany. "Want me to take Earl Grey out for a walk first?"

"Would you?" asked Theodosia.

"Love to," said Bethany.

"She really is in a wonderful mood," Drayton remarked in an offhand manner to Haley.

Bethany stood stock-still in the middle of the tea room, and her eyes searched out the three of them. "You all have been talking about me!" she declared. "Haley, you told!" She admonished Haley's retreating back as Haley decided to quickly disappear into the safe confines of her kitchen.

"What is with that girl?" declared Bethany. Her face was pulled into a frown, and she was vexed over Haley's obvious revelation about her previous night's date.

Theodosia put a hand on Bethany's damp shoulder to reassure her. "She's happy for you, dear. That's all."

"I suppose she told you it was Tanner Joseph. We only went to a gallery opening. The Ariel Gallery over on George Street had a show of black-and-white photography. By Sidney Didion, a local photographer."

"Did you enjoy yourself?" asked Theodosia. She had read a review of the Didion exhibit, and it had sounded quite good. Titled "Ghosts," the show consisted of moody black-and-white photo essays of old plantations.

"I did." Now Bethany's eyes shone brightly. "Did you know Tanner spent an entire year in the Amazon? He has a master's degree in ecology from the University of Minnesota, and he went down to South America to study the ecosystem of the rain forest."

"Yes, he mentioned that to me."

"Isn't it fascinating?" Bethany's face had taken on a curious glow.

Why, she seems to really care for this young man, thought Theodosia. *It's heartening to see her coming out of mourning and actually take an interest in someone.*

"Tanner spent a week living in a six-by-eight-foot tree house in the rain forest canopy," said Bethany. "Apparently he had this whole system of pulleys and harnesses and long ropes that allowed him to ride from one treetop to another and collect samples. Of course, I have acrophobia and absolutely *die* if I venture more than four feet off the ground, but it does sound like an amazing adventure."

"I've seen photos of researchers doing that in *National Geographic*," said Theodosia. "You really do need to be fearless about heights."

"There's a whole microcosm of plant and animal life up in those trees!" Bethany went on. "Insects, botanicals, birds. Most of them never touch the ground. Tanner told me all about these weird little green frogs."

Hairs suddenly prickled on the back of Theodosia's neck. "What did he tell you about frogs, Bethany?"

"Just that there's a certain type of frog the natives collect. They're very beautiful, bright green and yellow, but they're venomous. So the Indians dip the tips of their arrows into the frog's venom, then use those arrows for hunting. And Tanner told me about the most amazing orchids that grow up there, too. Bromeliads, actually. Orchid cousins. He says some of them have blooms that are ten inches across. Isn't that amazing?"

"It is," agreed Theodosia, but her mind was elsewhere. For some reason, she had gotten a terribly uneasy feeling the moment Bethany mentioned the frogs. Uneasy, she supposed, because it meant Tanner Joseph had a working knowledge of a certain kind of poison. And, she realized that the first time she had met Tanner Joseph, he had been outspoken about having a problem . . . no, make that a fairly substantial grudge . . . against Hughes Barron.

After Bethany left on her walk with Earl Grey, Theodosia sat in her office alone, pondering this new information. Could this just be a bizarre coincidence? Was truth, indeed, stranger than fiction? Take your pick, she thought. If it was a coincidence, it certainly was an odd one. And if Tanner Joseph was somehow *not* the mild-mannered eco-crusader he portrayed himself as (and she suddenly remembered how Tanner Joseph had shown a cold satisfaction when he'd spoken of Hughes Barron's karmic death), then it meant Bethany could be in serious danger.

And she was the one who'd put her in harm's way.

Theodosia lowered her head into her hands and rubbed her eyes tiredly. Damn! In her eagerness to get her tea labels done, she seemed to have opened up yet another can of worms.

Worse yet, if Bethany was still a suspect in the eyes of Bert Tidwell, and Tanner Joseph was somehow connected . . . Well . . . the possibilities weren't good at all.

Theodosia sighed heavily and gazed about her office distractedly. A piece of paper sitting on the corner of her desk caught her attention. It was the sheet she'd begun two days ago. The sheet that looked like a family tree. But instead of family names she had written "Hughes Barron" and "Poison?" at the top and the names "Timothy Neville" and "Lleveret Dante" underneath.

Theodosia picked up a silver pen. Purposefully, but with a good deal of anguish, she added a third name to her sheet: the name of Tanner Joseph.

29

By evening, the rain still showed no sign of letting up. A tropical disturbance had swept in from the Atlantic and hunkered down over the grand strand and the sea islands. Its fury extended a hundred miles in either direction, north to Myrtle Beach, south to Savannah.

Above the tea shop, in her little apartment just six blocks from Charleston Harbor, Theodosia could feel the full fury of the storm. Rain pounded the roof, lashed at the windows, and gurgled noisily down drain spouts. At moments when the storm's saber rattling seemed to abate slightly, she swore she could hear a foghorn from somewhere over near Patriots Point.

Lighting a fire in the fireplace in the face of so much wind would have meant losing precious warmth. Instead Theodosia lit a dozen white candles of varying sizes and placed them inside the fireplace. Now they danced and flickered merrily. Maybe not imparting warmth in terms of temperature, but certainly lending a cozy, tucked-in kind of feeling.

Curled up on her couch, a handmade afghan snuggled around her,

Theodosia sipped a cup of Egyptian chamomile. The taste was slightly sweet, reminiscent of almonds and apples. A good evening calm-you-down tea.

Calming was exactly what she needed, because instead of conducting a quiet investigation and perhaps discovering a lead on Hughes Barron's murderer, she seemed to have uncovered a number of potential suspects.

Timothy Neville hated Hughes Barron with white-hot passion, despised the man because of Barron's callous disregard for historic buildings and architecture. Somehow Timothy had known that Hughes Barron was making a play for the Peregrine Building. Timothy's assumption had been that Hughes Barron would have made significant changes to it. Would that have enraged Timothy Neville enough for him to commit murder? Perhaps. He was old, inflexible, used to getting his way. And Timothy Neville had a bottle of sulfuric acid in his study.

She had told Drayton about her discovery last night, after they'd departed Timothy Neville's house. He'd reinforced the notion that sulfuric acid was, indeed, used to remove rust and corrosion from old metal. But Timothy Neville going so far as actually pouring a dollop in Hughes Barron's teacup? Well, they didn't really have the toxicologist's report, did they? And neither of them could recall Timothy Neville's exact movements the night of the Lamplighter Tour. They only remembered that, for a short time, he'd been a guest in the back garden at the Avis Melbourne Home.

Then there was Lleveret Dante. From the conversation she'd overheard outside Sam Sestero's office, Hughes Barron's portion of Goose Creek Holdings fell neatly into Lleveret Dante's hands as a result of Barron's death. Plus, the man was obviously a scoundrel, since he was under indictment in another state. Theodosia wondered if Dante had fled Kentucky just steps ahead of an arrest or, like so many unsavory business characters today, had a slick Kentucky lawyer working on his behalf, firing off a constant barrage of appeals and paperwork until the case all but faded away.

Finally, there was Tanner Joseph, executive director of the Shorebird Environmentalist Group. *She* had brought him into their lives, had invited Tanner Joseph into the safety and security of their little tea shop. Could an environmentalist be overzealous? Consumed with bitterness at losing a battle?

Theodosia knew the answer was yes. The papers were full of stories about people who routinely risked their own lives to save the whales, the dolphins, the redwoods. Did those people ever kill others who stood in the way of their conservation efforts? Unfortunately, the answer was yes on that point, too. Redwoods were often spiked with metal pieces that bounced saw blades back into loggers' faces. Some animal rights activists, bitterly opposed to hunting, actually opened fire on hunters. It wasn't inconceivable that Tanner Joseph could be such a fanatic. History had proven that passion unchecked yields freely to fanaticism.

Theodosia shucked off her afghan, stretched her long legs, and stood. She padded to the kitchen in her stocking feet. From his woven rag rug in front of the fireplace, Earl Grey lifted his fine head and gazed at her with concern.

"Be right back," she told him.

In the kitchen, Theodosia took an English shortbread cookie from one of the pretty tins that rested on her counter. From a red and yellow tin decorated with pictures of noble hunting dogs she took a dog biscuit.

Doggy biscotti, she thought to herself as she returned to the living room where the two of them munched their cookies companionably. *Could be a profitable sideline.* Just last month she'd seen a magazine article about the booming business of gourmet dog treats.

Finishing off her cookie, Theodosia swiveled around and scanned the floor-to-ceiling bookshelf directly behind her. She selected a small, leather-bound volume and settled back comfortably again to reread her Agatha Christie.

The book she'd chosen was a fascinating primer on poison. She read eagerly as Agatha Christie described in delicious detail a "tasteless, odorless white powder that is poorly soluble in cold water but excellent to dissolve in hot cocoa, milk, or tea."

This terrible poison, arsenic, Theodosia learned, was completely undetectable. But one tablespoon could administer ten to thirty times the lethal dose.

As if on cue, the lights flickered, lending a strange magic lantern feel to the living room. Ever the guard dog, Earl Grey rose up a few inches and growled in response. Then there was a low hum, as though the generators at South Carolina Light and Power were lodging a mighty protest, and the lights burned strong and steady again.

When the lights had dimmed momentarily, Theodosia's startled reaction had been to close her book. Now she sat with the slim volume in her lap, staring out the rain-spattered window, catching an occasional flash of lightning from far away.

She considered what she had just read. Arsenic was amazingly lethal and extremely fast acting. Death occurred almost instantaneously.

But from what she had been able to piece together, Hughes Barron had walked into the garden under his own power and probably sat at the far table, drinking tea, for a good half hour. So Hughes Barron must have died slowly, perhaps not even knowing he was dying. Poisoned, to be sure, but some type of poison that deliberately slowed his heart until, like a pocket watch not properly wound, it simply stopped.

30

Drayton was deep in thought behind the counter, his gray head bent over the black leather ledger. He scratched numbers onto a yellow legal pad, then added them up using a tiny credit card–sized calculator. When he saw the total, he frowned. Painstakingly, he added the numbers again. Unfortunately, he arrived at the same total the second time through.

Sighing heavily, Drayton massaged the bridge of his nose where his glasses had pinched and looked out at the tea shop. Haley and Bethany were doing a masterful job, pouring tea, waiting on tables, coaxing customers into having a second slice of cream cake or taking home a few scones for tomorrow's breakfast. But once again, only half the tables were occupied.

Clearly, business was down, and his numbers told him they were down almost 40 percent from the same week a year ago. Granted, Thanksgiving was two weeks away, Christmas just around the corner. With the holidays would come the inevitable Christmas rush. But that rush should have showed signs of starting by now, shouldn't it?

The tourist trade brought in revenue, to be sure, as did the special tea parties they catered, like the bridal shower tea yesterday or the various birthday celebration teas. But the real bread and butter for the Indigo Tea Shop was repeat customers from around the neighborhood. For whatever reason (although in his heart Drayton was quite confident he knew the reason) many of the locals were skittishly staying away.

"We need to talk." Drayton's quiet but carefully modulated voice carried above the light jazz that played on the radio in Theodosia's office.

When she saw Drayton standing in the doorway, trusty ledger and sheaf of papers clutched in hand, she snapped off the music. "Rats. You've got that look on your face."

Drayton crossed the faded Oriental carpet, hooked a leg of the upholstered side chair with his toe, and pulled it toward him. He deposited his ledger and papers atop Theodosia's desk and sat down heavily in the chair.

"It's not good," she said.

"It's not good," he replied.

"Are we talking tailspin or just awfully slow?" asked Theodosia.

Drayton chewed his lower lip thoughtfully.

"I see," said Theodosia. She leaned back in her high-backed leather chair and closed her eyes. According to the Tea Council of the USA, tea was a five-billion-dollar industry, poised to boom in much the same way coffee had. Tea shops and tea salons were opening at a dizzying rate. Coffee shops were hastily adding tea to their repertoire. And bottled teas, although she didn't care for them personally, were highly popular.

All of that was great, she mused. Tea was making a comeback, big time. But all she wanted to do was make a secure little living and keep everyone here on the payroll. Would that be possible? Judging by the somber look on Drayton's face, perhaps not.

Theodosia pulled herself up straight in her chair. "Okay, what do we do?" she asked. "Try to roll out the Web site fast? Open up a second front?" She knew the battlefield analogy would appeal to Drayton, since he was such a World War II buff.

"We probably should have done exactly that earlier," said Drayton. His eyes shone with regret rather than reproach.

Theodosia's manicured fingers fluttered through the cards in her Rolodex. "Let me call Jessica at Todd & Lambeau. See what can be done." She dialed the phone and, while waiting for it to be answered, reached over to her bookcase and grabbed the stack of Web designs. "Here. Pick one." She thrust the storyboards toward Drayton.

"Hello," said Theodosia. "Jessica Todd, please. Tell her it's Theodosia Browning at the Indigo Tea Shop." She covered the mouthpiece with her hand. "They're putting me through," she said.

Drayton nodded.

"Hello, Jessica? I'm sorry, who? Oh, her assistant." Theodosia listened intently. "You don't say. An online brokerage. And you're sure it won't be any sooner? No, not really. Well, have Jessica call me once she's back in the office."

Theodosia grinned crookedly as she set the phone down. "Plan B."

Drayton lifted one eyebrow, amused at the magnitude of his employer's energy and undaunted spirit. "Which is?"

"Until this entire mess is cleared up, a dark cloud is going to be hanging over all of us." Theodosia stood, as if to punctuate her sentence.

"You're probably right, but you make it sound terribly ominous," said Drayton. "What is this plan B that you spoke of?"

Theodosia flashed him a brilliant smile. "I'm going to a funeral."

31

It isn't for naught that Charleston has been dubbed the Holy City. One hundred eighty-one church steeples, spires, bell towers, and crosses thrust majestically into the sky above the low-profile cityscape, a testament to Charleston's three-hundred-year history as well as its acceptance of those fleeing religious persecution.

The First Presbyterian Church, known as Scots Kirk, was founded in 1731 by twelve Scottish families.

Saint Michael's Episcopal Church, established in 1751, was where George Washington and the Marquis de Lafayette worshiped.

The Unitarian Church, conceived as the Independent Church in 1772, was appropriated by the British militia during the Revolutionary War and used briefly to stable horses.

It was in this Unitarian Church, with its stately Gothic design, that mourners now gathered. Heads bowed, listening to a sorrowful dirge by Mozart echo off the vast, vaulted ceiling with its delicate plaster fantracery that painstakingly replicated the Henry VII Chapel at Westminster Abbey.

Theodosia stood in the arched stone doorway and shivered. The weather was still chilly, not more than fifty degrees, and this great stone church with its heavy buttresses never seemed to quite warm up inside. The stained glass windows, so beautiful and conducive to contemplation, also served to deflect the sun's warming rays.

So far, more than three dozen mourners had streamed past her and taken seats inside the church. Theodosia wondered just who these people were. Relatives? Friends? Business acquaintances? Certainly not the residents of Edgewater Estates!

Theodosia knew it was standard police technique to stake out funerals. In cases of murder and sometimes arson, perpetrators often displayed a morbid curiosity, showing up at funerals and graveside services.

Would that be the case today? she wondered. Just hanging out, hoping for someone to show up, seemed like a very Sherlock Holmesian thing to do, outdated, a trifle simplistic. Unfortunately, it was the best she'd been able to come up with for the moment.

"My goodness, Theodosia!"

Theodosia whirled about and found herself staring into the smooth, unlined face of Samantha Rabathan. She noted that Samantha looked very fetching, dressed in a purple suit and jaunty black felt hat set with a matching purple plume.

"Don't you look charming in your shopkeeper's black velvet," Samantha purred.

Theodosia had made a last-minute decision to attend Hughes Barron's funeral, hadn't had time to change, and, thus had jumped into her Jeep Cherokee dressed in a black turtleneck sweater, long black velvet skirt, and comfortable short black boots. She supposed she might look a trifle dowdy compared to Samantha's bright purple. And it certainly wasn't uncharacteristic of Samantha to insinuate so.

"I had no idea you were friends with Hughes Barron," began Theodosia.

Samantha smiled sadly. "We made our acquaintance at the Heritage Society. He was a new board member. I was . . ."

She was about to say long-term member but quickly changed her answer.

"I was Lamplighter chairperson."

Theodosia nodded. It made sense. Samantha was always doing what was proper or decorous or neighborly. Even if she sometimes added her own special twist.

The two women walked into the church and stood at the rear overlooking the many rows of pews.

Samantha nudged Theodosia with an elbow. "I understand," Samantha whispered, "that woman in the first row is Hughes Barron's cousin." She nodded toward the back of a woman wearing a mustard-colored coat. "Lucille Dunn from North Carolina."

The woman sat alone, head bowed. "That's the only relative?" Theodosia asked.

"So far as I know," Samantha whispered, then tottered up the aisle, for she had already spotted someone else she wanted to chat with.

Slipping into one of the back pews, Theodosia sat quietly as the organ continued to thunder. From her vantage point, she could now study the funeral attendees. She saw several members of the Heritage Society, the lawyer, Sam Sestero, and a man who looked like an older Xerox copy, probably the brother, Edward, of Sestero & Sestero. There was Lleveret Dante, dressed conservatively in brown instead of a flashy white suit. And Burt Tidwell. She might have known.

But no Timothy Neville. And no Tanner Joseph.

The service was simple and oddly sad. A gunmetal gray coffin draped in black crepe, a minister who talked of resurrection and salvation but allowed as to how he had never really acquainted himself with Hughes Barron.

Struck by melancholy, Theodosia wondered who would attend her funeral, should she meet an early and untimely end. Aunt Libby, Drayton, Haley, Bethany, Samantha, Delaine, Angie and Mark Congdon of the Featherbed House, probably Father Jonathan, and some of her old advertising cronies.

How about Jory Davis? Would he crowd in with the other mourners? Would he remember her fondly? Should she call and invite him to dinner?

Theodosia was still lost in thought when the congregation launched into its final musical tribute, a slightly off-key rendition of "Amazing Grace."

As was tradition at funeral services, the mourners in the front rose first and made their way down the aisle, while those folks in the back kept the singing going as best they could. That, of course, put Theodosia at the very end of the line for expressing condolences to Hughes Barron's only relative, Lucille Dunn.

She stood in the nave of the church, a small woman with watery blue eyes, pale skin, and brownish blond hair worn in a tired shag style. The mustard color of her coat did not complement her skin tone and only served to make her appear more faded and worn out.

"You were a friend?" Lucille Dunn asked, her red-rimmed eyes focused on a point somewhere over Theodosia's right shoulder.

"Yes, I was." Theodosia managed an appropriately pained expression.

"A close friend?" Lucille Dunn's pale blue eyes suddenly honed in on Theodosia sharply.

Lord, thought Theodosia, *where is this conversation going?*

"We had been close." Close at the hour of his death, thought Theodosia, then was immediately struck by a pang of guilt. *Here I am,* she told herself guiltily, *lying to the relative of a dead man. And on the day of his funeral.* She glanced into the dark recess of the church, almost fearful that a band of enraged angels might be advancing upon her.

Lucille Dunn reached out her small hand to clutch Theodosia's hand. "If there's anything you'd like from the condo, a memento or keepsake, be sure to . . ." The cousin finished with a tight grimace, and her whole body seemed to sag. Then her eyes turned hard. "Angelique won't want anything. She didn't even bother flying back for the funeral."

"Angelique?" Theodosia held her breath.

"His wife. *Estranged* wife. She's off in Provence doing God knows what." Lucille Dunn daubed at her nose with a tissue. "Heartless," she whispered.

From a short distance away, Lleveret Dante made small talk with two commercial realtors while he kept his dark eyes squarely focused on the woman with the curly auburn hair. It was the same woman he'd seen acting suspiciously, trying to stake him out at Sam Sestero's office. The same one he'd followed back to that tea shop. And now, like a bad penny, she'd turned up again. Theodosia Browning.

Oh, yes, he knew exactly who she was. He enjoyed an extensive network of informants and tipsters. Highly advantageous. Especially when you needed to learn the contents of a sealed bid or there was an opportunity to undercut a competitor. His sources had informed him that the Browning woman had been in the garden the night his ex-partner, Hughes Barron, had died. Wasn't that so very interesting? The question was, what was she suspicious about? Obviously something, because she'd been snooping around. She and that overbearing fool, Tidwell. Well, the hell with them. Just let them try to put a move on him. He knew how to play hardball. Hell, in his younger days, he'd done jail time.

Gravel crunched loudly on the parking lot surface behind her, and Theodosia was aware of heavy, nasal breathing. It had to be Tidwell coming to speak with her, and she was in no mood for a verbal joust.

She spun around. "What are you doing here?" she demanded. She knew she was being rude, but she didn't care.

"Keeping an eye out," Tidwell replied mildly. He pulled a small packet of Sen-Sen out of his jacket pocket, shook out a piece and stuck the packet back in his pocket without bothering to offer any to her.

"You should keep an eye on *him*." Theodosia nodded sharply toward Lleveret Dante. Down the line of cars, Dante had pulled himself apart from a small cluster of people and was hoisting himself up into a chocolate brown Range Rover. Theodosia noted that the SUV was tricked out ridiculously with every option known to man. Grill guard, fog lights, roof rack, the works.

Tidwell didn't even try to hide his smirk. "There's enough people keeping an eye on him. It's the quiet ones I worry about."

Quiet like Bethany, Theodosia thought angrily. "When are you going to get off Bethany's case?" she demanded. "The more you continue to harass her, the more you look like a rank amateur."

Bert Tidwell guffawed loudly.

"Oh, Theo!" a voice tinkled merrily.

Theodosia and Bert Tidwell both looked around to see Samantha bearing down upon them.

"What is it, Samantha?"

"I was going to ride with Tandy and George Bostwick, but they're going to go out to Magnolia Cemetery, and I need to get back for an appointment. Can you be a dear and give me a lift? Just a few blocks over, drop me near your shop?" she inquired breathlessly.

"Of course, Samantha. I'd be delighted." And without a fare-thee-well to Burt Tidwell, Theodosia wrenched open the passenger door for Samantha, then stalked around the rear of her Jeep and climbed in.

"What was *that* all about?" Samantha asked as she fastened her seat belt, plopped her purse atop the center console, and ran a quick check of her lipstick in the rearview mirror.

Theodosia turned the key in the ignition and gunned the engine. "That was Bert Tidwell being a boor." She double-clutched from first into third, and the Jeep lurched ahead. "Thanks for the rescue."

"It is you who . . . Oh, Theodosia!" cried Samantha with great consternation as the Jeep careened onto the curb, swished perilously close to an enormous clump of tea olive trees, then swerved back onto the street again. "Kindly restrain yourself. I am in no way ready for one of your so-called off-road experiences!"

32

By the time she dropped Samantha at Church Street and Wentworth, Lucille Dunn's words, "If there's anything you'd like from the condo, a keepsake, a memento," were echoing feverishly in her brain. So Theodosia sailed right on by the Indigo Tea Shop and drove the few blocks down to The Battery.

Pulling into one of the parking lots, Theodosia noted that the wind was still driving hard. Had to be at least twenty knots. Flags were flapping and snapping, only a handful of people strolled the shoreline or walked the gardens, and then with some difficulty.

Out in the bay, there was a nasty chop on the water. Overhead, a few high, stringy gray clouds scudded along. Squinting and shielding her eyes from the hazy bright sun, Theodosia could see a few commercial boats on the bay, probably shrimpers. But only one sailboat. Had to be at least a forty-footer, and it was heeled over nicely, coming in fast, racing down the slot between Patriots Point and Fort Sumter. It would be heaven to be out sailing today, gulls wheeling overhead, mast creaking and straining, focusing your efforts only on pounding ocean.

"If there's anything you'd like from the condo, a keepsake, a memento."

Enough, already, thought Theodosia as the thought jerked her back to the here and now. Lucille Dunn had obviously mistaken her for a close female friend of Hughes Barron. Of that she had no doubt. Okay, maybe that wasn't all bad. It gave her a kind of tacit permission to go to Hughes Barron's condo.

Well, *permission* might be an awfully strong word. At the very least, Lucille Dunn's words had bolstered her resolve to investigate further.

But what condo had Lucille Dunn been referring to? Had Hughes Barron actually lived at that ghastly Edgewater Estates? Or did he have a place somewhere else? She vaguely recalled Drayton saying something once about the Isle of Palms.

Theodosia sat in the patchy sun, watching waves slap the rocky shoreline and tapping her fingers idly on the dashboard. Only one way to find out.

She dug in the Jeep's console for her cell phone, punched it on, and dialed information.

She told the operator, "I need the number for a Hughes Barron. That's B-A-R-R-O-N." She waited impatiently as the operator consulted her computer listings, praying that the number hadn't been disconnected yet and there'd be no information available. But, lo and behold, there was a listing, the only listing, for a Hughes Barron. The address was 617 Prometheus on the Isle of Palms. It definitely had to be him.

Grace Memorial Bridge is an amalgam of metal latticework that rises up steeply from the swamps and lowlands to span the Cooper River. The bridge affords a spectacular view of the surrounding environs and offers a bit of a thrill ride, so sharply does it rise and then descend.

Theodosia whipped across Grace Memorial in her Jeep, reveling in the view, grateful that the one- and sometimes two-hour backup that often occurred during rush hour was still hours away.

Twenty minutes later, she was on the Isle of Palms. This bedroom community of five thousand often swelled to triple the population in the summer months when all hotels, motels, resorts, and beach houses were occupied by seasonal renters, eager to dip their toes in the pristine waters and enjoy the Isles of Palms' seven unbroken miles of sandy beach.

Hurricane Hugo had hit hard here back in 1989, but you'd hardly know it now. Little wooden beach homes had been replaced by larger, sturdier homes built on stilts. Shiny new resorts and luxury hotels had sprung up where old motels and tourist cabins had been washed away.

Theodosia had little trouble locating Hughes Barron's condo. It was just off the main road, a few hundred yards down from a cozy-looking Victorian hotel of gray clapboard called the Rosedawn Inn.

Located directly on the beach, Hughes Barron's condo was part of a row of approximately twenty-four contemporary-looking condos. Judging from their low-slung, beach-hugging design, they were far more town-house than condo.

After consulting the mailboxes and finding Hughes Barron's unit number, Theodosia headed for Barron's condo via a wooden board-walk that zigzagged through waving clusters of dune grass. Pretty, she thought, and certainly a lot more upscale than his development, Edgewater Estates.

Had Hughes Barron developed these condos, too? she wondered. Or had he purchased a unit here because he saw it as a good investment? Just maybe, Theodosia thought, Hughes Barron was smarter than anyone had given him credit for. The over-the-top garishness of Edgewater Estates and its apparent success meant he had thoroughly understood the taste of his audience.

The front door of unit eight stood open on its hinges.

Slightly unnerved, Theodosia rapped loudly on the doorjamb. "Hello," she called. "Anyone home?"

A juggernaut of a woman wearing yellow rubber gloves appeared at the door. Had to be the cleaning lady, Theodosia immediately guessed.

"You with the police?" the woman asked.

Theodosia noted that the cleaning lady's tone was as dull as her gray hair and as nondescript as her enormous smock.

"I've been working with them," replied Theodosia, crossing her fingers behind her back at the little white lie.

"Private investigator?"

"You could say that," said Theodosia.

"Um hm." The cleaning lady bobbed her head tiredly. "I'm Mrs. Finster. I come in twice a week to clean. Course, I don't know what's going to happen now that Mr. Barron is gone." She retreated into the condo, and picked up a crystal vase filled with dead, brackish-looking flowers. "They already took some things, left me with a nice mess," she said unhappily.

By "they," Theodosia presumed Mrs. Finster meant the police.

Theodosia followed Mrs. Finster into the condo. It was a spacious, contemporary place. Low cocoa-colored leather couch, nice wood coffee table, wall filled with high-tech stereo gear, potted plants, lots of windows. She watched as Mrs. Finster halfheartedly moved things about in the kitchen.

"You just come from the funeral?" asked Mrs. Finster. She flipped the top on a bottle of Lysol and gave the counter a good squirt.

"Yes."

"Nice?"

"It was very dignified."

"Good." Mrs. Finster set the Lysol down, pulled off her rubber gloves, and brushed quickly at her eyes. "The man deserved as much. Me, I don't attend any kind of church service anymore. My first husband was an atheist."

Theodosia thought there might be more of an explanation for that somewhat strange statement, but nothing seemed to be forthcoming.

"Had you worked for Mr. Barron a long time?" she asked.

"A year, give or take," replied Mrs. Finster. "Him and the Missus."

Theodosia could barely contain her excitement. "His wife lived here, too?"

Mrs. Finster looked at her sharply.

"I only say that," said Theodosia, "because I had heard his wife was overseas."

Mrs. Finster considered her statement and shrugged. "Well, *someone* lived here with him. At least her things were always around. I never met the lady personally. People are funny that way. Most of 'em get out of the house when it comes time for someone to clean. Probably embarrassing for them. Having somebody else scrub their toilets or wipe toothpaste drips and drops out of the sink."

"Could be," agreed Theodosia.

"Anyhoo," continued Mrs. Finster, "now her stuff's gone. Moved out, I guess."

"Did you tell the police that?" asked Theodosia.

"That the lady moved out?"

"Yes," said Theodosia.

"Why?" Mrs. Finster planted her hands on her formidable hips. "They didn't ask."

The revelation of a lady friend was news to Theodosia. She pondered the ramifications of her new discovery on her drive back to Charleston.

Obviously, the woman who'd been living at the Isle of Palms condo wasn't the wife, Angelique, who was still languishing in Provence somewhere. Yet Hughes Barron had obviously been playing house with someone. Someone who might be able to shed considerable light on his death. Or maybe even know of a motive for his murder.

How involved had this mystery woman been in Barron's business dealings? Theodosia wondered. And where was she now? Had she been in attendance at the funeral today? Or was she hiding out for fear she might be the next victim?

33

Soft background music played as Bethany and Haley leaned over the counter, giggling. At the large table in the corner, Drayton sat with three guests, presiding over a tea tasting. For some reason, the women had wanted to focus only on Indian teas, so Drayton had brewed pots of Kamal Terai, Okayti Darjeeling, and Chamraj Nilgiri.

Now, as Theodosia sat at a small table near the window, ruminating over the events of the day, she could hear the four of them using tea-taster terms such as *biscuity,* a reference to tea that's been fired, and *soft,* which meant a tea had been purposely underfermented.

Indian teas were all well and good, but today Theodosia needed a little extra fortification. She'd opted for a pot of Chinese Pai Mu Tan, a rare white tea from southern China, also known as White Peony. With its soft aroma and smooth flavor, it was also known to aid digestion. After the roller-coaster ride of the past week, and the surprising revelations of today, Theodosia figured her digestive system could use a little settling.

"Bethany," Theodosia called quietly from where she was seated.

Bethany immediately came over to Theodosia's table and favored her with a wan smile.

"Sit with me for a minute."

Bethany's smile slipped off her face. "Am I fired? I'm not fired, am I?" She twisted her head around to peer at Haley. "I know it looks like we were goofing off over there, but I've got a—"

"Bethany, you're not fired. Please, try to relax." Theodosia smiled warmly to show Bethany she really meant it.

"Sorry." Bethany cast her eyes downward. "You must think I'm some kind of paranoid goose."

Theodosia poured Bethany a cup of tea. "No, I think you were treated unfairly at the Heritage Society, and it stuck in your craw. The experience has left your confidence more than a little shaken."

"You're right," Bethany admitted shyly. "It has."

"But I want to ask you something," said Theodosia, "and I don't want you to read anything more into it than the fact that it's just a simple, straightforward question, okay?"

"Okay," said Bethany, looking nervous again.

Theodosia leaned forward. "Bethany, you got into an argument with Hughes Barron, is that correct?"

"I spoke up to him at one meeting at the Heritage Society, but I wouldn't call it arguing. Really. You can ask Drayton."

"I believe you," said Theodosia. "And later, after that same meeting where Timothy Neville took offense at Hughes Barron and verbally chastised him—"

"He certainly did," Bethany agreed.

"You talked to Hughes Barron again. *After* the meeting?"

"I . . . I did. To tell you the truth, I felt kind of sorry for him. He was a new board member who had made a generous donation and then was treated badly. I know it wasn't my place, me being the new kid, but I kind of apologized to him. I didn't want him to think we were all maniacs. After all, *he* wasn't the one who lost his temper, it was Timothy Neville."

"Bethany, I have to ask this. Are you . . . did you have any dealings with Hughes Barron outside the Heritage Society?"

The stricken look on Bethany's face was the only answer she needed.

"I never talked to him alone except for that one time, after the meeting. That was the one and only time. On the night of the Lamplighter Tour, I didn't serve him. Haley did. I only . . ." Her voice trailed off.

Theodosia nodded and sat back. In her wildest dreams she hadn't believed that Bethany could be the mysterious girlfriend. But she had to ask. And if Bethany *had* spoken to Hughes Barron after that meeting, *apologized* to him like she said, maybe Timothy Neville had overheard her

words and been enraged. That would certainly account for her being summarily fired. *Fired for an act of kindness,* thought Theodosia. *What is the
world coming to?*

Bethany was smiling shyly at Theodosia. "Haley and I were working
on a new idea."

"What's that, Bethany?" My God, the girl had looked so stricken.
How could she have even *thought* she might have been involved with
Hughes Barron?

"At the photo exhibition the other night, I ran into a friend. We got
to talking, and I told her I was working here. Anyway, she called this
morning and asked if we could cater a teddy bear tea. For her daughter's
eighth birthday party."

Theodosia considered the request. She'd heard of teddy bear teas for
children. They'd just never done one.

"I said we could do it." Bethany paused. "Can we do it?"

Theodosia smiled at Bethany's hopeful eagerness. "I suppose so. Have
you talked to Drayton yet? He's major domo in charge of all catering."

"I have, and he suggested I take a shot at working up a menu and a
few party activities, then submit a proposal to my friend."

"Bethany, I think that's a fine idea."

"You do?"

"Is that what you and Haley were working on?"

"Yes, we've already got three pages of notes."

"Good for you." Theodosia smiled.

The bell over the door suddenly tinkled merrily.

"Two for tea?" asked Tanner Joseph as he stood in the doorway smiling at the two women seated at the small table.

Bethany rose awkwardly. "Hello, Mr. Jo—Tanner. Could I get you a
cup of . . . Oh, excuse me." She suddenly spotted the stack of art boards
under his arm. "You're here on business. The labels." She suddenly bolted,
leaving Theodosia to contend with an amused Tanner Joseph.

"She's a wonderful girl," he said, sitting down.

"We think so," agreed Theodosia. She was determined to play it cool
and carry on with her review of his label ideas.

Tanner set a stack of art boards on the table between them. "Tea labels, as promised," he said. "But I must confess, I took them a bit beyond the pencil stage."

"Whatever you did, it certainly didn't take you long," said Theodosia.

"You could say I threw myself into it." He favored her with a grin.

Dressed today in dark green slacks and a green military-looking sweater with cotton shoulder epaulets, Tanner Joseph looked rather dashing and every inch an eco commando. Though Theodosia had the distinct feeling he used his good looks to leverage every possible advantage, she could certainly see why Bethany had accepted a date with him. He was a handsome young man.

"Let's take a look at what you've got," said Theodosia. For the next few minutes, she banished all thoughts of poison frogs from her head as she studied the four label illustrations Tanner Joseph had created.

They were good. Better, in fact, than anything Theodosia had hoped for. Rendered in black and white, they were punchy and strong. They weren't just sketches but finished art, beautifully finished at that. Theodosia knew that once Tanner received approval from her, it was a simple matter of adding a bit of color.

"These are wonderful," declared Theodosia. She was particularly delighted by the free-flowing brushstrokes and the calligraphy he had managed to incorporate.

"I tried to capture a bit of a Zen feeling," said Tanner, "but still convey the zest of your flavors."

"Drayton." Theodosia raised her voice just a touch.

Drayton looked over at her and held up a finger. His tea-tasting group was jabbering amongst themselves, and it looked like he would be able to extricate himself for a few moments.

"How long will it take to add color?" asked Theodosia.

"Not long, a few hours," said Tanner. "Oh, hello." He smiled up at Drayton. "I guess you're the gentleman who created the tea blends."

He extended his hand, and Drayton shook it even as his eyes roved over the drawings.

"I like these," Drayton declared. "I've not seen anything like this before. Most tea labels are flowery or carry coats of arms or clipper ships or drawings of tea leaves. These are like . . ." Drayton searched for the right words. "Like the wood-block prints I saw in Kyoto when I was there on a buying trip."

Tanner Joseph smiled. "I'll admit Japanese prints were in the back of my mind. Indian manuscript paintings, as well."

Drayton's eyes shone. "Well, that really makes it perfect then, doesn't it?"

"I'd say so," agreed Theodosia.

"And when will these be ready to go to the printer?" asked Drayton.

Theodosia and Tanner gazed at each other.

"Tanner thinks he can add the color in a matter of hours," said Theodosia.

Drayton half closed his eyes as he calculated the time frame. "The printer needs at least a week to do the adhesive-backed labels. Theodosia, did you order the tins yet?"

"Yes," she replied.

"Gold or silver?"

"Gold."

"Two more days to sticker the tins and fill them," said Drayton. "So perhaps seven or eight working days at the outset."

"That's right," said Theodosia.

Drayton smiled at Tanner Joseph. "I think you've done a masterful job, young man. You certainly have my blessing."

Tanner bobbed his head, looking pleased. "Great." He smiled at Theodosia. "It's been a labor of love."

The bell over the door rang again, and a half dozen people entered the tea shop. Four immediately seated themselves at a table, and two began oohing and ahing over a display of Russell Hobbs tea kettles. At that same moment, both phone lines began to ring.

"Looks like your tea shop just got busy," declared Tanner. He began to collect his art boards. "I'd better get out of here and let you folks tend to business."

"Theodosia," called Haley from the counter, "telephone. A Mrs. Finster. Said she talked to you this morning. Something about Hughes Barron?"

Tanner Joseph's lip curled at the mention of Hughes Barron's name, and his eyes fastened on Theodosia. "The infamous developer," he spat out. "I wasn't aware Hughes Barron had been a friend of yours."

"He wasn't," replied Theodosia evenly, "but *you* certainly seem to have a strong aversion to the man. Or at least to his memory, since he's now deceased."

"Hughes Barron was a charlatan and an environmental pirate," Tanner declared vehemently. "I'm delighted he came to a well-deserved end."

"I see," said Theodosia, and a cold chill touched her heart. Their polite, enthusiastic meeting of a moment ago seemed to have rapidly deteriorated into a nasty go-round concerning Hughes Barron.

"Excuse me," said Theodosia. She rose from her chair and stalked off to take Mrs. Finster's call.

What an extraordinary woman, Tanner Joseph thought to himself as he quietly departed the Indigo Tea Shop. Confident, worldly, so full of energy. Since the moment she'd first walked into his office at the Shorebird Environmentalist Group, he had longed to learn everything there was to know about Theodosia Browning. Where had she grown up? What had she studied in college? What kind of man did she find attractive?

He had always found the simplest way to obtain a reliable dossier on someone was through their friends and acquaintances. So he had invited Bethany, her employee, to the gallery opening the other night. Of the two young women he had met in the tea shop, she had seemed the most needful, the most eager to talk. So he had flattered the girl, plied her with a few questions, appeared interested in her problems and her work. It had been simple enough.

Tanner Joseph glanced back at the brick-and-shingle facade of the Indigo Tea Shop and smiled to himself. What a fine joke that Hughes Barron had succumbed at the Lamplighter Tour's garden tea with a cup of Darjeeling clutched in his money-grubbing hand. Now he, Tanner Joseph, was designing a set of tea labels. It was those little touches of irony that made life so delightful.

Yes, he would keep an eye on this extraordinary creature, Theodosia. She was like some wonderful, rare tropical bird. But you couldn't just walk up and grab something like that. You had to charm it, woo it, make it feel safe. Only then could you hope to possess it.

34

"Hello, Mrs. Finster." Inwardly, Theodosia was shaking with anger from her conversation with Tanner Joseph.

"Miss Browning," said Mrs. Finster in her flat voice, "you asked me to call if I remembered anything that might pertain to the woman who lived with Mr. Barron."

"Yes," replied Theodosia, her voice almost a whisper, so upset was she.

"Well, I haven't," said Mrs. Finster.

"Then why—" began Theodosia.

"Because another detective came by after you."

"Tidwell," said Theodosia.

"That's right," said Mrs. Finster rather crossly, "and he showed me a badge. He had *credentials*."

Theodosia didn't say a word, but apparently Mrs. Finster wasn't that upset by her ruse because she continued after a moment.

"This Tidwell character acted like a bull in a china shop," she said. "At least you were polite. You showed concern for Mr. Barron."

"Did he ask many questions?" asked Theodosia.

"A few. Wanted to know if the woman living with Hughes Barron was a much *younger* woman."

"Thank you, Mrs. Finster," said Theodosia. "I really appreciate your calling."

Theodosia replaced the receiver in the cradle and glanced at the door. Drayton was shepherding his tea-tasting ladies outside, bidding them farewell. Theodosia tried to stifle the rising tide of anxiety inside her. She knew Drayton's good-byes were always prolonged.

DEATH BY DARJEELING 147

When he finally approached the counter a good five minutes later, she beckoned him to follow her into her office.

"Drayton." She closed the door softly. "I fear I've made a terrible mistake."

"What is it?" he said, instantly concerned.

"With Tanner Joseph."

His face had started to mirror her anxiety, but now it relaxed. "Oh, no, the labels are going to be perfect," he reassured her. "True, they are a trifle beyond the realm of traditional, but that's what makes them so charming. They're—" Drayton stopped midsentence and peered at Theodosia. Amazingly, he had detected a quiver to her lower lip, and her eyes seemed to sparkle a little too brightly. Could those be tears threatening to spill down her cheeks? He couldn't remember ever having seen Theodosia quite this upset. She was always so strong, so spunky.

"You weren't referring to the labels, were you?" Drayton asked.

Theodosia pursed her lips and shook her head. "No," she said hoarsely, finally getting her emotions under control.

He pulled out her desk chair. "Sit, please."

She did, and Drayton sat on the edge of her desk, facing her.

"Now tell me," he said quietly.

She looked up at him, worry clouding her blue eyes. "Drayton, Tanner Joseph is hiding something. Every time Hughes Barron's name is mentioned, he gets this hard, calculating look."

Drayton stared at her for a moment and stroked a hand across his chin. "I thought you were casting your suspicions toward Timothy Neville. Or Hughes Barron's awful partner. What was his name again?"

"Lleveret Dante. Yes, I have been," Theodosia said. "But that was before Tanner Joseph reacted so oddly."

"Oddly like a murderer?"

"I'm not sure," answered Theodosia. "But my main concern right now is with Bethany."

"She went out with him," Drayton said, suddenly catching on to why Theodosia seemed so upset.

"Yes, she did," said Theodosia.

"Then let's talk to her," Drayton urged. "See if we really do have something to fret over." He rose from the desk, moved swiftly to the door, and opened it. "Bethany," he called.

Haley appeared in the doorway. "We just sold two of those Hobbs teakettles, isn't that a scream? Two of them!" she announced delightedly. "One stainless steel, one millennium style." She paused, staring at the grim faces on Drayton and Theodosia. "What's wrong?"

"Everything," snapped Drayton.

"For gosh sakes, Drayton, lighten up a little," said Haley. She smiled brightly at Theodosia. "Hey, don't quote me on this, but I think business is turning around."

"We're not pulling our hair out over business," said Theodosia. "It's about Bethany. And Tanner Joseph."

"Oh," said Haley. She frowned quizzically and stared at the two of them.

"Theodosia thinks there's something a trifle off about Tanner Joseph," said Drayton.

"More than a trifle, Drayton," interjected Theodosia.

"In particular," said Drayton, "his attitude toward the late Mr. Hughes Barron."

Haley sobered immediately. "I think Bethany really likes that guy Tanner."

"What time is it?" asked Theodosia.

Drayton consulted his wristwatch. "Four-twen . . . four-thirty."

"Let's close early," suggested Theodosia. "Haley, would you latch the front door? And send Bethany back."

Haley glanced from one to the other, knowing something was up. "Sure."

Bethany had gathered her notes from her earlier brainstorming session on the teddy bear tea, fully prepared to present what she thought were some fun, innovative ideas. But the moment she set foot inside Theodosia's office, she knew the conversation was going to be a serious one.

"We want to ask you a few questions, Bethany," Theodosia began.

"Okay," said Bethany. She awkwardly shifted from one foot to the other.

"Do you want to sit down?" offered Theodosia.

"I'm fine." Bethany tilted her chin up, preparing for whatever was about to come her way.

Theodosia fumbled about, trying to figure out just where to start. Finally she plunged right in. "When you were with Tanner Joseph the other night, did he ask questions about Hughes Barron's death?"

"Not exactly," said Bethany slowly. "I mean, Tanner was already aware Hughes Barron had died. And we did sort of chat about it, but I think he could see it made me uncomfortable."

Bethany's eyes sought out Theodosia's and silently appealed to her. *See,* her eyes pleaded, *this makes me uncomfortable, too. This makes me relive that terrible night.*

"Did Tanner Joseph ask probing questions?" asked Drayton.

Bethany frowned. "No. At least they didn't feel probing. We talked, that's pretty much it." She stared unhappily at the two of them. "What is this really about?"

"We think Tanner Joseph had a slightly unhealthy interest in Hughes Barron's death," said Theodosia.

"Theodosia," returned Bethany, "I think *you* have more than a passing interest in Hughes Barron's death."

"Tell Drayton about the frogs, Bethany."

Now Bethany just looked confused. "The frogs?"

"You know, the rain forest frogs," prompted Theodosia.

"Oh, God," said Drayton.

"Tanner Joseph just told me about his work in the Amazon rain forest. Studying the ecosystem up in the canopy."

"And he told you about poison frogs, Bethany. Frogs that exude toxins. Tanner Joseph knows all about toxins," said Theodosia determinedly.

Haley had suddenly appeared back in the doorway, anxious to know what was being said. Each time Theodosia's voice hit hard on the word *toxins,* she grimaced.

"There have to be dozens of plants and animals in the Amazon that are toxic," countered Bethany. "So what! To even *think* that Tanner Joseph had something to do with Hughes Barron's death is so unfair!"

"No, Bethany," said Theodosia. "Unfair is Bert Tidwell thinking *you* killed Hughes Barron."

Tears streamed down Bethany's face, and Haley quickly went to her side and put an arm around her.

"There, there," Haley tried to reassure Bethany. "Don't cry," she cooed softly. She gazed up at Theodosia. "You don't need to do this!" Her voice was strident, defensive.

Drayton's face blanched white. "Please!" he cried out. "I cannot stand to have us all squabble and argue. This terrible thing is wrenching us apart!" His hands were outstretched, as if imploring them all to calm down.

"Drayton's right," said Theodosia finally. "I'm so sorry, Bethany. I truly didn't mean to upset you." She slipped out of her chair and squeezed around her desk. Putting her hands on Bethany's glistening cheeks, she stared raptly into the girl's troubled eyes. "Know this, Bethany. I did not mean to push this so far."

Tears continued to stream down Bethany's face, and she hiccuped softly. Haley continued to pat her back and murmur, "There, there." Drayton twisted his hands in anguish at this display of feminine angst.

Finally, Bethany was able to stem her flow of tears and blow her nose. She took a deep breath, held her head up high. "I'm not upset that you think Tanner Joseph might be a murderer," she declared.

The three stared at her in stunned surprise.

"You're not?" said Theodosia.

Bethany stared at Theodosia. "I'm upset because he asked so many questions about you!"

35

While spaghetti noodles bobbed and swirled in a pot of boiling water, Theodosia heated butter and olive oil in a large skillet.

"How are you coming with the pancetta, Drayton?" she asked.

He was bent over the cutting board, knife in hand, chopping the pancetta into thin strips.

"Done," he said, stepping away. "Want me to add it to the skillet?"

Theodosia checked the wall clock. Everything seemed to be timing out just right. "Yes."

Through the arched doorway they could hear Haley and Bethany talking quietly, setting the table. Ever since Theodosia had made the suggestion that everyone come upstairs for dinner and all had enthusiastically agreed, the mood had been considerably calmer and more copacetic.

Theodosia popped the cork on a bottle of Vouvray and measured out a third of a cup.

Drayton peered at the label. "You use this for *cooking?* This is awfully good wine."

Theodosia interrupted her stirring to reach overhead for two wineglasses. She poured each of them a half glass. "That's the whole idea," she said.

"Salut." Drayton tipped the glass toward her, took an appraising sip. "Excellent. Love that dry finish."

Theodosia poured her one-third cup of white wine into the skillet and watched it hiss and bubble.

"Now reduce it to half?" asked Drayton.

Theodosia nodded as she stirred the mixture that was beginning to exude an enticing aroma.

"And you really use eggs instead of cream?"

She nodded again. "Egg yolks."

"I think I'm going to *adore* this spaghetti carbonara," said Drayton. "Of course, it's not exactly the cholesterol-buster's version."

"That's where the wine comes in," said Theodosia. "Supposed to have a neutralizing effect. Well, at least we hope it does."

"You mean like the French paradox," said Drayton. He was making reference to the staple diet in France that consists of bread, rich cheeses, eggs, cream, and lots of chocolate desserts. Yet, because of their almost daily consumption of wine, the French have an extremely low incidence of heart disease.

"My God," declared Haley as she tasted her first bite of the creamy spaghetti carbonara. "This is incredible!"

"It's amazing how far a little cheese, butter, olive oil, pancetta, and egg yolks will go toward making mere noodles palatable," said Drayton as he passed a loaf of crusty French bread across the table to Haley.

"That's what's in this?" asked Bethany. "Yikes! I'm going to be on lettuce and water for a week."

"Two weeks," said Theodosia.

"Isn't it worth it?" Drayton grinned.

The four of them, their squabbles put aside and forgotten, sat around Theodosia's dining table. They were dining on Theodosia's good china, the Picard, with tall pink tapers glowing in the center of the table. Looking through the French doors, the diners could observe a fire crackling in the fireplace and hear light jazz as it poured from the CD player. Earl Grey lay under the table, snoring softly. It was hard to believe that just an hour ago they had been upset, angry, suspicious.

"This was worth blowing off night school for," declared Haley as she wound the creamy pasta around her fork and took a final bite.

"Which class was it?" asked Bethany. Candlelight danced on her cheeks, and she certainly didn't look as though she'd been sobbing her heart out earlier.

"Abnormal psychology," said Haley.

There was silence around the table, then Theodosia spoke up. "I didn't realize you were taking a psych course, Haley."

Haley nodded brightly. "It's my second one."

"I thought you were majoring in communications," said Drayton.

"I changed my mind," said Haley.

"I'd like to propose a toast," said Bethany. She held up her glass of wine, and the other three followed suit.

"To friendship," she said.

"To friendship," they repeated.

"And solving mysteries," added Haley.

They all gazed at her quietly, not sure she was even being serious.

"Hey, come on," urged Haley. "We opened Pandora's box. Or at least Theodosia lifted the lid and peeked in. Now we've got to see it through."

"Haley's right," agreed Drayton. "Let's lay it all out on the table right now."

"You mean everything we know about the suspects?" said Theodosia.

"Yes. If you shared the information you've been able to gather," he said, "maybe working together, we could all add our perspective and come up with something."

"That's a great idea," said Haley. "Kind of like a mystery dinner."

"Or a mystery tea," spoke up Bethany. "Wouldn't that be a unique thing to offer! If you can do bridal shower teas and teddy bear teas and Valentine teas, why not mystery teas?"

Theodosia had to chuckle. Right in the middle of a serious conversation, Bethany had come up with a terrific marketing idea. Themed teas. And why not? Why not mystery teas or book lovers' teas or chamber music teas? Such catered affairs—downstairs at the tea shop, in local inns, in people's homes—would open up whole new directions for profitability.

"I positively adore the idea, Bethany," said Theodosia. "And I cheerfully pass the torch of marketing director along to you!"

"Oh, no! When all this is cleared up, I'm going back to the museum world. It's a lot quieter than a tea shop."

"A lot safer, too, I'll warrant," said Haley. "Now, Theodosia, fill us in on what you've found out about Hughes Barron. Share your suspicions concerning Timothy Neville and Tanner Joseph, too. And who's that weird partner again?"

"Lleveret Dante," said Drayton, carefully enunciating every syllable. "Anyone for a cup of Chinese Hao Ya?"

Everyone nodded, and Drayton scooted into the kitchen. Measuring four teaspoons of the smoky black Chinese tea into a teapot, he splashed in hot water and returned to the table.

Theodosia leaned forward and, in her quiet voice, shared her suspicions as well as the subsequent discoveries she'd made during the past few days. She spoke uninterrupted for at least thirty minutes. When she finished, the group was wide-eyed with wonderment, literally sitting on the edge of their chairs.

"Wow," whispered Haley. "You actually went to the morgue?"

Theodosia nodded.

"And you snooped in Timothy Neville's medicine cabinet?" asked Bethany.

"I can't say I'm proud of that," said Theodosia.

"How brave you were," Bethany replied. "I would have been scared to death."

"Lleveret Dante is really the wild card in all this, isn't he?" said Haley.

"What do you mean?" asked Theodosia.

"He's the one we don't know all that much about."

"I suppose you're right," said Theodosia.

"How do we go about changing that?" asked Drayton.

"Spy on him," piped up Haley matter-of-factly. "Run a background check, ask around, follow him if need be. Try to put together a profile."

"You go, girl," urged Bethany.

"Haley," said Theodosia, "are you sure you're not taking classes in criminology?"

"What about Tanner Joseph?" said Drayton. He gazed evenly at Theodosia. "He's still working on our tea labels."

"Leave him to me," said Theodosia.

It was eight o'clock when they all trooped down the stairs, a yawning Earl Grey padding after them. Everyone still felt sated from the rich dinner, talked out, yet heartened by a renewed sense of camaraderie.

"Someone's pinned a note to the door," remarked Drayton.

"I bet it's for me," said Haley as she slipped her sweater on. "One of the delivery services probably arrived late and found us closed."

Drayton pulled the paper from the door, where one corner had been stuck into the wood trim that framed the small window. "Let me put on my spectacles." He pulled wire-rim glasses from his jacket pocket, hooked the bows behind his ears, and studied the note. "Oh, no," he said, his face crumpling in dismay.

"What is it?" asked Theodosia, instantly on the alert. She snatched the note from Drayton's hand and scanned it quickly. When she looked up, she was white as a sheet.

"Someone's threatened Earl Grey," she said softly.

"What!" exclaimed Haley. "Threatened . . . How do you mean?"

"The note," said Theodosia in a strangled voice, "threatened him with . . ." But her throat had closed up, and she wasn't able to finish.

"With poison," whispered Drayton.

"Oh, God!" Haley put a hand to her mouth, shocked.

Theodosia dropped to her knees and pulled Earl Grey close to her, placing her head against his own soft head. "I can't believe it," she murmured softly. "I don't know what I'd do if something happened to Earl Grey."

"Theodosia." Above her, Drayton's lined countenance was grave. "This threat has hit too close to home. I know what we talked about . . . agreed to . . . earlier, but now . . . Well, perhaps the prudent move is to bow out of the investigation entirely."

"Drayton, we haven't really been *in* the investigation," Theodosia shot back. "Up till now, we've only been on the periphery."

"You know what I mean." Drayton dropped his large hand to gently touch Earl Grey's sleek head reassuringly. "We would all be heartbroken should something happen to this fine fellow."

"Something's already happened," said Theodosia tightly. Her fingers kneaded at the dog's soft fur.

"But, Theodosia—" Haley began.

"When someone threatens anyone close to me, people or pet, they're threatening *me*," continued Theodosia, her voice shaking. "I take it personally. However, I do not take it well. So this *will* end. And *I* shall be the one who brings it to a crashing conclusion."

"My God, Theodosia, you can't be serious," implored Drayton. "After this terrible note—"

"I've never been more serious, Drayton," she said in a hoarse whisper. She stared up at him, fire smoldering in her eyes, her breath coming in short, choked gasps, her cheeks flushed with color.

Drayton gazed back at his beloved employer, knowing the depth of her emotions and the firmness of her resolve. "All right, then," he said finally. "Good for you. Damn good for you. You know we're all in this with you."

All hands reached down to touch Earl Grey, a silent acknowledgment of solidarity.

Upstairs in her apartment, alone with Earl Grey, Theodosia shook with rage. She had promised everyone she would lock the door and set the alarm. And, yes, she had done exactly that. But she had another idea cooking in her head. A good idea that would insure Earl Grey's safety and allow her to focus all her energy, once and for all.

Take Earl Grey to Aunt Libby's. Tonight. Right now.

Then, tomorrow morning, when she could think with a clear head and a lighter heart, she'd figure something out. Maybe even get in touch with Burt Tidwell. Who knows.

But she knew she had to do something. She couldn't just sit idly by, feeling scared and impotent. If some sick individual had threatened an innocent dog with poison, what would they do to a person?

Of course, she already knew that answer. They'd already done it once before. To Hughes Barron.

36

Bundled in a wool sweater, sipping a cup of tea, Theodosia sat on the wide wooden porch, enjoying the warmth of the early-morning sun. Secure in the knowledge that Earl Grey was safe, feeling comforted by the familiar old surroundings of Libby's house, she had slept well last night, had enjoyed deep, restful sleep for the first time in two weeks.

Now, her body refreshed and spirits slightly buoyed by the sun peeping over the trees, Theodosia gazed contentedly at the golden woods and fields spread out around her. Birds chirped dozens of melodies and darted about. Some even fluttered hopefully just above Aunt Libby's head as she poured thistle and cracked corn into large ceramic dishes set on the lawn.

Earl Grey, deliriously glad to be running off his leash where there were such interesting places to explore and things to sniff, circled around Libby exuberantly.

Now that the weather had turned cooler, Libby had switched to high-oil-content sunflower seeds. She claimed that migratory birds would soon be arriving exhausted from their long flight from the north and needed extra oil to restore their energy.

Theodosia wondered what it would take to restore *her* energy. The preparations to bring Earl Grey to Aunt Libby's last night had been nerve-racking. She'd had to make three trips just to get the dog bed, canister of food, aluminum food and water bowls, and Earl Grey, himself, down to her Jeep.

Then, just on the off chance that she was being watched or even followed, she'd circled through the historic district a few times, scanning her rearview mirror for any suspicious cars. She spent another fifty minutes driving and, upon arrival, giving a careful explanation to Aunt Libby so she wouldn't be thrown into hysterics.

But Libby hadn't gone into hysterics. She had listened with a sort of dead calm to Theodosia's disclosure of her sleuthing efforts following the death of Hughes Barron, as well as her explanation as to exactly why she'd brought her companion animal out to the plantation.

Libby had stretched a hand out to Earl Grey and patted him on the head. "It will do him good to spend time on the plantation," she'd said. "Let him stretch his legs and chase critters in the woods. He can be a country dog for a while."

Now Theodosia had to figure out her next move, and it had to be a careful one. Judging from the note last night, someone had been angered by her snooping around. Somehow, some way, she had rattled the cage of Hughes Barron's murderer.

It was a terrifying thought, one that chilled her to the marrow. At the same time, it also gave her an odd feeling of pride at the success of her own amateur sleuthing efforts.

"Breakfast's served." Margaret Rose Reese, Libby's live-in house-keeper, set a yawning platter of food down on the small pine table that sat outside on the porch.

"My goodness, Margaret Rose, breakfast's ready so soon?" said Libby as she climbed the stairs to the porch. Dressed in a tobacco-colored suede jacket, khaki slacks, and old felt hat, she looked like a seasoned plantation owner, even though she no longer grew her own crops.

Margaret Rose was a white-haired, rail-thin woman who seemed to have the metabolism of a gerbil. Between Libby and Margaret Rose, Theodosia didn't know which one exuded more nervous energy. In fact, if that energy were to be harnessed, it could probably generate enough power to keep the lights burning in the entire state of South Carolina.

"I swear," said Libby, pulling off her leather gloves and sitting down to the table laden with orange juice, tea, fresh fruit, croissants, and a platter of bacon and scrambled eggs. "The older you get, Margaret Rose, the earlier you get up. Pretty soon you'll have us eating breakfast at four a.m."

Margaret Rose grinned. She had been with Libby for almost fifteen years. In fact, Libby had hired her right after Theodosia went off to college and Margaret Rose's former employer, the Reverend Earl Dilworth, passed away.

Theodosia had always suspected Libby's reasons for hiring Margaret Rose were twofold. First, Margaret Rose didn't really have a place to go after old Reverend Dilworth died, and Libby was too kindhearted to see her left at odds and ends. Second, Libby finally realized how lonely she was, rattling around in that huge old house by herself.

True, Libby had two neighbors, good friends, who leased much of her land for growing crops and spent time around the house and old barn (now the equipment shed) on an almost daily basis. But that wasn't the same. The house would still have been empty.

"You're driving back to Charleston this morning?" asked Libby as she helped herself to juice, coffee, and a small serving of scrambled eggs.

Theodosia nodded.

"You know that Leyland Hartwell at your father's old law firm would be delighted to assist you in any way," said Libby.

She was trying not to show her deep-seated worry, but concern shone in her eyes.

"I've already spoken with Leyland," said Theodosia. "He helped me obtain some information I needed. He and another lawyer, Jory Davis."

Theodosia wondered if she shouldn't perhaps call Jory Davis and see if he could give her a referral on a good private security company. It might not be a bad idea to have someone keep an eye on the tea shop as well as Haley and Bethany's apartment across the alley. She decided she'd better include Drayton's house, too. His place was so old, over 160 years, that a clever person could easily pick one of the ancient locks or pry open one of the rattly windows. And, because any restoration Drayton had done had been to make it as historically accurate as possible, she knew there was no way he'd ever install a security system.

Their breakfasts eaten, Theodosia and Libby watched as an unsuspecting woodchuck lumbered out of the woods to go facedown in a platter of seeds. Then, abruptly startled by a playful, pouncing Earl Grey, the woodchuck was forced to beat a hasty retreat and hole up in a hollow log. Nonplused, Earl Grey circled the woodchuck's temporary hideout with a mournful but proprietary air.

"Walk with me for a while, dear," invited Libby, and the two descended the wooden steps and slowly crossed the broad carpet of lawn.

"So peaceful," murmured Theodosia as they wandered past the small family cemetery surrounded by a low, slightly tumbledown rock wall. In one corner of the family plot was a grape arbor with decorative urns underneath. The grapes from the thick twining vines had long since been carried away by grackles, and dry, papery leaves rustled in the gentle wind. An enormous live oak, that sentinel of the South, rose from another corner and spread its canopy over the small area.

"It's comforting to know our family is still nearby," said Libby. "Oh, look." She stuck her gloved hand into a large, dark green clump of foliage and pulled out a cluster of white blossoms that resembled delicate butterfly wings. Smiling, she held out the branch to Theodosia.

"Ginger lily," murmured Theodosia. It was a tropical plant that had long ago been brought over from Asia to grace Southern gardens. It was also one of the few plants that flowered in the autumn. Theodosia accepted the blossoms, inhaling the delicate fragrance so reminiscent of gardenias.

"Just a moment," she whispered, and slipped through the archway into the small cemetery to lay the blossoms on the simple marble tablet that marked her mother's grave.

Libby smiled her approval.

Circling around the pond with its shoreline of cattails and waving golden grasses, past the old barn that decades ago had held prize cattle and fine Thoroughbred horses, they came to a cluster of small, dilapidated wood-frame buildings. The elements had long since erased any evidence of paint, and now the wood had weathered silver. Redbrick chimneys had begun to crumble.

These were the outbuildings that long ago had been slave quarters.

When one of Libby's neighbors had once suggested to her that the buildings were an eyesore and should be torn down, Libby had steadfastly demurred and explained her strong feelings about preserving them just as they were.

"No," she'd said, "let people see how it really was, no tearing it down, no disguising the issue. Slavery was a disgrace and the worst kind of black mark against the South."

And so Aunt Libby's dilapidated slave quarters remained. Every so often, a group of schoolchildren or a history professor, filmmaker, or TV station would call and ask permission for a visit or to shoot film footage. Libby always said yes. She knew it was an abomination, but she also knew it was an irrefutable part of Southern history.

"Theodosia." Libby Revelle stopped in her tracks and turned to face her niece. Her wise, sharp eyes stared intently into the younger woman's face. "You will be very careful, won't you?"

37

"*You'll never guess* what happened!" exclaimed Haley.

Theodosia held her breath. She had just driven back from Aunt Libby's and quietly let herself in through the back door of the Indigo Tea Shop. Now, judging by the curious, startled look on Haley's face, it would appear that an event of major proportion had just taken place.

"Mr. Dauphine died!" Haley announced in hushed tones.

"Oh, no, how awful!" cried Theodosia, sinking into a chair. "The poor man." She let the news wash over her. Of course, she had just been to see Mr. Dauphine three days ago, checking with him about offers he might have received on the Peregrine Building. They'd had a pleasant enough discussion and Mr. Dauphine had seemed in good spirits. He may have been a little tired, and his coughing hadn't been good, but he certainly hadn't looked like a man who was about to die.

"They just took his body away," said Haley. "Did you see the ambulance?"

"No, I parked in back," said Theodosia.

"That's where the ambulance was," said Haley. "Miss Dimple had them pull around to the back. She didn't want to upset the tourists. Wasn't that sweet?"

"How did he . . . ?" began Theodosia.

Haley shook her head sadly. "Miss Dimple found him on the second-floor landing. She went looking for him when he didn't show up for work. Apparently, he was always punctual, always arrived by nine a.m. Anyway, by the time she got to him, he wasn't breathing. She phoned for an ambulance, but it was too late. The paramedics thought Mr. Dauphine might have had a heart attack."

Perhaps the four flights of stairs *had* finally done him in, thought Theodosia. How awful. And poor Miss Dimple; how awful to find her beloved employer of almost forty years crumpled in a sad heap, no longer able to breathe. Now there would be yet another funeral in the historic district.

The sudden memory of Hughes Barron's recent funeral service caused Theodosia to chase after Haley, who, shaking her head at the sad incident, had wandered out front to exchange additional bits of information with Drayton. Right after the ambulance had arrived, Drayton had gone up and down Church Street, chatting with the other shopkeepers, clucking over the sad news.

"Haley," said Theodosia, catching up to her, "they're sure it was a heart attack?"

There was an immediate flicker of understanding in Haley's eyes. "Well, everyone's saying it was a heart attack. But . . ."

"But what if it was something else that *caused* a heart attack?" asked Theodosia.

"My God," whispered Haley as she put a hand to her mouth, "you don't think someone bumped off Mr. Dauphine, do you?"

Theodosia reached for the phone. "Right now I don't know what to think."

"Who are you calling? The hospital?"

"No," replied Theodosia. "Burt Tidwell."

38

Burt Tidwell didn't show up at the Indigo Tea Shop until midafternoon. Even then, he didn't make his presence known immediately.

He sauntered in, sampled a cup of Ceylon white tea, and scarfed a cranberry scone, all the while keeping Bethany in a state of near panic as she waited on him. Finally, Burt Tidwell told Bethany that she could kindly inform Theodosia of his arrival. Told her to tell Miss Browning that, per her invitation to drop by the tea shop, he was, voilà, now at her disposal.

"Mr. Tidwell, lovely to see you again," said Theodosia. She arrived at his small table by the window bearing a plate of freshly baked lemon and sour cream muffins drizzled with powdered sugar frosting. Haley had just pulled them from the oven, and the aroma was enough to tempt the devil. The way to a man's heart may be through his stomach, Theodosia had reasoned, but you could just as often tap his inner thoughts via his stomach, too. And Burt Tidwell had a very ample stomach.

"And pray tell what are these?" Tidwell asked as Theodosia set the plate of muffins on the table between them. His nose quivered like a bunny rabbit, and his lips puckered in delight. "I declare, you folks certainly offer the most delightful repertoire of baked goods."

"Just our lemon and sour cream muffins," said Theodosia, waving her hand as if the pastries were nothing at all. In fact, she had instructed Haley to knock herself out.

"May I?" asked Burt Tidwell. He was just this side of salivating.

"Of course," said Theodosia in her warmest, coziest tone as she inched the plate and accompanying butter dish closer to him. Aunt Libby would have laughingly told her it was like dangling a minnow for spottail bass. "I'm glad you could drop by," she said. "I wanted to find out how the investigation was going and ask you a couple of peripheral questions."

"Peripheral questions," Tidwell repeated. "You have a gift for phrasing, don't you, Miss Browning? You're able to make unimportant data seem important and critical issues appear insignificant. A fine tactic often used by the police."

"Yes," she continued, trying to ignore his jab but being reminded, once again, of just how maddening the man could be.

"Such goings-on you've had in your neighborhood," chided Tidwell. His pink tongue flicked out to catch a bit of frosting that clung to his upper lip.

"Enjoying that, are you?" Theodosia asked archly.

"Delicious," replied Tidwell. "As I was saying, your poor neighborhood has endured more than its share of tragedy. First, Mr. Hughes Barron so inelegantly drops dead at your little tea party. Now Mr. Dauphine, your next-door neighbor in the Peregrine Building, has succumbed. Could you, perchance, be the common denominator?"

There's my opener, thought Theodosia. *As infuriating and off base as Tidwell's implication is, there is my opener.*

"But no one from the Indigo Tea Shop was *near* Mr. Dauphine when he died," said Theodosia. "And I was under the impression the poor man suffered a heart attack."

"But *you* were with Mr. Dauphine three days ago," said Tidwell. "His very capable associate, Miss Dimple, keeps a detailed log of all visitors and all incoming phone calls. And"—Tidwell paused—"she has shared that with me."

Good, thought Theodosia, *now if you'll just share a little bit more of that information with me.*

"Yes, I did go to Mr. Dauphine's office," said Theodosia, struggling to control her temper. "We *are* neighbors, and I was talking to him about the offer Hughes Barron put forth on his building." Theodosia took a deep breath. "Have *you* learned anything more about someone trying to buy the Peregrine Building?" She knew it was a stab in the dark.

Tidwell's huge hands handled the tiny butter knife with the sureness of a surgeon. Deftly he sliced a wedge of unsalted butter and applied it to a second muffin. "I understand the surviving business partner, Mr. Lleveret Dante, made an offer on the building only yesterday," he said.

"That's very interesting," said Theodosia. *Now we're getting somewhere,* she thought.

"Not that interesting," replied Tidwell mildly. "Hughes Barron had already made an overture to purchase the Peregrine Building. That was fairly common knowledge. It's only logical to assume that the remaining partner would follow up on any proposition that had already been put into motion."

"And you think Dante made a legitimate offer?"

Tidwell pursed his lips. "Highly doubtful. A leopard doesn't change his spots, Miss Browning. Mr. Lleveret Dante had many nefarious dealings in his home state of Kentucky."

The door to the shop opened, and Delaine Dish walked in. She took one look at Theodosia, deep in conversation with Burt Tidwell, and sat down at the table farthest from them.

Oh, dear, thought Theodosia, *just what I don't need right now—Delaine Dish making the rounds, whispering in hushed tones about the death of Mr. Dauphine.*

"Of course," continued Tidwell, "it makes no difference if Lleveret Dante offered three times market value on the Peregrine Building. He shall never own it now."

"Why do you say that?" asked Theodosia. She snapped her attention from Delaine back to Tidwell. *He knows something,* she thought with a jolt. Why else would his sharp eyes be focused on her like a cat doing sentry duty outside a mouse hole?

Tidwell rocked back in his chair. "Because Mr. Dauphine left a very specific last will and testament." He paused for a moment, then continued. "Mr. Dauphine's will clearly stated that, should he die before disposing of the Peregrine Building, ownership of it passes to the Heritage Society."

39

"*Theodosia, please,*" *began* Delaine, "someone's got to tell you, and it may as well be me."

"Tell me what, Delaine?" Theodosia slipped into the chair across from Delaine Dish. She was still rankled by Tidwell's attitude and shocked at his revelation that the Heritage Society was suddenly on the receiving end of poor Mr. Dauphine's generosity. This certainly was a surprising turn of events.

Delaine cocked her head in mock surprise. "Surely you're aware of Timothy Neville's mudslinging campaign. It has reached epidemic proportions."

So Delaine hadn't come here to talk about Mr. Dauphine. She still had a bee in her bonnet over Timothy Neville. Theodosia settled back in her chair and gazed at Delaine. She was dressed head to toe in cashmere, pale pink cowl-neck sweater that draped elegantly, and matching hip-skimming skirt. Even her handbag was cashmere, a multicolored soft baguette bag in coordinating pinks, purples, and reds. Theodosia slid her chair back a notch and peeked at Delaine's shoes. Ostrich. Holy smokes. The clothing business must be good these days, very good. Certainly far better than the tea shop business.

"Delaine," said Theodosia tiredly, "I have so much going on right now. I appreciate your concern, but——"

"Theodosia, I cannot stand idly by and tolerate this much longer. The man is spreading lies. Lies!"

Theodosia smiled and nodded as Angie Congdon from the Feather-bed House entered the shop. "Hello, Angie," she called, then turned back to Delaine. "What kind of lies?" Theodosia asked, the smile tight on her face.

Delaine Dish leaned forward eagerly. "Innuendoes, really. About the night of the Lamplighter Tour."

"Oh, that," said Theodosia.

"About your snooping around inside his house during one of his concerts." Delaine's cupid lips were curled in a smile, but her look clearly questioned the truthfulness of this allegation.

"He said that?" Theodosia tried her best to appear injured and innocent.

"That's what Timothy told George Harper when he stopped by the Antiquarian Map Store."

"Really," said Theodosia. *So maybe Timothy Neville had been the one who'd opened the door that night,* she thought. Come to check if she was snooping about. And she cowering in the dark. Truly, another proud moment in what had been an insane last couple weeks. "What else, Delaine?" Theodosia asked.

Delaine looked pained. "Something about the young woman who served as an intern at the Heritage Society. Now works for you."

"Bethany."

"That's the one."

"Let me guess, Delaine. Timothy Neville is convinced Bethany had some kind of *relationship* with Hughes Barron."

"Yes, he is!" said Delaine, enormously pleased that Theodosia seemed to be finally getting into the spirit of this juicy discussion.

"Forget it," said Theodosia. "It's not true. None of it's true." Well, she reluctantly admitted to herself, the snooping part was true, but she wasn't about to confess her sins to Delaine Dish. If she did, they'd be headline news all over Charleston.

"I know that, Theodosia," assured Delaine. "But Timothy Neville carries a lot of clout around here. You do, too, of course. Your family is almost as old as his. But *he* is being verbal. *You* remain silent."

"I do not need to dignify his lies with a rebuttal."

"Oh, *hello,* Angie," said Delaine excitedly. She turned in her chair, the better to greet Angie Congdon. "Wasn't it a *shame* about Mr. Dauphine?

Such a pity. Dear, do you have just a *moment?*" Delaine stood in a swirl of perfect pink and reached out to catch Angie's arm. "I just received the most *tantalizing* shipment of silks in the most *amazing* jewel tones and, of course, I *immediately* thought of your olive complexion and dark hair." Delaine was off and running.

Theodosia rose and began clearing the table, all the while pondering what Delaine had just related to her. As much as she wanted to, perhaps she couldn't ignore these issues any longer. Maybe she had to do something about Timothy Neville. The question was, what?

If he had been the one who left the note last night, it meant he was truly dangerous, a threat to everyone at the tea shop. But she still didn't have any hard evidence to use against him.

It was obvious now that Timothy Neville had been secretly fearful that Hughes Barron's offer on the Peregrine Building would be accepted. If the Peregrine Building had been sold before the event of Mr. Dauphine's death, the Heritage Society would have lost out completely.

Was that motive enough to do away with Hughes Barron? Perhaps.

And now, with Mr. Dauphine's very convenient death, the deed to the property slid over to the Heritage Society, no questions asked. Timothy Neville would, once again, look like a shining star in the eyes of his board of directors and roster of high-profile donors.

So did that make Timothy Neville a double murderer? It was a chilling thought.

There was yet another dark possibility. Only yesterday, Mr. Lleveret Dante had put forth an offer on the Peregrine Building. But what if Mr. Dauphine had turned him down flat? Could being rebuffed have sent Lleveret Dante into a vicious rage? A rage that prompted him to kill Mr. Dauphine?

Not knowing about Mr. Dauphine's will, Lleveret Dante might have assumed that, with the aging owner's death, the property would have been sold off hastily. He was already the likely suitor, already in a position to pounce on the Peregrine Building!

Her theories reminded Theodosia of the logic course she'd taken in college. If A equals D, then B equals C. Logic hadn't made any sense to her then, and her suppositions on Hughes Barron's murder or Mr.

Dauphine's death weren't yielding anything constructive, either. They were just puzzles within puzzles that made her head spin.

The phone shrilled on the counter next to her, and Theodosia automatically reached for it. "Indigo Tea Shop, how may I help you?" she said.

"Theodosia, Tanner Joseph here. Good news. I've just finished your labels."

"Wonderful," she said in a flat voice.

"Hey, don't sound so excited."

Tanner Joseph's tone was upbeat and breezy. A far cry, Theodosia thought, from the anger and hostility he'd radiated when she'd made mention of Hughes Barron the day before. She suddenly wondered if *he* knew something about the Peregrine Building. Everyone else certainly did.

"Will you be home this evening?" Tanner asked her. "I'm driving into the city, and I could easily drop them—"

"No," interrupted Theodosia. "Don't bother. I prefer to come pick them up." She thought quickly. "You'll be at your office tomorrow morning?"

"Yes," Tanner said, "but there's really no need to—"

"It's no trouble," said Theodosia and hung up the phone.

The labels. Damn. She'd forgotten about them for the moment. They were one more futzy detail to follow up on, one more reminder that she wasn't really tending to business here. Theodosia stared out into the tea shop where Delaine was still deep in conversation with Angie Congdon.

"Do we need to talk?" Drayton, reaching for a fresh jar of honey, saw consternation mingled with weariness on Theodosia's face.

Theodosia nodded. "My office, though."

When the two were alone, Theodosia related her conversation with Delaine.

"Pay no attention," counseled Drayton. "Everyone knows Delaine is a confirmed gossip." He peered at her, knowing something else was gnawing at her. "Did Burt Tidwell say something to you as well?"

"Drayton," said Theodosia, "you're on the board of directors of the Heritage Society. Were you aware that Mr. Dauphine had willed the Peregrine Building to the Heritage Society?"

"He did?" Drayton frowned. "Seriously? No, I knew nothing. It's news to me."

"So board members aren't privy to such information?"

"That kind of thing comes under the category of directed donation. So usually just the board president, in this case Timothy Neville, and the Heritage Society's legal counsel are privy to details."

"I see."

Drayton gazed at her. "You're getting frown lines."

"Not now, Drayton," she snapped.

"Oh, we're going to be that way, are we?" he said. "Once again, you have assumed the entire weight of the world on your small but capable shoulders." He continued even as she glowered at him. "As you wish, Theodosia. I shall play along, then." He crossed his arms and tried to appear thoughtful. "Let me guess. Suddenly you are envisioning a scenario where Timothy Neville also decides to hasten the death of Mr. Dauphine?"

"It's a possibility," admitted Theodosia.

"Perhaps. Or a second scenario might place our mystery man, Lleveret Dante, at the scene of that crime as well. Mr. Mustard in the library, so to speak."

"It's no joking matter, Drayton."

"No, it's not, Theodosia. I'm as concerned as you about everything that's gone on. And I certainly don't take the threat against Earl Grey lightly, either. I hope you informed Detective Tidwell about that incident."

He took her silence as a no.

"That's what I was afraid of," he said wearily.

"Last night, you said you were in this with me," she cried.

"That was before Mr. Dauphine turned up dead!" He rolled his eyes skyward as if to implore, *Heaven help me.*

"I'm not afraid," murmured Theodosia. "I'm not afraid of anything."

"Really," said Drayton. He planted both hands on her desk and leaned toward her. "Then, pray tell, why did you spirit Earl Grey off to your Aunt Libby's in the middle of the night?"

40

Tanner Joseph heard the muffled slam of the car door outside his office. She was here, he told himself excitedly. Theodosia Browning had arrived to fetch the tea labels. Evening before last, he had worked long into the night, adding subtle touches of color to the black-and-white drawings, so intense had been his desire to please Theodosia and see her again.

After his call to her yesterday, when she told him she wanted to wait till morning, preferred to drive out to Johns Island and pick up the labels herself, he had been terribly dismayed. But when the day had dawned and a gloriously sunny day revealed itself, his spirits had greatly improved, and he saw now that he might turn her visit to his advantage. He simply had to convince Theodosia to stay. To spend the rest of the day with him. And, he hoped, the evening. That would finally give the two of them the time and space they needed to really get to know each other.

The door flew open, and Tanner Joseph greeted Theodosia with a smile. It was the boyish grin he had practiced many times in his bathroom mirror. It was also a grin that, more often than not, worked rather well on girls.

Only Theodosia was not a girl, he reminded himself. She was a woman. A beautiful, enchanting woman.

"Hello, Tanner." Theodosia stood in front of his desk, gazing down at him. She wore a plum-colored pant suit and carried a slim leather attaché case. Her face was impassive, her voice brisk and businesslike.

Theodosia had to remind herself that this young man who sat before her, looking rather innocuous and innocent, had quite possibly used Bethany to obtain information about her. She wasn't certain why Tanner

Joseph wanted to collect this information but, since she still viewed him as a wild-card suspect in Hughes Barron's murder, his attempt at familiarity was extremely unsettling. As she met Tanner Joseph's piercing blue eyes, she assured herself this would be a quick, by-the-book business transaction.

Tanner Joseph took in her business garb and snappy attitude, and his hopes slipped a bit. Perhaps Theodosia hadn't taken time to fully appreciate the thousand-watt glow of his boyish grin. No, he could see she obviously hadn't. She was all but tapping her toe to get going.

"Here are the finished pieces, Theo." He held the art boards out to Theodosia and watched as she took them from his hands. Their fingers touched for a moment. Could she feel the spark? The electricity? He certainly could.

Theodosia quickly shuffled through the four boards, studying the finished art. "These are very good," she declared.

Tanner Joseph frowned. The gush of compliments he'd hoped for didn't seem to be forthcoming. Instead, her comment was more a calculated, measured appraisal. A pro forma "job well done."

"You finished them in tempera paint?" Theodosia asked. She tapped at one of the drawings with a fingernail.

"Colored markers," replied Tanner Joseph. He eased himself back in his chair. She was pleased, he knew she was. He could read it in her face.

Theodosia laid her attaché case on Tanner Joseph's desk and opened it.

"Drayton is going to love these," she said. "You did a first-class job." She placed the art boards carefully in her case, closed it, snapped the latch.

"That's it?" he inquired lazily.

"That's it," replied Theodosia. "Send me your invoice, and I'll make sure you receive samples as soon as everything's printed." She spun on her heel, heading for the door.

Tanner Joseph stood up so quickly his chair snapped back loudly. "Don't rush off," he implored. "I was hoping we could—"

But Theodosia was already out the door, striding across the hardpan toward her Jeep.

"Hey!" Tanner Joseph slumped unhappily in the doorway of the Shorebird Environmentalist Group headquarters and waved helplessly at her.

"Bye!" called Theodosia as the Jeep roared to life. The last thing she saw as she pulled into traffic was a forlorn-looking Tanner Joseph, wondering how things had gone so wrong.

41

"What are you drinking?" asked Bethany.

Drayton answered her without looking up from his writing. "Cinnamon plum."

He sat at the table nearest the counter, working on his article. It was 2:00 p.m., and Bethany and Haley were bored. The lunchtime customers had left, and afternoon tea customers hadn't yet arrived. Baked goods cooled on racks, shelves were fully stocked, and tables were set.

"Cinnamon plum sounds awfully sweet. I thought you said you never drink sweet teas," responded Bethany.

"I consider it more flavorful than sweet," said Drayton as he continued writing.

"What are you working on?" asked Haley.

"I *was* working on an article for *Beverage & Hospitality* magazine," said Drayton as he sighed heavily and put down his pen.

"About tea?" said Haley.

"Yes, about tea. I can't seem to put my finger on the precise reason, but I seem to have completely lost my train of thought."

"No need to get snippy, Drayton." Haley peered over Drayton's shoulder. "You always write your articles in longhand?"

"Naturally. I'm a Luddite. I abhor modern contraptions such as computers. No soul."

"Is that why you live in that quaint, rundown house?" asked Bethany.

"The dwelling you are referring to is neither quaint nor rundown. It is a historic home that has been lovingly and authentically restored. A time capsule of history, if you will."

"Oh," said Haley, and the two girls burst out giggling.

Drayton turned to face them. "Instead of plaguing me, ladies, why don't you just come right out and admit it? You're nervous about Theodosia's errand."

When he saw their faces suddenly crumple and real worry appear, Drayton immediately changed his tune. "Well, don't be," he replied airily. "She's highly capable, I assure you."

"It's just that everything's been so topsy-turvy around here," said Haley. "And now with that awful note . . ." Her voice trailed off. "I wish it hadn't been typed. If it was someone's handwriting, we'd have something to go on."

"Listen to yourself," scolded Drayton. "You're *still* talking about investigating. Don't you know we may be in real danger? Dear girl, there's a reason Theodosia hired a private security guard."

"She did?" Bethany's eyes were as round as saucers. This was news to her!

The doorknob rattled, then turned, and they all held their breath, watching.

But it was Miss Dimple.

Drayton rose from his seat and rushed over to greet her. He extended an arm to lead her to a table. "Get Miss Dimple a cup of tea, girls."

He sat down next to her, patted her arm. "How are you doing, dear?"

Miss Dimple's sadness was apparent. Her shoulders were slumped, her usual pink complexion doughy. "Terrible. I was just up in the office and I kept waiting for Mr. Dauphine to come clumping up the stairs." A tear trickled down her cheek. "I can't believe he's really gone."

Drayton pulled a white linen handkerchief from his pocket and passed it to her. She accepted it gratefully.

Bethany and Haley arrived with a steaming teapot and teacups. "Tea, Miss Dimple?" asked Haley.

"Don't mind if I do," she said, blotting her tears.

Drayton poured a cup of tea for Miss Dimple and, without asking, added a lump of sugar and a splash of cream.

"Thank you," she whispered and took a sip. "Good." She smiled weakly, glancing around at the three of them.

"We were all very sorry to hear about Mr. Dauphine," volunteered Haley. "He was such a nice man. He parked his car in the alley outside our apartment. He was always worried that he'd disturb us or something. Of course, he never did."

"I came to tell you all," said Miss Dimple, "that there will be a memorial service for Mr. Dauphine. Day after tomorrow."

"At Saint Philip's?" asked Drayton.

"Yes," Mrs. Dimple squeaked, and a few more tears slid down her cheeks. "He loved Saint Philip's," she said tremulously.

"As do we all," murmured Drayton.

Thirty minutes later, when Theodosia walked in, Drayton was back at his table working on his article, while Haley and Bethany were waiting on customers. Even though almost all the tables were filled, the mood in the tea shop seemed somber and quiet.

"Who died?" asked Theodosia, sitting down across from Drayton. Then she remembered. Mr. Dauphine had. "Oh, dear," she said contritely, "how could I have even said that! How thoughtless of me. Forgive me, Drayton." She went to pour a cup of tea and spilled it, so flustered was she by her inappropriate remark.

Drayton waved a hand. "Not to worry. I think the stress is getting to all of us. And of course it didn't help that poor Miss Dimple stopped in here awhile ago. She's going around to all the shops. Well, the ones up and down Church Street anyway. Telling folks that Mr. Dauphine's funeral will be held day after tomorrow."

Theodosia nodded.

"You picked up the artwork?" Drayton pointed his pen toward her attaché case.

"Already dropped it by the printer. They're probably making color plates even as we speak."

"No problems out there?" he asked, a pointed reference to Tanner Joseph.

"None at all."

"Excellent. FedEx delivered the tea tins while you were out. There are ten cartons in back stacked floor to ceiling. Your office now resembles a warehouse. All you need is a hard hat and forklift."

"Let me get you a fresh cup, Theodosia." Bethany reached over and carefully retrieved Theodosia's cup and saucer with its overflow of tea.

"Thank you, Bethany," murmured Theodosia.

Bethany transferred the cup and saucer to her silver serving tray. She hesitated. "Everything was fine with the artwork?"

Theodosia nodded. "Bethany, you wouldn't go out on a date with Tanner Joseph again, would you?" Theodosia asked the question as gently as possible.

"No chance of that," declared Bethany.

"I'm glad," said Theodosia, "because there is something decidedly unsettling about his—"

"I think so, too," whispered Bethany as she hurriedly slipped away to the kitchen.

"Theodosia. Telephone!" Haley called from the counter.

Theodosia hurried to the counter and picked up the phone. "This is Theodosia."

"Hi, it's Jory Davis," said the voice on the other end.

"Oh, *hello.*"

"I just wanted to tell you that your private security guard has reported no unusual incidents over the last two days."

"He's been watching us for two days? Are you sure? Because I haven't seen hide nor hair of anyone."

Jory Davis chuckled. "You're not supposed to. That's the whole point."

Theodosia considered his remark. "You're probably right. I certainly appreciate your arranging for this. I'm not entirely convinced it's necessary, but still it feels comforting."

"Again," said Jory, "that is the point." He hesitated. "Theodosia, I have two tickets for the opera tomorrow evening. *Madame Bovary,* to be exact."

She smiled, her first genuine, heartfelt smile in days.

"Realizing this is a rather late invitation, I offer, by way of explanation, that they are my mother's season tickets, actually quite excellent seats, and she is just now unable to attend. But I would love it if you'd accompany me."

"As it so happens, Mr. Davis, I am free."

"Wonderful. Black tie, of course. There's a cocktail party preceding the performance and afterwards a number of small parties to choose from. I shall call for you at precisely six-thirty p.m."

"I look forward to it."

Theodosia hung up the phone and whirled about to face the tea shop. So genuine was the smile that graced her face that two elderly ladies seated near the door smiled back at her.

What a delight! she told herself. *A date with Jory Davis. And to the opera, which was always fabulous. With parties before and after!*

"You look energized, Theodosia," commented Haley. "Your face is absolutely glowing."

"Drayton." Theodosia fairly skipped over to where he was sitting. "Why don't we start filling the tea tins with the holiday blends? Get a jump on the whole process?"

"Today? Now?" he asked, surprised by her shift in mood.

"As soon as the customers leave. I've been dragging everybody down with my snooping and sleuthing, and all it's done is put us farther and farther behind. Jeopardize business."

He was still staring at her.

"Where's the tea?" she asked. "Over at Gallagher's?"

"Of course."

Drayton always used the extensive food-prep facilities at nearby Gallagher's Food Service to blend his teas. Now they were stored there as well, all four of the holiday blends, in their twenty-gallon airtight canisters.

"Can they deliver today?"

"With their fleet of delivery trucks, they can probably have the tea here in thirty minutes."

"Perfect," said Theodosia.

42

Tables pushed together, empty gold tins laid out upon them, glinting under overhead lights, the group was ready to begin.

"Okay," began Drayton, "this is going to be assembly-line style. Haley and I will begin at opposite ends. She'll measure out the black currant blend, and I'll do the Indian spice. You two—" he nodded at Theodosia and Bethany—"have to keep tabs and let each of us know when we've filled two hundred fifty tins. Then we'll put covers on and restack the filled tins back in their original cartons to await the labels."

Bethany looked at the daunting task that loomed ahead. "Machines can't do this?" she asked.

Drayton snorted disdainfully. "Can machines create the perfect blend? Can machines add just the right touch of bergamot oil? Can machines impart care and love into each tin? I hardly think so." Drayton dipped a glass scoop into the twenty-gallon canister, filled it to equal approximately six ounces of tea, and began pouring tea into tins at his end of the table.

"Trust me, dear," said Theodosia. "It won't feel like love an hour from now. It will just feel like a sore back."

"You got that right," agreed Haley, who'd done this chore for the last two years.

"And remember," warned Drayton, "when you close up the filled tins and put them back into the cartons, mark each carton carefully as to the blend. We don't want to mix them up!"

"Yes, Drayton," said Theodosia obediently, and the two girls chuckled.

They worked quickly and efficiently. Soon the aroma of the spicy teas filled the air, and bits of loose tea clung to their clothing.

"This is like working in an aromatherapy factory," joked Haley. "There are so many different essences and aromas swirling around, I don't know whether to feel relaxed or invigorated."

"Just feel diligent," said Drayton. His personality was so task-oriented that, once he started a project, he doggedly kept at it until he finished.

"My back is killing me," complained Haley. She had just added a fourth layer of filled tins to one of the cartons and was bending over it, about to close it up.

"We're almost done," said Drayton. "It can't be more than . . ." He carefully surveyed the table of empty tins. "Perhaps forty more tins to fill with cranberry orange blend."

"Tell you what," said Theodosia. "Why don't you let me finish up?"

"Okay," agreed Haley. She was tired and ready to throw in the towel.

"But we're almost done," protested Drayton.

"Exactly," said Theodosia. "It's late. It's been a long day. I don't mind finishing myself. It'll be fun."

"Well . . ." said Drayton. "Be sure to mark each . . ."

"I'll mark each carton, Drayton," she assured him. "Now, you folks scoot!"

Theodosia breathed a sigh of relief as she turned the latch on the door.

It was nice to be alone in the tea shop, she decided. Nice to be able to finish this chore at her own pace instead of whipping along, trying to keep up with Drayton's production line.

She turned on the radio and found a station that was playing a whole set of songs by Harry Connick. She sang and hummed along, thoroughly enjoying herself. It took her almost an hour to finish filling the tins, replace the lids securely, pack them up, and stack the boxes in her office. When she was done, she enjoyed a real sense of accomplishment. All that was needed now were the printed labels.

Drayton was right, Theodosia decided as she surveyed the wall of floor-to-ceiling cartons. She did need a hard hat and forklift. What a huge amount of tea to sell. She definitely had to buckle down to business!

Once upstairs in her apartment for the evening, Theodosia's thoughts turned to her date tomorrow night. She was determined to find just the right moment to tell Jory Davis all about her private sleuthing and what she'd uncovered. He was a smart man, a lawyer. It would be valuable to get his input and hard-nosed advice. She certainly didn't seem to be making much headway. Maybe Jory Davis would see an angle that had eluded her.

Now, she asked herself, what would she wear? Jory Davis had specified black tie, so that narrowed it down. And the weather was still cool, so that was a factor, too. Were we talking black cocktail dress and beaded jacket or long gown with velvet opera cape? she wondered. Even though a long gown was technically not black tie, women in Charleston did tend to favor them. Especially for opening night at the opera. Oh, and there was that wonderful hand-painted velvet jacket hanging in her closet, too. Could she wear it with black velvet slacks and get away with it? Hmm . . . probably not. Might be just a tad casual. Better to go with the black dress and beaded jacket. That outfit would be classy and slimming.

Now, what about jewelry? Small, tasteful diamond stud earrings or glitzy drop earrings?

Just as she was beginning to think she should get Delaine on the line and do a quick consultation with the fashion police, Theodosia straightened up, cocked an ear. She'd heard a noise downstairs. A slight rattle. Subtle. Surreptitious.

Rattle? Like someone trying to open the back door? Maybe the same someone who left a threatening note two nights ago?

Panic gripped her heart. Her hand flailed for the light switch and hit it, dousing the lights. Now she pressed her face up close against the window and peered down into the alley.

There was a car down there, all right. Its lights were off, but she could hear the low throb of an engine. It sounded almost as loud as the pounding in her chest.

She contorted her head, trying to see more. A shadowy figure moved from her doorway to the car and climbed inside.

What to do? Where was the security guard? She had a phone number to call—should she dial it? Yes!

She scurried into the living room, fumbled through her purse, and found the number. Grabbing the phone, she punched in digits.

Someone picked up on the first ring. "Gold Shield Security."

"This is Theodosia Browning at the Indigo Tea Shop." Her words tumbled out, one on top of the other. "Someone's downstairs in the alley. Right behind my shop. Someone who shouldn't be."

"Calm down," replied the voice. "Let me check my screen." There was a pause. "Miss Browning, the security guard patrolling your area is about three blocks away. I've flashed him a message. Is the prowler still in the alley?"

"Just a minute." Clutching the cordless phone, she scurried back into the bedroom and pressed her face against the window. "Yes," she whispered into the phone.

"Stay on the line, please. I'll get back to you as soon as I get a response. Can you do that?"

"Yes. Of course."

Then Theodosia was standing there in the shadows, watching the dark car in the alley below, hoping the prowler hadn't ducked back in his car for a lock pick or sledgehammer, praying he wasn't going to step across the alley to Haley's and Bethany's apartment and knock on the door. Because, trusting souls that they were, they'd probably let him in!

"Miss Browning, our guard should be there any moment. Do you see anything?" asked the voice on the phone.

"No . . . yes!" She suddenly saw a car turn in to her alley, glide swiftly toward her shop. But now the prowler's car below suddenly flashed its lights on and gunned the motor. The driver hit the accelerator, and the tires screeched horribly for a few seconds, then found purchase on rough cobblestones. Roaring ahead, the prowler's car fishtailed, gaining speed. But the response car was right behind, searchlight on, accelerating full bore.

The words *in hot pursuit* formed in Theodosia's brain, then she sat down heavily on the bed.

"Miss Browning, everything okay there?" came the voice again in the phone.

"Yes, your security guard is in pursuit."

"We have him on our screen. A second security guard is en route and should be there within two minutes. He will remain parked outside your home through the night. If we get any information on your prowler, we'll call you."

"Thank you," said Theodosia gratefully.

She went to the window again and waited for what seemed like an eternity, although it probably was just two minutes, until the second security guard pulled up.

She flipped the bedroom lights back on and looked at the black dress hanging on her closet door. Well, at least she'd have an interesting story to tell over cocktails tomorrow night!

❧ 43 ❧

"These mugs are neat," said Haley. Federal Express had just delivered a large carton, and Haley was unearthing bubble-wrapped mugs from their nest of plastic peanuts.

"Did Drayton order these?" asked Bethany.

Haley nodded. "Gearing up for the holidays. We usually sell a lot of gifty items." She held a ceramic mug in each hand, one a pink peony pattern, the other a Chinese dragon design. "Look," she exclaimed, "matching tops to keep your tea warm. Pretty slick." She pushed the carton across the counter to Bethany. "Why don't you do one of your pretty arrangements while I pull my pumpkin scones out of the oven. See there, you can slide those trivets and candles over on that middle shelf."

"Sounds good," agreed Bethany as she admired the peony tea mug. "Has Theodosia seen these yet?"

"No, she's still on the phone."

Theodosia was bent over her desk, head cocked to the left, phone cradled in the crook of her neck. Her right hand clutched a black felt-tip pen. "Give me that plate number again," she said. Nodding to the disembodied voice on the other end of the phone, she wrote AUY372 on a sheet of paper. She tapped the tip of the pen against the paper sharply, making a series of zigzag doodles around the number. Nervous doodles.

"And you *did* get a response from the Motor Vehicles Department? Oh, they're faxing it now? Yes, of course I'll hold."

Theodosia continued tapping her pen nervously, and her gaze roved the room. It fell upon bookshelves filled with paperwork that demanded her attention. A chair heaped with storyboards that weren't going anywhere for a while. Cartons filled with tins of holiday teas. She groaned inwardly. That tea alone represented almost 20,000 dollars in potential gross profit. Could she sell it and jump-start business? That remained to be seen.

"Yes?" She fairly bounced out of her chair when the voice came back on the line. "I didn't realize a leased auto made a difference. Yes, it is interesting, isn't it?" she said, although she was clearly disinterested. "You have the name?" She sat up straight, eyes riveted on the plate number she'd written on her paper. "Yes? Tanner Joseph," she repeated in an odd, flat tone. "Thank you."

She slammed the phone down so hard the receiver bounced back out of its cradle.

"Damn!" she cried.

Drayton was in Theodosia's office in a heartbeat, easing the door closed behind him.

"Shhh." He held a cautionary finger to his lips. "We've got customers!"

She whirled to face Drayton, chest heaving, complexion mottled with anger, auburn hair in a mad swirl. "It was Tanner Joseph!" She spat the name out with anger and disgust.

"What was Tanner Joseph?" Drayton asked quietly. He figured the surest way to calm someone was to remain calm yourself, although he could certainly be proved wrong in this case. Theodosia seemed absolutely infuriated.

"Last night!" she raged and began pacing the confines of her small, cluttered office. "Out in the alley!"

"Someone was in the alley last night?" asked Drayton. Now his voice rose a few octaves as well. "Theodosia, did something happen after we left?" he demanded.

"That idiot, Tanner Joseph, was out there. Gold Shield Security just called. One of their security guards got a read on his plate number." She stomped her foot. "Of all the nerve!"

"But why would he . . . ?" Drayton let his sentence hang there, searching for a logical explanation. He tried again. "But you already picked up the labels, so . . ."

His eyes met hers and realization dawned. "Tanner Joseph was stalking you," whispered Drayton.

"No kidding," she said glumly.

❧ 44 ❧

For the first time in years, Theodosia did not find herself calmed by the simple act of sipping a cup of tea. As she gazed across her desk at Drayton, she realized he wasn't exactly the poster child for serenity either.

"What are you going to tell Haley and Bethany?" asked Drayton. He had experienced his own mini-meltdown upon hearing that Tanner Joseph had been Theodosia's unwelcome caller the night before, and now his hair was ruffled from running his hands nervously through it, his tie askew. And Drayton was gulping his tea rather than sipping it.

"I suppose I'll have to tell them the truth," said Theodosia. "Even though we still have the security guard, they need to be on the alert. We don't know what this character Tanner Joseph is capable of."

"We also don't know if he was the one who left the note the other night," said Drayton.

"He could have," said Theodosia. "But I'm more inclined to believe this was the first time Tanner Joseph has shown up. My guess is he was colossally ticked that I picked up the labels and didn't hang around to schmooze with him. Although I'm afraid he might have had more on his mind than just schmoozing."

Drayton gazed at her glumly. "If that's the case, it means there are *two* nutcases walking around."

Theodosia put both hands to her temples and massaged them. "Chilling thought, isn't it?"

A gentle rap on the door interrupted them.

"What?" called Drayton.

The door cracked open no more than an inch.

"Tidwell just came in," said Haley. "He wants to speak with Theodosia."

"Get out in front right now," ordered Drayton. "You know Bethany is scared to death of that man!"

"Okay, okay," grumped Haley. "Take a chill pill. I can't be in two places at once!"

Theodosia gazed wearily at Drayton. "Everything is falling apart," she murmured. "Ever since the murder of Hughes Barron, nothing's been the same."

Drayton grabbed her hand in his, held it firmly, and met her sad-eyed gaze with genteel fervor. "Hear me, Theodosia. We *will* get to the bottom of all this. We *will* unravel this mystery. And when we do, we shall both look back on this and laugh. That's right; we will find this all terribly droll and amusing, mark my words. Now, Miss Browning, I suggest you smooth your hair and blot your eyes. That's it," he said with encouragement. "Can't have terrible Tidwell thinking anything's amiss, can we?" He fell in step behind Theodosia. "Bear up, dear girl," he whispered.

Theodosia unleashed a warm smile on Burt Tidwell that she somehow managed to dredge from the depths of her soul. "Good morning, Detective Tidwell." Her voice, still husky from anger, passed for throaty.

"Miss Browning." Tidwell favored her with a quick grimace, his rendition of a smile, and Theodosia wondered if there was a Mrs. Tidwell attached to this quaint, quirky man. Pity the poor woman.

Tidwell half stood as Theodosia seated herself, then crashed down heavily into his chair. They both kept tight smiles on their faces as Haley set cups and saucers, spoons, milk, and a pot of Dimbulla tea in front of them. But no goodies. Theodosia intended to keep this visit brief.

Tidwell's bullet-shaped head swiveled on his beefy shoulders, appraising customers at surrounding tables. "Business good?" he asked.

Theodosia raised her shoulders a notch. "Fine."

"As you know, our investigation into Hughes Barron's death has been ongoing." Tidwell paused, pursed his lips, and took a tiny sip of tea. "Where is this from?" he asked.

"Ceylon."

"It would go well with a sweet."

"It would." Theodosia sat patiently with her hands in her lap. By now she was familiar with Tidwell's oblique tactics.

Tidwell blotted his mouth and favored her with a mousy grin.

Unless . . . she thought as she watched him carefully. *Unless the man has something up his sleeve.*

"To assure ourselves of a *thorough* investigation," Tidwell continued, "we focused much of our attention on Hughes Barron's business office here in town as well as his place of residence." He peered at Theodosia over his teacup. "You may be familiar with his beach condominium. Located on the Isle of Palms?"

Theodosia gave him nothing.

"Moving along," Tidwell continued, "I should tell you that we discovered an object at said condominium. An object that carries the fingerprints of one of your employees."

"Is that a fact."

"Yes, indeed. And I'm sure you won't be at all surprised when I tell you the fingerprints—and we obtained a rather excellent four-point match—belong to Bethany Sheperd."

Theodosia fairly spat out her next words. "Why don't you rock my world, Detective Tidwell, and tell me what *object* Bethany's fingerprints were found on."

"Miss Browning." His eyes drilled at her. "*That* information remains confidential."

45

Burt Tidwell sat in his Crown Victoria and stared at the brick-and-shingle facade of the Indigo Tea Shop. He had purposely not informed the Browning woman that her dear departed neighbor, Harold Dauphine, had, indeed, died of a heart attack. A myocardial infarction, to be exact.

He knew Theodosia was probably lumping the deaths of Mr. Hughes Barron and Mr. Dauphine together. Putting two and two together, he mused. A trifle off base in this instance. But overall, she hadn't performed badly for an amateur.

Burt Tidwell sighed, reached down to his midsection, fumbled for his belt buckle, and released it one notch. There. Better. Now he could draw breath. Now he could even begin to contemplate stopping by Poogan's Porch for an early lunch. Perhaps some shrimp Creole or a bowl of their famous okra gumbo.

Tidwell turned the key in the ignition. The engine in the big car caught, then rumbled deeply.

Theodosia Browning had proved to be highly resourceful. True, she was snoopy and contentious toward him, but she had made some interesting connections and suppositions.

Best of all, she'd rattled more than a few cages here in Charleston's historic district. That had certainly served his purpose well. After all, Theodosia was an insider. He was not.

46

"*Did you let* the police fingerprint you?" Theodosia paced back and forth in her small office while Bethany sat perched on a chair. Bethany's knees were pulled up to her chin, and her hands worked constantly, nervously twisting her long skirt.

"Yes," she said in a small voice. "Leyland Hartwell said it was okay. Anyway, the police explained that it was to rule me *out*."

"Bethany, you don't have to be so defensive. I'm not cross-examining you."

"No, that will come later," replied a glum Bethany.

"We don't know that at all," said Theodosia. *Honestly,* she thought to herself, *the girl could be positively maddening.*

The phone on Theodosia's desk buzzed, and she snatched up the receiver, almost welcoming a diversion.

"I understand you had some excitement last night," said Jory Davis.

"The security company called you?" said Theodosia, surprised.

"Of course. I hired them." There was a long pause, then Jory Davis asked quietly, "Theodosia, are you in over your head on this?"

She waited so long to reply that Jory Davis finally answered his own question. "Sometimes no answer *is* an answer," he said.

"I promise," Theodosia said, "to share absolutely everything with you tonight. And to listen carefully to any lawyerly advice you choose to impart." She paused. "Truly."

"Fair enough," said Jory Davis, seemingly appeased by this. "I await our evening with bated breath." His voice was tinged with faint amusement.

"Can I please go back to work?" Bethany asked. She noted that

Theodosia had long since hung up the phone but was standing there in the strangest way, staring down at her desk, seemingly lost in thought.

Theodosia looked up. "What? Oh, of course, Bethany."

Bethany jumped up to make her escape.

"You don't have any idea what Tidwell was talking about, do you?" Theodosia called to her back.

Bethany spun on her heel. "About my fingerprints? No. Of course I don't." She gazed at Theodosia, the expression on her face a mixture of hurt and humiliation. "I think . . . I think this should probably be my last day here," sniffled Bethany.

"Bethany, please." This was the last thing she wanted, to upset Bethany in any way, to foster more bad feelings.

"No. My being here has become entirely too problematic."

"As you wish, Bethany," said Theodosia. She waited until Bethany pulled the door closed behind her, then sat down in her chair and sighed. What in her wildest dreams had told her she could possibly solve Hughes Barron's murder? She had followed her leads and hunches and ended up . . . nowhere. If anything, there were more unanswered questions, more strange twists and turns. Now some mysterious object had been found at Hughes Barron's condominium, something the police had run tests on and found smatters of Bethany's fingerprints!

Theodosia pulled her desk drawer open and hoisted out the Charleston phone directory. As the book thudded on top of her desk, she quickly flipped through the front pages. Just past the directory assistance and long-distance calling pages, she found the number she wanted. The Charleston Police Department.

She dialed the number nervously, knowing this was a long shot.

"Cletus Aubrey, please," she told the central operator when she came on the line.

"Which department?" asked the disinterested voice.

"Computer records," said Theodosia.

"You don't have that extension?" The operator seemed vexed.

"Sorry, I don't," said Theodosia, feeling silly for apologizing to an operator whose job it was to look up numbers.

Cletus Aubrey was a childhood friend. He had grown up in the low-country on a farm down the road from the Browning plantation. As children, she and Cletus had spent many summer days together, romping through the woods, wading in streams, and tying pieces of string around chicken necks and trolling creek bottoms to catch crabs. Interested in law enforcement early on, Cletus had received encouragement from her father, Macalester Browning. And when Cletus graduated from high school, he went on to a two-year law enforcement program, then joined the Charleston Police Department.

"Mornin', Cletus Aubrey."

"Cletus? It's Theodosia. Theodosia Browning."

She heard a sharp intake of breath and then rich, warm laughter.

"As I live and die, I don't believe it. How *are* you, Miss Browning?"

"Cletus, exactly when did I become Miss Browning?"

"When you stopped running through the swamp barefoot and started running a tea shop. Listen, girl, it *pleases* me to call you *Miss* Browning. Reminds me of how you followed in the graceful footsteps of your Aunt Libby. And, by the way, how *is* Aunt Libby?"

"Very well."

"Still treating her feathered friends with all manner of seed and millet?"

"She's extended her generosity to woodchucks, raccoons, and opossum, too."

Cletus Aubrey chuckled again. "The good things in life never change. Theo, *Miss* Browning, to what do I owe this blast from the past, this walk down memory lane?"

"Cletus, I have a favor to ask."

"Ask away."

"You used to work in the property room, am I correct?"

"For three years. Before I went to night school and turned into a computer nut."

"How big a deal would it be to snoop around in there?"

"No big deal at all if I had a general idea what I was on the lookout for."

"Let's just call it a mysterious object found in the home of a Mr. Hughes Barron."

"Uh-oh, the old mysterious object search. Yeah, I can probably pull that off. What was the name again? Barron?"

"Yes. B-A-R-R-O-N."

"The first name is Hughes?"

"That's it," said Theodosia

"One of the guys who works in property owes me twenty bucks from a bet he lost on last week's Citadel game. I'll harass him and have a look around. Kill two birds with one stone."

"Cletus, you're a gem."

"That's what I keep telling my wife, only she's not buyin' it."

Theodosia was deep in conversation with one of the sales reps at Frank & Fuller, a tea wholesaler in Montclair, New Jersey, when the other phone line lit up. It was Cletus calling back.

"You ain't gonna like this, Miss Browning," he began.

"What was it, Cletus?"

"Some tea thingamajig."

"Describe it to me," said Theodosia.

"Silver, lots of little holes."

"A tea infuser."

"You sell those?" asked Cletus.

"By the bushel," Theodosia said with a sigh.

47

The last six months of sales receipts were laid out on Theodosia's desk. Haley had tried to stack them, month by month, in some semblance of order, but there were so many of the flimsy paper receipts they kept sliding around and sorting into their own piles.

"This is everything?" asked Theodosia. In an effort to gain some control and a slight appearance of tidiness, she had pinned her hair up in a bun, much to Haley's delight.

"You look like a character out of a William Faulkner novel," Haley quipped. "All you need are Drayton's reading glasses perched on the end of your nose."

Theodosia ignored her. "These are all the sales receipts, correct?"

"Should be, unless you want me to pull computer records, too." Haley sobered up. "We don't need to do that, do we? I think it would just duplicate efforts."

"If the two of us go through these, we should be able to sort out sales receipts on everyone who purchased a tea infuser."

Because the Indigo Tea Shop maintained a customer database for the purpose of sending out newsletters and direct mail, customer names and addresses were almost always entered on sales receipts.

Haley looked skeptical. "Which kind? Spoon infusers, mesh ones with handles, tea ball infusers?"

"All of them," declared Theodosia. "You take these three stacks, I'll take the others."

"What about infuser socks?" asked Haley.

"Anything having to do with tea infusers means infuser socks, too."

"Okay, okay. I'm just double-checking. I'm worried about Bethany, too." Haley bent diligently over her stacks of papers.

"You're sure Bethany didn't fill in here before six months ago?" asked Theodosia. She was concerned about the window of time they were checking.

Haley squinted thoughtfully. "Before last May? No, I don't think so."

Two hours later, they had sifted through all the receipts and found, amazingly, that the Indigo Tea Shop had sold almost fifty tea infusers in the last six months.

"Now we've got to try to rule some people out," said Theodosia, overwhelmed at the sheer number of receipts just for tea infusers.

"Such as?" said Haley.

"Tourists, for one thing. People who stopped by for a cup of tea and made a few extra purchases."

"Okay, I get it," said Haley. "Let me go through these fifty then. See what I can do."

Fifteen minutes of work produced a modicum of progress.

"I think we can safely rule out about thirty of these," reasoned Haley. She indicated a stack of receipts. "These customers are all from out of state and fairly far-flung. California, Texas, Nevada, New York . . ."

"Agreed," said Theodosia. "So now we're down to local purchases. Who have we got?"

Haley passed the remaining handful of receipts to Theodosia. "Those two sisters, Elmira and Elise, who live over the Cabbage Patch Needlepoint Shop. Reverend Jonathan at Saint Philip's. A couple of the B and Bs."

Theodosia studied the culled receipts. "Mostly friends and neighbors," she said. "Not exactly hard-core suspects."

"Lydia at the Chowder Hound Restaurant down the street bought *three* of them," said Haley. "Do you think she had it in for Hughes Barron?"

"I doubt she even knew him," murmured Theodosia. "Okay, Haley, thanks. Good job."

"Sorry we couldn't come up with something more definitive." Haley hesitated in the doorway, feeling somehow that she'd let Theodosia down.

"That's all right," said Theodosia. "Thanks again."

Theodosia reached for the clip that contained her thick hair and yanked it out. As her hair tumbled about her shoulders, she thought of all the things she had left undone at the shop, how she'd even missed this week's therapy dog session with Earl Grey.

Her heart caught in her chest. Earl Grey. The dog she'd found cowering in the alley out back, the dog that was her dear companion. Someone, quite possibly the person who had murdered Hughes Barron, had threatened to poison Earl Grey if she didn't back off.

Okay, Theodosia thought to herself. Following up on these sales receipts was going to be her last effort. And if it didn't pan out, she *would* back off.

Sitting in her chair, trying to focus, Theodosia leafed through the stack of twenty or so receipts Haley had culled out.

Lydia at the Chowder Hound. Could she have had any sort of

connection to Hughes Barron? Or, for that matter, any of the possible suspects? Her gut feeling told her probably not.

And Samantha Rabathan had bought a tea infuser a few months ago. Theodosia pondered this, thought about probable connections. What if, just what if Samantha purchased the tea infuser for the Heritage Society?

Samantha was kind of a goody-goody that way. When she wasn't out winning a blue ribbon for her spectacular La Reine Victoria roses or flitting about being a social butterfly, she spent a good portion of her time as a volunteer with the Heritage Society. She worked in the small library and helped the development director entice new donors.

So it *was* possible that Timothy Neville might be behind this after all.

Timothy Neville could have done away with Hughes Barron and somehow planted the tea infuser with Bethany's fingerprints as false evidence. He knew her prints would have thrown the police off the track. That is, if the police ever got onto that track in the first place.

Well, there was only one way to find out. She would go and ask Samantha if she'd bought a tea infuser for the Heritage Society. Samantha might think it a strange question, but she'd probably be too polite to say so.

48

Paved in antique brick and bluestone, accented by a vine-covered arbor, Samantha Rabathan's garden was a peaceful, perfect sanctuary. Flower beds arranged in concentric circles around a small pool had lost much of their bloom for the season but, because of the great variety of carefully selected greenery, still conveyed a verdant, pleasing palette.

"Yoohoo, over here, dear," called Samantha.

She had seen Theodosia approach out of the corner of her eye, had heard her footfalls. Still on her hands and knees, Samantha looked up, a smile on her face and pruning shears in her hand.

"Artful pruning in autumn makes for healthy flowers in spring," said Samantha as though she were lecturing a garden club. She was wearing a broad-brimmed straw hat, even though the afternoon sun kept disappearing, without a moment's notice, behind large, puffy clouds.

Theodosia gazed about. The garden was beautiful, of that there was no doubt. At the same time, Samantha's garden always seemed a trifle contained. So many of Charleston's backyard gardens felt enchanting and mysterious because of their slightly wild, untamed look. Vines tumbling down crumbled brick walls, tree branches twining overhead, layers of lush foliage with statuary, rockery, and wrought iron peeking through. These were the places Theodosia thought of as secret gardens. And there were many in the old city.

"How is everyone at the tea shop?" Samantha inquired brightly.

"Good," said Theodosia. "Busy. We're right in the middle of inventory, so everything's a muddle." She thought this little story might help deflect any flak concerning her tea infuser inquiry.

"Sounds very tedious," said Samantha as she picked up a trowel, sank it deep into the rich turf, and ousted an errant weed.

"Only way we can get a handle on reorders," said Theodosia as Samantha tossed the weed into a carefully composed pile of wilted blooms and stems.

"Samantha," continued Theodosia, "did you purchase a tea infuser for the Heritage Society?"

Samantha finished tamping the divot she'd created, stood up, and gave a finishing stomp with her heel.

"Why, I think perhaps I might have. Is there a problem, Theodosia? A product recall?" Now her voice was tinged with amusement. "Tell you what. Come inside, and we'll have ourselves a nice cup of tea and a good, friendly chat."

Without waiting for an answer, Samantha stuck her steel pruning shears and trowel into the webbed pockets of the canvas tool belt she wore cinched around her waist, linked her arm through Theodosia's, and pulled her along toward the back door of her house.

"Look, over there," Samantha said, pointing, "where I planted my new

La Belle Sultane roses last year. What do you bet that in five months I'll have blooms the size of your fist!"

Samantha fussed about in her kitchen, clattering dishes, while Theodosia seated herself in the small dining room. Samantha had an enviable collection of Waterford crystal, and today it was catching the light that streamed through the octagonal windows above the built-in cabinets in a most remarkable way.

"Here we are." Samantha bustled in with a silver tea service. "Perhaps not as perfect as you serve at the Indigo Tea Shop, but hopefully just as elegant."

Theodosia knew Samantha was making reference to her silver tea set. Not just silver-plated, the teapot and accompanying pieces were pure English sterling, antiques that had been in Samantha's family for over a century.

"Everything is lovely," murmured Theodosia as Samantha stood at the table, held a bone china cup under the silver spout, and poured deftly.

Theodosia accepted the steaming cup of tea, inhaling the delicate aroma. Ceylon silver tips? Kenilworth Garden? She couldn't quite place it.

As Theodosia lifted her cup to take a sip, her eyes fell upon the livid purple flowers banked so artfully on the cabinet opposite her. Funny how she hadn't noticed them before. But then the sun had been streaming in and highlighting the crystal so vividly.

The purple blooms were like curled velvet and bore a strange resemblance to the cowled hood of a monk's robe, she noted. Pretty. But also somewhat unusual.

Images suddenly drifted into Theodosia's head. Of flowers she'd seen elsewhere. Purple flowers that had graced the wrought-iron tables the evening of the Lamplighter Tour. Mrs. Finster at Hughes Barron's condominium holding a vase of dead flowers. Deep purple, almost black. Papery and shriveled.

Theodosia put her teacup down without taking a sip. The fine bone china emitted a tiny *clink* as cup met saucer. Suddenly she understood what kind of poison had been used to kill Hughes Barron and how easily the deed had been accomplished.

As understanding dawned, the chastising voice of Samantha Raba-than echoed dreamlike in Theodosia's ears.

"You're not drinking your tea," Samantha accused in a peevish, sing-song voice as she slipped quickly to Theodosia's side.

Theodosia, stunned, gazed down at the teacup filled with deadly liquor, blinked, lifted her head again, and stared at the steel-jawed prun-ing shears with their curved Bowie knife blade and sharp tip poised just inches from her. In a single, staggering heartbeat she saw anger and tri-umph etched on Samantha's face.

"Hughes Barron," whispered Theodosia. "Why?"

Samantha's mouth twisted cruelly as she spat out her answer. "I loved him. But he wouldn't divorce her. Wouldn't divorce *Angelique*. He prom-ised he would, but then he wouldn't do it."

"So you poisoned him." It was a statement, not a question.

"Oh, please. At first I only tried to make him sick. So he would need me. Then I . . ." Samantha's eyes rolled crazily in her head as she jabbed with the pruning shears, the sharp tip pressing in, dimpling the skin of Theodosia's neck again and again.

She's having some sort of breakdown, thought Theodosia. *The nerves that connect her thoughts with her actions have somehow short-circuited. She's divorced herself from reality.* At the same time, Theodosia knew she had to try to keep Samantha talking. Keep Samantha communicating and engaged, seeing her still as a person. Theodosia shuddered, trying to keep at bay the thought of those nasty carbon steel pruning shears slicing into her neck.

"What are they?" Theodosia's voice was hoarse. "The purple flowers."

"Monkshood," snapped Samantha.

"Monkshood," repeated Theodosia. She'd learned something about this plant in the botany class she'd taken back when she first became seri-ous about the tea business. Monkshood contained the deadly poison aco-nite. It had been used for centuries. The Chinese dipped arrows and spears in aconite. In England the plant was called auld wife's huid. And, indeed, the potent petals had turned many an old wife into a widow.

"Don't be impolite," taunted Samantha. "Drink your tea." The sharp point traced a circle on Theodosia's neck, slightly below and behind her left ear.

Theodosia flinched at the needlelike pain. *That's where the carotid artery is,* she thought wildly.

"The tea," spat Samantha. "You are fast becoming a rude, unwelcome guest who has severely stretched my patience!" The last half of her sentence came out in a loud, shrill tone.

Anger flickered deep within Theodosia, replacing fear. This woman, with cold, cunning calculation, had poisoned Hughes Barron. Had gone on to threaten Earl Grey. And now, this same deranged creature was within an inch of inflicting bodily harm on her! Smoldering outrage began to ignite every part of her body.

Theodosia raised her right hand slowly, extending it tentatively toward a tiny silver saucer where a half dozen cubes of sugar rested.

"May I?" asked Theodosia.

Samantha's laugh was a harsh bark. Her head jerked up and down. "What's that silly song? A spoonful of sugar helps the medicine go down? Go on, help yourself, you prim and proper little simp."

Theodosia reached for two cubes, clutched them gently between her thumb and forefinger. Feeling the fine granulation of the sugar cubes between her fingers, she was also keenly aware of cold steel pressed insistently against her neck.

As she drew her hand back, Theodosia suddenly dropped the sugar cubes as if they were a pair of hot dice. Her right hand wrapped around the handle of Samantha's handsome silver teapot, clutching it for dear life. With every bit of strength she could muster, Theodosia swung the heavy teapot, filled to the brim with hot, scalding tea, toward Samantha. The silver lid flew forward, cutting Samantha in the cheek. Then hot tea surged out and met its intended target, splashing directly into Samantha's face.

Samantha threw back her head and howled like a scalded cat. "My face! My face!" she shrieked. The garden shears flew from her hand and clattered to the floor as her hands flailed helplessly. "You nasty witch!" She gnashed her teeth in pain and outrage. "What have you done to my face!" Samantha tottered back unsteadily, eyes blinded by the viciously hot liquid, her hair drenched.

Theodosia bent down and snatched up the pruning shears. Then she reached over and plucked the steel trowel from Samantha's webbed belt as well. Like disarming a gunslinger, Theodosia told herself recklessly.

Samantha had one hand on the wall now, hobbling along, trying to cautiously feel her way toward the kitchen. "Help me!" she yowled. She was stooped over and bedraggled. "Cold water . . . a towel!"

Theodosia pulled her cell phone from her handbag and dialed Burt Tidwell's number. Tidwell's office immediately patched her through to his mobile phone.

Theodosia barked Samantha's address at Tidwell, admonishing him to get here *now*, even as she stepped outside and stood on the front porch to finish their terse conversation. Then she collapsed tiredly on the steps and dropped her head in her hands. She tried not to listen to Samantha's pitiful cries.

49

"You all right?" Tidwell peered inquisitively into Theodosia's face. He had arrived ten minutes earlier, breathless and bug-eyed, gun drawn. Two patrol cars, lights flashing, sirens screaming, had been just seconds behind him.

Theodosia took a deep breath, then blew it out. "I'm okay." Tidwell had led her gently from her perch on the front steps to more comfortable seating on the porch's hanging swing.

"You're sure?" One of Tidwell's furry eyebrows quivered expectantly. "Because you look awfully pale. Ashen."

"It's just my post-traumatic stress look," Theodosia said slowly. "Comes from confronting murderous maniacs." There was a slight catch in her voice, but there was a touch of humor, too.

Tidwell cocked his head, studying her. "You're right. You do project a certain been-to-the-edge look." He grinned crookedly, but his manner was respectful.

Theodosia sat silently for a few moments, staring at Tidwell's big hands fidgeting at his side. "Did you talk to her?" she finally asked.

Tidwell nodded gravely. "She wasn't making a lot of sense, but, to answer your question, yes, I did."

"I was so off base," fretted Theodosia. "I was so sure Timothy Neville was the murderer. And that was only after I'd cast suspicions toward Lleveret Dante and Tanner Joseph as well."

Burt Tidwell pulled himself up to his full height, sucked in his stomach, and gave her a look dripping with reproach. "I beg your pardon, madam. Kindly do not denigrate or underestimate your efforts. Justice will be served precisely because of your actions."

As if on cue, the front door snicked open, and two uniformed officers led a handcuffed Samantha out onto the porch. The officers had allowed her to pull a pink wool blazer over her gardening clothes and tie a matching paisley scarf, turban style, around her head. Even though the scarf was pulled down across her ears, angry red blotches, the beginnings of blisters, were visible on one side of her face.

Samantha, hesitating at the top of the steps, looked around dazedly. As she suddenly spotted Theodosia, something akin to recognition dawned.

"Theodosia." Her mouth twitched in a slightly vacant smile. "Be a dear and water that basket of plumbago, will you? And do take care with the sun."

50

"*She held a* knife to your throat?" squealed Haley.

"Haven't you been listening?" Drayton returned snappishly. "Theodosia just told us it was *pruning shears.*" Still shaken to the core by Theodosia's recent brush with danger, Drayton stretched an arm across the table and clasped his own hand warmly atop Theodosia's. "Anyone knows a tool like that is a deadly, dangerous weapon!"

Drayton, Haley, and Bethany had sat incredulous and openmouthed as Theodosia related the bizarre string of events that had unfolded at Samantha Rabathan's house. In fact, when Burt Tidwell led Theodosia into the tea shop some ten minutes earlier, pale and still slightly shaken, Tidwell had pulled Drayton aside for a hastily whispered conversation. Drayton listened to the amazing story and thanked Tidwell profusely. Then the usually unflappable Drayton had fairly kicked the few remaining customers out of the shop. As Haley declared later, this was the one time Indigo Tea Shop customers got the bum's rush!

"And I was beginning to believe Timothy Neville was the guilty party," spoke up Haley. "He's such an arrogant old curmudgeon."

"Timothy topped my list, too," admitted Theodosia. "I was even worried that he might have been involved in Mr. Dauphine's death. But Detective Tidwell assured me the poor man did suffer a heart attack."

"I thought it must be Tanner Joseph," said Bethany quietly. "Drayton confided to us earlier that he was snooping around outside your apartment last night."

"He really has a thing for you, Theodosia," Haley said, rolling her eyes.

"Well, he's terribly misguided," Drayton replied with indignation. "Crass fellow, sneaking around like that, peering in windows and such. I daresay he was probably planning to leave some kind of mash note until the security guard rousted him."

Bethany put a hand on Theodosia's shoulder. "So good to have you back safely," she said, her eyes glistening with tears.

"It's good to have *you* back," said Theodosia.

"Nobody cast their vote for Lleveret Dante?" asked Drayton.

"As the murderer?" said Haley. "Not hardly. But I think that's because we never knew enough about him to get really suspicious," she added.

"Burt Tidwell does," replied Theodosia. "He told me that Dante is in as much trouble here as he was in his home state of Kentucky."

"Well, I hope he gets indicted and shipped back there," said Drayton. "Good riddance to bad rubbish. We don't need unsavory chaps like that in Charleston."

"Right," declared Haley. "We've got enough of our own."

"Drayton," said Theodosia, "what time is it?"

He wrinkled his nose and peered at his ancient Piaget. "Twenty to four."

"Which means it's really ten to four," said Haley.

"Would you drive me out to Aunt Libby's?" asked Theodosia. "I want to pick up Earl Grey."

"Hear, hear," said Haley, pounding on the table. "Let's *all* drive out to the low-country and pick up Earl Grey. We can stop at Catfish Jack's on the way and celebrate with beer and blackened catfish."

"I love the idea," said Theodosia. "But can we save it for another time? Tonight I've got to get right back."

"Of course you do," said Drayton graciously. "You've just been through a terrible ordeal. Best thing for you is to spend a nice cozy evening at home."

Drayton's right, Theodosia mused to herself. I should take it easy, give myself a little quiet time. And I will. Tomorrow night for sure. As for tonight, however . . . tonight I'm going to the opera!

A RECIPE FROM
The Indigo Tea Shop

Theodosia's Tea-Marbled Eggs

A nice summer hors d'oeuvre

3 cups water
8 small eggs
2 Tbs. loose-leaf black tea or 4 tea bags black tea
1 Tbs. kosher salt

PLACE eggs in pot with cold water, cover, and bring to a boil. Reduce heat and simmer 10–12 minutes. Carefully remove eggs and reserve water. Place eggs in cold water, and when they're cool enough to handle, gently tap eggs all around with the back of a spoon to make cracks. Add tea leaves to the reserved water and place eggs back in. Add the salt and simmer, covered, for one hour. Remove pot from stove and allow eggs to soak in tea water an additional 30 minutes. Then remove eggs and cool. Eggs will now have a brown marbleized design. To serve, slice eggs in half and sprinkle with paprika and minced parsley.

GUNPOWDER GREEN

ACKNOWLEDGMENTS

Heartfelt thanks to all the wonderful people at Berkley. Thanks, too, to my husband, Dr. Robert Poor, for all his ideas, suggestions, and support.

1

Theodosia Browning reached up and removed the tortoiseshell clip that held her auburn locks tightly in place. As if on cue, the brisk wind from Charleston Harbor lifted her hair, just as it did the graceful, undulating flags that flew from the masts of the yachts bobbing in the harbor.

It won't be long now, Theodosia decided, shading her eyes against the brilliance of the midafternoon sun. Off in the distance, she could see dozens of sleek J-24s hurtling down the slot between Patriots Point and Fort Sumter. Masts straining, spinnakers billowing, the yachts and their four-man crews were fighting to capture every gust of wind, coaxing every bit of performance from their boats. Twenty minutes more, and the two hundred or so picnickers gathered here in White Point Gardens at the tip of Charleston's historic peninsula would know the outcome of this year's Isle of Palms Yacht Race.

Theodosia noted that most of the picnickers had drawn into cozy little circles of conversation, lulled by the warm April weather, sated by an abundance of food and drink. There had been a crazed hubbub when the sailboats from the competing yacht clubs took off, of course: cheering throngs, glasses held high in toasts, and loud boasts from both sailing teams. But once the flotilla of sailboats had zigzagged their way across Charleston Harbor and rounded the outermost marker buoy on their way toward the Isle of Palms, they were out of sight.

Which also meant out of mind.

The remaining yacht club members, with their abundance of friends, families, and well-wishers, most of whom lived in the elegant Georgian, Federal, and Victorian homes in the nearby historic district, had settled down to a merry romp in the verdant gardens that made Charleston's Battery so utterly appealing.

As proprietor of the Indigo Tea Shop, located just a few short blocks away on Church Street, Theodosia had been invited to cater this "tea by the sea" for the Charleston Yacht Club, the host for this year's race. She'd been pleased that Drayton Conneley and Haley Parker, her dear friends and employees, had displayed their usual over-the-top creativity in event and menu planning, and had enthusiastically jumped into the fray to lend a hand on this spectacularly beautiful Sunday afternoon.

Gulls wheeled gracefully overhead, and fat, pink clouds scudded across the horizon as Theodosia cinched her apron tighter about her slim waist and let her eyes rove across the two long tables that were draped with white linen tablecloths and laden with refreshments. Satisfied that everything was near perfect, Theodosia's broad, intelligent face with its high cheekbones and aquiline nose finally assumed a look of repose.

Yes, it *was* perfect, Theodosia told herself. Wire baskets held golden breadsticks, while fresh cracked crab claws rested on platters of shaved ice. Smoked salmon on miniature bagels was garnished with cream cheese and candied ginger. And the chocolate-dipped strawberries with crème fraîche were . . . oh my . . . disappearing at an alarming rate.

Hoisting a silver pitcher, Theodosia poured out a stream of pungent yellow green iced tea into a glass filled with crushed ice. She took a sip and savored the brisk, thirst-quenching blend of Chinese gunpowder green tea and fresh mint.

Drayton Conneley, her assistant and master tea blender, had created the tea especially for this race-day picnic. The Chinese gunpowder green tea was aptly named since, once dried, the tiny leaves curled up into small, tight pellets resembling gunpowder, unfurling only when subjected to boiling water. The fresh mint had been plucked yesterday from her aunt Libby's garden out in South Carolina's low country.

Theodosia had decided to name the new tea White Point Green, a nod to the tea's debut today in White Point Gardens. And judging from the number of pitchers that had already been consumed, this tea would definitely be packaged up and offered for sale in her tea shop.

"Your table reminds me of a still life by Cézanne: poetic, elegant, almost too beautiful to eat." Delaine Dish, owner of the Cotton Duck Clothing Shop, hovered at Theodosia's elbow. Her long, raven-colored hair was wound up in a Psyche knot atop her head, accenting her heart-shaped face.

Theodosia sighed inwardly. Cotton Duck was just a few doors down from the Indigo Tea Shop, and Delaine, though a kindhearted soul and true dynamo when it came to volunteering for civic and social events, was also the acknowledged neighborhood gossip.

"I mean it, Theodosia, this is an amazing bounty," cooed Delaine. Ever the fashion plate, Delaine was turned out today in a robin's egg blue silk blouse and elegant tapered cream slacks.

Theodosia wiped her hands on her apron and peeked down at Delaine's feet. They were shod in dyed-to-match robin's egg blue python flats. Of course Delaine would be coordinated, Theodosia decided. She was *always* coordinated.

Dipping an enormous ripe strawberry into a bowl of crème fraîche, Delaine stood with the luscious fruit poised inches from her mouth. "Did you ever think of switching to full-time catering, Theodosia?" she said as if the thought had just struck like a bolt from the blue. "Because you'd be *brilliant* at it."

"Abandon my tea shop? No, thank you," Theodosia declared fervently, for she had literally created the Indigo Tea Shop from the ground up. Starting with a somewhat dreary and abandoned little shop on Church Street, she had stripped away layers of grime and decades of ill-advised improvements such as cork tile, fluorescent lights, and linoleum. Somewhere along the way, Theodosia's vision took hold with a vengeance, and she sketched and dreamed and haunted antique shops for just the right fixtures and accoutrements until the results yielded a gem of a shop. Now her little tea shop exuded an elegant, old-world charm. Pegged wooded floors highlighted exposed beams and brick walls. Antique tables and chairs, porcelain teapots, and copper teakettles added to the rich patina and keen sense of history.

Floor-to-ceiling wooden cubbyholes held tins and glass jars filled with loose teas. Coppery munnar from the southern tip of India, floral keeman from China's Anhui province, a peaches and honey–flavored Formosan oolong. All the tea in China, as Drayton often remarked with pride. Plus teas from Japan, Tibet, Nepal, Turkey, Indonesia, and Africa. Even South Carolina was represented here with their marvelous, rich American Classic tea grown on the Charleston Tea Plantation, just twenty-five miles south on the subtropical island of Wadmalaw.

The tea shop had been Theodosia's exit strategy from the cutthroat world of media and marketing. She'd spent fourteen years in client services, years that had taken their toll. She grew exhausted working for others and not for herself. Theodosia was determined never to climb aboard that merry-go-round again.

"I bet you'd make more money in catering," cajoled Delaine. "Think of all the social tête-à-têtes that go on here in Charleston."

"A foray into food service just isn't for me," said Theodosia. "I've got my hands full just running the tea shop. Plus our Web site is up, and Internet sales have been surprisingly brisk. Of course, Drayton is constantly blending new teas to add to our line, and he's making plans to offer specialty tea events, too."

"Pray tell, what are specialty tea events?" asked Delaine.

"Chamber music teas, bridal shower teas, mystery teas—"

"A *mystery* tea!" exclaimed Delaine. "What's that?"

"Come and find out," invited Theodosia. "Drayton's got one planned for next Saturday evening."

Theodosia knew that she and Delaine Dish were a breed apart. She had abandoned the fast track of competing for clients and was deliciously satisfied with the little oasis of calm her tea shop afforded her. Delaine, on the other hand, thrived on spotting new trends and employed sharklike techniques with customers. When a woman walked into Cotton Duck for a new blouse, Delaine had a knack for sending her home with a skirt, shoes, handbag, and jewelry, too. And if Delaine had really worked up a full head of steam that day, the woman's purchase would probably include a couple of silk scarves.

"Hello, Drayton," purred Delaine as Drayton Conneley, Theodosia's right-hand man, approached, bearing a silver tray. "Aren't you just full of surprises."

Drayton Conneley arranged his face in a polite smile for Delaine, exchanging air kisses with her even as he raised an eyebrow at Theodosia.

"I was telling Delaine about your upcoming mystery tea," explained Theodosia.

"Of course." Drayton set his tray down and grasped Delaine's hands in a friendly gesture. "You must come," he urged her.

Theodosia smiled to herself. Drayton could schmooze with the best of them. But then again, he'd had years of experience. Drayton had worked as a tea trader in Amsterdam, where the world's major tea auctions were held. He had been hospitality director at a very prestigious Charleston inn until she'd talked him into coming to work for her. And Drayton Conneley was currently on the board of directors for the Charleston Heritage Society.

Of course, what Drayton did best was conduct tea tastings, educating their guests on the many varieties of tea and their steeping times, helping them understand little tea nuances such as bake, oxidation, and fermentation.

As much as Theodosia knew the tea shop was her creation, she often felt that Drayton was the engine that drove it. And, at sixty-one years of age, he reveled in his role as elder statesman.

Delaine reached out and brushed her French-manicured fingertips across the lapels of Drayton's sport coat. "Egyptian linen. Nice." She threw an approving glance toward Theodosia. "You can always tell a gentleman by the way he's turned out," she drawled.

"Drayton's straight from the pages of *Town and Country*," Theodosia agreed wryly, knowing that Delaine's affectations were beginning to set Drayton's teeth on edge.

"Theo, are there any more cucumber and lobster salad sandwiches?" asked Drayton as he rummaged through the wicker picnic hampers and coolers that had been stuck under the tables. "Oh, never mind, here they are." Drayton pulled out a fresh tray of the tiny, artfully prepared sandwiches. "We've been getting requests. And"—he paused, the first real look of genuine pleasure on his face—"would you believe it, Lolly Lauder just located an artisan from Savannah who assures her he can restore the molded wooden cornices on her portico and still preserve their integrity!"

Drayton adjusted his bow tie, smiled perfunctorily at the two women, then sped off, eager to exchange architectural gossip. He looked, Theodosia thought to herself, all the world like the perpetually hurried and harried White Rabbit from *Alice in Wonderland.*

Besides tea and gardening, Drayton's mission in life was historical preservation, and he enjoyed nothing better than to share tales of tuck pointing and tabby walls with his friends and neighbors who lived in the elegant old mansions that lined Charleston's Battery. Drayton himself lived in a tiny but historically accurate Civil War–era home just blocks from White Point Gardens.

"Do you see who's sitting over there?" asked Delaine in a low voice. Her violet eyes were fairly glimmering, her perfectly waxed brows arched expectantly.

Theodosia had been busy refilling tea pitchers and arranging more strawberries on the platter. "Delaine," she said, struggling to keep her sense of humor, "in case you haven't noticed, I've been working, not socializing."

"No need to get snippy, dear. Just look over my shoulder and to your left. No, a little more left. There. Do you see them? That's Doe Belvedere and Oliver Dixon."

"That's Doe Belvedere?" exclaimed Theodosia. "My goodness, the girl can't be more than twenty-five."

The Belvedere-Dixon wedding had been the talk of Charleston a couple months ago. Doe Belvedere and Oliver Dixon had staged a lavish wedding in the courtyard garden of the splendidly Victorian Kentshire Mansion. They had utterly dazzled guests with their horse-drawn carriages, champagne and caviar, and strolling musicians costumed like eighteenth-century French courtiers. Afterward, the newlyweds had dashed off to Morocco for a three-week honeymoon, leaving all of Charleston to relive the details of their sumptuous wedding in the society pages of the *Charleston Post and Courier.* Aside from those grainy black and white photos, this was the first time Theodosia had laid eyes on the happy couple.

"She's twenty-five," purred Delaine. "And Oliver Dixon is sixty-six."

"Really," said Theodosia.

"But honey," continued Delaine, "Oliver Dixon supposedly has piles of money. Did you read where he's about to launch a new high-tech company? Something to do with those handheld wireless gizmos that let you make phone calls or get on the Internet. That's probably what kept him in the running for Doe, don't you think?"

"I'm sure she loves him very much," said Theodosia generously.

Delaine gazed speculatively at the couple. "Yes, but money does give a man a certain, shall we say, *patina*."

"Who are you two whispering about?" asked Haley as she came up behind Theodosia and Delaine. Haley Parker was Theodosia's shop clerk and baker extraordinaire. At twenty-four, Haley was a self-proclaimed perpetual night school student and caustic wit. She was also the youthful sprite who ran the small kitchen at the rear of the Indigo Tea Shop with the precision and unquestioned authority of a Prussian general, turning out mouthwatering baked goods that drew customers in by the carload. Haley carefully supervised the choice of flour, sugar, cream, and eggs, and often went down to Charleston's open-air market herself to select only the finest apples, currants, sourwood honey, and fig syrup from local growers. And her unflagging high standards always paid off. Haley's peach tarts and apple butter scones were in constant demand. The poppy seed stuffing she infused in her lighter-than-air profiteroles was to die for.

"We were discussing Doe Belvedere," said Delaine conspiratorially. "You know, she just married Oliver Dixon."

Haley squinted in the direction of the pretty young woman with the flowing blond hair who sat chatting animatedly with well-wishers, even as she grasped the hand of her new husband.

"So *that's* Doe Belvedere," exclaimed Haley. She narrowed her eyes, studying the girl. "I've certainly heard enough about her. I mean, she's virtually a *legend* on the University of Charleston campus. Doe Belvedere was homecoming queen, prom queen, and magnolia princess all in one year. Talk about popular." Haley sniffed.

"That's nothing," said Delaine. "Doe was Miss South Carolina three years ago."

"Sure beats Miss Grits or Miss She-Crab," said Haley with a wicked laugh.

"You got that right," said Delaine with a straight face.

"As I recall," said Haley, "Doe Belvedere was offered a contract to model in New York."

"With the Eileen Ford Agency," said Delaine with delight. "But she passed on it. For *him*."

"I guess Oliver Dixon is one lucky guy, huh?" said Haley in a dubious tone.

"Oliver is supposed to be filthy rich," drawled Delaine. "How else could he afford that enormous house on Archdale Street?" Delaine nodded in the direction of Oliver Dixon's yellow-brick mansion. "I bet Timothy Neville positively had a *cat* when Oliver Dixon bought a mansion bigger than his, then built on another huge wing!"

Haley squinted at Doe and Oliver. "Think they're planning a family?" she asked.

"Haley!" said Theodosia.

"Hey, I was just wondering." Haley shrugged with a mischievous look.

"Genteel women do not wonder about such things in public," teased Theodosia as Haley's blush spread across her freckled cheeks.

"Who told you I was a genteel woman?" quipped Haley, with typical youthful bravado.

"Your mother," said Theodosia.

"Oh." Tears sprang quickly to Haley's eyes, for her mother had passed away just two years ago. "You're right. Sometimes I'm a little too . . ." Haley fumbled for the correct word. ". . . forthright . . . for my own good."

"We love you just the way you are, dear." Theodosia put an arm around Haley's slim shoulders. Although Theodosia was only thirty-five herself, she often felt very protective of her young employee. Haley was prone to plunging ahead, often before formulating a clear plan. A case in point, she'd already shifted her college major four times.

"Come along," urged Delaine, "I'll introduce you. Maybe that roving photographer from the *Post and Courier* will even snap your picture." She reached out and grabbed Haley's hand.

"Okay," Haley agreed and scampered off with Delaine.

Well, I'm not going to stand here like a bump on a log, decided Theodosia.

She picked up a plate of tiny, crustless sandwiches and was about to set off into the crowd, when a man's voice called to her.

"Say there, ma'am?"

Theodosia whirled about, finally glancing down toward the shore. One of the workers, a young man with dark, curly hair, the same one who'd helped set chairs up earlier, was struggling with a metal folding table. One end of the table seemed fine, but the legs on the other end were locked in place. "Do you have . . ." the man gave the table a disgusted kick. ". . . another of those cloths?"

Theodosia set her tray down, wandered a few steps closer to him. "You mean a tablecloth?"

"Yeah," he said, swiping an arm across his brow. "I'm supposed to set up the trophies and stuff here."

Theodosia walked back to her picnic hampers and snatched up the extra tablecloth she'd tucked in with her catering gear, just in case.

Wandering back down the bank, she saw that the worker had finally stabilized the table amid the sand and rocks. "This should do nicely," she said, unfurling the white linen tablecloth, letting the wind do most of the work. It settled gently atop the metal table.

"It's a warm day," said Theodosia. "Can I offer you a glass of iced tea, Mr. . . . ?"

"Billy," said the man. "Billy Manolo. I work over at the yacht club." He gestured toward a faraway cluster of bobbing masts barely visible down the shoreline. "I better not; lots to do yet." And off he strode.

Grabbing her tray of sandwiches again, Theodosia wandered among the picnickers, offering seconds. The day was a stunner, and White Point Gardens never looked as beautiful as it did this time of year. Magnolia, crape myrtle, and begonias bloomed riotously, and palmettos swayed gracefully, caressed by the Atlantic's warm breezes. In the early days, when Charleston had been known as Charles Town, pirates had been strung up here on roughly built gallows, and wars had been played out on these grounds. Now hundreds of couples came here to get married, and thousands more came to stroll the peaceful grounds that seemed to provide nourishment for the soul.

"This kingdom by the sea," Theodosia murmured to herself, recalling the famous line from Edgar Allan Poe's poem "Annabel Lee," which had so aptly and romantically described the city of Charleston.

For Charleston truly was a kingdom. No fewer than 180 church spires, steeples, and turrets pierced her sky. Across from White Point Gardens, crowding up against The Battery, shoulder to elegant shoulder, was a veritable parade of enormous, grande dame homes. Like wedding cakes, they were draped and ornamented with cornices, balustrades, frets, and finials. Most were painted in pastel colors of salmon pink, alabaster white, and pale blue; a romantic, French palette. Behind these homes lay another twenty-three-block tapestry of historic homes and shops, Charleston's architectural preserve, complete with cobbled streets, wrought-iron gates, and sequestered gardens.

"You're the tea shop lady, aren't you?" A rich, baritone voice interrupted Theodosia's reverie.

Theodosia turned with a smile and found herself staring into alert, dark brown eyes set in smooth, olive skin. A neatly clipped mustache draped over full, sensuous lips.

"You have the advantage, sir," she said, then realized immediately that she sounded far more formal than she'd intended.

But the man wasn't a bit put off and swept his Panama straw hat off his head in a gallant gesture that was pure Rhett Butler. "Giovanni Loard, at your service, ma'am."

The name sounded faintly familiar to Theodosia as she stood gazing at this interesting man who smiled broadly back at her, even as he dug hastily in the pocket of his navy blazer for a business card.

Theodosia accepted his card, squinted at tiny, old English type. "Loard Antiquarian Shop. Oh, of course," she said as comprehension suddenly dawned. "Down on King Street."

"In the antiques district," Giovanni Loard added helpfully.

"Drayton Conneley *raved* about your shop," she told him enthusiastically. "He said you had the finest collection of eighteenth- and nineteenth-century paintings in all of Charleston. Wonderful estate jewelry, too. I keep meaning to get down there but never seem to find the time," Theodosia lamented. "I've got this one wall—"

"That's *begging* for a truly great painting!" finished Giovanni Loard.

"Exactly," agreed Theodosia.

"Then, dear lady, you simply must *make* time," Giovanni admonished. "Or better yet, come open a second tea shop in our neighborhood. It would be a most welcome addition."

"I'm not sure I've got the first one under control yet," Theodosia admitted, "but it's a fun idea to entertain." Theodosia smiled up at Giovanni Loard, amused by this colorful, slightly quirky fellow and suddenly found him gazing in the direction of Doe and Oliver Dixon.

"My cousin," Giovanni Loard offered by way of explanation. "The groom."

"Oliver Dixon is your cousin?" asked Theodosia.

"Actually, second cousin," said Giovanni. "Oliver is my mother's first cousin."

Theodosia maintained her smile even as her eyes began to glaze over. In Charleston, especially in the historic district, it often seemed that everyone was related to everyone else. People literally went on for hours explaining the tangled web of second cousins, great-great-grandparents, and grandaunts.

Thankfully, Giovanni Loard didn't launch into a dissertation on his lineage. Instead, he gently plucked the tray of sandwiches from Theodosia's hands.

"Allow me," he said with a twinkle in his eye. "I'm sure you have other items to attend to." And Giovanni wandered off into the crowd, an impromptu waiter.

So surprised was Theodosia that she stood rooted to the spot, blinking after him.

"At sixes and sevens?" said Drayton's voice in her ear. She whirled to find him clutching two empty pitchers in one hand, a tray bearing a single, lonely sandwich balanced in the other. He gazed at her quizzically.

"That antique dealer you told me about, Giovanni Loard?" Theodosia gestured after Giovanni. "He offered to help. *Nobody* ever offers to help."

Drayton peered through the crowd. "Remarkable. Do you know that the Center for Disease Control in Atlanta has rated South Carolinians as having the most sedentary lifestyle in the country?"

"Hey," said Haley as she joined them, "I'm about ready for a sedentary lifestyle. My feet are tired, and I think I just got my first sunburn of the year. But first things first. Who *was* that cute guy, anyway?"

"Giovanni Loard," said Theodosia. "He runs an antique shop down on King Street."

They watched Giovanni pick his way through the crowd, dispensing sandwiches, talking animatedly with guests. "Personable chap, isn't he?" remarked Drayton.

Giovanni wound his way to Doe and Oliver Dixon's table, where Delaine was still seated, and offered sandwiches all around.

Suddenly, a man with flaming red hair swaggered up behind him. Although Theodosia, Drayton, and Haley were far enough away that they couldn't hear the exact words spoken, they could obviously see that the red-haired man was angry. Very angry. Oliver Dixon whirled about to confront him, and now both men were talking excitedly. A low murmur ran through the crowd.

"The guy with the red hair," said Haley. "What's his problem?"

"Don't know," said Theodosia.

"Do you know who he is?" asked Drayton as he pursed his lips and peered speculatively at the two men whose argument appeared to escalate by the second.

"That's Ford Cantrell," said Theodosia. She knew him, knew *of* him, anyway. Ford Cantrell was from the low-country, that vast area of woods, old rice plantations, and swampland just south of Charleston. He was a farmer by trade, although his ancestors would have been called plantation owners.

"He's been drinking," hissed Drayton. "Have you ever seen anyone drunk at an afternoon tea?"

Theodosia's eyes flickered back to the hotheaded, swaggering Ford Cantrell. He had one hand stuck out in front of him as he spoke angrily to Oliver Dixon. Then he gave Oliver Dixon a rough shove and stalked off.

"Yes," she finally answered. "I have."

Now another excited voice rose from a small group of onlookers gathered down by the shore. "Here they come!"

Two hundred people jumped from their chairs en masse and began pushing toward the water.

No, thought Theodosia. *Make that one hundred ninety-nine.* Ford Cantrell was hustling off in the opposite direction. She watched as he veered around a group of Civil War cannons, then set off toward the bandstand. Ford Cantrell appeared to be walking steadily, not staggering, but the back of his neck glowed red. A been-drinking-too-much red, not an out-in-the-sun red.

Why had the seemingly mild-mannered Oliver Dixon been embroiled in an argument with Ford Cantrell? An argument that looked like it could have erupted into a knock-down-drag-out fight? *What got those two men so fired up?* wondered Theodosia.

"Theodosia, come on," called Haley. "The sailboats are heading for the final markers!"

Theodosia shook off her consternation with Ford Cantrell and turned her attention to Charleston Harbor. She could see that a half-dozen boats had managed to gain a commanding lead and were bearing down on the two red buoys that pitched wildly back and forth in the billowing waves.

Somewhere out there, Jory Davis was skippering his J-24, Theodosia told herself. Jory was an attorney with her father's old firm, Ligget, Hume, Hartwell, and she'd been dating him off and on for the past few months. She hoped his yacht, *Rubicon,* was one of the handful of boats jockeying for finishing-line position.

Theodosia strode across the newly greened grass, picking up dropped napkins and flatware as she went. When she finally caught up with the crowd, they were packed into a tight knot near what was left of the old seawall that had been pummeled by Hurricane Hugo back in 1989. The onlookers were whistling and cheering as the sailboats fought their way through the strong crosscurrents that marked the confluence of the Ashley and Cooper rivers.

Theodosia cleared the half-dozen empty platters from the long buffet table and glanced toward the sailboats again. Once this race ended, and it looked like it would end soon, folks would wander over to the Charleston Yacht Club for cold beer, fried catfish, or she-crab soup. Some would retire to private courtyard gardens in the historic district for mint juleps and, later, enjoy elegantly prepared dinners on bone china. Her task here was almost done.

"Oliver, over here!" An officious-looking man with a shock of white hair and a too-tight white commodore's blazer trimmed in gold braid waved broadly to Oliver Dixon. He took the wooden box that had been tucked carefully under one arm and laid it on the table Billy Manolo had set up down at the shore. Then the man motioned to Oliver Dixon again. "C'mon, Oliver," he urged insistently.

Theodosia paused in her cleanup to watch as the highly excited commodore opened a rather lovely rosewood box and gently removed a pistol. It was old, she decided, antique, with brass fittings that glinted in the sun and a long, curved barrel. How nice, she thought, that Oliver Dixon was being given the honor of officiating at the finish line.

All the yachts had rounded the markers now, and two yachts had pushed out in front, gaining a substantial lead. One of the leaders flew a white mainsail that read *Topper*; the other had a blue and white striped sail printed with the numbers *N-271*. Neck and neck, they bore down toward the finishing-line buoy.

More cheers rose from the crowd. The wind had risen and was driving the two boats furiously toward the finish line.

Thirty feet to Theodosia's left, Oliver Dixon stood poised on the rocky shore, next to the table. His fine silver hair riffled in the wind, his eyes were fixed on the boat with the blue and white striped sail, *N-271*. That yacht seemed to have gained a slight advantage over *Topper* as it skimmed across the waves.

Now everyone on shore could see the crews working madly to fine-tune the trim of their sails even as they hung out over the sides, using body weight to balance their craft.

The two lead boats were closing in, *N-271*, the boat with the blue and white striped sail, still enjoying its small lead. So close were they now that Theodosia could even see the faces of the crew members pulled into grimaces, betraying their hard work and exhilaration.

Oliver Dixon stood at the ready, poised to fire the pistol as the winner hurtled across the finish line.

Theodosia picked up a silver pitcher and was about to empty it, when the finish-line gun sounded with a tremendous explosion.

A sudden hush swept through the crowd, as though someone had pulled the plug.

Then a single, anguished cry pierced the stillness. Beginning as a sob, Doe Belvedere Dixon's voice rose in a horrified scream as blood poured forth from Oliver Dixon's head, and she watched helplessly as her husband of nine weeks crumpled to the ground.

2

Drayton staggered toward Theodosia and grabbed her arm roughly. "No one's doing anything!" he said in a choked whisper.

Theodosia gazed about as the ghastly scene seemed to reveal itself in slow motion. Drayton was right. Everyone was just standing there. Picnickers who had been in such high spirits moments earlier seemed frozen in place. Most of the crowd gaped openly at Oliver Dixon's splayed-out body; a few grimaced and covered their eyes.

Out of the corner of her eye, Theodosia was aware of a woman collapsed on the ground. She considered the possibility that the young wife, Doe, had fainted and figured her hunch was correct.

Theodosia found her voice. "Someone call 911!" she yelled. Her words rang out loud and commanding.

Giovanni Loard was suddenly next to her, frantically punching buttons on his cell phone. He barked into it, a harsh, urgent request for the operator to dispatch an ambulance and medical team to White Point Gardens.

Frustrated, feeling the need to do something, anything, Theodosia rushed over to where Oliver Dixon's body lay. Staring down, she inadvertently flinched at the sight of silver hair flecked with drops of blood. The poor man had pitched face forward onto the table, then slithered down. And, while his head now rested on the sandy shore, the lower half of his body was partially submerged. Water lapped insistently, gently rocking him back and forth in the surf.

Seconds later, Theodosia pulled herself together. Bending down, she gently touched her index and middle fingers to the side of Oliver Dixon's throat. There was nothing. No throb of a pulse, no breath sounds.

"The ambulance is on its way. What else can we do?" Giovanni Loard had joined her again. His breath was coming in short gasps; he was pale and seemed on the verge of hyperventilating.

"Nothing," replied Theodosia as she stared at the bright crimson stain on Oliver Dixon's mortally wounded head. "I'm afraid there's nothing we *can* do."

What seemed like an eternity was really only three minutes, according to Drayton's ancient Piaget watch, before screams from the ambulance erupted just blocks away.

"Theodosia, come over here."

"What?" Theodosia looked up into Drayton's lined countenance. He bore the sad look of a betrayed bloodhound.

"Come over here while they tend to him," Drayton urged.

She was suddenly aware that her feet were cold, and her long, silk skirt had somehow gotten wet and now trailed sadly. Drayton pulled her away from Oliver Dixon's body as a team of paramedics pushed past them, kicking the table out of their way. White blankets fluttered, and Theodosia heard the clatter of the metal gurney against rock. It made an ugly, scraping sound.

Drayton led her to one of the chairs and forced her to sit down. *Minutes earlier, carefree revelers had sat here,* she thought to herself. People had been enjoying iced tea and hors d'oeuvres—*her* iced tea and hors d'oeuvres. The crowd began to disperse and mill around. People spoke in hushed tones, but still no one seemed to know quite what to do.

Delaine wandered over and collapsed in a chair across from Theodosia. Her teeth were chattering, and her hair swung down in untidy tendrils. Eyes the size of saucers, she stared at Theodosia. "My God," she moaned, "did you see that poor man's *face*?"

"Hush," snapped Drayton. "Of course she saw it. We all did."

Theodosia turned away from Delaine and gazed toward the rocky shore where Oliver Dixon's body still lay. The paramedics had arrived with a bustle, looking very official and snappy in their bright blue uniforms. They'd brought oxygen canisters, defibrillating equipment, IV needles, and bags of saline. Though they'd been working on Oliver Dixon for some time now, Theodosia knew there wasn't a single thing the paramedics could pull out of their bag of tricks that would make a whit of difference. The situation was completely out of their hands. Oliver Dixon was with his maker now.

Of course, the Charleston police had also arrived on the heels of the paramedics. Squealing tires had bumped up and over curbs, chewing across soft turf and leaving tire treads in their wake. In many spots, grass and newly sprouted flowers had been completely torn up.

Theodosia put her head in her hands and tried to shut out the low buzz of the crowd as the police began asking questions. She rubbed her eyes hard, then looked back at the minor furor that was still taking place over Oliver Dixon's body. One of the paramedics, the husky one, had inserted a tube down the poor man's throat and was pumping a plastic bag furiously.

Two men, obviously police, detached themselves from a cluster of onlookers and joined the paramedics.

Theodosia squinted, trying to protect her eyes from the glare of sun on water, and tried to sort out what exactly was going on between the paramedics and the police. When one of the policemen turned sideways, Theodosia realized with a start that she recognized that ample silhouette.

It was Burt Tidwell.

Theodosia sighed. Burt Tidwell had to be one of the most arrogant, cantankerous detectives on the entire Charleston police force. She'd run up against Tidwell last fall when a guest at one of the Lamplighter Tours had been poisoned. He'd been the investigating detective, obtuse in his questioning, brash in his demeanor.

At the same time, Tidwell was a star player. He was the Tiger Woods of detectives.

Theodosia watched as Tidwell took command of the scene. His

physical presence loomed large, his manner was beyond take-charge, veering toward overbearing. The paramedics, finally resigned to the fact that all their heroic efforts were in vain, quit what they were doing and stepped back. It was no longer their show. Now it was Tidwell's.

Finally, Theodosia could stand it no more.

"Where will you be taking him?" Theodosia plucked at the sleeve of Tidwell's tweed jacket. It was just like Tidwell to be wearing wool on the first really hot day. On the other hand, Tidwell wasn't the kind of man who concerned himself with matters of fashion. His was a more focused existence. Two things seemed to hold Tidwell's interest; crime and food. And not necessarily in that order.

Tidwell's bullet-shaped head swiveled on his broad shoulders until he was staring straight at Theodosia. His lower lip drooped, and his bushy eyebrows spread across his domed forehead like an errant caterpillar. Only his hooded eyes, clear and sharp, reflecting keen intelligence, registered recognition.

"You," he finally growled.

"You'll have to step back, miss." A uniformed officer with a name tag that read Tandy grabbed Theodosia by the elbow and began to apply pressure, attempting to pull her back. He was instantly halted by Tidwell's angry gaze.

"Leave her alone," Tidwell growled. His voice rumbled from his ample stomach like a boiler starting up.

Startled, Officer Tandy released Theodosia's arm and stepped back. "Yes sir," he said politely.

Tidwell eyed Theodosia. He took in her wet skirt and slippers, registered her obvious distress. "Probably not to the hospital," Tidwell said quietly as he watched one of the paramedics begin to pull a sheet up over Oliver Dixon's body. "This poor devil is most assuredly dead."

Once again, Theodosia took in the mud and bloodstains. Then her eyes strayed to something she hadn't noticed before. Pieces of the exploded pistol lay scattered about. An embossed grip sat on wet sand a few feet from where they were standing. Another piece of twisted gray metal was nestled in a crack between two nearby rocks.

"But then, you knew that, didn't you?" Tidwell gazed at her

pleasantly. "The paramedics said you were first on the scene. They said you were the first one to reach him." Tidwell had a maddening way of phrasing questions as statements.

"Yes, I guess I was," said Theodosia. It suddenly occurred to her that she might be experiencing a mild case of shock. It wasn't every day that someone was killed right before her very eyes.

"I believe I am correct in stating that the unfortunate Mr. Dixon was killed instantly when the pistol misfired," said Tidwell. He gazed across Charleston Harbor, his eyes seeming to search for something on the distant shore. "Hell of a thing, these old pistols," he murmured. "Thing works fine for years, decades it would seem in this case. Then one day . . . *ker-bang*." Tidwell's hands flew into the air in a gesture that seemed to communicate a randomness of fate.

"Sir." Officer Tandy handed a pair of latex gloves to Tidwell.

Wordlessly, Tidwell accepted the gloves, then worked the tight rubber over his chubby hands. He leaned down and began collecting the remnants of the pistol.

As Theodosia watched him, her normally unlined brow suddenly puckered into a frown. "You're going to have those pieces examined by a ballistics expert, aren't you?" she asked.

Burt Tidwell's hooded eyes blinked slowly, like a reptile contemplating its prey.

Tidwell dropped two pieces of the pistol into a plastic bag, handed the task off to Tandy, who hovered nearby. Then he hooked a large paw under Theodosia's elbow and began leading her away. Theodosia was aware of pressure on her arm and the crunch of tiny white seashells underfoot. And two hundred sets of eyes watching her.

When they were a good forty paces from the shore and Oliver Dixon's body, they stopped under a giant live oak tree and faced each other. Spanish moss waved in lacy, gray green banners above them. Warm, languid breezes off the bay caressed Theodosia's face, reminding her it was still Sunday afternoon. But the day no longer felt glorious.

"Tell me." Tidwell cocked an eye toward her. "Are you always filled with such suspicion and unbridled skepticism?"

"Of course not," said Theodosia defensively. *Lord,* she thought, *here we go again. Burt Tidwell has to be the most obstinate, obtuse cuss that ever roamed the face of this earth.*

Last October, during the Lamplighter Tour, Tidwell had kept them all on pins and needles for weeks with his suspicions and vexing accusations when Bethany Shepherd, one of Haley's friends who filled in occasionally at the tea shop, had come under scrutiny. Of course, Tidwell had been unapologetic, even after Theodosia had been the one to discover that it was Samantha Rabathan and not Bethany who had perpetrated the deadly deed.

That death in the garden of the Avis Melbourne Home had appeared accidental, too. Now Theodosia had learned to be a bit more skeptical and exercise a modicum of caution.

She also knew Tidwell could be an irritant or an ally. Today, she wasn't sure which one he'd be. That coin was still up in the air.

"Miss Browning," began Tidwell, "I have already spoken with one of the yacht club's board members. He is an attorney of note and is of the opinion that this was simply an unfortunate accident."

"Did he tell you where the pistol is usually kept?" pressed Theodosia.

"I presume at the yacht club," replied Tidwell. His smile was the kind tolerant adults often reserve for children. "Where it has always been kept under lock and key."

"Which club?" asked Theodosia.

There was a sharp intake of breath as Tidwell hesitated.

Aha, Theodosia thought to herself, *he doesn't know.*

"There are two yacht clubs," Theodosia informed Tidwell. She hesitated a moment before she continued. "And they are rivals."

❦ 3 ❧

Teakettles chirped and hissed, and the aroma of freshly brewed teas permeated the air: a delicately fruited Nilgiri, a sweet Assam, and a spicy black Yunnan from southwest China. Sunlight streamed in through the antique panes, bathing the interior of the tea shop in warm light and lending a glow to the wooden floors and battered hickory tables that were, somehow, just the right backdrop for the dazzling array of teapots that ranged from Cordon Bleu white porcelain to fanciful hand-painted floral ceramics.

Haley had been up early as usual, working wonders in the oversized professional oven they'd managed to squeeze into the back of the shop. Now benne wafers, blueberry scones, and lemon and sour cream muffins cooled on wooden racks. When the tea shop's double doors were propped open, as they so often were, Drayton swore the tantalizing aromas could be enjoyed up and down the entire length of Church Street.

By nine a.m., the day's first customers, shopkeepers from Robillard Booksellers, Cabbage Patch Needlepoint Shop, and other nearby businesses, had already stopped by for their cup of tea and breakfast sweet. All had pressed Theodosia, Drayton, and Haley for details on the terrible events of yesterday, shaking their heads with regret, murmuring about the dreadful turn of events, and wasn't it a shame about the young widow, Doe.

Then there was a lull before the next wave of customers arrived. These were usually regulars from the historic district, who were wont to stop by for tea and a quiet perusal of the morning's newspaper as well as tourists who arrived via horse-drawn carriages and colorful jitneys.

It was during this lull that Theodosia, Drayton, and Haley had gathered around one of the round tables to sip tea and rehash yesterday's tragic events. They'd been joined by Miss Dimple, their elderly bookkeeper, who'd dropped by to pick up last week's receipts.

"And the pistol just exploded?" asked Miss Dimple with awe as the story unfolded once more for her benefit.

"With a cataclysmic crash," said Drayton. "Then the poor man simply collapsed. But then, what else would you expect? I'm sure he was killed instantly."

"And nobody did anything," added Haley, "except Theodosia. She ran over and checked the poor man out. Oh, and that nice antique dealer, Giovanni Loard, called the paramedics."

"Good girl," said Miss Dimple, glancing at Theodosia approvingly. "But you must still feel a bit shaken up."

"A little," admitted Theodosia. "It was a terrible accident."

Miss Dimple leaned back in her chair and took a sip of Assam. "Are they sure it was an accident?" she asked.

Haley frowned and gave an involuntary shudder. "Miss Dimple," she said, "you just gave me chills."

"What makes you say that, Miss Dimple?" asked Theodosia.

"Well," she said slowly, "it seems like they've been using that old pistol for as long as I can remember. When I was a little girl, back in the forties, my daddy used to take us down to White Point Gardens to watch sailboat races. Not just the Isle of Palms race, either. Lots of different races. They used that same old pistol back then, and there was never a problem. Not until now, anyway."

"That's what Burt Tidwell said, too," remarked Theodosia. "But he said you could never tell about those old things. One day they just backfire."

Mrs. Dimple smiled, apologetic that her idle speculation had caused Haley such consternation. "Well then, you *see.* An expert like that, he's probably right."

"I think Theodosia wants to solve another mystery," piped up Haley.

"Haley," Theodosia protested, "I've got better things to do than run around Charleston investigating what was undoubtedly an accidental death."

Drayton peered over his half glasses owlishly and studied Theodosia. "Oh you *do*," he said. "I can tell by the look on your face."

Theodosia's bright eyes flashed. "I'm merely curious, as I'm sure you all are. It isn't every day someone as prominent as Oliver Dixon dies right before our very eyes."

"Before four hundred eyes," added Haley. "If someone had murder in mind, it was cleverly done."

"What do you mean?" asked Drayton.

"Too many witnesses is what she means," said Theodosia. "With so many sets of eyes, you'll get endless versions of the story, none of which will jibe."

"Now it's you girls who are giving me chills," said Miss Dimple, who had set down her pencil and closed the black leather ledger she'd been peering into.

"But does that really track?" asked Drayton. "Oliver Dixon was fairly well liked, right? He wasn't a scoundrel or a carpetbagger or anything like that."

Theodosia slid her teacup across the table, allowing Drayton to pour her a second cup of Nilgiri. "Delaine was saying something about Oliver Dixon launching a high-tech company," she said.

"Oh, I read about that in the business section," said Haley.

"Since when do you read the business section?" demanded Drayton.

"Since I decided to pursue an MBA," said Haley. "I want to run my own business someday. Like Theodosia." She smiled companionably at Theodosia.

"Haley, I think you're already a whiz at business," said Theodosia. "But tell us about this new company of Oliver Dixon's. And don't interrupt, Drayton."

"Yes, dear." Drayton hunched his shoulders forward, assuming a henpecked attitude, and they all giggled.

"Oliver Dixon had just swung a pile of venture capital money to launch a new company called Grapevine," said Haley. "You know, as in 'heard it on the grapevine.' Anyway, Grapevine is set to manufacture expansion modules for PDAs."

"Pray tell, what is a PDA?" asked Drayton.

"Personal digital assistant," explained Haley. She reached into her apron pocket and produced a palm-sized gizmo that looked like a cross between a cell phone and a miniature computer screen. "See, I've got one. Mine's a Palm Pilot. I keep notes and phone numbers and recipes and stuff on it. It even interfaces with my computer at home. According to *Business Week*, PDAs are the hottest thing. The world is going wireless, and PDAs are the newest techie trend."

"I don't like to hear that," shuddered Drayton. He was a self-proclaimed Luddite who strove to avoid all things technological. Drayton lived in a 160-year-old house that had once been owned by a Civil War surgeon, and he prided himself on maintaining his home in a historically accurate fashion. Drayton may have bowed to convention by having a telephone installed, but he drew the line at cable TV.

"Anyway," said Haley, "Oliver Dixon received his venture capital from a guy by the name of Booth Crowley. Grapevine was going to produce revolutionary new pager and remote modules that would make certain PDAs even more versatile."

"Oh my," said Miss Dimple. She was suddenly following the conversation with great interest.

"What?" asked Theodosia.

"Booth Crowley is a very astute businessman," said Miss Dimple. "Apparently he doesn't let a penny escape his grasp unless he's got a carefully worded contract that his lawyers have put under a microscope. Mr. Dauphine, God rest his soul, was on the Arts Association committee with Booth Crowley and told me the man was *extremely* mindful of how funds were dispersed."

Mr. Dauphine had been Miss Dimple's longtime employer. He had owned the Peregrine Building next door and had passed away last fall, while they were in the middle of trying to solve the mystery of the poisoning at the Lamplighter Tour.

Theodosia nodded. She'd heard about Booth Crowley. Certainly nothing bad, but his business dealings bordered on legendary. He was a very powerful man in Charleston. Besides heading Cherry Tree Investments, one of Charleston's premier venture capital firms, Booth Crowley sat on the board of directors of the Charleston Symphony Orchestra, the Gibbes Museum of Art, and Charleston Memorial Hospital. He was certainly a force to be reckoned with.

The bell over the door tinkled merrily, and a dozen people suddenly poured into the shop. Haley and Drayton instantly popped up from their seats and swept toward them, intent on getting their visitors seated, settled, and served. Theodosia watched with keen approval as Haley adroitly addressed the group.

"How many? Three of you?" Haley asked. "Why don't you ladies take this nice table by the window. There's lots of sunshine today."

Drayton was just as charming. "Party of five?" he asked. "You'll like this round table over here. I could even put several teapots on the lazy Susan and do a tea tasting, if you'd like. Now, I'll be just two shakes, and then I'll be back with tea and some complimentary biscuits."

And the rest of the day was off and running at the Indigo Tea Shop.

"I'll be back on Wednesday, dear." Miss Dimple put a plump hand on Theodosia's arm.

"Thank you, Miss Dimple. I'm so glad you've been able to help out here at the tea shop. Now that Bethany's got a job at the museum in Columbia, we've been woefully shorthanded."

"It's you who deserves the thanks," said Miss Dimple. "Not everyone would take a chance on a creaky old bookkeeper. Seems like the trend these days is to hire young."

"Trends don't concern us here at the tea shop," said Theodosia warmly. "People do."

"Bless you, dear," said Miss Dimple. And she toddled out the door, a barely five-foot-tall, plump little elf of a woman who was still sharp as a tack when it came to tabulating a column of numbers.

4

"Theodosia." Drayton had a teapot filled with jasmine tea in one hand and a teapot of Ceylon silver tips in the other. "As soon as we get our customers taken care of, I need to speak with you."

Theodosia glanced out over the tables. Their customers had already settled in and were munching benne wafers and casting admiring glances at the shelves that held cozy displays of tea tins, jellies, china teapots, and tea candles.

"What's up?" she asked.

He cocked his head to one side and gave a conspiratorial roll of his eyes. "The *mystery* tea," he told her in a quavering, theatrical voice.

Theodosia grinned. Drayton was certainly in his element planning all his special-event teas. But this mystery tea had really seemed to capture his imagination. It would appear that Drayton, the straitlaced history buff and Heritage Society parliamentarian, had a playful side, after all.

Anyway, Theodosia decided, Drayton certainly had an astute business side. His mystery tea was already shaping up as a success. Counting the two calls they'd received earlier this morning, they now had twelve confirmed reservations for Saturday night. And Drayton had audaciously put a price of forty-five dollars per person on the event.

"Okay, Drayton," she said, "I'll be in my office."

Theodosia disappeared behind the panels of heavy green velvet that separated the tea shop from the back area, where the tiny kitchen and her even tinier office were located.

• • •

Sitting at her antique wooden desk, thumbing through a catalog from Woods & Winston, one of her suppliers, Theodosia had a hard time keeping her mind on carafes and French tea presses. Her thoughts kept returning to yesterday afternoon, to Oliver Dixon's demise and to her subsequent conversation with Burt Tidwell.

She had taunted Tidwell a bit with her crack about rival yacht clubs. She'd been testing him, trying to ascertain what his suspicions had been, for she knew for a fact that, Burt Tidwell being Burt Tidwell, he'd certainly harbor a few thoughts of his own.

But had she really thought that members from one yacht club would plot against another? No, not really. She knew the Charleston Yacht Club and the Compass Key Yacht Club competed against each other all the time. And relations had always been friendly between the clubs. Besides the Isle of Palms race, they also ran the Intercoastal Regatta and some kind of event in fall that was curiously dubbed the Bourbon Cup.

What she *was* interested in knowing more about was Oliver Dixon and his new start-up company, Grapevine.

Then there was the obviously intoxicated Ford Cantrell, who had staged a somewhat ugly scene in front of Oliver Dixon and Giovanni Loard. What had that been about?

Haley had mentioned something earlier about her looking for a mystery to solve. Perhaps she had found her mystery.

"Knock, knock," announced Drayton as he pushed his way into her office, tea tray in hand. "Thought you might like to try a cup of this new Japanese Sencha. It's first flush, you know, and really quite rare," he said as he set the lacquer tray down on her desk.

Theodosia nodded expectantly. Any time you were able to get the first picking of a tea, you were in for a special treat. The new, young shoots were always so tender and flavorful.

Drayton perched on the overstuffed chair across from her desk, the one they'd dubbed "the tuffet," and fussed with the *tetsubin,* or traditional iron teapot. Moments earlier, he'd used a bamboo whisk to whip the powdered green tea, along with a dollop of hot water, into a gentle froth. Then he'd poured more hot water over the mixture, water that had been heated until it was just this side of boiling.

Now Drayton poured a small amount of the bright green tea into two teacups. Like the tea, the teacups were Japanese, tiny ceramic cups with a decorative crackle glaze that held about two ounces.

Savoring the heavenly aroma, Theodosia took a sip and let the tea work its way across her tongue. It was full-bodied and fresh, with a soothing aftertaste. Green tea was usually an acquired taste, although once a tea drinker became captivated by it, green tea soon found a place in his tea-drinking lexicon. It was a tea rich in fluoride and was reputed to boost the immune system. In a pinch, green tea could also be used on a compress to soothe insect bites or bee stings.

"Splendid," exclaimed Theodosia. "How much of this tea did we order?"

Drayton favored her with a lopsided grin. "Just the one tin. It's priced sky high, a lot more than most of our customers are used to paying. What say we keep it for our own private little stash?"

"Okay by me," agreed Theodosia. "Now, what's up with this mystery tea?" Drayton had worked out the concept on his own, distributed posters up and down Church Street and in many of the bed-and-breakfasts. But, so far, no one at the tea shop had been privy to his exact agenda.

Drayton whipped out his black notebook and balanced his reading glasses on the tip of his nose. "Twelve customers have signed up so far, and we have room for, oh, maybe ten more. We'll begin with caviar on toast points and serve Indian *chai* with a twist of lemon in oversized martini glasses. Then, as the program proceeds, we shall . . ." He glanced up to find a look of delight on Theodosia's face. "Oh," he said. "You like?"

"I like it very much," she replied. "What else?"

Drayton snapped his notebook shut. "No, all I really wanted was to gauge your initial reaction. And I'm extremely heartened by what I just saw. Now you'll have to wait until Saturday night to find out the rest."

"Drayton!" Theodosia protested with a laugh. "That's not fair!"

He shrugged. "I guess that's why they call it a mystery tea."

"But it sounds so charming," she argued. "At least the snippet you shared with me is. And you certainly can't do it . . . I mean, you *shouldn't* do it all by yourself. You'll need help."

Drayton shook his head firmly as a Cheshire cat grin creased his face. "Nice try," he told her. "Now I've got to get back out there and give Haley a hand." He took a final sip of tea and set his teacup back down. "Oh, and Theodosia, can you figure out what to do with the leftovers from yesterday? They're absolutely jamming the refrigerator, and I'm going to need space for my . . ." He dropped his voice. ". . . *mystery* goodies."

After he had gone, Theodosia leaned back in her chair, a wry smile playing at her lips. *All right, Drayton,* she thought, *I'll go along with your little game. We'll just wait and see what excitement you've cooked up for Saturday night.*

She took another sip of Sencha tea and thought for a moment about the dilemma inside the refrigerator. Drayton was certainly correct; there were packages of finger sandwiches that had been in the hamper from yesterday, and now they'd been crammed into the refrigerator. What could she do, aside from tossing them out and wasting perfectly good food?

I know, she decided, *I'll pack everything up and take it to the senior citizen home with me. After all, I'm going there tonight with Earl Grey.*

Her heart melted at the thought of Earl Grey, the dog she'd dubbed her Dalbrador. Part dalmatian, part Labrador, Theodosia had found the dog cowering in her back alley two years ago. Hungry and lost, the poor creature had been rummaging through trash cans in the midst of a rainstorm, trying to find a morsel of food. Theodosia had taken the pup in, cared for him, and opened her heart to him.

And Earl Grey had returned her kindness in so many ways. He'd turned out to be a remarkable companion animal. One who was personable and gentle and a perfect roommate for her in the little apartment upstairs. Earl Grey had taken to obedience training extremely well, delighted to learn the essentials of being a well-mannered pooch. He'd also shown a keen aptitude for work as a therapy dog.

Attending special therapy dog classes, Earl Grey had learned how to walk beside a wheelchair, how to gently greet people, and to graciously accept old hands patting him with exuberance. When one elderly woman, with tears streaming down her face and a mumbled story about a long-remembered pet dog, threw her frail arms about Earl Grey's neck, he calmly allowed her to sob her heart out on his strong, furry shoulder.

Upon graduation from therapy dog classes, Earl Grey had received his Therapy Dog International certification and was awarded a spiffy blue nylon vest that sported his official TDI patch and allowed him entry to the O'Doud Senior Home two nights every month.

"Hey." Haley stood in the doorway. "What's the joke between you and Drayton? He looks like a cat that just swallowed a canary."

Theodosia waved a hand. "It's the mystery tea thing."

"Oh, that," said Haley. "He's driving me crazy, too. Gosh, I almost forgot why I came in here. You've got a phone call. Jory Davis. Line two."

Theodosia grabbed for the phone. "Hello?"

"Theodosia?" came a familiar voice.

"What happened?" she asked. "Where were you? Your boat never finished the race."

"You wouldn't believe it," said Jory Davis. "When we got out of the shelter of the harbor, just past Sullivan's Island, the wind was so strong it blew out our genoa sail. We had to scrub the race and pull in at the Isle of Palms. By the time we found a place to moor the boat and hitched a ride back to Charleston, it was after ten. But we *did* hear all about Oliver Dixon. Poor fellow, what a terrible way to go. Kind of shakes you up. One day he's glad-handing at the clubhouse, and the next day he's gone. Do they have a handle yet on how the accident happened? Anybody examined that old pistol? I mean, it *was* an accident, right?"

That's funny, thought Theodosia. Jory Davis was the second person she'd spoken with who'd made a casual, questioning remark about whether it had been an accident or not. Correction, make that the third person. She, herself, had implied the same thing to Tidwell yesterday.

"Apparently, the pistol just exploded," said Theodosia.

"Wow," breathed Jory Davis. "Talk about a bad day at Black Rock for the Dixons."

"What do you mean?" she asked, her radar suddenly perking up.

"Oliver Dixon's two sons, Brock and Quaid, were supposed to be in the race with us, but they got disqualified."

"Why was that?" asked Theodosia.

"They had an illegal rudder on their boat. They're claiming that Billy Manolo, the guy who does maintenance on some of the boats at the yacht club, tampered with it. Frankly, I think those guys probably sanded the rudder down themselves in an attempt to streamline it. Anyway," continued Jory, "I don't want to trash those guys after their father just died so tragically."

"No, of course not," murmured Theodosia.

"And I didn't want to call you last night and risk waking you up. Especially in light of the kind of day you probably had. I understand you were the first person to reach Oliver Dixon's body."

"Yes," she said.

"That's pretty tough, kiddo. You doing okay?"

"I think so," said Theodosia. "I can't help thinking about Doe, however. I mean, they'd only been married something like nine weeks."

"It's a tragedy," said Jory. "I saw Doe and Oliver together at Emilio's Restaurant a week or so ago, and they were absolutely gaga over each other. Of course, the saving grace in all this is that Doe is still young. She'll be a lot more resilient and able to bounce back."

"Bounce back," repeated Theodosia absently. "Yes."

"But, listen," Jory continued, "I didn't call to rehash this misfortune. People have probably been stopping by the tea shop all morning to do that. I really called to tell you I'm flying to New York this afternoon."

"New York!" Theodosia exclaimed. She'd been hoping she could get together with Jory Davis and coax a little information from him. Being a longtime yacht club member, he'd undoubtedly have an inside track. And with his keen lawyer's perception, he might just notice if something seemed a little out of alignment. He could also fill her in on that historic old pistol they supposedly kept under lock and key at the yacht club clubhouse. Well, all that might have to wait.

"Our firm is representing some fast-food franchises who really got hosed by the parent corporation," he said. "I've got to depose witnesses, then file papers for a class action suit. Listen, I'll be staying at the

Waldorf. If you need me for anything, anything at all, just leave a message at the desk, okay?"

"Okay. Good luck." Theodosia hung up the phone, feeling slightly out of sorts. Gazing at the wall that faced her desk, her eyes scanned the montage of framed photos, opera programs, tea labels, and other memorabilia that hung there.

There was a photo of Earl Grey taken when she'd first found him, all ribs and scruffy fur. There was her dad posed jauntily on his sailboat. That had been taken just a year before he passed away. Another photo, one of her favorites, showed her mom and dad at Cane Ridge Plantation. That photo had been taken back in the early sixties, right after they'd gotten married. They looked so young and hopeful and so very much in love, with their arms entwined around each other. Six years after that photo had been taken, she had been born. Her mother had lived only eight more years.

Heaving a giant sigh, Theodosia told herself not to feel sad but to feel lucky. She had known unconditional love and support from her parents. Her parents' ultimate gift to her had been to fix firmly in her mind the notion that she could accomplish anything she set her mind to.

And she had.

Stop being a goose, she scolded herself, *just because Jory Davis is taking off for New York. You can always give him a buzz. He said as much, didn't he? And you've got lots of other friends and plenty of pressing business to keep you busy.*

Haley had accused her of wanting to solve another mystery. *Is that true?* she wondered. Is that why she felt so unsettled and restless? And did she really believe Oliver Dixon's death had been anything other than a terrible, unfortunate accident?

Theodosia let the idea tumble around in her brain as she reached for one of the catalogs and slowly thumbed through it, contemplating all manner of teapots and trivets.

5

A furry brown muzzle poked over the metal rails of the bed.

"Hello doggy." A tiny, birdlike woman reached out and gently rested her blue-veined hand on Earl Grey's forehead. He snuggled to her touch, and the old lady squealed with delight.

"You're a good doggy to come visit me," she told him. "A very good doggy."

Standing ten steps back, allowing Earl Grey the freedom he needed to interact with the residents, Theodosia beamed. This was what it was all about. Affording older folks the joy of touch and connection with an animal that demanded nothing of them, yet offered a warm, furry presence that inexplicably seemed to render a calming effect.

Tonight, Earl Grey and Theodosia had spent most of their time visiting the rooms of residents who were bedridden. Earl Grey, who was often exuberant when chasing a ball tossed by one of the residents down the wide hallways, seemed to understand that these types of visits required considerably more restraint. And Theodosia was pleased that Earl Grey had conducted himself with a great deal of doggy decorum.

"Theodosia? Can you bring Earl Grey into the TV room?" Suzette Ellison, one of the night nurses who had worked at the O'Doud Senior Home for more than fifteen years, stood in the doorway.

"What's up, Suzette? Another liver brownie cake for Earl Grey?"

Suzette grinned. "What else? But this is a special occasion. Your anniversary. It's been two years since you and that nice dog of yours have been coming here, and some of our ladies and gentlemen want to thank you."

"Surprise!" The group called out in unison as Theodosia and Earl Grey walked into the room.

Theodosia threw her hands up in surprise, and Earl Grey, immediately homing in on the liver brownie cake that rested on a low table in the center of the room, shook his head in anticipation and let out a sharp *woof.*

"Happy anniversary, Earl!" one of the ladies called out with exuberance. "Thanks for always making us smile."

Suzette had laid out all the sandwiches Theodosia had brought with her on a long table and rustled up a bowl of punch. The residents wasted no time in helping themselves to snacks, and the room suddenly buzzed with the makings of a party.

Theodosia grabbed a cup of punch for herself and wandered among the residents. They smiled and nodded at her, but Earl Grey was, of course, the real star. He was the one they wanted to talk to and pet. He was the one they looked forward to seeing.

"This is a lovely picnic you brought, Miss Browning."

Theodosia smiled down at an elderly man in a wheelchair. Freckles covered his bald head, and deep wrinkles cut into his face, but his eyes shone bright with interest.

"Glad you're enjoying it," she said.

"Kind of different from yesterday afternoon, eh?" said the old man.

Surprised, Theodosia sank down on one knee so she was eye level with him. He smiled at her then, a kind, knowing smile that suddenly took years off his tired, lined face.

"Oh yes," he told her as he wagged a finger, "I heard all about the accident from my son. He was there."

"Your son was in White Point Gardens yesterday?" asked Theodosia.

"Yup," said the old man. "Course, he didn't just phone me out of the blue and tell me. I read about it in the newspaper this morning. Then I called him so I could get the real poop. My son used to race Lasers with the yacht club," he explained.

The old man stopped abruptly, as if all this talking had been a considerable effort for him.

"Would you like something to drink?" asked Theodosia. She thrust her cup of punch toward him. "Here, take mine."

The old man eagerly grasped her drink and helped himself to several good swallows. "Good," he croaked. Setting the empty cup aside on a nearby table, the old man stuck out a withered hand. "I'm Winston Lazerby."

"Theodosia Browning," she said, shaking his hand. "And your son is . . . ?"

"Thomas Lazerby. He's a cardiologist at Charleston Mercy Medical. You know, a heart doctor." Winston Lazerby thumped his own skinny chest as if to demonstrate his son's specialty. "The minute I saw that article about Oliver Dixon," Winston Lazerby continued, "I thought of the feud."

Tiny hairs on the back of Theodosia's neck rose imperceptibly. "What do you mean, Mr. Lazerby?" she asked.

"The Dixon-Cantrell feud," Winston Lazerby said, staring at Theodosia intently. "Those two families have been going at it for almost seventy years."

Theodosia glanced around quickly. No one seemed to be paying the two of them a bit of attention. *Good,* she thought. "Tell me more, Mr. Lazerby," she urged him.

The old man leaned forward. "They been fighting with each other ever since the thirties, when Letitia Dixon up and ran off with Sam Cantrell."

"This Letitia Dixon, how was she related to Oliver Dixon?"

Winston Lazerby thought for a moment. "Aunt," he said. "Letitia would've been Oliver's mother's sister."

"And Sam Cantrell?" asked Theodosia.

Winston Lazerby nodded. "Related to all them Cantrells. Don't know the full story there. But I do know Sam was a smooth-talkin' feller, and Letitia was a young gal, eighteen years old at most, and wilder 'n seven devils."

"What happened to them?" asked Theodosia, intrigued. "Where did they run off to?"

"Nobody knows," replied Winston Lazerby. "There was rumors that Letitia ended up in Portland, Oregon, and died of rheumatic fever a few years later. But I personally think they was just rumors. People always think the worst when something like that happens."

"And there's still bad blood between the two families?" said Theodosia.

Winston Lazerby nodded knowingly. "Very bad blood."

"So that might explain why Ford Cantrell was so hot under the collar in front of Oliver Dixon and Giovanni Loard," murmured Theodosia.

"Giovanni Loard," giggled the old man suddenly. "Ain't that a fancy new name. Fellow's Christian name was George Lord. Guess he figured calling himself Giovanni would play better with the tourists. Or adding an *a* to his last name. Folks might mistake him for a real Southern gentleman."

"Do you know what the Dixons and Cantrells have been fighting over recently?" asked Theodosia.

"You name it, they probably fight over it," said Winston Lazerby. "Those two families have wrangled over business, over real estate, over *women*." He shook his head. "Crazy."

Theodosia glanced up and saw that many of the residents had begun to move off toward their rooms. It was eight-thirty and getting late for these older folk.

"Mr. Lazerby, could we talk again sometime?" Theodosia asked.

"Sure," he agreed. "Come on over any time. You know where I live." He gave her a wink.

Warm breezes caressed her face and carried delicious scents for Earl Grey's inquisitive nose as Theodosia sped home through the night, the windows of her Jeep Cherokee rolled down. She'd purchased the Jeep two years ago against the advice of Drayton and had immediately fallen in love with it.

When summer's heat and humidity hit full bore, wrapping Charleston in its smothering grip, Theodosia loved nothing better than to escape to the low country. Crashing down shady, narrow roads that were lush and overgrown with twining vines, she'd maneuver long-forgotten trails, confident in her Jeep's nimbleness and four-wheel drive. There were old rice dikes to bump over and moss-covered mounds that were remnants of old, abandoned phosphate mines. In the tangle of sun-dappled woods and myriad meandering streams guarded by live oaks, those grand sentinels of the South, Theodosia would find cool refuge and tranquility.

Tonight, however, Winston Lazerby's words weighed heavily on her mind. As she flipped a left turn onto Beaufain Street, past R. Pratt Antiques and Campbell's Architectural Supply, Theodosia wondered if he had been correct in his recollection, wondered if perhaps there really *was* something to Mr. Lazerby's story concerning a Dixon-Cantrell feud.

Well, she decided, as she pulled the Jeep in close to the rear of her little building and eased into her parking spot, *there's only one way to find out. Do a little research.*

Above the tea shop, Theodosia had created a cozy little abode for herself. Filled with a mélange of antiques and choice hand-me-downs, it was an airy little apartment with windows that not only pushed open to catch the harbor breezes but also afforded a spectacular view up and down Church Street and across Meeting Street toward The Battery.

While Earl Grey padded off to cuddle up on his bed, an oversized chintz cushion tucked into the corner of her bedroom, Theodosia fixed herself a cup of Orange Elixir tea. One of Drayton's custom blends, Orange Elixir wasn't really a tea per se, since it was not derived from *Camellia sinensis,* the tea plant. Rather, it was a delicious infusion of orange peel, hibiscus, gingko, and linden blossoms. Perfect for stimulating the mind but not the nerves.

Sitting down at her spinet desk, Theodosia turned on her iMac and clicked on Netscape Navigator. When the site came up, she typed *"Charleston Post and Courier"* into the search engine.

She took a sip of the flavorful fruit and herb drink and waited, hoping she'd be able to peruse their newspaper morgue.

No, the *Post and Courier* was archived back only to 1996. Theodosia tapped her fingers on the keyboard. What else could she try? The Heritage Society? Why not? They'd been around for well over a century, and their mission was to preserve written records as well as historic buildings and objects.

Theodosia typed "www.charlestonheritagesociety.org" into the browser. Within seconds, the Heritage Society's home page offered up a colorful photo montage of historical buildings and a menu with a dizzying array of choices.

Theodosia studied that menu, then clicked on "Historical Records."

Another menu spun out before her listing "Deeds," "Marriages," "Maps and Plans," "Military," "Civil War," "Ships' Logs," and "City Planning."

No, she told herself, *the last thing I want to do is rummage, hit or miss, through hundreds of individual documents.*

Theodosia scrolled to the bottom of the page and clicked on "Search." Now she could type in the name *Cantrell* and, if it was mentioned somewhere on the Heritage Society's Web site, the search engine would pull it up as a hit.

Five hits came up, each with a one-line descriptor. The first three were duds as far as Theodosia was concerned, since they all dealt with someone named Cora Cantrell, who'd been a schoolteacher in the town of Eutaville during the late 1800s.

Clicking on the fourth hit, Theo pulled up an article about the defunct Cantrell Canal that had been used by barges laden with indigo, cotton, and rice.

The fifth hit was far more enlightening. This was a newspaper clipping from the *Colton Telegraph*, a defunct newspaper from a now-defunct village. The article chronicled an altercation that had taken place in 1892 between one Jeb Cantrell and one Stuart Dixon. During a duel in the woods near Pamlico Hill Plantation, Jeb Cantrell had shot Stuart Dixon to death.

Were these two duelists the long-dead ancestors of Ford Cantrell and Oliver Dixon?

Had to be.

So this duel was perhaps the kindling that had sparked the nasty Dixon-Cantrell feud. Not a scandal concerning runaways from the two families like Winston Lazerby had thought. That had come later.

Historical dueling had always sounded so romantic, mused Theodosia. And yet, the heads of these two families had tragically fought each another over some point of honor. And one had been mortally wounded.

Theodosia lifted her eyes from the computer screen and stared across her living room at the moody seascape painting that hung above her fireplace.

She thought about how history had taught so many cruel lessons, one of them being that families, tribes, and often countries are rarely able to surmount a blood feud. Rather, the feud perpetuates itself, growing like a foul mushroom in the dank recess of a forest, feeding off decay.

Even when descendants are unclear about circumstances that led to the feud or had never personally known the ancestors who'd first spilled blood, these terrible blood feuds seemed to persist. An eye for an eye, a tooth for a tooth.

Theodosia stretched both arms over her head until she felt the tension in her shoulders ease. Then she placed her hands at the base of her neck and rubbed gently. If the Dixon-Cantrell feud *was* still going on—and hostility certainly seemed to have been roiling inside Ford Cantrell yesterday afternoon—then the whole situation certainly bore looking into.

Shouldn't Ford Cantrell be questioned? Not so much to ask him flat out if he'd somehow engineered an exploding pistol but to perhaps eliminate him as a suspect?

Theodosia rose swiftly from her chair, walked to a pine cabinet that displayed a small, tasty collection of Wedgewood, and pulled open one of the narrow drawers. Thumbing through a brown leather card case, Theodosia found Burt Tidwell's business card. She held it between her thumb and index finger as she continued to turn her question over in her mind.

Finally, she carried the card back to her computer, sat down, and composed a short E-mail message to Burt Tidwell. It was both an invitation and a request to stop by the Indigo Tea Shop tomorrow to discuss an important concern.

She paused for a moment, wondering if she was doing the right thing. Then she clicked "Send."

6

"Mariage frères teas," Theodosia told her three guests, "are blended in France. This particular tea, Mirabelle, is a Chinese black tea scented with the tiny but exquisite mirabelle plum that grows in northern France. Hence the mildly sweet aroma."

It was Drayton, for the most part, who conducted tea tastings. But this group of women, all women of a certain age and residents of the historic district, had specifically requested Theodosia's assistance. The three had met her while serving on a committee for Charleston's Garden Fest Tour and had been enthralled with Theodosia's knowledge of tea, her vibrancy, and her sweet nature.

That was just fine with Drayton this morning. Working as a backup for Haley, he'd been holding down the fort at the little table nearest the counter where the old cash register and various sweetgrass baskets filled with tea tins and tea goodies sat. Working diligently, he'd been able to put the finishing touches on all his ideas for summer teas.

"Need any help?" he asked Haley as she brushed past him with a second plate of apple tartlets for a group of five giggling tea shop regulars who seemed to be enjoying their morning tea immensely.

"Oh please," said Haley as she put a hand on her hip and tossed her head. "This is child's play."

Haley was incredibly task oriented and competitive, and once she'd decided to handle the morning's customers single-handedly, it was woe to anyone who tried to interfere.

"Just checking," Drayton assured her. "I wouldn't *dream* of interfering."

"Oh Drayton," she commented dryly, "I love your oratorical excess, but not as much as you love my cranberry scones." It was a pointed reference to the fact that Drayton had already consumed two of the giant pastries.

"When you get to be my age, you don't have to watch your girlish figure quite so much," quipped Drayton.

Drayton swiveled his head suddenly as Theodosia's group of ladies rose from their chairs and headed his way. He got to his feet immediately and stepped deftly around the counter to face them. "Ladies," he greeted them.

"I am in need of a tea press," said a lady in a yellow straw hat.

"And I have several marvelous ones to show you," replied Drayton as he plucked samples off the shelf and placed them on the counter.

The other two ladies immediately picked up sweetgrass baskets and began to coo over them. "These are wonderful," exclaimed one. "I had a sweetgrass basket that I used for years as a summer handbag. When it got tattered and worn, my granddaughter begged me to give it to her. She said they have some of these baskets on display at the Smithsonian."

"Indeed, they do," proclaimed Drayton. "A collection of South Carolina sweetgrass baskets resides in the Smithsonian's permanent collection, a fitting tribute to our low- country craftspeople."

Drayton held up one of the elegant, woven baskets that had been resting on the countertop. "These," he said enticingly, "were made from a sweetgrass crop cultivated on Johns Island. Would any of you ladies care to take one home?"

Two heads nodded, and Drayton beamed.

"You're a natural-born salesman, Drayton," Theodosia told him with unabashed admiration as she sat down across from him. Even though they'd been together almost three years, she was still slightly in awe of Drayton's prodigious sales talent. True, she had huckstered food products and computer peripherals on a national scale when she'd been in the advertising business. But selling one-on-one was still slightly disconcerting to her. She tended not to *sell* an item per se but, instead, let the item speak for itself.

Theodosia reached a hand across the table and tapped the black leather-bound ledger that Drayton had come to regard as his bible. It contained most of his tea-tasting notes and all of his ideas for tea blends, special events, and tea promotions.

"You've been working on the summer teas," Theodosia said with appropriate seriousness.

Drayton nodded.

"Your White Point Green was certainly a hit at the picnic, so we'll want to package that for sale," Theodosia said.

Drayton nodded again. "I agree. And I came up with one more iced tea." He paused. "I call it Audubon Herbal, a tribute to our nearby Audubon Swamp Garden."

Theodosia nodded. "Where John Audubon chronicled South Carolina's waterbirds."

"Right. The tea's a scant amount of black tea with hibiscus, lemongrass, and chamomile added. Mild, refreshing, not too stimulating."

Theodosia's eyes sparkled. "I like it. The tea and the tribute. What else?"

"Two more teas that veer decidedly toward the exotic," said Drayton. Then he added hastily, "But we've seen time and again that people *like* exotic teas."

"You won't get any argument from me, Drayton."

"The first one I call Ashley River Royal. It's a Ceylonese black tea with a pear essence."

"You're right, it *is* exotic."

"No, *this* one's the coup de grâce. Swan Lake Iris Gardens. Again, an homage to the elegant gardens that are home to . . . what? Seven species of swans? And you know how much everyone enjoys visiting the gardens in spring when the Dutch and Japanese iris are blooming."

"Of course," said Theodosia. "And what's the blend?"

"Four different teas with a top note of smoky lopsang."

"Drayton, you're not just going to capture the hearts of tea lovers, you're going to endear yourself to bird lovers and gardeners, too. And in Charleston, that's just about everyone."

"I know." Drayton smiled.

"Hey," interrupted Haley, "we're not going to package this stuff ourselves, are we? Remember last fall when we did holiday teas? My back gets sore just *thinking* about it."

"No, we'll have Gallagher's Food Service handle all that," said Drayton. "Frankly, I thought it was fun when we all worked together, but apparently no one else shared my enthusiasm. You all seemed to have mutiny on your minds."

"Last fall we had an extra pair of hands," said Haley. "But now that Bethany's moved to Columbia, who else could we shanghai? Miss Dimple?"

"Now *she's* a sport," said Drayton. "I bet she wouldn't complain half as much as you did."

"Drayton, don't you dare ask poor Miss Dimple to package tea," laughed Theodosia.

"One more thing," said Drayton, closing his book and getting up. "New packaging." He reached around to the back of the counter and pulled out a shiny, dark blue box with a rounded top that folded over. "Indigo blue boxes," said Drayton.

"They're the exact same color as the gift paper we use!" Theodosia squealed with delight. "Aren't you clever. Where did you find them?"

"Supplier in San Francisco," said Drayton. "We can have Gallagher's package the tea in our regular foil bags, then pop those bags into the blue boxes. From there we just need to add a label. I took the liberty of getting samples of gold foil labels from our printer. All you have to do is pick a label style and a typeface," said Drayton. "Then it's a done deal."

"Easy enough," said Theodosia.

"Don't look now," said Haley under her breath, "but that boorish cop just came in. Wonder what he wants?"

"I invited him," said Theodosia.

"You *invited* him?" Haley was stunned.

"Run and put together a nice pastry sampler, will you, Haley? And Drayton, could you do a fresh pot of tea? Maybe that Dunsandle Estate?"

"Of course, Theo," agreed Drayton. Then he turned to Haley. "Are you rooted to the floor, dear girl? Kindly fetch the pastries Theodosia requested."

"Okay," Haley agreed grudgingly. "But you know I can't stand that guy. He almost drove Bethany to a nervous breakdown with all his questions and nasty innuendos. He's a bully, pure and simple."

"He's a detective first grade," corrected Drayton under his breath. "Now the pastries, please?"

"Right," said Haley.

"Detective Tidwell," Theodosia greeted him warmly. "Sit here by the window."

"Nice to see you again, Miss Browning," said Tidwell as he lowered his bulk into a wooden captain's chair. "Good of you to drop me a note, even if it was of the electronic version."

He gave a cheery smile that Theodosia knew contained very little cheer. Tidwell's chitchat and tiny pleasantries were opening salvos that could be a steel-jawed trap for the unsuspecting.

"I wanted to talk to you about Oliver Dixon," said Theodosia.

"You mean Oliver Dixon's death," corrected Burt Tidwell.

"Since you put it that way, yes," agreed Theodosia.

She sat quietly as Haley placed teacups, plates, knives, and spoons in front of each of them, then Drayton followed with a steaming pot of tea. Theodosia poured some of the sweet elixir into Tidwell's cup and smiled with quiet satisfaction as his nose twitched. Then Haley delivered her plate of baked goods, and Tidwell brightened considerably.

"Oh my, this *is* lovely," he said as he scooped a raspberry scone onto his plate. "Is there, perchance, some jelly to accompany this sweet?"

But Haley was already back at the table with a plate of butter, pitcher of clotted cream, and various jars of jelly.

"Detective Tidwell," began Theodosia, "have you learned anything more about the pistol that killed Oliver Dixon?"

Tidwell sliced a sliver of butter and applied it to his pastry.

"Some," he said. "The pistol was American made, manufactured in the mid-1800s to Army specifications, and used as a sidearm by officers. Stock is curly maple and there's an acorn design on the trigger guard.

Graceful lines but a crude weapon. It was really only effective at close range."

But effective enough to mortally wound Oliver Dixon, Theodosia thought to herself.

"By the way," Tidwell said, "the pistol *was* kept at Oliver Dixon's yacht club. In friendly territory. So it's doubtful anyone would have tampered with it."

"Who loaded the pistol?" asked Theodosia.

"Fellow by the name of Bob Brewster. Been doing it for years. Apparently, you take a pinch of gunpowder and twist it inside a little piece of paper. Not unlike a tea bag," Tidwell told her. "Then you place the little packet in the barrel. Brewster's just sick about it, by the way."

"But Oliver Dixon *could* have had an enemy there," said Theodosia.

Tidwell stroked his ample chin. "Most people I've spoken with were highly complimentary of Oliver Dixon. He was a past commodore and had contributed a considerable amount of funds for the betterment of the place. He paid to have the boat piers reinforced and a clubhouse fireplace installed." Tidwell pulled a spiral notebook from his breast pocket and glanced at it. It was the same kind of notebook children purchased from the five-and-dime store. "Oh, and Oliver Dixon underwrote a sailing program last summer for inner-city youth. Kids Can Sail, or something like that."

"Dixon was known for his philanthropy?" asked Theodosia.

"And for being an all-around good guy," replied Tidwell. He smiled at her, then helped himself to an almond scone. "Lovely," he muttered under his breath.

He's not given me an ounce of useful information, thought Theodosia. *But then, did I really think he would?* She sighed inwardly. Conversations with Tidwell were always of the cat-and-mouse variety.

"You realize," she began, "there is a long-standing feud between the Dixons and the Cantrells." She watched him as her words sank in. He gave her nothing.

"The feud dates back to the 1880s," she said. "The heads of the two families fought a duel to the death."

"Mm-hm." Tidwell took another bite from his pastry, but Theodosia knew she had his attention.

"Sometime during the thirties, Oliver Dixon's aunt ran off with a Cantrell. Apparently, the two families have been openly hostile toward each other ever since."

"So you suspect young Ford Cantrell?" Tidwell's bright eyes were riveted on her.

"If I had a suspect in mind," Theodosia said slowly, "that would imply I believed a criminal act had been committed. And I have no proof of that."

"Aha," said Tidwell, "so this conversation is simply neighborly gossip."

Theodosia stared at him unhappily.

Seeing her displeasure, Tidwell's eyes lost their merriment, and he suddenly turned serious. "Yes, I have heard rumblings about this so-called Dixon-Cantrell feud. Although you seem to have gained the upper hand as far as specific details."

Though large in girth, Tidwell's words could be spare and pared down when he wanted them to be.

"Do you know much about antique pistols?" she asked him.

He looked thoughtful. "Not really. Obviously, our ballistics people are taking a look at it, but their forte, as one might imagine, really lies in modern weapons."

But I know an expert, thought Theodosia. *And I just might take a chance on talking to him.*

Tidwell seemed to contemplate helping himself to a third pastry, then thought better of it. "Ah well." He struggled to his feet, brushed a fine sheen of granulated sugar from his jacket lapels. "Time to be off. Thank you for your kind invitation and the lovely tea."

And he was out the door, just like that.

Theodosia gathered up the dirty dishes and carried them into the back of the tea shop. "Drayton," she called over her shoulder, "is Timothy Neville in town? The symphony was invited to perform in Savannah. Do you know if he's back?"

"He's back." Drayton popped his head through the curtains. "I spoke Timothy yesterday."

"Oh," was all Theodosia said. Contemplating a visit with Timothy Neville and actually *talking* to Timothy Neville were two different things.

"Do you think he still hates me for suspecting him of poisoning that real estate developer?" she asked.

"Nonsense," said Drayton. "Timothy Neville doesn't hate you; he hates everyone. Timothy has always been an equal-opportunity curmudgeon. Don't give his ill humor a second thought."

Timothy Neville *was* going to celebrate his eightieth birthday next month. But he wasn't about to spill the beans to the wags in the historic district. No sir, his DOB had long been a hot topic of conversation, and he wasn't going to spoil the fun now. Some folks put him at eighty- five; others kindly deducted ten years.

What did it matter?

He was in excellent physical condition except for a touch of arthritis in his hands. And that came from playing the violin these many years and bothered him only when the temperature dipped below fifty degrees.

Fact was, he had outlived two of his doctors. Now he rarely even bothered with doctors. He had Henry, his butler, take his blood pressure twice a day, and he swallowed a regimen of supplements that included ginkgo biloba, coenzyme 10, choline, and vitamins B_1, B_6, C, and E.

True, he had made a few concessions in his diet, switching from predominantly red meat to fish and from bourbon to wine. He still smoked an Arturo Fuente cigar occasionally but, more and more, that was becoming a rare treat.

Genetics. Timothy Neville chalked it all up to genetics. His mother had lived to ninety and had taken to her bed only on the day prior to her death. Her ancestors, most of whom dated back to the original Huguenots who fled religious persecution in France during the mid-1600s, had been a determined and hardy lot. They had endured the hardships of an ocean voyage, worked tirelessly to help colonize Charles Town, fought off the greedy English crown, then managed to survive the War Between the States. Today, his ancestors were numbered among the founding fathers of Charleston and considered social aristocracy.

Timothy Neville smiled to himself as he studied the landscape painting he held in his hands. It had been painted in the late thirties by Alice Ravenel Huger Smith, a watercolorist famed for her moody renditions of low-country rice plantations. The piece had sustained some damage. One corner had been gnawed by insects, and a brown splotch of water damage shot through the sky. The painting hadn't been preserved in acid-free paper, either, so it was slightly faded. It would take considerable conservation skills to restore the little watercolor, but the piece was well worth it. Huger Smiths were few and far between these days, and most people who held one in their possession preferred to sell it at auction in New York rather than donate it to a museum.

"Mr. Neville? There's someone to see you?" Claire, one of the secretaries, hovered in the doorway.

Timothy didn't look up. "Who, please?"

"Theodosia Browning?" *Claire has a way of making everything sound like a question. Why is that?* he wondered. He'd heard other young women speak in that same maddening way. Were they too insecure to spit out a simple declarative statement?

It didn't matter. Timothy knew he was merely stalling for time, letting the idea that Theodosia Browning had come to call upon him ruminate in his mind. There was certainly nothing wrong in allowing her a brief cool-your-heels period in the anteroom. After all, she had harbored suspicions about him being involved in the death of that real estate developer last fall and had helped herself to a merry snoop in his home during a music recital. Since that incident, he felt that she had been more cool and aloof with him than he with her. Embarrassment? Remorse over her actions? Had to be.

"Show her in," Timothy said finally.

Theodosia Browning entered his office in a whisper of silk. He heard the slight rustle of the fabric, could detect a pleasant, slightly floral scent about her. He wondered if it was perfume or tea.

Timothy laid the painting down on the table in front of him and turned to face her. He did not make any indication for her to take a chair.

She smiled at him, looking, he decided, rather pretty in her aqua silk slacks and jacket with that mass of curly auburn hair framing her head like a friendly Medusa.

"Mr. Neville . . ." began Theodosia.

"Call me Timothy," he said in his clipped, no-nonsense manner. "We are well acquainted with each other, are we not?"

Theodosia flinched slightly, and her cheeks flared pink from embarrassment.

"Timothy, then," said Theodosia. She was beginning to regret her impulsiveness at coming here. Timothy Neville had clearly not forgotten her actions of a few months ago. She swallowed hard, determined to get through this. "You're an expert in antique weaponry," she began. "Guns, pistols, the like. Would you be able to help me understand how a pistol might explode on its own?"

"Snooping again, are we Miss Browning?" Timothy Neville favored her with a remote smile.

"One could call it investigating, Mr. Neville," she replied. *To heck with calling him Timothy,* Theodosia decided. Addressing him as Mr. Neville was far more preferable. The formality kept him at arm's length, which was probably where she should keep this strange little man.

"One could," Timothy replied. "But then one would have to be a duly sworn investigator. I don't recall that you are."

Theodosia ignored Timothy's remark. "My interest is in Oliver Dixon's death . . . the terrible accident that befell him. You are—"

"Yes, of course I'm aware of what took place," murmured Timothy. "Terrible tragedy. He was a fine fellow." Timothy's bright eyes bore into her. "And you think because I have a collection of antique weapons that I know about exploding pistols and the like, is that it?"

"I rather thought you might be able to offer some type of explanation," said Theodosia.

"An explanation for an accident," said Timothy slowly. "I'm not sure I follow your logic. Or that I see there's any logic to follow."

"But if it wasn't accidental, then . . ." She stopped abruptly. "You're not going to help me, are you?" said Theodosia. This conversation wasn't going the way she'd hoped. She knew her feelings of regret for snooping on Timothy were a huge obstacle for her to overcome. That and the fact that Timothy Neville's brilliance made her feel like a plodding schoolchild.

Timothy Neville shrugged imperceptibly.

"Well, it might interest you," said Theodosia out of frustration, "that I have discovered a few clues of my own on the Heritage Society's Web site."

Timothy just stared at her.

"That's right," Theodosia continued. "Thanks to old newspaper clippings that reside on *your* Web site, I've discovered a few things about the Dixon-Cantrell feud."

"Good for you," said Timothy. He hadn't meant to sound flippant and harsh, but it came out that way. He knew he was a crusty old man, prone to caustic remarks and pronouncements, and he regretted his sarcastic tone instantly.

But his words cut Theodosia to the quick and made her spin on her heel.

It's definitely time to leave, she decided. *Timothy Neville is not going to give me one iota of cooperation.*

She had already retreated through the doorway when Timothy began to speak. "Miss Browning, if I were to hazard a guess, I'd say you might possibly have the right church but are looking in the wrong pew." His words, meant to appease, tumbled out in a rush. He'd also spoken so softly that Theodosia was barely able to register all his words. It had been like listening to a faulty record or tape and catching only fragments.

"What?" Theodosia asked, unsure of what he was trying to tell her.

But Timothy Neville had turned back to his painting.

8

"*Did you find* out what you wanted?" Drayton asked. After Theodosia returned to the tea shop, he had waited the better part of an hour before approaching her. She'd retired to her office immediately, and he'd heard her tapping away on her laptop computer. Probably working on some marketing ideas. Between the shop and the Web site and the specialty teas and her new idea for tea bath products, Theodosia was awfully busy. And a little distracted, too. "You were gone long enough," Drayton added.

Theodosia leaned back in her chair and exhaled slowly. "The meeting with Timothy didn't last all that long. But I was so darned upset afterward that I had to take a cool-down stroll behind Saint Philip's."

The cemetery behind Saint Philip's was one of those hidden places in Charleston, a spot not too many tourists found their way to. Filled with fountains and sculpture and fascinating old tombstones, it was a quiet, restful place where one could usually find solace.

"Timothy said something to upset you?" asked Drayton. He knew Timothy was old and crusty, but he also knew the man could be handled. Of course, you had to use kid gloves.

"Timothy Neville hates me," declared Theodosia. "I'm sure of it. He gave me that hard-eyed, calculating look that just seems to pierce right through you. I know all of you folks on the board at the Heritage Society think he does a masterful job, raising money and helping save old buildings by securing landmark status for them, but I don't see him as anything but rude and dismissive." She put her elbows on her desk and dropped her chin in her hands. "That's it," she said. "It's as simple as that. He hates me."

"Theodosia, I think you're being paranoid," said Drayton.

"I'm not. He really is an abominable little man."

"Who can also be quite charming," argued Drayton. "Besides, if Timothy hated you, he wouldn't have invited you to his Garden Fest party."

Charleston's annual Garden Fest started next week, a weeklong event where more than three dozen backyard gardens in the historic district were open for public viewing. Many would-be garden enthusiasts had been working on their gardens for years, adding fountains and cultivating prize flowers in an attempt to get on the venue. But it was a select number that were chosen every year. And it was a great honor. Of course, Timothy Neville's courtyard garden at the rear of his enormous Georgian-style mansion on Archdale Street topped the list.

"He didn't invite me," said Theodosia, "he invited *you.*"

"Yes, but your name went back on the RSVP, as you had agreed to accompany me."

Theodosia wrinkled her nose. "Do I have to go?"

Drayton looked stern. "Of course you do. I certainly can't cancel at this late date. Not very gentlemanly. Plus it's an important event."

"Okay," Theodosia sighed. She stuck her legs out straight and kicked off her loafers. They were exquisitely thin leather and perfectly matched her aqua silk outfit. Delaine, her fashion guardian angel, had seen to that. "I just hope Timothy doesn't toss me out on my ear."

"Timothy didn't give you any information at all?" Drayton prodded gently. "That's not like him. He might toy with you a bit, but Timothy is generally flattered when asked to lend his expertise."

Picking up a fat black pen, Theodosia began to make doodles on the art pad that sat front and center on her desk.

Drayton decided it might be advantageous to change the subject. "You've been working on your bath teas."

"Yes."

"Any ideas?"

Theodosia brightened. "Actually, lots. What would you think of an entire line of bath products? Tea bags for the bath, so to speak. So many green teas are excellent for relaxing sore muscles, and herbals like lavender, jasmine, calendula blossoms, and rose petals are soothing to the skin.

The bath care market, especially those products with natural ingredients, is taking off like crazy, and I think soothing tea products would fit right in."

"So do I," agreed Drayton.

They batted ideas back and forth for the better part of an hour, Theodosia taking notes like mad, finally switching to her laptop computer because, she contended, she could get the ideas down faster.

At five o'clock, Haley came in.

"I'm going to lock up, okay?" said Haley.

"Sure, fine," waved Theodosia, completely out of her funk now. "Have a terrific evening."

"You, too," said Haley. "Bye, Drayton."

"Good night," he called.

Theodosia and Drayton sat quietly for a moment, listening as Haley snapped off lights, then exited the front door, locking it behind her. The only light on in the tea shop was the glowing Tiffany lamp that sat on Theodosia's desk.

"Drayton," said Theodosia slowly, "Timothy Neville *did* say something to me."

He stared at her patiently.

"Timothy mumbled something about 'right church, wrong pew.' I think he was referring to the Dixon-Cantrell feud. You've heard about that?"

Drayton nodded. "Dribs and drabs over the years."

"That's what I was talking to Detective Tidwell about today."

"That's kind of what Haley and I figured. You think Ford Cantrell . . . ?"

Theodosia shrugged. "Maybe . . . You saw how irate he was at the picnic."

"Howling mad," agreed Drayton.

"Of course, Timothy could have been trying to send me off in the wrong direction, too," said Theodosia.

"That doesn't sound like Timothy," said Drayton. "He usually prides himself on being rather insightful and precise."

They stared at each other for a moment.

"So," said Drayton, *"are* you going to keep investigating?"

Theodosia's blue eyes were as lovely and unpredictable as the nearby Atlantic. "Count on it," she told him.

§ 9 §

"Isn't it a cunning little piece? See how the light catches the gray green glaze? I'm so hoping it was crafted by one of the Edgefield potters."

Theodosia carefully placed hot blueberry muffins on her serving tray and listened to that voice. She knew that voice. At least she *thought* she did.

Parting the curtains and stepping out into the tea shop, she was mildly surprised to find Giovanni Loard, cradling a teapot in his hands and talking animatedly with Drayton.

"Yes," Drayton was saying, "the Edgefield provenance is correct, and I'd definitely date it to the early nineteenth century."

Theodosia noted that Drayton had allowed his glasses to slip halfway down his nose and was speaking in what Haley called his Heritage Society voice. Timothy Neville may have loved to be called upon to lend his expertise, but Drayton wasn't far behind.

"Good morning," Theodosia greeted the two men after she'd dropped off pastry baskets at the various tables. Drayton smiled absently while Giovanni Loard jumped up from his chair and eagerly took her hand.

"Miss Browning, so nice to see you again," Giovanni gushed. "And so lovely to finally visit your tea shop."

"Delighted to have you," she replied. "My condolences again on the death of your cousin."

Giovanni's smile crumpled. "Thank you. It's been a difficult time for all of us. Especially Doe. Thank goodness for small kindnesses from people like you."

"Look at this," said Drayton, delivering a sturdy little ceramic into Theodosia's hands.

"Your absolutely brilliant colleague here has been kind enough to take a look at this teapot," said Giovanni. "He's quite sure it's an Edgefield."

Edgefield pottery came from a rich supply of heavy clay found in Edgefield County, northwest of Charleston and located along the Savannah River. In the 1800s, Edgefield potters had crafted pitchers, storage jars, bowls, and teapots as well as little jars with faces molded into them.

"Lovely," said Theodosia as she turned the little clay vessel over in her hands. "These things are getting hard to find. Did you just pick this up for sale in your shop?"

"Oh, no," said Giovanni, "it was one of Doe and Oliver's wedding gifts. Poor girl can't bear to even look at any of these objects now. It breaks her heart to have them in the house. She's kindly asked me to handle the sale of several pieces for her."

"I'm sure she's utterly shattered," said Theodosia, even though she found it strange and almost improper for Doe to be selling off wedding presents so soon after Oliver Dixon's death. For goodness sake, the man's funeral wasn't until tomorrow!

"There hasn't been any forward progress in determining what happened to Oliver," Giovanni said with a long face. "Everyone's clucking about what a terrible accident it was. But, of course, I suspect the pistol was tampered with. So does Doe."

"The police are investigating, are they not?" said Drayton.

"Yes," said Giovanni slowly. "And I have asked them to take a rather hard look at Ford Cantrell. He's a rotten egg, that one." Giovanni shifted an earnest gaze at Theodosia. "Thank you again for your quick action at the picnic."

Theodosia waved a hand. She would have done the same for anyone.

"Let me keep this teapot for a day or two," offered Drayton, "and I'll consult with an acquaintance of mine. He collects Edgefield pieces and might be able to provide us with some idea on price."

"That would be wonderful," murmured Giovanni Loard. His face eased into a smile as Haley approached their table, bearing a pot of tea. "Hello," he greeted her.

"Ah, here's the tea now," said Drayton. "Thank you, Haley." He poured cups of munnar tea for Giovanni, Theodosia, and himself.

But Haley didn't budge, and Giovanni continued to smile warmly at her.

"Giovanni Loard, this is Haley Parker," said Theodosia.

"Pleased to meet you," said Haley. "Could I offer you a sweet? I have some lemon tarts I just took out of the oven."

"That would be lovely," smiled Giovanni, and Haley dashed off to fetch the pastries.

"Pretty girl," remarked Giovanni as he took a sip of tea. "Oh, this is excellent," he exclaimed. "And I know nothing about tea. I couldn't tell you if this was Japanese or Chinese."

"Actually," said Theodosia, "it's from India."

"You see, what did I tell you," said Giovanni. "Oh my!" he exclaimed as Haley returned and set a plate of pastries in front of him. "You all are just bowling me over with your care and hospitality! I can't believe I didn't find my way to your tea shop sooner."

"You recently purchased a house nearby, didn't you?" asked Theodosia. She'd recalled that Delaine had said something to her about it.

"Yes," said Giovanni. "Over on Legare. It's one of those old Victorian single houses. You know . . . charm, carved balustrades, and absolutely *everything* in desperate need of a repair? I'd have to characterize it as a money pit so far, but I'm holding out hope that I'll be able to return it to classic status someday."

"I'm familiar with that particular row of houses," said Drayton. "Most of them have lovely gardens."

Giovanni nodded eagerly. "The garden has been my saving grace. The brick patio, small fountain, and statuary are in almost perfect condition. All I really had to do was update a few plantings. Don't laugh," Giovanni said in a conspiratorial tone, "but my garden is actually included in next week's Garden Fest."

"That's wonderful," exclaimed Drayton. Besides historical restoration,

Drayton was also passionate about gardening. He had cultivated an elegant garden in his small backyard and had even ventured recently toward becoming a bonsai master. "But I didn't realize you were a member of the garden club, much less that your garden was on this year's tour."

"My garden *open house* is Friday evening," said Giovanni, "the night after Timothy Neville's big kickoff party. I'd be honored if you all would drop by."

"I think Giovanni Loard wants to date Haley," said Drayton afterward.

Haley blushed all the way down to her toes. "No way," she said. "He's just a nice guy. A gentleman."

"Do you really think so?" said Theodosia. She had remained fairly quiet during Giovanni Loard's visit. Everything that had seemed charming about him during their initial encounter last Sunday now seemed a trifle forced. On the other hand, he might have been nervous being thrust in among the three of them. Their chattiness *could* be a little overpowering.

"Does it seem strange to you that Doe is selling her wedding presents?" Theodosia asked Haley as she stacked jars of DuBose Bees honey and Dundee's Devonshire cream on the shelves.

"It's tacky," agreed Haley. "And I'm beginning to suspect that Doe is a bit of a social climber. Why else would she have married someone so much older? I think Delaine was probably right about the money part."

Is Doe just an out-and-out fortune hunter? Theodosia wondered to herself. *Is that the bottom line?*

Doe appeared harmless enough, more youthful than anything. A pretty young woman who had fallen in love with an older man. Then again, her husband had just been killed and, Oliver's sons not withstanding, Doe stood squarely in line to inherit a good deal of his money. Which suggested she could also be regarded as a suspect.

Theodosia had been turning the idea of attending Oliver Dixon's funeral over in her head. She had pretty much made up her mind to go.

Why not? she asked herself. Oliver Dixon had lived in the historic district, and that made him a neighbor. Going to his funeral would be a neighborly thing to do.

And, of course, she'd been present at the time of Oliver Dixon's demise. True, she'd merely played a walk-on role, but that was more than most folks had done that terrible afternoon in White Point Gardens.

"Is this a good time?" Miss Dimple hovered in the doorway to Theodosia's office. "I can come back a little later if you'd like. No problem."

"Oh, Miss Dimple," said Theodosia, pulling herself out of her thoughts. "I really was lost in thought there for a moment. Come in."

"I brought you the spreadsheet for last month," Miss Dimple said, smiling at Theodosia. "Things are looking fairly good, even with start-up costs on the Web site."

"Miss Dimple," said Theodosia, a germ of an idea flickering in her brain, "you're an accountant. Is there some way to run a check on a company's finances without them finding out?"

"We could run a D and B. You know, a Dun and Bradstreet."

"Is that fairly easy to do?"

"I used to do it all the time for Mr. Dauphine. Now I understand it can be done even faster over the Internet."

"The Internet? Really?" Theodosia beamed. Here was territory she was familiar with. "Terrific suggestion. Let's do it."

❧ 10 ❧

"Have you heard the news?" Delaine Dish swept through the front door of the tea shop and planted herself at a table with all the aplomb of a Romanoff grand duchess.

"What news is that, Delaine?" Theodosia asked with a slightly resigned air. They had been frantically busy over lunch and had run out of sandwiches. Haley had bravely saved the day by whipping together a dozen fruit and cheese plates and tucking in mini stacks of water biscuits. Those fruit and cheese plates had seemed to do the trick for the folks who came in late, but Theodosia was still trying to catch her breath and wasn't completely sure she could fully cope with Delaine and her accompanying histrionics today.

"Remember that nasty man at the picnic?" asked Delaine. She whipped out a gold compact and lipstick. "Ford Cantrell?" Now she gave her lipstick a good twist and aimed it at her lips, confident she had everyone's attention. "I heard he was taken in for questioning," she murmured in an offhand manner as she held her mouth rigid and applied her signature pink.

Dropping her makeup into her handbag, Delaine aimed a dazzling smile at Theodosia and Drayton. "Isn't that something?" she asked, as though she were somehow acutely involved.

"Well, I can't say that I'm surprised," said Drayton. He grabbed a freshly made pot of tea, teacups, and what remained of his lunch, set it all down on Delaine's table, then eased himself into a chair across from her. "Whew, after the busy lunch we had, I'm almost done in," he declared. "I'm getting too old for this."

"Nonsense," said Delaine. "You're a man in his prime. Barely middle-aged."

"That's right, Drayton's planning to live to a hundred and twenty," said Haley as she brushed past him.

"Oh, shush," said Delaine. "Don't go getting Drayton all upset. I happen to know he's got another birthday coming up."

"Don't *you* have another birthday coming up, too, Delaine?" asked Haley.

"Good heavens no," she said. "That's a long way off yet." She eyed the fruit and cheese plate Drayton was picking at. "Do you have another one of those sweet little luncheon plates?" she asked Haley.

"Sure," Haley grinned. "Hang on." And she scampered into the small kitchen to fix a plate for Delaine.

"How did you hear about Ford Cantrell?" asked Theodosia.

"Oh, honey, the news is all up and down Church Street. Monica Fischer told me this morning when she stopped by the shop. Then I ran into Dundy Baldwin on the street. Anyway, that Cantrell boy embarrassed us all at the picnic, picking an argument with Oliver Dixon and that handsome cousin of his."

"Do you know what they were arguing about?" asked Theodosia.

"I don't know," said Delaine, waving a hand dismissively, "some silly thing. Fishing, I think. Did you know that Ford Cantrell's great-uncle ran off with Oliver Dixon's aunt a long time ago?" Delaine arched her eyebrows with disapproval. "People *still* talk about that."

"Do they really?" asked Drayton. "It's been an awfully long time, and Charleston has had some rousing good scandals since then."

Delaine leaned forward in anticipation. "Has something else happened I should know about?"

"One fruit and cheese plate, madam." Haley placed a pink and white bone china plate piled with slices of Camembert, cheddar cheese, grapes, and apple slices in front of Delaine. "Oh, and I was checking E-mails before and printed out this stuff for you," Haley continued. She thrust a handful of sheets at Theodosia. "I think they're for you. Some kind of financial profile on Grapevine?" She gave Theodosia a questioning glance.

"Grapevine?" piped up Delaine. "Isn't that the company Oliver Dixon started? Whatever would you want with *financial* information? Are you planning a little merger and acquisition we don't know about, Theodosia?"

"Try this tea, Delaine," offered Drayton. "It's a lovely Darjeeling."

"Why, thank you, Drayton." Delaine favored him with a dazzling smile as he carefully served her, then she speared a small piece of cheese on her plate and nibbled it delicately. "Oh, this Camembert is *heavenly*, simply *melts* in your mouth. I don't even want to *think* about butterfat content!"

"*Theodosia, I am so sorry*," said Haley. She shifted nervously from one foot to the other, and her face betrayed her anguish. "Mentioning that E-mail in front of Delaine like that . . . I just didn't think!"

"It's not your fault. You were just trying to be helpful," said Theodosia as she slid a stack of papers into her attaché case. She wasn't pleased about the incident either, but what could she do? Haley was usually very careful and discreet. This had been a slipup. It was just too bad the slipup had occurred in front of Delaine Dish.

On the other hand, Drayton had rushed in to distract Delaine by offering her a cup of Darjeeling. Maybe he had been successful. She'd just have to wait and see.

"I feel like such a jerk," said Haley.

"Don't," said Theodosia. "It could've happened to any one of us."

"You really think so? No, you're just saying that."

"Haley," said Theodosia. "Enough. Don't make yourself crazy over this."

"I was trying to save you some time by printing out E-mails, and I'd just been skimming this article," replied Haley. She held up a section of the *Charleston Post and Courier* for Theodosia to see.

"Which article is that?"

"Well, it's not really an article," amended Haley. "It's mostly photos from the picnic last Sunday. The Oliver Dixon thing has been in the forefront the last couple of days, so I guess the *Post and Courier* just now got around to covering the sailboat race. It's more society gabbing than news. Who was there, what friends were visiting from out of town, that kind of thing."

Theodosia took the page from Haley and scanned the article. Haley was right; it was soft news, society fluff. "That's right," said Theodosia, "they had one of their photographers there to cover the picnic, didn't they?"

"Yes. Seemed like he took gobs of pictures. Course, they only printed but three of them."

Theodosia stared at Haley intently. "I sure wish I could take a look at the rest of those photos."

"You do?"

Theodosia put a hand to her cheek and stroked it absently, thinking. "The photos might, you know, *chronicle* what happened," she said slowly.

"From what Tidwell says, nobody seemed to see anything out of the ordi-nary. And nobody's completely sure how many people handled the pistol once it was removed from its rosewood box."

Haley was suddenly grinning like a little elf. "Let me try to make up for my little faux pas," she exclaimed. "Let me see if I can get my friend Jimmy Cardavan to get us a look at the photos. He's a copy intern there."

"Really?" asked Theodosia. "How would we do that? Go down there? I have to run out to a Spoleto marketing meeting right now, but maybe we could swing by afterward."

Haley's grin stretched wider. "I've got a better idea. Let me E-mail Jimmy and see if he's got access to the *Post and Courier*'s intranet. If so, he can pull the photos up from their site and send them to us in a pdf for-mat. That way you could look at the photos on your computer and print the ones that interest you. That is, if one or another *does* interest you."

"Haley, you're a genius," declared Theodosia.

11

Spoleto Festival USA was Charleston's big arts festival, an annual gala event highlighting dance, opera, theater, music, art, and even literary presentations. Beginning each Memorial Day, Spoleto ran for an action-packed two weeks, launching an invasion of visiting directors, dance troupes, and theater companies that comingled with Charleston's already-strong arts scene and created a rich fusion of performance, visual, and literary arts.

Theodosia had served on Spoleto's marketing committee for six years. Originally, she'd been "volunteered" by her boss, but after the first year had found the experience so rewarding and enjoyable that she'd stayed on, even after she left the advertising agency.

This year, she'd produced a fast-paced thirty-second TV commercial, using snippets of footage from past events set to a jazz track. Then she negotiated favorable rates with the five commercial TV stations in Charleston, some of the TV stations in Columbia and Greenville, and those in Savannah and Augusta, Georgia, as well. The idea being that Spoleto's appeal would extend to arts-minded folk in neighboring cities and states as well as those in Charleston.

Now, as Theodosia meandered the broad corridors of the Gibbes Museum of Art, she decided to treat herself to a side trip into a couple of the smaller galleries. She'd arrived about ten minutes early and was, after all, heading in the general direction of the conference room where the marketing committee was scheduled to meet.

In the Asian Gallery, Theodosia studied the exquisite collection of Japanese wood-block prints. Many were by revered masters such as Hiroshige and Hokusai, but there were contemporary prints, too, by new masters such as Mitsuaki and Eiichi. These were artists who played with color, technique, and style, and sought to push the boundaries of Japanese printmaking. Fascinating, she thought, what a lovely, hazy feel they had, almost like twilight in the low country.

Glancing at her watch, Theodosia saw it was almost three o'clock. Hustling out of the Asian Gallery, she turned right and headed down the main corridor. At the entrance to the museum's administrative offices, she paused to shut off her cell phone, a small courtesy that she wished more people would observe. When she glanced up, a woman was staring at her, a woman with washed-out blue eyes and a frizzle of red hair shot with strands of gray.

"Do you have a moment?" the woman asked in a low voice.

"Pardon?" Theodosia stared quizzically at the woman.

The woman cocked her head to one side. "I'm Lizbeth Cantrell," she announced bluntly. "And you're Theodosia Browning."

"Yes, hello," said Theodosia, completely taken aback.

"I saw your name on the marketing committee list," announced

Lizbeth Cantrell as she stuck out her hand. "I was just here for a meeting, too. I'm on the ticket committee."

Theodosia accepted Lizbeth Cantrell's hand as she studied her. *What is this all about?* she wondered. Had Lizbeth Cantrell somehow gotten wind of the fact that she'd done a little investigating into the Dixon-Cantrell feud? No, couldn't be. That would lead back to Tidwell, and Tidwell would never divulge a source of information. You'd have to hand-cuff the man and beat it out of him. Then what did Lizbeth Cantrell want?

As Lizbeth Cantrell shuffled her feet and ducked her head, Theodosia realized the woman had to be at least six feet tall. Long-boned and angular, she had a face that seemed all cheekbone and jaw.

"Can we talk privately?" Lizbeth Cantrell asked.

"Of course," agreed Theodosia, finding herself all the more curious about this casual encounter that had no doubt been staged.

When they'd retreated to one of the conference rooms and pulled the double doors closed behind them, Theodosia studied Lizbeth Cantrell. All the qualities that made her brother, Ford Cantrell, tall and good-looking seemed to work against Lizbeth Cantrell. She was obviously older than her brother and appeared far more subdued and faded, as though her red hair had somehow leached all color and emotion from her.

Truth be known, Lizbeth Cantrell was a woman who was both plain and plainspoken, at her happiest when she was whelping a litter of puppies or crashing through the woods atop a good horse.

"You're a smart woman," began Lizbeth Cantrell. "A businesswoman. That makes you a breed apart from a lot of ladies."

"Thank you . . . I think," said Theodosia. "But what do—"

Lizbeth Cantrell held up a hand. "This isn't easy for me," she said. "I'm not used to asking for help."

"You want my help?" said Theodosia. This conversation was getting stranger by the minute, she decided.

"I know you were at White Point Gardens last Sunday when Oliver Dixon was shot," said Lizbeth Cantrell. "And I also hear that you know how to track down a murderer."

"I think you've got me confused with someone else," said Theodosia.

"No, I don't," said Lizbeth Cantrell firmly. "Your aunt Libby told me all about you. Last fall, the police thought maybe the girl who worked in your tea shop was responsible for the death of that man at the Lamplighter Tour. But you stood behind her. You figured it all out."

Realization was not dawning quickly for Theodosia. "My aunt Libby told you . . . ? Excuse me, exactly what are you asking me to do?"

"I want you to help clear my brother's name," said Lizbeth Cantrell. "He didn't tamper with that old pistol. Folks just think he might have because he acts so crazy most of the time. And because he collects guns and likes to hunt. But I know Ford is a good man, an honest man. He's no killer."

Let's not be so hasty, thought Theodosia. It was, after all, Ford and Lizbeth's great-great-grandfather, Jeb Cantrell, who shot Stuart Dixon to death back in 1892 and set the Dixon-Cantrell feud in motion.

On the other hand, even though Ford Cantrell had looked awfully suspicious at first, Theodosia wasn't so sure blame should be laid entirely at his feet. Doe was fast earning a place on her list of suspects, too. And Oliver Dixon's two sons, Brock and Quaid, bore looking into as well.

"Can you help me?" asked Lizbeth Cantrell. Her pale eyes transfixed Theodosia with their intensity. "I know you're a good lady. A smart lady."

"You live at Pamlico Hill Plantation," said Theodosia. "A few miles down the road from my aunt Libby's."

"That's right." Suddenly, a ghost of a smile played on Lizbeth Cantrell's plain face, bringing with it a softness and quiet animation that hadn't been visible earlier.

"I know you, don't I?" said Theodosia. Somewhere, in the depths of her memory, a faint recollection stirred.

"Yes, ma'am, you do," Lizbeth replied.

Theodosia stared at Lizbeth as though she were a distant shadow and tried to conjure up the memory. "You were there when my . . . my mother died," she finally said.

"Yes," Lizbeth replied softly. "You were just a little bug of a thing back then, couldn't have been more than seven or eight years old."

The flashback of that long-ago summer rushed at Theodosia in a Technicolor whirl and exploded in her brain. And along with it, came a wash of memories. The oppressive heat, her father's hopeful whispering, her heartbreaking sadness.

"My mother helped take care of your mother," explained Lizbeth. "And sometimes I came along."

"You came along," said Theodosia, as though she were in a trance. "You were older than I, and you took me swimming on hot days."

"That's right," said Lizbeth. "We went to Carpenter's Pond." Her smile was gentle, and she waited patiently as Theodosia's brain processed everything.

"Yes, I remember you," said Theodosia slowly. Her initial shock now over with, she was able to look back and slowly replay the memory. Her mother's last summer on this earth, spent at Cane Ridge Plantation in the low-country. Her mother had wanted more than anything to be able to watch sunlight play across the marsh grass, to gaze upon pink sunsets over shadowy, peaceful pine groves. And, finally, to be laid to rest in the old family cemetery there. Theodosia stretched one hand out tentatively, touched Lizbeth's sleeve. "You were so kind."

"You were so sad."

The conference room's double doors rattled noisily.

"I got to go," Lizbeth said as she began to gather up her purse and notebook. "I think your meeting's about to start." She paused and gave Theodosia a look filled with longing. "Will you help?" she asked.

The door burst open, and a half-dozen people crowded into the room. They swarmed around the table, paying little heed to Lizbeth and Theodosia, totally unaware of the highly charged atmosphere that seemed to permeate the room.

Theodosia dropped her arms to her sides and nodded. "I'll try," she said. She didn't know exactly what she was promising. Or why. But how could she not?

Lizbeth blinked back tears. "Thank you," she said simply.

12

A pot of lentil soup simmered on the back burner; popovers baked golden and fluffy in the oven. Although Theodosia's upstairs apartment was not overly large, it possessed that rare trait so often lacking in many newer apartments: style. Aubasson rugs in faded blue and cinnamon covered the floors. French doors gave the appearance of a living and dining room that flowed together flawlessly, while cove ceilings gave the rooms a cozy, architectural ambiance. Draperies and sofa were done in muted English chintz and prints.

Earlier, Drayton had gone next door to Robillard Booksellers and borrowed one of their oversized magnifying glasses on the pretext of trying to decipher some old Chinese tea labels. Now Theodosia held the magnifying glass in her hand as she sat at her dining room table, studying the black and white printouts. They'd been transmitted electronically just as Haley had promised, sliding, as if by magic, from her laser printer.

The photos were interesting in that they did, indeed, chronicle the events of that Sunday afternoon. Here were photos of sailboats jostling in the harbor at the beginning of the race. Then photos of the two dozen or so boats, sails filled with wind, setting off toward the Atlantic. The photographer had then concentrated on shots of the crowd. There were photos of people talking, people shaking hands, people hugging and exchanging air kisses. Delaine was in a couple shots; Drayton showed up in a few as well.

Here was Billy Manolo standing next to the table that held the rosewood box containing the pistol. And the commodore in the ill-fitting jacket with all the gold braid.

Theodosia shuffled through the printouts. They were interesting but a little disappointing at the same time. She hadn't expected anything to jump right out at her; that would've been too easy. But she felt the rumblings of a low-level vibe that told her there must be *something* to be learned.

That hope spun dizzyingly in her head as Theodosia decided to shift her attention to the Dun & Bradstreet report that had arrived so speedily this afternoon. There were just four pages, but they contained what looked like a good assessment of Grapevine: a rundown on its products and the company's growth potential. Just as Haley had mentioned a few days ago, Grapevine had started production on a number of different expansion modules for PDAs. Although competition was stiff in this area, the report seemed to indicate that Grapevine had done its homework and was about to launch a very viable product.

Theodosia finally took a break when the oven timer buzzed. Ambling out into the kitchen, she slid her hand into a padded mitt and pulled the popovers from the oven. They were perfect. Golden brown and heroically puffed. Haley's recipes were the best. They always turned out.

After pouring the lentil soup into a mug, Theodosia carried everything back to the dining room table on a tray, sliding the printouts out of the way before she set her food down. Earl Grey was immediately at her elbow, giving a gentle nudge, lobbying for a bite of popover.

"Leftovers when I'm finished," she told him, and he assumed that worried look dogs often get.

Theodosia had finished her soup and was plowing through the printouts a second time, when she stopped to study the single photo of Oliver Dixon lying facedown, half in, half out of the water.

The photographer must have snapped the shot just moments before she reached down to check for a pulse, because the tip of her right hand was slightly visible. They hadn't printed that photo in the paper because it was, undoubtedly, too gruesome, but they'd retained it in their collection of shots from that day.

Closing her eyes, Theodosia tried to recall her impression of that single, defining moment. She had a strong, visceral recollection of the hot, pungent aroma of exploded gunpowder, chill water lapping at her ankles, and a sense of unreality, of feeling numb, as she stared at Oliver Dixon's still body.

What had Tidwell told her about loading the old pistol? Theodosia searched her memory. Oh yes, Tidwell had said you put a pinch of gunpowder on a little piece of paper and twist it. Kind of like creating a miniature tea bag.

Theodosia held the magnifying glass to the printout. It was extremely grainy and hard to discern any real detail. She could just make out the back of poor Oliver Dixon's head, dark against a lighter background.

Theodosia sighed. There just didn't seem to be anything here.

13

April heralds spring in Charleston. Flickers and catbirds warble and tweet, flitting among spreading live oaks, searching out twigs and moss for building nests. Days become warmer and more languid and, ever so gradually, the tempo of Charleston, never moving at breakneck speed anyway, begins to slow.

On this extraordinarily fine morning, the fresh Charleston air was ripe and redolent with the scent of magnolias, azaleas, and top notes of dogwood.

But no one took notice.

Instead, mourners walked in somber groups of twos and threes into the yawning double doors of Saint Philip's Church. Overhead, the bells in the steeple clanged loudly.

There is no joy in those bells, thought Theodosia as she walked alongside Drayton. There were so many times when those bells had rung out in exaltation. Easter Sunday, Christmas Eve, weddings, christenings. There were times when they tolled respectfully. But today, the bells clanged mournfully, announcing to all in the surrounding historic district that one of God's poor souls was being laid to rest.

Choosing seats toward the back of the church, Theodosia and Drayton sat quietly, observing the other mourners. Most seemed lost in their own private thoughts, as is so often the case when attending a funeral.

Marveling at the soaring interior of Saint Philip's, Theodosia was reminded that it had been designed by the renowned architect Joseph Nyde. Nyde had greatly admired the neoclassical arches of Saint Martin-in-the-Fields church in London and had transferred those airy, sculptural designs to Saint Philip's.

With a mixture of majesty and pathos, the opening notes from Mozart's *Requiem* swelled from the pipe organ, and everyone shuffled to their feet. Then the funeral procession began.

Six men, all wearing black suits, white shirts, and black ties, and walking in perfect cadence, rolled Oliver Dixon's bronze casket down the wide center aisle. A good ten steps behind the casket and its catafalque, head bowed, hands clasped tightly, Doe Belvedere Dixon, Oliver's wife of nine weeks, solemnly followed her husband's body. Oliver Dixon's two grown sons, Brock and Quaid, followed directly behind her.

In her black, tailored suit and matching beret, her blond hair pulled back in a severe French twist, Doe looked heartbreakingly young.

"The girl looks fetching, absolutely fetching," murmured Drayton as she passed by them. "How can a woman look so good at a funeral?"

"She's young," said Theodosia as the choir suddenly cut in, their voices rising in a litany of Latin verse, "and blessed with good skin."

Reverend Jonathan, the church's longtime pastor, stepped forward to deliver his eulogy. Then a half-dozen other men also took the podium. They spoke glowingly of Oliver Dixon's accomplishments, of his service to the community, of his impeccable reputation.

As the service grew longer, Theodosia's mind drifted.

Staring at the backs of Brock and Quaid, Oliver Dixon's two sons, she wondered if their disqualification from the race was in any way related to this.

She recalled the strange walk-on scene Ford Cantrell had staged at the picnic. Wondered what his feelings would be today. *Had he shown up here today?* She ventured a look around. *No, probably not.*

Theodosia thought about the printouts she studied last night, the ones she'd hoped might be helpful. The final printout, the one where Oliver Dixon's upper body was silhouetted against a somewhat stark background, seemed burned in her memory.

Theodosia shifted on the hard pew, crossed her legs.

Stark background.

Theodosia suddenly sat up straight, uncrossed her legs. What *was* that background, anyway? Rocks perhaps? Or wet sand? She searched her memory.

It had to be her tablecloth.

Her tablecloth. The idea came zooming at her like a Roman candle. And on the heels of that came the realization that whatever residue might still be left on the tablecloth—gunpowder, exploded bits of metal, or even blood—it could just offer up some semblance of a clue.

A clue. A genuine clue. Wouldn't that be interesting?

As the final musical tribute came to a crashing conclusion, Theodosia managed to catch herself. She'd been about to break out in a smile, albeit one tinged with grim satisfaction.

Goodness, she thought, struggling to maintain decorum, *I've got to be careful. People will think I'm an absolute ghoul. Smiling at a funeral!*

"Let's go," Theodosia whispered to Drayton as she bounded to her feet.

"Yes, let's do express our condolences," said Drayton.

They waited in line a good twenty minutes, watching as Doe Belvedere Dixon hugged, kissed, and clutched the hands of the various mourners. She seemed to converse with them in an easy, gracious manner, accepting all their kind words.

"Does she seem slightly vivacious to you?" asked Drayton, studying her carefully. "Do you have the feeling she's a bit like Scarlett O'Hara, wearing rouge to her own husband's funeral?"

"I think the poor girl was simply blessed with good looks," said Theodosia. "She seems heartbroken."

"You're right," amended Drayton. "I should be ashamed."

"Should be," whispered Theodosia and aimed an elbow toward Drayton's ribs. She, too, had been watching Doe carefully, getting the feeling, more and more, that Doe might be wearing her mourning much the same as she would another beauty pageant title.

Finally, Theodosia and Drayton were at the head of the line, clasping hands with Brock and Quaid, Oliver Dixon's two sons. "So sorry," she and Drayton murmured to them in hushed tones. "You have our condolences."

Then Theodosia was eye to eye with Doe.

Drayton's right, she suddenly realized. The girl looked appropriately sad and subdued but, at the same time, she seemed to be playing a role. The role of grieving widow.

"My deepest sympathy," said Theodosia as she grasped Doe's hand.

"Thank you." Doe's eyes remained downcast, her long eyelashes swept dramatically against pink cheeks. Theodosia idly wondered if they were extensions. Eyelash extensions were a big thing these days. First had come hair, now eyelashes. These days, it seemed like a girl could improve on almost anything if she wanted to. And had enough money.

"As you may know," said Theodosia, "I was the first to reach him."

Doe's eyes flicked up and stared directly into Theodosia's eyes. Her gaze didn't waver. "Thank you," she whispered. "How very kind of you."

Theodosia was aware of Drayton gently crowding her. It felt like he was beginning to radiate disapproval. She knew it was one thing to speculate on Doe's veracity, another to push her a bit. Still, Theodosia persisted.

"Anyone would have done the same," Theodosia assured her. "Such a terrible thing . . . the pistol . . ."

Doe had begun to look slightly perturbed. "Yes . . ." she stammered.

"After all, your husband was an avid hunter, was he not? He was extremely familiar with guns?"

"Yes, I suppose . . . as a member of the Chessen Hunt Club he . . . I'm sorry, I don't see wha—"

"Shush," said Theodosia, patting the girl's hand. "If there's anything Drayton or I can do, please don't hesitate to call."

• • •

"That was expressing condolences?" hissed Drayton when they were out of earshot. "You just about browbeat the poor girl. She didn't know what to think." They walked a few steps farther. "I assume you were testing the water, so to speak? Trying to ascertain if Oliver Dixon knew anything about guns?"

"Drayton . . ." Theodosia grabbed his sleeve and pulled him out of the stream of people passing by. "I think Oliver Dixon was set up."

He pursed his lips and gazed at her with speculation. "Set up. You mean—"

"Someone *caused* that pistol to misfire," Theodosia said excitedly.

"You know, I really don't like where you're going with this," Drayton said irritably.

"Hear me out," said Theodosia. If someone tampered with that pistol, and I've really come to believe that's exactly what happened, then hard evidence might also exist. Like explosives or—"

"Hard evidence," said Drayton with a quizzical frown. "Hard evidence *where?*"

"On the tablecloth," said Theodosia.

Drayton just stared at her.

"One of my tablecloths was on the table that Oliver Dixon fell onto. He tumbled onto the table, then slid down into a heap. Remember?"

Drayton hesitated a moment, trying to fix the scene in his mind. "Yes, I do. You're right," he replied finally.

"So there could be particles of gunpowder or explosives or whatever still clinging to that tablecloth," prompted Theodosia.

"Oh," said Drayton. Then, "*Oh,* I see what you mean!"

"Now, if I could only figure out what happened to that darned table-cloth," said Theodosia. "In all the hubbub and commotion, I'm not entirely sure where it ended up." She stared out the open doors of the church toward the street.

"I have it," said Drayton.

She whirled toward him in surprise. "*You* have it?"

"I'm almost certain I do. At least I have a vague recollection of untangling it and packing it up with the other things."

"So where is the tablecloth now?"

"Probably still in the trunk of my car. I was going to drop all the dirty linens at Chase's Laundry yesterday, then I got busy with the Heritage Society. I received a call that someone had brought in this old, wooden joggling board . . . you know, they were used for crossing ditches on rice plantations? They're so terribly rare now and I—"

"Drayton . . ."

"Yes?"

"I'm so *glad* you have your priorities straight," Theodosia said as they strolled out into the sunlight. "Because you very nicely *preserved* what could amount to *evidence.*"

Suddenly, Theodosia's smile froze on her face and she stopped dead in her tracks. "Oh rats. That's Burt Tidwell over there."

Drayton frowned. "Why do you suppose *he's* here?"

"Why do you think?" she said, squinting across the way at him.

"Investigating?" squeaked Drayton. "Looking for suspects?"

"Same as us," said Theodosia. She bit her lip, debating whether or not she should go over and talk to him.

"Well, are you going to talk to him?" Drayton asked finally.

She hesitated a moment, then made up her mind. "Why not? Let's both waltz over there and see if we can push his buttons before he starts to push ours."

"All right," agreed Drayton. "But nothing about the—"

Theodosia held an index finger to her lips. "Mum's the word," she cautioned.

They strolled over to where a bank of memorial wreaths was displayed. Theodosia decided that Oliver Dixon must have been extremely well liked and respected to have garnered a church full of flower arrangements as well as a huge assortment of memorial wreaths that had spilled outside.

Burt Tidwell was studying one of the wreaths. "Look at this," he said to them. "Wild grapevine entwined with lilies, the flower symbolizing resurrection. So very touching." Tidwell inclined his head slightly. He'd captured Theodosia in his peripheral vision; now his eyes bore into her. "Miss Browning, how do. And here's Mr. Conneley, too."

"Hello," said Drayton pleasantly.

"You took Ford Cantrell in for questioning," said Theodosia without preamble.

Tidwell favored her with a faint smile. "My dear Miss Browning, you seem somewhat surprised. I thought you'd be absolutely *delighted* that I followed up on your so-called *tip*." Tidwell pronounced the word *tip* as though he were discussing odiferous compost in a garden.

Theodosia turned her attention to the memorial wreaths as Burt Tidwell rocked back on his heels, enormously pleased with himself. Here was a lovely floral wreath from the Heritage Society, she noted. And here was . . . Well, wasn't this one a surprise!

"You might also be interested to know," Tidwell prattled on, "that we discovered Ford Cantrell has a rather extensive gun collection. And that our Mr. Cantrell has recently turned his old plantation into a sort of hunting preserve."

Tidwell suddenly had her attention once again. "What kind of hunting?" Theodosia asked.

"He claims to be appealing to all manner of wealthy sportsmen, promising prizes of deer, turkey, quail, and wild boar," answered Tidwell.

"My aunt Libby has lived out that way for the better part of half a century," said Theodosia, "and the wildest critters she's ever encountered have been possum and porcupines." She paused. "And once, when I was a kid, we ran across a dead alligator. But I don't suppose that really counts."

"No one ever characterized Ford Cantrell as being an honest man," said Tidwell.

"Or hunters as being terribly bright," added Theodosia with a wry smile.

Their conversation was suddenly interrupted by loud voices.

"What are you doing here?" came an angry scream.

Theodosia, Drayton, Burt Tidwell, and about forty other people turned to watch the beginnings of a shouting match on the lawn of Saint Philip's.

"Who on earth is that?" asked Theodosia. She didn't know his name, but she recognized the angry man with the flopping white hair, florid complexion, and hand-tailored pinstripe suit as the very same man from the yacht race. The commodore in the tight jacket swathed in gold braid.

"That's Booth Crowley," Tidwell told her.

"*That's* Booth Crowley?" said Theodosia, stunned. Booth Crowley had been the one who'd been beckoning to Oliver Dixon that fateful Sunday. Booth Crowley had handed him the pistol.

And just look at who he's yelling at, she thought. *Billy Manolo, the worker from the yacht club who asked to borrow the tablecloth. Wasn't this a strange little tableau?*

"Hey buddy, cool your jets," Billy Manolo cautioned. Lean, dark-complected, and a head taller than Booth Crowley, Billy stood poised on the balls of his feet, glowering back and looking as dangerous as a jungle cat.

Still, Booth Crowley persisted in his tirade.

"Is there some *reason* you're here?" Booth Crowley thundered. "Don't you think you've caused *enough* problems?"

"Hey man, you're crazy." Billy Manolo curled his lip scornfully and waved one hand dismissively at Booth Crowley. "Take it easy, or you'll put yourself into cardiac arrest."

Indeed, thought Theodosia. Judging from Booth Crowley's beet-red face and frantic antics, it looked as though he might go into cardiac arrest at any moment. She wasn't sure she'd ever seen anyone quite so worked up. Booth Crowley was putting on a rather amazing show. And in front of the church at that.

"Do you know the fellow Crowley's yelling at?" asked Drayton, mildly amused by the whole spectacle.

"That's Billy Manolo," replied Theodosia.

Drayton's eyebrows shot sky high. "You *do* know him?"

"Met him," said Theodosia. "He apparently works at the yacht club, taking care of the boats and doing odd jobs, I guess."

The three of them watched Billy Manolo stalk off while Booth Crowley continued to rage at no one in particular.

"So that's the Booth Crowley who's a major donor to the symphony *and* the art museum *and* the hospital," commented Drayton. "He doesn't *look* like a mover and a shaker. Well, maybe shaking mad."

"Ssh, Drayton, he's heading this way," cautioned Theodosia.

Booth Crowley looked like a furnace that had been stoked too high. He strode across the green lawn purposefully, both arms pumping furiously at his sides, his nostrils flared, his mouth gaping for air.

"You . . . Tidwell," Booth Crowley hollered. "A word with you."

Tidwell stood silently, a look of benign amusement on his jowly face.

Booth Crowley came puffing over to Tidwell. "I want you to keep an eye on that one." Booth Crowley gestured wildly at the empty street behind him. "Billy Manolo. Works at the yacht club. Things have been missing. Manager had to dress him down last week, threatened to fire him if things don't improve. Boy is a hoodlum. No good."

Theodosia stifled a grin and wondered if Booth Crowley's sentence structures were always this staccato and devoid of nouns and prepositions. A strange man. With a strange way of talking, too.

Drayton put a hand on Theodosia's arm and began to steer her away from Tidwell and Booth Crowley. Crowley had eased back on the throttle a bit but was still sputtering. Tidwell was nodding mildly, listening to him but not really favoring Booth Crowley with his complete and undivided attention.

"Exit, stage left," Drayton murmured under his breath.

"I agree," said Theodosia. "But first . . ." Theodosia turned her focus on the bank of memorial wreaths she'd been studying earlier. *Where is that wreath?* she wondered. There was one composed of only greenery and purple leaves that had caught her eye earlier. *Ah, here it is.* She reached out and plucked a cluster of leaves from it even as Drayton propelled her away from one of the strangest memorial services she'd ever witnessed.

"What are you up to with that?" he asked.

Theodosia fingered the snippet of leaves. "They're from the wreath that was sent by Lizbeth Cantrell."

"Good Lord, you're not serious. She sent a wreath and her brother is the prime murder suspect?"

"I promised to help her," said Theodosia.

Drayton peered at her. "You did?" He shook his head. "You never fail to amaze me."

"Do you know what this is? The greenery, I mean."

Drayton pulled his half glasses from his jacket pocket and slid them onto his nose. "Coltsfoot," he declared. "I'm awfully sure it's coltsfoot."

"What a strange thing to use for a memorial wreath. It's not all that attractive," Theodosia mused. "Maybe that's why Lizbeth chose it. She was making a statement. Or anti-statement."

"It's more likely she chose it for the symbolism," said Drayton.

Now it was Theodosia's turn to give Drayton a strange look. "What symbolism might that be?"

"Coltsfoot represents justice," said Drayton.

"Justice," repeated Theodosia, now highly intrigued by Lizbeth Cantrell's use of symbolism.

"It seems to me that more and more people are paying attention to certain symbols or talismans," said Drayton. "I think it's a symptom of unsettled times."

"I think you may be right," said Theodosia.

❧ 14 ❧

"*What do you* think this could be?" asked Theodosia. They had waited until late in the afternoon when the tea shop was finally empty before they brought out the tablecloth. Drayton had fished it out of the trunk of his Volvo, and now they were staring at the stains and splotches that traced irregular patterns across what had once been pristine linen.

"Yuck," said Haley. "It's blood. What else would it be?"

"No, look here." Theodosia scratched at a brownish gray stain with her fingernail. "It could be powder marks," she said. "Gunpowder."

"Perhaps," said Drayton with a frown. Using the borrowed

magnifying glass, he studied the tablecloth carefully. "What about some variety of seaweed?" he proposed. "One end of it did end up dragging in Charleston Harbor. Isn't there some kind of microorganism that might have washed over it and caused this mottled effect?

"You mean like plankton?" asked Haley. She had quizzed the two of them at length about the funeral, then listened with rapt attention as they told their story of the raging Booth Crowley and the disdainful Billy Manolo.

"Well, it *could* be," replied Drayton, not entirely convinced by his own theory.

"What about schmutz?" countered Haley.

They both stared at her.

"You know," said Haley. "Dirt, pollution, oil . . . schmutz."

"Should the EPA ever offer you a position," Drayton told her, "I'd advise you to turn them down."

"All right, smarty, what do you think it is?" she said. "The darn thing slid onto the ground, some poor guy bled all over it, and then it knocked around in your trunk for a few days. Anything could have gotten on it."

"Whatever's on this tablecloth is from the picnic and not my trunk," replied Drayton. "But, like Theodosia, I'm getting more and more fascinated." He favored Theodosia with a serious look. "I do think you're on to something." He pulled a handkerchief from his pocket and cleaned his glasses. "You're still adamantly against mentioning anything about this to Tidwell?"

"Absolutely," said Theodosia. "I'm sure he's running his own investigation. For all we know, he could have an entire team of forensic experts poring over Oliver Dixon's clothing right now." She gave a sharp nod, as if to punctuate her sentence, then momentarily shifted her attention from the tablecloth to the printouts of the picnic photos. She had laid them out on the table earlier and was now sifting through them, still hoping to piece together some answers.

Haley picked up one of the printouts. "Who's this guy?" she asked.

Drayton peered at the photo. "That's Billy Manolo, the fellow we saw getting chewed out this morning by Booth Crowley."

"Hmm," mused Haley. "He looks kind of tough. You know, work-with-your-bare-hands kind of tough."

"He's the one who set up the table and borrowed the tablecloth," said Theodosia.

"So he handled the box with the pistol in it," said Haley.

Theodosia thought about it. "Probably. Then again, several people did. Booth Crowley, the fellow Bob Brewster, who Tidwell told us did the actual loading of the gun, and probably a few people at the clubhouse."

"How about Oliver Dixon's two sons, Brock and Quaid?" said Drayton.

"You don't think they wanted to do away with their own father, do you?" asked Haley.

"I don't know," said Theodosia slowly. Brock and Quaid didn't seem like viable suspects, certainly not as viable as Doe. On the other hand, Billy Manolo could be in the running, too. He had, after all, been seen handling the box that contained the mysterious exploding pistol.

Could he have tampered with the pistol? she wondered. Billy certainly would have had easy access. He worked at the clubhouse and did maintenance on the boats. It's possible he could have resented Oliver Dixon for any number of reasons. They could have had an argument or some misunderstanding. Of course, the big question was, why had Billy Manolo shown up at Oliver Dixon's funeral at all? Had he come to gloat? Or simply to mourn?

Theodosia reached out with both hands, pulled all the printouts to her, tamped them into one neat stack like a deck of playing cards.

One thing she knew for certain. She had to get this tablecloth analyzed.

"Theodosia," said Drayton in a cautionary tone, "if this should lead to something more, I don't want you to put yourself in harm's way. A man has been killed. What we all took to be an accident, what the *police* took to be an accident, could just be a clever charade."

"Maybe I need to speak with Timothy Neville again," said Theodosia.

"He knows more about antique pistols than anyone I know," agreed Drayton.

And so does Ford Cantrell, interestingly enough, thought Theodosia.

"Hey, give me that!" Haley suddenly snatched the tablecloth from where it lay balled up on the table. "Turn those printouts over," she ordered as she suddenly caught sight of a familiar face outside the window. "Delaine is heading for the door!" Haley warned as she scrambled for the back room.

Theodosia flipped the printouts facedown in a mad rush and flutter as Delaine Dish pushed through the door of the Indigo Tea Shop.

"Theodosia, Drayton, I'm so glad you're both still here, I have the most wonderful news," she gushed.

"What's that, Delaine?" said Theodosia. She put a hand to her chest to calm her beating heart.

"Alicia Abbot's seal point Siamese had kittens a few weeks ago, and she's giving me one!"

"That's wonderful, Delaine." Theodosia knew that when Delaine's ancient calico cat, Calvin, died almost a year ago, Delaine had been bereft. It had taken her a long time to get over Calvin's death.

"What are you going to call him? Or is it a her?" asked Haley as she emerged from the back, empty-handed now.

"It's a little boy kitty," smiled Delaine. "And I haven't settled on a name yet. Maybe Calvin II?"

"Catchy," said Haley.

"Or Calvin Deux," added Drayton, giving Haley a cautionary look as he scooped up the printouts and headed for Theodosia's office in back.

"Maybe I'll just call him Deux," said Delaine. "I don't know. What do you think, Theodosia? You were in advertising. You used to come up with names for all those products. And you dream up such wonderful names for all your teas." Delaine moved across the tea shop and peered at a row of silver tea canisters. She began reading off labels. "Copper River Cranberry, Tea Thymes, Lemon Zest, Black Frost . . ."

So that's what this is all about, thought Theodosia. *Naming her cat.*

"Let me think about it," said Theodosia. "I'll knock it around with Drayton, too. He's really good at that kind of thing," she added, noting that Haley had to clap a hand over her mouth to stifle a chuckle.

But Delaine wasn't ready to leave just yet. She hung around the tea shop, finally forcing Haley to offer her a cup of tea and a shortbread cookie.

"It's nice you can be gone from your store so long," said Haley.

"Oh, Janine's taking care of things. Besides, business is slow today. I think it's fixing to storm. The sky was so blue this morning, and now it's starting to cloud up." She wrinkled her nose. "I hope it's not going to rain. My hair will frizz."

"Mine, too," remarked Haley, patting her stick-straight brown locks. "Theo, you went to the service this morning, right?"

"Yes, Delaine."

"Heard anything more about that awful Cantrell fellow?"

"Just that he's turned his plantation into a hunting preserve."

"A *hunting* preserve? That sounds awful," said Delaine. "Killing poor, defenseless animals." She shuddered. "That's a terrible thing. Makes a person upset just hearing about it."

Theodosia smiled sympathetically, but she also knew that many Southerners grew up with a shotgun clutched in their hot little hands. Shooting varmints was a rite of passage in the South. She'd certainly done it herself and, while she no longer chose to hunt, she wasn't about to condemn those who did.

"Besides," said Delaine, still outraged at Ford Cantrell's new enterprise, "isn't that a concept at odds with itself? Hunting and *preserve?*"

"Like educational TV," said Haley. "No such thing, really."

"Or army intelligence," added Delaine, with a giggle. "Oh, ladies, I could sit here and chat for hours, but I really have to get back to the store now."

"Bye, Delaine," said Theodosia.

"Whew," said Haley after she'd left. "That lady can really take it out of you."

15

Rain spattered down in oversized droplets, drumming on roofs and turning city streets and sidewalks into miniature levees. Colorful horse-drawn carriages that plied the markets, antique district, and historic sites were abandoned as tourists sought shelter by the droves in shops and cafés.

From the steamed-up confines of her car, Theodosia punched in the phone number for the tea shop.

Drayton picked up on the second ring. "Indigo Tea Shop, Drayton speaking."

"Drayton? It's Theodosia. How are things going?" Theodosia had decided she'd better check in and make sure everything was running smoothly at the tea shop. Now she held her cell phone up to her ear while she drove one-handed through the pelting rain. It wasn't easy. Her defrosters didn't seem to be doing the job, the Jeep's windshield was hopelessly fogged, and traffic was in a nasty snarl.

"We're busy," said Drayton. "Lots of tourists trying to wait out the storm, but nothing we can't handle. Where are you? Better yet, are you coming in?"

But Theodosia had one thing on her mind. "Drayton, remember Haley's schmutz?" she asked excitedly.

"The tablecloth," Drayton said with an edge to his voice. "Oh dear, I was afraid that's what your little errand was about." He sighed disapprovingly. "What exactly did you do with the ghastly thing?"

"Remember Professor Morrow?"

"Morrow . . . Morrow . . . the botany professor at the University of Charleston?"

"That's the one."

"As I recall, you spoke quite highly of him when you took his classes. Back when you were still a tea initiate."

"He's agreed to analyze the tablecloth," said Theodosia. There was a note of triumph in her voice.

"What has poor Morrow gotten himself into?" asked Drayton. "Did you persuade him to turn his botany lab into a crime lab?"

"No, but he's got the same electron microscopes and apparatus for analyzing bits of metal or soil samples that a crime lab does. Let's just say I'm curious about whether what's on that tablecloth is animal, vegetable, or mineral."

"And poor, unsuspecting Professor Morrow has agreed to do this for you?"

"Yes, of course."

"Let's hope he doesn't lose his tenure over this," said Drayton.

"That's being a trifle overdramatic, don't you think?"

"Overdramatic, my dear Theodosia, is looking for murder at every twist and turn."

"Drayton, I knew this call would cheer me up. Oh, would you look at that!"

"Theodosia, please tell me you didn't sideswipe someone," Drayton cried with alarm.

"Hang on a minute." There was silence for a few moments, then Theodosia came back on the line. "You know where George Street crosses King Street?"

"Yes," said Drayton. "Of course."

"I just passed Loard Antiquarian Shop. I'm going to run in. Pay Giovanni Loard a surprise visit. Do a little snooping."

"*Then* you'll be back?"

"Yes . . . no . . . I don't know."

"Well, when you see Giovanni, tell him my friend authenticated the teapot. Definitely an Edgefield, estimated worth between eight and twelve hundred."

"Okay, Drayton. Bye."

Theodosia came around the block again, swerved across a lane of traffic, and headed, nose first, into a vacant parking space. It was pure impulse that had made her decide to stop in and pay Giovanni Loard a visit. And luck, she noted, that the rain had let up slightly, allowing her a chance to make a mad dash from her Jeep to the antique shop.

Loard Antiquarian Shop was one of over three-dozen antique shops in a two-block area. Situated on the first floor of a three-story Italianate redbrick building, the large front display window was filled with seventeenth- and eighteenth-century English furniture as well as a tasty selection of majolica, pewter, and antique clocks. The name, Loard Anti- quarian Shop, was painted prominently on the window in ornate gold script.

Giovanni Loard looked up hopefully as the bell over the front door rang merrily. He had been touting the merits of an antique brass spyglass to a woman from West Ashley for almost half an hour now, and she still showed no hint of wanting to buy. The woman had come in searching for a "fun" anniversary gift for her stockbroker husband and had alternately been captivated by an antique clock, a carved wooden box and, finally, the brass spyglass.

Business had been slow lately, and the brass spyglass, purchased at an estate sale in Summerville for 85 dollars, would yield a tasty profit with its new price tag of 450 dollars.

When Giovanni recognized Theodosia, a smile creased his handsome face.

"Miss Browning," he called out. "Be with you in a moment."

Giovanni turned back to the lady from West Ashley. "Perhaps you want to think it over." He reached for the brass spyglass, but the woman, sensing another customer behind her, a customer who perhaps might be interested in the very same piece, suddenly made up her mind.

"I'll take it," she declared. "It's perfect."

Giovanni nodded. "An excellent choice, ma'am. I'm sure your husband will be thoroughly delighted."

Giovanni accepted the woman's MasterCard and zipped it through his machine. *What luck,* he thought to himself, *that Theodosia Browning walked in when she did.* So often, customers were pushed into purchasing when it became apparent they would no longer enjoy a shopkeeper's undivided attention.

While Giovanni finished up with his customer, Theodosia wandered about the shop. She paused to admire a small collection of Coalport porcelain and a tray of vintage watches. It was a nice enough shop, she decided, but the inventory seemed a trifle thin. *Hard times?* she wondered. *Or just an owner who preferred a few tasty items to the usual overdone pastiche of furniture, silver, rugs, candlesticks, and porcelains?* On the other hand, in a town that was almost wall-to-wall antique shops, it must be awfully hard to remain competitive.

"Hello again." Giovanni Loard turned his hundred-watt smile on Theodosia once he'd shown his customer to the door.

"I was just driving past and spotted your sign," said Theodosia. "I decided this was the day to come in and look at those paintings I've heard so much about."

"For that special wall," he said.

"Exactly," said Theodosia, smiling back at him and wondering why she suddenly felt like she was playing a role in a drawing room comedy.

Giovanni Loard beckoned with an index finger. "Back here," he told her. "In my office."

Theodosia followed him obediently to the back of the store, waited as he unlatched a door, then stepped into a small wood-paneled office.

"Wow," was all she said.

The office was relatively small, perhaps twelve by fifteen feet, but its walls were covered with gleaming oil paintings. There were portraits, landscapes, seascapes, and still lifes. Some were dreamy and ethereal, others were incredibly realistic. All were exceedingly well done.

"What a lovely collection. Why don't you have some of these paintings on display in your shop?" she asked.

He shrugged with what seemed feigned indifference. "Once in a while I do," he said, and reached forward to straighten a small landscape painting that was slightly crooked. "But mostly, I keep them in here to admire for myself. And to save the very best pieces for special customers.

"This one . . ." Giovanni extended an arm pointed toward a small gem of a portrait. "This one reminds me of you."

Theodosia gazed at the painting, mindful of Giovanni's gaze upon her. The painting was of a woman in a full-skirted, corseted dress reclining on a chaise. The style invoked the antebellum period and the predominant colors were muted pinks and purples, with alabaster skin tones.

"It's beautiful," said Theodosia. The painting was a beauty, but there was an ethereal quality about it that was oddly disquieting.

"Thank you for coming to the funeral yesterday," Giovanni said, changing the subject abruptly. "I saw you during the service, but with everyone milling about afterward, we never did get a chance to say hello."

"How is Doe holding up?" asked Theodosia.

"Better than expected," replied Giovanni. "Her friends and family are being very supportive, and she's a brave girl, although I have to say, she's feeling a tremendous amount of frustration about the ineptitude and total inactivity of the police. They've gone absolutely nowhere in their investigation."

"Is there somewhere to go?" asked Theodosia.

Giovanni lifted an eyebrow. "They took Ford Cantrell in for questioning."

"I take it you're fairly convinced that Ford Cantrell somehow tampered with the pistol?" said Theodosia.

"Yes, I am," said Giovanni. "I simply don't believe it was an accident."

"Could someone else have tampered with it?"

Giovanni frowned as though the idea had never occurred to him. "I can't think of another soul who would have wanted to harm Oliver Dixon."

"Oliver Dixon was heavily involved in a new start-up company," said Theodosia. "There could have been someone who did not want him to succeed."

"I see what you mean," said Giovanni. "Oliver was a truly brilliant and gifted man. The ideas he was bringing to Grapevine would have helped revolutionize how people use PDAs." He paused. "Or so I'm told.

I, unfortunately, function at a relatively low technology level. The fax machine is about the most I can manage," he added ruefully.

"But it sounds like there was a tremendous amount at stake," said Theodosia. "Competition in business has been known to trigger volatile deeds. A fearful competitor, angry supplier, skittish investor . . . any one of them could have resented Oliver Dixon mightily."

"Highly doubtful," said Giovanni. "As you may or may not know, Booth Crowley was Grapevine's major underwriter, and he's known to have an impeccable reputation around here."

"I'm sure he does," said Theodosia, wondering if Giovanni had also witnessed Booth Crowley's over-the-top display of anger yesterday. "However," she continued, "that doesn't mean someone didn't have it in personally for Oliver Dixon."

Giovanni's face clouded. "I suppose you could be right," he conceded.

"Too bad about the disturbance yesterday."

"Pardon?" said Giovanni. He'd turned his gaze toward the painting he'd indicated had reminded him so much of Theodosia.

"At the funeral. The somewhat ugly scene between Booth Crowley and a fellow named Billy Manolo. Do you know him? Billy, I mean?"

"No, not really. Well, only by reputation. Fellow does odd jobs at the yacht club, I believe."

"Do you think he could have had a grudge against Oliver Dixon?"

"I don't see how he could have," said Giovanni in a condescending tone. "I mean, the man was hired help. They didn't exactly mix on the same social level."

That's precisely the reason why Billy Manolo might carry a grudge, Theodosia thought to herself.

Giovanni drew a deep breath, let it out, concentrated on trying to refocus his energy and his smile. "Shall I hold the painting for you?" he asked brightly.

"No, I don't think so," said Theodosia.

16

"I've been watching the weather channel, and it looks like there's a storm moving in," said Jory Davis.

"There is," agreed Theodosia. After five days in New York, Jory had finally phoned her. "It's been raining all day, and everything just seems to be building in intensity. Something's definitely brewing out in the mid-Atlantic. I spoke with Drayton earlier, and he's worried sick that all the flowers will get blown about and smashed. Which means next week's Garden Fest will be an absolute bust."

Theodosia was cozied up in her apartment above the tea shop. Even though it was Friday evening, it was far too rainy and miserable to contemplate going out anywhere.

"I'm worried about my boat," said Jory. "Eldon Cook, one of my sailing buddies, went over to the Isle of Palms a couple days ago and brought it back, so it's moored at the yacht club now. But if there's an even worse storm blowing in . . ."

"What can I do to help?" offered Theodosia.

"Could you stop by my office and pick up the second set of keys? I know Eldon locked up the boat, so if you could take the keys to the yacht club and give them to Billy Manolo—"

"Billy Manolo?"

"Yeah," said Jory, "he works there. He's a kind of handyman."

"I know who he is," replied Theodosia. "I met him yesterday morning. Well, I didn't actually meet him, I saw him. At Oliver Dixon's funeral."

"Of course," said Jory. "I'd completely forgotten that the funeral was yesterday. How was it?"

"Sad," said Theodosia. "But nicely done. A lot of his friends stood up and said some wonderful things about him."

"That's good," said Jory. "Oliver deserved it."

"So take the keys to Billy and have him do what?" continued Theodosia.

"Secure the boat, turn on the bilge pump. Probably check to make sure the sails are stored properly. Your basic hurricane preparedness."

"You trust this guy to do this?"

"Yeah. Sure I do. It's his job to do this kind of stuff." Jory paused. "Is there some problem, Theo? Something I don't know about?"

"No, of course not. Don't worry about a thing," said Theodosia. "I'll take care of everything. How are things on your end? How are the depositions going?"

Jory sighed. "Slow."

Theodosia hung up the phone and peered out her kitchen window as rain thudded heavily on the roof and sloshed noisily down drain spouts. She could barely make out the little garden apartment across the cobblestone alley where Haley lived, so strong was the downpour.

Shuddering, she buttoned the top button of her chenille sweater. Charleston was usually engulfed in warm weather by now, and everyone was enjoying a lovely, languid spring before the buildup of summer's oppressive heat and humidity. But this was a whole different story: nasty weather and a chill Atlantic breeze that seemed to whip right through you.

The tea kettle on the stove began its high-pitched, wavering whistle, and Theodosia quickly snatched it from the back burner. Pouring boiling water over a teaspoon of Darjeeling, she let it steep for three minutes in the tiny one-cup teapot. It was funny, she thought, the biggest enemies of tea were air, light, heat, and dampness. And, so often, Charleston's climate offered up abundant helpings of all of these!

Theodosia retreated to her living room and stretched out on the couch. Earl Grey, already well into his evening nap, lifted his head a few inches, eyed her sleepily, and settled back down.

As Theodosia sipped her tea, she thought about Lizbeth Cantrell, the woman who had implored her for help just a few days ago.

She still didn't know why she'd promised Lizbeth that she'd try to clear Ford Cantrell's name. After all, she was the one who'd been suspicious of Ford in the first place.

She supposed it was the connection between Lizbeth Cantrell and her mother that had triggered her answer. The bittersweet flood of memories had been a strange, slightly mind-altering experience.

And, deep down, she knew that she also felt beholden to Lizbeth. In the South, with its curious code of honor, when you were beholden to someone, you helped them out when they needed you. No questions asked.

But what would she do if she couldn't keep her promise to Lizbeth?

What if more investigating proved that Ford Cantrell really had tampered with that old pistol? Ford was, after all, the one with an extensive gun collection. So he had expertise when it came to antique weapons. And the man had recently turned his plantation into a hunting preserve. She wasn't exactly sure what that proved, but it was the kind of thing that could carry nasty implications in court.

But Lizbeth had seemed utterly convinced of her brother's innocence. Then again, Lizbeth was a believer in signs and portents. Like the wreath of coltsfoot. What was it supposed to symbolize again? Oh, yes, justice.

And exactly what justice had Lizbeth been making reference to? Theodosia wondered. *Justice for her brother, Ford Cantrell? Or the type of justice that might have already been meted out against Oliver Dixon?*

Theodosia stared at the bone china cup that held her tea. She had begun collecting individual coffee, tea, and demitasse cups long before she'd opened the tea shop. She'd found that when she set her table for a dinner party, it was fun to arrange it with mismatched pieces, pairing, for example, a Limoges plate with a Lilique cup and saucer.

Now the information she'd managed to collect so far on the people surrounding Oliver Dixon also seemed like mismatched pieces. But unlike the eclectic table settings her guests often raved over, none of these pieces seemed to fit together.

Theodosia stood, stretched, and tried to shake off the chill. She'd been avoiding turning on the heat—it seemed kind of silly to still be using heat in April—but her apartment felt like it was growing colder by the minute.

Relenting, Theodosia walked across the room and flipped the lever on the thermostat. She was immediately rewarded by an electrical hum followed by a small puff of warm air.

Okay, she asked herself, *what am I missing?* She stood, staring at the droplets of water that streamed down the outside of the windows, reminding her of tears. Like Doe's tears for her dead husband, Oliver Dixon?

She believed fervently that Oliver Dixon was more than just the victim; he was also the linchpin in all this. If she could figure out why someone wanted Oliver out of the way, she could establish motive.

And when you found motive, you usually found the murderer.

Theodosia went to her computer and sat down. She had looked at the financial and start-up information on Oliver Dixon's new company, Grapevine, and nothing seemed particularly out of the ordinary. They'd spent a lot of money on research and development, but that was fairly typical. And because Grapevine was a start-up high-tech company, their burn rate, or rate of spending for the first few months, had been high but certainly not unexpected.

She wondered what the media had written about Grapevine. Haley had quoted from an article in the business section of the *Post and Courier.* But, from the rah-rah sound of it, the article had probably been reedited from a press release that the company itself had prepared. That was usually how those things worked. Lord knows, over the years she herself had written enough press releases that got turned into newspaper articles or sidebars in trade publications.

But what had the hard-nosed business analysts said about Grapevine? The techie guys from Forrester or the business mavens at Arthur Andersen? Or even the reviewers at some of the vertical trade pubs?

Easy enough to check, she thought, as she clicked on Netscape and typed in the key word "Grapevine."

Forty-seven thousand hits came up for Grapevine, everything from rock bands to a restaurant in Napa Valley. *Oops. Definitely got to narrow the search,* Theodosia decided.

Now she added the term PDA to the search parameter. That yielded sixty-three hits. Far more manageable.

Theodosia scanned down her new list of hits, searching for a company profile, analyst's report, anything that might give her an outsider's snapshot view of Grapevine.

She clicked open an article from *Technology Voyage*, a well-respected publication that reported on new products and trends in E-commerce and provided top-line analyses of various new high-tech companies. She had actually placed advertising in *Technology Voyage* and met with its editors when she worked on the Avanti account, a company that manufactured semiconductors.

The *Technology Voyage* article was titled "PDAs on the Fast Track." It began with a good overview of the PDA market. Sales were erupting, topping three billion dollars with projections of more than six billion dollars by next year. And just as Haley had said, PDAs were touted as portable, pocket-sized devices that let you magically keep track of appointments, addresses, phone numbers, to-do lists, and personal notes. More full-featured PDAs could even be used to send and receive E-mail, surf the Internet, or support digital cameras.

The article went on to list the various PDA manufacturers, manufacturers of PDA applications, chips and inner workings, and PDA wireless service and content providers.

According to the article, Grapevine was a manufacturer of flash memory cards, thirty-two and sixty-four-megabyte SD cards for storing data in those PDAs that used the Palm operating system.

Wow, thought Theodosia. *What with working on computers, setting up a Web site, and trading stocks on-line, I'm fairly well versed in technology, but this is getting slightly complicated!*

The article went on to list the burgeoning number of PDA manufacturers that included such companies as Casio, IBM, Hewlett-Packard, Royal, Compaq, and Handspring, and briefly detailed Microsoft's competing operating system, Pocket PC.

Theodosia put two fingers to her forehead, kneaded gently at the beginnings of a techno headache. Better to quit while she was ahead? She scanned the rest of the article quickly, then became caught up again. As she read the "Editors Choice" thumbnail sketches of several different PDAs, she wondered how she'd ever gotten along without a Blackberry to deliver wireless E-mails. Then she changed her mind in favor of an Ericsson that boasted handwriting and voice recognition. And finally, Theodosia decided the daVinci, with its tiny folding keyboard, had to be the slickest thing yet.

Would one of these minicomputers work for her? Perhaps so. A whiz-bang PDA might help her keep better track of all manner of things. Tea party commitments, shopping lists and—she pulled her face into a wry grin—a list of murder suspects? She shook her head. Time to give it a rest. She was starting to obsess, and that wasn't good. That wasn't good at all.

❧ 17 ❧

"*Haley, where are* the tea candles?" barked Drayton.

"Top shelf," she called from the kitchen.

"Not the colored ones, I want the beeswax candles in the little Chinese blue and white containers." Drayton stood behind the counter, frowning, studying the floor-to-ceiling shelves.

"Bottom shelf," came Haley's voice again. "On the left."

Mumbling to himself, Drayton bent down and began pulling rolls of blue tissue paper, small blue shopping bags, and corrugated gift boxes from the cupboard in a mad rush to find his candles.

"Stop it." Haley, ever vigilant and slightly phobic about tidiness, appeared behind him and admonished him sharply. "You're getting everything all catawampus."

She knelt down. "Better let me do it," she said in a kinder tone.

Opening the cupboard door on the far left, she pulled out the candles Drayton had been searching for. "Here," she said as she put two boxes into his outstretched hands. "Candles. Far *left*."

"Thank you," Drayton said sheepishly. "Guess I really am in a twitter today."

"You got that right," Haley grumped as she stuffed everything back into the cupboard. "Good thing this mystery tea thing isn't a weekly event. I'd be a wreck. We'd all be a wreck."

"Who's a wreck?" asked Theodosia as she let herself in the front door.

"Drayton is," joked Haley. "In his sublime paranoia to keep everything a secret, he's ending up doing most of the prep work himself. Although he has *deigned* to allow me to bake a few of his menu items," she added with a wicked grin.

"Like what?" asked Theodosia. "I'm in the dark as much as you are," she explained as she slipped off her light coat and shook raindrops from it.

"Oh, let's see," said Haley. "*Cannelles de Bordeaux, croquets aux pignons*, and *fougasse*. Which is really just pastry, cookies, and breads. Except when you say it in French, it sounds exquisite. Of course, anything said in French sounds exquisite. A case in point: *boudin noir*."

"What's that?" asked Theodosia.

"Blood sausage," replied Haley.

Drayton rolled his eyes. "A bit bizarre for one of my teas," he declared as his eyes went to his watch, a classic Piaget that seemed to perpetually run a few minutes late. "Haley, it's almost nine. Better unlock the door."

"Theodosia already did," Haley shot back, then threw Theodosia a questioning glance. "You did, didn't you?" she whispered.

Theodosia gave a quick nod.

"I heard that, Haley," said Drayton.

"I don't know how many customers we'll have today," said Theodosia. "It's still raining like crazy out there."

"Oh, there'll be a few brave souls who'll come out to tromp the historic district," said Drayton. "And when they find their way to us, there's a good chance they'll be hungry."

"And cold," added Haley as she gave a little shiver.

"Right," agreed Drayton. "Which is why you better get back there and finish your baking," said Drayton.

"You don't need me to help out here? Set tables and things?"

"I'll set the tables and brew the teas, you just tend to baking."

"Okay," Haley agreed happily.

Standing at the cash register, fussing with an arrangement of tea canisters, Theodosia was aware, once again, of how much she loved their mix of personalities and the easy bantering that went on among the three of them. Anyone else walking in might think they were being slightly argumentative, but she knew it was the unrestrained familiarity that was usually reserved just for family members. Yes, they joked and pushed one another at times, but at the first sign that someone was feeling slightly overwhelmed or even provoked, they rallied to that person's defense.

The door flew open, and cold, moist air rushed in. A bulky man in a nondescript gray raincoat lowered his umbrella and peered at them.

"Detective Tidwell," Theodosia greeted him as she closed the door quickly and ushered him to a table. "You're out and about early. And on a Saturday yet."

"Tea?" offered Drayton as he approached Tidwell with a freshly brewed pot of Kandoli Garden Assam.

Tidwell lowered himself into a chair and nodded. "Thank you. Yes."

Drayton poured a cup of tea, then stroked his chin thoughtfully. "Perhaps I'm being presumptuous, Detective Tidwell, but you look like a man who might possibly be in need of a Devonshire split."

Tidwell's beady eyes gleamed with anticipation. "Pray tell, what is a Devonshire split?"

"A traditional little English sweet bun that we serve with strawberry jam. Of course, if we were in England's lake country, we would also serve it with clotted cream."

"Pretend that we are," Tidwell said. "Especially in light of this hideous wet weather."

Slipping into the chair across from Tidwell, Theodosia studied the man carefully. Tidwell had obviously come here bearing some type of information. Would he be forthright in telling her what was on his mind?

Of course not. That wasn't Tidwell's style. He preferred to play his own maddening little games.

But today Tidwell surprised Theodosia. For, once his pastry and accompaniments arrived, he became quite talkative.

"We've finished most of our ballistics tests," he told her. "Regretfully, nothing's jumped out at us." Tidwell sliced his Devonshire split in half, peered at it expectantly. "At first we thought the bullets in the pistol might have been dumdums."

"What exactly are dumdums?" asked Theodosia. She'd heard the term before, but had no idea what dumdums really were.

"A nasty little trick that originated in India," said Tidwell as he lathered clotted cream onto his pastry. "Put succinctly, dumdums are expanding bullets. When they impact something, they expand."

"And you thought these tricky little bullets might have impacted Oliver Dixon's head?" she said.

"Well, not exactly," said Tidwell. "The pistol would have to have been pointed directly at him for that to occur. And from everything we know, from interviews with fairly reliable people, Oliver Dixon was holding the pistol at shoulder level and pointing it up into the air. If it had been loaded with dumdums, they could have exploded and dealt a fatal wound, but something would've been needed to make them explode."

"So your tests revealed nothing," said Theodosia.

Tidwell took a sip of tea and set his tea cup down with a gentle clink. "Let's just say our tests were inconclusive."

"What about Oliver Dixon's jacket?" asked Theodosia. "I would imagine you ran forensic tests on that?"

Tidwell sighed. "Spatters of blood, type B positive, which is somewhat rare, maybe only ten percent of the population. Definitely belonging to Oliver Dixon, though; we checked it against his medical records. On the sleeves and jacket front, residue from Charleston Harbor showing a high nutrient concentration and a low N-P ratio. And a small amount of imbedded dirt. Probably from the shore."

Theodosia thought about the blood-spattered, dirt-smeared linen tablecloth that now resided in Professor Morrow's botany lab. "Probably," she agreed, trying to keep any sign of nervousness from her voice. If Tidwell knew what she was up to, she'd be in deep trouble, and the table-cloth would undoubtedly be confiscated by the police.

They both fell silent as the front door opened with a whoosh and two couples, obviously tourists, pushed their way in.

"Can we get some coffee and muffins?" asked one of the men. He wore a yellow slicker and spoke with a Midwesterner's flat accent.

Theodosia was up and out of her chair in a heartbeat. "How about tea and blackberry scones?" she invited. "Or a plate of lemon tarts?"

"Tea," mused the man. He turned to the rest of his party, who were all nodding agreeably, pulling off wet outerwear and settling into chairs. "Why not," he said, "as long as it's hot and strong."

Tidwell sat at his table, happily sipping tea and eating his pastry while Theodosia and Drayton quickly served the new customers.

Like many tourists who wandered into the Indigo Tea Shop, they seemed eager to embrace what would be a new experience for them.

On the other hand, Theodosia had to remind herself that, after water, tea was the most popular drink in the world, a much-loved, long-established beverage that had been around almost 5,000 years. Sipped, savored, or tossed back hastily, the peoples of the world consumed more than 700 billion cups of tea in a single year.

"Detective Tidwell." Theodosia put her hands on the back of one of the creaky, wooden chairs and leaned toward him. "Do you remember the fellow who was involved in the terrible scene at Oliver Dixon's funeral the day before yesterday?"

"You mean Booth Crowley?" he asked.

"No, I mean Billy Manolo," she said. *Do not allow him to fluster you*, she cautioned herself. *The man is obstinate only because he relishes it as great sport.*

"You realize that Billy Manolo works at the yacht club," she said. "He had access to the pistol."

"Of course he did," said Tidwell. "In fact, his fingertips were found on the rosewood box that the pistol was kept in."

"What do you make of that?" asked Theodosia.

Tidwell shrugged. "A half-dozen other sets of fingerprints were also found on that box."

"Was Ford Cantrell's among them?" she asked.

"Do you really think Ford Cantrell would be foolish enough to leave his prints on the box if, in fact, he tampered with the pistol?" asked Tidwell. He picked up a silver spoon, scooped up yet another lump of sugar, and plunked it into his teacup.

Theodosia stared at Tidwell. *He has a unique talent for deflecting questions,* she decided. *And answering questions with another question designed to throw you slightly off track.*

"I take it you have elevated Billy Manolo to suspect status?" said Tidwell.

"The notion of Billy as suspect is not without basis," said Theodosia.

Tidwell shook his great head slowly. "Doubtful. Highly doubtful. Billy Manolo seems like a troublemaker, I'll grant you that. And he has a past history of being involved in petty thievery and nefarious dealings. But is our Billy cool enough, calculating enough, to plan and execute a murder? In front of two hundred people? I hardly see even a flash of that type of required brilliance. I fear Billy Manolo exhibits only limited capacity."

Theodosia knew what was coming and steeled herself for it. She had sent Tidwell careening down this path, and she regretted it mightily. To make matters worse, her commitment to Lizbeth Cantrell felt pitifully hollow, as though there wasn't a prayer in the world that her brother's name could be cleared.

"Ford Cantrell, on the other hand, is a man with a grudge," continued Tidwell. "A man who manufacturers his own munitions. Yes," Tidwell reiterated when he saw Theodosia's eyes go large, "Ford Cantrell makes a hobby of packing gunpowder into his own cartridges. If anyone knew how to rig that old pistol to explode, it would be someone with the critical knowledge that Ford Cantrell possesses. I am confident of a forthcoming arrest."

18

A lone tern rode the crazed thermals, wheeling high above the yacht club where J-24s, Columbias, and San Jose 25s creaked up against silvered wooden pilings and tugged at their moorings as they pitched about in the roiling sea. The only sound, save the howling wind, was a sputtering bilge pump, somewhere out on the end of the long main pier.

Nobody home, thought Theodosia as she cinched her trench coat tighter about her and stepped onto the pier. In some places, the weather-beaten boards had two-inch gaps between them, so she had to really watch her footing. There didn't appear to be anybody on this long, wet pier today, and the water looked cold and unforgiving. A misstep was unthinkable.

She'd first tried the door to the clubhouse and found that locked. Even pounding on the door and punching the doorbell hadn't roused anyone. It was conceivable no one was here at all, that Billy Manolo didn't work on Saturday or hadn't come in because of bad weather or might be planning to show up later.

Theodosia did hold out a faint hope that someone might be hunkered down on the sailboat at the far end of the pier where the bilge pump sounded so noisily. It could be Billy Manolo, she mused, pumping out a leaky boat, working down below, trying to elude the wind's nasty bite.

Halfway to the end of the pier, Theodosia gazed out toward Charleston Harbor. Only two ships were visible through the gray mist. One appeared to be a commercial fishing vessel; the other looked like a Coast Guard cutter, probably from the nearby Coast Guard station located just down from The Battery at the mouth of the Ashley River. It certainly was a far cry from almost a week ago, when the harbor had been dotted with boats, when the promise of spring had hung in the air.

"Anybody there?" She reached the end of the pier and saw that the pump was running full tilt, pouring a steady spew of frothy green water from a twenty-five-foot Santana into the harbor. She stepped down to the smaller pier that ran parallel to the moored boat. These side piers weren't anchored by deep pilings like the main pier. Instead, they floated on top of barrels. Now, with the wind whipping in from the Atlantic at a good ten knots, the smaller, auxiliary pier pitched about precariously.

"Billy?" Theodosia called, fighting the rising panic that was beginning to build inside her as the small pier bobbed like an errant cork.

Get a grip, she admonished herself as she extended both arms out to her sides for better balance, then picked her way carefully back to the safety of the main pier. *You've walked up and down piers your whole life. This is no time to get spooked.*

Jory Davis's boat was moored at slip 112, more than halfway back in the direction of the clubhouse, with side piers that were considerably more stable since they were sheltered. Theodosia walked out to *Rubicon*, the J-24 that he loved to pilot around Charleston Harbor and up and down the Intracoastal Waterway, put her hands on the side hull, and clambered aboard. Standing in the cockpit, she felt the rhythm of the boat, heard the noisy overhead clank of halyards against the mast. She leaned forward, stuck the key in the lock for the hatch, and turned it. Grabbing the handle, she braced herself and tugged it open.

Theodosia peered down into the boat. Jory had been right. *Rubicon* was seriously taking on water. At least three inches of green seawater had managed to seep inside and was sloshing around.

She searched for a bilge pump, found one, then wasn't exactly sure how to connect the darn thing and get it started.

No, she finally told herself, *leave well enough alone.* The best thing to do was follow Jory's advice. Find Billy Manolo and have him take care of this.

Still crouched on the deck, Theodosia searched for a clue that might tell her how to get in touch with the elusive Billy Manolo.

Flipping open one of the small storage bins, she found a clear plastic pouch that contained the boat's user manual and a clutch of maps. Following her hunch, she unsnapped the pouch and rummaged through the papers.

On the inside cover of the user manual was a hand-written list of names. The fourth one down was Billy M. There was a phone number listed and an address: 115 Concannon.

Could this be Billy Manolo? The yacht club's Billy Manolo? Had to be.

❧ 19 ❧

Upriver, on the west bank of the Cooper River, sits the now-defunct Charleston Naval Base. Decommissioned some ten years ago, it is technically situated in North Charleston, an incorporated city of its own and the third-largest city in South Carolina.

With sailors and officers gone, the economy forever changed, real estate had become more affordable, zoning more forgiving.

Theodosia drove slowly down Ardmore Street, searching each street sign for the cross street, Concannon. Here was an older part of Charleston, but not the part that showed up in glossy four-color brochures sent out by the Convention & Visitors Bureau. Instead, these small, wood-frame houses looked tired and battered, many in dire need of a coat of paint. Yards were small, often with more bare patches than tended lawn. Those places that were better kept were often surrounded by metal fences.

Just past a tire recycling plant, Theodosia found Concannon Street. She made a leap of faith, put the Jeep into a right turn, and searched for numbers on the houses.

She had guessed correctly. Here was 215, here 211. Billy's home at 115 Concannon was in the next block.

A vacant, weed-filled lot bordered Billy Manolo's house, a one-story home that was little more than a cottage. Once-white paint had been ground off from years of wind, rain, and high humidity, and now the weathered wood glowed with an interesting patina. As Theodosia strode up the walk, she noted that, aside from the paint, everything else appeared sturdy and fairly well kept.

Grasping a black wrought-iron handrail, she mounted the single cement step and rang the doorbell.

Nothing.

She hit the doorbell again, held it in longer this time, and waited. Still no one came to the door. Perplexed, Theodosia stood for a moment, let her eyes wander to an overgrown hedge of dogwood, then to a small brick walkway that led around the side of the house.

Why not? she decided, as she crossed wet grass and started around the house.

It was like tumbling into another world.

Sections of beautifully ornate wrought-iron fences and grilles danced before her eyes. Elegant scrolls, whimsical corn motifs, and curling ivy adorned each piece. Wrought-iron pieces that had been completed leaned up against wood fences and the back of Billy Manolo's house. Other pieces, still raw from the welder's torch and awaiting mortises and hand finishing, were stacked in piles and seemed to occupy every square foot of the small backyard.

Sparks arced from a welder's torch in the dim recess of a sagging, dilapidated garage that appeared slightly larger than the house.

Billy Manolo lifted his welder's helmet and glared at Theodosia as blue flame licked from his torch. "What do you want?" he asked. His voice carried the same nervous hostility he'd exhibited the other day at Oliver Dixon's funeral.

Still in a state of delighted amazement, Theodosia peered past him, her eyes fixing on even more of the beautifully crafted metalwork. Most was stacked in hodgepodge piles, a few smaller pieces hung from the ceiling.

"These are wonderful," she said.

Billy Manolo shrugged as he flicked the switch on his oxyacetylene torch. "Yeah," was all he said.

"You made all these?" she asked.

Billy grunted in the affirmative. His welder's helmet quivered atop his head like the beak of a giant condor.

"They're beautifully done. Do you do a lot of restoration work?" Theodosia knew that Charleston homes, especially those in and around the historic district, were always in need of additions or repairs.

"Who wants to know?" Billy Manolo demanded.

"Sorry." She colored slightly. "I'm Theodosia Browning. We met at the picnic last Sunday? You borrowed the tablecloth from me." She moved toward him to offer her hand and almost tripped on a stack of metal bars.

"Careful," Billy cautioned. "Last thing I need around here is some fool woman falling on her face." He stared at her. "How come you came here?" he asked abruptly. "I don't keep no pictures here. You got to go to Popple Hill for that."

"Popple Hill?" said Theodosia. She had no idea what Popple Hill was or what Billy was even talking about.

"The design folks," Billy explained impatiently as though she were an idiot child. "Go talk to them. They'll figure out size and design and all. I just make the stuff." Billy Manolo shook his head as though she were a buzzing mayfly that was irritating him. He leaned forward, slid a grimy hand into a leather glove that lay atop his forge. There was a hiss of air and immediately flame shot from his welder's torch again.

"I see," said Theodosia, averting her eyes and making a mental note to ask around and find out just who these Popple Hill designers were. "Actually, I just came from the yacht club," she explained. "Jory Davis in slip one twelve wanted me to give you these." She reached into her purse, grabbed the keys, and dangled them at Billy. "The keys for *Rubicon.*"

Billy Manolo sighed, switched the torch off again.

"He wants you to turn on the bilge pump," said Theodosia, this time putting a tinge of authority into her voice. "He's stuck out of town on business, and he's afraid his boat is taking on water. Actually, it is taking on water. I was just there."

Billy Manolo pulled the welder's helmet from his head and strode toward her. He reached out and snatched the keys from her outstretched hand and stared stolidly at her.

"Great," she answered, a little too heartily. She gazed about the back-yard, realizing full well that Billy Manolo was an ironworker by trade, that he'd probably made some of the gates, grills, and balcony railings that adorned many of Charleston's finer homes.

And along with that realization came the sudden understanding that Billy Manolo, with his knowledge of metals and stress points and such, could easily have been the one who had tampered with the old pistol. Billy Manolo, whose fingerprints had certainly turned up on the rose-wood box that the old pistol had been housed in.

"Look," Theodosia said, caught somewhere between losing her patience at Billy's rudeness and a small insinuation of fear, "the very least you can do is be civil."

He tilted his head slightly, gave her a surly, one-eyed glance. "Why should I?"

Theodosia lost it. "You might want to seriously consider working on your people skills," she told him. "Because should you be questioned by the Charleston police, and the possibility is not unlikely, the inhospitable attitude you have just shown toward me will not play well with them."

Billy Manolo snorted disdainfully. "Police," he spat out. "They don't know nothin'."

"They are not unaware of your little public to-do with Booth Crowley two days ago," said Theodosia.

"Booth Crowley has a lot to hide," snarled Billy.

"From what I hear, Billy, *you* might have a few things to hide," Theodosia shot back. She was fishing, to be sure, but her words were more effective than she'd ever thought possible.

Stung by her innuendo, Billy bent down, picked up an iron rod, and glared at her dangerously. "Get lost, lady, before you find yourself floating facedown in Charleston Harbor!"

20

Dozens of small white candles flickered on every table, countertop, shelf, nook, and cranny of the Indigo Tea Shop. Muted paisley tablecloths were draped elegantly across the wooden tables, and the overhead brass chandelier had been dimmed to impart a moody aura.

"It looks like someone unleashed a crazed voodoo priestess in here," declared Haley.

"What?" Drayton's usually well-modulated voice rose in a high-pitched squawk. "It's *supposed* to look mysterious. I'm trying to create an atmosphere that's conducive to an evening of high drama and new experiences in the realm of tea."

"And it does," Theodosia assured him. "It's very atmospheric. Haley," she cautioned the young girl, "ease up on Drayton, will you? He's got a lot on his mind."

Haley's needling banter was usually welcome in the tea shop and easily parried by the often erudite Drayton, but tonight Drayton did seem a little discombobulated.

Haley sidled up to Drayton and gave him a reassuring tap on the shoulder. "Okay. It's cool."

"You *do* think the shop has a certain dramatic, stage-setting appearance, don't you?" Drayton peered anxiously at Theodosia.

"It's perfect," declared Theodosia. "Our guests will be thrilled." She gazed at the lineup of Barotine teapots borrowed from one of Drayton's antique dealer friends. The fanciful little green and brown glazed teapots were adorned with shells, twining vines, and snail-like shapes, and lent to the aura of mystery.

Then there were the centerpieces. Here again, Drayton had gotten a few choice antique pieces on loan and let Hattie Boatwright at Floradora run wild with them. An antique ceramic frog peeked from behind clusters of purple hydrangeas, a bronze sculpture of a wood nymph was surrounded by plum blossoms, a jade statue of the Buddha sat amid an artful arrangement of reeds and grasses.

"You've managed to instill elegance as well as a hint of mystery in our little tea shop," praised Theodosia, "and I, for one, can't wait to see what's going to happen tonight!"

Truth be told, Theodosia wasn't exactly sure what was going to take place, but she had complete confidence in Drayton and knew that, whatever menu and program unfolded, he'd pull it off with great style and aplomb. Besides, while she'd been out this afternoon, getting drenched at the yacht club and then insulted by Billy Manolo, four more people had called, begging for last-minute reservations. That meant they'd had to slip in extra chairs at a few of the tables.

As Theodosia laid out silverware and linen napkins, Haley placed tiny gold mesh bags at each place setting.

"What are those?" asked Theodosia.

"Favors," said Haley. "Drayton had me wrap tiny bricks of pressed tea in gold fabric, then tie them with ribbons."

"Drayton's really going all out," said Theodosia, pleased at such attention to detail.

"You don't know the half of it," whispered Haley. She glanced around to make sure Drayton was in the back of the shop. "He's got five actors from the Charleston Little Theater Group coming in tonight. They're going to do a kind of one-act play while they help serve tea and goodies. And, of course, they'll drop clues as they go along. At some point in the evening, one of them will have a mysterious and fatal accident, and the audience has to figure out who perpetrated the dastardly deed!"

"You mean like Mr. Mustard in the library with the candlestick?" asked Theodosia.

"Something very close to it," said Haley.

Drayton emerged from the back room, carrying a tray full of teacups. "Listen," he instructed, one finger aimed at the ceiling.

Theodosia and Haley stopped what they were doing and listened to gentle drumming on the roof.

"It started raining again," said Drayton. "Sets the mood perfectly, don't you think?"

"Quoth the raven . . . nevermore," giggled Haley.

Halfway through Drayton's mystery tea, Theodosia found herself perched on the wooden stool behind the counter, utterly charmed and fascinated by what was taking place before her. True to Haley's prediction, five members from the Charleston Little Theater Group, all amateurs and friends of Drayton, had shown up. Upon serving the first course, a hot and sour green tea soup, they immediately launched into a fast-paced, drawing room type play that, except for the murder, bordered heavily on comedy and kept their guests in stitches.

The audience had been swept up in the drama from the outset. Chuckling in all the right places, oohing and ahing as tiny candles sputtered out at strategic times during the play, gasping when Drayton suddenly doused the overhead lights and the "murder" took place.

Theodosia had been delighted that Delaine Dish had shown up with her friend Brooke Carter Crockett, who owned Heart's Desire, a nearby jewelry shop that specialized in high-end estate jewelry. Miss Dimple had brought her brother, Stanley, a roly-poly fellow who, except for being bald as a cue ball, was the spitting image of Miss Dimple. Plus there were tea shop regulars and lots of friends from the historic district. In all, twenty-five guests sat in the flickering candlelight, enjoying the mystery tea.

And they'd had a couple surprise guests, too: Lizbeth Cantrell and her aunt Millicent.

Theodosia hadn't expected to see Lizbeth Cantrell so soon, and especially not tonight. But the ladies had slipped in at the last moment, Lizbeth nodding knowingly to Theodosia, then found their seats and settled back comfortably to enjoy the play.

The actors, down to four now, were serving the main course, chicken satays with a spicy sauce of Sencha tea and ginger, and playing their roles rather broadly. Theodosia had her money on the Theodore character as the murderer. He was a pompous patriarch who certainly *looked* like he could whack someone on the head with a bronze nymph. (Now she knew why Drayton had gone to all that trouble with table centerpieces!)

On the other hand, you never could tell when it came to spotting suspects. First impressions weren't always that reliable. Look how she'd pinned her suspicions on Ford Cantrell. He'd certainly appeared to be the perfect suspect, and now she wasn't sure at all.

But Theodosia did know one thing for sure. She was going to get to the bottom of Oliver Dixon's murder. If she discovered the real killer and was able to clear Ford Cantrell, she'd have done a great kindness for Lizbeth Cantrell. On the other hand, if Ford Cantrell wasn't the innocent man his sister professed him to be . . . well, then at least the truth would be out. And knowing the truth was always better than not knowing at all.

Loud clapping and shouts of "Bravo!" brought Theodosia out of her musings and back to the here and now. Drayton was extending a hand toward the four remaining actors as they took a collective bow and then struck exaggerated poses.

"I present to you, the suspects," announced Drayton, obviously pleased with the crowd's reaction. "As they have dropped bold clues and broad hints throughout the evening, we shall now pass ballots around the table so *you* can be both judge and jury and hopefully solve our murder mystery."

The guests' voices rose in excited murmurs as the amateur actors, obviously still relishing their roles, walked among the tables, passing out paper and pens.

"And," added Drayton, "while you ponder the identity of the perpetrator of the crime, we shall be serving our final course, tea sorbet with miniature almond cakes."

"What's the prize for solving the mystery?" called Delaine.

"Haley, care to do the honors?" asked Drayton.

Haley stepped to the front of the tea shop and cleared her throat. "The winner or winners, should there be a tie, will receive a gift basket filled with teas and a half-dozen mystery books."

"Perfect!" exclaimed Miss Dimple. "Then you can have your very own mystery tea . . . any time you want."

"But our evening is far from drawing to a close," said Drayton. "After dessert, we shall be offering tastings on a number of select estate teas." He paused dramatically. "And we have a special guest with us, Madame Hildegarde. Using her fine gift of divination, Madame Hildegarde will read your tea leaves."

There was a spatter of applause, and then chairs slid back as people stood up to stretch their legs, move about the tea shop, and visit with friends at other tables.

Lizbeth Cantrell wasted no time in coming over to speak with Theodosia.

"I don't know if you've ever met my aunt," said Lizbeth Cantrell. "Millicent Cantrell, meet Theodosia Browning."

Theodosia shook hands with the diminutive woman who also had a no-nonsense air about her and gray hair that must have also been red at one time.

"Hello," Theodosia greeted her. "I hope you've enjoyed the evening so far."

Millicent Cantrell smiled up at Theodosia. "I've never been to a mystery tea before. Went to a mystery dinner once at the Hancock Inn over in Columbia, but everything was terribly overdone and not very good."

Theodosia smiled at the old woman, even as she wondered if Millicent Cantrell was referring to the play or the cooking.

Millicent Cantrell's hand groped for Theodosia's. "You're a real dear to help us."

Theodosia searched out Lizbeth Cantrell's eyes.

Lizbeth met her gaze. "I told her you had pledged to help clear my brother's name."

"Pledged, well, that might be . . ." began Theodosia, feeling slightly overwhelmed. These ladies seemed to have pinned all their hopes on her. It suddenly felt like an overwhelming responsibility.

"You're a good girl, just like your momma," Millicent Cantrell told her as tears sparkled in her old eyes.

"And she's smart," added Lizbeth. "Theodosia's not thrown off by the occasional red herring, to use an old English fox hunting term."

"Isn't this cozy? I had no idea you all knew each other." Delaine Dish had slipped across the room and now raised a thin, penciled brow at Theodosia. She seemed to be waiting expectantly for some sort of explanation. Theodosia wondered how much Delaine had overheard.

"Hello, Delaine," said Lizbeth pleasantly. "Nice to see you again. Theodosia and I are getting pretty excited about the upcoming Spoleto Festival. She and I are both serving on committees."

"Spoleto," purred Delaine. "Yes, that does happen soon, doesn't it?"

"It's my third year on the ticket committee," said Lizbeth smoothly.

"The ticket committee," said Delaine in her maddening, parrotlike manner. "Sounds terribly interesting."

"It is," said Lizbeth, ignoring the fact that Delaine's comments, delivered in a bored, flat tone, implied it wasn't interesting at all. "As you probably know, tickets for the various Spoleto arts events are sold in packages."

"Mn-hm." Delaine leaned in close and narrowed her eyes.

"And our committee works out the various pairings." Lizbeth ducked her head and grinned, and Theodosia could see that she was having a little fun with Delaine now. "Actually," continued Lizbeth, "it's kind of like seating guests at a dinner party. You try to pair the interesting ones with the shy ones. In this case, we pair the real blockbuster events with some of the events that people might perceive as sleepers but are, of course, really quite stimulating."

"What a quaint analogy," murmured Delaine.

"Delaine, come have your tea leaves read." Drayton appeared at Delaine's elbow. "Be a darling and go first, would you?" he whispered to her. "Help break the ice for the other guests."

Theodosia grinned as Delaine reluctantly allowed herself to be led over to Madame Hildegarde, a sixtyish woman in a flowing purple caftan, who was now ensconced at the small table next to the fireplace.

Some forty minutes later, most everyone had departed. Angie Congdon, who owned the Featherbed House, one of the most popular B and Bs on The Battery, shared the honors for correctly guessing the murderer along with Tom Wigley, one of Drayton's friends from the Heritage Society.

"Drayton," Haley urged, *"you* come have your tea leaves read."

"Oh, all right," he agreed reluctantly.

"Don't be such a curmudgeon," Haley scolded as she slid her chair over to make room for Drayton. "Madame Hildegarde just told me I was going to meet someone *verrry* interesting. Maybe she'll have something equally exciting for you."

"Maybe she'll predict when this storm will end and I can get out and work in my garden," fretted Drayton.

Madame Hildegarde gazed at Drayton with hawklike gray eyes. "Drayton doesn't care for prognostication," she said with a heavy accent. "Doesn't want to look ahead, only behind." She laughed heartily, taking a friendly jab at his penchant for all things historical.

"You know how it works," Madame Hildegarde told him as she poured a fresh cup of tea. "Your teacup represents the vastness of the sky, the tea leaves are the stars and the myriad possibilities. Drink your tea." She motioned with her hand. "And turn the cup upside down. Then I read."

Drayton complied as the remaining guests gathered round him to watch.

"An audience," he joked. "Just what I don't need."

But Lizbeth Cantrell and her aunt Millicent, Theodosia, Delaine Dish, and Miss Dimple and her brother crowded around him, anyway. The rain was pelting against the windows now, and there was no question of leaving until it let up some.

"You want to ask a question or just have me read?" Madame Hildegarde asked Drayton.

"Just read," he said. "Give it to me straight."

"Oh," cooed Miss Dimple, "this is so interesting."

Madame Hildegarde flipped over Drayton's cup and carefully studied the leaves that clung to the bottom inside the white porcelain cup.

"Oh, oh, a love triangle," joked Haley.

Madame Hildegarde held up a hand. "No. The leaves predict change. A big change is coming."

Drayton frowned. "Change. Goodness me, I certainly hope not. I detest change."

Madame Hildegarde was undeterred. "Change," she said again. "Tea leaves don't lie. Especially not tonight."

Drayton cleared his throat somewhat uneasily. "Someone else try," he urged. He was obviously unhappy being the center of attention and having a spotlight placed on his future.

"I'll try," volunteered Lizbeth Cantrell.

"Excellent," said Drayton as he slipped out of his chair and relinquished it to Lizbeth Cantrell. "Another brave soul hoping to have her future divined."

Madame Hildegarde poured a small cup of tea and passed it over to Lizbeth. She drank it quickly, then, without waiting to be told, flipped the teacup upside down and pushed it toward Madame Hildegarde.

"I'd like to ask a question," she said.

Madame Hildegarde locked eyes with Lizbeth as the fire crackled and hissed behind her. "Go ahead," she urged.

Theodosia held her breath. In that split second, she knew what was coming. She knew what Lizbeth Cantrell was going to ask. And she wished with all her heart that she wouldn't. Because, deep inside, Theodosia was afraid of what Madame Hildegarde's answer would be.

"Who killed Oliver Dixon?" Lizbeth Cantrell asked in a whisper.

A hush fell over the room. Madame Hildegarde reached for the cup, her opal ring dancing with fire, and began to turn the cup over slowly.

As she did, the tea shop was plunged into sudden darkness.

A heavy thump at the front door was followed by a loud crash. Then Haley screamed, "Someone's at the window!"

"What's happening?" shrieked Miss Dimple. "What was that noise? Where are the lights?"

A second crash sounded, this time right at Theodosia's feet.

"No one move," commanded Theodosia as she began to pick her way gingerly across the room. Guided by the flickering firelight and her familiarity with the tea shop, she headed unerringly toward the counter. "There's a lantern behind the cash register," she told everyone. "Give me a moment and I'll get it."

Within seconds, the lantern flared, illuminating the tea shop like a weak torchère and catching everyone with surprised looks on their faces.

Haley immediately rushed to the door and threw it open. There was no one there.

"They're gone," she said, confusion written on her face.

"Who's gone?" asked Theodosia as she came up behind her and peered out. Up and down Church Street not a single light shone. The entire street was eerily dark.

"The shadow, the person, whatever was here," Haley said. "It just vanished."

"Like a ghost," said Miss Dimple in a tremulous voice.

"There's no such thing as ghosts," spoke Drayton.

"It *looked* like a ghost," said Miss Dimple rather insistently. "I saw something at the window just before we heard that thump. It was kind of wavery and transparent. Did you see it, too, Haley?"

Haley continued to gaze out into the street, a frown creasing her face. "*Someone* was here," she declared.

Theodosia spun about and turned her gaze on Madame Hildegarde. "The teacup, what was the answer in the teacup?" she asked.

Madame Hildegarde pointed toward the floor and, in the dim light, Theodosia could see shattered fragments strewn across the wood planks.

"Gone." Madame Hildegarde shook her head with regret. "All gone."

21

Sunday morning dawned with swirls of pink and gold painting the sky. The rain had finally abated, and the few clouds remaining seemed like wisps of cotton that had been tightly wrung out.

The slight haze that hung over Charleston Harbor would probably burn off by noon, but by ten a.m., tourists who'd been hunkered down in inns, hotels, and bed-and- breakfasts throughout the historic district, fretting mightily that their weekend in Charleston might be a total wash-out, began emerging in droves. They meandered the sidewalks, taking in the historic houses and antique shops. They shopped the open air market and bought strong, steaming cups of chicory coffee from vendors. And they strolled cobblestone lanes to gaze upon the Powder Magazine, one of the oldest public buildings in the Carolinas, and Cabbage Row, the quaint area that inspired *Porgy and Bess*, George and Ira Gershwin's beloved folk opera.

Whipping along Highway 700, the Mayfield Highway, in her Jeep, Theodosia was headed for the low-country. She told herself she was mak-ing a Sunday visit to her aunt Libby's, but she also knew she'd probably do a drive-by of Ford Cantrell's place, too. Sneak a peak, see what all this game ranch fuss was about.

Earl Grey sat complacently beside her in the passenger seat, his long ears flapping in the wind, velvet muzzle poked out the open window as he drank in all manner of intoxicating scents.

With all this sunshine and fine weather, the events of last night seemed almost distant to Theodosia. Of course, even after the power had come back on some ten minutes later, Haley had insisted that someone had been lurking outside. And Miss Dimple had clung hopefully to her notion that a ghost, possibly induced by all the psychic energy they'd generated, had paid them all a visit last night.

Theodosia was fairly sure that if anything had been at the window last night, it had been a window peeper. A real person. Which begged the question, *Who in his right mind would be sneaking about on a cold, rainy night, peeping in windows?*

On the other hand, maybe the person hadn't been in his right mind. Last night's peeper could have been angry, worried, or just frantically curious about someone who'd been attending the mystery tea.

Theodosia frowned and, just above her eyebrows, tiny lines creased her fair skin. Then she made a hard right, jouncing onto County Road 6, and her facial muscles relaxed. She was suddenly engulfed in a tangle of forest, a multihued tapestry of green.

Years ago, more than 150 thousand low-country acres had served as prime rice-growing country, producing the creamy short-grain rice that had been Carolina gold. Fields had alternately been flooded and drained as seasons changed and the cycle of planting, growing, and harvesting took place. Remnants of old rice dikes and canals were still visible in some places, green humps and gentle indentations overgrown now by creeping vines of Carolina jessamine and enormous hedges of azaleas.

Many of these rice fields had also reverted to swampland, providing ideal habitat for ducks, pheasants, and herons. And over the years, hurricanes and behemoth storm surges, the most recent wrought by Hurricane Hugo in 1989, had forged new courses in many of the low-country creeks and streams.

As a child visiting her aunt Libby, Theodosia had explored many of the low-country's tiny waterways in a bateau, or flat-bottomed boat. Poling her way along, she had often dabbled a fishing line into the water and, when luck was with her, returned home with a nice redfish or jack crevalle.

"Aunt Libby!" Theodosia waved wildly at the small, silver-haired woman who stood on the crest of the hill gazing toward a sparkling pond.

"You've brought the good weather with you," said Libby Revelle as she greeted her niece. "And none too soon. Hello there, Earl Gray." She reached down and patted the dog, who spun excitedly in circles. "Come to tree my poor possums?"

Libby Revelle, who loved all manner of beast and bird, spent much of her time feeding wild birds and setting out cracklins and pecan meal for the raccoons, foxes, possums, and rabbits that lived in the swamps and pine forests around her old plantation, Cane Ridge. Of course, when Earl Grey paid a visit, the critters she had so patiently coaxed and cajoled suddenly went into hiding and all her goodwill gestures went up in smoke.

Theodosia put her arm around Libby as they started toward the main house. Theodosia's father, Macalester Browning, had grown up here at Cane Ridge, and her parents had lived here when they were first married.

Built in 1835 near Horlbeck Creek, Cane Ridge had been a

flourishing rice plantation in its day. Now it was an elegant woodland retreat. With its steeply pitched roof and fanciful peaks and gables, the main house had always reminded Theodosia of a Hansel and Gretel cottage, although the style was technically known as Gothic Revival.

"Tell me the news," coaxed Libby as they settled into creaking, oversized wicker chairs and looked out toward the woods from the broad piazza that stretched around three sides of the house. "How are Drayton and Haley?" Libby asked. "And did you ever decide to hire that sweet little bookkeeper?"

"Drayton and Haley are fine," said Theodosia. "Like oil and water sometimes, but they're delightful and caring and keep things humming. Our new bookkeeper, Miss Dimple, is an absolute whiz. What a load off my mind since she's been handling payables and receivables. Why did I ever think I could handle the books myself?"

"Because, my dear, you believe you are capable of handling just about anything. In most cases, you can, but when it comes to the business of accounting, I think that's best left to an expert."

Theodosia smiled to herself. When her mother passed away, Aunt Libby, newly widowed, had stepped in and helped with so many things in the realm of child rearing. One of those was homework. Theodosia had excelled in subjects such as English and composition and history but had foundered at math. Algebra was gut-wrenching, geometry a foreign puzzle. Libby had seen her consternation and struggle with numbers and encouraged her gently. But Theodosia had never really gained complete mastery in that area.

"You heard about Oliver Dixon," said Theodosia.

"I've heard about Oliver Dixon from the horse's mouth," said Libby.

"What do you mean?"

"Lizbeth Cantrell stopped by this past week," said Libby. "Told me that her brother was being questioned, asked lots of questions about you."

"I figured as much," said Theodosia.

"Did she ask you to help?" asked Libby.

Theodosia sighed. "Yes."

"Are you going to?"

"I told her I'd try. I'm not sure there's much I can do, though," said Theodosia.

Libby leaned forward in her chair and grasped Theodosia's hands. "Don't sell yourself short," she said. "You have a relationship with the investigating officer."

"You mean Tidwell?"

"Yes. Of course."

"I'm not sure I'd call it a relationship," said Theodosia, who considered their standoffish treatment of each other as bordering on adversarial.

"Then call it a nodding acquaintance," said Libby. "But you *are* in a position to affect and impact his thinking."

"I suppose so," said Theodosia, not quite convinced.

Libby smiled. "Good." She released Theodosia's hands and sat back in her chair. "Then do what you do best. Nose about, ask questions, trust in your instincts. You're *good* at solving mysteries, Theodosia. We all know that."

"And if Ford Cantrell really is guilty?" asked Theodosia.

"Then he's guilty," said Libby. "But at least you tried. At least you put forth your best efforts. I know Lizbeth would appreciate that."

Theodosia stared toward the pond. With the sun a great golden orb in the sky now, it caught each gentle ripple and cast diamonds across the water. Around the edge of the pond, bright green fronds of saw grass waved gently in breezes that carried just a hint of salt.

Theodosia shifted her gaze to the left of the pond, to the small family cemetery. Dogwoods were beginning to bloom, and crape myrtle poked over the crumbling stone wall that surrounded the small plot. Her mother and father both rested here, under the ancient live oak that spread its sheltering branches above them. Her mother had died when she was eight, her father when she was twenty. The sorrow she had once felt had long been replaced by gentle sadness, tempered with warm memories that would always be there, always live on.

"Lizbeth Cantrell was around when Mother was so sick, wasn't she?" said Theodosia.

"Indeed she was," said Libby.

"I'd forgotten a lot of that, but now it's coming back to me."

They sat and watched as Earl Grey emerged from the woods, plunked himself down in a sunny spot, and set about chewing at a clutch of cockleburs that clung stubbornly to his left shoulder. There was no need for the two of them to talk. Over the years, they'd said it all. They were all the other had; there were no other relatives. They knew in their hearts how important they were to each other and cherished that knowledge. Their kind of love didn't require words.

Finally, Libby pushed herself up from her chair. At seventy-two, she still had a lithe figure and proud carriage, still walked with a bounce in her step.

"I think it's time we thought about lunch. Margaret Rose baked cranberry bread yesterday, and I threw together some chicken salad earlier. Why not fix trays and eat out here where we can enjoy the view? It'll be ever so much nicer."

Theodosia hit the wooden bridge on Rutledge Road much too hard, almost jouncing her and Earl Grey out of their seats.

"Sorry, fella," she murmured as the dog looked up with questioning eyes. Earl Grey had played and chased and worried critters for the better part of three hours and then fallen asleep on the backseat, which Theodosia had laid flat for this second part of their trip.

"I know the turn for the Cantrell place is *somewhere* along here," she said out loud. "I just haven't been down this particular road in fifteen years, so it's all a little foggy."

Twenty minutes ago, she'd passed the restored Hampton Plantation where Archibald Hampton, the former poet laureate of South Carolina, had lived. She was pretty sure the old Hampton place was on the way to the Cantrells' place, so she had to be on the right track.

"There is it. . . . Oh mother of pearl!" Theodosia cranked the wheel hard to the left and still overshot the turn. Slamming on the brakes, the Jeep shuddered to a halt. At the same exact moment, she felt the right side of her vehicle sink down into squishy soil.

"Nuts," she said. She sat for a moment, staring out the front window, then jumped out and walked around the back of the Jeep to see how bad the damage was.

Not terrible. She'd overshot the turn, and her right front wheel was off the gravel road and sunk midway in oozing mud. Remembering horror stories of quicksand in the area, Theodosia quickly decided her wisest move would be to simply shift into four-wheel drive and muscle her way out.

That would work, of course it would.

She stood by the side of the road, batting at gnats, feeling the heat begin to build around her.

She studied the road and the turn she'd just attempted. This *had* to be the turn to the Cantrell place, she decided.

Woof.

Earl Grey peered out the window, wagging his tail expectantly.

"No, you stay there, fella. I'll have us out in—"

Circling around the back of the Jeep, Theodosia stopped dead in her tracks. Off in the nearby underbrush, she'd heard a rustle. A slight whisper. It was probably nothing. Then again . . .

She began moving quietly, softly, but with purpose, creeping toward the driver's side.

There it was again. Not a rustle, more a soft gush of air. Couldn't be an alligator, they were few and far between out here. Plus those critters barked and moaned and made a terrible racket. No, this was more like . . . a snort?

By the time her brain registered the sound, a new movement was under way.

Hoofs clicking on gravel. Quick, precise, and moving toward her. Fast.

Theodosia scrambled for the car door, pulled at the handle, fumbled, pulled at it again. As the Jeep's door swung open and she struggled to climb in, the boar appeared on the road, not more than twenty feet away. It ran easily, almost mechanically, dainty feet carrying the wild pig with awesome swiftness. Theodosia saw that the creature's sharp, beady eyes were focused directly on her.

Theodosia slammed the door shut and grabbed for the ignition key. As the engine turned over, a loud report sounded.

Wham.

Confusion for a split second, not comprehending what had just happened. Jeep backfiring? Wild pig crashing headlong into her front fender?

Theodosia peered out the window and saw the pig lying motionless on the gravel not six feet from her. Then a pair of dusty boots came into view.

Ford Cantrell. Casually hefting a rifle in one hand.

Theodosia remained in her seat and, with shaking hands, pushed the button to lower the driver's-side window.

"Sorry about that," Ford Cantrell called to her. He waved at her casually, as though he were out for a stroll in the park.

Sinking back against the soft leather of the Jeep's upholstery, Theodosia breathed out slowly. Aunt Libby had once told her the Cantrells weren't happy with a thing unless they could ride it, shoot it, or stuff it. She might have been right.

"This bugger got away from us," called Ford. "I had a mind it might be headed this way. Hope it didn't cause you any problem."

Theodosia climbed down from the Jeep. "Quiet," she told Earl Grey, who was barking at the dead pig and at Ford Cantrell. "Settle down."

"Those things bite?" she asked, pointing toward the dead boar.

"They can take a chunk out of a fellow," Ford Cantrell replied mildly. "Although if you'd let that dog of yours out, he probably would of shagged it away. Most pigs are pretty scared of dogs."

As if to underscore Ford's remark, Earl Grey let loose with a throaty growl.

"Most pigs," repeated Theodosia. Fresh in her mind was the look of *intent* on the boar's curiously intelligent face.

"What are you doing this far from town?" Ford Cantrell asked her.

"I was visiting my aunt Libby." Theodosia waved an arm in the direction she'd just come. "At Cane Ridge."

Ford Cantrell seemed to accept her explanation. "Guess you heard I turned Pamlico Hill into a game ranch, huh?"

Theodosia nodded. She was surprised that Ford seemed to know exactly who she was. Introductions at this point would seem superfluous.

He nudged the dead pig with his boot. "This here's one of my main draws. A classic American razorback. Breeder I got 'em from said they's descended from the swine that Ponce de León brought from Spain. Supposed to be real smart."

"I'll bet," said Theodosia.

"Hear you're pretty smart, too. You've been asking questions about me."

Theodosia didn't back off. "A lot of folks have," she said.

Ford Cantrell squinted in the direction of the sun and swiped his hand roughly at the stubble on his chin. "And I guess they always will. Appears I've always been a lot more welcome out here in the low-country than in town."

When Theodosia didn't say anything, Ford Cantrell continued. "Yeah, I'm gonna be moving my boat over to McClellanville. Those guys at the yacht club are just too snooty for my taste."

Theodosia nodded. A sleepy little fishing village on Jeremy Creek would be quite hospitable to a low-country denizen like Ford Cantrell. And he certainly had to be persona non grata at the yacht club these days. Maybe the board of directors had even forced Ford to resign. She'd have to call Jory Davis's friend Eldon Cook, and ask him if he'd heard anything to that effect.

Ford Cantrell swept his broad-brimmed straw hat off his head and ran his broad fingers through a tangle of red hair. "Funny thing about that to-do," he said, finally looking Theodosia directly in the eye. "Everybody thinks Oliver Dixon and me were on the outs. But I was working for him."

Theodosia stared at Ford Cantrell, stunned by his words. "You were working for him!" she exclaimed. "What are you talking about?" she fumbled. "You mean Oliver Dixon was a partner in the hunting preserve?" That didn't sound quite right, but it was the best she could come up with at the moment.

"No, no," Ford said. "I was doing some work for his new company, Grapevine." He laughed harshly. "Well, not *his* company, the whole thing's very tightly controlled by the investors. Anyway, I had worked on some of the fault-tolerant disk arrays for Vantage Computers. You know, the company over in Columbia that has a lot of contracts with the military? Anyway, Oliver asked me to serve as an outside consultant. As it turned out, Oliver and I didn't see eye to eye on many things. That's why we were arguing that day in White Point Gardens. I'm sure everybody thought it was the old family feud but, in truth, I'd just told him he was a damn fool if he didn't think streaming video would be critical."

"You were working *together?*" Theodosia knew she must look totally unhinged, caught so off guard as she was by this new revelation. And here she'd gone and sicced Burt Tidwell onto Ford Cantrell. Tidwell had followed up, so he had to know about the two men's business relationship.

Had Tidwell been able to find some hard evidence that implicated Ford in Oliver Dixon's death? Or was Tidwell laughing merrily behind her back because she was a rank amateur who had jumped to a wild conclusion?

Theodosia watched as Ford Cantrell carefully leaned his rifle up against a tree stump, then grabbed the boar by its hind feet and dragged it to the side of the road.

"Be back to pick up this big boy later," he told her.

"You worked together," Theodosia murmured again.

"Yes," responded Ford, "but it's a moot point now. The investors have decided to shut Grapevine down."

"I hadn't heard anything about that." *Goodness,* she thought, stunned, *things are happening fast.*

"I just got word late Friday. Come tomorrow, the employees are on the street, and any existing inventory of raw materials is scheduled to be sold off." His eyes, pale blue like his sister's, like a sea captain who'd stared at too many horizons, met hers sadly. "I suppose any technology developed so far will also be sold or licensed."

"But why?" asked Theodosia. "I thought Grapevine was beginning to get noticed as a player in the market."

Ford shrugged. "Who the hell knows why these things happen? Could be a jittery board of directors with zero confidence, now that Oliver Dixon's gone. Or maybe the investors found a better place to make a fast return on their buck." Ford Cantrell traced the toe of his boot in the sand. "Hell, maybe somebody has inside information on what's *really* happening with PDAs and is executing a cut-bait maneuver."

Theodosia nodded. She understood there could be any number of reasons. Business start-ups and spin-offs were constantly being shut down or sold off at a moment's notice. Sometimes there was a solid reason; often it was done on a whim. She'd once developed a marketing plan for computer voice recognition software that showed great promise, only to find the entire project shut down because the product manager resigned to take a job with another company.

"Did your sister know you were working with Oliver Dixon?" asked Theodosia.

Ford Cantrell shook his head slowly. "Nope. Less Lizbeth knows, the better."

"What are you going to do now?" she asked him.

Ford Cantrell grinned crookedly, then shifted his gaze toward the dead boar. "Have a barbecue."

On her way with little more than a muddy fender to show for her mishap, Theodosia drove back toward the city, lost in thought. She wasn't sure if Ford Cantrell's business relationship with Oliver Dixon clearly meant the man was innocent, or if it gave Ford all the more reason to want Oliver Dixon out of the way. Maybe Ford Cantrell had somehow ingratiated himself with Oliver Dixon, gotten the consulting project, then conspired to move himself into the senior slot. If Oliver Dixon were out of the picture, the door would have been wide open. In the high-stakes world of business and technology, a power play like that wasn't unheard of.

But now Ford Cantrell was out of a job, too. Correction, out of a consulting job. For all she knew, his part could have been done. He could have already been paid.

Or fired by Oliver Dixon?

She thought back to what Delaine had said a week ago. She had told everyone at the tea shop that the two men were arguing about fishing, which had sounded exceedingly strange at the time, unless you knew Delaine. But Ford Cantrell had just told her the argument was over video *streaming*. Had Delaine somehow gotten fishing and streaming mixed up?

Theodosia knew that the answer was yes. Probably yes.

Theodosia eased off on the accelerator as the Jeep approached Huntville, a small, sleepy village on the Edisto River. Creeping across a one-lane wooden bridge, she found the way partially blocked by a sheriff's car.

Coming to a complete stop, Theodosia waited as a barrel-chested man dressed in a lawman's khakis crossed the road and ambled over to her.

"Looks like you had yourself a spot of trouble." The man with the sheriff's badge pointed to her mud-caked front fender.

"Overshot a turn back there."

"Yeah, that's easy to do." The sheriff grinned widely, revealing front teeth rimmed in gold. "Good thing this jobby's got four-wheel drive." He put his big paw on her door. "Lots of muck and quicksand around."

And then, because her curiosity usually got the better of her, Theodosia asked him, "Is there some kind of problem here, Sheriff?"

The sheriff shifted his bulk to face the river. "Nah, not really." He pointed to where the river narrowed to a sort of canal that flowed under the bridge. A skinny, young deputy in thigh-high waders was poking around down there. "Somebody come through here last night in a hell of a hurry," he said. "Must of been a big power launch 'cause he clipped the wood where the sides is shored up, then completely knocked out one of the bridge pilings."

Theodosia looked in the direction the sheriff was pointing and saw two timbers peeled back from the bank, rough edges exposed.

"Probably some good old boys got liquored up, then couldn't steer their way clear," continued the sheriff. "Only reason we're checkin' it out is 'cause we got a heads-up from the Coast Guard. They got tipped some two-bit smugglers might be workin' around this area and decided old Sheriff Billings didn't have enough to do. Send *him* on a wild-goose chase the first nice Sunday when he could be havin' a nice time at the car races over in Summerville."

Theodosia nodded, amused by the sheriff's peevishness. She knew there was a maze of rivers and inlets and swamps to navigate out here.

Lots of back country that only the locals were familiar with. "They'd have to know this territory pretty well," she said.

"Sure would," agreed the sheriff.

"Sheriff Billings, if it *is* smugglers, what would they be bringing in?" asked Theodosia.

"If it *is* smugglers, most likely goods from somewhere in the Caribbean. Booze, cigars, cigarettes. Folks just love to avoid that federal excise tax." The sheriff peered down over the embankment. "You find anything down there, Buford?" he hollered to his deputy.

"Nothin'," the deputy yelled back. "Seen a darn cottonmouth, though."

"Well, leave it be," advised the sheriff.

❧ 22 ❧

"*All you serve* is tea?" asked the young woman with a frown.

"Come on," said her companion, a young man in blue jeans and a Save the Redwoods T-shirt, "there's gotta be a coffee shop down the street."

"If you don't care for tea, you might find something you like on our Tea Totalers Menu," offered Haley.

The young woman accepted the slip of parchment paper tentatively. "Chamomile, Ginseng, Orange Spice," she read as she scanned down the list. "But these are teas, aren't they?"

"Actually," explained Haley, "they're infusions. Therapeutic fruits and herbs that don't contain leaves from the tea plant."

"Are they good for you?" asked the girl.

"Rose hips and hibiscus are extremely high in vitamin C, while ginseng and peppermint are energy boosters," said Haley. "Tell you what, I just brewed a pot of rose hips. You can have a taste and judge for yourself."

Haley went behind the counter and poured two small cups of rose hips. It was early Monday morning, and no other customers had come in yet. She could hear Theodosia and Drayton talking quietly in Theo's back office. Her scones and honey madeleines were baking in the oven, and she could afford to spend a little time with this young couple.

Their eyes lit up at the first taste.

"This is good," declared the boy. "But I think I'd like to try the plum. It sounds refreshing. Interesting, too."

"I'll stick with the rose hips," said the girl. "And you serve pastries here, as well?" Her nose had picked up the aromatic smells emanating from the back room.

"Have a seat, and I'll bring a pastry tray out," said Haley. "That way you can see everything."

Drayton stared at Theodosia from across her desk. "They were working *together?*"

"It would appear so," said Theodosia.

"I can hardly believe it," said Drayton. "Everyone and his brother has been so sure those two were still engaged in some dreadful eye-for-an-eye feud."

"Including me," said Theodosia. "I feel terrible about jumping to such a hasty conclusion."

"Don't beat yourself up over it," advised Drayton. "Tidwell certainly believed you and, in fact, seemed to confirm your thoughts. And, as you pointed out earlier, Ford Cantrell could have been secretly scheming to oust Oliver Dixon. He could have been seeking a permanent solution, if you get my drift."

"I suppose," fretted Theodosia.

"Frankly, I think you should speak with Tidwell again," urged Drayton. "About Ford Cantrell *and* Billy Manolo. Just the fact that Billy Manolo showed up at Oliver Dixon's funeral—and Tidwell was a witness to that—is somewhat suspicious. And I'm very uneasy about the fact that he threatened you."

"Who threatened who?" asked Haley as she stuck her head in the door.

"It's nothing, really," said Theodosia. She didn't want Haley to get upset over Billy Manolo's cruel remark about her floating facedown in Charleston Harbor.

"When our Theodosia went to Billy Manolo's house last Saturday, he picked up a piece of pipe and threatened her," said Drayton.

"Did you call the cops?" asked Haley. "Any guy looks cross-eyed at me these days, I call the cops."

"What about that Hell's Angel with the overpowered motorbike who hung around here all last summer?" Drayton asked. "He frightened off half our customers."

"Teddy wasn't threatening," said Haley. "He was simply in the throes of an identity crisis. Anyway, he's back in school now."

"Studying what," asked Drayton, "anarchy?"

"If you must know, he's studying to be a paramedic," said Haley. "But tell me more about this Billy Manolo character. Maybe he was the one who was peeking in our window Saturday night."

"You're still convinced someone was up to no good," said Drayton.

"I don't know what they were up to, but *somebody* was out there," replied Haley as the timer on her stove gave a loud ding. "Oops, got to pull this batch out," she said as she sailed around the corner.

By ten o'clock, every table in the tea shop was occupied. Drayton had predicted they'd have a busy morning, even though it had started out slowly, and had readied at least two dozen teapots. Now they were being filled with keeman, puerh, and Darjeeling, and being dispatched to the various tables occupied by tourists as well as tea shop regulars.

Theodosia was behind the counter, manning the old brass cash register and, in between cashiering and handing out change, was scribbling notes she could add later to the "Tea Tips" section of her Web site. When it didn't appear that the Indigo Tea Shop could hold one more customer, she looked up to see the door swing open and Doe Belvedere Dixon walk in followed closely by Giovanni Loard.

"Hellooo . . ." Drayton flew over to greet them, had an obvious moment of panic when he realized there wasn't an available table, then demonstrated signs of palpable relief when he saw that two women were just getting up to leave. "I'll have your table ready in a moment," he assured Doe and Giovanni.

Theodosia waited until Doe and Giovanni had been seated and served before she went over to their table to greet them. Things had settled down somewhat—all the customers were sipping and noshing—and Drayton seemed to be in a perpetual hover mode near Doe and Giovanni's table.

For someone who'd recently lost her husband, Doe appeared to have done an admirable job of pulling herself out of her grief. Theodosia watched as she chatted animatedly with Drayton, then with people at two other tables.

"They say Coco Chanel always took her tea with lemon," said Doe as her elegantly manicured fingertips gently pushed back a swirl of blond hair. "And that she always ordered in toast and jam from the Ritz." Doe glanced up as Theodosia approached. "Hello," she said, sipping delicately from her teacup. "I love your tea shop; it's so quaint."

"Thank you, how nice to see you again," said Theodosia, "although it's unfortunate our first meeting was under such sad circumstances. How are you doing?" Theodosia wondered if Doe would remember that she was the one who'd pushed her about Oliver's knowledge of guns the day of the funeral. No, probably not, she decided.

"I'm feeling so much better," replied Doe. "Everyone has been so kind." She turned luminous eyes toward Giovanni and smiled.

Giovanni fumbled for Doe's hand and patted it gently. "She's a strong girl, a real survivor," he said.

Doe shifted her hundred-watt smile to Drayton, and Theodosia wondered just how long this girl figured she could get by on her mesmerizing beauty. Perhaps until she married a second time? Then again, Doe also possessed enormous self-confidence. She might just sail through life, as some people did, secure in the knowledge that the world would always deliver its bounty to them.

"Can you sit with us a moment?" Giovanni asked Theodosia and

Drayton. "I was just telling Doe what a lovely time I had here last week. How helpful Drayton was with the Edgefield teapot and what a gracious hostess Theodosia had been." He smiled warmly at the two of them. "I feel as though you all are good friends already."

"We were surprised to hear that your husband's business was shutting down," said Theodosia to Doe. First thing this morning, she had scanned the business section of the *Charleston Post and Courier*. There had been a short article, and details had been fairly sketchy, but it did confirm what Ford Cantrell had told her yesterday. Grapevine was being shut down. Not with a bang but a whimper.

Doe blinked slowly, and a tiny furrow appeared just above the bridge of her nose. "The board of directors has been very kind, particularly Mr. Crowley."

"Booth Crowley?" asked Theodosia.

"Yes," said Doe. "He came to inform me in person that it was a business decision prompted solely by Oliver's death." She sighed. "It's comforting to know that Oliver was held in such high esteem and that the company is unable to function without him."

"Oliver Dixon was a brilliant man," said Giovanni. "One our community isn't likely to forget for a long time."

"It's a shame the company is being shut down entirely," continued Theodosia. "To keep Grapevine going, to build it into a success, would have been a tremendous testament to your husband."

"Unfortunately, it's just not to be," said Giovanni. His eyes seemed to have taken on a hard shine, sending a not-so-subtle warning signal to Theodosia.

Giovanni's overprotectiveness rankled Theodosia and gave her the impetus she needed to continue.

"Well-planned companies usually have a number of capable executives who can take over at the helm," said Theodosia. "For example—" Under the table, she felt a subtle kick from Drayton. Obviously, he thought she was going too far, pushing a little too hard, as well. "For example," she continued, "it turns out Ford Cantrell was doing some consulting work with your husband. As a former VP at Vantage Computers, perhaps he could have provided the needed interim leadership."

Doe frowned and cast her eyes downward, while Giovanni stared at Theodosia with a cold fury. "I'm afraid we'll be leaving now," he announced. He stood abruptly, and Doe, tight-lipped and grim, stood up as well.

Then Giovanni Loard headed for the door without uttering another word and Doe, bidding them a clipped good-bye, followed on his heels.

"*Well, you certainly* got a rise out of them," said Drayton as they huddled at the counter. "And some might say exceeded the boundary of good manners."

"I take it you disapprove?" asked Theodosia.

Drayton put one hand to the side of his face and patted it absently. "Not entirely," he said. "Like you, I get a very queasy feeling about a number of people."

"And your suspicions are focused on . . ."

"The girl, yes," said Drayton. "Such a pretty thing. But I can't help feel that beneath that radiant exterior is a very tough cookie."

"A girl who arranged to have her own husband murdered?" asked Theodosia.

"It's true, Doe didn't pull the trigger," said Drayton. "Poor Oliver did that all by himself."

"Rather convenient, wasn't it?" said Theodosia. "And now sweet young Doe has inherited Oliver Dixon's home and all his worldly assets." She turned to arrange a stack of saucers and cups. "Did you get the feeling that Doe knew Ford Cantrell had been working with Oliver Dixon?"

"Hard to tell," muttered Drayton, "hard to tell."

Over lunch at her desk, Theodosia reread the *Post and Courier* article. The byline at the end of the article said J. D. Darling. She knew J. D. Darling wasn't one of the regular business writers and, from the tone of the piece, the whole thing sounded like a quick rewrite of a press release. Probably one that had been issued hastily by Cherry Tree Investments over the weekend, then reworked by one of the copy cubs who pulled the Saturday to Sunday shift.

Theodosia drummed her fingers on her desk. The last line of the article intrigued her. It said that Cherry Tree Investments would continue to focus its efforts on several new high-tech start-ups.

Close down one high-tech company to start another? It happened, but it still sounded strange. Especially in light of all the gut-wrenching front-end work that had probably gone into Grapevine; months or perhaps even years of product development, writing a business plan, creating marketing and media strategies, finding a distribution chain, and developing a sales force strategy.

And, truth be known, high-tech companies weren't exactly the darlings of the venture capital world these days. It wasn't that long ago that the whole dot com thing experienced a disastrous shakeout on Wall Street, and skeptical analysts, probably the most vocal being those who got burned themselves, had stuck dot coms with the kiss-of-death label "*dot bombs.*"

Theodosia set her tuna fish sandwich down and dialed information. Within seconds, she'd obtained the number for Cherry Tree Investments and was dialing it.

"Hello," Theodosia greeted the woman who answered Cherry Tree's phone, "this is Judith Castleworth at the *Post and Courier.* I'm calling to clarify a few facts for one of our business writers, Mr. J. D. Darling?"

"Of course," said the receptionist.

"In Cherry Tree's recent press release regarding the closing of the company Grapevine, you mention that Cherry Tree is undertaking financing for several new high-tech companies. Can you give me the names of those companies?"

"You're talking about our newest underwritings," said the receptionist, not sounding completely sure of herself.

"Yes," said Theodosia.

"Let me see if I even have that information," said the woman. "Shirlene, the regular girl is at lunch, I'm Marilyn. Can you hold for a moment?"

"Of course," said Theodosia.

There was a rustle of papers, and Theodosia could hear the woman coughing gently. Then she was back on the phone.

"Miss Castleworth? I have those names for you."

"Go ahead," said Theodosia.

"The companies are Deva Tech, that's D-E-V-A Tech, two words. And Alphimed, A-L-P-H-I-M-E-D, one word."

"Deva Tech and Alphimed," repeated Theodosia.

"Yes," said Marilyn. "Deva Tech manufactures scanners for the warehouse industry, and Alphimed is a franchised medical testing company. Interim financing for both has already gone through, and Cherry Tree will be issuing a complete story to the media . . . oh, probably next month."

"Would it be possible to speak with your president, Mr. Booth Crowley?" asked Theodosia.

"I'm sorry, Mr. Crowley's at lunch. Could I have him return your—?"

"Thank you anyway, Marilyn," said Theodosia.

Theodosia replaced the phone in the cradle and leaned back in her leather chair. So Booth Crowley was financing two more high-tech companies. And from the way things sounded, they were very close to launching.

Booth Crowley. He was the man who'd handled Oliver Dixon the pistol. He was the man who'd been so hostile toward Billy Manolo at Oliver Dixon's funeral. And Booth Crowley was the big-time venture capitalist who launched Grapevine by virtue of his financing, then pulled the plug after Oliver Dixon was killed.

"You look like you've got a headache," said Haley.

"Getting one, anyway," said Theodosia, her head spinning with possibilities. She was hungry but had only eaten a quarter of her sandwich.

"I have the perfect antidote," said Haley. "Just give me a sec."

Theodosia stared out the window, thinking that *everybody* had suddenly begun to look suspicious.

Haley returned with a teacup filled with pale yellow liquid. "Drink this," she urged.

"What is it?"

"Meadowsweet tea."

"Perfect," declared Theodosia. Meadowsweet was a plant that had been used for centuries to fight fever and tame headaches. Its derivative, salicylate, was the compound that had been chemically formulated to produce aspirin.

"Drayton told me about your genteel conversation with Giovanni and Doe," Haley said, very tongue-in-cheek. "You don't think *she* had anything to do with Oliver Dixon's death do you?"

"I'm not sure what to think anymore," replied Theodosia. "First Ford Cantrell looked suspicious, then Billy Manolo. Although Billy just seems a little crazy."

"But crazy people do crazy things," said Haley.

"Yes," said Theodosia slowly, "they do. And now I'm also having second thoughts about Doe. It would appear she had a lot to gain from Oliver Dixon's death."

"You think the prom queen whacked her own hubby? Gosh, it sounds like tabloid fodder, doesn't it? Or a plot for a B movie."

"It doesn't stop there," sighed Theodosia. "I'm also curious as to what Booth Crowley is up to. It still seems strange to me that he just closed down Grapevine." Theodosia sipped her tea as Haley stared placidly at her. "Haley, tell me more about PDAs."

"What do you want to know?"

Theodosia paused. "There are different kinds. . . ." She wasn't sure where she was going with this.

Haley frowned at Theodosia, as if trying to decipher her thoughts. "You mean different operating systems?"

"I think so, yes," nodded Theodosia.

"Oh that," said Haley. "There's two kinds duking it out right now. Palm versus the Pocket PC."

"And your gizmo uses Palm," said Theodosia.

"Right," said Haley, "because I've got a Palm Pilot."

"What was Grapevine designing applications for?" said Theodosia.

"Not really applications, more like expansion modules."

"For the Palm," said Theodosia.

"Yes," said Haley.

"And now Booth Crowley is going to underwrite Deva Tech, a

company that manufactures warehouse scanners. What kind of computer systems do big warehouses generally use?"

"Big stuff, networks," she said.

"No Palm operating system?" asked Theodosia.

Haley smiled. "Hardly."

"So maybe Grapevine was small potatoes," said Theodosia.

"Or Booth Crowley didn't want to tick off the powers that be, the Microsofts of the world. It was just easier to dump Grapevine."

"Or dump Oliver Dixon," said Theodosia.

"Chilling thought," said Haley.

"Which means I need to find out a whole lot more about Booth Crowley," said Theodosia.

"How about tapping into radio free Charleston down the street?" suggested Haley.

"You mean Delaine?"

"Who else? She always seems to have the latest word on everything. Just don't let on that you're *too* interested," warned Haley.

⁊ 23 ⁊

"*Theodosia, I just* got in the most *marvelous* green silk jacket," exclaimed Delaine. "It is to *die* for." Delaine bustled over, delivered a quick air kiss in Theodosia's general vicinity, then scampered off, leaving an aromatic cloud of Joy in her wake.

"Janine!" Delaine yelled to her overworked assistant. "Where did we hang those silk jackets? Or are you still steaming them?"

Janine came rushing out from the back room, bearing silk jackets on padded hangers. Janine always looked a trifle red-faced and out of breath, and Theodosia often wondered if the poor woman had borderline high blood pressure or if her state of nervous excitement was due to six years of working for Delaine. She suspected the latter.

"Here, try this." Delaine pulled at Theodosia's black cashmere cardigan, trying to wrest it off, while she held out the green silk jacket for her to try on. "No, this is a medium, Janine, get Theodosia a small. These jackets run a tad generous, and our girl seems to have lost a couple pounds. Did you, dear?" she asked pointedly.

Theodosia ignored Delaine's question and, instead, slid into the smaller-size jacket. She adjusted it, buttoned a couple buttons, pirouetted in front of the three-way mirror.

"Oh, with your hair, *très élégant*," gushed Delaine.

Theodosia gazed at herself in the mirror. The jacket was a stunner, she had to admit. Sleek, lightweight, and a very bewitching green. She could see herself wearing it to any number of upcoming outings and parties. Accompanied, perhaps, by Jory Davis?

"I have it in jade green, pomegranate, and, of course, black," said Delaine. "Very limited quantities, so you won't see yourself coming and going." She plucked at one of the sleeves. "And so light, gossamer light, like butterfly wings. Perfect for a cool spring evening."

Theodosia snuck a peek at the price tag and decided she'd have to sell a good sixty or seventy cups of tea to finance her purchase.

"Let me think about it, Delaine," she said, slipping the jacket off and delivering it into the waiting arms of Janine.

Delaine wagged a finger at her. "Don't wait too long, Theo. These jackets will go like hotcakes."

"I know, I know." Theodosia picked up a beaded bag.

"Those are all hand-stitched in Indonesia," Delaine told her. "They come in that leaf pattern or there's a star motif."

"Lovely," said Theodosia as she examined the bag, then set it back down on the little display table. "Doe and Giovanni stopped by the tea shop this morning," she said.

Delaine brightened immediately. "Did they really? How is Doe getting along?"

"Seems to be bearing up quite well," said Theodosia. She didn't want to confide to Delaine that Doe and Giovanni had both exited the tea shop in a somewhat hasty huff. Delaine would probably learn about that soon enough. "And you heard about Grapevine, Oliver Dixon's company? Booth Crowley closed it down."

"Mmm, yes," said Delaine as she fussed over a tray of scarves, arranging them in artful disarray. "I saw something about that in the paper this morning."

"You haven't heard why, have you?"

"I just assumed the company couldn't get along without him."

"But you haven't heard anyone mention a specific reason," said Theodosia as she fingered the beaded bag again.

"Mmm . . . no," said Delaine as she straightened a stack of cotton sweaters. "Gosh," she said, peeling an apple green sweater off the top, don't you adore this color? Can't you see it paired with white slacks? Yummy."

"Pretty with your coloring," said Theodosia.

Delaine held it up. "You're right." She preened in the mirror. "Anyway, Theo, to get back to what you were saying, Booth Crowley certainly must know what he's doing. He's had his hand in enough different businesses."

"Yes, I guess he has," said Theodosia.

"Do you know his wife, Beatrix?" asked Delaine.

"No, not really."

"Delightful woman, patron of the Children's Theater Company. She buys quite a lot of her clothing here. Of course, she also flies to New York and Paris. I believe she even attends some of the *collections*."

"Wow," said Theodosia, trying to look suitably impressed for Delaine's sake. She wandered over to an antique armoire set against a cantaloupe-colored wall. The doors of the armoire were open, and it was stuffed with a riotous array of silk camisoles, jeweled pins, antique keys strung on ribbons, and Chinese ceramic cachepots. A turquoise silk sari hung down from one side.

"Delaine, your decor is absolutely delightful," began Theodosia. "I've been thinking about giving my shop a bit of a face-lift. Maybe even go for a touch of exotica." Theodosia watched as interest flickered on Delaine's face. "One of the design firms that's been recommended to me is Popple Hill. Are you familiar with them?" She'd tucked Billy Manolo's Popple Hill connection in the back of her brain and now figured it might be worth seeing what Delaine knew.

"My dear, Popple Hill is *extraordinary*," gushed Delaine. "It's headed by two absolutely brilliant women, Hillary Retton and Marianne Petigru. I know them because they also shop here whenever they can. Both are cultivated beyond belief and *so* multitalented. Do you know Gabby Stewart, who lives over on Lamboll?"

"I think so."

"She's the pretty blond with the really good face-lift whose husband gave her the black Jaguar XKE for her last birthday, which nobody's bothering to count anymore."

"Now that you've described her so precisely, I do recall her," said Theodosia, smiling.

"Well, the Popple Hill ladies took *her* house from early Dumpster to utterly dazzling. Gabby and her husband, Derwood or Dellwood or something like that, inherited that great old house and all the furniture. The wooden pieces were okay, so-so seventeenth-century French that could be refinished and touched up a bit, but most of the dining room chairs were absolutely bedraggled. And *nothing* had been done to the interior, not a speck of paint nor snippet of wallpaper, in ages. Now it's stunning, an absolute showpiece. I wouldn't be surprised if *Town and Country* or *Southern Accents* wanted to do a big spread on it."

"What about the exterior?"

Delaine wrinkled her nose. She wasn't too keen on having her stories interrupted. "Yes, Hillary and Marianne masterminded a restoration on that, too."

"They used wrought iron?"

"Oh, *tons* of it," said Delaine, "because of the huge garden courtyard out back. You know that house, don't you? You've been inside and seen that marvelous oversized fireplace?"

Theodosia ignored Delaine's question. "Do you know any of Popple Hill's craftspeople?" she asked.

Delaine frowned. "Their *craftspeople*? No, I wouldn't know about that.

I imagine they're just ordinary workers. Hillary and Marianne are the real genuises." Delaine paused. "I love that you're thinking about updating your look."

"Mm-hm," said Theodosia, knowing she'd *never* let anyone tinker with the cozy interior she loved so much.

"Come to think of it, Popple Hill did some recent restoration work on Doe and Oliver's home, too," said Delaine as the ring of the telephone perfectly punctuated the end of her sentence.

"Chloe Keenland is on the phone," Janine called to Delaine. "She wants to know if you're still on for this afternoon."

Delaine pushed back her sleeve, glanced at her watch, a Chopard rimmed with sparkling jewels. "Gosh, I'd forgotten all about Chloe." Delaine chewed her lower lip as she gazed at Theodosia. "Garden Fest starts this Friday, and I'm on the opening night refreshment committee," she explained. Swiveling her head toward Janine, Delaine smiled winningly. "Janine, could you be an absolute *angel* and work until five today?"

Janine looked glum. "I suppose," she said.

"Wonderful," declared Delaine. "Perfect."

Back at the tea shop, Theodosia felt more confused than ever. Her somewhat strange and rambling conversation with Delaine hadn't yielded much. And none of the theories she'd been tossing around seemed to make sense, either.

"Haley, did you—" began Theodosia, but her sentence was cut short.

"Don't look now, but it's the prom queen again," Haley muttered under her breath.

Theodosia looked up to see Doe Belvedere Dixon striding into the Indigo Tea Shop for the second time that day.

"Miss Browning," said Doe in a breathless, little-girl voice, "can we talk?"

Theodosia nodded and quickly steered the girl to one of the far tables. "Of course," she said, her curiosity suddenly hitting a fever pitch.

Doe waited until they were both seated and was positive no one was in earshot before she began. "I came back to apologize," she said.

"Giovanni is still very touchy about Oliver's death, and he often overreacts rather badly. But you have to understand, he was so very fond of his cousin."

"Second cousin," said Theodosia, watching Doe closely, wondering what the real agenda was.

"Yes, of course," said Doe as she picked a tiny fleck of lint from the sleeve of her perfect buttercup yellow sweater. "But the two of them were extremely close. Giovanni's mother died when he was very young, and Oliver was always like an older brother to him."

"I'm sure he was," said Theodosia, wondering again why Doe had come back. Her apology didn't seem all that heartfelt.

Then Doe leaned forward across the small wooden table and her taffy-colored hair swung closely about her face. "Frankly, I think Giovanni was upset because I told him about Ford Cantrell and me," she said.

Now it was Theodosia's turn to lean forward, the better to catch every word.

"Ford and I met a few years ago at the University of Charleston," explained Doe. "He was a grad student in computer engineering, and I was a Tri Delt pledge." She stopped and smiled wistfully at Theodosia. "Were you ever in a sorority?"

Theodosia stared at Doe. "No," she said.

"Best time of my life," she declared. "Anyway, Ford and I dated a few times, and then I broke it off."

"You *dated* Ford Cantrell?" Theodosia said in a loud whisper.

Doe frowned, as though she were unused to any type of critical remark. "Honestly, Theodosia, it was no big deal." She shrugged. "I *said* I broke it off. If you ask me, Ford Cantrell has never accepted being rejected."

"*She dated him?*" Drayton tucked his chin down and stared over his glasses. His right eyebrow twitched crazily; he did not look amused. "You're making this up," he finally declared in a flat voice. "In a brazen attempt to completely muddle my poor mind."

Theodosia shook her head. "Doe told me so herself."

"Is that what you two were whispering about?" said Haley. "A date she had with Ford Cantrell in college? Hmm, she certainly holds herself in high regard, doesn't she?"

"I think she was just trying to explain why Giovanni got so upset when I started talking about Ford Cantrell this morning," said Theodosia. "In her own way, Doe was trying to be nice."

"She's got a funny way of being nice," grumbled Haley.

"Indeed she has," agreed Drayton.

Theodosia was inclined to agree with them, if the whole situation hadn't been so bizarre. Bizarre bordering on Ripley's Believe It or Not!

And when you tried to look at Oliver Dixon's murder from the standpoint of pure motive, it was also terribly confusing.

Ford Cantrell supposedly harbored a grudge against Oliver Dixon, yet he'd worked for the man as a consultant. Ford had motive only if you took into account the long-standing family feud and their somewhat strange business arrangement, which could have been far from amicable.

Booth Crowley and Billy Manolo had both handled the antique pistol minutes before Oliver Dixon was killed by it. Both men impressed Theodosia as being short-tempered and snappish.

But as far as motive went, the only connection Billy Manolo seemed to have to Oliver Dixon was through the yacht club and as an ironworker, possibly creating some decorative wrought-iron pieces for Doe and Oliver's home via the Popple Hill people.

Would you kill someone because he might have criticized the scrollwork on your garden gate? She didn't think so.

Booth Crowley was a suspect by virtue of his peripheral connections. He'd handed the pistol to Oliver just moments before he was killed and had put up most of the money for Grapevine. On the other hand, if Oliver Dixon had somehow gotten wind that Booth Crowley was going to shut the company down, he might have been forced to retaliate. That was a theory that certainly warranted more investigating.

As far as Doe Belvedere Dixon was concerned . . . well, Theodosia wasn't sure where Doe fit into the equation, other than the fact that she stood to inherit a lot of money.

Of course, to make things all the more confusing, Ford Cantrell,

Booth Crowley, Oliver Dixon, and Billy Manolo were all members of the same yacht club. Well, Billy worked there, but he was still at the club a lot of the time.

So what did all that information add up to? As far as Theodosia was concerned, it totaled a big fat zero.

Puttering about the tearoom for the rest of the day, Theodosia fretted about her inability to draw any kind of conclusion. She was unwilling to let it go by the time evening rolled around and she found herself upstairs with Earl Grey in her little apartment.

As though Earl Grey had psychically picked up on her restlessness and disquietude, the dog paced about the apartment, toenails clicking against kitchen tile and hardwood floors.

They'd already taken their evening walk through the historic district. Starting on Church Street, they'd jogged up Water Street, then wended their way down Meeting Street to The Battery. After Earl Grey had romped in the park, they'd even walked home past the Stewart home on Lamboll Street, where Billy Manolo, according to Delaine, had supposedly created *tons* of wrought iron to enclose their backyard garden.

And still Theodosia was restless.

What to do? she wondered. *Take another walk? Sip some chamomile tea? Fix a tisane of Saint-John's-wort to calm me down?*

No, she finally decided, there was something far better that she could do. She could put it all down on paper. Or rather, computer. She would compose and organize her thoughts, making notations if she was seriously bothered by any glaring facts or strange coincidences. Then she could hit a single key and E-mail the whole shebang to Detective Burt Tidwell. She could put him on the same page with her, so to speak. Get him alerted to or caught up on all the details. After all, she told herself, two heads were better than one. And from the looks of things, her head seemed to have borne the brunt of worrying about Oliver Dixon's death these last nine days. Not even Oliver's wife, Doe, seemed to think the accident hadn't really been an accident.

That resolved, Theodosia sat down at her computer and began the task of putting it all down.

The writing and rewriting took her a good while. But when she was finished and the information sent, it felt like a great weight had been lifted from her shoulders. And Theodosia, sleepy at last, padded into her cream-colored bedroom and slid into bed between indigo cotton sheets that were cool and featherlight and infinitely conducive to pleasant dreams.

❧ 24 ❧

"Theodosia? It's Bernard Morrow."

Clenching the phone tighter, Theodosia straightened up in her chair. "Professor Morrow, hello. I've been hoping to hear from you." She glanced out across the tearoom. Haley was sliding gracefully between the small tables with a tray that held samples of their new South African Redbush tea. Drayton was chatting with two regulars who came in every Tuesday morning, dressed to the nines and wearing hats and gloves. Sunlight streamed in through the heavy, leaded panes, lending a shimmering glow to everything. With the morning's sunlight came a ray of hope as well.

"Yes, well, I meant to get your little project dispatched with sooner," said Professor Morrow, "but I've been serving on this confounded academic search committee. Everyone on it worries endlessly about adding new, untenured faculty to the department and pontificates over their own specialized area. All in all, it gives you the sense that your career is drawing to a close, and it's time to take a final bow."

"You're not thinking about retiring, are you?" Theodosia asked in alarm. Professor Morrow was one of the most caring, humane professors she had ever encountered. It would be a profound loss to the University of Charleston if he were to retire.

"Considering it, but not planning my exit in the near future," said

Professor Morrow. "Anyway, I didn't call to tell you my problems. You asked me to analyze the material on the linen tablecloth, and I did exactly that. Not the blood, of course, you'd need a chromatograph to do that, and our lab is simply not equipped that way."

"I understand," said Theodosia.

"Anyway, I took a look at the ground-in matter. It's dirt, all right."

"Dirt," repeated Theodosia.

"Not flecks of metal or gunpowder as you had initially suspected. Just garden-variety dirt." He paused. "I could run a couple more tests, see if I can break down the compounds, measure phosphorous and potassium, things like that."

"Would you?"

"No problem. Those are simple chemical analyses I can do with reagents we have right here in the lab. Take me a day or two."

"Thank you, Professor Morrow."

Theodosia hung up the phone and hastily replayed their conversation in her mind. It wasn't what she'd wanted to hear. She'd been fairly convinced that the pistol had been tampered with in some way and that the fine dust on the linen tablecloth would reveal metal shavings or some type of unusual gunpowder.

But *dirt*? What the heck did that mean? Had someone kicked it around in the mud before Drayton snatched it up and stuck it in the trunk of his car?

"You look as though someone just delivered some bad news," said Drayton.

"Professor Morrow just called with his analysis of Haley's schmutz," replied Theodosia.

"And?"

"Dirt," she replied.

Drayton looked skeptical. "Dirt? That's it?"

"That's it. Now you can see why I'm disappointed."

"You're disappointed? *I'm* disappointed," said Drayton. "I've been envisioning endless scenarios involving strange resins or chemicals that could be traced, by means of sophisticated forensics, to a particular suspect who would then be summarily apprehended."

"Drayton, you watch too much crime TV," said Haley, who had been filling teapots and eavesdropping at the same time.

"I rarely watch television," he said with an imperious lift of his gray head.

"I stand corrected. Then you read far too many mysteries," said Haley. She furrowed her brow as if to lend solidarity to Theodosia's dashed hopes. "Sorry the tablecloth didn't lead somewhere," she said.

Theodosia nodded.

"What's next, then?" asked Haley. Boundlessly optimistic, Haley was never one to be discouraged by a little bad news. She was always ready to move on, explore another angle.

"I think I've got to pay another visit to Timothy Neville," said Theodosia.

"You mentioned that a couple days ago, but I haven't seen any forward progress yet," Drayton commented in a dry tone.

Theodosia undid her apron, balled it up, thrust it into Drayton's hands. "On my way."

"Mr. Neville?"

Timothy Neville looked up from the antique map he was studying, a schematic diagram of old Fort Sumter. "Yes, Claire?"

"Miss Theodosia Browning is here to see you?"

"Is that a statement or a question, Claire?"

Flustered, Claire just stared at him. She loved working at the Heritage Society but had long since decided that Timothy Neville was the strangest little man she'd ever encountered. "Perennially puckish" was how Theresa, one of the longtime curators, had described him, and Claire had the feeling that Theresa had hit the nail squarely on the head.

"It's both," said Claire finally. "She's here. Do you have time to see her?"

Timothy Neville smiled to himself. "Kindly show her in."

"Yes, sir."

"And Claire?" said Timothy.

Claire hovered in the doorway. "Yes?"

"Thank you." Timothy Neville smiled to himself as he carefully rolled up the fragile parchment map and slid it into a cardboard storage tube. He waited until he heard the Browning woman enter his office and cross over to his desk before he looked up. When he did, he was struck by the keen intelligence in her eyes.

"Hello," he said to Theodosia.

Theodosia stared back at Timothy Neville, noting that his eyes were the sad, unblinking eyes of an old turtle. "Hello, Mr. Neville," she replied.

Timothy Neville lifted his gnarled fingers slightly, inviting Theodosia to be seated in one of the French deco leather club chairs that flanked his desk. She did.

Watching her closely, Timothy Neville was somehow pleased that the woman sat poised so straight in her chair and kept her eyes focused directly on him.

"You have questions," he said. "About antique pistols."

"Yes," she said.

Timothy bobbed his head and managed a half smile. "Drayton called just a few moments ago. Begged me to be civil to you."

"Will you be?" she asked.

"Of course. I'm generally civil to everyone. It's false benevolence I abhor."

Timothy Neville sat down at his desk and faced her. Theodosia noticed that they were at eye level with each other and suspected that the small-of-stature Timothy had adjusted his chair to a higher level, the better to be on an equal parity with visitors.

"You have considerable knowledge about the workings of antique pistols," said Theodosia.

"I have a collection of them, a small collection. Two dozen at most. But I've been collecting for more than fifty years, so I have a couple choice pieces that are now exceedingly rare."

"Can you tell me how a person might cause an antique weapon to explode?" she asked him.

"I take it the antique weapon you so coyly refer to is the offending pistol that brought Oliver Dixon's life to a crashing conclusion?"

"That's right," she said, wondering why Timothy Neville seemed to want to footnote everything. She supposed it was his lifelong involvement in all things historical.

"As chance would have it, I have a pistol of the same ilk. Crafted by the old E. R. Shane Company in Pennsylvania. It's not a perfect mate, but it's very, very close."

"Have you ever fired it?" asked Theodosia.

"Not recently," said Timothy. "But to answer your question, the simplest way to cause a pistol to explode is to overpack it." Timothy folded his arms protectively across his thin chest and posed gnomishly, awaiting her next question.

"With gunpowder?" she asked.

Timothy Neville gave her a thin smile. "That's one way. Not the best, though."

"What else could you use?" Theodosia asked. "Dirt?"

"Pack a pistol with dirt, and you're almost guaranteed it will explode," said Timothy.

Pinwheels of color flared in Theodosia's cheeks. *Dirt,* she thought. *Simple dirt.* She leaned back in her chair slightly and envisioned the scenario. You take an old pistol that had been hand-wrought almost two hundred years ago. You pour in a handful of Carolina dirt, pack it in tight, tamp it down. When the trigger is pulled . . . *boom.* The amazing exploding gun trick.

What was it Professor Morrow had called the residue he'd found on the linen tablecloth?

Garden-variety dirt.

Okay, that had to be it. Then, the next big question that loomed in front of her was: Dirt from whose garden?

"Theo, there's someone here to see you," said Haley.

Theodosia had let herself in the back door that led directly from the alley to her office.

"Who is it?" she asked as she tucked her handbag into the desk drawer.

Haley shrugged. "Beats me. Some guy who came in about twenty minutes ago. I gave him a cup of tea and a scone and tucked him at the small table by the fireplace."

Taking a quick peek in the tiny mirror that hung on the back of her door, Theodosia smoothed her hair and decided to pass on the lipstick. The six-block walk back from the Heritage Society had infused her complexion with a natural, rosy glow, infinitely better than anything packaged cosmetics could deliver.

She emerged through the green velvet curtains with a smile on her face and confidence in her step. But her smile froze when she saw who it was waiting to see her: Booth Crowley.

She recovered quickly. "I'm Theodosia Browning," she greeted the man at the fireside table. "How can I help you?"

Booth Crowley stood and faced her. He was a big man to begin with, but wearing a coal black, three-piece suit, he looked even more imposing. His shock of white hair bristled atop his head, a crooked mouth jagged across his square-jawed face.

"I'm Booth Crowley," the man said as he took her hand in his and clamped down roughly. "We need to talk."

Booth Crowley released Theodosia's hand only when she was half seated. By that time, a single word had bubbled to her brain: *bully*. She'd been in Booth Crowley's immediate presence for all of thirty seconds, and already he impressed her as a bully of the first magnitude. But, then again, hadn't she seen him bullying Billy Manolo that day at the church? It certainly looked like he'd been.

"A very unpleasant man, that Burt Tidwell," said Crowley in his strange staccato manner. "Stopped by to see me this morning." His upper lip curled as he spoke, and his pink face seemed to become increasingly florid.

Tidwell, thought Theodosia. *He had received my E-mail and must have found some merit to it. Obviously he had, since he'd already had a chat with Booth Crowley.*

But would Tidwell have confided to Booth Crowley that she was the one who harbored suspicions about him? Doubtful, highly doubtful. If anything, the pendulum swung in the other direction with Tidwell. He was extremely tight-mouthed about investigative details.

But Booth Crowley wasn't nearly finished. "My wife attended a meeting yesterday," he snarled at her. "Ran into a friend of yours. Delaine Dish."

Theodosia groaned inwardly. Leave it to Delaine to chatter about anything and everything. And to Booth Crowley's wife yet! Unfortunately, there was no way she could have known that Delaine sat on the same committee that Booth Crowley's wife did.

Booth Crowley narrowed his eyes at her. "You've been talking about me. Asking impertinent questions," he said accusingly.

"Actually," said Theodosia, deciding to play it absolutely straight, "my questions have been about Oliver Dixon."

"And Grapevine," Booth Crowley shot back, "which most certainly *does* concern me."

"I was sorry to hear you closed it down," said Theodosia, keeping her voice light. "Good thing you have two more companies ready to come out of the chute. What are they? Oh, yes, Deva Tech and Alphimed."

"What do you know about those?" he snapped.

"Probably no more than anyone else," said Theodosia, "unless you'd care to enlighten me." There, she had jousted with him and obviously struck a nerve. Now it was his turn.

Booth Crowley smiled at Theodosia from across the table, but the vibes weren't particularly warm. "You know," he said, suddenly changing the cadence of his voice and adopting a silky, wheedling tone, "my wife, Beatrix, has always wanted to open a tea salon."

"How nice," said Theodosia. *Give him nothing,* she thought, *nothing. Never let them see you sweat.*

"Right now, she owns that lovely little sweet shop Le Bonbon. Down on Queen Street. She has a couple of ladies—dear, trusted souls—who've been with her for years. They make handmade truffles similar to the ones you find at Fauchon in Paris." Booth Crowley took a long sip of tea, wiped his mouth with a napkin, and tossed it down haphazardly on the table. "But a *salon de thé* that serves high tea is her absolute dream." He looked around imperiously. "Of course, it would be far more formal than what you have here. And I have the perfect name for it. Tea with Bea."

"Cute," said Theodosia.

"Yes, she's always wanted a little shop. Somewhere here in the historic district," said Booth Crowley. "I do so love to indulge my wife."

Theodosia knew that Booth Crowley and his wife, Beatrix, could squash her like a bug if they wanted to. Booth Crowley's net worth had to be high, almost astronomical. As CEO of Cherry Tree Investments, he smooth-talked countless investors into providing millions in venture capital for dozens of companies. More importantly, Booth Crowley sat on the Charleston Chamber of Commerce. If he decided to *indulge* his wife, as he had rhapsodized, he could easily persuade the Charleston tour buses to stop at his wife's tea shop instead of hers. It wasn't good, she decided, it wasn't good at all. She'd stirred up a hornet's nest, and now she might have to face the consequences.

Booth Crowley stood up abruptly and, reluctantly, Theodosia stood, too. "Good day," he told her, his grin hard, his gray eyes filled with menace. "If you hear of any vacancies on your block, be sure to let me know. In the meantime, I'll consult with one of the commercial Realtors my firm has on retainer." He spun away from her, heading for the door, then stopped in his tracks and looked back over his shoulder. "I wouldn't go signing any long-term leases, if I were you," he spat out. "Especially with the economy so uncertain and competition breathing down your neck." Then he slammed out the door and was gone.

Theodosia was aware of Drayton hovering behind her.

"What did he want?" Drayton asked quietly. He put a hand on Theodosia's shoulder, gently steering her over to the counter, where they could have some privacy.

"He came here to rattle my cage," Theodosia told him. "To intimidate me." She tried to keep her remark light, but she realized that, deep inside, she *was* rattled and intimidated.

"Who *was* that big boor?" asked Haley as they all crowded behind the counter, whispering.

"That was Booth Crowley," Drayton told her.

Haley's eyes went wide. "*Really?* Darn. If I'd known who he was, I wouldn't have been so pleasant to him when he first came in." She meant her remark to be humorous, but she saw the look of consternation on Theodosia's face. "Just how did Booth Crowley try to intimidate you?" Haley asked.

"Oh, it was rather indirect at first," said Theodosia. "He talked about how his wife has always wanted to have a tea salon somewhere in the historic district. Then he escalated things, told me not to sign a long-term lease or anything." She struggled to maintain an outward calm, but she still came across shaken.

"You've had competition before," said Drayton, trying to be practical. "It hasn't made a whit of difference."

"Not *real* competition," said Theodosia.

"What about Tea Baggy's over on Wentworth?" Drayton offered.

Theodosia looked thoughtful. "That's different. Tea Baggy's is retail, and all the charm is in the name. Besides, they only stock a few canisters of so-so tea. Most of their sales are in candy and glassware. And gobs of giftware."

"They just added a line of teddy bears," said Haley helpfully.

"You see?" said Theodosia to Drayton. "It is more retail. Booth Crowley was talking about something entirely different."

"How much you want to bet he was just bluffing," said Haley.

"How did your meeting with Timothy go?" asked Drayton, deciding it might be best to change the subject and try to get Theodosia's mind off Booth Crowley's threats.

Theodosia stared at Drayton as though she wasn't sure what he was talking about. Then she blinked, and understanding came back to her face. "My goodness, I forgot to tell you! I came back here and went rushing into that awful meeting."

"So Timothy was helpful?" said Drayton.

"Actually, he was extremely helpful. And so were you," said Theodosia. "Thank you for calling ahead and smoothing the way."

Drayton waved a hand airily. "Just making sure the ferocious Timothy didn't make mincemeat out of you."

"So what did Timothy Neville say?" asked Haley.

"Basically, he told me it's fairly easy to rig a pistol to explode," said Theodosia. "All you have to do is overpack it."

"Overpack it?" frowned Haley. "With what?"

A sly smile crept onto Theodosia's face. "I think somebody over-packed the yacht club's pistol with dirt," she said.

"Which tracks with what Professor Morrow told you," Drayton exclaimed excitedly. "He said the tablecloth had *dirt* on it."

"Does somebody want to give me the complete story?" asked Haley impatiently.

"Haley," said Theodosia, "Professor Morrow analyzed the tablecloth and said the smudge, or schmutz, as you called it, was garden-variety dirt. Then I talked with Timothy, and he said that if you stuffed a pistol full of dirt, it would probably explode."

"Holy smokes," said Haley. "So maybe the garden-variety dirt—"

"Is really from somebody's garden," finished Drayton.

The three exchanged knowing glances.

"Sounds like we might have to slip into our ninja costumes tonight and visit a few gardens," suggested Haley.

Drayton rubbed his hands together in anticipation. "Like Booth Crowley's, Billy Manolo's—"

"Let's hold off on that for the time being," said Theodosia. "Professor Morrow is going to try to break down the compounds. He thinks he can get a lot more specific than telling us it's just dirt."

"You mean he'll determine pH balance or nitrogen content?" asked Drayton. "That would be fabulous! In fact, it would help launch us in a very specific direction. For example, if we found out the soil was acid-based, we'd look for someone who had, say, a rose garden."

"Pretty slick," agreed Haley. "That would really help narrow it down. When do you think your professor will have those test results for us?"

"Hopefully, tomorrow," said Theodosia.

"Isn't it serendipitous," said Drayton, "that the Garden Fest kicks off in two days?"

"Kind of gives us an excuse to poke around in the dirt," said Haley with an impish grin.

25

The next morning, they all fluttered about nervously, waiting for Professor Morrow's phone call. But when the good professor hadn't called by ten a.m., Drayton suggested they put their heads together and work on some ideas for an artists' tea.

"I've heard of garden teas and teddy bear teas and, of course, we just had our mystery tea," said Haley, "but what the heck is an artists' tea?"

Drayton's eyes skimmed across the tea shop. Only three tables were occupied, and the customers sitting at them had all been served. Business was a tad slow but, then again, it was midweek.

"I was thinking of holding an artists' tea in conjunction with Spoleto," explained Drayton. "Theme the tearoom with Art Deco table decor, offer a creative menu, invite a few performing artists in. Maybe a jazz trio or string quartet. Or we could have a poetry reading."

"Sounds neat," said Haley.

"Theo?" asked Drayton. She had been arranging sets of miniature teapots on the wooden shelves and seemed lost in thought. "What do you think?"

"Judging by the success of your mystery tea, I think you could expect standing room only," she said, producing a grin that stretched ear to ear on Drayton's venerable face.

"What if one of the teas we served was badamtam," suggested Haley. "Really make it special."

Drayton feigned mock surprise. "My goodness, our little girl has actually been paying attention. Badamtam is, indeed, a grand Darjeeling."

"We could even invite some fine artists in," suggested Theodosia.

"Display their work or actually have them sketching or painting during the tea. You know, in the manner of a plein aire artist, where a small painting is begun and completed in the field, so to speak, all in one sitting."

"How about using sheets of classical music as place mats?" suggested Haley.

"That's the spirit," crowed Drayton as his black Montblanc pen fairly flew across the pages of his notebook. "Now, if I can just jot all these great ideas down—"

"Yoo-hoo."

They all spun on their heels. Delaine was standing there, smiling in her maddeningly, self-important manner.

"Can I get a quick cup to go?" she asked. "Assam, if it's not too much trouble."

"We've got ten different kinds of Assam," said Drayton as he deftly ran his fingertips across the lineup of tea tins that were shelved on the nearby wall. "But this golden tips is by far the best," he said, pulling down one of the shiny brass tins.

"Theo, I'm still holding that jacket for you," said Delaine.

"I know you are. And I'm still thinking about it." Theodosia paused. "Delaine, did you by any chance say something to Booth Crowley's wife the other day?"

Delaine smiled coyly. "Whatever are you talking about?"

"Booth Crowley stopped in here yesterday afternoon. To say he was unhappy would be putting it mildly. He was under the impression that I've been asking probing questions about him." She paused. "When in fact, we were just making conversation, were we not?"

Delaine hesitated for a moment, and Theodosia could see her mind working to formulate a plausible, Delaine-deflecting answer.

Theodosia sighed inwardly. Really, it *had* been her own fault. She knew that Delaine's true nature was to dish out as much information as she could, and still she'd kept pressing her for answers.

"Good heavens, Theodosia," Delaine said finally, "I ran into Booth Crowley's wife a couple days ago, that's all. Beatrix and I are on the same committee. I suppose I *might* have mentioned that her husband's name came up in conversation, but certainly nothing beyond that."

Theodosia gritted her teeth. She *really* should have known better. Delaine thrived on gossip and adored passing it on.

"Drayton," said Delaine, eager to change the subject, "are you terribly excited about Garden Fest? Is there any chance we'll get a peek at your Japanese bonsai trees this year?"

Drayton filled an indigo-colored paper cup with the freshly brewed Assam and snapped on a white take-out lid. "Actually, Timothy Neville has invited me to display a few of my bonsai on his patio," Drayton told her. "You know his garden is very dramatic and Asian-inspired. Of course, there'd be no judging involved, the bonsai would be purely for fun."

"So you'll have your bonsai at Timothy's Garden Fest party!" Delaine exclaimed. "How delightful. You know what? You folks should serve some of your yummy Japanese tea as well. Make it a *themed* affair."

"Yummy isn't the precise term I'd use to describe Japanese green tea, but, yes, Delaine, the idea had occurred to me," answered Drayton.

"We have to *work* at Timothy's party?" asked Haley.

Delaine turned probing eyes on Haley. "You're on the guest list, dear?"

"Well, not exactly," stammered Haley.

"Then serving tea would be an ideal way for you to be in attendance at a major social function, would it not?" said Delaine. "Give you a chance to hobnob with *café* society?"

"It's still work," grumbled Haley as she turned to answer the ringing phone. "Hello?" she said. "Yes, she's here." Haley put her hand over the receiver. "It's for you, Theodosia."

"I'll take it in my office, Haley," said Theodosia, chuckling at Delaine's somewhat pompous reference to café society. It was hard to stay angry with Delaine. She was a sweet woman and a rich source of entertainment. Still, there was no way she was going to have this conversation, or *any* conversation, in front of Delaine Dish. She'd learned her lesson for good.

"Hello?" said Theodosia as she kicked back in her comfy leather chair.

"Theodosia, it's Lizbeth Cantrell."

"Hello, Lizbeth," said Theodosia.

"My brother just told me." Lizbeth Cantrell's words spilled out in a rush.

"Told you what?" said Theodosia.

"That he's been doing consulting work for Oliver Dixon." She hesitated. "I feel like . . . I'm sure I put a great imposition upon you. Not knowing all the facts and then still pushing you . . . Well, anyway, it's over, isn't it? I feel like a great load has been lifted off my shoulders."

"Lizbeth, what do you mean?" asked Theodosia.

"There's no way anyone could be suspicious of Ford now," said Lizbeth, her voice filled with relief.

Theodosia stared at a bright little spot of sunlight that fell at her feet. "Lizbeth, I hate to say this, but your brother is not entirely off the hook."

There was silence for a moment. "I don't understand," said Lizbeth. "He and Oliver Dixon were working *together.* Surely, anyone could see they had a business relationship. Why would anyone believe that Ford wished harm to the man?"

"Yes, but it's not clear what *kind* of relationship they had," said Theodosia. She hated to say it, but she had to. "For all we know, it could have turned adversarial. Your brother made a recommendation that Oliver Dixon didn't agree with. . . . The result was friction between the two of them. . . ."

"Oh," said Lizbeth in a small voice.

"A man like Booth Crowley might even tell police that it reached the point of severely damaging the company," said Theodosia. "Then, what with Oliver's, uh, accident . . . Well, they might just read any business problem as motive."

"Booth Crowley would say something like that?" asked Lizbeth.

Oh yes, thought Theodosia. *The man would lie through his teeth if he thought it would gain him a centimeter's advantage.* Instead, Theodosia said, "There was a lot at stake. An investor might have an entirely different perspective."

"And the issue of the pistol still hangs over my brother's head," said Lizbeth. "All because Ford's an avid collector, because he knows guns. . . ."

Yes, thought Theodosia, *and gun collectors often know tricks. If Timothy*

Neville knew how to mastermind an exploding pistol, chances are, Ford Cantrell did, too.

"I had no right to involve you," said Lizbeth Cantrell. "I feel awful." She sounded as though she were ready to break down sobbing.

"Lizbeth," said Theodosia in as gentle a manner as she could, "you didn't involve me. Truth be known, I involved myself. And, please, also know this. . . . I intend to see this thing through to the bitter end. I will uncover some answers."

"You're going to keep investigating?" asked Lizbeth.

"Yes," said Theodosia.

"In cooperation with the police?" asked Lizbeth.

"That depends on how cooperative the police are," said Theodosia.

"Who's Drayton talking to?" asked Theodosia as she slid behind the counter and poured herself a cup of lung ching.

"Don't know," said Haley. "The other line rang the minute you went in back to take your call. Whoever he's on the line with has been doing all the talking, though."

Drayton hung up the phone, looking sober.

"What's with you?" asked Haley.

"I just had a very strange conversation with Gerard Huber, the manager of the Saint James Hotel," said Drayton.

Haley gave a low whistle. "That's a pretty hoity-toity place. What the heck did they want with you?"

"They just offered me a job," said Drayton unhappily.

"What?" exclaimed Haley.

"You heard me," snapped Drayton. "Gerard Huber asked if I had any interest in coming to work there."

"Doing what?" asked Haley.

Drayton turned a clouded face toward Theodosia. "Executive director of their food and wine service." He reached a gnarled hand out, rested it gently atop Theodosia's. "You know what this is all about, don't you?" he asked.

"Change!" declared Haley boisterously. "This is what Madame Hildegarde predicted the night of the mystery tea!"

Theodosia shook her head slowly. "I'm afraid not, Haley. But what it does mean is that Booth Crowley has started to come after us."

"Booth Crowley?" said Haley, scrunching her face into a quizzical frown. "What does *he* have to do with this?"

"He's one of the owners of the Saint James Hotel," said Drayton. "One of their silent partners, so to speak."

"Oh," said Haley, absorbing this latest information. "Did they offer you a lot of money?"

"Haley," said Theodosia, "that's Drayton's—"

"It's okay," said Drayton as his gray eyes sought out Theodosia's blue eyes. "They said they'd double what I was making now."

Haley gave a low whistle. "Double the salary . . . imagine that."

Drayton's face settled into a look of indignation. "As if I could be bought. What absolute rubbish!"

26

Detective Burt Tidwell finally showed up midafternoon. Theodosia knew he would. He almost had to, given the fact that her earlier missive to him, her E-mail spelling out her roster of murder suspects, had undoubtedly prompted him into having a talk with Booth Crowley.

Tidwell grasped a floral teacup in his huge paw, took a delicate sip of amber-colored dimbulla tea. "Ah, Miss Browning," he said as he settled back in his wooden chair, "such a civilized respite." Tidwell took another sip and gazed placidly about the tearoom. "With such lovely environs as this, why do you continue to involve yourself in such unpleasantness?"

"You're referring to Oliver Dixon's death?" she said.

"That and your persistent penchant for investigating," said Tidwell. "Why risk exposing yourself to unnecessary danger?"

"Do you think I'm in danger?" Theodosia asked with genuine curiosity.

"Anyone who goes about asking probing questions will, sooner or later, find their popularity severely compromised," said Tidwell.

What a maddening answer, thought Theodosia as she stared across the table at him. *Tidwell is, once again, jousting with words. He's trying to determine who I think should be at the very top of the list that I sent him.*

"So you believe my questions have exposed a few sensitive areas?" said Theodosia.

Tidwell waited a long time to answer. "Yes," he finally replied. "Although your Mr. Booth Crowley seems to be a tad hypersensitive." Tidwell's eyelids slid down over his slightly protruding eyes in the manner of one who is relaxed and ready to fall asleep. "Interesting man, Mr. Crowley. Did you know he can trace his ancestry back to John Wilkes Booth?"

Theodosia ignored Tidwell's remark. It seemed like everyone in the South could trace their ancestry back to someone who was famous, infamous, or had played some sort of walk-on role in the course of the nation's history. Her own mother had been a great-great-grandniece of Aaron Burr.

"How hard have you looked at Doe?" Theodosia asked him.

"Ah," said Tidwell as his eyes snapped open like a window shade. "Doe Belvedere Dixon. Grieving widow, toast of the town, belle of the ball."

"Don't forget Magnolia Queen," added Theodosia.

Tidwell pursed his lips delicately. "The girl *did* seem to collect beauty pageant crowns much the same way a Girl Scout does merit badges."

"The question is," said Theodosia, "was Oliver Dixon one of her merit badges?"

"Miss Browning, you have a nasty habit of thinking the worst of people."

"As do you, Detective Tidwell," said Theodosia, smiling at him.

"Touché," said Tidwell. "Here's what I *will* share with you, Miss Browning. According to a recent study conducted by our wise friends at the Justice Department, forty percent of so-called family murders are committed by a spouse."

"Do you think this was a family murder?"

"Hard to say," said Tidwell.

"Was there life insurance?" asked Theodosia.

"There was considerable life insurance as well as accidental death insurance."

"Accidental death," said Theodosia. "Interesting." She thought for a moment. "Did anything turn up during Oliver Dixon's autopsy?"

Tidwell lifted one furry eyebrow, and a knowing smile spread across his chubby, bland face. "Your line of reasoning follows that if Oliver Dixon suffered from an incurable disease, the possibility exists that he might have staged his own accidental death?"

"It wouldn't be the first time someone tried to do it," said Theodosia.

"Nor the last," agreed Tidwell. "But no, I studied the medical examiner's report with great care, I assure you. Aside from a small degree of hardening of the arteries and the onset of osteoarthritis in his hands, Oliver Dixon was in relatively good health for a man of sixty-six."

Theodosia reached for the teapot and poured them each another half cup of tea. "Would you tell me about your visit with Booth Crowley?" she asked.

"I think not," he said.

"But you find him a suspicious figure in all of this?" she said.

"I once told you that I regard everyone as a suspect."

"And I once told you that cannot be efficient."

"If efficiency is what you seek, I suggest you cease and desist from your amateur sleuthing," Tidwell told her. "Since the modus operandi of an investigator is dependent on tedious fact-finding and repetitive questions."

Theodosia decided to try another approach. "Your talking to Booth Crowley indicates you may have shifted your focus away from Ford Cantrell."

"I didn't say that," said Tidwell.

"No, but your actions indicate that," said Theodosia.

"Why do I have the nagging feeling that you're trying to clear Ford Cantrell?" asked Tidwell.

Theodosia sighed. What harm would it do to tell Tidwell, even if he was closemouthed with her? "If you must know, I told his sister I'd do everything in my power to help her."

"Why?" asked Tidwell.

"It's personal," said Theodosia, standing up. "It turns out we go back a long way together. Now, if you'll excuse me, Detective . . ." And she hurried over to where Drayton was folding napkins.

Tidwell continued to sit at the table, sipping tea, enjoying the aromatic smells and the bubble and hiss surround-sound that enveloped him like a warm cocoon. He lived alone, police work filled his days and most of his nights, so it wasn't often that he was able to be part of an environment that felt so pleasant and relaxed.

So the Browning woman had made some sort of promise to Lizbeth Cantrell, Tidwell mused to himself. That was unfortunate, because he still had doubts as to Ford Cantrell's complete innocence. And it especially didn't look good that Billy Manolo was involved.

Or, at least he *thought* Billy Manolo was involved.

He'd instructed the patrol cars in Billy Manolo's neighborhood to keep tabs on the hotheaded young man. Most of the time, when Billy went out at night, it was to drink a couple beers at a desultory little bar called the Boll Weevil. But on two separate occasions, and rather late at night, they'd observed Billy's old Chevy pickup heading out the 165 toward the low country. And the low country was where Ford Cantrell lived.

Had Billy Manolo somehow aligned himself with Ford Cantrell? Tidwell wondered.

Possibly.

Of course, he was still questioning personnel from the now-defunct Grapevine, but he'd heard his share of stories about disagreements between Oliver Dixon and Ford Cantrell. So Ford *could* have had motive. And Billy *could* have done the dirty work.

Tidwell had studied the shots that the *Post and Courier*'s photographer had taken that day in White Point Gardens. That lovely Sunday afternoon when he'd been home in his postage stamp–sized backyard, trying to coax some life from the tulip bulbs he'd planted last fall.

They'd all been watching the sailboat race, the whole cast and crew. Oliver Dixon, Doe Belvedere Dixon, Ford Cantrell, Billy Manolo, and Booth Crowley. And Theodosia Browning.

Tidwell took a final sip of tea, pushed his chair back, and stood, economical movements for a man so large. Removing a five-dollar bill from his wallet, he laid it gently on the table. Theodosia had never charged him for tea, yet he felt paying for it was the honorable thing to do. He knew the young girl Haley probably didn't like him, but she was always polite and took great pains to serve him properly. In a world gone mad with indifference, that counted for something.

"*Miss Dimple, you're* doing the bookkeeping for a couple other shops on Church Street, aren't you?" asked Theodosia. Theodosia knew she was, but it seemed like a good way to kick off the conversation she wanted to have.

It was late afternoon, and the last customers had just left. Miss Dimple had her ledgers spread out on one of the tables and was slowly going through the last few of the day's receipts.

Miss Dimple beamed. "Indeed I am. Monday mornings I tally the weekend receipts for the Chowder Hound, and Tuesday afternoons I'm at Pinckney's Gift Shop. Once in a while I even work behind the cash register. It's so pleasant to be around all that Irish linen and crystal."

"Have you heard any rumors about Doe Belvedere Dixon? How she's doing, what she's doing?" asked Theodosia.

Miss Dimple placed the tip of her Ticonderoga number-two yellow pencil between her lips and thought for a moment. "I heard she was selling off some of her art and collectibles. But, then, you already know about that."

"Right," volunteered Haley, who had been unpacking Chinese blue and white teapots from a newly arrived shipment. "Giovanni Loard brought in that Edgefield pot last week."

"I *did* hear something about her changing her name," said Miss Dimple.

"Changing her name?" asked Drayton. He'd obviously been listening, too, as he double-checked the order forms for some covered tea mugs that had caught his eye in a supplier's catalog.

"Yes," said Miss Dimple, her memory coming back to her now. "Word is out that Doe is going back to being just Doe Belvedere."

"You know why I think she's doing it?" asked Haley. "Because Doe Dixon sounds like an exotic dancer."

"Nonsense," said Drayton, a smile playing at his lips. "You determine your exotic dancer name by combining your pet's name with your mother's maiden name."

"Oh, my God!" screamed Haley. "Then mine would be Lulu Rendell!"

"See?" said Drayton.

"You two!" said Miss Dimple, shaking with laughter.

27

Wynton Marsalis played on the CD player, and she was deep into Pearl Buck's *Pavilion of Women* when Professor Morrow called.

"Miss Browning," he said in his somewhat distracted manner, "I hope I've not phoned too late."

Theodosia glanced at the baroque brass clock that sat on the pine mantel, saw that it was just half past eight.

"Not at all, Professor Morrow," she said, sliding a bookmark between the pages and closing her book. Her heart seemed to thump an extra beat in anticipation of his news. "I'm delighted you called. In fact, I've been looking forward to hearing from you," she told him.

"Good, good," he said. "Took me longer than I thought. But then, everything takes longer these days, doesn't it? I'm teaching a two-week interim course this June, and Kiplinger, our department head, just now suggested I develop an on-line syllabus. So of course I had to scramble—"

"What's the course?" asked Theodosia, trying to be polite.

"Herbaceous perennials," said Professor Morrow. "Simple to teach, not a lot to prepare, and students always seem to like it."

"Great," said Theodosia. "I really want to thank you for taking time to do this soil analysis."

"Right," said Professor Morrow, "the analysis."

Theodosia had a mental picture of Professor Morrow adjusting his glasses and thumbing through his notes, ready to deliver a short lecture to her.

"I ran a standard micronutrient test, measured levels of sulfur, iron, manganese, copper, zinc, and boron. As far as pH level goes, I'd have to say your dirt came from an area where the soil was quite acidic."

"What kind of plants grow in acidic soil?" asked Theodosia.

"Are we talking flowers or shrubs?" asked Professor Morrow.

Theodosia made an educated guess. "Flowers." In her mind's eye, she could imagine someone stepping out into his garden, shoving the point of a trowel into soft, black dirt, then scooping that dirt into a plastic bag to carry to the yacht club.

"Flowers," said Professor Morrow, weighing the possibilities. "Then you're talking something like verbena, marigold, calliopsis, or nicotiana. Of course, those varieties are all annuals. In perennials, you'd be looking at baptisia, coreopsis, platycodon, or silene."

"Wow," said Theodosia, feeling slightly overwhelmed.

"Of course, roses are also notorious for preferring acidic soil, but you can't have it *too* acidic. The demanding little darlings prefer a pH balance somewhere between 5.5 and 6.5. Any more than that, and they get chlorotic."

"What does that mean?"

"Their leaves mottle," said Professor Morrow.

28

"It's a good thing he faxed you his notes," said Drayton, "otherwise this would be *really* complicated."

For the last hour, Drayton had been poring over Professor Morrow's jottings, checking them against three different gardening books that he'd borrowed from Robillard Booksellers next door. Books, faxes, and pages torn from Drayton's ledger were strewn on one of the tea shop's tables. In between waiting on customers and serving fresh-from-the-oven pastries, Haley hovered at the table where Drayton and Theodosia had set up headquarters.

"I'm going to end up buying these books," Drayton announced. "They're very good, and I don't have them in my collection. Just look at this tabular list of garden perennials and this lovely chapter on bridge grafting. You don't run across information like this every day."

Earlier, Theodosia had shared Professor Morrow's findings with Drayton and Haley, and they had both jumped at the chance to be involved in the investigation. Although it felt like they were heading down the right trail, their task also felt slightly daunting. Professor Morrow had given them so many details and possibilities that one almost needed a degree in horticulture to figure everything out.

"Haley, we're going to need litmus paper," said Drayton. "Can you run down to the drugstore later and pick up a packet?"

"Sure," she agreed. "You're still convinced we can get a handle on who might have overpacked that pistol by testing soil from various gardens?"

"And the yacht club," said Theodosia. "Let's not forget the yacht club."

"Right," said Drayton, then added for Haley's sake, "this is a gamble that *could* pay off. We've got the results from Professor Morrow's tests, so that becomes our baseline. Now what we do is check the various soil samples using the soil testing kits we got from Hattie Bootwright's floral shop down the street."

"So how exactly are we going to pull this off?" asked Haley. She was almost dancing in place, excited at the prospect of being involved in a full-blown investigation and, at the same time, keeping a watchful eye on her tea shop customers.

"Drayton and I already talked about that," said Theodosia. "We'll all be at Timothy Neville's tonight, so that will serve as a kind of home base."

"Right," agreed Drayton. "We'll work from there. Doe lives half a block away, so we can easily scout her garden and obtain a sample."

"You're sure she'll be at Timothy's tonight?" asked Haley.

"Absolutely," said Drayton. "In fact, she'll be attending with Giovanni Loard. He called me yesterday about a silver teapot someone brought into his shop, and he mentioned that he'd be there. If you remember, his garden is on tomorrow night's tour. So he's very excited about the entire Garden Fest event."

"He's not still mad about the other day?" asked Theodosia.

"Never mentioned it," said Drayton.

"Okay then," said Theodosia, getting back to business. "Booth Crowley lives two blocks away on Tradd Street, so his garden should be an easy hit as well. We know he'll be there tonight, since his wife Beatrix serves on one of the Garden Fest committees with Delaine."

"Perfect," said Drayton, rubbing his hands together.

"What about Billy Manolo and Ford Cantrell?" asked Haley. "I thought they were on your hot list, too."

"They are," said Theodosia, "but Billy Manolo doesn't really have a yard. Well, he does, but almost every square inch is littered with pieces of iron or covered with finished metalwork. We can drop by the yacht club, though, that's easy enough."

"And I guess it would be difficult to check Ford Cantrell's place, since he lives on a huge plantation," said Haley. "You wouldn't even know where to start." She turned to scan the tearoom, saw out the window that one of the yellow tour jitneys had just let off a load of tourists, and they were making a beeline for the tea shop.

"I guess we'll just work with what we've got," said Haley as she headed for the door to greet their new customers.

"Actually," said Theodosia, once Haley was out of earshot, "it's *not* all we've got."

Drayton turned his head sharply to stare at Theodosia. Something in her tone told him she might be hatching another idea. "What do you mean?" he asked warily.

Theodosia bent close to Drayton's ear and began to whisper. And as she did, a look of astonishment flickered across his face. When she was done, he gazed at her with admiration.

"It's a jolly good brazen plan, all right," said Drayton. "The question is, will it work?"

Theodosia lifted her shoulders imperceptibly. "It might flush out a fox or two."

"It's also dangerous," he said, adding a sober note to the conversation.

"Agreed," said Theodosia, "But that's also why I like it." She frowned. "Trouble is, the whole plan would hinge on Timothy Neville's cooperation. Do you think we can persuade him to go along with us? And especially at such short notice?"

"You leave Timothy to me," advised Drayton. "I can be very convincing when I have to. And since elections at the Heritage Society are coming up soon, and Timothy is lobbying strongly for reelection as president, he might just listen carefully to what I have to say. So you go call Lizbeth Cantrell and arrange for her to come up with some creative ruse to have her brother present at the party tonight. And leave Timothy Neville to me."

• • •

Theodosia tapped her fingers on the telephone. This wasn't going to be easy, she told herself. Because she *could* be setting Ford Cantrell up for a terrible fall. Then again, if Ford really was instrumental in engineering Oliver Dixon's death, justice would be served.

The word *justice* echoed in Theodosia's brain. Lizbeth's wreath of coltsfoot had been intended to connote justice. Funny how that single word seemed to hang over this entire investigation like a sword suspended from a single thread.

Taking a deep breath, Theodosia opened the phone directory, ran her finger down a fairly long list of Cantrells, spotted Lizbeth Cantrell's phone number, and punched it in.

Lizbeth Cantrell was in today; she picked up on the first ring.

"Lizbeth," said Theodosia, the words tumbling out, "can you bring Ford to a party at Timothy Neville's home tonight?"

"What's going on?" asked Lizbeth, her antennae already at full alert.

"Hopefully, a plan that will reveal Oliver Dixon's killer," said Theodosia.

Lizbeth hesitated. "A plan you want my brother's participation in."

"Yes," said Theodosia, "but I'm afraid I can't share the exact details."

"And if this plan backfires?"

Theodosia had heard fear and worry in Lizbeth's voice and knew exactly what she was thinking. *Backfiring* was Lizbeth's euphemism for Ford being proven guilty. She knew Lizbeth was utterly heartsick over the possibility.

I've got to strongly dissuade her of that thought, Theodosia decided. *Keep her thinking positive.*

"Hopefully," said Theodosia, "this plan will help *clear* Ford's name, once and for all. But it will only work if he's in attendance tonight. At the Garden Fest kickoff party." Theodosia listened to dead air for a moment. "You know where Timothy lives?" she asked hopefully.

"Yes," said Lizbeth.

"So we can count on your attendance?"

"We'll be there," said Lizbeth finally. "Ford won't like it, but I'll think of something."

Breathing a sigh of relief, Theodosia hung up the phone. That hadn't been as difficult as she'd thought it might be. But, then again, Lizbeth Cantrell was one tough lady, made of fairly stern stuff.

It would all play out tonight, Theodosia decided, once her plan was set into motion. Of course, her plan also hinged on a number of critical pieces: all the right people showing up and Timothy Neville's supreme cooperation. Was that too much to ask? She surely hoped not.

Gazing at the wall of photos across from her desk, Theodosia's eyes were drawn to an old black and white picture of her dad rigging one of his old sailboats, a Stone Horse. And her thoughts turned to Billy Manolo, the surly part-time handyman at the yacht club.

It would be perfect if she could somehow get Billy Manolo to show up tonight as well. Then they'd have all the players. . . .

Yes, it would be perfect, she decided. It was certainly worth a try. But how exactly would she . . . ?

Theodosia punched in the phone number for the yacht club. A crazy idea had popped into her head that, on closer inspection, might not be so crazy after all.

"Yacht club," answered a youthful male voice.

"Is Billy Manolo there?" she asked.

"Oh, he's . . . I think he's out working on one of the boats. I saw him on one of the piers an hour or so ago, but I couldn't say where he is now. I just stopped by the clubhouse to grab a drink of water, and the phone rang. I can't really help—"

"Could you take a message?" asked Theodosia.

"A message. Yeah, I suppose so. Hang on a minute. Gotta get a pencil and paper."

There was a fumble and a clunk as the phone was set down, then the young man came on the line again.

"Okay, go ahead," he said.

"This is for Billy Manolo," said Theodosia. "The note should say, please be at Timothy Neville's home tonight at eight. Address is 413 Archdale."

Theodosia could hear the man softly repeating the message to himself as he wrote it down. "Anything else?" asked the young man.

"Add that it's urgent Billy show up and make a note that it's at the request of Booth Crowley."

"How do you spell that? I got the Booth part, I'm just not sure on Crowley."

"C-R-O-W-L-E-Y," said Theodosia.

"Okay," said the young man. "And who is this?"

Theodosia ransacked her brain for the name of the woman she'd spoken with the day she phoned Booth Crowley's office. Marilyn, the woman's name had been Marilyn.

"This is Marilyn from Booth Crowley's office."

"Gotcha," said the young man. "I'll leave the note in his mailbox."

"Yes, that's perfect," said Theodosia, remembering a line of four of five wooden mail slots that were used by employees, handymen, yacht club commodores, and other folks who spent time there.

29

Timothy Neville adored giving parties. Holiday parties, charity galas, music recitals. And his enormous Georgian mansion, a glittering showpiece perched on Archdale Street, was, for many guests, a peek into the kind of gilded luxury that hadn't been witnessed in Charleston since earlier times.

Although not an official Garden Fest event, Timothy had been staging his Garden Fest kickoff party for more years than anyone could count. It was a way to bring all the Garden Fest participants together in one place, and it served as a kind of unofficial marker that heralded the arrival of spring. Days were becoming warmer, deep purple evenings held the promise of fluttering luna moths and night-blooming nicotiana. And, once again, everyone in Charleston was more than ready to treat their gardens as an extended room of their house. For Charlestonians adored their gardens, whether they be tiny, secluded brick patios surrounded by slender columns of oleander or one of the enormous enclosed backyards in the historic district, lavishly embellished with vine-covered brick walls, fountains adorned with statuary, and well-tended beds of verdant plant life.

Poised on his broad piazza, dressed in impeccable white, Timothy Neville greeted each of his guests with a welcoming word. Flickering gaslights threw a warm scrim and lent an alabaster glow that served to enhance the complexions of his female guests.

Just inside, Henry Marchand, Timothy's valet of almost forty years, stood in the dazzling foyer. Attired in red topcoat and white breeches, Henry solemnly directed newly arrived ladies to the powder room and gentlemen toward the bar with the grace and surety of a majordomo secure in his position.

"Even though it's not entirely black tie, it's certainly creative attire," exclaimed Drayton as he and Theodosia surveyed the chattering crowd. Most of Timothy's guests were also residents of the historic district and, thus, nodding acquaintances to the two of them. Many were descended from Charleston's old families and had lived in the surrounding neighborhood for years. Others had been drawn to the historic district by their love of history, tradition, and old-world charm and had scrimped and saved to buy their historic houses with an eye toward full restoration. For in the historic district, restoration was always big business. And a major boon to the plasterers, wallpaperers, chimney sweeps, gardeners, designers, and various other tradespeople and craftsmen who were so often called upon to keep these grande dame homes in working order.

Earlier, Drayton and Theodosia had helped Haley get her tea service set up outside in Timothy's lush garden. Ten of Drayton's bonsai had been arranged on simple wooden Parsons tables, creating an elegant, Zen-like atmosphere. Haley was now busily pouring Japanese tea into small, blue-glazed tea bowls and passing them out to those guests who'd come outside to admire Timothy's elegant garden and Drayton's finely crafted bonsai.

"I do love this house," declared Theodosia, as she gazed in awe at the Hepplewhite furnishings, glittering crystal chandeliers, and carved walnut mantelpiece signed by Italian master Luigi Frullini. She'd only given a cursory glance to the oil paintings that lined the walls but had already recognized a Horace Bundy and a Franklin Whiting Rogers. She also knew that the china Timothy displayed in illuminated cases in one of the two front parlors was genuine Spode.

"Timothy's got taste, all right," said Drayton, "and the man has demonstrated a remarkable amount of class. I couldn't believe how willing he was to take part in our little plan."

"I'm relieved that he's agreed to help," said Theodosia. "But I must admit I'm a little nervous about the whole thing."

"Me, too," said Drayton. "But if we stick to our plan . . . Oh, talk about perfect," said Drayton under his breath.

"You bought the jacket!" Delaine Dish's strident voice rose above the buzz of conversation in the solarium where Theodosia and Drayton had wandered in to visit the bar and get flutes of vintage champagne. Clutching an oversized goblet of white wine and wearing a frothy wrapped dress of pink silk, Delaine pushed her way through the crowd to join them.

"When?" she asked Theodosia, her eyes all aglow. "Today?" Her dark hair was done up in a fetching swirl and held in place by a pink barrette. Her shellacked pink toes peeped out of matching pink sandals.

"About two hours ago," said Theodosia. "Suddenly, the jacket seemed like the absolute perfect thing to wear to this party. So I phoned your shop and talked with Janine and, lo and behold, I was in luck. You still had the green."

"And so pretty with your ring," giggled Delaine, noting the cluster of peridots that sparkled on Theodosia's hand. "Is that a family heirloom?"

"My grandmother's," replied Theodosia.

"Inherited jewelry," murmured Delaine, "always the best kind." She turned glittering eyes on Drayton. "No strings attached. Unlike a gift from a gentleman."

"Delaine, any gentleman worth his salt would be quite content to lavish gifts upon you, nary a string attached."

"Oh, Drayton," she cooed.

Drayton bowed slightly. "Now, if you ladies will excuse me, I'm going to head out to the garden. Timothy has asked me to do a short, impromptu talk on the style merits of the windswept bonsai."

"Such a gentleman," said Delaine. She smiled at Theodosia with a slightly glassy-eyed look, and Theodosia knew Delaine was wearing her tinted contact lenses tonight. She was terribly nearsighted and, at the same time, loved to enhance and sometimes change the color of her eyes.

"Delaine," Theodosia began, feeling a tiny stab of guilt at what she was about to set into motion. "You know I've been asking more than a few questions about Oliver Dixon's death. . . ."

Delaine blinked and moved closer to her. "Has something new turned up?" she asked.

"In a way, yes," said Theodosia. "I probably shouldn't—"

"Oh, you can tell me, dear," said Delaine. She put a hand on Theodosia's arm, pulled her protectively away from the throes of the crowd. "I'm as concerned about all this as you are."

"The thing of it is," said Theodosia, "I've stumbled upon the most amazing clue."

"Whatever do you mean?" asked Delaine.

"Remember the linen tablecloth?"

Delaine's face remained a blank.

"The one that Oliver Dixon sort of fell onto during the . . . uh . . . accident?"

Remembrance suddenly dawned for Delaine. "Oh, of *course*. The *tablecloth*."

"Well, I had it analyzed."

"You mean like in a crime lab?" asked Delaine. She glanced around to make sure no one was listening in on their conversation.

"No, a private analysis. But by an expert."

"How fascinating," said Delaine, her face lighting up with excitement, "tell me more."

"One of the theories about that old pistol exploding was that someone *meant* for it to explode. Someone packed it chock-full of gunpowder and dirt."

"How awful," said Delaine, but her face held a smile of anticipation.

"The analysis I had done broke that dirt down into specific compounds. In theory, if we can match the dirt from the weapon with the dirt in someone's garden, we'd have Oliver Dixon's killer."

Delaine's mouth opened and closed several times. "That's amazing," she finally managed. "Astonishing, really."

"Isn't it?" said Theodosia.

"When are you going to do this matching of dirt?" asked Delaine.

"We're working on it right now," said Theodosia.

"So you could know *tonight*?"

"In theory . . . yes," said Theodosia.

"Do the police know? That Detective Tidwell fellow?"

"All in good time," said Theodosia.

Delaine let loose a little shiver. "I'm getting goose bumps. This is just like one of those true-crime TV shows. On-the-spot investigating . . . very exciting."

Theodosia stared across the room into the crowd. She could see Booth Crowley standing at the bar. He had just gotten a martini or a gimlet or something in a stemmed glass with a twist of lemon and was staring glumly at his wife, a small, sturdy woman with hair teased into a blond bubble.

At the opposite end of the room, Ford Cantrell had just walked in with his sister and was glancing nervously toward the bar, probably hoping he could get three fingers of bourbon instead of a glass of champagne and wondering why on earth Lizbeth had seen fit to drag him to this stuffy party where he was probably highly unwelcome.

Across the wide center hallway, Theodosia could see Doe Belvedere Dixon reclining on a brocade fainting couch in Timothy's vast library. Doe was dressed in a sleek cranberry-red pantsuit and was gossiping and talking animatedly with three other young women. Giggling like a schoolgirl, not a decorous widow.

Scanning the rest of the crowd, Theodosia hoped Billy Manolo had gotten the message she'd left him and would also put in an appearance some time this evening.

Theodosia knew that any one of them could have overpacked that pistol. Any one of them could be a cold, calculating killer. And tonight was the night to set a trap and see who stumbled in.

❧ 30 ❧

The hiss of the oxyacetylene torch was like a viper, angry and menacing. It was exactly how Billy Manolo felt tonight as he wielded his welding equipment.

He was angry. Angry and more than a little resentful. First of all, he was supposed to have this stupid gate finished by tomorrow morning. He'd been following a classical French design and using mortise joinery, and the project seemed to be taking forever. Marianne Petigru had made it perfectly clear to him that if he missed one more deadline, he could forget about getting any more work from Popple Hill. But Marianne was a snotty, rich bitch, he told himself, who could go stick her head in a bucket of swamp water for all he cared.

At the same time, he genuinely *liked* working on these projects. They were good jobs, substantial jobs, and they usually involved design challenges. It also didn't hurt that he was able to earn several hundred bucks a crack.

And, face it, he told himself, there was no way in hell he could ever *parlaz vous* with those rich folks by himself and convince them to hire a guy like him to create wrought-iron gates, fence panels, and stair rails for their fancy houses. Hell, if he were a rich guy, he wouldn't hire a guy like himself!

The other problem that gnawed at him was the fact that he was supposed to have gone out on another job tonight. And if he wasn't along to practically hold the hands of those dumb yahoos, they'd sure as hell get lost. Because not one of those good old boys was smart enough to find his backside in the hall of mirrors at high noon. That was for sure.

But everything had changed when he received that stupid message from Booth Crowley. Old jump-when-I-say-so Crowley wanted him to meet him tonight at some guy's house. What was *that* all about? Had the plan changed completely? Was he no longer honchoing their little clandestine operation?

Billy reached down with a leather-gloved hand and shut off the valve for the gas. He let the blue white flame die before his eyes before he tipped his helmet back.

Eight o'clock, the note had said. Eight o'clock. He guessed he'd better not cross a guy like Booth Crowley. Crowley was one important dude around Charleston, and Billy knew firsthand that he could also be a pretty nasty dude. Right now, he regretted ever getting involved with Booth Crowley.

Billy Manolo carefully laid his equipment on the battered cutting table. He shut off the lights in the garage, pulled down the door, and locked it.

As he picked his way across the yard, he told himself he had barely enough time for a quick shower.

31

"*Did you get* the samples?" Drayton asked quietly.

Triumphantly, Haley laid three plastic Baggies full of dirt on the table next to Drayton's bonsai trees. "I did just as you said," Haley told him. "Used the litmus paper first in a half-dozen places. Then, when I found what seemed like a fairly close match for the soil's pH level, I collected a sample."

"Good girl," breathed Drayton as he pulled two little plastic petri dishes out of the duffel bag that held his bonsai tools and copper wire. "You're sure nobody noticed the light from your flashlight?"

"Positive. The yacht club was a cinch, 'cause nobody was there. And when I went into the two backyards, I only turned the flashlight on for a moment when I had to read the litmus paper. And then I cupped my hands around it."

"Sounds like an excellent cat burglar technique," said Drayton.

But Haley was still riding high from her little adventure. "Doe's yard was easy," she chattered on. "Nobody home at all. But I had to scale a pretty good-sized fence in order to get into Booth Crowley's backyard. I had a couple hairy moments that definitely brought out my inner athlete." She paused. "You're going to test the soil samples right now?"

"That's the general idea," said Drayton as his fingers fluttered busily, measuring out spoonfuls of soil from each bag and dumping them into their own petri dishes.

"So we'll know right away?" asked Haley.

Drayton slid the three petri dishes out of sight, behind a large, brown, glazed bonsai pot that held a miniature grove of tamarack trees. "Haley," he said, "*everyone* will know right away if you persist in asking these questions."

"I thought that was the general idea," she said.

Drayton smiled tolerantly. "All in good time, dear girl, all in good time."

Lights blazed, conversation grew louder, the string quartet that Timothy Neville had brought in, fellow symphony members, played a lively rendition of Vivaldi's *Four Seasons*. Theodosia moved from room to room, dropping a hint here, a sly reference there. She was following in Delaine's wake, so all she really had to do was toss out an innuendo for good measure. It was surprisingly simple. And since this was a party where conversation groups constantly shifted and re-formed, it was easy to mix and mingle and get the rumor mill bubbling.

In one of two front flanking parlors, Theodosia ran into their genial host.

"Enjoying yourself, Miss Browning?" Timothy pulled himself away from a group of people that was heatedly discussing the pros and cons of faux finishes and peered at her hawkishly.

"Lovely evening, Mr. Neville," she said.

"I noticed you've been flitting about," Timothy said, pulling his lips back to reveal small, square teeth, "and chatting merrily with my guests. The old marketing instinct dies hard, eh? Fun to be a spin doctor again." His voice carried a faint trace of sarcasm, but his eyes danced with merriment. Then Timothy leaned toward her and asked quietly, "Drayton working his alchemy with the soil testing?"

"Should be," she said, taking a sip of champagne, feeling slightly conspiratorial.

"Why not scoot out and check for results then. If it's a go, we'll launch part two of your little plan."

Theodosia was suddenly captivated by Timothy's quixotic spirit. "Why, Mr. Neville, I do believe you're rather enjoying this," she told him.

"It's a game, Miss Browning, a fascinating game. Truth be known, Drayton didn't have to twist my arm much to get me to play along. But"—Timothy Neville suddenly sobered—"at the same time, Oliver Dixon was a decent man and a friend. He was a generous benefactor to the Heritage Society and lent support to several other worthwhile charities here in Charleston. It was a terrible fate that befell him, and if someone *was* responsible for masterminding such a frightful, premeditated act, that person should be made to pay. If the police haven't figured something out by now, I see no reason why the fates shouldn't intercede. Or at least receive a helpful prod from us." Timothy paused, removed a spotless white handkerchief from his inside jacket pocket, and blotted his brow gently. "Now, when you have an answer, Miss Browning, be sure to tell Henry immediately. He's the one charged with rounding up the troops for my little spectacle here tonight." Timothy reached for a glass of champagne from the tray of a passing waiter, held it up to Theodosia in a toast. "Henry is also who most of my guests fear more than me." He chuckled.

• • •

"Drayton, Timothy wants to know if you have any results yet," Theodosia asked somewhat breathlessly. She'd hurried from one end of Timothy's house to the other, then fairly flown down the back staircase into Timothy's elegant garden.

How delightful it is out here, she thought suddenly as she felt the gentle sway of palm trees and bamboo around her, caught the moonlight as it shimmered on the long reflecting pool. *How cool and quiet after the closeness and social chaos inside.*

But Drayton was peering at her with a glum expression. "I've got results, but not the kind you want to hear about," he said, a warning tone in his voice.

Theodosia was instantly on the alert. "What's wrong?"

"What's wrong is that none of our soil samples match with what Professor Morrow took off your tablecloth," he said. He drummed his fingers on the tabletop, obviously irritated.

Theodosia stared at Drayton and saw his vexation and frustration. Haley, who stood poised with a Japanese teapot in her hand, suddenly looked ready to cry.

"I did it just the way you told me to, Drayton," Haley said.

He held up a hand. "I'm not questioning your methodology. The preliminary matches looked good. It's just that . . ."

"What is it?" asked Theodosia.

"When we run a full analysis," said Drayton, "we come up empty."

"So Doe, Booth Crowley, and Billy Manolo are all innocent?" said Haley.

"Innocent of using soil from their own backyards," said Theodosia. "Or the yacht club, in Billy's case." She was bitterly disappointed as well. At the same time, she'd known this whole soil business had been a long shot.

"So that's it?" asked Haley. "We've come this far just to hit a dead end?"

"Not quite," said Theodosia. "The soil samples were really only the lure. Now it's time to have Timothy dangle the bait."

32

Billy Manolo heard the laughter and conversation from half a block away. It drifted like silver strands out the open windows and doors of Timothy Neville's enormous home and seemed to rise into the blue black sky.

Billy stopped for a moment and stared upward, half expecting to see something tangible in the night sky above him. Then he shook his head and resumed walking toward the big house on Archdale Street. *Foolishness,* he told himself. *Just plain foolishness.*

Henry met him at the door before he had a chance to knock or ring the bell.

"Mr. Manolo?" Henry asked in his dry, raspy voice.

Billy stared at him. The old guy in the red and white monkey suit had to be ninety years old. He also looked like somebody out of an old movie. A silent movie at that.

"Yeah, I'm Billy Manolo," he answered, his curiosity ratcheting up a couple notches. "Is there some kind of problem?"

"Not in the least," smiled Henry. "Fact is, we've been expecting you."

"Is that so?" Billy eyed Henry warily as he stepped into the foyer and glanced hurriedly around. "Looks like you all have a party going on."

"Indeed," said Henry.

"This is quite a place. You could park a 747 in this hallway."

"Thank you," said Henry. "I shall convey your rather astute observation to Mr. Neville, I'm sure he'll be pleased."

"Booth Crowley around?" Billy asked. "I got some weird message to meet him here."

"Yes, that was nicely arranged, wasn't it," said Henry.

"Huh?" asked Billy sharply.

"If you'll follow me to the music salon, sir," beckoned Henry. "It's time we get started."

The thatch of white hair atop Booth Crowley's head bristled like a porcupine displaying its quills. Then his small, watery gray eyes focused on Billy Manolo, dressed in faded jeans and a black T-shirt, swaggering down the center of the Oriental runner that ran the length of the hallway. Strangely enough, he followed in the wake of Timothy's man, Henry.

"Damn that boy," Booth Crowley muttered under his breath, immediately tuning out the two women who'd been making a polite pitch to him concerning funding for their beloved Opera Society's production of *Turandot*.

Their eyebrows shot immediately skyward. Swearing was not unknown to them, but neither was it customary for a man to display such rudeness in a social situation like this. The eyes of the volunteer coordinator flashed an immediate signal of those of the board member: *Uncouth. Not much of a gentleman.*

But committing a social faux pas was the furthest thing from Booth Crowley's mind right now. His was a personality hot-wired for anger, one that accelerated from rational behavior to utter rage with no stops in between, no chance for a safety valve.

Booth Crowley bulled his way across the room. Leading with his barrel of a chest, he shoved himself between Henry and Billy in an attempt to physically block Billy's way.

"Get the hell away from here," Booth Crowley snarled. His lips curled sharply, his Adam's apple bobbed wildly above his floral bow tie. Several people standing nearby paused to watch what seemed to be an ugly spectacle about to unfold.

Billy gazed at Booth Crowley in disbelief and decided the old fart had to be bipolar or whatever the current pop psycho term was. First Booth had left him a note that was practically a presidential mandate to meet him here tonight. Now the crazy fool was trying to toss him out! *What an idiot,* thought Billy as he shook his head tiredly. But then, everything felt nuts these days, like the world was crashing down around him.

The high tinkle of a bell cut through the raw tension and the sudden buzz of excitement.

"Everyone is kindly requested to convene in the music salon, please." Henry's normally papery voice had suddenly increased by twenty decibels, ringing out strong and clear and authoritative. He sounded like a courtier announcing the arrival of the queen to parliament.

"You old fool," spat Billy to Booth Crowley as the two men were suddenly jostled, then engulfed as bodies flowed past them.

Party guests pushed toward the music room, flushed with excitement, their spirits buoyed by the free flow of the excellent Roederer Cristal Champagne. Billy Manolo and Booth Crowley could do nothing but let themselves be carried along with the crowd. The most they could manage were furious scowls at each other.

Out on the patio, Drayton, Theodosia, and Haley also heard the high, melodious tinkle of Henry's bell.

Theodosia turned bright eyes to Drayton. "This is it," she whispered excitedly. "Keep your fingers crossed."

"Is *somebody* going to tell me what's *really* going on?" complained Haley. "I feel like I'm the last person on earth to—"

Drayton grabbed her by the hand and pulled her forward. "Come on then. Timothy's going to do his little speech. In about two minutes, you'll see exactly what we're up to!"

The three of them scampered up the back staircase into Timothy's house and pushed down the main hallway with the rest of the crowd. Once inside the vast music salon, they jockeyed for position.

Standing center stage, in front of an enormous marble fireplace, Timothy Neville waited as the crowd continued to pour into the room and gather around him. High above him, set incongruously against gold brocade wallpaper, hung a scowling portrait of one of his Huguenot ancestors.

It was a full minute before all the murmurs, coughs, and whispers quieted down. Finally, Timothy looked over toward Henry, who nodded slightly at him. Timothy gazed serenely out into the crowd, found Drayton and Theodosia, but did not acknowledge them. Then he pulled himself into his usual ramrod posture and began.

"Thank you all for coming tonight," he greeted the crowd in a ringing, impassioned voice. "It's always an honor to host a party for a delightful crowd such as this."

There was exuberant applause and several shouts of "Hear! Hear!"

Again, Timothy waited for the noise to die down. "Our Garden Fest event continues to grow each year," he told them. "This year alone we've added six additional garden venues to our program. That gives us a grand total of thirty-eight private gardens in our beloved historic district that will be open, over the next three days, for the public's sublime viewing pleasure."

More applause.

"On a more personal note," continued Timothy, "I sincerely regret that the garden of my friend and neighbor, Oliver Dixon, will no longer be included on the Garden Fest roster. As you all know, we lost Oliver recently, and the memory of his accident still haunts us."

With those few words, Timothy had suddenly gained the complete and rapt attention of the crowd.

"Oliver Dixon was a generous contributor to the Heritage Society," said Timothy. "And more than a few years ago, when I was a younger and far nimbler fellow, I sailed against Oliver Dixon in several of the yacht club's regattas: the Isle of Palms race, the Catfish Cup, the Patriots Point Regatta. Oliver was a true gentleman and a fine competitor. I know in my heart that he would not wish the yacht club's reputation or any of its longstanding traditions to be tarnished by what was truly a senseless accident."

Timothy paused, much the same way a minister would when asking for a moment of silence. The crowd seemed to hold its collective breath, sensing something big was about to happen.

"To celebrate Oliver Dixon's vast contributions and help continue the yacht club's time-honored customs, I am making a special donation in his memory."

The inimitable Henry now strode forth, bearing in his arms a large wooden box. Turning to face the crowd, Henry paused for a moment, then slowly lifted the lid.

Catching the gleam from the overhead chandelier, a silver pistol glinted from its cradle of plush red velvet.

There was a hush at first, an initial shock, as a visceral reaction swept through the crowd. They were surprised, slightly stunned. Then a smattering of applause broke out among several of the men standing near the front. The applause began to build steadily until, finally, almost everyone had politely joined in.

"You were right," Drayton whispered to Theodosia, "it *was* a shocker."

But Theodosia had turned to face the crowd, and her eyes were busily scanning faces.

She caught the look of initial shock, then supreme unhappiness that spread across Doe's young face.

Ford Cantrell, pressed up against the back wall, retained a mild smile that seemed to barely waver. But Theodosia had caught a spark of something else behind Ford's carefully arranged public face: curiosity. Ford Cantrell had taken in the entire scenario and was trying to figure out exactly what was going on, what con was being run.

Booth Crowley's sullen countenance bobbed among the crowd like an angry balloon. He had applauded perfunctorily but seemed nervous and distracted. His wife, Beatrix, at his side, maintained the look of mild bemusement she'd worn all night.

And Billy Manolo, looking like an angry rebel in his black T-shirt among a sea of dinner jackets and tuxedos, kept an insolent smirk on his face.

"What kind of pistol is it?" asked a young man at the front of the crowd. His eyes shone brightly, and he seemed pleased with himself for asking such a bold question.

Timothy's grin was both terrifying and curiously satisfying. "A Scottish regimental pistol. Manufactured by Isaac Bissell of Birmingham, England. See the engraved RHR? Stands for Royal Highland Regiment."

Delaine stood nearby, fanning herself nervously. "Is it loaded?" she asked with a mixture of alarm and fascination.

"Of course," said Timothy, hefting the weapon in one hand and pointing it toward the ceiling. "The cartridge is a traditional hand-rolled cartridge, loose powder and a round ball wrapped in thin, brown paper. It was crafted in the British tradition by Lucas Clay, one of the foremost munitions experts in the South today." Timothy held the pistol aloft for a moment, then put it reverently back in its box.

There were whistles of appreciation and murmurs as several people pressed forward to gaze at it, lying there, shiny and dangerous, on a bed of red velvet.

They are drawn to it like the hypnotic attraction of a cobra to a mongoose, thought Theodosia. The pistol was troubling yet difficult to resist, on display for all to admire on the library table next to the fireplace.

But the crowd was also beginning to dissipate now, moving out into the center hallway where it was cooler. Most folks were shuffling down the hall toward the solarium for drink refills at the bar.

Booth Crowley had shoved his way through the crowd again and stood talking with Billy Manolo. Or, rather, Booth Crowley was doing all the talking. Billy stared fixedly at the floor while the tips of Booth Crowley's ears turned a bright shade of pink.

Almost as pink as Delaine's dress, thought Theodosia, wishing she were a little mouse who could scamper across the floor and listen in on the tongue-lashing Booth Crowley seemed to be inflicting upon Billy Manolo.

"What do you think?" Drayton asked eagerly as he hovered at her elbow.

"Jury's still out," replied Theodosia.

"I'm going to dash over and grab a word with Timothy," he said. "Be right back."

As the room emptied rapidly, Theodosia moved along with the crowd, straining to keep everyone in view. Just ahead, Doe held an empty champagne glass aloft and, with a deliberate toss of her blond mane, handed it over to Giovanni Loard.

Giovanni Loard.

The thought struck Theodosia like a whack on the side of the head. *Maybe we should have taken soil samples from his garden,* she thought suddenly. After all, Giovanni seemed to get awfully cozy with Doe right after

Oliver's death. On the other hand, Giovanni was Oliver's cousin, so he was expected to be sympathetic and solicitous.

She looked back to see where Drayton was, but he and Timothy were nowhere in sight.

"Theodosia!" Delaine's troubled face appeared before her. "Did Timothy not *transcend* the boundaries of good taste tonight?"

Delaine wore a mantle of pious outrage, but Theodosia knew she would deliciously broadcast and rebroadcast tonight's events for days to come.

"Timothy's a true eccentric," admitted Theodosia. "You never know what he's got up his sleeve."

"Eccentric isn't the word for it," sputtered Delaine. "He's downright . . ." She searched for the right word. "Intemperate."

Amused, Theodosia glanced back into the music salon. It appeared to be completely empty now. Drayton and Timothy must have exited via another door, she decided.

"And what's with those soil samples you've been collecting?" asked Delaine. She nudged closer. "Any results you'd care to share?"

Soil samples, Theodosia thought again. *Should get one from Giovanni's garden, just to be safe.*

"Oh my gosh," gasped Delaine suddenly, "there's Gabby Stewart." She craned her neck to catch a glimpse of a pencil-thin woman in a short black cocktail dress. "Will you look at her face; not so much as a single line. Oh, Gabby . . ." And Delaine elbowed her way frantically through the crowd.

Theodosia stood by herself for a moment, watching the last of the guests amble toward the solarium and out onto the enormous front portico. Then she made a snap decision.

Giovanni lived nearby. His garden was highlighted on the map in the Garden Fest program that had been passed out earlier to all the guests.

She'd go there right now and take a soil sample. What harm would it do? After all, she'd be back in five minutes.

33

Flaming torches illuminated Timothy's backyard garden, although it was completely deserted at the moment. Beginning life as a classical Charleston courtyard garden, it had, over the years, veered toward an Asian-inspired garden. Now indigenous flowering trees and shrubs rubbed shoulders with thickets of bamboo, stands of lady fern, and Korean moss. The long, rectangular pond was overgrown with Asian water plants. Along the paths, stone lion-dogs and Buddhas stood guard.

Cool breezes swept through the garden as Theodosia stepped hurriedly down a stone walkway. In a far, dim corner, a small waterfall splashed noisily. Arriving at the back wall, Theodosia put a hand on the ancient wooden gate that led to the alley. Pushing outward, the old metal hinges creaked in protest. And in that same instant, Theodosia heard something else, too: light footsteps in front of her.

She hesitated, then turned to peer into the darkness.

A silver moon slid out from behind a bank of clouds and cast faint light on the man standing ten feet in front of her.

Theodosia put a hand to her chest. "Giovanni, you frightened me."

"I meant to," he said.

Theodosia caught her breath. Giovanni's voice was cold and menacing. He was no longer playing the role of the charming and witty antique dealer. Her eyes went immediately to the pistol Giovanni had clutched in his hand. It was the same pistol Timothy had just presented in the music room. Theodosia decided that Giovanni must have waited until everyone had left, then snatched it from the wooden box that looked so eerily like a miniature coffin.

"You think you're so smart," Giovanni snarled at her. "Why couldn't you just mind your own business?"

"And let you get away with murder, Giovanni?" Theodosia faced him with as much bravado as she dared. "Killing your own cousin. What a coward you turned out to be."

"*Second* cousin," corrected Giovanni. He waved the pistol menacingly at her. "But what does it matter how we were related? The fact is, Oliver signed his own death warrant by staunchly refusing to give me any help at all."

"Help with what?" asked Theodosia, determined to draw him out.

"Money," sneered Giovanni. "I needed money. Some very nasty men were demanding immediate payment of a debt. But Oliver, righteous citizen and uptight businessman, wouldn't *give* it to me. Wouldn't even *lend* it to me. Said I was incapable of managing my finances."

"What did you need the money for?" she asked him, knowing full well that greed was a motivator that often outweighed a pressing need for money.

"What does it matter?" Giovanni said petulantly. "The shop, gambling debts . . . Anyway, my problems are almost behind me now."

"And you think you'll get control of Oliver's money by wooing Doe," said Theodosia. *Keep him talking,* she told herself. *Drayton has to come looking for me.*

"Doe has the mind of a child," said Giovanni scornfully. But she *listens* to me, she *trusts* me. It won't be long before *I'm* calling the shots."

"You think you can make her fall in love with you? Marry you?"

Giovanni shrugged. "Sure, why not?"

"She's not that much of a child," said Theodosia.

"Shut up!" he said with a harsh bark. All pretense of Giovanni's carefully cultured voice had long since been abandoned.

"What have you got in mind?" Theodosia goaded Giovanni. "Another accident? Another exploding pistol?" Fury shone brightly in her eyes; her cheeks blazed high with color.

"Not necessarily," said Giovanni, and suddenly his voice was smooth and hard as ice. "I'm sure this pistol will fire quite nicely all on its own. We have our host, Timothy Neville, to thank for that. Quite the expert when it comes to weapons." Giovanni's eyes darted about the dark garden, but only golden koi peeped at them from the pond. The woman had been stalling for time, Giovanni decided, and he knew he'd better bring this to a rapid conclusion.

"Unlatch that gate." He gestured with the pistol. "You and I are going to take a little stroll down to Charleston Harbor. The water's awfully chilly this time of year but . . ." He chuckled nastily. ". . . You won't be in any condition to notice."

Theodosia faced him square on. "I don't think so," she told him.

Her obstinance infuriated him. "You foolish, snooping woman," he hissed. "Very well, have it your way. You hear them in there?" He gestured toward Timothy's house. "No one's going to come to your rescue. Everyone is having a merry old time, sipping champagne and whispering about your silly soil samples. I'm sure they all think you're quite mad. Especially when they find out you were sneaking about at night, snooping in people's gardens. No wonder you met with such an unfortunate accident."

Theodosia stared at him. Giovanni had become so enraged he was spitting like a cat, and his eyes were pulled into narrow slits like an evil Kabuki mask.

Oh dear, Theodosia suddenly thought to herself as her heart began to pound a timpani solo inside her chest. *Did I push him too hard? I hope he—*

Giovanni's finger tightened about the trigger.

"Giovanni . . ." said Theodosia, extending a hand.

Giovanni Loard squeezed the trigger, flinching slightly as a loud *whomp* echoed in the courtyard. At the same instant, Theodosia's hands flew up in surprise, and she uttered a tiny cry of dismay.

"You fool!" Timothy Neville's voice rang sharply across the garden, bouncing like shards of glass on cobblestones.

Startled, Giovanni whirled to find the grim face of Timothy Neville staring at him from above the barrel of a pistol, a sleek contemporary pistol that looked far more menacing than the one Giovanni held in his hand.

"Miss Browning?" Timothy called. "Still in one piece?" He looked past Giovanni, but his gun never wavered. It remained pointed squarely at Giovanni's heart.

Giovanni snapped his head around toward Theodosia. "What?" he gasped, amazed to find her still standing.

"You're a pitiful excuse for a man," said Timothy, his upper lip curled in disgust.

Giovanni was thoroughly stunned that his shot had been without effect. "It was supposed to be loaded," he stammered. "You said—"

"Assuming you are still in one piece, Miss Browning, would you care to enlighten the recalcitrant Mr. Loard?"

Theodosia lifted her chin in triumph. Her eyes bore into Giovanni, and her hair flowed out around her like a vengeful wraith.

"We created a special type of ammunition," she told him. "Gunpowder green."

"That's right," added Timothy. "We figured once our killer knew that soil samples were being tested, it was only a matter of time before he, or she, erupted into a full-blown panic and attempted something foolish." Timothy smiled with smug satisfaction. "Witness your own folly just now."

Giovanni Loard's face was black with fury. "You put *what* in the pistol?" he bellowed.

"Gunpowder green," said Theodosia. "Actually a rather pungent and flavorful Chinese tea. But then, what would you know?" Her eyes blazed like a huntress who'd just claimed her prize. "You yourself admitted you were unable to distinguish between Chinese and Japanese blends. We simply assumed your inadequacies ran to gunpowder, as well."

"And we were correct." Timothy smiled.

"You pompous old blowhard," menaced Giovanni. His hands clenched and unclenched, and his eyes sought out the pale skin of Theodosia's neck.

In a split second, Timothy read the cold, calculating menace on Giovanni's face.

"You're not nearly as smart or as quick as you think you are," Timothy warned him. "Consider the fact that this Ruger is loaded with .22 caliber hollowpoints." Timothy's eyes gleamed, almost daring Giovanni to make a move.

When Giovanni continued to stare at Theodosia, Timothy Neville pulled his face into a tight smile and cocked the hammer back. The loud click reverberated off the stone garden walls.

"Timothy . . ." cautioned Theodosia. Fear suddenly gripped her. She was afraid that Timothy Neville, fiery old rebel that we was, might well escalate this standoff into something extremely foolish.

Timothy's dark eyes glittered with cold, hard rage. "Go ahead, Giovanni, why not make a grab for her? With my arthritis and advanced age, my reflexes probably aren't what they used to be, so we could make a game of it, you and I. Never mind that I've cocked the hammer back, which puts you about a nanosecond away from meeting your maker."

Giovanni almost seemed to consider the possibility for a moment. Then there were sudden, fast footfalls across cobblestones as men rushed toward them, and shapes emerged from the darkness. Much to Theodosia's delight, Tidwell's big belly bobbed across the garden courtyard. She'd never been so happy to see that protruding form in all her life.

Along with Tidwell were two uniformed police officers, one with his gun drawn, the other brandishing a set of handcuffs. At the sight of the three lawmen, Giovanni Loard seemed to collapse within himself.

"Detective Tidwell," said Theodosia, surprised and a little breathless, "what are you doing here?"

"I took the liberty of calling him, ma'am," said Henry, Timothy Neville's highly competent old butler, as he stepped out from behind Tidwell. For all his part in tonight's drama, Henry still seemed relatively unfazed.

"Good work, Henry," crowed Timothy, seemingly happy now to relinquish the task of dealing with Giovanni to the police. "Fine work."

Henry turned baleful eyes on Timothy. "Sir, your guests are departing. Perhaps you should come up to the house and bid them a proper good night?"

34

"*You're making a* terrible mistake!" screamed Booth Crowley as a pair of handcuffs was clamped tightly about his chubby wrists. "One call to Senator Wilbur and your career is finished!"

"Yeah, sure," said the police officer calmly. He turned as Tidwell entered the house. "These two go to central booking?" he asked.

Tidwell nodded. "ATF's been alerted, they're aware they're being brought in."

"Tidwell, you idiot!" screamed Booth Crowley, "I'll have your head on a platter. When I'm finished, you won't be able to get a job as a crossing guard!"

Theodosia couldn't believe the bizarre scene being played out inside Timothy's home. She had just witnessed Giovanni Loard's arrest out in the garden. Now two more uniformed officers had just apprehended and handcuffed Booth Crowley and Billy Manolo and were about to lead them away. And while Billy seemed subdued and cooperative, Booth Crowley was in a vile rage.

"B. C.?" Beatrix Crowley made pitiful little bleating sounds as she ran helplessly alongside her husband. "What's going on?" she pleaded. "Tell me why this is happening!"

"Shut up with your fool questions and get on the phone to Tom Breedlaw," Booth shouted at her. "Tell that good-for-nothing lawyer he'd better move heaven and earth on this one! Go on, what are you waiting for?" he sputtered.

"What *is* going on?" Theodosia asked Tidwell as a bemused crowd of onlookers, the remains of Timothy's party guests, gawked and whispered as the two men were led away.

Tidwell favored Theodosia with a benevolent smile. "Yet one more piece of business taken care of, Miss Browning. Not to steal credit from Henry, but we were en route, anyway." He paused for a moment to scrawl his name on a piece of paper a uniformed officer had presented to him. "We were coming to pick up those two chaps." Tidwell waved after the departing Booth Crowley and Billy Manolo. "And we ended up with your Mr. Loard, too. A lucky strike extra, I'd have to say."

Theodosia's brows knit together as she stared earnestly at Burt Tidwell. "Explain please," she said as Drayton, Haley, and Timothy crowded around them.

Drayton and Haley had rushed out into the garden just in time to see Giovanni Loard taken into custody. Now they were equally amazed by the arrest of Booth Crowley and Billy Manolo. But, of course, everyone was.

Tidwell gazed into their eager faces. Drayton looked like he was about to collapse, Haley was boundlessly enthusiastic, and Theodosia and Timothy seemed to await his words with a peculiar calm.

"A sheriff and his deputy apprehended a group of smugglers over near Huntville," Tidwell told them. "Not more than an hour ago. The sheriff had been alerted by the Bureau of Alcohol, Tobacco and Firearms working in conjunction with the Coast Guard. Everyone was pretty sure there'd be some activity tonight; they just weren't sure where. Then, when the smugglers ran their boat aground, the sheriff and his deputies nabbed them. Being caught red-handed with the goods, the four smugglers rolled on their ringleader in about five minutes flat."

"Let me guess," said Theodosia, "the ringleaders being Booth Crowley and Billy Manolo." In her mind, Theodosia could see Sheriff Billings questioning the confused smugglers in his laconic, low-key manner. She was glad he'd been the one to bring them down.

"Booth Crowley was the kingpin," said Tidwell. "Billy Manolo was really just hired help. Apparently, Billy was born over in that area, near Shem Creek. He knew the coastal waters and could thread his way through the inlets and channels like a swamp rat. Billy was supposed to serve as guide tonight, but for some strange reason, he ended up here." Tidwell swiveled his bullet head and turned sharp eyes on Theodosia. "Funny turn of events, wouldn't you agree?"

"It is strange, isn't it," she said.

Haley was grinning from ear to ear. "I love it when people get their comeuppance. Leading Booth Crowley out in handcuffs sure had to bring him down a peg or two."

"It couldn't happen to a more deserving chap," commented Drayton. He'd loosened his bow tie and was fanning himself madly, using a palmetto leaf as a makeshift fan.

"But why smuggling?" asked Theodosia. "Booth Crowley had money, a successful company—"

"For a person with a true criminal mind, that's not enough," said Tidwell. "It's never enough. A person like Booth Crowley is constantly looking for a new angle, a new money-making scheme. And this isn't the first time he's run afoul of the law. He and several of his investors are under close scrutiny by the Securities and Exchange Commission because of possible insider trading."

"That's amazing," said Drayton. "And after the big show he made about supporting the arts—"

"I must commend you, Miss Browning," continued Tidwell. "Wresting a confession from Giovanni Loard was an admirable piece of work."

"I couldn't have done it without Timothy's help," said Theodosia. "He helped set the snare with his donated pistol and impassioned speech."

Timothy beamed. "Thank you, Miss Browning," he said, "the pleasure was all mine. I enjoyed being complicit in your little scheme because I sincerely meant what I said earlier in the music room. Oliver Dixon was a fine neighbor and a good friend. If I helped put temptation in front of Giovanni Loard in the form of that pistol, then so be it. I'm a firm believer in poetic justice."

"And Ford Cantrell's name is cleared after all," said Drayton as he grasped Theodosia's hand tightly, almost as though he were fearful some terrible fate might still befall her. "His sister will be eternally grateful to you, I'm sure. Although you gave us all a nasty fright!"

"His sister is more than eternally grateful," said Lizbeth Cantrell, as she approached the group, her brother Ford in tow. "Thank you, Theodosia, you are an interceding angel, truly heaven-sent."

The two women embraced as Ford looked on sheepishly. "Thank you, Miz Browning," he told her. "You're very kind. Very smart, too. If you ever decide to get into computers . . ."

Theodosia shook her head. "Judging by tonight's events, the tea business holds more than enough intrigue for me." She laughed.

"And Doe was proved innovent, too," mused Haley as Theodosia smiled after the departing Lizbeth Cantrell. "Now I feel a little sheepish thinking she might have had a hand in killing Oliver Dixon."

"It doesn't appear Doe was in collusion with Giovanni Loard," said Tidwell. "She'll be questioned, but I doubt we shall find any ties. I doubt there are any ties."

"Giovanni offered a lot of false sympathy," said Theodosia. "I can see where it was easy for her to lean on him."

"Say," said Haley, "do you suppose that was Giovanni Loard prowling around outside the night of our mystery tea?"

"I'm almost positive it was," said Theodosia. "He had to have been curious about our investigation and worried about how much we knew."

"Goodness, I need a cup of tea," declared Drayton.

"Come," urged Timothy. "Come sit out on the side piazza and relax. We've all had enough high drama for the night."

They all followed Timothy the few steps outside, then collapsed into comfortable wicker chairs and chaise lounges. A few feet from where they sat, a whippoorwill called mournfully from where it had tucked itself among sheltering bows of live oak, and streamers of Spanish moss wafted gently in the night breeze.

"Teakettle's on," Henry announced to the group. "Should only be a moment."

"I couldn't believe Booth Crowley's face when he was led out in handcuffs," said Drayton.

"It was bright red," chortled Haley.

"Like keeman tea," said Drayton.

"I guess Booth Crowley's wife won't be starting that tea shop any time soon," said Haley.

"Right," agreed Drayton, "he's going to have to put his money to better use, like paying attorney's fees."

"And he'll need to focus on mounting a strong legal defense," added Tidwell. "Smuggling is a federal crime. It's not much fun going up against the Justice Department. Those boys do their job because they love it and because they're true believers. They're not in it for the money because, Lord knows, there *isn't* that much money."

Just like you, Theodosia thought to herself. *Just like you, Detective Tidwell.*

Teacups clattered as Henry approached, bearing a silver tray laden with a lovely blue ceramic French tea service. Henry poured steaming cups of tea for everyone, then passed them around.

"Delicious," declared Tidwell, taking a loud slurp. "And what kind is this?"

They turned inquisitive faces to Henry. He had, after all, brewed the tea.

"Why, I prepared the tea Mr. Conneley brought over," Henry said in his papery, proper voice, even as a faint smile tugged at his mouth.

"The gunpowder green!" exclaimed Drayton and Haley together.

Timothy rose to his feet and held his teacup aloft. "I'd like to propose a toast," he announced. "To Theodosia."

"To Theodosia," everyone chimed in.

"Just like her marvelous tea," said Timothy, "you discover what she's really made of when you put her in hot water."

"Hear! Hear!" cried Drayton. "Describes our girl perfectly."

Theodosia just smiled and sipped her tea.

RECIPES FROM
The Indigo Tea Shop

Theodosia's Earl Grey Sorbet

An especially refreshing dessert

1¼ cups water
1 Tbs. sugar
Freshly squeezed juice from 2 lemons plus rind
2 Tbs. Earl Grey tea leaves
1 egg white

BRING water, sugar, lemon juice, and lemon rind to a boil in saucepan and allow to boil for four minutes. Add tea leaves, cover, remove from heat, and let steep until cool. Strain into a bowl, cover, and place in freezer until mixture is slushy and half frozen. Beat egg white until stiff, then fold into mixture. Freeze until sorbet reaches desired consistency. To serve, scoop sorbet into parfait dishes and garnish with fresh fruit or a lemon cookie.

Theodosia's Tea Scones

1 Tsp. baking p.owder
1 Tsp. granulated sugar
1 cup all-purpose flour

¼ tsp salt
1 Tbsp. orange juice
½ cup milk
½ cup raisins

MIX dry ingredients together in bowl, add orange juice and milk. Mix into a dough, then add raisins. Place 8 scoops onto a greased baking sheet, bake in preheated 425 degree oven for 15 to 20 minutes. Serve hot with plenty of butter and jam. Yields 8 scones.

Apricot Tea Sparkler

1⅓ cups strong Irish Breakfast Tea
1⅓ cups apricot nectar
1⅓ cups sparkling water

COMBINE tea, apricot nectar, and sparkling water. Pour into ice-filled glasses. Make 4 servings.

Theodosia's Chocolate Dipped Strawberries

2 large chocolate bars (Ghiradelli or Dove work well)
12 large, fresh strawberries

WASH and dry strawberries, leaving stems on. Break chocolate bars into bits and place in microwave safe bowl. Heat in microwave on high for 30 seconds or until melted completely. Hold each strawberry by its stem and dip into melted chocolate. Place on waxed paper to cool.

Drayton's Cucumber and Lobster Salad Sandwiches

1 lb. cooked lobster meat
2-3 stalks celery
small onion
Prepared mayonnaise
1 cucumber

CHOP the lobster into small pieces. Chop and dice the celery and onion into very small pieces. Combine ingredients in a bowl and add a small amount of mayonnaise. If mixture seems dry, add a little more mayonnaise, then add salt and pepper to taste. Peel cucumber and slice into very thin slices. Spread lobster salad on slices of cocktail bread, top with cucumber, top each sandwich with another slice of bread. Carefully cut each sandwich into two triangles and arrange on platter.

Earl Grey's Liver Brownie Cake

(This is strictly for dogs!)

2 lbs. chicken liver
⅓ cup canola oil
2 eggs
1 fresh clove of garlic
3 cups wheat flour

MIX chicken liver, oil, eggs and garlic in food processor. Pour into mixing bowl and combine with flour. Pour into well-greased 9" x 11" pan. Bake 350 degrees for 40 minutes. When completely cool, cake can be lightly frosted with low fat cream cheese.

Easy tea time treats you can whip up in your own kitchen.

SERVE as many of these as you'd like, but always in small quantities. This is the time to use your fancy glass plates or two-tiered serving tray.

Cream cheese balls rolled in chopped walnuts
Tiny cucumber sandwiches (buy small loaves of
    bread and remove crusts)
Thin slices of Swiss or jarlsberg cheese
Wedges of brie or camembert
Deviled eggs garnished with pimento
Cranberry or zucchini bread
Chicken salad on small croissants
Chutney or honey butter on toast points
Crab salad on English muffins
Macaroons
Scones with jam

Setting your tea table.

UNWRAP grandma's teapot, round up all your mis-matched cups, saucers and tiny plates. Set out thin slices of lemon, sugar cubes, a tiny pitcher of milk, and a small pot of honey. Gather fresh flowers from your garden or adorn your table with pots of ivy. Light the candles, play a favorite CD, indulge in the relaxing ritual that is tea time.

SHADES OF EARL GREY

ACKNOWLEDGMENTS

Heartfelt thank-you's to Mary Higgins Clark for her kindness and gentle *noodge* into mystery writing; my agent, Sam Pinkus; everyone at The Berkley Publishing Group; friends from Malice Domestic, MWA, and Bouchercon; the wonderful tea hostesses (tireless entrepreneurs, all of them!) at countless tea shops around the country who have embraced my series; all the marvelous booksellers who have kindly recommended my books; the writers and reviewers who have generously featured my books in their magazines, newspapers, newsletters, and websites. Much gratitude to my husband, Dr. Robert Poor, to Jennie, Mom, and Jim Smith, and the many readers who continue to be charmed by Theodosia and the Indigo Tea Shop. Tea and trouble keep brewing in Charleston because of you!

Find out more about the author,
her Tea Shop Mysteries,
and her Scrapbooking Mysteries
at www.laurachilds.com.

1

Scurrying across the Italian marble floor of the Lady Goodwood Inn, Theodosia Browning glanced up at the gleaming painting of the inn's venerable founder and matriarch. Harriet Beecher Goodwood gazed down at her guests from her lofty perch. With her glowing porcelain skin, heavy necklace of blue topaz, and pale peach organza gown cinched tightly about her waist, she was the very picture of Southern femininity. A woman with a properly demure manner who also conveyed a fine aristocratic bearing. Yet her watchful eyes seemed to betray a certain wistfulness, as though Lady Goodwood would prefer to step out of her formal portrait and mingle with the carefree throng that milled about below.

In her black satin slacks and figure-skimming smoking jacket, Theodosia breathed a silent prayer of relief that modern-day Charleston women were no longer bound by strict social constraints or uncomfortable, tightly corseted gowns. How on earth would she ever be able to fly about the Indigo Tea Shop, greeting guests and brewing tea, if she were costumed in ankle-length skirts, pantalets, high button boots, and a whalebone corset? Better yet, how would she even draw breath in an outfit like that? Especially when summer's heat and humidity crept in from the lowcountry and turned the city into a real cooker!

"Theodosia! Over here!" Drayton Conneley, Theodosia's dear friend and right-hand man at the Indigo Tea Shop, gave a casual wave to her from the spot he'd staked out near the potted palms. Sixty-two years old, with a head of grizzled gray hair, Drayton was dashingly attired in a cream-colored cashmere jacket, dove gray slacks, and trademark bow tie. Theodosia noted that, for this late autumn party, Drayton had chosen a muted paisley bow tie. Plu-perfect, of course, and the signature touch that always made Drayton the picture of elegance and charm.

Theodosia grinned at Drayton as she pushed her way through the crowd. What a sport he was to accompany her here tonight in lieu of her usual boyfriend, Jory Davis. Especially when Drayton didn't even know the bride-to-be! But then, Drayton was always a gentleman and a good sport. Intrigued by her vision of starting Charleston's first authentic tea shop in the historic district, Drayton hadn't hesitated to resign his rather lofty position at one of Charleston's major hotels and leap at the opportunity to become her master tea blender and majordomo.

Theodosia had a great admiration for risk takers. Of course, she'd been one herself. Just three years ago, she'd bid a hearty *arrivederci* to job security at one of Charleston's major advertising agencies when she'd resigned *her* job as vice president of client services.

A long-abandoned, dusty little tea shop on Church Street had quietly beckoned. Along with a yearning for a far more independent lifestyle and a desire to chart her own course, make her own business decisions. Theodosia knew she would get out of the tea shop exactly what she put into it, and she was fine with that. More than fine, in fact.

And Drayton and Haley Parker, dear friends and willing accomplices, had been there with her from the very beginning.

Drawing upon his years spent in Amsterdam as a master tea blender, Drayton had immediately set about stocking the Indigo Tea Shop with an enviable selection of loose teas. Pungent, orange-red Assams. Smoky, slightly sweet Ceylon teas. Fragrant Darjeelings from the steep slopes of the Himalayas. There were also sparkling emerald green teas from Japan, gyokos and senchas, that were a touch puckery and a bit of an acquired taste. Plus a robust assortment of Indonesian, Malaysian, Turkish, and African teas, as well as the enticing black tea grown at the Charleston Tea Plantation located some twenty-five miles south of Charleston on Wadmalaw Island in the low-country.

Haley, Theodosia's young pastry chef, was a sometime student who was still trying to determine her way in the world. How lucky for the Indigo Tea Shop, however, that Haley delighted in baking her infamous blackberry scones, cream muffins, gingerbread cakes, and shortbread in the tiny little aromatic kitchen at the back of the tea shop. Lately, Haley had even come up with her own recipe for marvels, those deep-fried cookies so peculiar to South Carolina.

And all the elements had come together. Beautifully. The Indigo Tea Shop had fast become a charming little gem of a shop, one stitch in the elegant tapestry of restaurants, shops, museums, and historic homes that made up Charleston's famed historic district.

The tea shop's interior, stripped of its former cork ceiling panels and indoor/outdoor carpet, now gleamed richly with original pegged wooden floors, exposed beams and redbrick walls. Antique hickory tables and chairs, some Theodosia had salvaged from the outbuildings of her Aunt Libby's farm, contributed to an atmosphere that was authentically cozy and inviting. Shelves that weren't laden with copper canisters and sparkling jars filled with tea, were crowded with Yi-Hsing teapots, tea presses, jars of DuBose Bees Honey and Devonshire cream, and their own house brands of packaged teas such as Cooper River Cranberry and Britannia Breakfast Blend. The Indigo Tea Shop was a setting filled with authenticity and grace, and it tantalized guests. And luckily for Theodosia, those guests descended upon her tea shop in droves. The shopkeepers from up and down Church Street, residents of the historic district who had been anxious to adopt a charming little tea shop as their own, visitors to Charleston who strolled the nearby walkways and hidden cobblestone paths.

Theodosia hurried over to Drayton and grabbed his arm. "So good of you to come," she told him.

He smiled down at her. "You're looking lovely," he told her.

"To be perfectly honest," she said, turning her blue eyes upon him and patting her auburn hair self-consciously, "I feel rather tossed together. Delaine called at the last minute to ask if she could borrow my baroque silver card receiver to use as a stand so she could display Camille's wedding ring. So, of course, I had to scoot over here, where I immediately got roped into helping with a few *more* last-minute details. Then I had to make a mad dash home, give Earl Grey a quick run around the block, and get myself all fixed up. And then it started to pour buckets," Theodosia added breathlessly.

The Delaine that Theodosia was referring to was Delaine Dish, a friend of Theodosia's and Drayton's who owned the clothing boutique, Cotton Duck, just a few doors down from the Indigo Tea Shop. Earl Grey was Theodosia's dog, a mixed breed she'd found cowering in the alley behind the tea shop one rainy night. Theodosia had promptly adopted the bedraggled pup and dubbed him a purebred dalbrador. The very grateful and loving Earl Grey had been Theodosia's constant companion ever since. He had taken to obedience and agility training like a duck to water and had also earned his Therapy Dog International certificate, which gave both of them the privilege of making regular visits to nursing homes and children's hospital wards.

Tonight's *soiree* was an engagement party for Delaine's niece, Camille Cantroux. Camille was engaged to marry a young Marine captain, Corey Buchanan from Savannah, Georgia. In fact, the wedding was just a few weeks away, set to take place the Saturday after Thanksgiving.

"Here's Haley," said Drayton as a young woman in a swirl of black crepe hurried to join them.

"Hey, you guys," said Haley in a breathless rush, "tell me if this dress looks okay." As she executed a self-conscious little twirl, her long straight hair swirled out in a wedge around her. "I borrowed it from my cousin, Rowena."

"Terrific," piped up Drayton immediately, without so much as a look in her direction.

Haley rolled her eyes.

Theodosia, however, took Haley very seriously and studied her little black cocktail dress with an appraising eye. In her short, fun dress she looked like an updated Audrey Hepburn. Coltish, very much the gamin. Except, of course, for her long, straight hair and slightly impudent nature. That was pure Haley.

"You look adorable," Theodosia reassured her. "Youthful, very fresh. I'm confident every young man here tonight will have his eye on you."

"Do you really think so?" asked Haley. She glanced around quickly at the crowd of young people. "There *are* lots of good-looking guys here, aren't there? Do you think they're all Marines?"

"I'd say there are more than a few good men," said Drayton, who never failed to delight in teasing Haley.

Haley, on the other hand, simply ignored his jibes. "How come Delaine is throwing an engagement party here in Charleston when her niece and her fiancé are getting married in Savannah?" she asked.

"Besides the fact that Delaine lives here, Camille also attended school here at Charleston College," explained Theodosia. "So Camille has loads of friends in the area. You know, she graduated this past summer with a B.A. in English literature."

"Cool," nodded Haley. "I was an English lit major once."

"Haley," said Drayton, "you were also a studio arts major, women's studies major, and . . . let's see . . . what was your most recent foray? Business?"

"Hey, smarty," Haley shot back, "I'm *still* taking classes in business administration. This time I will get my degree."

"Of course you will," Theodosia assured her.

"Thanks, Theo," said Haley. "Hey, your hair looks great tonight," she exclaimed as an afterthought.

"No, not really," said Theodosia, nervously patting her hair again.

"Batten down the hatches," said Drayton under his breath. "Here comes Delaine."

Delaine Dish, proud aunt and planner extraordinaire of tonight's engagement party, came plowing through the throng of guests like an ocean liner entering New York Harbor. Delaine's long, dark hair was swept into an updo and she wore a midnight blue chiffon dress with a beaded camisole bodice and frothy skirt. With her slightly upturned eyes, Delaine looked tall, dark, and elegant.

"Delaine, darling," said Drayton, greeting her. "You're looking lovely."

Delaine rubbed a bare shoulder against Drayton. "Such a way with women you have, Mr. Conneley."

Theodosia sighed. Delaine was a sweet soul. No one could touch her fiery zeal when it came to raising money for the Heritage Society, campaigning for the Charleston Humane Society, or selling tickets for the Lamplighter Tour. But Delaine did have a certain fondness for men.

Delaine finally turned her gaze toward Theodosia and Haley. "Having a good time, you two?"

"Everything is lovely," replied Theodosia. "The Lady Goodwood Inn was a perfect choice."

"So was the string quartet," added Drayton, nodding toward the group of musicians tucked off in the corner.

Theodosia let her gaze wander, taking in the small, elegant ballroom with its color palette of cream and pale blue, the multitude of vases overflowing with fresh flowers, the tuxedo-clad waiters who bore silver trays with crystal flutes of champagne. "It's nice to be a guest for once and not the caterer," she told Delaine.

In the past year, the Indigo Tea Shop had catered a multitude of engagement teas, garden teas, and wedding receptions. So being a guest here tonight really *was* a luxury for Theodosia.

"Tell us about Captain Corey Buchanan," Haley urged Delaine. "I love the idea that he's a captain in the Marines. Just the thought of it is so dashing and romantic."

"Well, I don't know him all *that* well," replied Delaine. "In fact I've really only met the dear fellow twice. But I *can* tell you he's a graduate of Annapolis and the Basic School in Quantico, and that Captain Corey Buchanan is one of *the* Buchanans from Savannah." Delaine's eyes sparkled with excitement. "They're a very old family. Terribly well-to-do."

"I'm sure he's a fine young man," said Theodosia, choosing to ignore Delaine's somewhat tactless implication of wealth and riches. "And that he and Camille are very much in love."

Haley nodded in agreement. "In the scheme of things, that's what really counts."

"Have you seen Camille's ring?" asked Delaine, still in a twitter.

"Gorgeous," replied Drayton.

"Oh, no," Delaine was quick to protest. "Not the *engagement* ring. Of course, that's beautiful. Stunning, really. But wait until you-all get a gander at Camille's *wedding* ring. I just put it on display in the Garden Room a few minutes ago. It's what you'd call a *killer* ring. Estate jewelry, don't you know?"

"Estate jewelry," repeated Haley. "What exactly does that mean?"

Delaine looked pleased at Haley's question. "Honey," she said in a hushed tone, "it means the ring has been in Captain Buchanan's family for *decades!*" She took a quick sip of champagne to fortify herself, then continued. "The ring is an emerald-cut diamond flanked by six smaller round diamonds. The center stone came from a distant relative, Angelique Delacroix, who was a French noblewoman married to a minor Austrian archduke back in the mid-eighteen-hundreds. The archduke reputedly purchased the diamond when one of Marie Antoinette's crowns was sold off!"

"Wow!" said Haley, impressed now. "Sounds like the kind of ring a girl could lose her head over."

"Oh yes," Delaine bubbled on. "Wait until you see it." She glanced around. "Captain Buchanan and the rest of the boys should be here any moment. A couple of the groomsmen had tuxedo fittings this afternoon." She rolled her eyes. "You know how young men are. They probably stopped at Slidell's Oyster Bar for a celebratory drink. I certainly hope they won't be indiscreet."

"Or delayed," added Theodosia. All the guests had been sipping cocktails for the better part of an hour now and there seemed to be a restless hum in the tightly packed room. Probably, Theodosia decided, most of the guests were as ready as she was for dinner in the more spacious Garden Room, which had once been the inn's greenhouse. Delaine had been huddling with the Lady Goodwood's head chef for weeks and had finally decided upon an appetizer of she-crab soup, a salad of baby field greens, and an entrée of smoked duck breast, cranberry relish, and fried squash blossoms.

"So when do we get a peek at this showstopper of a ring?" asked Haley, looking around in great anticipation.

Delaine glanced nervously at her watch again, a jewel-encrusted Chopard. "Hopefully we'll be going in for dinner any minute now. We're really just waiting for Captain Buchanan." Delaine drained the last of her champagne. "Until this afternoon," she explained, "Brooke had been storing the ring in her vault at Heart's Desire. For safekeeping, of course."

Located on Water Street in the historic district, Heart's Desire was one of Charleston's premier estate jewelry shops. It was owned and lovingly operated by Brooke Carter Crockett, a woman who could trace her ancestry all the way back to the famous frontiersman, Davy Crockett.

Over the years, Heart's Desire had become the premier jeweler for buying and selling estate jewelry. So much fine jewelry was still available in Charleston, owing to the many French and English families who had settled in and around the area during the seventeen-and eighteen-hundreds. And over the years, their rice, indigo, and cotton plantations had yielded enormous wealth and all the trappings that came with it.

"Camille and Captain Buchanan have even agreed to allow the wedding ring to be displayed in the Heritage Society's Treasures Show," Delaine prattled on.

"That starts this weekend?" asked Haley.

"The members-only part is this Saturday evening," explained Drayton, who currently served on the board of directors of the Heritage Society as parliamentarian. "Then the grand opening for the public will be the following weekend."

"Of course," said Delaine, "the wedding ring is not quite as showy as some of the pieces in the European Jewel Collection, but it's a quality piece, just the same." The European Jewel Collection was a special traveling show that was being brought in to augment the Heritage Society's own pieces.

"It was a lovely and generous gesture on the part of Camille and Captain Buchanan to allow their ring to be displayed," said Drayton.

"Oh, Coop, over here!" chirped Delaine. She waved at a tall, lanky man, beckoning him to come join their foursome. "You-all know Cooper Hobcaw, don't you?" she asked.

"Hello, Mr. Hobcaw," said Theodosia, shaking hands with the silver-haired, hawk-nosed Hobcaw.

"Coop. Just Coop," he told her. Glancing at Drayton and Haley, Cooper Hobcaw nodded hello.

Cooper Hobcaw was a senior partner at Hobcaw McCormick and one of Charleston's premier criminal attorneys. He was smart and tough and wily and had a reputation for playing hardball. Last year he'd defended an accused murderer and had succeeded in getting him acquitted. That had made Cooper Hobcaw slightly unpopular among Charleston's more politically correct set and had greatly rankled Burt Tidwell, the homicide detective who was an on-again off-again friend of Theodosia's.

But a person shouldn't be defined by what they do, decided Theodosia. Cooper Hobcaw had been squiring Delaine around for quite a few months now, and Delaine seemed completely and utterly charmed by him.

"Would you like another drink, honey?" Cooper Hobcaw asked Delaine solicitously.

"Please," she said, handing over her empty glass. "But this time . . . maybe a cosmopolitan?"

"Ladies?" Hobcaw threw a questioning glance at Theodosia and Haley, who both shook their heads. Their champagne glasses were still half-full.

"I'll come with you," offered Drayton.

"No, no, please. Allow me," said Cooper Hobcaw. "You stay with the ladies and keep them amused. I'll bring you a . . . what is it you've got there? Bourbon?"

"Right," nodded Drayton.

"Good man," said Hobcaw with a crooked grin. "I can't stand that bubbly stuff either."

"Okay," said Haley after Cooper Hobcaw had moved off, "tell me which one is Camille Cantroux. There are so many pretty girls here, I don't know one from the other."

"Over there," said Theodosia. "Standing by the baby grand piano. With the short blond hair." She indicated a young woman in a champagne-colored slip dress whose tones just happened to perfectly match her short-cropped and ever-so-slightly-spiked hair.

"The one who's about a size *two?*" said Haley. "My, she *is* pretty, isn't she."

"Camille's adorable," gushed Delaine, who was fairly gaga over her young niece.

"Did you help pick out her wedding gown?" asked Drayton, who had finally assumed an *if you can't beat 'em, join 'em* attitude about the wedding discussion.

"Of course," said Delaine. "But being that Camille is so tiny,

I suggested breaking from traditional style. Instead of her being overpowered by a big flouncy dress and flowing veil that would make her look like a human wedding cake, I found the most adorable little French creation. It has a bodice with just the tiniest bit of rouching, and a tulle ballerina skirt. *Très elegant*—but, of course, not in white."

"Not in white?" said Drayton. "Then what . . . ?"

"*Ivory*," said Delaine, as though she'd single-handedly invented the color. "Ivory is so much more elegant than white. White has become awfully" she paused, searching for the word "passé."

"I'm particularly fond of ecru myself," said Haley. "On the other hand, I wouldn't entirely rule out alabaster . . ." Haley suddenly stopped short as a deafening crash echoed through the room. At the exact same moment, a flash of lightning strobed in the tall, cathedral-style windows that lined one end of the ballroom, illuminating the night sky.

Startled, Theodosia took a step backward and turned toward the nearest waiter, fully expecting to see an entire tray of champagne glasses dumped on the floor. But no, the waiter was still clutching his tray, looking around in alarm.

The string quartet had stopped mid-note and the musicians were also glancing about with nervous looks. A strange hush had fallen over the room as the guests milled about, mumbling quietly and looking profoundly unsettled.

As if on cue, a second crash suddenly rocked the room. This time, the noise was louder still. And there was no mistaking the direction from which it came.

Camille Cantroux broke from the crowd and ran to the double doors that led to the Garden Room, where the sit-down dinner was supposed to take place. Grabbing the ornate door handles, Camille tugged at the doors, struggling to pull them open. The heavy doors seemed to resist for a moment, then they suddenly flew open, revealing the interior of the Garden Room.

But instead of elegant linen-draped tables alight with blazing candles, the Garden Room was a disaster! Half of the roof had seemingly collapsed. Rain poured in from above, drenching tablecloths, place settings, floral arrangements, and gifts. Sheets of glass mingled with smaller, dangerously pointed shards. Twisted metal struts, once part of the roof, poked up from the rubble.

And underneath it all lay Captain Corey Buchanan.

Camille's voice rose in a shrill scream. "Corey! Corey!" she cried as she ran to him and threw herself down on the floor, ignoring the shattered glass and jagged metal.

Facedown, arms flung out to his sides like a rag doll, poor Corey Buchanan lay motionless. Camille plucked frantically at the back of his damp uniform as blood gushed from Captain Buchanan's head and rain poured down from above. Desperate, needing to do *something,* Camille struggled to work her arms under and around Captain Buchanan, ignoring the debris that tore at her, wanting only to cradle her fiancé's bloody head in her arms.

Following directly on Camille's heels, Theodosia had raced across the room, covering the short distance in a heartbeat. She'd hesitated in the doorway for a split second, taking in the roof with its gaping hole, the wreckage of glass strewn everywhere, and the one enormous shard of glass that had imbedded itself deep in the back of Captain Buchanan's neck, right near the top of his spine.

And Theodosia knew in her heart there was no hope.

Kneeling gingerly to avoid the needle-like slivers of glass and pointed metal, Theodosia gently placed her index and middle fingers against Corey Buchanan's neck. Hoping against hope, she held her breath and prayed. But there was no pulse, no sign of life in this poor boy.

Captain Corey Buchanan, eldest son and proud warrior of the Savannah, Georgia, Buchanans, would never again serve his country as a United States Marine, would never walk with pride down the church aisle in his dress white uniform. Now the only service poor Captain Buchanan would take part in would be his own funeral.

Wailing in helpless despair, Camille rocked her dead fiancé back and forth in her arms. "Now who'll place the wedding ring on my finger?" she sobbed.

Theodosia turned her gaze to the black velvet ring box that was perched atop the silver card receiver she'd brought over earlier. Captain Buchanan had obviously slipped in the back door with the intention of putting the ring on display. But the velvet box sat empty. There was no ring to be seen.

2

From a scene that seemed to unfold in slow motion, activity suddenly accelerated with warp speed. Police and paramedics arrived to load Captain Corey Buchanan onto a gurney and hustle him out to a waiting ambulance. A sobbing Camille Cantroux was aided to her feet by Theodosia and Drayton. Then Delaine, shell-shocked and shaking, led her away, presumably to follow the ambulance to the hospital.

The rest of the partygoers pressed through the double doors into the Garden Room. They crunched across glass, gaping at the enormous hole in the ceiling and talking in hushed tones about the horrible turn of events.

At one point Theodosia was aware of Cooper Hobcaw arguing with Frederick Welborne, the manager of the Lady Goodwood Inn. Hobcaw's once-elegant suit was now dripping wet. He had apparently run out into the street to flag down the ambulance and guide the paramedics to the nearest entry.

As he loudly harangued poor Frederick Welborne, the man looked as though he might suffer a heart attack on the spot.

Cooper Hobcaw's slipped into his role as lawyer, Theodosia thought to herself. Probably talking about liability and personal injury suits. She decided she wouldn't want to be in Frederick Welborne's shoes tonight. No way, no how.

"I can't believe this," wailed Haley. She was pale and shivering. "Do you think Captain Buchanan will be okay?"

Theodosia pulled Haley aside and out of the way of the gawkers. "It doesn't look good," she told her in a quiet voice.

Haley bobbed her head rapidly, obviously experiencing more than a little stress. "That's what I was afraid of. Oh, that poor, poor man, did you see the glass sticking out of . . . ?"

Drayton put a hand on Haley's shoulder. "*Shhh* . . . it's okay. Try to calm down."

Haley stared at him with sadness in her eyes. "But it isn't okay," she whispered. "Theo thinks he might be *dead!*"

"We'll phone the hospital later and see what news there is," said Drayton. He kept his voice calm and soothing, and his reassuring tone seemed to work on Haley, seemed to calm her down considerably. "Delaine and Camille went on to the hospital," he added, "so we'll be able to speak with them later and see what's going on."

"We need everyone to exit this room, please!" rang out a loud, authoritarian voice. Cooper Hobcaw stood in the doorway, gazing imperiously at the crowd. When he seemed to command everyone's attention, he clapped his hands together loudly. "Please, we need you-all to leave . . . immediately!"

The crowd seemed to hesitate for a moment, torn between their fascination with the terrible accident that had just occurred and doing what they knew was the proper thing. Then, slowly, people began to depart the room.

Cooper Hobcaw watched as the crowd trickled past him, then strode over to the head table where Theodosia, Drayton, and Haley were still gathered.

What once had been festive and romantic now seemed macabre. The head table had been set with enormous bouquets of white roses and elegant sterling silver candlesticks. Now, one bouquet was knocked over, another completely flattened by a pane of falling glass. Candles had been knocked out of their holders, dishes lay spoiled and broken. Only the large silver teapot and matching cream and saucer pieces seemed to remain unscathed. Set on a matching oval tray, the tea set lent the only hint of normalcy to the entire table.

"Miss Browning, may I have a moment?" Cooper Hobcaw asked. "I . . . I need your help."

Theodosia turned to Cooper Hobcaw, concern on her face. "Of course," she said.

"This may seem a strange thing . . ." Cooper Hobcaw hesitated. ". . . but Delaine is terribly concerned about the wedding ring. Strangely enough, it appears to be . . . missing."

"Yes," said Theodosia. "I noticed that, too." She had immediately seen that the wedding ring was no longer nestled in the black velvet ring box that had been prominently displayed at the head table. *The ring must be . . . where?* she wondered. *Had it been knocked out of the ring box and now it was under one of these tables?* She looked around at the terrible chaos. *Probably.*

"Since you are such a dear friend to Delaine," Hobcaw said, "could I impose upon you to . . ."

"You'd like us to stay here and search for it?" Theodosia finished the sentence for him.

Cooper Hobcaw's face seemed to sag with relief. "Yes," he said. "Would you?"

Drayton suddenly jumped feetfirst into the conversation. "Of course we will," he said graciously. "You go on to the hospital and lend what support you can to Delaine and Camille. We'll stay behind and find that ring. Don't worry about a thing."

Cooper Hobcaw clutched Drayton's hand and pumped his arm mightily. "Thank you, thank you so much," he said. Then he grabbed Theodosia's hand and did the same. "You are a dear lady," he told her, then strode quickly out of the room.

Theodosia turned toward Haley. "Haley, why don't you go home now."

"You don't want me to help?" she asked, her eyes still wide with concern. She still seemed rather jumpy.

"No need," said Theodosia. "I'm sure the ring simply rolled under one of these tables." She looked around the Garden Room, noting what an absolute mess it was.

"Okay," said Haley, relief palpable in her face, "but call me the minute you find something out about poor Captain Buchanan, okay?"

"We'll do that," Drayton assured her.

With the Garden Room empty of guests, Theodosia and Drayton stared at each other, unsure of where to begin.

The rain had thankfully let up, but the room was a soggy mess with glass and debris scattered everywhere. In the paramedics' haste to extract Captain Buchanan, they had rolled towels about their hands then shoved the larger hunks of glass aside. Smaller pieces had been ground under the wheels of the gurney and now glistened dangerously.

"The ring must have just rolled out of the box, don't you think?" said Drayton. He sounded positive, but looked a trifle dubious.

"I assume it did," replied Theodosia. "I think if we pull up the edges of these tablecloths, we'll probably find it soon enough."

But ten minutes of searching high and low, looking under tables, sliding back chairs, revealed nothing. Frustrated, Drayton found a broom and poked through the rubble. Still nothing.

"On top of one of the tables then?" said Drayton. He had removed his jacket and now his shirt was partially untucked and his bow tie hung askew. Theodosia had never seen him looking so frazzled.

"Maybe," Theodosia told him.

This time they sorted through all the table settings, pawed through the damp table linens and wrecked floral centerpieces, and rearranged all the wrapped gifts that lay in a soggy, bedraggled pile on the gift table. Still no ring.

"This is very strange," said Drayton. "I would have sworn the darn thing would turn up. A little thing like that couldn't have rolled all *that* far." He furrowed his brow and scratched his head, the picture of complete bewilderment.

"Do you think one of the guests might have picked it up?" he asked aloud, then gave a mumbled answer to his own question. "No, they were all good friends. Friends of Delaine's, friends of Camille and Captain Buchanan's. If someone found the ring, they surely would have *said* something."

Theodosia, meanwhile, had turned her attention to the gaping hole in the glass ceiling. The rain had completely abated and now there was just darkness and roiling clouds overhead.

Drayton saw her staring up at the ceiling and followed her gaze. "Do you think the roof just gave way?" he asked.

"I suppose it did," she said slowly, still staring upward. "It was an old greenhouse, after all. From before, when the Lady Goodwood used to raise their own orchids and camellias to pretty up the rooms and create centerpieces for the dining room." Theodosia paused, thinking. "Maybe it was hit by lightning. There was that enormous flash."

"It was positively cataclysmic," agreed Drayton.

Theodosia put her hand on the back of a wooden chair, dragged it across the sodden carpet until it was positioned directly beneath the jagged hole in the glass roof. She put one foot on the upholstered seat cushion. "Drayton, give me a boost up, will you?"

Drayton stared at her as though she'd lost her mind. "Good heavens, Theodosia, just what do you think you're going to accomplish?"

"I want to take a look at this greenhouse ceiling."

"Yes, I assumed as much. What I don't understand is *why*."

"Stop acting like a parliamentarian and just help me, would you?"

Drayton steadied the chair with one hand, extended his other hand to help Theodosia as she climbed up. "Don't I always?" he muttered, affecting a slightly pompous attitude.

"Darn," said Theodosia from above.

"What?"

"I can't really see anything. I'm not up high enough."

"Good. Then kindly hop down before you break your neck." Drayton moved to assist her and glass crunched underfoot. "This is dreadful," he declared. "Like walking on the proverbial bed of nails."

"You folks okay?" called a voice from across the room.

Drayton and Theodosia spun on their heels to find an older man in a gray jumpsuit staring at them. By the looks of the man's outfit, he was one of the inn's janitors.

"We're fine," said Theodosia. "You're from maintenance?"

"Yup," he nodded. "Harry Kreider, at your service."

"Would you by any chance have a ladder, Mr. Kreider?" asked Theodosia. "I'd like to take a peek at this ceiling."

"You from the insurance company or something?" he asked.

"No," she replied. "Just very curious. I was a guest here tonight." She raised a hand, indicated Drayton. "We were both guests."

Harry Kreider cocked his head, assessing her request. "Certainly was a terrible thing," he said. "I was sitting home watching reruns of NASCAR racing on TV when they called and told me the roof collapsed on some poor man." He paused. "You ever watch NASCAR?"

"No," said Drayton abruptly and Theodosia rolled her eyes at him.

"Yeah, I s'pose I could get you a ladder," the janitor said slowly, scratching at his jowly cheeks with the back of his hand. "Storage closet's just down the hall. Be back in a moment."

"Thank you," said Theodosia. "We really appreciate it."

"What is this about?" asked Drayton as they waited for the janitor to return with a stepladder. "What exactly are you looking for?"

"Not sure," said Theodosia.

"Well, you're up to *something*."

There was a *clunk* and a *thwack* as the janitor angled a twelve-foot ladder through the double doors, scraping them slightly. He eased the ladder in on its side, then, when he'd caught his breath, set the ladder up directly beneath the gaping hole.

"I'm sorry about this," Drayton said to the janitor.

"No problem. Got to rig up a temporary patch for this hole anyway. Can't have the rain coming in again. Whole place'll be damp by morning otherwise. That darned humidity just steals in and chills you to the bone. Gonna have to seal off this whole wing, I s'pose." The janitor gazed at the mess ahead of him and sucked air through his front teeth. "You two go ahead and take your look up there while I rustle up some tarps. Just don't fall off that darn thing and break your neck. There's been enough trouble here for one night."

"I'll be careful," Theodosia assured him as she scampered up the ladder.

"*Please* be careful," said Drayton as he stood below, clutching the ladder.

Theodosia climbed to within two steps of the top, put a hand gingerly on the metal strut that ran the length of the greenhouse roof. It felt solid and stable. It was the glass that had seemingly crumpled and given way.

She stuck her head up through the hole. The roof, or what was left of it, was still slick and wet from the earlier downpour. Light from below glowed faintly through it. *Okay, no surprises here,* Theodosia decided.

She felt beneath her with her right foot, took a step back down. Now she was eye level with the tangle of glass and metal. She reached out, flicked at a small oval-shaped piece of metal that hung there. It was weathered looking, once silvery, like the rest of the pieces.

"See anything?" Drayton called from below.

"Not really," she said.

"Then kindly come back down."

Theodosia began her climb back down.

"Here," said Drayton, grabbing for her hand once she was in reach, "let's get you back on terra firma."

Theodosia stood next to the ladder, looking thoughtful. "Drayton, let me ask you something. What if someone had their eye on Camille's wedding ring?"

Drayton's eyes widened as he caught the gist of what she was suggesting. "You think someone might have been up there? That this *wasn't* just an accident?"

"I'm not sure," said Theodosia. "Let's just suppose for a moment that a thief was prowling about . . ."

"Camille's ring would make quite a prize," he said slowly.

Theodosia's eyes flicked over the head table, where the silver tea set gleamed from the wrecked table top. "And the silver?" she asked.

"That's lovely, too," he agreed slowly. "Queen Anne style. Don't quote me, but I believe it was crafted by Jacob Hurd in the mid-seventeenhundreds. And of course, it's been in the Goodwood family for ages. You see that engraved cartouche on the body of the teapot?"

Theodosia nodded.

"That's the family crest. A heraldic shield on a bed of roses."

"So besides Camille's ring, which I believe Delaine told me had been valued at something like seventy grand . . ."

"Seventy grand!" exclaimed Drayton. "Good gracious."

"And all this silver would have been worth a good deal of money, too," ventured Theodosia.

Drayton nodded briskly, far more familiar with appraisals on antiquities than he was with jewelry. "Oh yes. The teapot alone might fetch ten or twenty thousand dollars. To say nothing of the creamer, sugar bowl, and that magnificent tray."

"Okay, then," said Theodosia, "follow my line of thinking for a moment, will you?"

Drayton cocked his head to one side in an acquiescing gesture.

"What if someone was scrambling across the top of the roof . . ." she began.

"It would have to be someone very skillful and limber," he said, gazing upward. "There are only those struts for support, everything else is glass."

"I agree," said Theodosia. "But it can be done. A case in point: the man who cleans my air conditioner does it every spring in my attic."

"Walks across the narrow wooden struts," said Drayton.

"Yes," said Theodosia. "But maybe tonight this person, whoever he was, got caught off balance. The storm, the pouring rain, a nearby lightning strike spooked him or unnerved him. Or maybe it was just terribly treacherous up there. Anyway, somewhere along the way, his foot just happened to slip."

They both gazed up at the gaping hole.

"And he came crashing through into the Garden Room," said Drayton.

Theodosia pointed to the remains of an elaborate pulley system that hung from the ceiling. "You see that chain and pulley right there? This roof was meant to crank open. It was designed that way back when it was a working greenhouse, before they pulled out the old wooden tables and sprinkler system and turned it into the Garden Room. But I imagine the system still works. You could still open the roof . . ."

"Someone scampered across the roof," said Drayton, still trying out the idea. "With the idea of making off with the ring and maybe even the silver. But instead, this person came crashing down on top of poor Captain Buchanan."

"Yes," said Theodosia, "that might explain the first crash we heard."

"And the second crash?" asked Drayton.

Theodosia hesitated. "I'm not entirely sure. But if someone crashed *through* the roof, wouldn't they have to go back up through it?"

"How?" he sputtered.

"I have no clue."

"Folks?" called the janitor. "Is one of you a The-o-dosia?" He pronounced the name slowly and phonetically.

"That's me," said Theodosia.

"Phone call," said the janitor.

Theodosia and Drayton hurried out to the lobby, where Mr. Welborne was talking excitedly with two staff members.

"I have a phone call?" she said.

The woman behind the front desk indicated a small, private phone booth just down the hallway.

Theodosia seated herself on a small round stool that was covered with a needlepoint cushion and picked up the receiver.

It was Cooper Hobcaw calling from the hospital. He spoke clearly but rapidly for a few minutes and Theodosia listened carefully. Afterward, she thanked him, then hung up the phone.

She stood, drew a deep sigh, and turned to Drayton. "He's dead," she told him sadly. "Captain Buchanan is dead."

3

Friday morning at 9:00 a.m., the Indigo Tea Shop was packed. Besides their Church Street regulars, a tour group led by Dindy Moore, one of Drayton's friends from the Heritage Society, had decided to begin their walking tour of the historic district with a breakfast tea. And now the group easily filled four of the dozen or so tables.

Drayton hustled back and forth, a teapot in each hand, pouring steaming cups of Munnar black tea and English breakfast tea. Haley had come in early, even though she'd been deeply upset by the news of Captain Corey Buchanan's death, and still managed to bake a full complement of pastries. This morning the customers at the Indigo Tea Shop were enjoying steaming apple-ginger muffins, blueberry scones, and cream muffins, which in any other part of the country would rightly be called popovers.

Standing behind the counter, Theodosia busied herself by handling take-out orders, always in big demand first thing in the morning.

After the horror of last night, she felt reassured and warmed by the atmosphere of the tea shop. A fire crackled in the tiny stone fireplace as copper teapots chirped and whistled. The scent of orange, cinnamon, and ginger perfumed the air around her.

Teas were like aromatherapy, Theodosia had long since decided. The ripe orchid aroma of Keemun tea from Anhui Province in China was always slightly heady and uplifting, the bright, brisk smell of Indian Nilgiri seemed to calm and stabilize, the scent of jasmine always soothed.

Finally, when the morning rush seemed to settle into a more manageable pace, Theodosia slipped through the dark green velvet curtains and into her office at the back of the shop.

This was her private oasis. Big rolltop desk wedged into a small space, wall filled with framed mementos that included photos, opera programs, and tea labels. A cushy green velvet guest chair faced her desk, a chair that Drayton had dubbed "the tuffet."

Sitting at her desk, Theodosia thought about the hellish events of last night. *Did someone actually crash through the roof and steal the antique wedding ring or am I just trying to rationalize a terrible event? When bad things happen to good people, that sort of thing?*

She thought about it, tried to dismiss her somewhat strange theory. But it wouldn't go away. Stuck in her mind like a burr.

All right, she thought to herself, *then I've got to tell someone. Who, though? The police? Hmm, seems a little alarmist. No,* she decided, *Delaine will come by. She always does. I'll run it by Delaine and then, if it still holds water, Delaine can take it to the police.*

She wasn't about to get pulled into this, was she? No, of course not.

Haley was always kidding her that she liked nothing better than a good mystery to poke her nose into. Well, she was going to leave this incident well enough alone, wasn't she?

Wasn't she?

Theodosia sighed. On the other hand . . . from the moment she'd climbed that ladder last night, she'd felt as if she was being pulled slowly and inexorably into what appeared to be a web of intrigue.

What was this strange fascination she had with murder? Why did she have this dark side?

Enough, she decided as she flipped open her weekly planner and studied her calendar. This weekend looked relatively quiet. Tomorrow, Saturday night, was the members-only party at the Heritage Society to celebrate the opening of next week's big Treasures Show. And then her calendar was fairly clear until the following Thursday afternoon when they were scheduled to have an open house at the tea shop.

The open house. She had to start thinking seriously about that. The Indigo Tea Shop was about to kick off its new line of tea-inspired bath and beauty products and she had to decide exactly what refreshments they'd be serving, what theme this little launch party should follow.

Theodosia had experienced a brainstorm not too long ago about packaging green teas, dried lavender, chamomile, calendula petals, and other tea and herb mixtures into oversized tea bags for use in the bath. She had commissioned a small batch to be manufactured by a highly reputable cosmetics firm and then tested the feasibility of those products on her web site. Much to her delight, the T-Bath products, as she had named them, had sold remarkably well, so she expanded the line to include lotions and oils as well. This coming Thursday, their open house would serve as the official product launch for the new T-Bath line. She'd already been interviewed by the *Charleston Post & Courier* and a fairly in-depth article about her new bath products would be running in their Style Section sometime next week.

"Theodosia?"

Theodosia looked up to find Haley standing in her doorway. She wiggled her fingers, gesturing for Haley to come in.

"Delaine's here," Haley told her. "She'd like to talk to you."

"How is she?" asked Theodosia.

"Sniffly. Subdued," said Haley. "Same as us."

"You're a real trooper for coming in," Theodosia told her. "Last night was pretty rough."

"That's okay," said Haley. "I feel better now. Sad for poor Camille, of course." Haley shook her head as if to clear it. "Strangely enough, Delaine is dressed to the nines. Anyone else would have thrown on a pair of jeans and a sweatshirt. I guess Delaine's brain doesn't operate that way."

"She probably just came from her store," said Theodosia. "So she had to dress up."

Delaine's store, Cotton Duck, was just down the block from Theodosia's tea shop. Over the past ten years, Delaine had built it into one of the premier clothing boutiques in Charleston. Cotton Duck carried casual cotton clothing to take you through the hot, steamy Charleston summers, rich velvets and light wools for the cooler months, and elegant evening fashions for taking in the opera, art gallery openings, or formal parties in the historic district. In just the last year, Delaine had begun carrying several well-known designers and was now featuring trunk shows several times a year.

"Don't think ill of Delaine," added Theodosia. "It's just her way. Whenever there's a crisis, she dresses up for the part."

. . . .

Delaine was sitting at the table by the fireplace, wearing a camel-colored cashmere sweater and matching wool slacks, sniffling into her cup of Assam tea. She looked up with red-rimmed eyes as Theodosia approached.

"Delaine," said Theodosia, "how are you?" She sat down across from her and clasped her hands, feeling a bit like a brown wren in her sensible workday gray slacks and turtleneck.

"Holding up," said Delaine. "Of course, last night was an absolute *horror.* First we couldn't find out *anything* from the doctors, then they informed us that Captain Buchanan had actually *died* en route to the hospital." She bit her lip in an attempt to stave back tears. "Apparently, his respiration and spinal cord had been affected."

"Oh, no," exclaimed Drayton. After taking a quick check of customers, who all seemed to be sipping tea and happily munching Haley's fresh-baked muffins and scones, he had joined them at the table. "How awful," he said.

"If Captain Buchanan had lived," said Delaine in a hoarse whisper, "he would have been a quadriplegic."

"Oh, my," said Drayton, shaking his head sadly.

"How's Camille doing?" asked Theodosia.

"Terrible," said Delaine. "She just sat next to Captain Buchanan's poor body and cried and cried all night. She wouldn't leave him, wouldn't even take a sedative when one of the doctors offered it. Poor lamb, she's absolutely heartbroken."

"And Captain Buchanan's family has been notified?" asked Drayton.

"Yes," said Delaine. "Cooper Hobcaw called and spoke with them first. He's not as . . . close . . . to this tragedy as we are, so he was able to maintain a certain calm and decorum. Then Camille got on the line, too." Delaine fumbled in her purse for a handkerchief, unfurled it, blew her nose loudly. "We're all just so sad. Camille is planning to accompany Captain Buchanan's body back to Savannah later today. That's where the funeral will be." Delaine blew her nose again and glanced about helplessly. "I'm sorry," she apologized. "I'm just so very upset."

Drayton reached over and patted her shoulder gently. "We know you are, dear."

"Thank you for staying last night," said Delaine. "I knew I could count on the two of you."

Theodosia and Drayton exchanged quick glances.

"Camille is planning to take the wedding ring back with her today and return it to the family," said Delaine. "Of course it's the only acceptable thing to do. After all, there won't be any . . ." Delaine's voice trailed off and she dissolved into tears once again.

Theodosia threw Drayton a quick *what do we do now?* glance.

He gave a helpless shrug.

Delaine, sensing the subtle exchange between them, suddenly looked up.

"You *did* recover the ring, didn't you?" she asked.

Drayton, usually eloquent, fumbled for a moment. "Actually, Delaine, we . . . uh . . ."

"There was a *problem?*" she asked. Now there was a distinct edge to her voice.

"The problem was," said Theodosia, deciding honesty was the best policy, "we never actually found the ring."

Delaine was incredulous. "But Cooper said you were going to *look* for it. Surely you . . ."

"We *did* look," Drayton assured her. "We searched high and low, practically tore the premises apart. But . . ." He hesitated, steepled his gnarled fingers together, then pulled them apart slowly, as if to indicate a lack of resolution. "Alas, no ring," he said.

One of Delaine's French-manicured hands fluttered to her chest. "My goodness, this *is* quite a shock."

"It was to us, too," said Theodosia. "We really did search everywhere."

"What do you suppose happened to it?" asked Delaine. She frowned, twisted her handkerchief in her hands, stared at the two of them, obviously expecting an answer.

"We think, that is, *Theodosia* thinks . . ." began Drayton.

"Spit it out, Drayton!" said Delaine suddenly. "If something's gone wrong, I have a perfect right to know!"

Theodosia glanced about the tea shop to make sure her guests hadn't overheard Delaine's somewhat indelicate outburst. "Of course you do,

Delaine," Theodosia assured her. "It's just that all we're going on right now is a sort of theory."

"Then kindly explain this *theory*," demanded Delaine. She arched her eyebrows, sat back in her chair with an air that was dangerously close to imperious, and waited for an explanation.

"It involves theft," said Drayton delicately.

"Of the *ring?*" said Delaine in a high squeak.

"Well . . . yes," said Theodosia. *Why is it so difficult to just come right out and say it?*

"Oh my goodness," cried Delaine, sinking back in her chair. "You think the ring has been *stolen?*" she said in a whisper.

"We're not positive," said Drayton, "but it looks that way."

Delaine's face crumpled and she was seconds from another outpouring of tears.

"Remember, this is just a wild supposition on our part," said Theodosia, "but from the looks of things, it's possible a thief might have had his eye on Camille's ring. After all, it was rather beautifully displayed on that baroque silver calling card receiver." *Now why did I have to say that?* Theodosia thought to herself. *Darn, this isn't going well at all.*

"And all that beautiful old silver was sitting right next to it," said Drayton. Old silver that'd been in the Goodwood family for generations.

"Crafted by Jacob Hurd," Theodosia added helpfully.

Delaine nodded tightly. "Of course, I remember the silver. It's all very old, very elegant. I specifically requested it for just that reason."

"Anyway," continued Theodosia, "we think someone might have been prowling across the roof top."

"And taken a misstep," said Drayton.

"Which caused him to come crashing down through the roof," added Theodosia.

"On top of poor Captain Buchanan," said Drayton, grimacing. He knew the two of them sounded like they were doing some kind of tag-team routine.

Delaine peered at Theodosia and Drayton in disbelief. "You're not serious," she said in a choked voice.

"And that's when the ring was stolen," said Drayton. "Or *might* have been stolen," he added. "We're still not sure."

Delaine sat stock-still as their words washed across her. She frowned, leaned forward, put a hand to her mouth. "Then Captain Buchanan was *murdered*," she whispered hoarsely.

"Oh, no, I wouldn't go that far," said Drayton hastily. "After all, the roof could just as easily have collapsed on its own."

"But the ring is gone," said Delaine slowly. "Nowhere to be found, as you say. Doesn't that *prove* your theory?" She leaned back in her chair again. "Oh my," she murmured to herself, "this is simply *awful*. We'll need to contact the *police*."

"That's probably a good idea," admitted Theodosia. She would have done it herself last night, but the idea of the thief on the roof hadn't completely gelled in her mind. It had been a theory, a decent one at that. But of course, there was no concrete proof.

Delaine suddenly clutched Theodosia's hand. "Theodosia, you've got to help me!"

"Oh, no . . ." protested Theodosia.

"Yes," said Delaine, clutching Theodosia's hand even more forcefully and digging in with her nails. "We need to get to the bottom of this, figure out what really happened. Like you, I simply don't want to believe this was all just a horrible accident." Delaine's pleading eyes bore into Theodosia. "Oh please, you're so terribly good at this kind of thing. You helped figure out who killed poor Oliver Dixon last summer when that horrible pistol exploded at the picnic."

"She did do a fine job with that, didn't she," said Drayton, admiration apparent in his voice.

Theodosia frowned at Drayton. "That was a very different set of circumstances," she protested. "I was standing right there and had just witnessed a rather strange argument between . . ." She hesitated, decided she'd better shift her line of conversation back to the here and now. "Delaine, I really wouldn't have a clue as to where to begin. If my theory does hold water, it really was a motiveless murder."

Delaine lifted her head and gazed at Theodosia mournfully. "But that's just it. It was murder!"

"No," said Theodosia, trying to back-pedal as best she could. "I stand corrected then. It was an *accident.* The kind of accident the police need to investigate. Let them determine if there were any suspicious people lurking about in the lobby last night. Any cars seen speeding away from the Lady Goodwood Inn. Any clues left on the rooftop. That sort of thing."

"But we've got to get that ring back!" shrilled Delaine. "Camille is my niece. *I'm* responsible."

"I'm sure Captain Buchanan's family won't hold you personally responsible," said Drayton.

"Of course they won't," added Theodosia. "Because there really is nothing to go on," said Theodosia. "No way to get a bead on this mysterious intruder."

"If there even was one in the first place," Drayton added.

Delaine sat there toying with her own ring, a giant moonstone that glimmered enticingly. "But there is a way," she said slowly. "At least, there might be."

Theodosia and Drayton exchanged startled glances.

"What do you mean, honey?" asked Drayton.

"You said the burglar was probably after the ring. Maybe even had his eye on the antique silver," began Delaine.

"*Probably* being the operative word," said Drayton.

"Well, what if this person really is a practiced thief," said Delaine. "Then this wouldn't be the end of it, would it? This person, this thief who prowls about in the night, wouldn't just stop cold turkey, would he? This, whatever-he-is, cat burglar, would keep stealing, wouldn't he?"

"I suppose so," said Theodosia slowly.

Drayton set his teacup down with a loud *clink.* There was a distinctly funny look on his face. "Where are you going with this, Delaine?"

"I was thinking about tomorrow night," she said. Now a sly look lit her face. "You know, the preview party at the Heritage Society. For the Treasures Show. There's going to be that whole cache of European jewelry on display."

"I was hoping you wouldn't go there, Delaine," said Drayton. He pursed his lips and his lined face assumed a pained expression. "*Really* hoping you wouldn't go there."

Delaine continued to toy with her ring. "Well, Drayton, honey, I just did. So there. And you two know exactly what I'm talking about." She looked up in triumph, then glanced back and forth, from Theodosia's face to Drayton's. "Don't tell me the same thought hasn't crossed your minds. You know darn well that any thief who was attempting to steal an heirloom ring might also have his eye on that European Jewel Collection!"

With that, Delaine put her handkerchief to her face and began emitting little sobs.

Theodosia sat back in her chair and studied Delaine. *Are these crocodile tears or genuine tears of sorrow and frustration? Probably a little of both,* she decided. Delaine was genuinely upset over the death of her niece's fiancé as well as the apparent loss of the antique wedding ring.

On the other hand, if Delaine thought she could goad her and Drayton into helping, then she would. She'd use every trick in the book.

Theodosia sighed. Problem was, Delaine's remark about the Treasures Show at the Heritage Society was a point well taken. *Would a cat burglar stop with just one item? No, probably not. Would the European Jewel Collection at the Treasures Show be enough of a lure to bring him out again? Hmm . . . that was the sixty-four-thousand-dollar question, wasn't it?*

"Drayton, what are you doing?" shrieked Haley in alarm.

Standing behind the counter, Drayton was dumping teaspoon after heaping teaspoon of Lapsang Souchong into a Victorian-style teapot.

"Hmm?" he asked. It was early afternoon and the luncheon crowd had just departed. Haley had whipped together chicken salad with pecans and served it mounded on lettuce cups with a wedge of banana bread spread with softened cream cheese. Every plate had sold out.

"You've dumped almost a dozen spoonfuls into that pot!" she told him. "Your tea is going to be so strong it'll take the finish off!"

Drayton gazed down in horror. "Good lord! I completely lost track there, didn't I?"

"Here," Haley said as she elbowed Drayton out of the way, ready to take charge. "Let me do this. You get out the step stool and pull a couple jars of DuBose Bees Honey down from the shelf. You see that lady over there in the yellow sweater?"

Drayton scanned the tea room then nodded obediently, still lost in thought.

"Well, she adored the DuBose honey so much on her scone that she wants to take a couple jars home."

"Okay," he agreed.

"Really," huffed Haley, "it seems like everyone's lost their mind today."

"Who's lost their mind?" asked Theodosia as she emerged from the back carrying a fresh plate of scones.

"Drayton has," said Haley. "He was about to make a superstrong pot of tea. As if that stuff isn't strong enough to begin with." She sniffed.

"Look at our little Haley," said Drayton. "Two years ago she didn't know a Darjeeling from a Yunnan. Now she's an expert."

"That's enough sarcasm, Drayton," Haley snapped. "I wasn't the one who was about to send one of our guests into anaphylactic shock with a gigantic overdose of caffeine."

The bell over the door tinkled as a group of tourists pushed their way into the shop. Haley, sensing that Drayton still wasn't himself, immediately hustled over to seat them.

"Still feeling discombobulated?" Theodosia asked Drayton.

He nodded. "I keep thinking about what Delaine said regarding the members-only party tomorrow night at the Heritage Society. Granted, the installation of the entire Treasures Show won't be completed until next weekend when the public opening occurs. But the traveling European Jewel Collection will be there tomorrow night. For all to see."

"Including our so-called cat burglar."

"Right," said Drayton. "And if this thief had his eye on Camille's ring, he might also be honed in on the European Jewel Collection. It certainly has received enough publicity."

Indeed, there had been a splashy write-up in the Arts Section of the *Charleston Post & Courier* and Drayton had even been interviewed on the *Good Morning, Charleston* radio show.

"If it makes you feel any better, Drayton, those same concerns have been bouncing around in my head, too," Theodosia told him.

"Unfortunately, there really isn't much we can do," said Drayton. He assumed a glum expression. "Something like this, you have to wait and see what happens." He paused, reached behind him for a cup of tea he had brewed earlier for himself, took a sip.

"Chamomile?" asked Theodosia. Chamomile was a tried-and-true remedy for nerves.

Drayton nodded. "Do you know if Delaine talked with the police yet?"

"I just got off the phone with her," said Theodosia. "She was on her way over to the Lady Goodwood Inn to meet with two detectives from the Robbery Division."

"Too bad your friend, Detective Tidwell, couldn't be of help."

"I wouldn't go so far as to call him a friend," responded Theodosia.

Burt Tidwell, one of the Homicide Detectives in the Charleston police force, had once insinuated that Bethany Shepherd, one of Theodosia's former employees, had been involved in the poisoning of a slightly shady real estate developer during a historic homes tour. Theodosia had worked with Detective Tidwell, if one could call it that, to resolve the case and bring the true culprit to justice.

"Besides, Tidwell's in the Homicide Division," added Theodosia. "Last night's event is being assessed as a robbery."

"Right," said Drayton. He set his teacup down, picked up the two jars of honey, balanced them in his hands as though he were weighing something. "Anyway, I'm still worried about tomorrow night."

"What if we spoke with Timothy Neville?" said Theodosia. "Suggest to him that the Heritage Society might want to take some extra precautions?"

Timothy Neville was the president of the Heritage Society and a good friend of Drayton's. Timothy's great-great-grandmother had been one of the original Huguenot settlers in Charleston back in the seventeenhundreds and her descendants had become wealthy plantation owners, growing rice, indigo, and cotton. Timothy resided in a magnificent Georgian-style mansion over on Archdale Street.

Drayton nodded. "Timothy might go along with the idea. *Should* go along with it, anyway. It would certainly be in his best interests."

"So you'll speak to him?" asked Theodosia. "Share our concern without completely alarming him?"

"Absolutely," said Drayton, making up his mind. "I'll call Timothy this instant."

4

"This," said the enthusiastic manager of Spies Are Us, "is the slickest little device this side of the DOD."

"What's the DOD?" asked Drayton.

"Department of Defense, my friend. And this little baby provides your first *wall* of defense."

Theodosia and Drayton stood in the high-tech electronics store gazing at a device that looked like a second cousin to a video camera. Around them were showy displays that featured motion detectors, security cameras, tiny cameras that fit into pens and lapel pins, as well as miniature microphones.

"How exactly does this work?" inquired Drayton. He had voiced his feelings to Timothy Neville about heightening security at the members-only party tonight and, surprisingly, had received a green light. The problem he and Theodosia now faced was to select the right security device from the hundreds for sale in the store. Security, it would seem, was very big business these days.

"This motion detector functions like the automatic range finder on a camera," said the young store manager whose name tag read RILEY. "Basically, you set the perimeter via this keypad." Riley's fingers tapped lightly on the shiny keypad. "Then, once the device is programmed, it emits sonar pulses and waits for an echo. But if someone breaks the electronic beam, say they walk through it or even pass a hand nearby . . . then *wham!* The alarm goes off!"

"How large an area will this secure?" asked Theodosia.

"What are we talking, warehouse or retail?" Riley asked.

"Think of a smaller retail space," said Drayton. "With glass cases."

"A smaller area, I'd say you should probably go with two," Riley told them. "If you decide later that you need to expand your protected area, you can always add a couple additional modules." Riley smiled and nodded over the top of Theodosia's head toward a customer. "Could you excuse me for a moment? I've got a customer who's here to pick up a security camera. Poor guy owns a couple liquor stores and is constantly getting ripped off."

Theodosia looked askance at the device in Drayton's hand. "How much is this thing?" she asked.

Drayton studied the price tag. "Ninety-nine dollars," he told her. "I'm amazed this stuff is so affordable."

"Me too. But you know how much technology has come down in price. Look at DVD and CD players."

Drayton stared at her blankly. As a self-professed curmudgeon who was scornful of all things technologic, he still preferred his old Philco stereo and vinyl record albums.

"Well, never mind," Theodosia told him, deciding this probably wasn't the best time to illuminate Drayton on the advances that had been made in the past ten years. "You think we'd need two of these?" she asked.

Drayton studied the brochure and did some quick math, figuring square footage while he mumbled to himself. "Two should do it," he decided. "The jewelry will be on display in the small gallery. That's really our key area of concern right now."

"And Timothy approved this expenditure?" Even though Timothy Neville lived in baronial splendor in a huge redbrick Georgian mansion, he was notoriously frugal when it came to expenditures for the Heritage Society.

"When I spoke with him yesterday, he certainly agreed there was a potential for trouble. So yes, he did approve this. Tonight's party is members-only, of course, and he didn't seem to feel we should expect any problems. I think Timothy's got more of an eye toward next weekend. That's when there could be a security issue. I suppose he views tonight as a sort of dry run."

"But he's agreed to security guards, too," said Theodosia. She wasn't about to pin all her hopes on two ninety-nine-dollar motion sensors.

"Two security guards will be posted. But realize, we had to employ them anyway," Drayton told her. "For insurance purposes. Anytime you have a traveling show like this European Jewel Collection, you're contractually obligated to provide a certain amount of security."

They stood there silently, eyeing the device.

"Are we overreacting?" asked Theodosia.

"Probably," admitted Drayton. "In the cold, clear light of day, when you stand in this store and see all this tricky-techy stuff that plays right into people's paranoias, our cat burglar theory does seem awfully far-fetched."

"Right," Theodosia nodded. Her hand reached out and touched the motion sensor. It had a black metallic surface with a matte finish. Very gadgety and *Mission Impossible* looking. "This *is* sort of crazy," she admitted. "You turn this little gizmo on and it generates supersonic detector beams."

"It's nuts," agreed Drayton.

"Maybe we shouldn't buy it then," said Theodosia.

"Of course we should," said Drayton.

Rain swept down in vast sheets, a cold, soaking late October rain that lashed in from the Atlantic. Spanish moss, heavy with water, sagged and swayed in the branches of giant live oaks like flotsam from the sea. Heroic last stands of bougainvillea and tiny white blooms from tea olive trees were mercilessly pounded, their blossoms shredded then pressed into the damp earth as though some careless giant had defiantly strode through and flattened everything in his wake.

Out in Charleston Harbor, waves slapped sharply against channel buoys as the Cooper and Ashley Rivers converged in Charleston Harbor to confront the driving tide from the Atlantic. The mournful sound of the foghorn out on Patriot's Point moaned and groaned, its low sound carrying to the old historic homes that crowded up against the peninsula, shoulder to elegant shoulder, like a receiving line of dowager empresses.

The lights inside the old stone headquarters of the Heritage Society glowed like a beacon in the dark as ladies clad in opera capes and men in tuxedos splashed through puddles in their evening finery and struggled frantically with umbrellas blown inside out.

Standing in the entryway, Theodosia shrugged off her black nylon raincoat, gently shook the rain from it, then handed it off to a young volunteer, who seemed at a complete loss as to what to do with all these wet garments.

Patting her hair and smoothing the skirt of her black taffeta cocktail dress, Theodosia composed her serene face in a natural smile as she made her way down the crowded hallway, trying to push her way through the exuberant throng of Heritage Society members.

"Theo!" cried an excited voice. "Hello there!"

Theodosia turned to see Brooke Carter Crockett, the owner of the estate jewelry store, Heart's Desire, smiling and waving at her.

"Brooke . . . hello," she responded. But then she was carried along by a crowd of people and eventually found herself at the end of the great hallway in the suite of rooms the Heritage Society used for receptions such as this and as galleries to showcase items pulled from their vast storage vault in the basement.

Making a mental note to get back to Brooke later when some of the initial hubbub had died down, Theodosia gazed around appreciatively at the interior of the building.

The old stone building that housed the Heritage Society was definitely one of Theodosia's favorite edifices. Long ago, well over two hundred years ago, it had been a government building, built by the English. But rather than exuding a residual bureaucratic aura, Theodosia felt that the building seemed more contemplative and medieval in nature. An atmosphere that was undoubtedly helped along by its arched wood beam ceilings, stone walls, heavy leaded windows, and sagging wooden floors.

It was, Theodosia had always thought, the kind of place you could turn into a very grand home. Given the proviso, of course, that you owned tons of leather-bound books, furnished it with acres of Oriental rugs and overstuffed furniture, and had a passel of snoozing hound dogs to keep you company.

It would be a far cry from her small apartment over the tea shop, she decided, which she'd originally decorated in the chintz-and-prints-bordering-on-shabby-chic school of design, and was now veering toward old world antiquities and elegance.

On her way to the bar, which turned out to be an old Jacobean trestle table stocked with dozens of bottles and an enormous cut-glass bowl filled with ice, Theodosia met up with Drayton. He was chatting with Aerin Linley, one of the Heritage Society's volunteer fund-raisers and cochair of the Treasures Show.

"Theo, you know Aerin Linley, don't you?" he asked.

"Of course," said Theodosia as she greeted the pretty redhead who looked absolutely stunning in a slinky scoop-necked, cream-colored jersey wrap dress and an heirloom emerald necklace that matched her eyes. "Nice to see you again."

"Besides cochairing the Treasures Show, Aerin authored the grant request that helped secure funding to bring in the European Jewel Collection," Drayton told her.

"I'm impressed," said Theodosia as the two women shook hands. "I've tried my hand at writing a few grant requests myself, mostly to try to obtain program support for Big Paws, our Charleston service dog organization, so I know grant writing is a fairly daunting task. Lots of probing questions to answer and hurdles to jump through."

"It's *awfully* tricky," agreed Aerin Linley. "And there does seem to be a language all its own attached to it, one that's slightly stilted and bureaucratic. Not really my style at all," she laughed. "I think I just got lucky with this one."

"You're still working at Heart's Desire?" asked Theodosia. She remembered that Brooke Carter Crockett, the shop's owner, had mentioned something about Aerin being her assistant.

Aerin Linley fingered the emerald necklace that draped around her neck. "Can't you tell?" she said playfully. "This is one of our pieces."

"It's gorgeous," said Theodosia as she peered at it and wondered just how many cups of tea she'd have to sell to finance *that* little piece of extravagance!

"Never hurts to show off the merchandise," laughed Aerin. "You never know when somebody's in the market for a great piece. But to answer your question, yes . . . and I'm absolutely *loving* it there. And now that I'm handling most of the appraisals, Brooke has been freed up to focus more on acquisitions and sales. She just returned from a sales trip to New York, where she made quite a hit with some of the dealers at the Manhattan Antique Center. They went absolutely *crazy* over our Charleston pieces. I think they were thrilled to get some pieces with real history attached to them as opposed to flash-in-the-pan nouveau designer pieces."

"Of course they were," said Drayton, the perennial Charleston booster.

"I also turned Brooke on to some rather prime buying opportunities for heirloom jewelry down in Savannah," said Aerin. "There are so many old families who have jewel boxes just brimming with fine old pieces. To say nothing of all the secret drawers and panels built into the woodwork of those old homes."

"Did you grow up in Savannah?" asked Theodosia. Savannah was just ninety miles south of Charleston. That great, vast swamp known as the low-country was all that separated the two old *grande dame* cities.

"I did," said Aerin. "But I moved here a few months ago after my divorce." She flashed a wicked grin. "Savannah's really an awfully small town when you get right down to it. And it certainly wasn't big enough for the two of us, once we called it quits."

"Then you know the Buchanans," said Theodosia.

"Quite well, actually," Aerin replied. "And such a tragedy about poor Corey Buchanan. Drayton's been filling me in. Brooke, too." She lowered her voice. "I can't say we're thrilled by these whispered allegations of a cat burglar. Heart's Desire has a well-earned reputation for offering a stunning array of estate jewelry, so we do make an awfully broad target," she said, widening her eyes in alarm.

"There you-all are!" Delaine Dish, with Cooper Hobcaw in tow, edged up to the group. "Look, Coop, here's our dear Theo and Drayton. And Miss Linley, too. Hello," she purred.

"Good evening," Cooper Hobcaw said politely. "Hello, Miz Browning, Drayton, Miz Linley." He executed a chivalrous half-bow in their general direction.

Delaine gazed up at Cooper Hobcaw with studied intensity, then actually batted her eyelashes at him. "Don't you just *love* a real Southern gentleman?" she cooed, seemingly entranced by his presence.

Cooper winced and gave a self-deprecating laugh. "Now Delaine, darlin', most Southern gentlemen are gentlemen," he joked and the rest of them laughed politely.

Aerin Linley put a hand on Cooper Hobcaw's arm to get his attention. "It was nice of you to call Lorna and Rex Buchanan the other night," she told him. "According to Drayton here, you handled a very intense situation with a good deal of care and grace."

Cooper Hobcaw bobbed his head modestly. "I'm sure any one of us would have been glad to do the same thing."

"I take it funeral arrangements have been made?" asked Drayton.

"Yes," said Theodosia, "when is the funeral?"

"Monday," replied Delaine. "In Savannah, of course. Apparently it took some time to notify all of Captain Buchanan's military friends. Some of them were out at sea, so they had to be pulled off their ships by helicopter."

"So sad," murmured Theodosia.

"It is," agreed Delaine, who seemed to have gotten some perspective on the death of her niece's fiancé. She was congenial, Theodosia noted, but her mood was tempered by a certain sadness.

"I'll be driving down Sunday night," Delaine told them. "Celerie Stuart is going with me. She was a dear friend of Lorna Buchanan's. They went to school together at Mount Holyoke."

"And what of Camille?" asked Drayton.

"She's down in Savannah now," replied Delaine. "Staying with the Buchanans." Delaine's eyes suddenly glistened as tears seemed to gather in the corners. "It's the best thing for her, really. To be surrounded by people who loved him."

Drayton nodded knowingly, reached out, and patted Delaine's hand.

The Treasures Show, once the installation was finally complete, would be a stunning display of some of the choicer pieces the Heritage Society had amassed over the years. Established as a repository for historical paintings, maps, documents, furniture, and antiques, the Heritage Society had been collecting antiquities for nearly 160 years. More recently, under the careful guidance of its president, Timothy Neville, the Heritage Society had staged several "appeal" campaigns, with subtle requests going out to Charlestonians asking them to kindly donate some of their more important paintings and pieces.

And certain residents of Charleston, especially those with homes filled to the rafters with inherited treasures, had responded generously. Especially those who had a relatively high tax liability and wanted to get that all-important museum tax credit.

That tax deduction loophole was perhaps one of the reasons the Heritage Society now had in its possession a tasty mélange of French empire clocks, eighteenth-century Meissen figurines, Queen Anne "handkerchief" tables, old pewter, fine sterling silver, and Early American paintings.

A handpicked assortment that included some of those very fine pieces would be installed during the coming week to make up the Heritage Society's much-heralded Treasures Show.

But for now it was the traveling exhibition of exquisite European jewelry that had captured Theodosia's eye. This collection of jewelry was pure ecstasy, the kinds of pieces a woman could truly dream over.

Here, on a mantle of black velvet, was a diamond brooch that had once nestled at the ample breast of Empress Josephine, Napoleon's one true love. And in this next case was a strand of giant baroque pearls that had reputedly been worn by the Duchess Sophia, when Archduke Ferdinand of Austria was assassinated in 1914. And Theodosia was utterly entranced by the jeweled flamingo pin that had been commissioned by the Duke of Windsor and worn by Wallis, his lifelong love and the Duchess of Windsor.

All thoughts of burglars and thieves creeping through the night vanished from Theodosia's mind as she gazed in wonder at the radiant treasures that occupied the glass cases in the small, dark room. Lit from above with pinpoint spotlights to highlight the radiance of the gemstones, the jewelry simply dazzled the eye.

As Theodosia gazed in wonderment, she was suddenly aware of Timothy Neville, the venerable old president of the Heritage Society, standing at her side.

At age eighty-one, Timothy was not just the power behind the Heritage Society, but also a denizen of the historic district, first violin of the Charleston Symphony, collector of antique pistols, and proud possessor of a stunning mansion on Archdale Street that was furnished with equally stunning paintings, tapestries, and antiques. And interestingly enough, all that knowledge and power was contained in a small man, barely one hundred forty pounds, who had a bony, simian face, yet possessed the grace and poise of an elder statesman.

"This is an absolutely stunning show, Timothy," said Theodosia.

Timothy Neville smiled, revealing a mouth full of small, pointed teeth. Any compliment directed at the Heritage Society was a personal triumph for Timothy. But it was not just ego that drove him, it was a sense of satisfaction that the Heritage Society had once again fulfilled its mission.

"The show will be even more spectacular once the complete installation is in place," replied Timothy Neville. "As you can see, we've only just utilized this one room. The furniture, decorative arts, and paintings will be displayed in the back two galleries."

Theodosia pointed to a necklace that featured an enormous pear-shaped sapphire accented by smaller sapphires. "This blue sapphire necklace is stunning," she told him.

"And the provenance is absolutely fascinating," replied Timothy.

Intrigued, Theodosia bent forward and read the description for what they were calling the Blue Kashmir necklace. "Originally worn by an

Indian maharajah, then purchased in the twenties and made into a neck-lace by Marjorie Merriweather Post, the breakfast cereal heiress," she read aloud. "Wow."

"Most people take jewelry at face value," said Timothy, smiling faintly at his small joke. "What they don't realize it that jewelry is often an intrinsic part of history as well. Jewelry speaks to us, tells a story."

Timothy pointed to a case that contained a stunning group of black and gold brooches and pins. "Take this mourning jewelry, for example. Belonged to Queen Victoria. After Prince Albert died of typhoid fever in 1861, the old girl was so distraught she went into mourning for the next three decades. In fact, her mourning policy was so strict that she allowed only black stones to be worn in the English court. Jet, onyx, bog oak, that type of thing, set in silver and gold."

"I had no idea," said Theodosia.

"Most people don't," replied Timothy.

Theodosia turned to face him. "I'm sorry if we alarmed you," she said. "About the possibility of a jewel thief."

Timothy grimaced, pulled his slight body to his full height. Dressed in his European-cut tuxedo, he looked like a martinet, but his eyes were kind. "Yes, Drayton was in a bit of a flap over the accident at the Lady Goodwood Inn the other night. Who knows what really happened, eh? The police are investigating, are they not?"

"Yes, they are," said Theodosia. "At least I *hope* they are."

"Then I suppose we'll have to wait and see what their assessment of the situation really is," replied Timothy. "And in the meantime, bolster our security around here. I actually like the idea of having electronic gizmos. We have security devices on our doors and windows, of course, but I never thought to use them in conjunction with our various exhibits. Of course, the Heritage Society doesn't put on all that many blockbuster shows that are advertised widely to the public. Mostly we're a quiet little place. People find their way to us in ones and twos." Timothy hesitated. "Sad about young Buchanan, though. I never met the fellow, but I knew his grandfa-ther. Fine family." Timothy shook his head and the overhead spotlights made his bald pate gleam. "Hell of a thing," he murmured quietly.

• • •

"Delaine," gushed Theodosia, "have you seen the jewelry yet?" She gestured over her shoulder at the small gallery she'd just emerged from. "It's absolutely fantastic!"

Delaine smiled wanly. "Not really. I've been gossiping with Hillary Retton and Marianne Petigru. You know, the two ladies who own Popple Hill Interior Design? Did you know they recently worked on the Lady Goodwood Inn? That superb tapestry in the foyer came all the way from France. I think it might have been hand-loomed by cloistered nuns or something."

"Are you okay, Delaine?" asked Theodosia. Delaine was looking decidedly unhappy and her voice had taken on a shrill tone. She was undoubtedly still upset from the other night. The fact that she'd been discussing the decor at the Lady Goodwood probably didn't help matters, either.

"I'm perfectly fine, Theodosia. I've just been trying to get another *drink!*" Delaine held up an empty glass and lifted her chin. "That fellow over there has been no help whatsoever. I've asked him twice now to bring me a Kir Royale and do you think I have *yet* to see my drink? Of course not!"

"Delaine," said Theodosia, "the man's a security guard, not a waiter."

Delaine furrowed her brow and pulled her face into a petulant expression. "Well, he's *dressed* like a waiter."

"That's part of the setup," Theodosia explained patiently. "Remember, we told you the Heritage Society would have extra security on duty tonight?"

"Oh." Delaine bit her lip as Drayton wandered up to join them, alone this time. "Yes, I guess you did mention that."

But from the look on Delaine's face, Theodosia knew she was still unhappy about not getting her drink. It was amazing that just yesterday morning Delaine had been worked up about possible thievery at tonight's event and now she was consumed with trying to get a drink. Theodosia sighed. Delaine *did* tend to be a bit self-centered.

"Where's Cooper?" Theodosia asked as Drayton joined them carrying a goblet half-filled with red wine.

Delaine shrugged helplessly. "Off somewhere. Mingling, I suppose." She turned to Drayton and eyed the goblet in his hand. "What's that?" she asked.

"A marvelous Bordeaux, Haute Emillion, 'ninety-two. Take it," he offered generously. "It's freshly poured and as yet untouched."

"No thanks," said Delaine. "I'm trying to get a *real* drink."

Drayton, sensing the impending onslaught of World War III, suddenly decided to take matters in hand.

"Pardon me," he said, flagging down a waiter who was hustling by with a tray of drinks in his hand. "Could you fetch us a drink?"

The young, ginger-haired waiter stopped in his tracks, bobbed his head. "Of course, sir."

"Here you go, Delaine. This young fellow here . . ." said Drayton.

"Graham, sir," said the waiter.

"Tell Graham what you'd like, Delaine. He'll take care of you." Drayton fumbled in his pocket for a few dollars, pressed them into the waiter's hand. "For your trouble, young man."

"No problem, sir," replied the waiter.

"I'd like a Kir Royale," Delaine told the waiter. "Cassis and champagne?"

The waiter nodded. "Of course, ma'am. Be back in a moment."

"Evening, ladies," **boomed** a rich male voice.

Jory Davis, Theodosia's on-again off-again boyfriend, grinned at them. Tall, well over six feet, with a square jaw, suntanned complexion, and curly brown hair, Jory Davis had a slightly reckless look about him. He didn't look the way a traditional lawyer was supposed to look, all buttoned up and slightly pompous. Instead, Jory Davis had an aura of the outdoors about him. Dressed in casual clothes, he could have passed for a trout fishing guide. Or maybe a wealthy landowner whose life's love was training thoroughbred horses.

Jory Davis snaked an arm around Theodosia's waist and pulled her close to him, touched his chin to the top of her head. Pleased, she snuggled in against him.

The move was not lost on Delaine. "I see you two are still very cozy," she said.

"Mmm," said Jory. "And why not?" He smiled down at Theodosia. "I was thinking about taking *Rubicon* out tomorrow. What do you think? Are you up for an ocean sail?"

Jory Davis's sailboat, *Rubicon,* was a J-24 that he kept moored at the Charleston Yacht Club. He was an expert yachtsman and regularly competed in the Isle of Palms race as well as the Compass Key yacht race.

"Isn't it still raining?" asked Theodosia.

"Tonight it is," said Jory, "but the weather's supposed to clear by tomorrow. If there's a chop on the water, it'll just make our sail all the more interesting. And challenging," he added.

Clear weather and a chance to clear my head, thought Theodosia. *Truly a heavenly idea.* The past two days had been fairly fraught with tension, what with the terrible accident at the Lady Goodwood and Drayton's fear that something might go wrong here tonight. Jory's suggestion of a sail in Charleston Harbor and the waters beyond would be a perfect way to put it all behind her.

"You're on," she told him.

"Good," he said. "I'll pick you up around nine, then we'll go rig the boat. And bring that goofy dog of yours along. We'll turn him into a sea dog yet."

"Sailing sounds like fun," said Delaine. The note of wistfulness in her voice was not lost on the two of them.

"Say," said Jory, "I'm going to slip across the room and have a word with Leyland Hartwell. He's representing the Tidewater Corporation in a zoning dispute and I'm second chair. Be back in a couple minutes, okay?"

"Sure," said Theodosia as she watched her tall, tanned boyfriend navigate his way through the crowd.

Ligget, Hume, Hartwell, the firm Jory Davis worked for, was also her father's old firm. He had been a senior partner along with Leyland Hartwell before he passed away some fifteen years ago. Her father had become a distant memory now, but he was always in her heart. As was her mother, who had died when Theodosia was just eight.

"What kind of law does Jory Davis practice again?" asked Delaine.

"Mostly corporate and real estate law," said Theodosia. "Deeds, fore-closures, zoning, leases, that sort of thing."

"So he's never faced off against Cooper in a courtroom," said Delaine.

The thought amused Theodosia. She could see Cooper Hobcaw with his arrogant stance arguing torts against a bemused Jory Davis. But no, that would never happen. Cooper Hobcaw was a criminal attorney, Jory Davis a real estate attorney.

"Cooper Hobcaw seems like a nice fellow . . ." began Theodosia when, suddenly, every light in the place went out. *Whoosh*. Extinguished like the flame on a candle.

Oh no, thought Theodosia, her heart in her throat. *Not again!*

Plunged into complete darkness, the room erupted in chaos. Women screamed, a tray of drinks went crashing to the floor. Across the room, something hit the carpet with a muffled thud. Disoriented by the dark, people began to lunge to and fro. Theodosia felt an elbow drill into her back, a sleeve brush roughly against her bare arm.

Suddenly, mercifully, from off to her left, someone flipped on a ciga-rette lighter and held the flame aloft like a tiny torch. There was a spatter of applause, then a deep hum started from somewhere in the depths of the building.

"Generator," murmured a male voice off to her right. "Emergency lights should kick on soon."

Ten seconds later, four sets of emergency lights sputtered on.

They blazed weakly overhead, yet did little to actually illuminate the room. The lighting felt unnatural and fuzzy, like trying to peer through a bank of fog.

"Hey!" called a voice that Theodosia recognized as belonging to Jory Davis. "Someone's down over here!"

Theodosia quickly elbowed her way through the crowd in the direc-tion of Jory Davis's voice.

Ten feet, fifteen feet of pushing past people brought her to just out-side the small gallery. In the dim light she could see one of the security guards sprawled on the floor. Jory Davis was already on his hands and knees beside the man, making a hasty check of his airways, trying to determine if he was still breathing.

"Is he okay?" asked Theodosia.

"He's still breathing," said Jory, "but he's for sure out cold." Jory put a finger to the top of the security guard's head, came away with a smear of blood. "Looks like he took a nasty bump to the noggin." Jory glanced up at Theodosia. "Somebody sapped this poor guy, but good," he added in a tight, low voice. Then Jory Davis scrambled to his feet. "Can someone please call an ambulance!" he shouted.

With Jory Davis's forceful lawyer voice ringing out across the room, no fewer than twenty people responded instantly. Cell phones were yanked from pockets and evening bags, and twenty fingers punched in the same 911 call, completely swamping the small crew that manned Charleston's central emergency line.

"Theodosia!" Timothy Neville was suddenly at her side and clutching her arm. "It's gone!" he told her in a tremulous voice. "Vanished!"

"What's gone?" she asked, momentarily confused.

"The Blue Kashmir," Timothy hissed. "The sapphire necklace. It's disappeared from its case!" Timothy clapped a wizened hand to the side of his face and seemed to collapse in on himself.

Theodosia stared at Timothy in disbelief. When the power went out, the sensor beams had stopped working, too, she realized. *Oh, no . . . we didn't even consider that possibility. Had someone cut the power deliberately? Or had the storm just knocked it out?*

No, she decided, if a guard's been injured, the power *had* to have been disabled on purpose.

In the dim light Theodosia could see that Timothy was dangerously on the verge of passing out.

"Are you okay, Timothy?" she asked.

"Yes, yes," he said hurriedly, although perspiration had broken out on his face and his breathing had suddenly turned shallow.

Ohmygosh, Theodosia thought to herself. *Heart attack? Not Timothy. Please, Lord, not Timothy. Not now.*

Pushing his way over to them, Drayton took one look at Timothy Neville's face, grabbed him firmly by the arm, and steered him to a nearby chair a few feet away. "Are you all right, Timothy?" he asked as Timothy sat down gingerly, looking paler than ever.

"Yes, I think so . . ." rasped Timothy, ". . . just let me catch my . . ."

Theodosia whirled about and threw herself down next to Jory Davis. He had once again taken up his position next to the fallen security guard and had bunched up his jacket and put it under the poor man's head. A woman whom Theodosia recognized as Dr. Lucy Cornwall, Earl Grey's veterinarian, was administering CPR to the downed security guard, while Jory Davis continued to monitor the man's pulse.

"There's something wrong with Timothy," Theodosia told them in a rush. "I think he's having a heart attack!"

On this lazy Sunday in late October, autumn was clearly in the air. The wet weather was temporarily held at bay by a warm front that had finally drifted up from the Gulf of Mexico. It seemed like a toss-up as to whether the day would dissipate into scattered thundershowers or weak sunshine would punch through the low-hanging clouds.

Down at Charleston Harbor, people strolled through White Point Gardens and Battery Park, delighted by the huge displays of Civil War cannons and gazing at the magnificent harbor where whitecaps rose like peaks of frosting. Out on the water, sailboats bobbed like corks, tossed about in the boiling froth, masts straining against strong twenty-knot winds.

But Theodosia was not out sailing today. She was not slicing through the waves, enjoying salty breezes and the exhilaration of navigating tricky crosscurrents.

Instead, she sat with Drayton and Timothy on the side piazza of Timothy Neville's home. The sun was warm and caressing, the view conducive to Zen-like contemplation since the piazza overlooked the bamboo groves, rocky paths, Chinese lanterns, and trickling fountain of Timothy's Asian-inspired garden. But the mood was not particularly serene.

Timothy hadn't experienced a heart attack last night after all. After rushing him to the hospital along with the security guard, an EKG had been administered, cardiac enzymes monitored, blood pressure taken every fifteen minutes.

Extreme stress, the doctor had ruled, once he'd studied the test results and learned of the strange events that had taken place at the Heritage Society's party. Extreme stress had triggered a rush of adrenaline and a flood of cortisol, which had produced *symptoms* that closely mimicked an all-out heart attack.

A shaken but stoic Timothy had put up with all the tests and ministrations at the hospital, but staunchly vetoed any notion of an overnight stay even if it was intended purely for observation.

The security guard hadn't fared as well. He lay in intensive care, his head swathed in bandages, fluttering in and out of a coma, hooked up to a host of beeping, glowing monitors.

"Have you seen this?" Timothy Neville winced as he held up the front page of the main news section of the Sunday *Post & Courier.*

"We've seen it," said Drayton. He sat in a wicker lounge chair facing Timothy, looking anything but relaxed. In fact, Drayton was wound so tightly it looked as though his bow tie was about ready to spin.

"Jackals," spat Timothy. "How do they get this stuff out so fast?"

A small article, mercifully positioned at the bottom of the page, led off with the headline GEMS NABBED FROM HERITAGE SOCIETY.

"At least it's not in seventy-two-point type," Drayton pointed out.

Timothy stared at him with a mixture of anger and disgust.

Nervously, Drayton crossed his legs then uncrossed them, deciding that perhaps humor *wasn't* the most practical approach here.

"We look like *idiots,*" raged Timothy. "This is going to cost us donors and then some!"

Theodosia knew that Timothy Neville was worried sick that this incident might also cost him his job as president of the Heritage Society. The man was eighty-one, she reasoned, and had done a masterful job for the past twenty-five years. But how long could he continue? Would this be the political scandal that brought about his downfall? She hoped not, but it was certainly possible.

"Timothy," began Drayton, "I know you have serious doubts about opening the Treasures Show to the public next Saturday. Please . . . just take into consideration how much promotion has already been done, how much publicity we've gotten."

Timothy gazed at the front page of the newspaper again. "Publicity," he snorted. "This kind of publicity we don't need. What's important now is damage control. This incident has been the worst kind of *blight* on the Heritage Society." Timothy spat out the word *blight* as though he were discussing manure.

"Which is why we should stay the course," pleaded Drayton. "Open the Treasures Show to the public next weekend as planned. Show everyone that it's business as usual, that we *haven't* been affected!"

Timothy sighed deeply. "I don't know. I'll have to speak with the insurance company. And our executive advisory committee, of course." Timothy sat quietly in his chair, staring out at the garden. "Any word on the poor fellow who got clobbered on the head?" he asked finally.

"The man's name is Harlan Wilson," said Drayton. "He was one of the security guards from Gold Shield who has been employed by us on several other occasions. As far as we know, he's still terribly groggy, in and out of consciousness. He has a rather nasty concussion as well as a hairline skull fracture. The results of his ECG, his encephalogram, looked very positive, however. There are no interruptions in brain activity, which is a very good sign. Doctors, being doctors, are remaining cautious, though. They haven't allowed the police to question Mr. Wilson as yet. They warn that it might be a day or two before he's well enough for that."

Timothy shook his head. "Such a terrible thing. Poor man getting hurt like that."

Theodosia had remained quiet during most of the exchange between Timothy and Drayton. She wasn't on the board of the Heritage Society like Drayton was. And she wasn't a close friend of Timothy's like Drayton was. But she *did* share their anger and frustration. After all, *she'd* also had a nervous rumbling about this. And had thought, mistakenly it would appear, that security guards and some newly purchased gadgets would be enough to ensure safekeeping of the European Jewel Collection.

Did that make her partially responsible for what happened last night?

With Theodosia's sense of fair play, the answer was a resounding yes. Yes, she was partially responsible. So, yes, she was determined to try to help resolve this problem.

Delaine had begged for her help in trying to find the missing wedding ring; now Drayton and Timothy seemed to be in a fairly tight situation as well.

Theodosia also knew that the one issue that desperately needed to be discussed remained unspoken.

"You know what this means, don't you?" began Theodosia quietly.

"Of course," said Timothy with an air of resignation. "It means our good name has been besmirched. How willing are people going to be to donate a silver tankard or a piece of Chippendale if they think the Heritage Society can't even offer decent security?" He shook his head. "I doubt they'll even trust us with a dog-eared *photo album* now."

"Timothy," Theodosia said slowly, "this second theft gives us a fairly good confirmation that some kind of special thief or cat burglar *is* operating in the historic district."

She watched as Timothy lowered his head in his hands.

"Why, oh why, didn't I take this more seriously?" he lamented. "I assumed that missing wedding ring had just rolled into a corner somewhere and was lying there in a puff of dust. I never thought any kind of serious *theft* would occur at the Heritage Society. Not in my wildest dreams!"

"Don't be so hard on yourself," spoke up Drayton. "I'd say you took our warning very seriously. When I spoke to you about the wedding ring disappearing from the Lady Goodwood Inn, you were *extremely* agreeable about taking precautions. You even approved the expenditure for the electronic equipment. Which means you did *everything* right, Timothy. No one could possibly fault you or hold you responsible."

Timothy grimaced, unwilling to meet Drayton's earnest gaze. "Oh, but I'm afraid they will," he replied, his voice quavering.

"Timothy," said Theodosia, determined to bring him back to the subject at hand, "we've got to face reality. Whoever is responsible for these thefts has to be one of our own."

Timothy's eyebrows rose like two question marks on his pale face as he stared at Theodosia with trepidation. "Explain," he said. One hand gestured at her weakly, urging her to continue.

"If it isn't someone from our own circle," said Theodosia, "then how else would they have known about Camille's wedding ring at the Lady Goodwood? Or the European Jewel Collection?"

"They read the paper? Studied their intended target?" proposed Drayton.

"The European Jewel Collection was written up in the paper, yes," said Theodosia. She thought for a moment. "But there was nothing about Camille Buchanan's wedding ring. That was . . . that was . . ."

"An accident?" proposed Drayton.

"You're not going to like this, but I'd say it's more likely an inside job," said Theodosia. "As far as the Lady Goodwood's silver goes . . . well, you'd just have to know about that."

"So whoever perpetrated the crime was right there," said Timothy slowly. "They were right there among us last night. Probably sipping drinks, chatting with guests."

They all sat in shocked silence for a moment, pondering the implications.

Finally, Theodosia spoke up. "There's something else, too."

"What's that?" asked Drayton.

"If the two thefts are related, and I think we have pretty much come to the very unsettling conclusion that they are, then poor Harlan Wilson could be in danger," said Theodosia. "Because he's probably the only witness we have."

"But he's still in a coma!" exclaimed Drayton.

"Which is very good news for our thief," said Theodosia. "Unless Mr. Wilson suddenly comes to and is able to provide the police with a careful description. Of course, we don't know for certain that Mr. Wilson even saw the robbery take place. Let's assume that he did, however, and act accordingly. Err on the side of caution."

"So what do we do now?" asked Timothy. He suddenly looked terribly defeated.

"Obviously we need reinforcements," said Theodosia. "And protection for Mr. Wilson."

"The police," said Timothy with resignation. "They're already on it. I spoke with two investigators this morning."

"Did you voice your concerns about a connection with the ring disappearing at the Lady Goodwood?" asked Drayton.

"No," said Timothy. "I guess I just didn't want to believe . . ." His voice trailed off.

"Then might I suggest we call in the big guns?" said Theodosia.

"You mean . . ." said Drayton, glancing sharply at her.

Theodosia nodded. "That's right. Detective Tidwell."

Henry Marchand, Timothy's butler and housekeeper for the last forty years, suddenly appeared behind them. For someone who was so advanced in years, Henry moved with amazing stealth. They had heard nary a footstep.

"Sorry to interrupt, sir, but you have a phone call," Henry said in his somber, papery voice.

Theodosia glanced down at Henry's feet. He was wearing a pair of Chinese shoes. Thin-soled slip-ons made of black cotton fabric. No wonder he moved like a Ninja.

Timothy waved a hand as though to dismiss the call. "Tell them to—"

"It's Mr. Bernard," said Henry with a grave face.

Timothy reluctantly pulled himself up from his wicker chair. "You hear that? Vance Bernard is *chairman* of our executive advisory committee. The committee *I* report to. I can assure you, Vance Bernard is not a happy man today. Which can result in just one thing—my head will be placed squarely on the chopping block!"

Timothy took a few steps to the door, hesitated, turned back toward

Theodosia and Drayton. "Once you speak with this fellow, Tidwell, you'll let me know, yes?"

"Of course," Theodosia assured him, then watched as Timothy turned back and entered the house. It was the first time she'd seen Timothy Neville walk without a spring in his step. It was the first time she'd really seen him looking old.

6

The notes from Pachelbel's *Canon* drifted through Theodosia's upstairs apartment, a cozy fire crackled in the bright fireplace, a chapter from a new mystery novel beckoned. But try as she might, Theodosia just couldn't concentrate, couldn't relax.

After that rather jarring meeting with Timothy Neville, she and Drayton had tried to formulate some sort of battle plan. But nothing had seemed to gel. There didn't seem to be any real clues. After all, if no one person stuck in their minds as a potential suspect, what exactly could they do? Nothing. Nothing at all.

Theodosia lay her book facedown on the sofa, kicked off the afghan she'd been snuggled under, and gazed about, a slightly disgruntled look on her usually serene face.

She loved her little place above the tea shop. It was elegant, cozy, and suited her perfectly. This past summer, she'd taken the big plunge and painted the walls. But instead of a conservative palette of eggshell white or cream, she'd opted for a rich ochre base coat, then sponged a second layer of flaxen yellow on top of it. The result was a sun-washed feel reminiscent of a Tuscan villa. Now the cinnamon and gold Oriental rug she'd always had in the living room really came alive. As did the gleaming seascape oil paintings on the walls. Flanking the double doorway that led to her small dining room, she'd installed two antique wooden columns as plant stands for her Boston ferns.

What had once been very shabby chic had suddenly become the picture of Southern elegance.

That's good, she had told herself. *The nature of a home should shift and mature along with its owner.*

But tonight, the upstairs apartment she'd worked so hard and lovingly on just felt confining.

Enough, she decided as she padded into her bedroom, rooted around in the bottom of the closet for her Nikes, and pulled a pair of leggings from a chest of drawers.

When in doubt, go for a jog.

Earl Grey, suddenly alert and convinced something wonderful was about to take place, sprang to his feet. Toenails clicking against hardwood floors, he circled her repeatedly, ears pitched forward, tail beating a doggy rhythm in double time.

"You got it, fella, let's go," said Theodosia as she grabbed his leather leash off the hook in the kitchen.

Ecstatic now, Earl Grey tumbled down the stairs ahead of her, ready to charge out and own the night.

Heading down Church Street past the Chowder Hound Restaurant, Cabbage Patch Needlepoint Shop, and Floradora, her favorite flower shop, Theodosia and Earl Grey cut over on Water Street to East Bay. The night was cool but not cold. The atmosphere, laden with humidity, lent a soft focus to the light that streamed from the old mansions, garden lanterns, portico and streetlamps. Charleston, always highly atmospheric to begin with, positively glowed at night.

The first six blocks they kept it down to a fast walk. Theodosia wanted to stretch her legs, ease out the kinks. She loved to run, had been a runner for some ten years now. But she also knew the cardinal sin in running was to skip the warm-up and zoom right into high gear. That was the absolute *wrong* way to do it. That's how muscles got pulled, tendons sprained.

But by the time she and Earl Grey hit Battery Park at the very tip of the peninsula, they were warmed up and ready to blow out the carbon.

Theodosia gave a fast look around, didn't see anyone who remotely resembled the pooch police. *Excellent,* she thought with a tiny stab of guilt as she unclipped Earl Grey's lead. And with that, the two of them bounded down the pathway that snugged the shoreline.

A salty wind whipped Theodosia's hair out in streaming tendrils, oyster shells crunched beneath her feet. They pounded past a trio of Civil War cannons, past a huge stack of old cannon balls, past the bandstand where so many weddings and wedding party photos had taken place. To their left was the surging harbor with its marker buoys and flickering lights, to their right loomed the dark city of Charleston, the Kingdom by the Sea that Edgar Allan Poe had immortalized in his poem *Annabelle Lee.*

Theodosia took a right where Legare Street intersected and Earl Grey bounded along beside her. They flew down the block, the dog maintaining his easy, loping stride in order to stay even with his beloved owner. Now they were deep in the heart of the historic district again. Streets were canopied over with trees, cobblestones paved a warren of narrow walkways and secret alleys, and large, elegant homes butted up against each other. Theodosia cut to the right, down Atlantic, and whistled softly for Earl Grey to follow. He did.

They skimmed past the tiny brick Library Society building with its ornate wrought iron fence, then turned down a narrow, hidden pathway that ran behind the building. Theodosia slowed her pace, then pulled to a stop just outside the Library Society's lush courtyard garden. In the dim light, she could make out the three-tiered fountain, columns of lush oleander, and large camellia bushes.

Time to reel her dog in, she decided. Time to start the cooldown. Theodosia knelt down, clipped the leash back onto Earl Grey's leather collar, and gave him a reassuring pat.

And in the moment of silence that followed, heard footsteps coming up behind her.

Had someone been following her?

She remained kneeling in the back alleyway, her breath coming faster now, her heart pounding.

If someone *had* been following her, she reasoned, they probably hadn't realized she'd stopped. Which meant they'd be coming around that corner any second. Hastily, she unclipped Earl Grey's leash and wound it around her right fist. The leather and metal snap would make a dandy weapon and Earl Grey would be far more effective as a guard dog if he were free to move about on his own.

Earl Grey stood expectantly now, as did Theodosia, listening to rapidly approaching footsteps.

Suddenly, the nighttime runner was upon them. Startled, obviously not expecting to see someone blocking the pathway, the man, a tall man, skidded to a stop and gaped at Theodosia, his breath coming in hard gasps.

"Theodosia?" he said.

Theodosia stared back, relief suddenly flooding her. The mysterious runner was none other than Cooper Hobcaw.

She put a hand to her heart. "Oh my goodness," she laughed, "you startled me."

Cooper Hobcaw looked equally rattled. "Yeah . . . sorry. Are you okay?" he asked.

Theodosia knew he was probably wondering just what she was doing here, standing in this dark pathway, looking like an idiot.

"I was just putting the leash back on Earl Grey," she explained, "and heard someone coming." When she'd realized who it was, she had quickly loosened the leather leash from around her hand. There was no reason to let Cooper Hobcaw know she'd been prepared to launch an all-out assault on him.

Now Theodosia bent down and clipped the leash onto Earl Grey's collar. "There," she said as it made a satisfying snap. "Sorry we startled you."

"Hey," he breathed, "same here. You can't be too careful after what happened last night."

"Exactly my thought," replied Theodosia.

"Strange goings-on," said Cooper Hobcaw. "Have you heard . . . is the fellow who got knocked on the head, the security guard, going to be okay?"

"I think so."

"Good," he said. Cooper Hobcaw peered at her in the darkness. "I thought I was the only nutcase who went running through the historic district at night."

"No," she said. "There are actually quite a few of us."

Cooper Hobcaw nodded. "The professional's dilemma, right? Work all day, exercise at night."

She nodded back. "'Fraid so."

"I like your buddy here." He reached out and rubbed Earl Grey behind the ears. Earl Grey responded by tossing his elegant head and inviting a scratch under the chin. "Nice dog," said Cooper Hobcaw. "Friendly, too. I like that."

It was only after Cooper Hobcaw had jogged off that Theodosia remembered he lived over on the other side of Calhoun and not in the historic district at all.

7

"*Once you taste* this Formosan Oolong," promised Drayton as he poured a steaming brownish-amber liquid into celadon green ceramic teacups for the three women seated at his table, "I think you'll understand why it's been dubbed the champagne of teas."

Heads bobbed forward, and here and there a delicate slurp was emitted.

"Delicious!" declared one of the women.

A second woman held up the small teacup. "Why no handles?" she asked.

"It's simply the convention for Chinese teacups, or tea bowls as they are often called," replied Drayton. "Same for Japanese teacups. Now if we were drinking a nice strong tea in Morocco or Russia, we'd probably be using a glass. And the English teacup, usually slightly fluted and with a delicate handle, is a derivation of the ale tankard which was often used for imbibing the proverbial hot toddy."

The ladies nodded happily, delighted with their tea tasting and with Drayton's fascinating bits of tea lore.

"This oolong does have a slightly sweet flavor," declared one of his tasters.

"Can you pick up a hint of peaches or honey?" he asked.

The three ladies tasted again, then nodded.

"And chestnuts," he added. "Very often an oolong will offer up a delicate nutty taste. That's a result of the shortened withering period. Freshly picked leaves are dried for only about four or five hours, then allowed to partially ferment. Once the outside of the leaves begin to turn greenish-brown, the tea is fired. Remember," he told them, "tea is one thing that *never* improves with age. Freshness does count."

"I'll never go back to orange pekoe again," declared one woman happily.

"Which, as you all know, is really a *grade* of tea, not a flavor at all," said Drayton as a quick aside. "Now if you'll excuse me, ladies," he stood up from the table, "I shall check to see if a certain batch of croissants are out of the oven yet."

The ladies beamed, caught up as they were in the fascinating world of tea. But then, whenever Drayton conducted one of his tea tastings, he was highly instinctive as well as delightfully entertaining. He was sometimes booked weeks in advance, and often, bed-and-breakfasts such as the Featherbed House or the Allister Beene Home would recommend to their guests that tea with Drayton was a "not to be missed" event.

Drayton hustled over to where Theodosia stood at the counter. "Are the croissants ready yet?" he asked.

"Should be just coming out of the oven," she told him.

Drayton stood for a moment and fidgeted.

"You're thinking of the funeral," she said, noting the suddenly somber look on his face.

"Yes," he said, "aren't you?"

"Here you are, Drayton," said Haley as she came through the curtains and delivered a plate of golden pastries into Drayton's waiting arms. "And some *pain au chocolat,* too. I had extra dough so I sweetened things up a bit." Haley suddenly paused, registering the looks on their faces. "Oh, gosh," she said, "the funeral's today, isn't it? I wonder how they-all are doing down in Savannah."

"Probably awful," said Drayton.

"That's what I figured, too," said Haley. "I mean, I only met Camille that one time but I really liked her a lot. She was a hoot. Well, you know what I mean."

"Of course, we do, dear," said Theodosia. "She's a lovely girl."

"You called Tidwell, right?" said Drayton.

"You're going to talk to *him?*" said Haley. She didn't care for Tidwell, thought him to be a boor and a brute.

"I sent him an e-mail last night," said Theodosia.

"Technology," Drayton said derisively. "It's going to be the downfall of Western civilization."

"You didn't think so the other day when you guys set up those tracker beams," said Haley.

"And they didn't work, did they!" argued Drayton.

"Hold everything," said Theodosia. "We all know the motion sensors didn't work because someone cut the power. It had nothing to do with a technological meltdown."

"Drayton, don't you have a table full of customers waiting for those?" Haley indicated the plate of baked goods in his hand.

"Don't you have today's luncheon to figure out?" he asked her.

"Tea-marinated prawns on Japanese noodles," she told him. "But I don't anticipate there'll be any leftovers."

"Tea-marinated prawns?" he said, suddenly perking up. "My, that *does* sound lovely. May I ask which tea you've chosen as a marinade base?"

Haley grinned. "You may not. But if any of our *customers* are interested, you may tell them it is Lapsang Souchong."

"Mmnn," said Drayton, considering. "Nice, rich, black tea from southern China. Smoky flavor. Should be highly complementary with seafood."

"Maybe there'll be a nibble left over," she told him.

"Let's hope so," he said.

Haley's tea-marinated prawns were an enormous hit. Theodosia wasn't sure exactly what seemed to be bringing the customers in these days—the cool, sunny weather, the hint of autumn in the air, or a sudden jump in the number of tourists—but they were packed for lunch once again. Standing room only, in fact. Giselle and Cleo, two regulars from Parsifal, a gift shop down the street, ended up getting their lunches packed to go in one of the Indigo Tea Shop's indigo blue boxes, rather than stand around and wait for a table.

"Maybe we should be putting tables on the sidewalk," Theodosia lamented to Drayton.

"We've talked about outside tables before and never done it," he said. "It would mean a little more work, but it would certainly increase our capacity as well."

"By capacity, you mean profits," she said.

"Of course I mean profits. Profits are the lifeblood of a business," said Drayton, ever mindful of the bottom line.

"What would we need to do?" she asked. "File something with the city for a permit?"

"I think so," he said. "Maybe your friend, Jory Davis, could look into it."

"Good idea," replied Theodosia, then added, "or is it too late in the year? We could get a cold snap any day now."

"Then we'll be well prepared for spring," Drayton assured her.

By two o'clock things had settled down to normal. Haley was rattling dishes in the kitchen, clearing away lunch, and had already put a couple pans of gingerbread in the oven in anticipation of the afternoon tea crowd. Drayton was seated at the table nearest the counter, munching his prawns and doing a highly adequate job of snaring the slippery Japanese soba noodles with his pair of wooden chopsticks. Theodosia was arranging antique teacups and muffin plates on the high shelf behind the counter where their old brass cash register sat.

She had collected dozens of teacups over the years, a hard-to-find Shelley Apple Blossom, several Limoges, and a pretty fan-handle Russian teacup from the Popov Porcelain Factory, to name just a few. And she'd decided it was a shame to keep so many stored away in boxes. Better to bring them downstairs and create a fanciful display.

"That's a lovely Shelley," called Drayton from his table.

Theodosia held up the Shelley Apple Blossom for him to admire. It was creamy white bone china covered in a riot of pink apple blossoms. It was also one of the cups and saucers that was most prized among the many avid Shelley collectors throughout the world.

"As you probably know," Drayton told her, "I've got the Shelley Dainty White in the Queen Anne style. Setting for eight. Hudgins Antiques offered me fifteen hundred for it just last year."

"Did you consider selling?" she asked.

"Absolutely not, it's worth twice that. Besides, I love those dishes. They were passed down to me by my dear Aunt Cecily."

When the front door fluttered open a few minutes later, it wasn't the first wave of afternoon customers come for tea. Instead, Detective Burt Tidwell strode forcefully into the room.

Burt Tidwell wasn't exactly one of Theodosia's favorite people. But then again, Burt Tidwell wasn't *anyone's* favorite person. An ex-FBI agent, Burt Tidwell lived in Charleston in what he considered a state of semiretirement. Which, for the driven, results-oriented, obsessive-compulsive man that he was, meant he was employed full-time, working a sixty-hour week as lead homicide detective for the Charleston Police Department.

Brash, bordering on boorish, Tidwell's physical being projected his inner personality. What you saw was what you got. A tall man, way beyond heavyset, Tidwell had a strange bullet-shaped head that seemed to rest directly upon his shoulders. Worse yet, Tidwell was a bulldog with steel jaws, tenacious, slightly ill-tempered, perpetually dubious.

Yet Burt Tidwell did have a certain way about him. When he chose to be, Tidwell could border on courtly, particularly in discussions with women. He was an avid reader and a keen admirer of Sartre, Hemingway, and Octavio Paz. Many years ago, back when FBI agents were also required to have law degrees, Tidwell had attended Harvard and so still had a keen sense of the written word.

Theodosia seated Tidwell at the table with Drayton, then quickly ferried over cups, saucers, a pot of tea, plates, napkins, silverware, and a tray of assorted goodies.

When she finally sat down next to Tidwell, Theodosia didn't mince words.

"What do you know about cat burglars?" she asked him.

But Tidwell wasn't about to let her slip into a prosecutorial mode quite so easily. He took a sip of tea, allowed his eyes to rove across the tray of baked goods. "Pray tell, what is this delightful-looking bread?" he asked with an inquisitive air as he hooked the plate with his index finger and pulled it toward him.

Realizing Tidwell wasn't going to be as forthcoming as she wished, Theodosia slid the butter plate toward Tidwell. "Persimmon bread," she told him.

"And the tea is . . ."

"Assam. Taste the sweetness?"

"I do. As well as a slightly malty flavor."

"Why, Detective Tidwell, I do believe you're becoming a tea connoisseur," said Theodosia as Drayton looked on, pleased.

Tidwell picked up the cloth napkin and daubed at his lips. "You never know, dear lady, you never know."

"Detective Tidwell," began Theodosia, "you received my e-mail and my slightly abbreviated account of the two thefts."

"The wedding ring and the gems at the Heritage Society. Yes, I did," he said. "Additionally, I spoke with the two investigators, Jacob Gallier and Peter Delehanty, who are currently working both cases. They're not convinced the two incidents are at all related."

This was surprising news to Theodosia. "How could they not look at them in the same context?"

Tidwell shifted his eyes from the persimmon bread to Theodosia's face. "What is your interest in this?" he inquired.

"My friends are involved," she said. "I'm worried about them."

"Ah," he said, "assuming the worries of the world again, are we?" Tidwell shook his great head slowly. "Oh, to be young and burning with such inner fire."

"You were saying," prompted Theodosia, "that Mr. Gallier and Delehanty do not think the two thefts are related?"

Tidwell chewed thoughtfully. "From their perspective, the first incident at the Lady Goodwood Inn seems more like an unfortunate accident."

"And the second incident?" asked Drayton, suddenly deciding to join the conversation. "The missing necklace at the Heritage Society?"

"That *is* a clear-cut robbery," said Tidwell. "No one's disputing that." He swiveled his head toward Theodosia and bore into her with small, intense eyes. "But according to the rather rambling e-mail you forwarded to me, *you* believe there is some mysterious cat burglar prowling the historic district."

"I think it's a distinct possibility," Theodosia said. "And I do think the two cases are related." She looked at Drayton, who hovered nearby, for confirmation.

"We both do," he said.

Tidwell sat back in his chair with an air of finality. "And you'd like me to expound on what I know concerning the phenomenon known as the cat burglar," he said with a sigh.

"Could you?" asked Theodosia with an encouraging smile.

Tidwell reached one paw up, absently brushed stray bread crumbs from the lapels of his tweed jacket. "Closest thing you can compare it to is a great white shark," he said.

"What a strange analogy," Theodosia said, looking perplexed.

Tidwell grimaced. "In my experience, which admittedly is quite limited, a cat burglar tends to be a territorial creature. If the feeding is plentiful in one place, he will tend to stay put."

"And the feeding should be mighty plentiful in Charleston," murmured Theodosia. "Think of all the estate jewelry that's here. Or the priceless antiques and oil paintings that grace so many of the homes in the historic district."

Tidwell nodded. "A tasty treasure trove, indeed. Old families, old money. There is a lovely synchronicity at work."

"So we have to just sit around and wait for this cat burglar to strike again?" asked Drayton somewhat peevishly.

Tidwell reached for a second slice of persimmon bread, took a large bite, chewed with great enthusiasm, swallowed. "If he strikes at all," said Tidwell. "Let me again emphasize that my experience is limited. However . . ."

"However what?" asked Drayton.

"There is another breed of cat burglar," said Tidwell. "And that is the migratory kind."

"Versus the territorial kind," said Drayton. Now his lined face betrayed a fair amount of skepticism.

"Exactly," said Tidwell. "This migratory version follows the goods."

Theodosia and Drayton exchanged puzzled looks. "Which means . . ." prompted Theodosia.

Tidwell rocked back in his chair and the ancient wood creaked in protest. "For openers, there's the summer social season in the Hamptons, opera season in New York, then a long stretch of charity balls in Palm Beach."

Drayton's mouth opened then closed. "Oh," he finally said. "I see what you mean."

Theodosia deftly slid the plate of baked goods closer to Tidwell. "If you had a gut feeling, how would you characterize our fellow?" she asked.

"If I listened to my gut, I wouldn't help myself to a third pastry," said Tidwell with a rueful smile. He reached for a croissant, slid it onto his plate. "Alas, dear girl, I can offer you no great insight."

Drayton and Theodosia sat there looking slightly deflated.

Tidwell saw their distress. "What I may be able to parcel out," he added, "is a small amount of information. The robbery division is working up a guest list from both functions. If something strange rears its head, I'll let you know. How would that be?"

"Good enough," said Theodosia. "Thank you."

Tidwell raised a furry eyebrow and cast a warning glance at her. "You can keep your eyes open," he told her, "but I warn you right now, do not make *any* attempt whatsoever to track, trail, or apprehend anyone you deem a potential suspect." He continued to gaze steadily at Theodosia. "Is that clear?"

"Of course," she said.

"Of course," Tidwell repeated. "Miss Browning, your voice carries such a tone of innocence. But why do I sense a certain degree of insincerity in your promise?"

"No, I'll be careful," Theodosia assured him. "Really I will."

"When are we going to talk about the open house?" asked Haley. She'd emerged from the kitchen and now stood hands-on-hips, staring at Theodosia.

Theodosia, standing up on tiptoes with her right arm extended, stopped in mid-stretch. She'd almost finished arranging her display of teacups.

The finished T-Bath products had all arrived, the shipping cartons stacked so high in her office it made it almost impossible to navigate her way to her desk. And the invitations for this Thursday's afternoon reception had been mailed out well over two weeks ago. So far almost three dozen people had responded with RSVPs and she was confident quite a few more people would just spontaneously drop by. But drop by for what? Their big event was now three days away and it still needed to be finalized!

"I'm sure nobody feels like planning this thing," continued Haley in a somewhat plaintive tone of voice, "but it *is* on our schedule."

"You're right," said Theodosia. "And it's not that we don't want to plan it, we've just been caught up in other things." She glanced across the room at Drayton. "Drayton?" she called.

He looked up from where he was pouring a warm-up cup of tea for two women seated near the front door and held up a finger. "Be there in a sec," he answered back.

"What I thought," said Haley moving into her take-charge mode, "was that we'd try for a kind of Zen-like atmosphere. Try to capture the feeling of relaxation and renewal that the T-Bath products are supposed to impart."

Theodosia nodded. "That sounds like a great idea. We could use a stress-free zone around here."

"And if we brought in some of Drayton's Japanese bonsai trees, they'd make cute accent pieces for all of the tables."

"You think he'll let us?" asked Theodosia. "He's awfully protective of those trees of his."

Drayton had joined them now and was nodding enthusiastically. "Only the Fukien tea plant and the jade tree stay at home. They're the most sensitive. As for the others, the maples, junipers, and larches . . . well, you know I never miss a chance to show off my bonsai," he added with a modest grin.

"Great," continued Haley. "Then, what if on the main table, the buffet table, we have a real knockout floral arrangement. Something very Asian looking. I don't know what you call those arrangements, but they're quite artsy and contemporary looking. I was thinking we could do something with orchids surrounded by stalks of bamboo?"

"I believe the correct term is ikebana," said Drayton. "It's Japanese flower arranging at its most fanciful. In fact, *ikebana* literally translated means 'fresh flower.' You might call it the bonsai of flower arranging."

"Okay," said Haley. "Great."

"We'll ask Hattie Boatwright over at Floradora to design something for us," suggested Drayton. "She took an ikebana workshop with me a few years ago and her arrangements turned out far better than mine." He pursed his lips, thinking. "But then, she's a professional."

Haley continued ticking off ideas in rapid-fire succession. "And the refreshments at our main table should include Japanese green tea, some sushi, nothing too exotic, maybe some California rolls, and some of those little kushiyaki sticks. You know grilled chicken and vegetables with teriyaki sauce?"

"Can you make the California rolls?" asked Theodosia, "or should we ask Miyako's Sushi to do the catering?"

"I can do it," said Haley. "Once I cook the rice and season it properly with wine vinegar, the rest should be a snap."

"Listen to her," said Drayton. "She doesn't even need *us*."

"Oh, yes I do," said Haley. "You two have to figure out where to display all our nifty products. Then you should probably make up some gift baskets for sale, probably using those extra sweetgrass baskets we have in back. And—" she looked around "—oh yeah, dig out those tiny little Japanese cups we've got stored around here somewhere."

8

In 1929, with an eye to the future and their collective hearts set squarely in the past, Charleston's city council passed the nation's very first zoning ordinance to protect many of their city's historic buildings. Two years later, they went a step further and set aside a full twenty-three square blocks of the peninsula—what is known today as the historic district—containing a rich assortment of historic homes as well as significant commercial, religious, and civic buildings.

The result is a breathtaking architectural preserve. The historic district is replete with Colonial, Georgian, Italianate, Greek Revival, and Federal-style buildings, as well as many examples of the ubiquitous Charleston single house, that have remained unchanged for well over a century. And even though the occasional hurricane blows in to rearrange things (such as Hurricane Hugo did in 1989), the streets are still lined with graceful live oaks, enormous mulberry bushes, and flowering magnolias, and the hundreds of hidden, backyard private gardens are nothing short of breathtaking.

As Theodosia stepped across the patio of the Heritage Society, she was delighted to see that some craftsperson had pieced together the beginnings of what would probably be a splendid-looking wrought iron bench.

Based on the design of a Victorian love seat, the bench was fashioned in a graceful S-curve, with one seat facing one way and another seat facing the opposite way.

Theodosia noted the sections where additional scrollwork would be added and decided the new bench was pretty and whimsical and would be a perfect addition to the patio outside the Heritage Society, since so many of their parties seemed to spill outside anyway.

"That's going to be a lovely bench," she told Claire Kitridge, one of the Heritage Society secretaries, who was seated at the massive wood reception desk. Claire had worked at the Heritage Society for several years and always seemed extremely dedicated.

Claire nodded her frizz of grayish hair. "Isn't it?" she responded. "I'm just crazy over anything that's wrought iron?" she said, allowing her voice to rise at the end of her sentence, making her statement sound like a question.

Sitting at the desk with her blue oxford shirt tucked into a plain navy skirt, Claire looked busy and efficient. She wore nary a speck of makeup and had her glasses strung around her neck on a practical silver chain. Theodosia had always thought Claire to be a straightforward, no-nonsense type of woman. But she also knew that Claire was a devotee of antique linens and had amassed a spectacular collection.

"Still sorting through flea markets, Claire?" Theodosia asked.

Claire fixed her with an eager gaze. "You wouldn't believe the luck I've had. I just stumbled upon some spectacular linen napkins? Damask, woven back in the twenties for the ocean liner, the *Queen Mary?* Wonderful," she declared. "So crisp and smart. They certainly don't make them like that anymore." Claire paused expectantly. "I found some old tea towels, too, if you're interested?"

"I am, but I'm going to have to find a bigger house," bemoaned Theodosia. Tea towels were another one of her passions. Just like her collection of teacups.

"Tell me about it," laughed Claire. "Between my linens, eiderdowns, and antique lace, it's *really* getting out of hand. My house looks like a Victorian parlor run amuck. Think I can stop, though? Hah!" She suddenly spun her chair a half-turn, snatched up the phone. "You're here to see Timothy?" Claire asked.

"Yes, would you see if he can spare a few moments?" Theodosia asked.

"Of course," said Claire. She punched a couple buttons. "Mr. Neville? Miss Theodosia Browning is here at the front desk? Could you . . . of course, I'll tell her." Claire hung up the phone and smiled at Theodosia. "Mr. Neville said to come right in. You know which office is his?"

"Yes, thank you," said Theodosia.

"Let me know about those tea towels," called Claire as Theodosia started down the hall.

"*What do you* think?" Timothy asked Theodosia as she stepped into his office. "An authentic Sully or a very good copy?" His arm made a sweeping gesture to indicate a portrait of a woman framed in gilt.

Theodosia took a few steps forward and studied the portrait that lay on Timothy's desk. She knew that Thomas Sully was a distinguished painter who had lived and worked in Charleston for many years. He had produced a fairly large body of work, but he'd had his imitators, too. Then again, what successful artist didn't?

Theodosia studied the surface of the painting. It was aged and the glaze crackled, that was for sure. So the painting certainly wasn't recent. The signature looked good and the subject, a young woman sitting beside a fireplace, did seem to emit a certain glow from within. Still . . .

"May I?" she asked. Timothy nodded abruptly as Theodosia picked up the portrait and turned it over. It had been painted on canvas, she noted, not just on a wooden board. And the wooden canvas stretchers looked old and weathered, which was often a good giveaway of authenticity.

"I'd say it's real," she told Timothy. "And a fine example, at that."

Timothy Neville beamed at her. "Well done, Miss Browning. May I ask what aspect of this painting most convinced you as to its authenticity?"

"The canvas looks old," she said. "A little dry, in fact. And the stretchers are the slot and groove kind. That usually indicates late-eighteenth or early-nineteenth century."

"Yes, this portrait is absolutely authentic," Timothy told her. "It's a recent donation and a welcome one at that." Timothy rocked back on his heels. "I don't know how popular we're going to be in the future, however. Our recent debacle last Saturday night may have sealed our fate as far as donations go."

He sat down heavily in his chair, as though he'd suddenly run out of energy and enthusiasm. "Sit, please," he told her.

Theodosia moved around his desk and seated herself in one of the oversized leather chairs that faced Timothy's desk.

"I talked with Tidwell," she told him.

"Good. And I spoke with our insurance company." He drew in a breath, held it, then blew out heavily. "But I'm getting ahead of myself. You obviously came here to share some news."

Theodosia nodded. She wasn't sure how pleased Timothy Neville would be with her news, however.

Timothy leaned forward in his chair. "You kept your meeting confidential?"

"It was just Drayton and myself, yes. Tidwell already knew about the two robberies, of course. But we spoke with him about the possibility of a cat burglar at work in Charleston."

"And what was his learned opinion?"

Theodosia gave Timothy a quick rundown of their conversation with Tidwell, including his territorial great white shark analogy.

When she was finished, Timothy grimaced. "Territorial. I don't like the sound of that at all. Especially with the Treasures Show about to open this weekend."

"Is it opening?" she asked.

"For now, yes," replied Timothy. "The decision's just been made." He hesitated. "Actually, truth be known, we arrived at a sort of compromise. The European Jewel Collection won't be part of it. Those pieces are being packed up even as we speak. They'll be shipped back to the organizing museum in New York. So the Treasures Show that the public will see this Saturday evening will consist only of selected pieces from the Heritage Society's collection. A pair of Louis the Fifteenth chairs, some excellent Meissen ware, this portrait by Sully . . . you get the general idea."

Theodosia nodded. "But no headliner pieces."

"Nothing outside the realm of what we already have. Unless you have something utterly spectacular stashed in your attic. No . . ." Timothy shook his head slowly. "We'll have to come up with something else to put in the small gallery. I don't exactly know what yet." Timothy cast his eyes about his office to the shelves that lined the walls. They contained rare books, old maps, some pewter ware. "Maybe our collection of antique sterling silver letter openers?" he offered, but he didn't sound totally convinced.

Theodosia smiled. "That sounds lovely."

"Still . . ." said Timothy. "There's no guarantee that the disaster of last Saturday night won't be repeated."

Timothy looked so bereft that Theodosia's heart went out to him. "I'm sure everything will be fine," she assured him. "On a more personal note, how are *you* feeling? You gave us all quite a scare the other night."

Tapping his chest, Timothy gave her a rueful look. "I didn't even have a regular physician and now it seems I've inherited a team of specialists. A cardiologist and some fellow who studies respiration. Don't need anyone, of course. I'm as healthy as you are."

Theodosia knew that Timothy adhered to a strict daily regimen of vitamins and minerals. Drayton had even told her once about some sort of life extension formula that he imported from Rumania. Considering that he was just past eighty and acted fifty, that formula just might be the real deal.

"Have you heard any more about the security guard who was injured Saturday night?" Timothy asked her.

"He's still in intensive care at Saint Anne's Hospital," said Theodosia. "I thought I'd stop by and visit him tonight. I was scheduled to go to Saint Anne's anyway. Earl Grey is paying a visit to the children's ward." She smiled warmly at Timothy. "I'll let you know."

"Do that," Timothy said. "We've sent flowers and such, but I'm sure he'd be pleased to see an attractive face such as yours."

"*Can you help* him?" asked Claire as Theodosia darted past the front desk.

Theodosia stopped in her tracks. "Can I . . ."

"Ever since that necklace disappeared Saturday night, Timothy hasn't been the same," said Claire. "He's been quiet and brooding all morning, hasn't looked good. I'm worried about him. Everyone here is." Claire leaned forward and dropped her voice to a whisper. "We're worried about his heart."

"So am I," confided Theodosia as she slipped out the door.

Goodness, she thought to herself as she hurried across the patio. *This really is a mess. Because no matter how valuable that missing necklace is, and the number has to edge up to almost half a million, it's nowhere near as important as Timothy's health. If he worries himself to death over this . . .* Theodosia suddenly stopped in her tracks, freeze-framing that thought. *No, she wasn't going to think like that. Nobody was going to die. She simply wasn't going to let that happen!*

9

Earl Grey poked his furry muzzle through the slats of the tiny patient's bed. Wearing his blue vest with his THERAPY DOG INTERNATIONAL insignia, he looked very official, acted very well behaved.

"Do you want to pet the doggy, Katie?" asked Angela Krause. Angela was a nurse and a friend of Theodosia's. She had worked at Saint Anne's Hospital for almost five years and was a fixture on the children's ward.

Katie, a tiny five-year-old who'd just undergone a round of chemotherapy for acute myeloid leukemia, nodded. Blue veins showed through her almost transparent skin and her head was covered by a small red kerchief. But she was still game to meet Earl Grey.

"Okay, then," said Angela, "put your hand out. He won't hurt you."

Katie stuck her hand tentatively through the slats of the crib. Gently, Earl Grey sniffed at the tiny hand.

There was a delighted giggle and then Katie's entire face was pressed up against the slats.

"Do you want to toss the ball?" asked Theodosia.

Katie reached out her small hand and Theodosia placed a red rubber ball in it. Winding up like an all-star pitcher, Katie flung the ball out the door of her room and Earl Grey bounded after it. Within seconds, he returned and gently placed the ball in Katie's hand.

"Good doggy," said Katie.

"His name is Earl Grey," said Theodosia.

"Earl Grey," said Katie, patting his head gently. "Bye bye, Earl Grey."

Out in the hallway, Theodosia and Earl Grey stopped in front of another patient room.

"What about this one?" Theodosia asked Angela.

Angela looked grim. "Billy Foster," she said. "He hasn't spoken since he underwent surgery three days ago to repair a collapsed lung." She shook her head sadly. "Poor little guy. First he gets banged up rather badly in a car accident, then he's traumatized by the ordeal of surgery. Plus both his parents are in the hospital, too." Angela made a rueful face. "Nobody wearing seat belts. Billy wasn't in a children's car seat." Gazing in the door of the little boy's hospital room, she said, "Sometimes these kids are as resilient as a rubber band, other times they're just incredibly fragile." Angela glanced again in Billy's room, where his small body lay immobile under the covers. "This one"—she looked about ready to cry—"just tears my heart out. The doctors say he should be able to take deeper breaths by now, but for some reason he can't. Or won't. His blood oxygen saturation is low and the poor guy is still on a nasal cannula."

Theodosia bit her lip. This was the hard part of volunteering with a therapy dog. Seeing little children who were so very, very ill.

"Maybe a dog would cheer him up?" Theodosia suggested.

Angela nodded. "We've tried just about everything else we could think of to get him to breathe on his own. She pushed open the doors to Billy's room. "Just hang on a minute, though. Let me go in and talk to him first."

Theodosia watched from the doorway as Angela walked quietly over to Billy's bed, knelt down beside him. She could hear her murmuring to him, gently, very quietly.

The little boy must have understood everything Angela had said, because he suddenly turned his head and stared directly at Earl Grey, his soft brown eyes suddenly big with interest. Angela motioned for Theodosia and Earl Grey to enter the boy's room.

Earl Grey entered slightly ahead of Theodosia, restrained by his leash, but still on his best behavior. When they got to Billy's bedside, Theodosia gave Earl Grey the *sit* command. Earl Grey responded immediately, sitting like a perfect gentleman, staring inquisitively at Billy even as the little boy stared back.

Suddenly, just as Billy leaned forward, Earl Grey thrust his head forward, too. Billy's face connected squarely with the tip of Earl Grey's soft muzzle and the dog planted a gentle kiss on the boy's cheek.

Surprised, the boy drew a sudden, swift intake of breath. Which immediately triggered a beep on the machine he was connected to.

"Oh my gosh!" exclaimed Angela.

"Should I run to get help?" asked Theodosia quickly. Her heart suddenly in her throat, she was convinced something had just gone terribly wrong.

"No, no. It's just that . . ." Angela said in a stunned tone of voice. "He took a breath. She knelt down beside the little boy. "Billy, you took a deep breath, didn't you? The doggy surprised you and you took a deep breath!"

Eyes bright, Billy nodded back at her.

"Can you take another one?" she asked.

Billy nodded and the machine at the bedside blipped happily again.

How could this visit have turned out any better? Theodosia thought to herself as she and Earl Grey strode back through the corridors of Saint Anne's.

Now they were one floor down and about to stop by to visit Harlan Wilson, the security guard who'd been injured at the Heritage Society. He'd been moved from the ICU to a regular patient room this morning. Theodosia figured that was a good thing. Must mean Mr. Wilson was showing real signs of improvement.

"Pardon me," said Theodosia as she approached the nurses' station. "I'm—"

"We know who you are," said a pretty African-American nurse whose name tag read CECILE RANDOLPH. "Angela just called to say you were coming by with your very gifted dog."

"He's just along for the ride now," laughed Theodosia. "Earl Grey's finished with *his* visiting."

Cecile nodded. "Angie said you wanted to look in on Mr. Wilson?"

"Yes, is he awake?"

"He wasn't when I checked ten minutes ago, but that doesn't mean he isn't now. He's been in and out all day."

"But he's getting better?" asked Theodosia.

"Absolutely," Cecile assured her. The phone on the desk in front of Cecile started to ring and she reached for it. "Go ahead on down. He's in room two-oh-seven."

Theodosia and Earl Grey walked down the hallway looking for room two-oh-seven. It was almost eight-thirty and the hospital was quiet, visiting hours almost over for the evening. Lights had been dimmed and the exit sign glowed red above the door to the emergency stairway at the end of the hallway.

Room two-oh-seven turned out to be the second to the last room. But the door was closed.

Should she go in?

Theodosia paused for a moment, wondering if it was too late for a visit. Glancing down at Earl Grey, trying to decide what to do, she saw that the dog had his head cocked, listening.

Suddenly curious, Theodosia listened herself. It *did* sound as though someone was moving around in there. Good. Probably Harlan Wilson was awake after all. Perhaps trying to manage a glass of water or reach the call button.

Knocking softly, Theodosia didn't wait for an answer. Instead she pushed the door open slowly. But as the door swung inward on its hinges, she could see that Harlan Wilson was still asleep in his bed. A shaft of light from somewhere—the bathroom?—played across his face.

Theodosia was ready to turn around and leave when Earl Grey suddenly gave a low growl.

She stopped in her tracks, still half inside the room. But now her eyes had had a few moments to get accustomed to the dark. And she was able to see that she wasn't alone. Just to her left, someone was pressed up against the wall of Harlan Wilson's room!

Who could it be? she wondered, her brain trying to process this strange information. *Hospital personnel?* No, no, no, her brain flashed a warning to her. *Not a nurse, someone who meant to do him harm!*

Suddenly, whoever it was, dove around the corner into the bathroom and slammed the door.

In a flash, Theodosia was pulling at the bathroom door.

It stuck for a moment, then flew open. Nobody there! Too late! It was a shared bathroom and the menacing visitor must have dashed into the room next door.

Theodosia and Earl Grey pushed through to the adjoining room, found it empty. Without hesitation, they charged out into the hallway . . .

. . . And got there just in time to see the door to the stairwell swing shut!

"Cecile, call Security," Theodosia yelled.

"What?" came a startled voice.

"Security!" yelled Theodosia as she dropped Earl Grey's leash and pushed the door to the stairwell open. "C'mon, fella. Downstairs! Follow him!"

As they charged down the stairs, Theodosia could hear the door at the bottom clang shut. *But which door?* Theodosia wondered as they hit the first-floor landing. *The door that led to the lobby or the emergency exit that opened outside?*

Has to be outside. Theodosia decided as she lowered a shoulder and hit that door hard.

Cool air greeted them as they rushed out.

They found themselves in back of the hospital. Dark and deserted, there appeared to be a thin line of trees and what looked like a small garden where patients could go and sit.

That garden was in deep shadows now, but Theodosia could just make out a figure slipping in among the trees.

"Go get him!" she told Earl Grey. "Stop him!" She'd never taught him *those* commands before, but the dog responded like a champion, dashing off toward the small woods.

Theodosia ran after her dog. *Just maybe,* she thought, *Earl Grey can catch him and run him down like a rabbit.* Because whoever had been lurking in Harlan Wilson's room had certainly been up to no good.

Dashing into the thin line of trees, Theodosia leapt over a fallen log, almost stumbled, then broke out of the woods into the parking lot of the Dixie Quick Market.

From somewhere nearby came the cough of a car ignition turning over, then a loud squeal of tires.

Theodosia ran out to the street. Earl Grey was standing there, tail low, hackles up, still growling. Together they watched as red taillights receded in the distance.

10

Drayton frowned as he carefully measured several spoonfuls of dragon's well tea into a blue willow teapot. Haley always chided him for wanting to "match" teas to teapots. *Well, so what if I do?* he thought to himself. *Would you really want to serve this fine sweet tea from central China in a Japanese tetsubin? No, of course not. No tea lover in their right mind would. The traditional metal tetsubin should be reserved for Japanese green tea like bancha or gyokuro. Or even better, a nice first-flush sencha.*

But Haley's good-natured chiding wasn't what was chafing at Drayton this morning. No, he decided, it was Theodosia's visit last evening to

Saint Anne's. And the fact that she had chased, actually *pursued*, some strange intruder down the stairwell and into the dark.

He'd always known Theodosia had a wild streak in her. But this last incident seemed positively reckless!

On the other hand, the fact that some lunatic had been lurking in Harlan Wilson's room seemed to confirm the fact that the guard had actually *seen* the thief at the Heritage Society the other night. So maybe they'd really have something to go on now. That would certainly be welcome news to poor Timothy Neville, who seemed to be waiting on pins and needles for the ax to fall on his head.

"I can't believe you actually chased this fellow," Drayton said to Theodosia. "Did you alert the security staff at the hospital, too?"

Theodosia nodded. "I went back afterwards and talked to them."

"And . . ." said Drayton.

"Someone had fiddled with Harlan Wilson's oxygen line."

Drayton's face blanched white. "Good lord! This intruder really did mean to do harm!"

"It looks that way," said Theodosia. "Apparently Mr. Wilson didn't exactly need the oxygen, it was supplemental, but the intruder didn't know that."

"So the intent was still to harm him," persisted Drayton.

"Looks like," said Theodosia. She glanced up from the counter, where she and Drayton had both been fixing pots of tea. Haley seemed to have all the tables under control. All she needed were the fresh pots of dragon's well and English breakfast tea that were now steeping.

"Has Mr. Wilson been able to say much of anything?" asked Drayton.

"I'm afraid not," said Theodosia. "He's still pretty woozy."

"And you didn't get a good look at the intruder?" asked Drayton.

Theodosia shook her head sadly. "Not really."

"Was he tall or short?"

"Not sure."

"Skinny or heavyset?"

Theodosia sighed. "I'm afraid I couldn't say either way. Sorry. I know if I'd been more alert, or a tad faster, we'd have something to go on."

"No, no," said Drayton. "I didn't mean to imply you'd done a poor job of it. You just got caught unawares. Usually when one enters a hospital room, there isn't a malevolent figure lurking in the dark." Drayton gave her a commiserating look. "You really should call Detective Tidwell again," he urged.

"Don't you think he already knows?" said Theodosia. "The hospital is going to put a guard on Mr. Wilson's room."

"But that doesn't mean Tidwell's in the loop," said Drayton. "He told us those two other fellows . . ." Drayton paused, trying to recall the names of the two men from the Robbery Division.

"Gallier and Delehanty," filled in Theodosia.

"Right," said Drayton. "Tidwell said they were handling the alleged robbery at the Lady Goodwood and the disappearance of the sapphire necklace. The various departments don't necessary communicate with each other."

"You're right," agreed Theodosia.

"Is that tea ready yet?" asked Haley.

Theodosia grabbed both teapots and passed them over to her. "Yes, sorry we're taking so long."

"I kind of heard what you guys were whispering about," said Haley. "This is all getting very frightening."

"I know what you mean," said Theodosia. "I was scared out of my wits Sunday night when Cooper Hobcaw came running up behind me in an alley."

"What?" said Drayton. "He must have strayed pretty far from home."

"He's kind of a weird guy," said Haley. "I'm not sure I trust him."

Drayton's eyes sought out Theodosia's. "You don't suppose . . ." he said.

"What?" asked Haley as she stared at the two of them. "You think *he's* somehow involved in all this?"

"Probably not," said Theodosia, although she couldn't seem to shake the notion from her head that Cooper Hobcaw seemed to conveniently appear in so many different places.

The bell over the door tinkled and all of them turned to look.

Drayton's face broke into a wide grin. "It's Brooke," he said. "From Heart's Desire. Oh quick, Theo, she's a true devotee of Goomtee Estate tea. Brew up one of those two-cup pots while I go and greet her, will you?"

Theodosia nodded even as she pulled a small silver tin down from the shelf and went to work. Goomtee Estate was a classic, smooth Darjeeling, light in color with a delicate, sweet aroma and gentle hint of muscatel flavor. Most people favored it as an afternoon tea, but Brooke was an exception. She liked it in the morning, hot and black, with no milk or sugar.

"This should steep another minute or so," said Theodosia as she delivered the small pot of tea to Brooke's table.

"Aren't you a love," said Brooke. "Drayton said you were brewing a pot of Goomtee just for me."

"And I have the perfect accompaniment," said Drayton as he hovered over her with a plate. "Fresh-baked baps."

"Scottish breakfast bread!" exclaimed Brooke. "My granny used to bake baps."

"Well, these are made according to one of Haley's traditional low-country recipes, or receipts as we South Carolinians like to say. Not too sugary, not too sweet, but always delightful with a pat of butter and some good sourwood honey." And Drayton scampered off to fetch more baps for the rest of the customers.

"Theo," asked Brooke as she pulled her pot of tea toward her. "Do you have a moment?"

Theodosia slipped into the chair opposite Brooke. "Certainly."

Brooke Carter Crockett was a self-reliant woman. She had owned Heart's Desire for some fifteen years and had seen it thrive as a small business. Brooke had also offered inspiration and invaluable help to Theodosia when she'd first opened the tea shop. It had been wonderful to receive mentoring from a small business owner who'd already endured her baptism by fire.

Now Brooke seemed to be searching for just the right words. She shook her sleek mane of white hair, brushed it back behind her ears, revealing a pair of canary yellow diamond stud earrings.

Have to be three full carats each, thought Theodosia. *And marquis cut at that. Stunning, really stunning.*

"Theodosia," began Brooke, "I'm just going to ask this flat out. Do you think there's a cat burglar at work in the historic district?" Brooke curled a hand delicately around the handle of the small teapot, poured a steaming stream of the golden-red liquor into her teacup, and waited for an answer.

"Honestly," said Theodosia, "I don't know. I *think* there might be, but it's just supposition. A hunch at best."

"Drayton mentioned something strange to my associate, Aerin Linley, the other night. At the Heritage Society's members-only party."

"What did he tell her?" asked Theodosia.

"Just that you didn't think the death of that poor Buchanan boy was any accident. That you suspected someone might have been up there on the roof."

"Well, the whole incident did have a strange feel to it. Not exactly *engineered*, but not a complete accident either." She knew exactly where Brooke was heading with this line of questioning. With Heart's Desire specializing in high-end estate jewelry, Brooke was understandably nervous about being a possible target. Theodosia wondered if she should tell Brooke about the hospital last night. *No,* she decided, *better to keep that little incident to myself.*

"Brooke," Theodosia said, suddenly getting a germ of an idea. "Do people just walk in off the street with jewelry and offer to sell it to you?"

"Oh, yes. Absolutely," said Brooke. "Dealers, antiquers, just regular folks. Of course, we get lots of locals. You'd be amazed at the people who come in. There are some folks who put on an impeccable appearance, yet are poor as church mice. They've been selling off inherited jewelry and heirlooms for years in order to maintain a certain standard of living. Naturally, Aerin and I try to be extremely discreet. We wouldn't maintain much of a customer base if we blabbed about who sold this or bought that."

"No, you wouldn't," said Theodosia. "But do you ever"—she hesitated, unsure of how to phrase her question—"do you ever get just a tiny bit suspicious of someone who's selling a very expensive piece of jewelry?"

Brooke hesitated. "Well, yes, I suppose I have in a couple instances. I don't really feel I can go into detail, though . . ."

"That's okay," said Theodosia hastily, "it was just a random thought. Forget I even brought it up."

But Brooke continued to pick at the thread of their conversation. "When a seller *does* act a bit nervous or suspicious, I try to get a quick Polaroid of the jewelry they're offering for sale. Then I check with the Police Department to see if anything similar has been reported stolen. Now, of course, there are several Internet web sites that specialize in the recovery of art and high-end jewelry. You can post stolen, suspicious, or recovered items with them."

"And there are also web sites where you can sell goods, no questions asked," said Theodosia.

"Yes," sighed Brooke, "there are *lots* of those. Antique auction sites, sellers' marts, what have you."

"Can I offer you a little more honey?" asked Haley as she deposited a small silver dish on the table filled with the sticky gold liquid.

"Thank you, Haley," said Brooke. "Your biscuits are delicious. Nice and light, and really great with this honey."

"It's from DuBose Bees," responded Haley. "They're one of our best suppliers and specialize in all different flavors of honey. Sourwood honey, apple honey, melon honey . . ."

"How on earth do you get melon honey?" asked Brooke.

Haley wrinkled her button nose and smiled. "It's really kind of neat. The grower puts his beehives right smack dab in the middle of a field of melons. Apparently, once the bees pollinate the flowers, their honey begins to take on this sweet melon flavor. Works the same way with apples and peaches."

"I never dreamed it was done that way," said Brooke, genuinely fascinated. "I always thought they just added flavoring or something."

Haley glanced up as the bell over the door tinkled. "Hey there, Miss Dimple," she said in a chirpy voice.

Short and plump, edging up into her high seventies, Miss Dimple flashed a big smile at Haley and Theodosia as she swished in wearing a purple wool poncho slung over her purple and red dress. She had worked in the building next door to the tea shop, the Peregrine Building, as a personal assistant to old Mr. Dauphine, the building's owner, for many years. When Mr. Dauphine died of a heart attack last year, Miss Dimple, in a state of anxiety and desperately needing a job, was encouraged by Theodosia to pursue freelance bookkeeping. Now Miss Dimple had a new career handling payables and receivables for several small businesses on Church Street such as the Chowder Hound Restaurant and Turtle Creek Antiques. She even worked behind the counter from time to time at Pinckney's Gift Shop.

"Miss Dimple," said Theodosia, popping up from her chair. "How was your vacation in Coral Gables?"

Miss Dimple toddled over to her in a pair of too-tight shoes and grasped Theodosia's arm. "Wonderful," she gushed. "Do you know they *still* have those water skiers? I saw them back in 1958 and they're still doing amazing stunts, standing on each other's shoulders and skiing backwards."

"Guess you're not a Six Flags kind of gal, huh, Miss Dimple?" said Haley with a mischievous grin.

"You're a wicked girl, Haley Parker," scolded Miss Dimple. "You know my brain would be in an absolute spin if I went on one of those topsy-turvy rides. No, just *watching* water skiers is excitement enough when you get to be my age," she said as she followed Theodosia into the back of the shop.

When they had passed through the green velvet curtains and were in Theodosia's private office, Miss Dimple said in a loud whisper, "I hear you've had some excitement around here again." Her old eyes sparkled. "That theft at the Heritage Society must have put Drayton in a dreadful state. Timothy Neville, too. Neither one has what you'd call a tranquil personality."

"They were both pretty upset," agreed Theodosia. "Still are." She rummaged through the stack of papers that had somehow accumulated with amazing speed on top of her desk, searching for the previous week's receipts so Miss Dimple could bring their books up to date.

"I was so sorry to hear about the death of Delaine's niece's fiancé, too." Miss Dimple paused. "That's a mouthful, now isn't it?"

"It was a tragedy," said Theodosia. "His death and the missing ring have us all on edge."

"Missing ring?" asked Miss Dimple, suddenly perking up. "I didn't hear about that."

Theodosia gave up looking for the receipts for a moment. "Camille's heirloom wedding ring is still unaccounted for. But keep that under your hat, will you? The fact that the ring might be related to the disappearance of that sapphire necklace at the Heritage Society is really just a theory we're going on."

"The theory being . . ." said Miss Dimple.

"Well . . . that the two incidents are related," said Theodosia.

Miss Dimple gazed at her with eyes big as saucers. "Do you know Chessie Calvert?" she asked suddenly.

Theodosia shook her head.

"Two weeks ago, just before I went on vacation, somebody broke into Chessie's house and stole her collection of Tiffany Favrile vases," said Miss Dimple. Favrile vases were among the early efforts of Louis Tiffany. Highly colorful and often fancifully shaped like flowers, Tiffany vases were renowned for their jewel-like brilliance.

"No kidding," said Theodosia. This *was* a bit of a bombshell.

"Now when I say collection, I mean a total of three vases," said Miss Dimple. "Still, they were gorgeous pieces. Inherited from her Grand-Aunt Polly and worth a pretty penny. Chessie was heartbroken."

"So there *have* been thefts before," said Theodosia. "Camille's ring wasn't the first."

"Could be a nasty trend," said Miss Dimple.

"Did your friend, Chessie, report this theft to the police?" asked Theodosia.

"Oh yes," said Miss Dimple. "And they sent a—what-do-you-call-it?—an e-mail to the folks at that Art Theft Association in New York. The police theorized that Chessie's pieces might show up at auction somewhere. Apparently there's a huge demand for Tiffany collectibles."

Theodosia drummed her fingers on her desk. "This isn't good."

"No, it's not," said Miss Dimple. She studied Theodosia with a cool, appraising look. "Let me guess," she said, her old eyes narrowing. "In light of the rather bizarre occurrences with Camille's ring and the necklace at the Heritage Society, you've decided to launch your own investigation."

She tossed the word *investigation* out as though she were Watson chatting it up with Sherlock Holmes.

"It's more just looking into things than anything," said Theodosia, offering a hasty explanation. "Delaine was awfully upset. And Timothy's worried sick about losing his job."

"Yes, but bully for you, dear," said Miss Dimple. "Besides jumping in to help, you show a real *intuition* for this line of work." She nodded approvingly at Theodosia. "If I were to place a bet, I'd put my money on you instead of the police."

"Thanks for your confidence, Miss Dimple, but like I said, I'm really . . . oh, here they are!" Theodosia grabbed the packet of receipts that had been clipped together and then somehow buried under a mound of tea catalogs, invitations, recipes, and marketing ideas.

Miss Dimple took the receipts from Theodosia and opened her purse to put them in. "I don't know if what I told you about Chessie Calvert's Tiffany vases has helped or hurt," she said.

"Definitely helped," said Theodosia. "It means there's been a pattern. That's not great news, of course, but it means my theory has credence."

"So you're going to keep investigating?" asked Miss Dimple.

"Absolutely," said Theodosia. *Three instances of valuables stolen, maybe more? You better believe I'm going to keep going.*

"Oh!" Miss Dimple suddenly exclaimed. "What's wrong with me? I almost forgot." She plunked herself down in the chair across from Theodosia and rifled through her handbag. "I found this in a darling little shop in Key Largo and thought it would be absolutely *perfect* for you!" Miss Dimple pulled out a gift wrapped in pink tissue paper and handed it to her.

Theodosia accepted the gift, peeled back the paper. It was a wrought iron trivet in the shape of a teapot.

"Thank you," said Theodosia as a smile lit her face. She was touched by Miss Dimple's thoughtfulness. "It's lovely. Perfect for the tea shop, too. We keep setting hot pots down and scorching our nice wooden counter."

"It's you who deserves the thanks," said Miss Dimple. "If you hadn't pushed me into this freelance gig, I'd be just another old gal sitting alone in her house conversing with fifty cats."

"You don't really have fifty cats, do you?" asked Theodosia in mock horror.

"No, just the two. Sampson and Delilah. But loneliness can drive a person to do strange things."

"Here," said Haley after Miss Dimple had left. She placed a tall, frosty glass filled with cinnamon-scented froth in front of Theodosia. "Try this." Pulling a postcard advertising the historic district's upcoming Lamplighter Tour from the mound of papers on Theodosia's desk, she added, "Use this as a coaster."

"And what is this?" asked Theodosia, intrigued by the interesting concoction that now sat before her.

"A tea smoothie," said Haley proudly.

Theodosia couldn't help but grin. Any smoothie she'd ever had usually consisted of fruit, low-fat milk, and yogurt. Trust Haley to come up with a smoothie using tea. "Okay, what's in it?"

"Take a sip and find out," said Haley. She was fairly dancing on the balls of her feet, waiting for Theodosia to taste her new recipe.

Obediently, Theodosia took a sip. "Mmn," she said. "Apples and cinnamon for sure . . ."

"That's Drayton's blend of apple-cinnamon tea," said Haley in a rush. "I whipped it in a blender with some frozen yogurt then added an extra dash of cinnamon." Her dark eyes sparkled as she gazed at Theodosia. "Like it?"

"It's terrific," said Theodosia. "I'll bet we could even sell these at lunchtime. Or as afternoon pick-me-ups." She took another sip, feeling pleased. This was what running a small business was all about. Everyone pitching in, everyone contributing new ideas. And doing it in an atmosphere that was fun, fluid, and not a bit stuffy or inhibiting.

"Actually," said Haley. "I *was* hoping to add a couple smoothie offerings to our menu. I've got an idea for a Moroccan mint tea smoothie and one with green tea and mango."

"They're a far cry from a little Victorian teapot filled with English breakfast tea, but I love the idea of showing people how versatile tea can be. After all, people all over the world have been improvising with tea for centuries, frothing it with milk, blending it with spices, adding dried fruits and herbs." Theodosia took another sip. "Plus, we'd be extending our product line."

"Kind of like what we're doing with the T-Bath products," said Haley.

"Exactly," agreed Theodosia. "When I worked in marketing, we called it brand extension."

"Okay then," said Haley, "what about chai?"

Chai was black tea with a blend of spices, usually cardamom, cloves, cinnamon, and ginger, steeped in milk, then sweetened and served hot.

"I can get Drayton to blend the spices, the rest is a snap," enthused Haley. "Well, we might have to get a small cappuccino machine to steam and froth the milk—but that would be it."

"Haley," laughed Theodosia, "this is the Indigo Tea Shop, not the International Food Corporation. Let's go with the tea smoothies for now and see what happens, okay?"

"Okay," Haley agreed. "Hey, is that from Miss Dimple?" She'd just noticed the wrought iron tea trivet that sat on Theodosia's desk.

"She brought it back from Florida for me," said Theodosia. "Wasn't that sweet."

"She's a neat old gal," said Haley as a low buzz suddenly issued from the kitchen next door. "Oops! There goes the oven timer. Gotta check my quiche." And Haley zipped out the door like a jackrabbit.

Theodosia took a few more sips of her tea smoothie with the intention of sorting through the stack of papers on her desk. Besides being a compulsive hoarder of junk mail, she found it difficult to toss out the various tea and tea ware catalogs that found their way to her on an almost daily basis. What if, at some point in time, she just *had* to have some of those pedestal mugs to sell in the tea shop? Or some of those neat wooden honey dippers. After all, they sold a tremendous amount of honey along with their packaged teas. And then there was this wonderful little biscotti company in North Carolina that offered dreamy flavors such as chocolate raspberry and lemon almond.

Better save these catalogs, she told herself. And as she gathered them up, her eyes fell once again on the wrought iron trivet Miss Dimple had brought her from Florida. She stared at the black wrought iron that had been heated then formed into a rounded teapot outline.

So Miss Dimple had known of another strange robbery that had a cat-burglar-like MO. *Have there been other robberies of valuables?* She'd have to check with the police.

Deep inside her a warning bell sounded.

She tried to push her unsettled feelings into the back of her mind, but couldn't.

There'll be more robberies to come, she told herself. *This isn't over. Not by a long shot.*

11

Haley pulled open the door of the large institutional oven and peered at her quiche. She had three pans of the stuff baking away inside the oven. And right now all of them were bubbling like crazy and turning a nice golden brown on top.

Looking good, Haley murmured to herself as she eased the oven door closed, then slipped the oven mitt off her hand.

The three pans of quiche would hopefully serve today's luncheon crowd. Hopefully. They were all double pans, but then again, their luncheon business had been increasing at an alarming rate.

Haley hummed to herself as she moved a stack of mismatched salad plates onto the serving counter. Plates that she and Theodosia had picked up at flea markets and estate sales. The fact that none of them matched seemed to contribute to the general feeling of cozy and chaos that reigned at the Indigo Tea Shop.

She remembered very well the day Theodosia had first opened her doors. They'd served fifteen customers that first day. Fifteen inquisitive souls who'd made their way down Church Street and ventured into the tea shop, intrigued by the sights, sounds, and smells.

That had been almost three years ago and business had grown in decisive spits and spurts ever since.

Haley turned back to the oven and flipped open the door. *Perfect.* She quickly pulled all three pans from the oven and set them on top of the large, institutional stove.

The aroma wafting from the quiche was heavenly, she decided. But then, her bacon and red pepper quiche was always a thing of pure joy. How did she know? Haley smiled contentedly to herself. Because lots of folks, oodles of folks, had *told* her so. And because she used a secret ingredient— almost a half-pound of cream cheese in every pan—to guarantee that her quiche would turn out extra smooth and creamy.

Why, just this morning, Brooke Carter Crockett had urged her to put together a recipe book. And Brooke hadn't been the first one to make that suggestion, either. Lots of folks, including Drayton and Theodosia, had brought up the idea.

Haley slid a knife through the first pan of steaming quiche, cutting it into even squares. The idea of a recipe book appealed to her. Heck, she decided, restaurants and church groups all over Charleston had put together recipe books. Some featured gorgeous four-color photos and were professionally printed and bound, others were typed on computers, laser-printed at home, then hand-punched and tied with ribbon.

What would mine look like? Hmm. Have to think about that.

"Haley," said Drayton as he stuck his head around the corner. "Our luncheon crowd awaits today's offering with bated breath."

"Then don't just stand there being erudite, Drayton, kindly *help* me. Nestle a small bunch of green grapes on each plate and let's get going." Haley saw him hesitate for a split-second. "Yes, *those* grapes," she snapped. "Right there in the basket." She shook her head good-naturedly, knowing she was a perfectionist and sometimes a little too hard-driving for her own good. For *anyone's* good. "What would you guys do around here without me to keep up my constant barrage of browbeating?" she added.

"Haley," said Drayton, who was now scrambling to place grapes on plates and slide plates onto trays, "I don't mind saying that sometimes you employ the iron-fisted tactics of a Prussian general."

She grinned as she topped each square of quiche with a bright sliver of roasted red pepper. "Why, thank you, Drayton. I'll take that as a compliment."

"Like hotcakes," marveled Theodosia. "Your quiche just went like hotcakes. How many pans did you bake?" she asked Haley.

"Three," said Haley, who was standing behind the counter, ringing up a final take-out order.

"So there were, what? A dozen servings in each pan?" asked Drayton.

"Yup," said Haley as she handed change across the counter. "Thank you so much," she told her customer. "Come back and see us again."

"Three dozen lunches in the course of an hour or so," said Theodosia. "And that's not counting the tea and scone orders. We don't usually do that many."

"Better get that permit for outside tables," chided Drayton.

"You're right," said Theodosia. "I'm definitely liking the way business is shaping up."

"Wait until the T-Bath products go on sale," warned Haley. "Business will be bonkers."

"You really think so?" asked Theodosia. She was hopeful the T-Bath products would take off, but then again, you never know. Business could be a real crapshoot.

"I think you're going to be pleasantly surprised," said Haley. She stretched her arms high above her head, bent slightly to the left. In her rust-colored long-sleeve T-shirt and long, filmy skirt of rust and blue, Haley looked like a ballet dancer, lithe and limber.

"In case you guys haven't noticed, tea is big business these days," pronounced Haley. "Look at all the green tea candles and tea-scented perfumes and lotions out there on the market. And every time you go into a gourmet shop or kitchen boutique, you find tons of teapots and tea infusers and boxed teas."

"She's right," said Drayton. "And while we may not always like some of the bottled teas or premixed jars of chai in the supermarket, *someone* is buying them. Which I guess is good for us."

"Speaking of business and products flying off the shelf," said Theodosia, "how exactly are we going to display the T-Bath products when we launch on Thursday?"

"I've got that covered," replied Drayton. "I found a marvelous old secretary at Tom Wigley's antique shop. Wooden, a little scuffed, but it still retains most of its original shelves. Not too deep, either. I believe it will fit flush to the wall over near the fireplace and work perfectly as a display case."

"Kind of like the wooden cabinet Delaine has in her store," said Theodosia. "The one holding scarves and purses and such."

Drayton furrowed his brow, trying to recall what was in Delaine's shop. "Something like that, yes. Tom said he'd bring the piece round tomorrow."

Much to everyone's surprise, Brooke Carter Crockett and her associate, Aerin Linley, were back in the tea shop that afternoon.

"Bet you didn't think you'd see me again so soon," laughed Brooke. "But we just had to come by for another cuppa."

"Dear lady, twice in one day is an absolute delight," assured Drayton. "Now let me share with you a Castleton estate tea. Still an Indian black tea, just not as buttery as your beloved Goomtee. This one is slightly fruity, but kindly reserve judgment until you've given it a fair shake."

"Who's minding the store?" asked Theodosia, as Drayton went off to prepare the pot of tea.

Aerin waved a hand. "Oh, business was slow, so we just hung a sign on the door. You know, one of those hand-scrawled notes that says, *Back in twenty minutes.*"

Theodosia nodded. It wasn't unusual to see signs like that up and down Church Street and at the little shops throughout the historic district. People were always running out for tea or coffee or a quick visit. It was one of the little quirks that made the neighborhood so charming and fun to be part of.

She was also glad that Brooke and Aerin had just casually dropped by. As Theodosia well knew, repeat customers are the bread and butter of any small business.

The importance of generating repeat business was also one of the main reasons Theodosia tried to maintain a database of all her regular customers' names and addresses. If you mailed out postcards on luncheon specials or invited folks to promotional events like the T-Bath open house they were staging Thursday, customers *would* continue to return.

"Say, Theo," began Brooke. "I was telling Aerin about our little talk this morning. You know, when you asked about people just dropping by Heart's Desire and offering items for sale? She remembered someone acted somewhat strangely while I was away in New York."

"That's right," said Aerin. "It was a woman who came in a few weeks ago with a very pretty brooch."

"There was something unusual about her behavior?" asked Theodosia.

Aerin Linley paused. "She just seemed nervous, a little on edge. I remember thinking it was odd at the time, but then I dismissed it."

"Did you buy the piece from her?" asked Theodosia.

"Yes, we did," said Aerin. "I knew our inventory was low and it was a rather lovely piece. An emerald cut citrine surrounded by ten small diamonds. Not a huge piece, mind you, but fairly tasty. Fine craftsmanship and it definitely had some age on it." She hesitated. "Now, thinking back, I guess *I'm* a little nervous about the entire transaction."

Brooke leaned forward in a conspiratorial manner. "I think you even know the seller, Theo. Claire Kitridge?"

"Claire from the Heritage Society?" asked Theodosia.

Claire? Theodosia thought to herself. *The Claire that always seems so buttoned up and straitlaced? The same Claire that collects antique linens?*

"Ladies," said Haley, arriving with their tea. "May I present Drayton's fabled Castleton estate tea. And one of my blackberry scones for each of you. The blackberries, I might add, are from a recent crop grown on nearby Saint John's Island."

There were oohs and aahs from the two ladies as Haley set teacups, teapot, and accoutrements on the table and they began helping themselves.

"Enjoy your teatime," said Theodosia as she slipped away. "I'll chat with you again later." Slightly unnerved, she went to the display shelves and began rearranging the antique teacups she had placed there just yesterday. In her heart, she knew Brooke and Aerin had to be mistaken. Claire Kitridge was above reproach. She'd worked at the Heritage Society for three or four years now. She'd even heard Timothy Neville, in one of his rare instances of magnanimity, praise Claire for her hard work and dedication.

"Oh no," said Haley under her breath. "Not *him*."

Burt Tidwell had just pushed his way through the door and seated himself at one of the smaller tables.

Theodosia squinted across the room at him. Tidwell didn't usually just show up unannounced unless he had something on his mind. The question was, *What was on the old boy's mind today?*

"Detective Tidwell," said Theodosia, trying her best to manage a lighthearted greeting. "Good afternoon, how can I help you?"

Tidwell arranged his mouth in a reasonable facsimile of a smile, but the vibes weren't particularly warm. "Tea and the prospect of polite conversation have drawn me to your little establishment today."

What a maddening oblique manner he has, she thought to herself. Studied, slightly formal, but still with that cat-and-mouse attitude he was so famous for. *Very well,* she decided, *I'll play along for now.*

Hastily brewing a pot of uva tea, a delicate, slightly lemony Ceylonese tea, she put a stack of madelaines on a plate and carried everything back to Tidwell's table.

"Sit a moment, will you?" he invited. "Join me?"

She turned back to the counter, grabbed the first teacup she could lay her hands on, a Delvaux porcelain. She balanced it atop a Spode muffin plate, another antique piece from her collection, and went back to join Tidwell at his table. Sliding into the chair across from him, she watched as Tidwell poured out a stream of the pale amber tea into her teacup first, then his.

"This is nice," he said with another quick twitch of a smile.

She wasn't sure if Tidwell was referring to her company or the tea. It didn't really matter. The sentiment didn't feel genuine.

"You've been busy," Tidwell began. His large fingers skittered across the plate of madelaines, stopped on one, gathered it up.

This time she knew exactly what he was referring to. And it had nothing to do with the increase in business at her tea shop.

"Saint Anne's Hospital the other night. Not a smart thing to do," he told her. Tidwell cocked a furry eyebrow, waited for a response.

That man can convey reproach with just the quiver of an eyebrow, Theodosia marveled to herself. *How must a true criminal feel when Tidwell focuses his beady-eyed gaze upon them? Nervous, probably. That's when they know the jig is up.*

"I wasn't aware I had to obtain your permission in order to visit people in the hospital," Theodosia told him, her manner deliberately cool.

"Visitation is not what I was referring to," said Tidwell. "Far be it from me to criticize you and your canine friend from bringing cheer to small, needful children. I was referring to the fact that you gave chase to someone." Tidwell took a sip of tea, then gave her yet another look of stern reproach. "I warned you not to get involved."

"I wasn't involved," said Theodosia. "I went into a hospital room to pay a visit. It wasn't my fault someone was lurking there. I wasn't looking for trouble."

Now Tidwell fixed her with a steady gaze. "I get the feeling, Miss Browning, that you don't ever go *looking* for trouble. It comes calling on you." His eyes bore into her. Then, just as quickly, flicked down to scan the plate. His fingers convulsed, but he did not reach for a second madelaine.

"Detective Tidwell," Theodosia began, "have you been able to look into the incident at the Lady Goodwood Inn? The break-in that led to the death of poor Captain Buchanan?"

"Ah, change of subject," said Tidwell. "Very well, it was done politely. Not the most graceful segue in the world, but adequate." He leaned back in his chair, hunched his shoulders, and crooked his head to the left, as though trying to dislodge a kink from his thick neck.

"I carefully reviewed the investigation report that Officers Gallier and Delehanty filed on the so-called break-in at the Lady Goodwood Inn. They did, in fact, check the roof and the various access points to it for fingerprints as well as signs of a disturbance. None were found." He paused. "I stand corrected—on one of the remaining panes of glass in the ceiling, they found fingerprints belonging to one of the maintenance men. A Mr. Harry Kreider."

Harry Kreider, thought Theodosia. That was the man she'd spoken with that awful night, the one who'd lent her the ladder. He certainly wasn't a viable suspect in her mind.

"So it's a dead end," said Theodosia. Frowning slightly, she reached for one of the madelaines, took a bite, chewed absently.

"It was never going anywhere to begin with," said Tidwell. He gazed at her, saw her apparent distress. "I'm sorry," he added, tempering his tone. "I don't mean to be so rude. It was a game try, you made a good guess."

Theodosia exhaled slowly. No, she decided, it was more than a guess on her part. It was a . . . what was it, exactly? A feeling? A visceral intuition that the two incidents were connected?

Tidwell was watching her closely, trying to get a read on her by using *his* natural instincts. She dropped her voice so Brooke and Aerin, sitting at the nearby table, wouldn't hear her. "Let me ask you about something," said Theodosia. She picked up her teacup, took a deliberate sip.

Tidwell continued to watch her expectantly.

"Other thefts in the historic district," she said as she balanced her cup on the muffin plate. "Have you heard of any?"

"Nearly half a dozen."

A loud crash sounded at her feet. Startled, Theodosia looked down to see the teacup and plate she'd been holding just moments earlier lying in smithereens on the floor. Without thinking, she bent down to pick up one of the pieces, immediately came away with a cut.

"Miss Browning," said Tidwell, reaching for her arm, gently pulling it back. "Do be careful." He looked into her eyes, saw what he took to be bewilderment and confusion. "I'm sorry," he said. "I didn't mean to startle or upset you in any way. Please do believe me."

In that same instant, Brooke Carter Crockett had jumped up from her seat at the table and now stood next to Theodosia, surveying the damage. "Oh, no," she mourned, gazing down at the shattered china. "Were they good pieces?"

Theodosia blinked back tears. *Silly,* she thought to herself, *it's only a plate and teacup. Lots more where that came from.* "The teacup, a Delvaux, it . . . was my mother's," she replied. She reached down again, but Haley was suddenly there with a broom and dust pan.

"Careful, Theo," Haley warned. "Those little shards are awfully sharp." She swept the larger pieces into the dust pan, went over the floor again to try to collect the smaller pieces. "These pegged floors are terrible," she complained. "Every little thing gets caught down in the cracks. I'm going to have to bring out the vacuum sweeper."

"Later, Haley, okay?" said Theodosia. She glanced at her watch. "We'll be closing in an hour or so anyway. Just let it go till then."

Haley, a compulsive cleaner and neatnik, wasn't pleased with what she viewed as a huge delay in putting things right. But she backed off anyway.

Tidwell rose suddenly from his chair. "Sorry if I caused you any distress," he said. "I just found out about this so-called rash of robberies myself a few hours ago. Very strange."

A half-dozen other robberies, Theodosia thought to herself. *Not good. Not good at all.*

"That's all right," said Theodosia, still feeling slightly distracted. "And this is my treat," she added when she saw him reach into his jacket pocket for his wallet. "Sorry to have been so clumsy." And she hurried off after Haley.

"Are you okay?" asked Drayton. He was ferrying empty teapots and teacups from the various tables. For some reason, the Indigo Tea Shop had cleared out rather suddenly. "You're white as a sheet," he told her.

Theodosia slid in behind the counter. She put a hand to her heart and found it was beating like crazy. "There *have* been other robberies," she hissed at Drayton.

"What?" He stared at her crazily.

"Tidwell just told me. A half-dozen other robberies!"

"Good lord. In the historic district?"

Theodosia nodded.

"Hey," said Haley as she emerged from the kitchen with a cardboard take-out carton in her hands. "What's with you two?"

"Tidwell delivered some fairly earth-shattering news," said Drayton.

"I gathered that," said Haley, glancing over to the spot where she just *knew* some tiny shards were still wedged between the floorboards.

"There have been other thefts," said Drayton in a low voice.

"Holy cow," said Haley. "A lot?" Now he really had her attention.

"A half-dozen or so. Plus Camille's wedding ring and the necklace at the Heritage Society," replied Drayton.

Haley shook her head. "Right under our noses. Imagine that."

"Strange, isn't it?" said Drayton. "I suddenly feel like I've been dumped into a vintage Alfred Hitchcock film. Twists and turns everywhere."

Theodosia nodded her agreement. "Drayton, you just said a mouthful."

12

From the first day she'd found Earl Grey in her back alley, a shivering, whimpering puppy that some heartless person had abandoned, Theodosia had struggled with his food.

At first, the poor dog had been so starved he gobbled anything and everything she put in front of him, barely pausing to take a breath. She'd fed him a standard dog food with a teaspoon of olive oil poured over it, in hopes of improving his coat. But as Earl Grey had gotten older and started to feel more secure, came to realize he was much loved, and had finally found a permanent home, the dog had become a trifle picky. From gourmand to gourmet.

And so Theodosia began to experiment. Adding cooked vegetables to Earl Grey's food and occasionally boosting his protein intake by giving him a raw turkey neck.

That had seemed to do the trick. The coat that Drayton continued to insist was salt and pepper but Theodosia saw as dappled gray had grown lush and thick, Earl Grey had added muscle tone in his chest area, too, but still remained properly lean so you could gently feel a faint outline of his ribs.

Tonight, Theodosia stirred a mixture of yogurt and steamed broccoli into Earl Grey's food, then heated up a carton of gumbo for herself that she'd pulled from her freezer that morning. Duck and sausage gumbo was a staple all across the South, and no one made it better than her Aunt Libby, who lived out in the low-country. Aunt Libby had prepared gallons of the hearty stew earlier this fall and had given Theodosia at least a dozen cartons. Suffused with smoked sausage, tender breast of duck, okra, rice, celery, onion, hot peppers, herbs, and spices, the gumbo was an aromatic, heartwarming dinner. Especially since Theodosia had grabbed one of Haley's blackberry scones to go along with it.

"What do you think the calorie content of that was?" she asked Earl Grey, who had fixed her with a baleful look as she finished her dinner. "Yes, I know," she told him. "You dined on low-fat yogurt and florets of broccoli while I sated myself with a high-fat, high-carb dinner. Life isn't fair, is it?"

Earl Grey sighed loudly, as if to say, *You're the one who said it, not me.*

"Only one thing to do, big guy," she told him. "Go for a run."

Ah, the magic word. *Run.* Although *walk, jog,* and *out* were big-time favorites in Earl Grey's lexicon, the word *run* seemed to evoke the most joy. For Earl Grey was instantly on his feet and pacing wildly as Theodosia dumped dirty dishes into the sink. He added a low whine to his repertoire as she changed into her running gear, and strained mightily as Theodosia struggled to clip the leash onto the overjoyed dog's collar.

Then they were down the steps and out the door into the dark night.

The historic district on this October night was a thing of beauty. The atmosphere, heavy and redolent with mist, lent a soft focus to everything. Lights became shimmery, hard edges obscured.

After a fast walk down their alley, Theodosia and Earl Grey picked up the pace. They settled into a good rhythm as they cut across the interior of the peninsula on Broad Street, covering a good eight or nine blocks. Popping out near the Coast Guard station, Theodosia could make out the faint silhouette of bobbing sailboats and towering masts at the Charleston Yacht Club far off to her right.

Jogging down Murray, Theodosia and Earl Grey rounded the tip of the peninsula. For some reason it seemed darker out here. And lonelier. Fog, not just mist, but real cottony, wispy fog, was rolling in now from the Atlantic. Across the parkway, houses and lights that had merely looked soft focus before were suddenly being swallowed up in a wall of gray.

Passing near the Featherbed House, a bed-and-breakfast run by Angie and Mark Congdon, four squat orange pumpkins glowed like beacons from the front steps. Tiny candles flickered inside their carved grins, broadcasting a sinister welcome.

Halloween, thought Theodosia. *It's only a few days away.*

Theodosia and Earl Grey slowed their pace, Theodosia deciding, at the last minute, to head down the Congdons' private alley. It was a narrow cobblestone lane that wound past their garage then connected up with another walkway. That walkway would bring her, in a roundabout manner, back to Tradd Street. It sounded complicated, but wasn't. The historic district was a maze of alleys, walkways, and connecting paths, the result of old carriage drives, servants' entrances, and tradesmen's lanes. Once you had it figured out, you were set.

As Theodosia slipped slowly past the Featherbed House with its second-story bridge that connected the main house with two rooms over the carriage house, Earl Grey gave a low growl. He strained at his leash, jerking Theodosia toward a nearby tree. Then the dog gazed sharply upward on full alert.

What is up there? Theodosia wondered. She hesitated, then approached the tree cautiously. It was an enormous old tree, a live oak, draped in banners of gray-green Spanish moss. It was the kind of tree that was easy to climb. Which meant *anything* could be up there. Squirrel, possum, porcupine, person.

Earl Grey gave a quick sniff at the base as though to once again confirm his suspicions, then rose up on his hind feet and planted his front paws on the base of the gnarled trunk.

Still curious as to what exactly had caught the old boy's attention, she peered up the gnarled base, expecting to see . . . what?

Glinting green eyes peered back at her.

A cat! There was a cat up the tree! Probably one of the old tabbies that lived at the Featherbed House. Angie was a soft touch for strays and always joked about how a network of hobo cats had put the word out on her. *Psst! Come to the Featherbed House for a little R and R. No kitty ever gets turned away.*

Theodosia whistled softly and Earl Grey turned his attention back to her. They continued down the alley past the carriage house and turned right where the alley connected with the back drive of another home, the Ebenezer Stagg House, an Italianate mansion that had once been a private boys' school. The two of them picked their way carefully on glistening cobblestones, taking care where they stepped. The fog really had them surrounded now, London style, and the only thing that kept Theodosia moving forward at a fairly good clip was her firsthand knowledge of these old alleyways.

As they passed behind the Stagg House, Theodosia could hear footsteps coming from the right. She stopped in her tracks and Earl Grey sat down, a move they'd both practiced during obedience training. But the person, whoever it was, crossed right in front of them without noticing them, and headed down a different alley, an alley that angled back toward King Street.

Who was that? she wondered. *Who else is out creeping around in this fog? Was it Cooper Hobcaw on one of his jogs? Maybe.* But this man, and she was pretty sure it *was* a man, hadn't been jogging. Even though the alley he'd gone down was a nice, even pavement that had been fairly well lit with glowing lamps.

An uneasy feeling began to steal over Theodosia and she shivered under her layers of sweatshirts. Cooper Hobcaw had joked that he went out jogging every night in the historic district. *Does he just prefer the historic district?* she wondered. *Does he drop in on Delaine every night?*

Or is he up to something else?

That last thought stunned her. *Does Cooper Hobcaw have another reason for prowling the historic district at night? Could Cooper Hobcaw be casing the area?*

Theodosia couldn't get home fast enough.

She reeled Earl Grey in close to her and kept to the middle of the pathways until she came upon the familiar lights and sights of Church Street.

So, of course, the phone was ringing as she climbed the back stairway.

"Hello?" she answered, slightly out of breath.

"Theo, it's Jory," came a familiar, upbeat voice.

"Oh, hi there," she answered. "Hang on a minute, will you?" She unclipped Earl Grey's leash, shrugged out of her sweatshirt, kicked off her running shoes. Then she settled down cross-legged on the overstuffed couch, comfy in her T-shirt and sweat pants.

"Okay, I'm back," she told him.

"Good. I called to see if we're still going to the symphony Thursday night. We talked about it, but I'm not sure we ever made it formal."

"The symphony. Thursday. Hmm . . . Thursday's the open house."

"Right," he said. "Your tea bag products."

"T-Bath."

"Exactly. But that'll be over . . . when?"

She considered this. "Maybe four-thirty, five at the latest."

"Excellent," said Jory. "The concert doesn't start until eight. Which should give you ample time to recoup, recover, and get gorgeous."

She laughed. Jory Davis *did* have a way with words. "I suppose you're right," she said.

"Hey," he cajoled, "this is supposed to be fun. We're talking major league date here."

Good heavens, she thought to herself, *I'm acting like an idiot. As Haley would say, this is one cute guy!*

"Sorry," she told him. "An evening at the symphony sounds wonderful. No, better than that . . . fabulous!"

"Over-the-top enthusiasm. That's more like it." He laughed, but a moment later turned sober. "Hey, this thing that happened at the Heritage Society last Saturday night . . . you're not getting all tangled up in Drayton's and Timothy Neville's problems, are you?"

How could she, really? she wondered. She hadn't found a solid clue to go on yet. All she had were hunches. "No," she told him. "Not really. You just caught me at the end of a busy day and a long jog."

514 Laura Childs

"I thought so," he said. "That dog is running you ragged. I told you to get a bulldog or a dachshund. Those guys have little, short legs. Means you'd travel a much shorter distance. But no, you had to go and hook up with a . . . what is he again? A doberarian?"

She giggled. "A dalbrador. Thanks, Jory. Good night."

"'Night, kiddo."

Hanging up the phone, Theodosia decided maybe the better part of valor was to turn in early. She paused, thinking of Jory and their date Thursday night. She was looking forward to spending time with him. As she meandered through her apartment, pulling the draperies across and turning off lights, her mind wandered back to the man she'd seen tonight. Had it been Cooper Hobcaw out loping along in the fog? She'd thought the figure had *looked* a little like him, long legs, slightly haggard frame. But now she wasn't sure. She supposed the fog could make anything a little hazy. Including her memory.

The one thing she *was* sure of, however, was the nagging feeling that something strange was definitely going on. That a cat burglar, or whatever you'd call him, was definitely on the loose out there.

So instead of turning in, Theodosia decided to do a little investigatory work. On the Internet. Surely she'd find *something* about cat burglars. Everything else was there, for goodness' sake.

As it turned out, the Internet search proved very productive. When she typed cat burglar into one of the search engines, hundreds of hits came up. A few were for a rock band and some for a kind of cat burglar game that sounded similar to the old Dungeons and Dragons-type fantasy game.

But she also found good, solid information, too. Newspaper articles about cat burglars who had struck in places like Malibu, New York, Palm Springs, and Palm Beach.

That chilled her. It was exactly what Burt Tidwell had said. The *migratory* type of cat burglar follows the goods.

There was information posted by different law enforcement agencies, too. And as she scanned the various MOs, one profile seemed to emerge. Cat burglars were bold, even fearless. They were adrenaline junkies who thrived on danger. Apparently, some cat burglars even preferred to ply their trade when a home, hotel room, or shop was *occupied.* The thrill of someone sitting downstairs, sleeping in the next room, or eating dinner nearby seemed to add an extra touch of danger, an extra dimension to a game they relished. It also appeared that cat burglars often circumvented security systems by scaling buildings or power poles and shutting off electricity.

Shutting off electricity.

That's what happened at the Heritage Society. Or had that been a storm-induced power failure that a thief simply took advantage of? She didn't know.

From everything she read, cat burglars also appeared to be smart. Very smart. One cat burglar, known as the dinner hour burglar, entered homes while the residents were downstairs eating their dinner. Another selected his targets by reading magazines like *Town & Country* and *Architectural Digest.* And still another savvy cat burglar with a predilection for gold and silver carried a test kit along with him. That way he could pass on the candlesticks and platters that were merely gold- or silver-plated and concentrate on stealing only the finer pieces!

Like Camille's wedding ring? Or the silver at the Lady Goodwood Inn? she wondered. *Holy cow.*

Theodosia quickly scanned the rest of the hits. Several law enforcement officials had gone so far as to speculate on the type of person who turns to cat burglary. They tended to be strong and agile, often with gymnast backgrounds, always bold.

She thought about this. Cooper Hobcaw was certainly bold enough. Bold bordering on brash. And as a criminal attorney, he courted danger in a manner of speaking. He could be looking for another outlet from which to get his thrills.

Was Claire Kitridge bold and agile? She wasn't that old, maybe late thirties. And she looked like she was in good shape. Maybe all those weekend jaunts into the countryside looking for antique linens were really . . .

No, not Claire. It couldn't be Claire, could it?

Tired now, eyes stinging from peering at the monitor so intently, Theodosia exited the Internet and shut down her computer.

Enough, she told herself. *Time to turn in.* Earl Grey was already snuggled in his dog bed, snoring softly. It was time she did the same.

But as cozy and comfortable as Theodosia's bedroom was, with the down comforter and the Egyptian cotton sheets, it was a long while before she was able to fall asleep.

13

Last evening's fog, which had grounded planes at Charleston International Airport in North Charleston, had been dissipated overnight by strong winds swooping in from the Atlantic. The sky was a deep cerulean blue with just a few wisps of errant clouds, and the sun shone brightly, gilding the brick facades, wrought iron artistry, and wooden shutters that made the shops of Church Street so very quaint and picturesque.

But as Delaine Dish strode down Church Street, past the Chowder Hound, the Cabbage Patch Needlepoint Shop, the Antiquarian Bookstore, and the Peregrine Building, which housed the newly opened Gallery Margaux, she barely noticed the magnificent day that had dawned in Charleston.

Delaine was a woman on a mission.

She had driven back from Savannah last night with her friend, Celerie Stuart, feeling upset and more than a little helpless. Captain Corey Buchanan's funeral had been a blur. She'd been introduced to a kaleidoscope of solemn-faced, tight-lipped Buchanans, who had all seemed to regard her with the same measure of cool detachment.

After all, it was *her* niece who had been engaged to Captain Buchanan. And the tragic accident had occurred at the engagement party *she* had thrown!

They had looked at her with accusing faces. Did they not know she felt positively tortured by the terrible circumstances? How could she ever forget what had happened? How could anyone forget?

As if the death of Captain Buchanan wasn't enough of a tragedy, the issue of the missing ring had also been a sore point. She'd been informed by one of the Buchanans that they had been in contact with the Charleston Police Department and were awaiting a complete report on the accident.

Thank goodness the entire Buchanan clan seemed to believe the whole thing had been an accident! Delaine thought to herself. A tragic accident that could be chalked up to an old greenhouse and an unfortunate lightning strike.

But the whole time she'd been in Savannah, the conversation she'd had with Drayton and Theodosia had spun hopelessly about in her head, playing like an endless loop on a VCR. She recalled their *hunch,* their *supposition*, that someone *could* have come crashing through the old greenhouse roof and landed squarely atop Captain Buchanan's head.

There were about a million times during the visitation, the funeral service, and the sad reception afterward when she felt she'd simply burst with this knowledge. There were a thousand times when she thought she should just sit down and *share* these terrible suspicions with Captain Buchanan's family.

But then what?

Then she'd have to prove everything. Maybe they'd even expect her to try to find the person responsible. And bring them to justice!

Delaine touched her right hand to her temple as if the very thought was enough to trigger a migraine.

She couldn't resolve any of this mess. Of course not. There was no *way* she could ever accomplish that type of Herculean task.

But Delaine had the proverbial ace in the hole. Theodosia and Drayton had searched high and low for the missing wedding ring and, in so doing, had become intrigued by the mystery of its disappearance.

Especially Theodosia. She had an adventuresome heart and a fearless soul, Delaine reminded herself. And Theodosia commanded the ear of Burt Tidwell, one of Charleston's finest detectives!

Thank goodness!

Tidwell, bless his snoopy, inquisitive little heart, had stopped by her shop this morning. Early, just after she'd first arrived, before she could even steam the wrinkles from that new line of hand-knit sweater jackets and get them out on the floor. Tidwell had pussyfooted around a bit, asking her this and that. Inquiring whether she remembered anything unusual, asking about any strangers hanging around that terrible night, and did she know the waiters who had worked the party?

Of course she hadn't. But Tidwell's probing had stirred in her a germ of an idea. And given her a ray of hope.

If Theodosia had been guardedly persuasive in her argument about a possible intruder—and now Burt Tidwell was snooping around—then there must be something to it!

Of course, Theodosia was completely convinced that Burt Tidwell hated her. That Tidwell regarded her as a bit of an airhead.

Delaine knew that nothing could be further from the truth. She'd seen the way Burt Tidwell looked at Theodosia Browning.

Not because he had any silly romantic notions. Oh no. Absolutely not. Burt Tidwell was far too professional for that. But Tidwell *did* admire Theodosia, did respect her thoughts and opinions. Valued her keen intelligence and remarkable intuition.

Which meant Burt Tidwell might just go out of his way to help her.

Delaine clutched her buttercup yellow cashmere cardigan around her as though it were protective garb. No, she couldn't venture to dream of getting to the bottom of this all by herself. But if she enlisted Theodosia's aid, really encouraged her to keep investigating, then . . . then she just might have a fighting chance.

"*Delaine, you're back* from the funeral." Haley stood holding a green Staffordshire teapot, pouring a stream of amber tea into white take-out cups.

Delaine smiled a sad smile, touched a delicately manicured finger to her lips in a gesture that said *shoosh.* Then, choosing the small table closest to the counter, she slid quietly into a chair. "I don't really want to talk about it with everyone in the place," she told Haley. "I'm keeping a low profile for now."

"Theodosia and Drayton have been worried about you," continued Haley. "We all have." *Gee,* Haley thought to herself, *this is one bristly lady when she wants to be. And what's this low-profile stuff? Delaine has never kept a low profile in her life!*

"But I *would* like to speak with Theo and Drayton," she told Haley. Delaine glanced down at the bare wooden table as though she expected to find a teacup, linen napkin, and silverware all set up for her. "Just a cup of black tea this morning, dear. Irish breakfast tea."

"Sure thing," said Haley.

"How was the funeral?" asked Theodosia. Sitting in her office, she had heard Delaine's voice and immediately come out to speak with her.

Delaine plucked a handkerchief from her leather bag and daubed at her eyes. "Heartbreaking. Captain Buchanan's mother and sisters never stopped crying for one instant."

"Oh, no," said Theodosia as she slipped into the chair across from Delaine.

"At the church, they had poor Captain Corey's casket covered with an American flag and a military honor guard standing by. The service was very somber, of course, and his brother read a poem by Walt Whitman. I think it was *In Paths Untrodden.* Afterwards, the honor guard escorted the casket out of the church to the cemetery. After the minister said his final words, they fired a twenty-one-gun salute. Then a lone bugler played taps. Such a mournful sound."

Theodosia nodded. On the few occasions she'd attended military funerals, the playing of taps at the end had always seemed so sad and lonely. The bugler's haunting notes a signal that the service was over, the deceased committed to the earth for eternity.

"What's Camille going to do now?" asked Haley.

Delaine glanced down at her wrist nervously and Theodosia noticed she wasn't wearing her usual jewel-encrusted Chopard watch. Probably left it at home for the funeral. Too showy.

"She's going to stay in Savannah for a while," said Delaine. "Captain Corey's sister, Lindsey Buchanan, runs a travel agency and Camille is going to work for her."

"That's nice," said Theodosia.

"It will give everyone a chance to heal," said Delaine. "Hopefully." Delaine reached for her teacup, finally took a sip of tea. "So sad," she murmured. "I was going through a few things at my shop late yesterday afternoon, after I got back. And I came across Camille's wedding veil." Tears welled up in Delaine's eyes and threatened to spill down her flawless pink cheeks. "The base of the veil was this tiny little feathery cap, like something a ballerina might wear if she were going to dance *Swan Lake*. So pretty and feminine, with just a bit of dainty lace in front."

"When did you get back from Savannah?" asked Theodosia, eager to guide Delaine to a more neutral and less heart-wrenching subject.

"Yesterday. Early afternoon," said Delaine. "I went to the store because we had a big shipment coming in. But then I couldn't seem to get my head back into it."

"That's understandable," said Theodosia. "You're still in shock. Still in mourning."

"I just let Janine tend to things," explained Delaine. Janine was her sales assistant who'd been with her for quite a few years. "I went out and took a walk. I ended up over at Heart's Desire, talking to Brooke and Aerin."

"Those two were in here yesterday," said Haley. "Very nice ladies."

"You know," said Delaine with careful deliberation, "they *are* saying there's a cat burglar at work."

"Who's they?" asked Theodosia. "Brooke and Aerin?"

"Not exactly," said Delaine evasively. "But everyone up and down the length of Church Street seems to have mentioned it in one way or another. And Brooke and Aerin are both scared to death their shop might be targeted."

"Yes, I know she's concerned," said Theodosia, recalling her conversation with Brooke yesterday.

"You know," Delaine added, "their vault is just *overflowing* with valuable estate jewelry. Brooke confided to me that she just received a shipment of fire opals from Brazil. And she's also a master goldsmith, so she plans to set them in eighteen-karat gold. Won't that make for an absolutely stunning necklace? Fire opals and gold? With matching earrings as well?"

"Delaine, maybe you shouldn't be talking about this," Theodosia cautioned.

"I'm only telling *you*," replied Delaine peevishly. "It's not like I'm dashing about the entire historic district telling everyone I run into!"

No, Theodosia thought to herself, *but you could let this information slip to someone like Cooper Hobcaw. And that might not be the most prudent thing right now.*

The fax machine on the counter next to them suddenly beeped sharply.

Startled, Delaine jumped at the intrusion, then put a hand to her heart. "What was *that?*" she asked.

"Lunch orders," announced Haley, who headed for the counter, suddenly all business.

"Listen, Theo," said Delaine, now that the two of them were alone. "Remember what we talked about a few days ago? The cat burglar?"

Theodosia nodded.

"Now I am convinced that you were right." Delaine peered at Theodosia, her green eyes sparkling with intensity.

"What changed your mind?" asked Theodosia. She was curious whether Delaine was having an emotional reaction after the funeral or if she'd actually obtained some useful information.

"If there isn't a cat burglar at work, why would everyone be talking about it? And why would Detective Tidwell have been at my shop this morning?" *There,* thought Delaine with satisfaction, *that will certainly throw open this whole mess now.*

"Tidwell came to your shop?" said Theodosia. This *was* an interesting turn of events.

"Indeed, he did," cooed Delaine. "And, I daresay, the ordeal was quite upsetting."

"Why was that, Delaine?" Theodosia tried to manage a note of sympathy even though her curiosity was at a fever pitch.

"Well, Tidwell played it very close to the vest, of course," replied Delaine. "You know how absolutely maddening the man is. He said he wasn't investigating *per se,* merely poking around, looking at things. But I got the very distinct impression that Detective Tidwell shares *your* sentiment. He does *not* view Captain Buchanan's death at the Lady Goodwood as an accident!"

Fascinated, Theodosia waited for Delaine to continue.

"You see," said Delaine, "he inquired about the *waiters.*"

So Tidwell has taken me seriously, thought Theodosia. *But the waiters, that was an angle I hadn't considered.*

"Delaine, what did Detective Tidwell want to know about waiters?" said Theodosia.

"Oh, he wanted to know who I'd hired to work at the reception, serving champagne and such. But of course, I told him the folks at the Lady Goodwood had taken care of all that. They'd hired the waiters."

"Did he ask about specific waiters, Delaine?"

"Not really. He just rattled off some names." Delaine dug in her purse. "I wrote down their names, though. It seemed like the right thing to do." She pulled out a scrawled list on a sheet of Cotton Duck stationery. "I guess not all of the waiters were working at the engagement party, but they were all on the premises that night. There was another function going on in the dining room. A sales meeting or something. For some computer company."

Theodosia scanned the list of names. There wasn't one she recognized.

"Can I keep this list, Delaine?"

"Well . . . I don't suppose it would hurt if you made a *copy* of it."

"Great," said Theodosia. "Be right back."

At the counter she literally bumped into Drayton, who had just let himself into the tea shop via the back door.

"I've got Hattie Boatwright working on the most delightful centerpiece for tomorrow," he told her excitedly. "It's part Japanese ikebana, part Southern luxe. That lady really has exceptional talent. Now if I could just convince her to join our bonsai group, I think she'd be a natural."

"I thought the whole idea of bonsai was that they *weren't* natural," quipped Haley as she emerged from the kitchen. "Stunted trees twisted into bizarre shapes and forced to live in tiny pots. What's natural about that?"

"It's a highly evolved art form," argued Drayton. "One that's been around for more than a thousand years. The style and context of bonsai are highly representational."

"Well, they're cute little things anyway," allowed Haley. She paused to watch Theodosia slide Delaine's list into the fax machine. "Are you trying to make a copy?" she asked.

Theodosia nodded.

"You have to hit the *function* button first, then press *copy*. Here, I'll do it." Haley's slim fingers flew over the keys and the piece of paper began to feed through.

"Tidwell asked Delaine about the waiters who worked at the Lady Goodwood the night of the engagement party," explained Theodosia. "Apparently he shared this list of names with her in the hope that something might pop out."

"You don't say," said Drayton as he watched a grayish page emerge from the bottom of the fax machine and slide into the waiting tray. But as he glanced at the list, his look of mild interest suddenly changed to one of alarm.

"*I* recognize a name on this list," he said quietly so Delaine wouldn't overhear.

"No way," said Haley.

Drayton slid his finger halfway down the list as Theodosia and Haley crowded in closer. "There. Graham Carmody. I think he might have been a waiter at the Heritage Society that night."

"*That* night?" asked Haley excitedly. "You mean last Saturday night when that fancy necklace disappeared?"

Drayton nodded gravely.

"You really think so?" said Theodosia. She was a little surprised that something had even come of Tidwell's list.

"I'm positive it was this fellow," said Drayton. "In fact, I think he was the one I asked to fetch a drink for Delaine."

"Did she ever get her drink?" asked Theodosia.

Drayton scratched his head. "I honestly don't recall."

• • •

Lunch was a rush again. They had a full house, then a gaggle of tourists who'd just been dropped off by one of the sightseeing jitneys came pouring in right in the middle of things. Because there weren't enough tables available, Haley had to pack up box lunches for the dozen or so tourists to carry to nearby White Point Gardens.

Delaine hung around for a while, looking alternately morose and sweetly sad, then finally wandered off after consuming a luncheon plate of chicken salad and marinated cucumbers.

And all the while Theodosia fretted. As if Cooper Hobcaw and Claire Kitridge didn't look suspicious enough, what about this waiter, Graham Carmody? He'd attended both functions! The engagement party and the Heritage Society's member's-only party. Well, not *attended* as a guest, but he'd been working there. Which gave him far more freedom and latitude than an ordinary guest. After all, a waiter could slip in and out and no one would really pay him any undue attention. Waiters were even *supposed* to be a trifle surreptitious, she decided.

In the early afternoon, the antique secretary that Drayton had ordered from Tom Wigley's antique shop was delivered and everyone crowded around to ooh and aah. It was a handsome piece, just as Drayton had promised. Handcrafted of a lovely burled walnut with a fine array of shelves, nooks, and cubbyholes. Theodosia decided it *would* make a perfect display case for the T-Bath products.

"And it doesn't take up a lot of space," said Haley, pleased with their new acquisition. "I won't be bumping my keester every time I lug a tray of tea to somebody's table."

"Haley," said Drayton, "if your attitude is such that you're merely *lugging* trays of tea, perhaps the time has come to investigate a new career path."

"All right, smarty, you know what I mean," she shot back. "I just meant that the secretary was an *economical* piece of furniture. It doesn't stick way out into the room." She gave an exaggerated frown and shook her finger at Drayton. She knew that *he* knew *exactly* what she meant.

"Oh, my goodness," said Miss Dimple as she arrived with an armload of ledger books. "Every time I stop by, you folks have something new going on."

"Hey there, Miss Dimple," called Haley. "I've got one plate of chicken salad left. It's got your name on it."

"Thank you, Haley," said the small, rotund woman. "Chicken salad sounds delightful."

"And maybe a muffin to go along?" tempted Haley. "We've got cranberry and orange blossom today."

"Orange blossom," announced Miss Dimple.

"Oh, Miss Dimple," said Theodosia, "you're going to have to sit out here today. My office is not only crammed with boxes, we're going to have to start unpacking and hauling things out."

"That's right," said Miss Dimple, settling herself down at a vacant table. "Your T-Bath products. I've heard so much about these products, I can't wait to try them for myself. There's nothing more rewarding for the soul than a good soak."

"You're coming tomorrow, right?" asked Haley as she set the chicken salad and muffin down in front of her.

"Wouldn't miss it," she said. "Jessica Sheldon from Pinckney's Gifts is planning to stop by, too."

"Good," said Theodosia. She gazed at the ledgers. "So everything's tallied and balanced?"

Miss Dimple put a chubby hand on one of the ledgers as she chewed a bite of chicken salad. She swallowed, cleared her throat, was suddenly all business. "Shipshape," she told Theodosia. "Profits are up and the only debt you're carrying is for the manufacture and production of the T-Bath products. As we've seen, they did extremely well when you test-marketed them on your web site, so there's no reason to believe they won't do just as well in a retail setting." And with that bit of good news delivered, Miss Dimple dove back into her chicken salad.

"Hey, guys," said Theodosia to Haley and Drayton. "Can you unpack those boxes without me? I've got to make a phone call, then step out for a bit."

Drayton glanced about the tea shop. Besides Miss Dimple, only one other table was occupied at the moment. "I don't know why not," he said.

"So . . . just stick the T-Bath products on shelves and stuff a few baskets?" asked Haley.

"Haley," said Drayton, "you make it sound so *artless*."

"In that case, my dear Drayton," said Haley, laying on her best boarding school accent, "we shall *artfully* stack products on shelves and *artfully* stuff baskets. How does that sound?"

"Much better, Haley, much better."

Theodosia looked up the number for St. Anne's Hospital, dialed the phone.

"St. Anne's, how may I direct your call?" came the receptionist's voice.

"I'm trying to get ahold of Cecile Randolph, one of the nurses who works on your second floor," said Theodosia.

"One minute," said the voice. There was a click and a buzz and Theodosia was on hold.

"This is Cecile," said a pleasant voice.

"Cecile? This is Theodosia Browning. We met the other night when my dog and I chased the intruder from Mr. Wilson's room?"

"Oh, yes," said Cecile, recognition dawning in her voice. "How are you?"

"Fine," said Theodosia, "but I'm more concerned about Mr. Wilson."

"He's been released," said Cecile.

"That's very good news," said Theodosia. "So he's at home now?"

There was a pause. "I think he's staying with a relative for now," said Cecile. "I'm not sure how much I'm allowed to say, but since you were directly involved in the incident of the other night, I think it's okay to tell you that the police suggested Mr. Wilson not go home for a while."

"But he's feeling better?" asked Theodosia. *This is interesting. Now Harlan Wilson is in hiding. Well, maybe not in hiding, but certainly incognito.*

"He was fine when he walked out," said Cecile. "Just fine."

14

The Lady Goodwood Inn was operating at about half-capacity. The hotel staff was at the ready, with desk clerks and concierge ready to check guests in, bell hops and chambermaids all available to tend to their needs. And in the kitchen, cooks, sous-chefs, prep workers, and waiters were ready to spring into action at a moment's notice. The two women who handled bookings for parties and event catering were waiting for the phone to ring. But it didn't. Business had slowed considerably since that fateful evening when the glass ceiling of the Lady Goodwood's Garden Room had collapsed atop Captain Corey Buchanan.

Frederick Welborne, the man who'd proudly served as general manager at the Lady Goodwood Inn for the better part of two decades, gazed about the empty lobby and sighed. This was not the venerable old inn's finest hour.

Tall and angular, balding and long of face, Frederick Welborne, a man who already appeared slightly burdened, now bore a look of perpetual sadness. The Lady Goodwood Inn was in a state of disrepair. And when the good lady was ailing, *he* was ailing, too.

In the past few days, yards of wet carpeting had been hauled from the ruined Garden Room. And despite the scented candles that had been burned, air fresheners that had been sprayed, windows left open, and contract cleaners who'd been brought in to work their magic with potions and sprays and ion machines, there still remained the unmistakable trace of mildewy odor.

Guests had grimaced at the sight of the wreckage. Two large Dumpsters were hunkered down in the parking lot, the repository for all that ruined carpet and glass.

And the question still remained: what would be done about the old greenhouse, the Garden Room? The owners, descendants of the original Goodwoods who didn't even live in the area anymore, wanted it repaired. The inn was, after all, a continuing source of revenue for them, what with the many wedding receptions, business meetings, club functions, and private parties that were booked there, to say nothing of the tourists who stayed in the guest rooms.

One of the contractors who'd been brought in to survey the damage had just shaken his head and recommended the Garden Room be torn down completely.

Now a second contractor had been brought in at the specific request of the absentee owners.

Frederick Welborne wouldn't be a bit surprised if that contractor recommended patching it up.

"Mr. Welborne, do you have a moment?"

Frederick Welborne turned with a slow smile to greet Theodosia and shake her outstretched hand.

"Miss Browning," he said, "nice to see you under slightly better circumstances." After that fateful night, Frederick Welborne had instructed his staff to continue searching for the missing wedding ring and had felt badly that no one had been able to recover it.

"I'm afraid I still don't have hopeful news regarding your friend's wedding ring," he told her. "We've been looking, we've *all* been looking. But alas, no luck."

Theodosia saw the sadness behind his smile, noted the empty corridors of the Lady Goodwood, and knew all was not well. But then again, how could it be?

"You've got quite a cleanup operation going on here," she told him. "I saw Dumpsters out in the parking lot."

"The sooner those are gone, the better," Frederick said. "Just a sad reminder."

"Any plans to rebuild the Garden Room?" she asked.

"Still up in the air." Frederick Welborne sighed. "That decision, I'm afraid, is being left to our attorneys, insurance agents, building contractors, and owners." He smiled sadly. "I am, when all is said and done, simply a humble manager, charged with running this establishment." He gazed around. "Such as it is."

"And a fine job you've done," said Theodosia with as much warmth as she could muster, for she and Drayton had catered several engagement teas, a New Year's Eve party, and even a children's teddy bear tea at the Lady Goodwood Inn over the last couple years. And on each occasion, arrangements at the inn had been impeccable.

"May I go in and take a look?" she asked.

Frederick Welborne held up a finger. "Yes, but give me a moment." He retreated quickly to his office, returned with two yellow hard hats.

"You'll have to wear one of these," he told her. "Regulations."

"No problem," said Theodosia as she slipped the hard hat on her head.

Frederick Welborne smiled faintly at the sight of all that auburn hair spilling out from beneath the yellow work hat. "It looks good on you, you're a natural," he told her as he led her into the Magnolia Room, where Camille and Captain Buchanan's cocktail party had been held, then through the doorway into the Garden Room.

"The room looks a bit different, doesn't it," said Frederick Welborne.

Theodosia gazed about. The Garden Room had looked awful the night the roof collapsed, but now it was barely recognizable. Carpet had been torn up and metal scaffolding crowded the room. The ceiling, which had formerly been a glass arch, had been rebuilt as a temporary flat ceiling of plywood.

"What's going to happen to this room?" asked Theodosia. She gave a little shudder. Now that she'd returned to the scene of Captain Buchanan's death, she was struck by the full magnitude of what had really happened here. *Or is it the scene of a crime?* she wondered.

"Mr. Welborne? Telephone." A bell hop in a burgundy uniform with matching cap stood at Frederick Welborne's elbow. They turned and followed the bell hop out into the hall.

"Joey here went through all the carpeting after it was torn up," Frederick told her. "Looking for the ring. But he didn't find anything."

"No, sir," said Joey with what seemed like genuine regret. "And I *really* did look."

"I believe you," said Theodosia. "Thank you, thank you both," she said, smiling at the two of them.

"We'll stay in touch," said Frederick as he scurried off down the hall to take his phone call.

"I take it business has been slow?" Theodosia said to Joey, noting that despite his youthful name, Joey wasn't exactly a kid. In fact, Joey looked like he might be in his early sixties.

"Glacial. I've been here twenty-six years and never seen anything like it. We had two big wedding parties cancel out on us. And then, yesterday, a ladies luncheon group just turned on their pointy little heels and left. Guess they got spooked because the workers were taking the roof down."

"The roof came off yesterday?" asked Theodosia.

Joey nodded. "What was left of it. That's what that second Dumpster's for. The metal struts and such. Got to separate stuff these days. Even landfills are getting particular. Or maybe it's because they recycle it, I don't know."

"Joey," said Theodosia, "is there a way for people to know about the events that go on here?"

Joey cocked an eye at her. "What do you mean?"

"When the Lady Goodwood has receptions and parties and such, is that information published? Or posted somewhere?"

Joey scratched his chin, thinking. "We have a newsletter," he told her.

"A newsletter," repeated Theodosia. "And your mailing list would be . . . how large?"

Joey shrugged. "I don't know, maybe a couple thousand." He stared at her intently, then his lined face seemed to light up as another idea dawned. He snapped his fingers. "We have a web site, too," he told her proudly. "That probably reaches a whole lot more folks."

I'm sure it does, thought Theodosia with grim determination. *Maybe even the person who came here that night and left with a diamond ring in his pocket instead.* "Thanks, Joey," Theodosia told him.

Joey touched his hand to the short brim of his cap. "No problem."

Walking across the parking lot to her Jeep, Theodosia found that her gaze was once again drawn to the two large brown metal Dumpsters. Jingling her car keys in her hand, she walked across the parking lot to the side of the building where the Dumpsters sat. One was piled high with glass and remnants of old carpet. The other, for all practical purposes, looked empty.

Intrigued, she walked up to that Dumpster, stood on tiptoes, and peered in. It wasn't empty at all. Joey had been right. This Dumpster was half-filled with metal struts and rails. The bones of the greenhouse roof, she thought to herself. The skeleton.

As she gazed at the twisted metal, Theodosia recalled the strange oval-shaped metal ring she'd seen attached to one of the ceiling struts. She hadn't given the metal ring a lot of thought. After all, she'd been balancing precariously on a monumentally tall ladder just moments after Captain Buchanan had been buried in rubble. More than a few things had been occupying her mind.

But as she stood with her hand on the rough edge of this heavy metal Dumpster, something prickled at Theodosia's thoughts.

If someone had crashed through the roof, had actually descended inside the Garden Room, then how did they get back up again?

How exactly did one manage an acrobatic feat like that?

She supposed you could use a pulley of some kind. Or something akin to the high-tech "spider" apparatus that filmmakers loved to feature in spy films like *Mission Impossible.*

Could the ordinary person just *buy* that type of equipment right off the shelf? Better yet, could an ordinary person even *negotiate* that type of equipment?

Did Cooper Hobcaw have the strength and flexibility to manipulate a Spiderman rig like that? she wondered. Maybe. He was a runner. Or at least he claimed to be a runner.

Could Claire Kitridge? She looked fairly lithe and limber.

And what of this Graham Carmody? Was he agile, too? Or didn't he have to be. Did he just show up as a waiter and then work his angle?

The questions burned in her mind like wildfire.

15

Graham Carmody sat at his Dell computer scanning the Internet auction site. This was the best part, he told himself. This was what made it all worthwhile.

Oh, finding the objects was exciting, he couldn't deny that. There was the thrill of the hunt, which always set his pulse to racing. But once the object was digitally photographed and put up on the web site, then things *really* got interesting. Because that's when he started making money.

Graham loved checking and rechecking the bids, especially when one of his choice items was reaching its final days. It was exciting to note when his reserve price had been met, even better when bidding heated up and competitors from all over the world began to play a cat-and-mouse game with each other, sneaking in new bids at three in the morning!

What a marvel the Internet was. And what a brilliant way to move merchandise. So fast, so inexpensive, and so highly anonymous. Whoever had *really* invented the Internet (and he was quite sure it hadn't been Al Gore, more likely a bunch of brainy military tech weinies) should be awarded a gold medal. Because the Internet had become the repository for all of civilization's accumulated knowledge. And an international marketplace for all of civilization's goods.

Graham Carmody stretched his long legs, scratched at the scruff of ginger-colored beard that sprouted on his face. He'd have to can it in a little while, get his shit ready for tomorrow. Starting tomorrow noon he'd be working nonstop for the next couple days. A docents' luncheon at the art museum, then the gig at Symphony Hall. Friday and Saturday evenings were booked solid, too. Working as a temp for Butler's Express didn't leave a lot of room for extracurricular activities, but it certainly got him into lots of interesting places. Oh well, hit it hard now, retire early . . .

Reaching for a cigarette, Graham Carmody stood up suddenly, letting his computer chair snap back. He glanced at the walls of his study, at the tasty antiques and oddities that occupied the wooden shelves. He didn't even remember where he'd picked up that pre-Columbian statue. Or that silver tray. Oh well. Didn't matter.

Overcome by fatigue now from too many hours spent staring at the computer screen, he paced the length of the room, glancing out the window into the back garden of the small single house he rented. What luck he'd had in finding this place. Mrs. Gerritsen, an older lady and recent widow, had been looking for a young man to rent the downstairs from her. Give her a sense of security, she'd told him. He gazed at his rumpled reflection in the window. Security. Him. Sure. You bet, Mrs. Gerritsen. Anything you say, babe.

A sudden movement outside caught his eye. He stepped closer to the window, cupped his hands to the glass, and tried to peer outside.

Is someone out there? Moving around in the alley?

He darted through the doorway into the kitchen and threw open the back door.

Hey! he called, leaping down the back steps, intent on throwing a good scare into whoever was sneaking around out back.

But all he saw were shadows. All he heard was the whisper of the wind through Mrs. Gerritsen's dead flower stalks.

Graham Carmody stood on the sidewalk in his bare feet. *Nothing,* he finally told himself. *Probably just a stray cat trying to paw its way into the garbage bag I set out earlier.* He'd seen the damn things around before, thought maybe Mrs. Gerritsen secretly put out food for them.

You're just feeling jumpy, kid. Time to log some serious sack time.

Graham Carmody turned and went back inside his house.

Graham Carmody, Graham Carmody. The name had played like a litany in Theodosia's head. He'd been one of the waiters at Delaine's party; he'd also worked at the Heritage Society the night the Blue Kashmir necklace disappeared. Coincidence or convenience?

And so it wasn't any surprise that at nine o'clock that night Theodosia pulled out the Charleston phone directory, paged through the *C*'s, and ran her finger down the index of names until she actually found the name, *Graham Carmody.*

Over on Bogard Street. Not all that far from here.

She'd stood in her hallway, gazing at her reflection in the mirror, debating how she could pull this off. Go for a jog and take Earl Grey along in case she needed a convincing ruse? Or just drive there and snoop?

In the end she jumped in her Jeep and drove there. Parked a block or so away. Flipped the switch that killed the dome light, then slipped quietly out the door.

Theodosia had scouted the house from the street first. It was your typical Charleston single house. Long and narrow, one room wide, butted up against the street. Charleston folklore held that residences had once been taxed according to how much street frontage they occupied. Hence the evolution of the conservatively narrow Charleston single house.

This one was clapboard, though many single houses were far grander and built of brick or stucco. Graham Carmody's house looked fairly well kept for its age, Theodosia decided. It had probably been built just before the turn of the century. The previous century.

And look, next to the front door. Two mailboxes. The house had obviously been turned into a duplex of sorts. *Is Graham Carmody the landlord or the renter?* she wondered.

Going around to the back of the house, walking down the alley, she'd seen him through the window, working on his computer.

Graham Carmody was surprisingly pleasant looking. Young, probably late twenties. A trifle scruffy, but still the kind of guy Haley would find attractive. Would call hunky.

Theodosia had been staring in at him from outside, drawn unconsciously forward, when the tip of her shoe had struck something.

A black vinyl garbage bag.

Was it his? she'd wondered. *Should she look inside? Better yet, should she take it?*

Feeling a trifle foolish, but still curious, she'd snatched up the black bag and slung it over her shoulder.

That's when the man in the window had reacted. Had bolted out of the room in a flash.

Theodosia had known he was coming after her. He'd seen something, her movement or shadow when she grabbed the bag, and was rushing out to check!

But she was down the alley and around the corner before Graham Carmody ever hit the flower beds. Then she crouched behind a huge clump of magnolias, trying to control her breathing, knowing Graham Carmody hadn't been wearing shoes, but praying he wouldn't run down the alley after her anyway.

He hadn't.

Theodosia waited a full five minutes, during which time she felt like a surreptitious Santa with a bag of who-knows-what thrown across his back.

She took a roundabout route back to her Jeep, unlocked the door, slid into the driver's seat.

Keeping one eye on the rearview mirror, she drove a circuitous route back to her apartment above the Indigo Tea Shop. Finally, when her breathing had returned to normal and she'd parallel parked in the spot behind her shop, she turned her attention to the black garbage bag that rested beside her on the passenger seat.

Digging a fingernail into the soft plastic, she ripped the bag open. But instead of the orange juice cartons, candy bar wrappers, and empty cereal boxes she'd expected to see, there were printouts. Computer printouts. Mounds of them.

Frowning, Theodosia snapped the Jeep's dome light on and stared at the sheets of paper.

They were activity printouts from an Internet auction site. Dates and times of bids. Amounts of bids.

She sat stock-still and stared out the front window of the Jeep. *If Graham Carmody is a cat burglar, what better way to fence his stolen goods than on an Internet auction site! It would be a way to draw millions of buyers from all over the world and still remain anonymous!*

Yes, she decided, this definitely bore looking into. And the sooner the better.

16

Timothy Neville had weathered many crises in his eighty years and many problems during his tenure as president of the Heritage Society. But neither he nor any of his people had ever come under such merciless scrutiny before.

He fairly shook with indignation as he strode down Church Street. Dressed in a double-breasted camel hair blazer and cocoa brown slacks, Timothy was the picture of style. His jacket with its nipped-in waist, his paisley yellow ascot, his highly polished shoes, had been chosen with great care this morning. But after the events of this morning, and his infuriating phone conversation with Vance Bernard, the chairman of the Heritage Society's executive advisory committee, Timothy Neville was beyond caring. In fact, he was positively livid. And when Nell Chappel of the Chowder Hound Restaurant waved hello to him as she collected her morning mail and headed into the kitchen to set a nice pot of she-crab soup to simmering, Timothy didn't even take notice.

"Drayton. A moment of your time, please," said Timothy as he strode into the Indigo Tea Shop like a martinet, ramrod stiff and utterly devoid of any extraneous pleasantries.

"Timothy . . . oh, of course," said Drayton. Clutching a teapot in each hand, his tortoiseshell half-glasses sliding down his aquiline nose, Drayton was completely taken by surprise. "Give me a minute," he told Timothy. "Take that table over there," he said, pointing with his chin, "and I'll be right with you."

Timothy strode over to the table, sat down. Even though he sat perfectly erect, with one leg crossed over the other, his pleated slacks falling elegantly, his face was a thundercloud.

"Timothy," said Theodosia as she rounded the corner from the kitchen. "Good morning, this *is* a surprise." Stopping in her tracks, she suddenly took a good look at him. "What's wrong?"

"Everything," he snapped. "I don't even know where to begin."

"Simply start at the beginning," said Drayton as he arrived at Timothy's table, somewhat breathless. "Haley," he called, "can you get a plate of scones for table three and another pot of Darjeeling for table two?"

She nodded.

"Now tell us," said Drayton. "What's happened to put you in such a state?"

"The Charleston Police came to the Heritage Society some forty minutes ago, that's what happened," said Timothy. "Apparently they received an anonymous tip that Claire Kitridge was somehow involved in the recent thefts that have plagued our neighborhood."

"That's absurd," said Drayton while Theodosia inwardly cringed.

Timothy held up a gnarled finger. "Wait," he cautioned, "it gets much worse. Because of the recent death and apparent theft at the Lady Goodwood and the theft of the Blue Kashmir necklace, the police took this tip rather seriously. Claire, on the other hand, did not take the police seriously." Timothy grimaced. "That was her mistake."

"What happened?" asked Theodosia, a sick feeling suddenly gripping her.

"Oh, they asked Claire a few routine questions. Where do you live? How long have you worked at the Heritage Society? That type of thing. Then they wanted to know if they could have a look inside her desk. Claire said yes, knowing she had nothing to hide."

"I still don't see the problem," said Drayton. "Didn't you tell them the notion of Claire as sneak thief was utterly ridiculous?"

"Of course I did," sputtered Timothy. "Until they rifled through the bottom drawer of Claire's desk and found Delaine Dish's missing watch."

"What!" said Drayton. Now it was his turn to sputter.

"You know, that fancy Chopard with all the diamonds," said Timothy.

"But Claire didn't steal it . . . wouldn't steal it," fumbled Drayton.

"Of course she wouldn't, she's above reproach. *You* know that and *I* know that, but the police . . ." Timothy shrugged. "Well, it isn't good. Obviously, the discovery of Delaine's expensive watch is very incriminating."

"They came looking for a watch without benefit of a search warrant," said Theodosia slowly, "and the whole thing's based on an anonymous tip? I'd say that's awfully fishy."

"So fishy it stinks!" declared Drayton.

"Doesn't it," said Timothy, his voice brimming with bitterness. "And now our illustrious executive advisory committee wants Claire Kitridge fired. Of course, they're calling it a temporary leave of absence, but it's just a matter of time before it becomes a formal disciplinary firing. Unless, of course, we *somehow* find the person responsible . . ." Timothy's voice faltered and he gazed at Theodosia in despair.

"This is awful!" howled Drayton, gazing at Theodosia with an equal degree of unhappiness.

Timothy reached for his handkerchief, blew his nose, cleared his throat. "Claire . . ." he began, "is a very *good* person. She's been with the Heritage Society for almost four years. In that time I've seen her diligence and kindness shine through." Timothy's voice faltered again. "I've seen Claire go out of her way to make people feel welcome and appreciated. People who've donated things to the Heritage Society, little things like an old letter or a small antique . . . they receive the same heartfelt thank-you letter from her as a million-dollar donor would. Claire is just that kind of person."

Theodosia stared at the two men unhappily. She couldn't help but remember Brooke and Aerin's conversation about Claire bringing in a citrine and diamond broach for sale. Was it possible Claire Kitridge *wasn't* what she appeared to be? That she was, instead, a sly fox in the weeds who took careful advantage of her position at the Heritage Society? Could she have heard about Camille's wedding ring through the grapevine or via Delaine's bragging and gone after it? Because Claire had inside access at the Heritage Society, could she also have snatched the Blue Kashmir necklace? Was she responsible for the other art thefts? The Tiffany vases, the half-dozen other thefts Tidwell had mentioned?

The thought of Claire Kitridge as a cat burglar was sickening to contemplate.

On the other hand, someone very wily and clever could have maneuvered to set Claire up. Someone who needed to deflect blame from themselves. Someone who had access to the Lady Goodwood Inn and the Heritage Society. Someone with a working knowledge of the historic district and all its wealthy residents.

Someone like Cooper Hobcaw or Graham Carmody.

The rest of the morning was a whirlwind at the Indigo Tea Shop. Customers had to be served, finishing touches put on the T-Bath display, sweetgrass baskets had to be stuffed to the brim with T-Bath products and stacked on the counter. And all the while, they worried about Timothy and Claire.

Drayton had decided they should close the Indigo Tea Shop at one o'clock in order to prepare for the afternoon's open house. And just as soon as Haley returned from Gallagher's Food Service, their favorite restaurant supply house, with ingredients for the California rolls, they'd push three of the tables together to form the head table for the buffet. Then, of course, they'd have to set everything up and decorate the rest of the tables with Drayton's bonsai.

"Drayton," said Theodosia, "I know this isn't a good time to ask, but when is Hattie bringing the centerpiece by?"

"Any minute," he said. "And you're right, it isn't a good time. Why does everything have to happen at once? Good things and bad things all mulled together."

She sighed. "Life does seem to unfold that way, doesn't it?"

"We worked so hard on these T-Bath products and looked forward to this day and now it . . ." He searched for the right word. "It feels *tainted.*"

"I know," said Theodosia. "The good shoulder to shoulder with the bad. Maybe it's a test of fortitude."

"Makes us stronger?" he asked.

"That's what my mother believed," said Theodosia. Her mother had passed away when she was eight, but she could always remember her saying something to the effect that problems can't be solved, but only outgrown.

"Hey, you guys!" The door flew open as Haley rushed in, her long hair streaming behind her, her arms filled with bundles.

"Good heavens, Haley," said Drayton. "You're a regular beast of burden with all those bags. Here, let me give you a hand."

"Thank you, Drayton," said Haley as she handed over her packages. "Hey, Theo, guess what? When I was on my way back from Gallagher's, I came back past Heart's Desire. Guess who I saw in there? Standing at the counter?"

"Claire Kitridge?" said Theodosia. For some reason the name just popped into her head and she blurted it out.

"Nope. Cooper Hobcaw."

"Really?" said Drayton with a frown.

"Oh, yeah," said Haley. "He was leaning across the counter, kind of flirting with that woman, Aerin, who works for Brooke. At least I think he was flirting. They had their heads together, talking awfully close." Haley paused. "I thought Cooper Hobcaw was sweet on Delaine."

"So did I," said Theodosia. She turned toward Drayton, raised her eyebrows as if to say *what's up?* But he appeared equally surprised.

"As far as I know, Cooper Hobcaw has been squiring Delaine around to various social functions," said Drayton. "They were at an art opening last week for that new painter who's showing at the Wren Gallery. And of course, Coop was her guest at the engagement party and the ill-fated Heritage Society members' party."

"So you don't think he'd two-time her?" said Haley.

"Honestly, Haley," said Drayton, "I don't know what to think anymore."

It wasn't until Theodosia was in her office later, unpacking the last of the T-Bath products, that she realized how heartsick she suddenly felt for Delaine. If her hunch or odd feeling or whatever it was about Cooper Hobcaw proved true and he *did* turn out to be a thief, it would be a devastating blow to Delaine. And if Cooper Hobcaw was merely getting cozy with Aerin Linley in anticipation of possibly dumping Delaine, she'd be equally traumatized.

Theodosia propped her elbows on her desk and rested her head in her hands, thinking. Cooper Hobcaw, the lanky, soft-spoken fellow who jogged through the historic district late at night, was a strange duck. Had he charmed Delaine in order to get closer to people and places of wealth in the historic district?

Was he flirting with Aerin at Heart's Desire because she might be a way to unload expensive merchandise? As one of Charleston's top attorneys, he wouldn't be viewed with suspicion if he waltzed into Heart's desire with expensive jewelry. It would just be assumed they were old family pieces.

Theodosia rubbed her eyes tiredly. Okay, what about all those print-outs she'd grabbed from Graham Carmody's back alley last night? She hadn't even mentioned them to Drayton and Haley yet. But she'd have to. In fact, she wanted to. She'd lay out what she knew, what she suspected, what appeared to be evidence, and get their opinions. After all, three heads were better than one!

17

"*Don't get the* seaweed wet!" warned Drayton. "If you do, the entire California roll will be soggy and completely inedible. And be sure to wrap cellophane around them so you can roll them snugly. Otherwise the darn things just crumble apart on you."

"I'm not going to blow the California rolls," scoffed Haley. "And stop being so futsy." She slapped the back of Drayton's hand as he reached over to poke an avocado and check its ripeness. "The rice has been cooked perfectly, the crab is delightfully pink and fresh, and the avocados are ripe. And by the way, Mr. Conneley, who appointed *you* chief cook and bottle washer in *my* kitchen? Theodosia!" Haley called at the top of her lungs. "Will you *pleeease* put Drayton to work somewhere else? He's making me crazy!"

"Drayton," said Theodosia, "I really could use your help out here." She scanned the room, noting the positions of the tables.

"What?" he said grumpily, emerging from between the green velvet curtains.

"What with all the moving about of tables, the proportions seem a little out of whack," she said. "Can you work some of your magic?"

Somewhat mollified by her request, Drayton scanned the room with an appraising eye. "Well, there's your problem right there," he told her. "You've got two tables absolutely *jammed* against the fireplace." He threaded his way through the mazes of tables, pulled two of them away from the fireplace. Then he looked about the room and made a few more adjustments. Tables were angled, chairs pushed in, the head table also angled slightly.

"Now for the bonsai," he said as he bent down and pulled bonsai trees from the two large black plastic trays he'd used to transport them. "Let's place the small Japanese junipers and dwarf birches on the smaller tables." He quickly began arranging pots of bonsai. "And the larger bonsai, like this elm forest and this taller tamarack, on the larger tables."

"It looks wonderful," said Theodosia once he'd finished his arrangement.

"What time do the guests arrive?" Drayton asked for about the fiftieth time.

"The invitations specified three. Of course, some folks always arrive a little earlier; a few will dash in late as usual. If we plan on serving our Japanese tea and goodies from about two-thirty to four, we should be right on."

"Maybe I should check on Haley again," said Drayton.

"Oh look," said Theodosia as the door to the shop swung open, "here's Hattie with your ikebana centerpiece."

And as Drayton rushed to greet her, Theodosia breathed a sigh of relief and thought to herself, *Saved by the bell.*

By three-fifteen, the reception was in full swing. Delaine had been the first to arrive, bringing with her Cordette Jordan, the woman who owned Griffon Antiques over on King Street.

Brooke Carter Crockett and Aerin Linley followed on their heels, and shortly thereafter, Miss Dimple and Jessica Sheldon from Pinckney's Gift Shop came rushing in.

There was about a five-minute lull and then a second influx of guests poured in. Angie Congdon from the Featherbed House, Lillith Gardner, one of the partners at Antiquarian Booksellers, Nell Chappel from the Chowder Hound Restaurant, and at least two dozen more friends from in and around the historic district.

Drayton was in his element, alternately pouring tea, answering questions about bonsai, and doing a major amount of schmoozing.

Theodosia stayed near the front door, where she could serve as official greeter, and Haley was kept busy restocking tidbits of sushi and kushi-yaki on the main buffet table, in between dashing to the cash register to ring up sales on their new T-Bath products.

The din of conversation rose, as did the clink of cups and the squeal of voices.

"Did you really design this cunning packaging?" asked Nell Chappel. She held up a package of T-Bath Green Tea Soak with its elegant celadon green wrapper and typography done in a Japanese dry-brush style. "It's so elegant and Zen-like," she exclaimed.

Then, just when it looked as though they couldn't squeeze one more person into the Indigo tea Shop, an entire jitney packed full of tourists stopped in front of the shop and a dozen women came tumbling in for tea.

Theodosia met them at the door. "I'm sorry, but we're having a reception here today."

They crowded around her, peering curiously over her shoulder.

"We were looking forward to a spot of tea," said one lady with a pouf of blue hair.

"Of course you're welcome to come in and help yourself to tea," Theodosia said, "but I'm not sure I can offer you a table and a quiet respite today."

"What's your reception for?" asked another lady and Theodosia quickly explained the concept of the T-Bath products.

There were cries of *How wonderful!* and *Can we buy, too?* and the ladies came pouring in to join the ranks of the already jostling throng.

"Theo!" cried Delaine. She waved frantically from across the room as she clutched a sweetgrass basket filled with T-Bath products. "I simply *adore* your new products," she said, making extravagant mouth gestures as she pushed her way through the crowd.

"Thanks, Delaine," said Theodosia. "Your praise is much appreciated." She hadn't been able to speak privately with Delaine earlier and decided to take the opportunity now. It was funny, she thought, sometimes conversations could be the most private when you were surrounded by a crowd of people who were busy paying attention to something else.

"Lavender Luxury Lotion," exclaimed Delaine, digging into her basket of products. "And Green Tea Feet Treat. Marvelous! You know, I wouldn't be averse to stocking a few of your T-Bath items in my shop."

"I appreciate the offer," said Theodosia, "but let's talk about it later, shall we?"

"Of course, Theo," said Delaine. "If you're too *busy* to discuss it now."

"Delaine," began Theodosia, "Timothy Neville tells me that your diamond watch was found in Claire Kitridge's desk at the Heritage Society."

Delaine knit her perfectly plucked brows together. "Yes," she said, "the police called me earlier about that. I meant to tell you. Isn't it strange? And all the time I've been volunteering there, I considered Claire to be an extremely honest and trustworthy person. Salt of the earth, really. It's funny how people can fool you. And disappoint you, too," she added.

"Do you really believe Claire stole your watch?" asked Theodosia.

Delaine was suddenly reluctant to meet Theodosia's gaze. "Well, *someone* did," she said vaguely. "Along with everything else."

By *everything else,* Theodosia knew Delaine was still stewing mightily about the missing wedding ring.

"When did you first decide your watch was missing?" asked Theodosia.

Delaine shrugged. "I don't know. Maybe before I went to Savannah for the funeral. Maybe the day I got back. I'm not exactly sure. It's all a little fuzzy. I certainly had *other* things on my mind."

"Is it possible you took your watch off while you were at the Heritage Society?" Theodosia knew that, as a volunteer for the Heritage Society,

Delaine spent countless hours there. "Could you simply have misplaced it? If you did, someone might have found your watch and put it in Claire's desk for safekeeping."

"Well . . ." said Delaine, "I *was* there Sunday morning for a while going over the numbers on ticket sales. And things were still in an uproar from the night before." She shrugged again. "I don't know, Theodosia. Don't let's get into it right now, there's so much that's still very painful for me."

"Please realize," said Theodosia, "that the Heritage Society's executive advisory committee wants to fire Claire."

Delaine looked surprised. "I thought she was just suspended."

"Delaine, *think,* please," urged Theodosia. "This is important."

Delaine suddenly turned flashing eyes on Theodosia. "My niece Camille was important, too. And her poor dead fiancé. And their wedding ring. What if Claire Kitridge was somehow involved in that tragedy?"

"You don't really believe Claire is a cat burglar, do you?" Theodosia asked gently.

Delaine pulled a hanky from her small baguette bag and daubed at her perfectly made-up eyes. "I don't know what to think anymore."

"Could someone have come into your house while you were in Savannah for the funeral?" asked Theodosia.

"Just Coop."

"*What,* Delaine?" said Theodosia loudly.

"I gave Cooper Hobcaw the keys to my house."

"Why?"

"Someone had to feed Sasha. I couldn't let my little darling go hungry now, could I?"

Sasha was Delaine's cat, a seal point Siamese that she absolutely adored.

"No, of course not," agreed Theodosia.

"Well then," argued Delaine, "don't you think Coop would have known if someone broke in or not? He's a lawyer." Delaine hesitated, rethinking what she'd just said. "Well . . . what I *meant* to say was that Cooper Hobcaw is extremely observant. He would certainly have noticed if a window was ajar or a door unlocked."

"You're right," said Theodosia. At this point she knew it was easier to agree with Delaine than argue with her. But she *was* mulling over the possibility that Cooper Hobcaw could have lifted Delaine's Chopard watch and somehow planted it at the Heritage Society.

"Theodosia, this is all so splendid," exclaimed Brooke Carter Crockett. Theodosia turned to find that Brooke and Aerin Linley were also loaded down with an assortment of T-Bath products.

"Isn't it just?" agreed Delaine, glad for the diversion. "And do you know, I'm actually *considering* carrying some of these marvelous products in my store?"

"Is she really?" asked Brooke as Delaine scurried off.

"I think we'll probably end up retailing everything here and on our web site," said Theodosia.

"Delaine *is* a bit of a dragon lady, isn't she?" said Aerin Linley with a wry smile.

"But a good customer of ours, too," said Brooke, in a tone that indicated enough had been said about Delaine Dish. "Oh, I almost forgot . . ." Brooke dug in her purse, pulled out a tiny gold box, and handed it to Theodosia. "For you."

"Brooke! What's this?" exclaimed Theodosia as she tentatively accepted the little box.

"Not much, really. Just a fun thing I put together."

"Go ahead, open it," urged Aerin.

Theodosia carefully lifted the lid on the box, then let out a squeak of surprise. "Is it my teacup?"

Brooke nodded. She had taken the colorful shards of Theodosia's shattered teacup of the other day, rimmed them with sterling silver and tiny bits of gold, and hung them on a charm bracelet.

Entranced, Theodosia lifted the bracelet from the box. The results of Brooke's efforts were spectacular. The broken pieces that had looked so sad when they were lying on the floor now gleamed and danced with a whole new life.

"It's spectacular," said Theodosia. She clutched Brooke's hand. "I don't know what to say."

"Don't say anything. Just wear it in good health," said Brooke. "As we shall continue to drink your tea in good health."

"But it must have taken so much time to create," Theodosia protested.

Brooke waved a hand dismissively. "Really, it's not that big a deal. I buy the silver in small, thin strips anyway and it's extremely malleable. It only takes a few minutes to outline each piece, then pinch everything into place. From there on it was just straight ahead soldering and jump rings. Jewelry Making 101."

"Well, it looks like a million bucks," said Theodosia as she watched the colorful teacup pieces dance and jingle in their reincarnation as charms.

"Think of it more as a priceless memory of your mother's china," said Brooke.

"Theo," said Aerin, who had been watching her with a barely contained smile. "I have an interesting proposal for you."

Theodosia turned inquisitive eyes on Aerin.

"I have a dear friend who's the producer for *Windows on Charleston* at Channel 10. She's always looking for interesting guests and I mentioned your name—"

"Oh, I don't think—" began Theodosia.

"And she mentioned that she'd *love* to have you on!" finished Aerin. "She saw the write-up on you and the T-Bath products in the Style Section and was really intrigued."

"Theodosia *would* be perfect, wouldn't she?" interjected Drayton. He'd come up behind the three of them and overheard part of the conversation. "There's been such an enormous resurgence in tea drinking. And of course, the Charleston Tea Plantation, the only tea plantation left in the United States, is practically in our backyard. Their American Classic Tea has been the official White House Tea since 1987 and has also been designated Hospitality Beverage of South Carolina."

Aerin clapped her hands together. "That's so *perfect,* Drayton. Exactly the kind of sound bite they're always looking for. Theodosia could expound on tea lore as well as talk about contemporary tea drinking. Maybe even share recipes."

"It *would* be a fun piece," agreed Brooke.

"We'll look into it," Drayton assured them.

"Be sure to mention my name," said Aerin.

"What are you doing?" Theodosia hissed at Drayton when she had him alone.

"Encouraging you to get a gig," he said with a poker face.

"What if I don't want to get a gig?"

"Think about it, Theo," said Drayton. "What if you could actually land a *segment* on a local TV show? Think what it could do for business!"

Theodosia glowered at him. "You're using a marketing strategy to try to persuade me. That's how I used to handle clients. Persuade them by pointing out the financial upside."

Drayton smiled. "Then you of all people should want to explore this opportunity. See if you can find out any more from Aerin, will you? She's really a great person to know, exceedingly well connected."

"Drayton . . ." Theodosia began. She still hadn't had a chance to tell him about her visit to Graham Carmody's house last night, and her strange discovery of the Internet auction printouts was percolating in her brain.

"Hmm?" he asked as he looked over her shoulder, his face suddenly lighting up. "Well, look who's here! Hellooo!"

"Oh, my gosh," exclaimed Theodosia as her Aunt Libby walked through the door. "What are *you* doing here?"

Libby Revelle squared her narrow shoulders and gave her niece a mildly inquisitive look. "You invited us, don't you remember?"

"Yes, of course. But I never expected you to show up."

Libby turned to Margaret Rose Reese, her companion and housekeeper. "It seems we're a bit of a surprise," she said dryly.

"You're a wonderful surprise!" exclaimed Theodosia as she suddenly threw her arms around Aunt Libby and planted a kiss on her smooth cheek. She released her, then repeated her motions with a slightly embarrassed Margaret Rose.

"Oh, honey," protested Margaret Rose, who struggled to maintain the stern facade she'd honed to perfection from years spent as a housekeeper for an aging Episcopalian minister, "you don't have to go all gushy. It's just us." But she was pleased anyway.

"We decided to make an evening of it," declared Aunt Libby.

"Margaret Rose and I have been stuck out at Cain Ridge for what feels like forever."

Cain Ridge was the former rice plantation out in the low-country where Aunt Libby and Theodosia's father had grown up.

"Our master plan," continued Aunt Libby, "was to drop by your little reception, then treat ourselves to dinner at the Women's Club. Afterwards, we're going to soak up a little culture at the symphony."

Theodosia stared at her. "*I'm* going to the symphony tonight. With Jory Davis."

"Good," declared Aunt Libby with a sly grin. "Then you and your gentleman friend can buy us both a nice Dubonet with a twist during intermission" And with that, Aunt Libby pushed her way into the crowd, eager to get reacquainted with old friends and enjoy a good chat.

❧ 18 ❧

The haunting strains of *Nessum Dorma* from Puccini's opera *Turandot* filled the auditorium as the symphony orchestra played their fourth piece of the night. Normally, the symphony offered three concert series over the course of their season—Chamber Music, Classical, and Pops. But tonight's gala was a special concert, an opera venue that featured a medley of work from such opera greats as Puccini, Verdi, and Rossini.

On the stage, Timothy Neville played first chair in the violin section. In the audience, sitting center stage, fifteen rows back from the orchestra, Theodosia and Jory Davis listened with rapt attention. Off to their left and a few rows down were Aunt Libby and Margaret Rose. Before the auditorium lights had dimmed, Theodosia had spotted Delaine and

Cooper Hobcaw over to her right, their heads together, whispering conspiratorially.

The conductor bobbed and wove with the sweetly lyrical music. Then, as the final elegant notes hung in the air, he spun on his heels, his baton held aloft, and bowed deeply. The packed house rose to its feet and thunderous applause flooded the hall.

Jory Davis gazed down at Theodosia. She could see in his eyes that he approved of how she looked tonight. She'd dressed in a short silver sheath and left her auburn hair loose so that it fell over her shoulders.

"Want to stroll down to the lobby for a drink?" Jory asked. "We've got a good twenty minutes before the second half of the concert begins."

Theodosia's shining face smiled up at him. "Love to," she said.

Everyone seemed to have the same idea, and by the time they'd elbowed their way to the small bar, it was six deep in thirsty customers. It seemed that almost every opera lover was also eager for a cold refreshment.

"I've got an idea," said Jory, taking Theodosia's elbow and steering her away from the knot of people. "Let's sit at one of those little tables over by the window. I actually believe there are waiters who'll shuttle drinks to us."

Theodosia followed Jory to a tiny black enamel table and seated herself on an even tinier black enamel folding chair.

"I wonder where Aunt Libby and Margaret Rose are?" said Theodosia, looking around, trying to peer over heads.

"Maybe they didn't come down for intermission after all? Oh, here we go," said Jory as a waiter dropped two white bar napkins on the table. "Theo, what would you like to drink?"

"White wine, please," she said as she continued to scan the crowd.

"Glass of white wine," Jory repeated to the waiter, "and a bourbon and water."

Theodosia glanced up just as the waiter finished making a note of their drink order and turned to leave. Recognition jolted her and she instinctively clutched at Jory Davis's arm. The waiter who'd just taken their drink order was none other than the young man she'd paid a surreptitious visit to last night! Graham Carmody!

Amazing, she thought to herself. *The very same waiter who was working at the Heritage Society the night the Blue Kashmir necklace disappeared and at the Lady Goodwood Inn when Captain Corey Buchanan was killed! And now he's turned up here.*

As Theodosia stared at the retreating back of Graham Carmody, she realized that, if the young man really *was* a cat burglar, his job as a waiter was the perfect ploy to put him in close contact with potential victims! What better way to check out which ladies were wearing diamond earrings or flashing an emerald bracelet or carrying a Judith Leiber jeweled purse? You could spot your mark and then pounce!

"It's perfect," Theodosia uttered aloud, surprised at the simplicity of it all. Because when you thought about it, working as a waiter for an upscale caterer really *was* a clever cover.

Jory Davis smiled at her, apparently assuming her remark referred to their evening together thus far. "Glad you're having a good time," he replied. "You seemed a bit distracted earlier, but I chalked it up to a hectic day."

"Jory," she said, "we need to talk."

Jory gazed at her anxiously. "Okay," he said slowly.

Theodosia saw the worried look on Jory's face and hastily reassured him. "No, this isn't about us. This isn't one of those *We need to talk because I just want to be friends* kind of things."

Exhaling with a mock sigh of relief, Jory suddenly turned sober. "Hey, you're really upset, aren't you?"

She nodded.

"Tell me what's going on," he urged. "Let me help."

"Okay," she agreed, "but let's get our drinks first. And move outside. You'll see why in a moment."

Once their drinks arrived, they carried them out to a small patio directly off the lobby. The night was cool and the beginnings of a full moon bobbed overhead. *Halloween's in two nights,* Theodosia reminded herself. A haunting night, a night filled with mystery. Then again, she just might have as much mystery and intrigue as she needed right now!

Settling down on a wide bench, Theodosia took a quick sip of wine, then held Jory's hand in hers as she slowly related to him the events of the past week.

She told him about the mysterious intruder she and Earl Grey had chased from Harlan Wilson's hospital room.

She told him about Cooper Hobcaw and his evening runs through the historic district. Explained that just when Cooper Hobcaw was given custody of the key to Delaine's house, her expensive Chopard watch suddenly turned up missing. Then she related how the watch had been discovered in Claire Kitridge's desk at the Heritage Society, thanks to an anonymous tip.

Theodosia's suspicions about the waiter, Graham Carmody, came as a complete surprise to Jory. So much so, in fact, that when the strains of the opening overture came wafting out, he asked Theodosia if she'd rather stay there and keep talking.

"Absolutely I would," she told him.

"You're sure you don't mind missing the second half?" he asked. "They're doing Bizet's *Carmen*."

"I've got it on CD. Besides, this is more important, don't you think?"

"It's fascinating as hell, I'll give you that much," said Jory. He frowned, set his empty drink glass down next to his feet. "Okay, let's go back to the first event. The engagement party. That's when everything seemed to kick into high gear."

"Right," said Theodosia. "That's when things came to *our* attention. Drayton's and mine. And Haley's and Delaine's, too, I guess. Then we found out that other valuables had been stolen previously." Theodosia took a final sip of her white wine. "Camille's wedding ring was appraised at something like sixty or seventy thousand dollars." She shrugged. "I don't know the value of the other items that have been stolen, but I'd say our cat burglar has been making quite a haul."

"Only the insurance companies know for sure," said Jory. "But let's see what kind of case we can build against Cooper Hobcaw. Do you remember seeing him after the ceiling crashed in at the Lady Goodwood?"

"Yes," replied Theodosia. "And he was absolutely soaked to the bone. Dripping all over the carpet. But he'd ostensibly run out to flag down the ambulance."

"So that's circumstantial evidence," said Jory. "And we know Cooper Hobcaw likes his nightly jaunts through the historic district. But we don't have proof as to whether he's casing homes or just stretching his legs."

Theodosia snuggled against Jory's shoulder. It was comforting knowing he was securely on her side.

"And this waiter . . ." Jory began. "The one that's here tonight."

"Graham Carmody," said Theodosia.

"He's a real wild card. Turns up like a bad penny." Jory Davis rubbed a hand through his curly hair. "Did you get a good look at those computer printouts you lifted?"

"Pages and pages of Internet auction bids."

"And all on the sale of antiques and jewelry," mused Jory. "I'd say that's fairly incriminating." He thought for a minute. "Let me run a check on this Graham Carmody, see what turns up. You never know, he could have an arrest record."

"What about Cooper Hobcaw?" asked Theodosia.

"We won't find anything there. If he had a record, he wouldn't be doing the kind of lawyering he is."

"There's one person we really haven't discussed," said Theodosia.

"The woman from the Heritage Society?"

"Right," said Theodosia. "Claire Kitridge."

"Doesn't feel right," said Jory.

"Doesn't to me, either," agreed Theodosia. "Why would Claire swipe Delaine's watch then plant it in her own desk? That hardly seems logical." On the other hand, Theodosia thought to herself, what was overtly illogical was often discounted by investigators. They often assumed criminals would act in a certain pattern or mode. So Claire could be dumb like a fox.

"Anyway," said Theodosia, "I get the feeling that any one of our suspects had the talent and wherewithal to snatch Delaine's watch and plant it in Claire Kitridge's desk. And the access," she added.

Jory nodded. "They're all clever enough, that's for sure."

"So what's next?" asked Theodosia.

"Not sure," said Jory.

Theodosia gazed up into the night sky. The moon was almost as round and orange as a wheel of cheddar. "If I had to put money on one of them," she mused, "I think I'd pick Graham Carmody."

"Why so?" asked Jory.

"Because of his familiarity with the layout at the Heritage Society. He's worked there several times as a waiter. Knows the kitchen and back hallways and such. Plus people don't usually give waiters a second glance. Especially when they're busy partying and schmoozing it up."

As the moon continued to rise, full and round in the night sky, they talked back and forth, tossing around various theories. Finally, people began spilling out of the concert hall.

"It's over?" said Theodosia. "We missed the entire second half?"

"Looks that way," said Jory.

Good heavens, she thought. *And we aren't any closer to finding an answer. But at least I feel better having talked it all over with Jory.*

"Isn't that your Aunt Libby over there?" asked Jory. "With her friend?"

Theodosia peered at the spill of people pouring down the steps. "Yup, that's her."

"Want to go say hi?"

Theodosia smoothed her skirt and stood up, took Jory's hand firmly in her own. Together they crossed the plaza toward the oncoming rush of concert goers.

19

Haley cast an appraising eye at the yellow froth that bubbled in the top pan of her double boiler. It looked good, she decided, was sticking together nicely. Grabbing a wire whisk, she added the last of the sugar and lemon zest, then continued to whisk the mixture as it cooked. Finally, when her concoction began to thicken, she removed the pan from the stove and began to add soft fresh cream butter, feeding it in a little at a time.

"My goodness, Haley," marveled Drayton as he stepped into the kitchen, "it smells absolutely divine in here. What magic are you whipping up this morning?"

She held up the pan for him to see. "Lemon curd. And it *does* smell wonderful, doesn't it?"

"You're making *real* lemon curd?" he asked in amazement.

"Sure. It's a snap, really. Just four simple ingredients. Eggs, lemon, sugar, butter."

"Yes, but you have to know exactly what to *do* with the ingredients. And it's not just proportions, the cooking times are quite exacting, too. And then there's the double boiler thing."

"Are you saying I don't know how to make fresh lemon curd?" Haley demanded with a crooked smile.

"No, I'm just saying it's a tricky proposition at best."

"Proof's in the tasting," said Haley as she held up a wooden spoon with a swirl of yellow gracing the end.

Obediently, Drayton tasted the dollop of lemon curd. "Oh my goodness!" he exclaimed. "This *is* good. Sweet but subtly tart, too. Layers of flavor."

"My grandmother's recipe," explained Haley. "And if it's any consolation to you, those are the same things *she* said. Awfully tricky, got to get the proportions just so, and a double boiler is a must."

"But you mastered it," said Drayton, still impressed.

"Of course."

"And you plan to serve it with . . ." prompted Drayton.

"There's a couple pans of shortbread in the oven," said Haley. "But lemon curd keeps for a good month once it's refrigerated, so when we do cakes for afternoon tea, it'll make a great topping."

"Morning, Theo," Drayton called as he heard the back door click open. "How was the concert last night?"

"Yeah," called Haley, "I bet it was great, huh?"

Theodosia stood in the doorway of the tiny kitchen and nodded enthusiastically. "Wonderful." She didn't have the heart to tell them she'd listened halfheartedly to the first half, then spent the second half outside, trading cat burglar theories with Jory Davis.

"Timothy was playing first violin, I take it?" said Drayton as he grabbed a silver tray and followed Theodosia into the tea shop.

"And doing a masterful job," Theodosia assured him.

"I'm baffled as to how the man does it," said Drayton. "Poor Timothy is worried sick about the public opening of the Treasures Show tomorrow night, yet there he was playing with the symphony," said Drayton. "He's really quite remarkable."

"I agree," said Theodosia as the two copper tea kettles Drayton had put on to boil just minutes earlier began to sing their high-pitched duet. "So what's on tap for this morning?" she asked him.

Drayton reached overhead and pulled down tins and jars of loose tea. "I thought I'd do pots of Earl Grey and Assam, which are nice and mellow and traditional, although this particular Assam *is* a trifle malty. Then I'll mix things up with a couple blends, perhaps a cinnamon spice and a ginseng plum. Of course, if someone has a special request, we'll oblige them as always."

"Wonderful," said Theodosia. She still felt a little discombobulated from last night. After her intense discussion with Jory Davis, she'd had dreams about cat burglars all night long. *Got to get my head in the game,* she told herself as the door swung open and the morning's first customers came drifting in. *Stop worrying about creepy cat burglars.*

"Oh," said Haley as she sped past Theodosia with plates of shortbread topped with her still-warm lemon curd, "I forgot to give you this." She handed over a large brown envelope. "I guess someone must have slipped it under the door. Anyway, it was lying on the floor when I opened up this morning."

Theodosia took the envelope from Haley and glanced at it curiously. The envelope was a number ten, business size, made of brown craft paper. Glued to the front was a white label with a single typed word, *Theodosia*.

"Wonder what it is?" she said.

Haley, who was busy gathering napkins and placing forks on plates, shrugged. "Don't know," she said, unconcerned. "Maybe a thank-you note from someone who attended yesterday afternoon's reception?"

Theodosia grabbed a butter knife, slipped it under the gummed flap of the envelope to open it. She pulled out a piece of paper and unfurled it. As she began to read, her brows knit together and a frown creased her normally placid face. It was a note all right, but not of the thank-you variety. Instead, a very strange message had been laser-printed on a sheet of plain white paper.

> *Twinkle, twinkle, little bat*
> *How I wonder where you're at.*
> *Up above the world you fly,*
> *Like a tea-tray in the sky.*

"What is it?" asked Haley, suddenly aware that Theodosia had gone silent.

Wordlessly, Theodosia handed the note to Haley and watched as she read it.

Haley's face changed from polite interest to utter confusion. "What the heck . . . ?" she said. "Is this crazy little ditty supposed to mean something?"

"It's a passage from *Alice in Wonderland*," said Theodosia.

"Yeah, great. Fun kids literature and all that. But why send it to you? And without a signature yet. Is this supposed to be some kind of inside joke?"

"I'm not exactly sure," said Theodosia. "But I get the feeling that it might be . . . it could be . . . some kind of challenge."

"Holy smokes!" exclaimed Haley, realization starting to dawn. "Because you've been poking around . . . Hey, Drayton!" She motioned frantically for Drayton to come over to the counter.

Drayton came hustling over immediately. "What's wrong?" he asked, taking in the very sober looks on both their faces.

Haley thrust the mysterious note into Drayton's hands. "Take a look. I found it stuck under the door this morning."

"Addressed to Theodosia?" he asked as he reached into his jacket pocket, pulled out his glasses, and slid them onto his nose.

They both nodded.

Drayton studied the note intently. Finally, he looked up and met their gazes. "It's a passage from Lewis Carroll's *Through the Looking Glass*," he said.

Haley bobbed her head eagerly. "That's what Theodosia said. Gosh, you two are so incredibly well read. Makes me want to change my major back to English lit."

"Haley . . ." warned Drayton with an owlish look. "I don't think this was intended as a lighthearted little note."

"Theodosia called it a challenge," Haley told him.

"Indeed, it could be," said Drayton. "Witness the teatime reference that clearly relates to us."

"And what about the *little bat* business and *up above the world you fly?*" asked Haley.

"I don't know," said Drayton. "It's strange, I'll give you that much. I get the feeling they're slightly left-handed inferences as to what's been going on around here lately. Flying around, looking around, something like that."

"Mm-hm," said Haley, not completely absorbing all of Drayton's words.

"In other words, a taunt," said Drayton, heavily enunciating the *t*'s.

"You mean someone might be *daring* Theo to take them on?" asked Haley. "Someone being this cat burglar guy?"

"I suppose one could interpret it that way," said Drayton.

"Whoooa," said Haley. "Ain't that a kick."

"It means you've struck a nerve," said Drayton, looking directly at Theodosia.

Theodosia managed a thin smile. "Gulp," she said. She meant her remark to be humorous, but nobody laughed.

Drayton refolded the note, handed it to Theodosia. "We'd better talk about this when we're not so busy."

Theodosia was still standing at the counter with the folded note in her hand when Aerin Linley came bustling in a few moments later.

"Hey there," she greeted Theodosia. "Can I get a couple cuppas to go? Anything you've got ready is fine. As long as it's not sweet."

"Absolutely," said Theodosia, sliding the note across the counter and putting a little green Staffordshire teapot on top of it for safekeeping.

"You okay?" asked Aerin.

Theodosia looked up sharply. "Pardon?"

"Oh, you looked a little worried there for a moment. I would think you'd be doing handsprings right about now. Folks really went gaga over your T-Bath products yesterday afternoon. I hope you've called in a big reorder to your supplier."

"Don't worry," said Theodosia as she poured streams of freshly made Assam tea into dark blue take-out cups. "That's at the top of my to-do list today." Aerin's good humor was contagious and Theodosia was suddenly caught up in her enthusiasm. "I'm so glad you and Brooke were able to stop by."

"You know, I was perfectly serious about the TV show idea," Aerin said as she cocked her head and smiled at Theodosia. In her pink cotton crewneck sweater, khaki slacks, and beige leather slip-on shoes, she looked very sporty, far younger than her thirty-six or thirty-seven years. "You'd be great on-air," Aerin said with encouragement. "You're so pretty and vivacious, I'm sure you could deliver a great segment."

"Actually," said Theodosia, warming up to the idea, "I'd *love* to do a tea segment. A few folks are still under the illusion that tea is the drink of choice for blue-haired ladies in pillbox hats. Nothing wrong with blue-haired ladies in hats, of course, but tea's really come into its own as a contemporary drink."

"You're darned right it has," said Aerin. "When kids are chugging premixed chai like water, you know tea has hit mainstream! Ohh . . ." she exclaimed as Haley rushed by with another tray of shortbread and lemon curd. "Is that lemon curd? *Real* lemon curd? The kind you slave over a hot stove for?"

So, of course, Theodosia had to fill a small, square jar with lemon curd for Aerin to take along with her.

Jory Davis didn't call until they were caught up in the whirlwind that was lunch. "Hello?" said Drayton, deftly balancing the phone, a tray stacked with fruit and cheese plates, and a pot of tea.

"Hi, Drayton," said Jory. "Is Theodosia around?"

Drayton peered out over the tearoom and crooked a finger at Theodosia. She caught his meaning and signaled back. "She'll be with you in a second," Drayton told Jory.

Theodosia hurried across the room and snatched the phone up. "Hello?"

"Hey there," said Jory Davis.

"Hey there, yourself," said Theodosia. "You realize everyone here thinks I was soothed by music from *Rigolletto* and *La Traviata* last night."

"Well, you almost were," he said. "And admit it, wasn't snuggling under a full moon better?"

"You'll get no argument from me. Like I said last night, I can always listen to it on CD."

"Say," said Jory, "I know you're busy, heck, we're *both* busy, but I was able to work in some fast investigating this morning."

"Terrific. What did you come up with?" she asked.

Jory Davis sighed. "Nothing."

"Even on Graham Carmody?" Theodosia asked with surprise.

"Nada," said Jory. "No record. The guy's clean as a whistle."

"That's weird. I had a feeling there might be something."

"I couldn't even find an unpaid parking ticket," said Jory. "He's a model citizen."

"Hmm." Theodosia gazed out over the tea shop, noting that every table was filled and that Drayton and Haley were running around like chickens with their heads cut off. "Listen, why don't you come by for dinner tonight." She wanted to clue Jory in about the note that had been slipped under the door this morning, but right now wasn't the best time.

"Great!" said Jory.

"Hold on," said Theodosia. "I'm thinking about inviting Drayton and Haley, too."

"Oh, a *working* dinner," said Jory, with no less enthusiasm.

"When we get this cat burglar thing figured out," said Theodosia, "I promise dinner for two. With a full complement of candlelight and wine."

"And I shall bring the roses," laughed Jory. "Although I think I'll bring wine tonight as well. What time shall I plan to arrive on madame's doorstep?"

"Eight. And since you volunteered to bring wine, kindly make it white."

"I'll spend the rest of my day pondering the merits of a fine Vouvray versus a Chenin Blanc."

"Bye bye," she told him, laughing.

"My gosh," said Drayton, "I must have looked like the juggler in Cirque du Soleil, what with teapots in one hand and fruit and cheese plates in the other. Sometimes I yearn for the good old days when we only served tea."

"Adding a lunch service really has livened things up," agreed Theodosia.

"And contributed nicely to our bottom line," added Drayton.

Theodosia was keenly aware that they had run in the red for more months than she cared to think about. Now, this last year, they had clearly been in the black, with the last six months veering toward very respectable profits.

"Today will be a push from now on," declared Haley. "Friday afternoons are never all that busy. I guess people must take off early or go shopping or something. Anyway," she looked over at the three tables that were still occupied, "they're not here."

"How would the two of you like to join me for dinner tonight?" suggested Theodosia.

"Really?" squealed Haley. "I'd love to. I didn't have anything special planned."

"What about you, Drayton?" asked Theodosia. "I've invited Jory Davis to dinner, too."

"I'd be delighted," he said. "May I bring anything. Or do anything?"

"That goes for me, too," said Haley.

"Drayton, you just get yourself to my place by eight o'clock. Haley, if there's some leftover shortbread and lemon curd, maybe you could package it up and bring it along for dessert."

"Oops," said Haley, cupping a hand to her mouth. "We just served the last piece of shortbread. But there's still tons of lemon curd to use as topping. How about if I pop a cake in the oven?"

"Fine idea," declared Drayton.

"Only if it isn't too much work," said Theodosia. "After all, we're all still recovering from yesterday."

"I'm sure Haley can manage just fine," offered Drayton. "And if I could interject a thought, might I suggest a coconut cake?"

"Haley, can you manage?" asked Theodosia, amused by Drayton's ravenous desire for cake.

"Seeing how much it means to Drayton," she said, assuming an exaggerated hands-on-hips stance, "I'll try."

Detective Tidwell pushed open the door, eased himself into the tearoom. He let the door close behind him, yet made no effort to move to a table, preferring to stand there in an ill-fitting tweed jacket and porkpie hat, surveying the premises with a slightly haughty air.

Haley noticed him first. "Uh-oh," she said under her breath. "That *detective* is here again."

Theodosia looked over and gave a quick wave.

"He looks like he's been shrink-wrapped in tweed," murmured Haley.

"Ssssh," warned Drayton as he tried to stifle a grin and Theodosia hurried forth to greet Tidwell.

"Detective Tidwell, nice to see you again," said Theodosia in her best tea shop hostess patois. "Won't you have a seat?"

Tidwell shuffled to a table, lowered his bulk carefully.

"Can I offer you some tea?" asked Theodosia. *Goodness,* she decided, *in the wake of Tidwell's sullenness, I sound hideously chirpy.*

Tidwell gave a faint nod.

"Do you have a taste for anything in particular?" she asked.

"Surprise me," said Tidwell in an uncharacteristic move.

Theodosia bustled into the kitchen to scrounge a muffin while Drayton busied himself with a fresh pot of tea.

"Surprise him," Drayton muttered under his breath. "I'd like to surprise that fellow, all right."

Tidwell was already sipping his tea when Theodosia came back with a reheated muffin and small pot of peach jam.

"And this tea is . . ." said Tidwell, still not wasting any time on pleasantries.

"Earl Grey," said Theodosia. "Taste the bergamot?"

Tidwell gave a perfunctory nod. "I do. And a hint of something else, too."

"A touch of white tips," said Theodosia. "Just to lighten things up." White tips meant, literally, the white tips or most prized leaf of the plant.

"Excellent," said Tidwell, finally uttering a positive word. "I take it this is one of your own special Indigo Tea Shop blends?"

"Drayton created it. He calls it Shades of Earl Grey."

"Rather pleasant," responded Tidwell.

Theodosia smiled patiently. She was getting used to these strange exchanges with the venerable detective. They so often started out adversarial then veered toward semipoliteness.

Tidwell dribbled a spoonful of jam onto his muffin. "Not that you'd be interested, Miss Browning, but there has been a report of another theft in your neighborhood."

"Is that a fact?" said Theodosia. *Play it cool,* she told herself. *He's bursting to tell you, but if you ask him outright, he'll probably clam up.*

Tidwell shook his jowly head. "A rather expensive collectible disappeared last night from the Hall-Barnett House."

Built in the mid-eighteen-hundreds and located over on Tradd Street, the Hall-Barnett House had first served as a convent and then a private home. Now it was a small museum, a period house, furnished with the trappings of the era and open to the visiting public.

"I only mention it to you," added Tidwell, "because one of the items missing is a tea caddy."

Theodosia stared at him. *The tea caddy from the Hall-Barnett House was missing?*

"Ah," said Tidwell, noting her surprise, "you're familiar with that particular piece?"

"Of course," said Theodosia. "It's a lovely tea caddy crafted from tortoiseshell and inlaid with ivory. It's probably from the mid-eighteen-hundreds yet still in excellent condition."

"Yes," agreed Tidwell. "Worth quite a pretty penny, I'm told."

Several thousand dollars, Theodosia thought to herself. "And it's disappeared?" she said to Tidwell.

"That's the strange thing," replied Tidwell. "Mrs. Roman, the woman who was guiding the tours yesterday afternoon, swears she saw the tea caddy sitting in its rightful place on the fireplace mantel. Right before she locked up late yesterday."

"Do you believe her?"

"No reason not to."

"Then what do you suppose happened to it?" asked Theodosia.

Tidwell's eyes burned brightly even as his face assumed a hangdog expression. "I suppose, Miss Browning, it could have caught the fancy of your cat burglar."

"The Hall-Barnett House was broken into?"

"Let's just say a window was open upstairs."

Theodosia conjured up a mental picture of the Hall-Barnett House. Built completely of brick, it was tall and stately, fashioned in the Italianate tradition. *Hard to clamber up the side of a brick building, though,* she decided.

"Did the police find a ladder anywhere?" she asked. "Lying in the yard or stashed in the carriage house out back?"

"Nothing," said Tidwell. "If I had to hazard a guess, although I prefer *not* to, I'd say your cat burglar probably scaled a nearby tree then made a rather heroic leap."

"Why do you keep calling him *my* cat burglar?" asked Theodosia, somewhat testily.

"Because you were the first one to put forth the cat burglar theory," said Tidwell. "Pray tell what's wrong? Aren't you pleased? Here I thought for sure that you'd be pleased."

"No, of course I'm not *pleased,*" she cried out, and the frustration that had built up inside her for the past week suddenly began to explode. "Poor Drayton and Timothy Neville are worried sick about the public opening of the Treasures Show tomorrow night. Captain Buchanan was *killed* at the Lady Goodwood Inn . . . probably in an accident caused by this very same cat burglar. And now, because someone, presumably this cat burglar, stole Delaine's watch and stashed it in Claire Kitridge's desk, Claire stands to lose her job! So no, Detective Tidwell, I am in no way pleased. I am angry, frustrated, and worried beyond belief, but the very last thing I am is pleased!"

Drayton, upon hearing Theodosia raise her voice to Tidwell, suddenly grabbed a pot of tea and hustled over to their table.

"Everything okay here?" he asked as he approached.

"Fine," said Tidwell, putting a chubby hand over his teacup. "No need for a refill."

Drayton pointedly ignored Tidwell and focused his lined countenance squarely on Theodosia. "Are *you* okay?" he inquired.

Theodosia shrugged and her voice was slightly tremulous. "Yes. I'm just feeling . . . embroiled . . . in this rapidly unfolding cat burglar mystery."

"I believe Haley needs you in the kitchen," said Drayton. Now he shifted his gaze to Tidwell.

Theodosia waved a hand. "Haley's fine, Drayton. She's doing . . . I don't know . . . the cake. Remember?"

"I am quite certain Haley is in need of your assistance," repeated Drayton. Now his stare turned into a glower and Tidwell seemed to squirm just a bit under Drayton's intense scrutiny.

"What's the problem?" asked Theodosia, still not picking up on his cue.

"There's a dire problem with the coconut," said Drayton. "A question of toasting or not toasting, I believe."

Now it was Tidwell's turn to look mildly disconcerted.

Theodosia rose from her chair suddenly. "Forgive me, Detective Tidwell, but there *is* a pressing business problem I must attend to."

"Very pressing, indeed. I understand," he said and walked out.

"Are you all right?" asked Drayton as he pushed his way into the kitchen. "Because that detective seemed far more annoying than usual."

"I'm fine, Drayton," replied Theodosia. She was sitting on a stool, sipping a cup of tea. "But thanks for the rescue, anyway. I was pretty much at the end of my rope."

"Glad to be of assistance," said Drayton. He reached over and picked up a small plate decorated with purple flowers that was sitting on Haley's small counter. "What's this?" he asked.

"Remember the muffin plate I dropped the other day?" said Theodosia. "Along with the teacup?"

Drayton nodded. As he studied the plate, recognition dawned. "Oh. This is the plate that broke in half!"

"Haley fixed it," said Theodosia.

"I superglued it," volunteered Haley. "I was going to toss the pieces out, but after I saw the charm bracelet Brooke created, and how delighted Theodosia was at her reclaimed treasure, I decided to try a little glue."

"It was very sweet of you, Haley," said Theodosia.

"Not bad," said Drayton, turning the muffin plate over. "You can hardly see the repair."

"Thanks," said Haley. "It turned out to be kind of a fun project."

"We might have to tap your services for the Heritage Society," grinned Drayton. "Put you to work in our restoration department. Maybe your talents run toward restoring old prints and photographs, too."

"Speaking of the Heritage Society," said Haley, "are you-all still going ahead with the opening tomorrow night?"

Drayton grimaced. "Yes, we are. Up until yesterday there were still nasty rumblings from the executive advisory committee about canceling or even delaying the public opening of the Treasures Show. But of course, Timothy Neville fought them tooth and nail. He's quite adamant about adhering to his predetermined schedule. Don't you know, all the invitations have been sent out and all the publicity done. So what else could Timothy do? Plus, he didn't want to look like an alarmist. After all, this cat burglar fellow could have moved on, just like Detective Tidwell suggested."

"He hasn't," spoke up Theodosia. "In fact, it seems there's been another break-in. Tidwell just told me about it. That's the reason I was so upset."

Drayton put a gnarled hand to his head, rubbed his gray hair. "Oh, no. Did he mention where?"

"The Hall-Barnett House," said Theodosia.

"Wow," said Haley. "What was snatched this time?"

"An antique tea caddy," said Theodosia.

Drayton and Haley just stared at her.

"Weird," said Haley finally.

"So, like the shark with his territorial feeding habits, this fellow is still circling the neighborhood," sighed Drayton.

"And it looks like he's making tighter circles," said Theodosia. "The Hall-Barnett House is just a couple blocks from here."

Haley shuddered. "That feels a little *too* close for comfort."

"This new information is absolutely appalling," declared Drayton, fingering his bow tie nervously. "Who else knows about this?"

"I honestly don't know," said Theodosia.

"If Timothy or the executive committee find out, they'll for sure cancel the opening," said Drayton glumly.

"Then don't tell them," piped up Haley.

They were all three silent for a moment.

"What if," said Haley finally, "what if we could concoct some kind of scheme? Something that would trap this guy for good?"

"We already tried that," snapped Drayton, obviously feeling dispirited and dejected.

"Not really," said Haley. "The electronic devices you set up weren't exactly a *trap*. You said yourself they were more of a security precaution."

"Which didn't work," said Drayton with a dispirited air.

"Because the *electricity* went off," offered Haley. "Not because you guys screwed up."

The timer on the oven suddenly emitted a loud *ding*. Startled, Drayton gave a little jump, then watched sheepishly as Haley slipped an oven mitt onto her hand and opened the oven door. The two round cake layers looked perfect. Beautifully golden brown and pocked with tiny bubbles like the surface of a miniature moon. Smiling, Haley pulled the two pans of coconut cake from the oven.

"Perfect," murmured Drayton as he gazed at the cakes.

Haley set the cakes to cool on the scarred wooden table. "You just said a mouthful, Drayton," said Haley. "Because what you need *this* time is the perfect plan."

He stared at her. "I'm sure I don't know what you're jabbering about."

Theodosia, deep in thought, suddenly spoke up. "Tell me, Drayton, what's the most valuable object that the Heritage Society has in their collection?"

Sidetracked by Theodosia now, Drayton scratched his chin thoughtfully. "I don't know. I suppose it would be a silver tray made by Paul Revere. The Calhoun family had it in their possession for ages until they donated it to us two years ago." He threw Theodosia a dubious glance, as though he knew exactly what she was thinking. "But I *hardly* think Timothy's going to allow us to use a valuable such as that for bait. Especially in light of how our efforts failed so miserably at protecting the Blue Kashmir in the European Jewel Collection."

"Exactly," said Theodosia. "Which means we're going to have to pull something out of a hat."

"What?" Drayton's voice rose in a squawk. "What are you talking about?"

"And," said Theodosia, "it's going to have to be a very tasty little item." She gazed at Drayton, her blue eyes sparkling, her enthusiasm suddenly back with a vengeance. "Drayton, your friend still writes the arts column for the *Post & Courier,* doesn't he?"

Drayton nodded. "Sheldon Tibbets? Yes, he's still doing a fine job of it. But I don't see what—"

"Do you think you could persuade Mr. Tibbets to compose a special little blurb for us?" Theodosia said in a rush.

"I suppose I could," said Drayton slowly.

"Excellent," said Theodosia as her energy seemed to increase by leaps and bounds. "Because we're going to take the liberty of *augmenting* the Heritage Society's collection."

Drayton narrowed his eyes. "What exactly do you mean by *augment?*" he asked.

Theodosia suddenly jumped down off her stool. "The three of us are going to come up with a glitzy, glamorous new objet d'art. Something that's utterly irresistible to a professional cat burglar. And as the icing on the proverbial cake, you, my dear Mr. Conneley, are going to persuade your good friend, Sheldon Tibbets, to give our fabulous new collectible a big write-up in tomorrow's paper!"

Drayton stared at her. "You've got to be kidding."

"I couldn't be more serious," said Theodosia. What had Timothy Neville said to her just a few days ago? She racked her brain. *Oh, yes, he said, "There's no guarantee the disaster of last Saturday night won't be repeated."*

"We're going to deliver a guarantee!" exclaimed Theodosia. "A treasure so tasty and utterly irresistible that it's *guaranteed* to attract every salivating cat burglar from here to Palm Beach!"

Drayton was shaking his head and his voice carried a dubious tone. "But what object could possibly do that?" he asked.

Theodosia thought for a moment, recalling an article about so-called investment collectibles that had run not too long ago in *Business Week* magazine. *Let's see,* she thought, *the article mentioned that sports memorabilia were very big today. As well as the ever-popular antiques and artwork. And gold coins. And what else?*

Theodosia suddenly pushed her way through the velvet draperies back into the tea shop. Puzzled, Haley and Drayton followed in her wake.

Theodosia stood poised in the middle of the Indigo Tea Shop, her eyes wandering as her mind struggled to spin out a plausible scenario.

Something rare, she told herself. Intriguing, mysterious, with a huge intrinsic value. As her eyes continued to wander, they fell upon the display of teas that sat on one of the wooden shelves behind the old brass cash register. There was a huge selection. Boxes of loose tea from Higgins & Barrow Tea, as well as from Toby & Sons, and Chelsea and Worther.

Suddenly, her eyes focused on the box of Dunsdale Earl Grey Tea. It bore a delightful label, pale green with a heraldic crest surrounded by elaborate flourishes. In the middle was a silhouette of some nobleman. Perhaps, she surmised, the founding Dunsdale himself.

Inspiration suddenly hit her.

"How about a postage stamp?" suggested Theodosia.

Drayton blinked. Any enthusiasm he seemed to be mustering suddenly drained out of him. "Theodosia, I'm sorry but I've been collecting postage stamps for almost thirty years and the rarest one I have is an 1861 two-cent Andrew Jackson with a double transfer on the top left corner. A delicious specimen, to be sure, but not quite in the lofty realm of rare stamps. Not in the ranks that might attract the attention of a cat burglar, anyway."

Theodosia smiled placidly as Drayton continued.

"And Timothy Neville's been collecting stamps for over *forty* years and the rarest piece in his collection is a block of four 1851 twelve-cent Washingtons." Drayton paused and pursed his lips, thinking. "We'd have to come up with something far, far better than those if we really wanted to tantalize our thief."

"Like what?" asked Haley.

Drayton thought for a moment. "The Pony Express collection is worth a fortune. But I can't imagine where we'd lay our hands on a set."

"What about a one-cent Z grill?" asked Theodosia.

Drayton stared at her. "The 1869 Benjamin Franklin with the Z grill background? Are you kidding?" he snorted. "*Nobody's* got a one-cent Z grill."

"Aunt Libby does," said Theodosia with sudden calm. Aunt Libby had inherited a very fine stamp collection from her grandfather, Theodosia's great-grandfather.

"Really?" squealed Haley. She grabbed for Drayton's arm, ready to do a little dance. "A Z grill!" She hopped up and down, did a quick shuffle, then stopped suddenly. "What's a Z grill?"

"An exceedingly rare philatelic specimen, that's what it is," said Drayton. He peered at Theodosia and cocked his head in disbelief. "Really? Your Aunt Libby has one?" Now he sounded like Haley. Incredulous.

Yes, Theodosia mused to herself, a rare postage stamp would be perfect. Stamps in general were escalating in value, sometimes even outpacing other collectibles. Besides, rare stamps were portable, easy to hide, and relatively easy to cash in. They were an easy sell to private collectors, who were often compulsive about completing their prized collections. Who knows, a rare stamp might even be the perfect bait to lure a cat burglar.

Drayton was still looking eagerly at her, waiting for an answer. "You're quite sure it's a Franklin Z grill?"

Theodosia nodded and a slow smile spread across Drayton's face.

"Yes," he murmured, "that's the ticket, then. A stamp so rare perhaps only a handful of top collectors know about it or have even seen one."

"What's the story?" asked Haley. "Why will it be on display?"

Theodosia thought for a moment. "We'll say it's part of Drayton's collection." She gazed at him, liking the sound of it. "Will that make good enough fodder for a newspaper article?" she asked.

"I'll call Sheldon Tibbets now," Drayton told her.

20

Chicken Perloo has long been a dinnertime favorite in Charleston as well as the surrounding low-country. Really a type of pilaf or jambalaya, Chicken Perloo, usually pronounced PER-lo and sometimes spelled pilau, is a homey one-pot meal that combines chicken, onions, celery, butter, tomatoes, thyme, and that ever-popular Carolina staple, white rice.

Simmering and bubbling on the stove in Theodosia's kitchen, the Chicken Perloo emitted enticing aromas as Theodosia, Jory, Drayton, and Haley sat around Theodosia's dining table. First course was a citrus salad topped with sliced strawberries and toasted almonds.

"Are you sure we shouldn't check on the Chicken Perloo?" asked Drayton. He was seated closest to the kitchen door and was the one most tantalized by the flavorful aroma.

"Don't you dare lift the cover on that kettle," warned Theodosia.

Haley shook her head. "Why do men always want to take a peak?" she asked.

"Because that's how men are," said Jory Davis. "It's inherent in our nature. We're compulsive lid-lifters and oven-door openers." He took a sip of wine. "Curiosity is a wonderful thing," he added.

"Not when it causes a cake to fall," said Haley. "Remember that angel food cake I made last month? Drayton just couldn't resist. Had to sneak the oven door open and take a look. And what were the results of his unbridled curiosity? Bam. A nasty mess. The poor thing crashed like the *Hindenburg.*"

"Why blame me, when the true culprit was the humidity," protested Drayton. "Everyone knows you can't bake angel food cake when the air is completely saturated with humidity."

"We hadn't had rain in days," said Haley. She slid out of her chair and began collecting the empty salad plates. "I'll help you serve, okay?" she said to Theodosia.

"Great," said Theodosia. "And if Jory could pour some more wine, I think we're set."

It was a perfect dinner. Morsels of fresh, plump chicken blended with the tomatoes, celery, onions, and moist rice in a rich milieu. Not quite a stew, not quite a gumbo. And with Jory's crisp white wine and a pan of fresh-baked corn muffins, nothing else was needed.

No one spoke of cat burglars or the dilemma at the Heritage Society until dessert, when Haley's cake and lemon curd were served. And then it was Theodosia who began the discussion by bringing Jory Davis up to speed on the strange note they'd received that morning.

"It does seem like a cryptic warning," he said as he held the note in his hands, studying it. "It's tempting to just blow it off or chalk it up to a disgruntled customer, but I don't think that's the case here."

"Neither do we," said Theodosia.

"So you think it's from this cat burglar guy, too?" Haley asked Jory as she began collecting plates.

"It's possible," said Jory. He stared across the table at Theodosia and concern was apparent in his face. "Tell me again about your idea for tomorrow night?"

Earlier in the evening, when Jory Davis had first arrived and she was still chopping celery, she'd mentioned her plan for putting a rare postage stamp on display at the Heritage Society tomorrow night. Now she filled Jory in about how Drayton had convinced his friend, Sheldon Tibbets, to write a short blurb about the Z grill to run in tomorrow's edition.

Jory Davis leaned back in his chair and chuckled. "Sounds good. Although I must say, you three have exceedingly *active* imaginations."

"But do you think it will work?" pressed Drayton.

"Why not," said Jory, suddenly switching to a more serious demeanor. "Of course, not being a stamp collector or . . . what's the technical term?"

"Philatelist," filled in Drayton.

"Not being a dedicated philatelist," said Jory, "the stamp sounds intriguing. But not something I'd risk life and limb for. However . . ."

He gazed across the table at Theodosia, bathed in the glow of pink candlelight.

"I think that professional thieves are probably also knowledgeable connoisseurs," continued Jory. "My guess is they have a fairly good grasp of today's market value for oil paintings and jewelry and stamps and such. That's what drives them." Haley set a dessert down in front of him and Jory immediately helped himself to a bite of cake. "Mmn, good. That might also be your cat burglar's Achilles' heel, by the way."

"What do you mean?" asked Haley, fascinated.

"My guess is their knowledge is their downfall. It's how they eventually get caught. A professional thief *knows* the value of his ill-gotten merchandise, yet often ends up trying to negotiate with fences or unsavory dealers who *don't.* If these dealers get an inkling that something *is* of real value, they could easily flip on their so-called customer, report it to the insurance company, and pocket a nice fat reward."

"And if a cat burglar sells his stolen goods on the Internet?" said Theodosia.

Jory Davis knew she was referring to Graham Carmody. "That's a different story," he said. He looked around the table. "Have you told them about Graham Carmody?" he asked her.

And so Theodosia quickly related her tale of going to Graham Carmody's house, snatching the black plastic garbage bag, and finding it stuffed with computer printouts from various Internet auction sites.

"Theodosia," chided Drayton, "you continue to trample the boundaries of what is prudent and safe. Going to this Graham Carmody's house alone was far too impulsive."

"Yeah," agreed Haley, "you should have asked us to go along with you. Make a real outing of it!"

Drayton glowered at Haley. "That's not what I meant and you know it!"

"But look at the valuable information she picked up," argued Haley. "Up until now, did you think this waiter was a viable suspect?"

Drayton shrugged. "It was anybody's guess," he said.

"Right," said Haley. "And look where we are now." She flashed a lopsided grin at Drayton, who did his best to ignore her.

"Let's talk about tomorrow evening," said Drayton. "I'm exceedingly nervous about pulling this off."

"I think we all are," said Theodosia. "But at least we'll have our whole cast of characters assembled there."

"Graham Carmody is on the list as one of the waiters?" asked Jory.

"His employers at Butler's Express assure me he'll be there," said Drayton.

"Are we keeping an eye on Cooper Hobcaw?" asked Haley. "I'm still suspicious of him after you told me about his nightly runs through the historic district."

"Cooper Hobcaw will be attending with Delaine," said Theodosia. "After all, she's on the committee for ticket sales."

"What if he's cooling off over Delaine and getting interested in Aerin?" asked Haley. "I mean, the two of them really had their heads together when I saw them. It looked fairly intense. Maybe he's up to something?"

"I'll stop by Delaine's store tomorrow morning and have a chat with her," said Theodosia. "See what I can find out."

"So who else needs to be covered?" asked Jory.

"Claire Kitridge," said Theodosia. "She's kind of a wild card in all this."

"Will she be at the opening?" asked Jory.

"Certainly not as an invited guest," said Theodosia.

"I hardly think Claire will be there," replied Drayton, "seeing as how the poor woman's been placed on suspension."

"I'll watch her," volunteered Jory. "I've always wanted to be on a stakeout anyway."

"I'll babysit Earl Grey," piped up Haley, "but if anything big happens, you guys better promise to call me."

"So we're set," said Theodosia. "Our bait will be in place, now all we have to do is see if anyone comes sniffing after it."

"To the hunt," said Drayton, raising his glass of wine in a toast.

Theodosia, Jory, and Haley raised their glasses to join him. "To the hunt," they chorused loudly, startling Earl Grey from his bed and prompting a hearty *woof.*

Haley giggled as their wineglasses came together in a mighty *clink.*

Only Theodosia did not join in the laughter. To her, this was no laughing matter.

21

Clip clop, clip clop. Two great gray Belgian draft horses dipped their noble heads and shuddered to a halt on Meeting Street. Behind them, sitting in the brightly painted red and yellow carriage, visitors perked up and listened with rapt attention as their guide began a slightly theatrical narration about two of Charleston's so-called "haunted" houses.

Halloween, or All Hallow's Eve, was tomorrow night and the various carriage tours that plied the lanes and cobbled streets of the historic district were making the most of the spooky legends and ghostly sightings that were so much a part of Charleston folklore.

Theodosia was out with Earl Grey this Saturday morning. Together they were enjoying the fine cool weather and stretching their collective legs. Today, however, Theodosia had opted not to jog, but rather to stroll leisurely through the historic district as she pondered what events might possibly transpire tonight at the Heritage Society's public opening of the Treasures Show.

She was both dreading and looking forward to tonight. Hoping they'd be able to smoke this cat burglar out of his lair, of course, but nervous about the possibility of putting anyone in harm's way.

Cutting through Gateway Walk back to Church Street, Theodosia passed by St. Philips's Cemetery. Tomorrow night children would dare each other to run through here, she thought. As if these poor departed souls could cause anyone harm. No, she decided, it was the living that threw a wrench into things. It was the living you had to watch out for.

"You be a good boy and wait here," Theodosia told Earl Grey as she clipped his leash to the wrought iron fence next to the building that housed Cotton Duck, Delaine Dish's clothing store. "I'll be back in a couple minutes."

Earl Grey plopped himself down on the sunny sidewalk and gazed up at Theodosia as if to say, *No problem, I could use a break anyway.*

"Well, lookie who's come to call," sang out Delaine as Theodosia entered the store. "Miz Theodosia Browning."

"Hi, Delaine," said Theodosia as she gazed about at the funkiness and opulence that characterized Cotton Duck. Racks overflowed with casual cotton outfits as well as elegant silks. Antique cupboards, their doors flung open, were filled with a luxurious array of cashmere sweaters, silk scarves, beaded bags, and sparkling costume jewelry. Delaine might be a little over the top, Theodosia decided, but she was utterly brilliant when it came to fashion merchandising. On every buying trip that Delaine made, she focused on a specific palette of colors. Sometimes the clothes and accessories she brought back featured brilliant jewel colors such as emerald, purple, and hot pink. Sometimes they were more subdued shades such as persimmon and mulberry and loden green. But whenever you shopped in Delaine's store, you were guaranteed to find fabulous outfits and accessories that matched and blended beautifully. It was quite a talent, Theodosia had to admit.

"I was just reading the *Post & Courier,*" said Delaine. "Sheldon Tibbits gave tonight's Treasures Show another nice write-up."

"Oh, did he?" said Theodosia with as much innocence as she could muster.

"I certainly had no idea Drayton's stamp collection was so . . . elaborate," said Delaine.

Theodosia decided *elaborate* was Delaine's code word for *valuable.*

"Drayton's been collecting for an awfully long time," said Theodosia.

Delaine reached out and straightened a display of leather handbags. "A Z grill stamp. Now that's something you don't see every day. Nice of Drayton to allow it to be shown tonight."

Theodosia turned her attention to a rack of skirts and grabbed a black skirt in an attempt to stifle a giggle. She was quite sure Delaine had never even *heard* of a Z grill stamp until this morning's article.

"Oh, no, not *that* one, dear," Delaine suddenly protested. "A long black skirt is far too somber for someone like you." She hurried to Theodosia's side, snatched the offending black skirt from Theodosia's hands, and pawed hastily through the rest of the rack.

"This is what you need," she declared triumphantly as she held up a long, elegant silver skirt cut from thin crinkley cloth. *"Très elegant?"* she asked.

"It *is* gorgeous," Theodosia admitted as she gazed at the shimmery skirt.

"Perfect for tonight," declared Delaine. "If you pair it with . . ." Her eyes roamed across the stack of sweaters. "Ah, here's the perfect match," she said as she pulled a sweater out. "A perfect pearl gray cashmere. Cool and understated, but still delivering a hearty dose of va-voom."

Theodosia stood back and appraised the outfit. It was gorgeous. Silver and pearl gray. Very ice maidenish. Or Swarthmore 'sixty-two. She could accent the clothing with what? A colored gemstone pin? Maybe her garnet earrings?

Delaine held the clothes out enticingly. "Want to try them on?" Then, without waiting for an answer, Delaine spun on her heel. "Janine," she shrilled loudly to her perpetually harried assistant. "Put Theodosia in the large dressing room, will you?"

Minutes later Theodosia was out of the dressing room and doing a pirouette in front of the three-way mirror.

"Lovely," declared Delaine.

"Lovely," parroted Janine, who was perennially red-faced from rushing around trying to follow Delaine's often contradictory directives.

Theodosia smiled at herself in the mirror. Never had she once heard poor Janine express an opinion of her own. Then again, Delaine was opinionated enough for an entire room full of people. Oh well. She peered in the mirror again. Hmm . . . the outfit *did* look good. The long silver skirt gave her a nice, lean silhouette and the pearl gray cashmere sweater, which was baby-bunny soft, made her auburn hair shine. Yes, she decided, she'd wear the garnet earrings Aunt Libby had given her. Definitely.

"You'll wear it tonight?" asked Delaine, vastly confident in her recommendation.

"Why not," said Theodosia, throwing up her arms in mock defeat.

"Janine, be sure to let Theo take the skirt on a hanger," Delaine told her. "Don't go folding it or anything," she cautioned.

"Yes, ma'am," said Janine.

"I imagine you're looking forward to tonight as well," said Theodosia, catching Delaine's eyes in the mirror.

"A lot of us have worked very hard on this exhibition," said Delaine who, Theodosia knew, had headed ticket sales. "So yes, I am. As long as there are no *unusual* surprises."

"Coop will be there with you tonight?" asked Theodosia.

"Wouldn't miss it," Delaine declared breezily.

22

"I hope you realize," said Timothy Neville as he pulled Drayton aside, "that philatelists all over Charleston are positively drooling!"

Drayton wrung his hands nervously. "This wasn't actually my idea . . ." he began.

Timothy stared back at him with hooded eyes.

"This rare stamp display was Theodosia's brainstorm," explained Drayton. "Honestly. The stamp isn't mine. The Z grill really belongs to her Aunt Libby," he whispered.

Timothy gave a sharp nod, then gazed over at Theodosia, who was busily engaged in conversation with Delaine Dish and Cooper Hobcaw. Suddenly, an uncharacteristic grin split Timothy's ancient, sharp-boned face. "So that's the story, is it? Well good. Now let's just hope her little plan works!" he declared, giving Drayton a firm thump on the back.

"Isn't this fun," drawled Delaine, giving a little shiver as she slid her wrap off her bare shoulders. "Can you believe how many folks have turned out? I knew ticket sales were going well, but this is absolutely splendiferous!"

Cooper Hobcaw gave her an approving grin. "That's my girl," he told her. "Hits a home run every time."

The first night of the Treasures Show looked very much like a rousing success as hundreds of people streamed into the Heritage Society's great stone building. The red-carpeted lobby was thronged with new arrivals making the requested fifteen-dollar donation, and a waiting line of previously ticketed guests had already formed in the hallway that led to the exhibition rooms.

"Theo," said Drayton as he put a hand on her shoulder, "a moment of your time, please."

"You're looking dapper tonight," cooed Delaine as Theodosia turned her attention toward Drayton.

"And you, Miss Dish, are as ravishing as ever," Drayton said to Delaine, favoring her with a genteel half-bow.

"Don't you ever get tired of being obsequious?" Theodosia asked him as they hurried down the corridor together.

"Me? Never," declared Drayton with a sly grin. "Obsequious is my middle name. Drayton Obsequious Conneley. In fact, you can just call me Drayton O."

At the end of the corridor, Drayton steered Theodosia around a corner, slipping past the purple velvet cord that kept visitors in line, and led her into the largest of the two galleries.

It was a sight to behold.

The large gallery, paneled in cypress wood, gleamed with a welcoming glow. Tables and glass cases displayed the finest treasures from the Heritage Society's sizable collection. A collection of antique pewter tankards rested on a Hepplewhite sideboard. Silver candlesticks and gleaming bowls adorned a revolving Sheraton drum table. On a French Empire card table reputed to have once belonged to Napoleon was an antique Japanese Imari bowl.

Entranced, Theodosia's eyes drank in the various displays. Here was a portrait by Alice Ravenel Huger Smith, an eighteenth-century painter who had immortalized many of the old Carolina rice plantations in her moody, sienna-tinged paintings. And here were a dozen original Audubon prints. And hung on the back wall, a half-dozen painted portraits from the mid-seventeen-hundreds done by Charleston artist Jeremiah Theus.

"Oh, my," said Theodosia, "this is very impressive. You and Timothy and the rest of the crew have worked absolute wonders."

"Tasty pickings, no?" said Drayton. "And look over here." He guided Theodosia to a fall-front mahogany Chippendale desk that was lit from above by pinpoint spotlights. On it sat a collection of antique desk ware— a silver inkwell and matching pen, an ornate French clock of gilded bronze, a silver snuffbox. Propped in front of those accoutrements was a bound leather stamp album and displayed on a tiny glass pedestal next to it was the one-cent Z grill stamp. In the dim room, with just the lights from above, the blue stamp with the somewhat stern portrait of founding father Benjamin Franklin did look rather tantalizing. Especially in light of the rather boastful write-up it had received.

Theodosia's mouth twitched in a grin. "It's perfect," she declared.

"Does it look like bait?" asked Drayton under his breath.

Theodosia nodded. "I'm itching to grab it myself."

Reaching into the pocket of his gray wool suit, Drayton pulled out an antique pocket watch. "Eight o'clock on the noggin," he said. "So everything is in place for our little game?"

"Jory Davis is stationed outside Claire Kitridge's house even as we speak," said Theodosia. "Jory's got his cell phone, so he'll call and let us know if anything's going on. We don't expect Claire to show up here tonight, but if she does leave her house and heads for the Heritage Society . . . or anywhere, for that matter . . . we'll be the first to know."

"Outstanding," said Drayton. He gazed about the room, let his gray eyes settle once again on the display case that held the rare postage stamp. "Well," he said. "We know that Graham Carmody is here tonight—"

"You've seen him?" interrupted Theodosia. "You're *sure* he's here?"

Drayton nodded. "Last I peeked he was restocking crackers and tidbits of cheese at the buffet table."

"And we know Cooper Hobcaw is here because we just saw him with Delaine."

"Right," said Drayton. "So . . . we've got all our bases covered."

"We *hope* they're covered," said Theodosia as her cell phone beeped from inside her beaded evening bag.

She fished the phone out and pushed the *receive* button. "Hello?"

"It's me," said a voice on the other end of the line.

"It's Jory," Theodosia whispered to Drayton. "You're still at Claire Kitridge's house?" she asked with a shiver of anticipation.

"Not exactly," replied Jory. "Claire came out of her house about twenty minutes ago and jumped in her car."

"She's headed here!" cried Theodosia.

"No," said Jory, chuckling. "I tailed her for a couple miles until she pulled into some church parking lot. The Divine Redeemer, I think it was. Anyway, I think Claire's in there with some women's tatting group."

"You're sure she didn't sneak out the back?" asked Theodosia.

"Her car's still here."

Theodosia suddenly felt deflated. She'd been sure that if Claire was on the move, she'd be heading for the Heritage Society. "You're positive she's still inside?" she asked, disappointment in her voice.

"Yes, I'm sure she's in there," said Jory. "There's lacy stuff spread out all over the place."

Theodosia slid her cell phone back into her purse and looked around for Drayton. He seemed to have disappeared somewhere, but Timothy Neville was standing nearby, giving a glowing history of the Napoleon French Empire card table to a young couple.

"Timothy," she called.

Timothy excused himself and came over to Theodosia.

"Everything looks wonderful," she told him.

"Appearances are so deceptive, are they not?" he said as he pulled a letter from his jacket pocket. "Because things are *not* wonderful in the least."

"Timothy, what's wrong?" asked Theodosia.

"I received an envelope via messenger a few minutes ago. From Claire Kitridge." He handed the envelope to Theodosia. "Perhaps you'd like to see for yourself."

Theodosia flipped open the envelope. Inside a folded letter was a faded photograph, a black-and-white photo of two women standing in front of what looked to be a car from the early sixties. Big hood ornament, fins on the rear fenders. Theodosia continued to study the photo carefully.

"Oh no," she said finally.

"Oh yes," said Timothy.

Theodosia stared into Timothy's old face and saw sadness. "She's wearing the antique brooch," said Theodosia.

"In a photo that appears to have some age on it," added Timothy.

"So this is pretty much proof positive that the brooch *did* belong to Claire Kitridge."

"Read the letter. She states how the brooch has been in her family for quite some time. Passed down from her great-aunt."

"This still doesn't explain why Delaine's watch was found in her desk drawer, but it certainly clears her on the rumor of possibly selling stolen goods," said Theodosia slowly. She bit her lip. Still . . . this was not good. Not good at all. A lot of people had jumped to conclusions and now Claire Kitridge was left to pay the price. Feeling a bit sheepish, she decided she'd have to call Jory immediately and tell him to abandon his vigil at the church.

"I should never have listened to the executive committee," lamented Timothy. "I feel totally responsible for this."

"It's not your fault, really," said Theodosia. "A lot of us jumped to conclusions."

Timothy continued to look unhappy.

"Do you think you could persuade Claire to return to her job at the Heritage Society?" asked Theodosia. "Once this watch business is cleared up?"

Timothy shrugged. "Claire may still be upset and feel that unfair accusations will always be hanging over her head."

"Then what?" asked Theodosia.

"Then it's our profound loss," said Timothy.

Two hours rolled by and still nothing happened. Graham Carmody and the rest of the waiters began packing up all the dirty serving platters and leftover food and carried everything out to a white caterer's van that said BUTLER'S EXPRESS on the side. Now, as Theodosia and Drayton peered out the window at Graham Carmody, he was standing in a puddle of light with two other waiters, smoking a cigarette.

Theodosia made a quick appraisal of him. His tie was loosened, his shock of ginger-colored hair slightly disheveled, and he seemed tired. In fact, Graham Carmody didn't look at all like a professional cat burglar who was biding his time, poised to strike. He looked like a slightly pooped waiter who was about to go home, put his feet up, and catch the late-night headlines on CNN.

584 Laura Childs

"You think he's going to make a move?" asked Drayton hopefully.

"Are you kidding? The man looks like he's barely *able* to move," said Theodosia.

Drayton yawned. "I know the feeling."

"What a washout," said Theodosia. "I was sure something was going to pop tonight."

"Let's go back and check the two galleries," said Drayton. "Make sure."

"Okay," agreed Theodosia.

On their way back through the kitchen and down the hallway, they ran into Delaine and Cooper Hobcaw. Delaine was still flitting about like a social butterfly, chitchatting with guests, bragging about ticket sales, but Cooper Hobcaw looked as if he was ready to pack it in for the evening.

"Having fun?" Theodosia asked him.

Cooper Hobcaw stifled a yawn. "I'm out on my feet and Delaine here is still going strong."

"No jogging tonight?" said Theodosia.

"No nothing tonight," he told her.

Timothy was suddenly at Theodosia's side, touching her arm. Pulling her aside, he cast a glance about. When he was sure no one would overhear their conversation, he spoke.

"That waiter you had suspicions about?" said Timothy. "I spoke with him just a few moments ago. He was telling me how much he enjoyed the Treasures Show. It seems he's an amateur antique dealer himself. Spends every free moment scouring estate sales and flea markets for various items."

"Yes . . ." said Theodosia, waiting for the other shoe to drop.

"Then he sells them on the Internet," said Timothy.

"Graham Carmody told you this?" asked Theodosia.

"Yes," said Timothy. "He mentioned that he used to have a booth in one of the North Charleston antique malls, but now he does far better selling his finds on the Internet auction sites."

Oh, lord, thought Theodosia. *Did we leap to conclusions about Graham Carmody, too?*

"Did you mention this to Drayton?"

Timothy nodded. "Yes, I just spoke to him." He cast a quick glance over Theodosia's shoulder. "Here he is now."

"So Timothy's told you?" asked Drayton. "About Graham Carmody?"

"Afraid so," said Theodosia.

The three of them drew deep breaths and stared at each other for a few moments.

"Let's look at the positive side," said Theodosia. "We've just eliminated Claire Kitridge and Graham Carmody as suspects."

"At least for tonight," added Drayton. "I suppose any one of them could *still* be our thief." If anyone could sound down but still hopeful, it was Drayton.

"What about this Cooper Hobcaw fellow?" asked Timothy. "You were so suspicious of his late-night jogs."

"Cooper Hobcaw didn't even seem to *notice* any of the objects," said Drayton. "He just followed Delaine around with a slightly morose look on his face." Drayton looked about quickly. "If you ask me, Hobcaw's not as charmed by Delaine as he once was."

"Maybe, just maybe," said Theodosia, "our cat burglar decided it was far too risky to hit the Heritage Society a second time."

"Maybe," said Drayton, but his heart wasn't in it.

"Thank God," said Timothy, relief apparent on his face.

Theodosia reached for the old man's hand. "Timothy," she said, "thank you for letting us set this up tonight. I know you took a terrible risk."

"Theodosia," Timothy replied, his eyes bright with intensity, "if you can do anything, and I do mean *anything* to help get the Blue Kashmir necklace returned, I will be forever grateful."

It was eleven o'clock by the time Theodosia made her way upstairs to her apartment above the Indigo Tea Shop. She'd talked with Jory Davis on her cell phone one last time, thanked him profusely for keeping tabs on Claire Kitridge, then bid him good night.

She unlocked the door at the top of the stairs and pushed her way into her kitchen before realization dawned that she'd forgotten to swing by Haley's apartment to pick up Earl Grey.

"Oh rats," she said out loud, then stopped suddenly in her tracks.

Did I leave the light on in the dining room?

She thought she'd turned everything off except for the little light over the kitchen sink. That light was still on, winking at her. But there was a definite glow coming from beneath the door that led to the dining room.

Okay, then. Maybe Haley already let Earl Grey in. And he's in there now, curled up on his bed. Or on the couch. That hadn't been part of their plan, but with Haley, who knew what could happen? She was like a miniature sidewinder, always going off in different directions.

Well, decided Theodosia, *only one way to find out.*

Her heart pounding mildly, she pushed open the swinging door that led from the kitchen to her dining room and stepped gingerly into the room.

Every light in the dining room and adjacent living room was on! The cut glass chandelier hanging above the polished oak dining table blazed brightly.

And there, in the dead center of her dining room table, sat a tea caddy!

Theodosia stared at it, barely daring to breathe. The mild pounding in her chest suddenly accelerated to double time.

Is that the tea caddy that was stolen two days ago from the Hall-Barnett House? she wondered. She stared at the highly polished tortoiseshell. *Has to be.*

What is it doing here? Better yet, how did it get here?

Figure all that out later, her brain suddenly flashed. Just get out! And get out now!

Theodosia whipped down the stairway, made a mad dash across the cobblestone alley, and pounded on the door of Haley's small garden apartment. Theodosia could see that a light was still on and she could hear faint music.

"Haley, let me in!" Theodosia called.

"Is that you, Theo?" came Haley's voice from the other side of the door.

"It's me," Theodosia answered. "Open up. Hurry!"

"Oh, hi," called Haley as the lock was unlatched and the chain unhooked from the door. The door swung open inward and Haley appeared, dressed in pajamas and fluffy slippers. "Come for your good dog, I suppose . . ." began Haley. Then she stopped, her smile frozen in place as she caught the look of fear and utter confusion on her dear friend and employer's face.

"Theodosia," she said. "What's wrong?"

"Remember that sleepover we talked about?"

Haley nodded.

"This is it. Someone's been inside my apartment."

"They broke in?" Haley asked, horrified, as she grabbed Theodosia by the arm and pulled her quickly inside.

"I . . . I think maybe the lock might have been picked," said Theodosia.

"Oh my god, we've got to call the police!" exclaimed Haley as she threw her apartment door closed, quickly turned the dead bolt, and scrambled to refasten the chain.

Theodosia watched as Haley dove for the phone. *I'm in a mild state of shock,* Theodosia decided. *Things seem a little hazy and it feels like everything's happening in slow motion.* She shook her head, tried to clear her brain.

"Do you remember the note that someone left yesterday morning?" Theodosia finally asked Haley.

"The *twinkle twinkle little bat* note?" said Haley. She stood, poised, ready to dial 911.

"I think it might have been the same person," said Theodosia. "Only this time they didn't leave a note. They left a tea caddy."

"What?" exclaimed Haley. She put a hand to her forehead in a gesture of incredulousness. "The one that . . . ?"

Theodosia pumped her head in agreement. "I think it's the *exact* same tea caddy that was stolen from the Hall-Barnett House."

"Wow," breathed Haley and her eyes were round as saucers. "This whole thing is getting very, very weird."

23

The knob rattled, then pounding sounded on the door of the Indigo Tea Shop. "Are you open?" called a voice from outside. "Can we come in for tea?"

Drayton went to the door, peered through the leaded pane at the little group of visitors that stood on the doorstep.

"I'm sorry," he told them. "We're closed today." He glanced over at Theodosia, who sat sprawled at the table nearest the little stone fireplace. The lights were on, a tea kettle was whistling and bubbling, but they were most definitely closed. He also had the distinct feeling that if these strange events didn't come to a head sometime soon, they might be closed for a few *more* days.

Last night had been a nightmare for Theodosia. The police had shown up and scouted through her apartment looking for signs of a forced entry. They had found none.

They'd been equally puzzled over the mysteriously appearing tea caddy that sat on her dining room table. Halfheartedly accepting Theodosia's story that it had been stolen earlier, they'd checked back with headquarters at her urging and confirmed that, yes, indeed, a tea caddy fitting that same general description *had* disappeared some two days earlier from the historic Hall-Barnett House.

Theodosia had been at a loss to explain the sudden appearance of the tea caddy in her home and the police hadn't pressed her for details. Just took the tea caddy into their possession and requested that she sign a receipt acknowledging their removing it as evidence.

She and Earl Grey had spent a restless night at Haley's. And first thing this morning, Theodosia had given Drayton a call. It had been his suggestion that they meet at the Indigo Tea Shop and try to figure out a next step.

"Did you call Jory about this?" Drayton demanded as he poured a cup of Assam for Theodosia.

"No, I didn't want to worry him," said Theodosia.

"That's precisely why you *should* call him," responded Drayton. "Because he will undoubtedly be very worried about you."

"I know," she said, taking a sip of the hot tea, letting the sweet, slightly malty flavor refresh and revive her. "Gosh, this is good. Really hits the spot."

"Towkok Estate," Drayton told her. "I thought we deserved to treat ourselves, today of all days."

Drayton knelt down, constructed a little pile of kindling in the fireplace, struck a match to it, and fanned the flames briskly. Once the kindling was crackling nicely, he added a couple of medium-sized logs to the fire.

"Drayton," said Theodosia, "I think that tea caddy was meant as another taunt."

He stood up, looking remarkably poised, and pocketed the matches. "I'm sure it was."

Theodosia peered at him anxiously. "Is it someone close to us?"

Drayton frowned. "Hard to say," he said, staring into the fireplace. "Maybe we miscalculated with the stamp," he said finally.

"What do you mean?" asked Theodosia.

Drayton rocked back on his heels, stuck his hands in his pants pockets, jingled his change. "Not enough of a lure?" He pulled his hands from his pockets, fidgeted some more. "To be perfectly honest, this whole charade made me extremely nervous. And people *did* ask a lot more questions than I thought they would last night. I felt like I had to keep *explaining* things."

Theodosia's brows knit together upon hearing this. "What do you mean, Drayton? What did you *tell* them?"

"Exactly what we rehearsed. The Z grill stamp, issued in eighteen sixty-nine, Benjamin Franklin, blah, blah, blah." He grimaced slightly.

"But I still felt like a fraud, seeing as how it's not really part of my collection."

"Did you tell people the stamp was staying on display?" Theodosia asked.

"Heavens no," exclaimed Drayton. "I made it quite clear that this was a onetime event. That I was returning the stamp to my personal collection the very next day." He shook his head. "I really *hated* saying that."

Theodosia stared at him. "That's what you told people? Really?"

"Awful, isn't it? I feel like such a liar when it's not even my stamp. What happens if a bunch of reputable collectors ever ask to see it? I'm cooked." He sat down at the table across from Theodosia, stared at his tea.

A smile suddenly formed on Theodosia's face. Her blue eyes began to twinkle. "Drayton, you're a genius."

He looked up from his tea sharply. "What?"

"You heard me. A genius."

"I am?" He looked pleased yet befuddled, quite unsure as to what his great brainpower status was being attributed.

"Don't you see?" began Theodosia excitedly. "Knowing it was on display for one night only, the thief might decide to come looking at *your* house."

Drayton's face suddenly dissolved into worry. "Oh no. That's not good at all. Especially when it won't even be there."

"Are you kidding?" said Theodosia. "This is a terrific break!" She grinned. Yes, she thought to herself, it suddenly made perfect sense. The bait had been there for the taking last night. But then Drayton, in all his nervousness about the stamp, had related his little story about the stamp being on loan just for the opening night. That it would soon be returned to his own private collection. So, if the thief had truly been intrigued by the Z grill stamp, he had to figure it would be much easier to break into Drayton's house than risk a second attempt at the Heritage Society!

Theodosia looked at her watch. "I'd say we've got some serious planning to do."

Drayton gave her a skeptical look. "For what, pray tell?"

"We've got to be ready in case that cat burglar decides to break into your house tonight."

"My house? Tonight?" His voice rose in protest. "Oh, no. I don't think so." He crossed his arms resolutely and shook his head.

"Oh yes," urged Theodosia. "This could be our big chance."

"I'd feel far more confident if we called the police," Drayton argued.

"I did that last night. They didn't seem to have any brilliant suggestions."

Drayton considered this. "True," he allowed.

"In fact, they seemed to have no clue as to how the cat burglar even got in my house," said Theodosia.

Drayton frowned. "I thought you said the locks had been picked."

"Actually, I think our cat burglar came across a series of rooftops, jumped a five-foot span, and snuck in through the dormer in my bedroom."

Drayton stared at her. "Have you suddenly gone psychic? Whatever made you compose *that* elaborate scenario?"

"There's a tiny scuff on my window ledge," said Theodosia. And indeed, there had been. Just the tiniest, minutest scuff. Nothing you'd really notice, unless you'd just dusted a couple days before and were quite sure it hadn't been there then.

Drayton continued to stare in surprise. "A scuff. You base your theory on a scuff?"

"And a hunch," said Theodosia. "A very weird hunch. Trust me on this, Drayton. There's someone out there who adores playing games. Leaving notes, planting clues, playing both sides. And I think there's a very distinct possibility they're going to show up tonight."

"Halloween night," he said. "Why on earth would they choose Halloween night to appear?"

Theodosia considered Drayton's question. "I think," she said, "it would appeal to their sense of play. Now . . . are you in or not?"

Drayton rolled his eyes, plucked nervously at his bow tie. "Of course I'm in," he replied finally. "After everything that's happened, how could I not be?"

24

The moon, still a fat round globe with barely a scant wedge missing from it, slid into the night sky above Charleston and shone down through skeletal tree branches. On most every step, stoop, and piazza of the elegant homes in the historic district, fat, orange pumpkins squatted, their innards replaced with flickering candles. Trick-or-treaters in fluttering capes and costumes ran wildly down cobblestone lanes, drinking in the excitement and magic that was All Hallows' Eve.

At exactly seven o'clock, Drayton exited his house, a one-hundred-sixty-year-old brick and wood home that had once been owned by John Underwood, a Civil War surgeon. He made a big production of locking his front door, then stepped jauntily down Montagu Street toward the Heritage Society. Two of his friends, Tom Wigley and Clark Dickerson, would be waiting for him there. He'd phoned them earlier and arranged to hold an elaborately staged meeting that had absolutely nothing to do with Heritage Society business.

The only thing the three men were going to do was talk, shuffle papers, and sit in one of the meeting rooms with the lights blazing like mad, maintaining the illusion of an important, productive meeting. Anyone peering in from the street would see Drayton participating in this meeting. And know that he was, therefore, not at home.

Theodosia, on the other hand, had been sequestered in the small closet in Drayton's study for the last half-hour or so.

She had assured Drayton that she was going to phone Detective Tidwell on her cell phone, explain exactly what they were up to, and request that he send over a couple of uniformed police officers to keep watch over Drayton's house.

But she hadn't.

Instead, Theodosia was crouched in the confines of the small closet with Earl Grey snuggled beside her, his elegant head resting gently in her lap.

Outside the closet, barely six feet from where she sat, was Drayton's desk where one of his stamp albums lay enticingly open. Rows of plastic-encased stamps that hearkened back to Revolutionary War days filled its pages. This album was propped up against a second leather-bound stamp album. Next to these albums was a smattering of first-day covers, rare stamps that had been postmarked on their first day of issue, and of course, Aunt Libby's Z grill stamp. At the last minute, Drayton had added a few extra props to make it look, as he put it, "not so much like a stage set." A pack of gum, silver letter opener, a leather box filled with paper clips, Haley's bottle of superglue, and a small notepad with some random scribbles on it.

This desktop still life was lit by a single Tiffany lamp that sat on Drayton's desk, which was not really a desk at all but a sturdy old oak library table. The rest of the small twelve-by-fourteen-foot room was lined with bookcases that sagged with all manner of books—fiction, history, poetry, gardening, and cooking. In one corner was an overstuffed leather chair. On the wall opposite the closet where Theodosia sat waiting was a small window that looked out over the back garden.

Theodosia knew that if their cat burglar was going to show tonight, there was a very good chance he'd come in through that window. On the other hand, because Drayton had a prize collection of Japanese bonsai trees, a tall wooden security fence had been constructed around the backyard to make it virtually impenetrable.

So . . . Theodosia told herself, the cat burglar would have to scale the wooden fence, *then* come in through the window. Not exactly a difficult feat for someone who had leapt to her window ledge or climbed the live oak tree outside the Hall-Barnett House or clambered across the glass roof at the Lady Goodwood Inn.

Minutes ticked by slowly as Theodosia sat in the darkness, wondering who, if anyone, might show up.

A few moments ago, there had been knocking at the front door. Small, tentative knocks at first that had escalated into a couple of real whaps. Unhappy trick-or-treaters, no doubt, who'd been hoping for a handout of candy bars or popcorn balls.

Now there was only silence.

Theodosia put her hand to the old brass doorknob on the inside of the closet door, turned it slowly, heard the catch release. Slowly, she pushed the closet door open. An inch at first, then two inches. Now she could see the desk and the little puddle of light that lit the stamp and the stamp albums. Next to it was the office clutter that Drayton had arranged.

Theodosia pushed the door open another two inches. Now she could see part of the window.

Better, she thought as she rested her head against the back wall of the closet and slid a piece of remnant carpet underneath her so the sagging old hickory floor wouldn't be *quite* so hard. Earl Grey, trying to get comfortable himself, had pushed away from her and snuggled himself into the far corner of the closet. Now the dog was curled up in a ball, nose to tail, behind an old leather footstool that had been shoved in the closet.

Theodosia had sat with her eyes closed for the better part of forty minutes when she heard a faint sound. She watched as the tips of Earl Grey's ears lifted slightly, then relaxed again.

Must be nothing, she told herself.

Scrtch scrtch.

There it was again. A faint scratching.

What is it? She strained to hear. Dry leaves sliding across patio bricks? Kids running down the back alley, their witches capes and superhero costumes rustling in the wind?

Probably.

And yet . . . there it was again. Not really footsteps. But . . . *something.*

Theodosia glanced over at Earl Grey. Now the top of his nose was visible above the footstool. She held her hand out toward him, palm forward. The hand signal that told him to stay. She could see one of his shiny brown eyes watching her intently.

Then she heard it. A small *creak*. The outside shutter on the window being moved just so? Moved by the wind? She thought not.

Fear suddenly gripped her heart and she had to remind herself that the window was locked. If someone intended to break in, they'd have to break the glass. And if *that* happened, she'd hit 911 on her cell phone.

Now a different sound. Faint, almost imperceptible.

The window in Drayton's office slid up with a low groan.

Ohmygod. Someone must have inserted some kind of tool in the lock and popped it. Probably the same kind of flexible metal bar that police use when you lock your keys in your car!

She hadn't counted on this. Now, any movement in the closet, any dialing of 911, would be immediately detected.

Theodosia held her breath. This was not good, she decided. Not good at all.

She leaned forward slowly, peering through the darkness at the window.

A leg eased itself slowly over the sill and down toward the floor. A leg encased in black lycra. Wearing a shoe of soft brown leather. The kind of shoe that looked very sporty, but could also be worn for rock climbing.

In that instant, Theodosia suddenly understood the identity of the mysterious cat burglar.

It wasn't Cooper Hobcaw, who'd roused her suspicions with his late-night runs through the historic district. And it sure as heck wasn't the waiter, Graham Carmody.

The realization of who had caused Captain Buchanan's death, who had stolen the Blue Kashmir necklace at the Heritage Society, who had been an intruder in her house last night, caused her to inhale sharply. And in that instant, she felt a subtle change in the room.

With a sickening realization, Theodosia knew her cover was blown. Frantically, she grappled for her cell phone, punched the numbers for the Heritage Society, frantically flailed to hit the *send* button. But even as her fingers finally found the button, the closet door was jerked open.

Aerin Linley, eyes hard as ice, peered into the darkness.

Theodosia raised a hand, palm out. Her signal to Earl Grey to stay put, to remain exactly where he was.

Aerin Linley took it as a gesture of surrender and smiled.

Reaching in, she snatched Theodosia's cell phone from her and threw it to the floor. The little black Star Tac smashed into a dozen pieces.

Theodosia stared up into a grim, determined face. *Aerin Linley,* she thought. *The trusted associate of Brooke Carter Crockett at Heart's Desire. The same woman who'd carefully planted nasty innuendoes against Claire Kitridge. Aerin Linley, who had once made mention of secret drawers and panels in the old homes of Savannah. Aerin Linley, who would have known all the details about the Buchanan family's heirloom ring!*

"Get up," Aerin snarled at Theodosia. Her eyes blazed with a slightly deranged look.

Theodosia rose to her feet. And as she did, a glint of light caught her eye. Aerin Linley had grabbed the letter opener from Drayton's desk and now clutched it menacingly in her hand. Honed from silver, the metal instrument looked extremely sharp.

Can it inflict a serious wound? Theodosia wondered. *Of course it can. No doubt about it.*

"Did you think I was so stupid?" Aerin hissed. "I could smell your pathetic trap a mile away."

Even as Aerin jabbed the letter opener toward Theodosia's throat, she pawed frantically with her other hand, trying to gather up the stamps that lay scattered atop Drayton's desk.

"You goody-goody," Aerin sneered at Theodosia. "With your proper little friends and your proper little tea shop." She stuffed the Z grill stamp into the pocket of her black fleece vest, then her hand went back and swooped up the pile of first-day covers. "You really thought you were *investigating,* didn't you? Hah," she barked sharply. "Little Miss Detective. Looks like the joke's on *you.*"

Theodosia stared at her evenly, praying that Earl Grey would continue to obey her command and remain in the closet. In the distance she could hear the shrill of a police siren. Her call *had* gone through. Drayton had known it was her and immediately phoned the police. Thank goodness.

Aerin saw Theodosia register the sound of the siren and sneered at her. "You think that police car will get here in time? I think not. No one's come close to me yet, no one ever will. I'll be out of here and out of this town so fast it'll make your head swim. And you'll look like a fool." She gave Theodosia the flat, slow-eyed blink of a reptile. A snake about to swallow its prey.

"You were on the roof of the Lady Goodwood Inn . . ." stuttered Theodosia.

"Piece of cake." Aerin sneered at her. "I grew up scaling rocks in the Blue Ridge Mountains. Only gear I needed for that job was an aluminum descender."

Theodosia suddenly recalled the metal ring she'd seen hanging from the strut of the Garden Room's roof. Aerin must have employed the same gear that sport rappellers and police and fire rescue units used.

"Pity the roof gave way," said Aerin in a cold, offhand manner. "And trapped that poor fellow underneath." She shrugged. "You never can tell about those old structures."

"I have to know," said Theodosia. *That's it, keep her talking.* "Did you snatch Delaine's watch and plant it in Claire's desk?"

"Oh please," snapped Aerin, "that was child's play. Delaine's house is a cat burglar's dream and the Heritage Society kindly invited me in on a jewelry appraisal. Convenient, no?" Smug and cold, Aerin's grin was hideous.

She turned suddenly and ripped five rows of plastic-encased stamps from Drayton's album. Still keeping an eye on Theodosia, Aerin backed slowly across the room until her hips connected with the window ledge. Then she sat down and swung one leg over the ledge with ease.

"I'd really love to stay and gab," she said. "But I've got far better things to do. My car's just down the block and the trunk's filled with loot . . . including that antique ring you've been so hot and bothered about."

Theodosia waited until Aerin had completely swung around and was about to drop to the ground.

"Earl Grey, attack!" she yelled at the top of her lungs.

Earl Grey came hurtling out of the closet like a silver streak. He rocketed across the room, his front paws barely skimming the windowsill as he sailed through the window frame. As Aerin Linley dropped to her feet, Earl Grey smashed into the back of her like a freight train. Eighty pounds of well-muscled canine heeding the command of his beloved mistress.

Aerin Linley screamed sharply even as she went down like a rock. The letter opener flew from her hand and made a dull *clink* on one of the patio stones.

As Theodosia ran toward the window, her hand instinctively reached out and grabbed the bottle of superglue from Drayton's desk. Then she had one foot on the window ledge and was clambering out herself.

On the ground below, Aerin was struggling mightily with Earl Grey, batting at him furiously, her hands balled into fists.

"Get off, you horrible mutt!" she screamed. "Get off!"

Theodosia dropped to the ground, stumbled forward, felt the sting of gravel cut into her palms and knees. She rolled, scooped up the letter opener that lay gleaming on the patio stones, found the bottle of super-glue that she'd dropped, and scrambled over to the struggling mass of dog and woman. Now she pointed her finger at Aerin's neck.

"Hold tight!" she commanded the dog.

Earl Grey promptly clamped his wide jaws around Aerin Linley's neck. He didn't sink his teeth into her flesh, but he held her very, very firmly, just as Theodosia had commanded.

"Get this mangy creature off me!" Aerin Linley was screaming and carrying on like a banshee. Her face was beet red, her words a garbled cry. Her heels beat furiously against the pavement as her body squirmed and thrashed, struggling to throw the dog off.

Popping the top off the tube of superglue, Theodosia aimed the tip at Aerin's hair. She squeezed, watched as a huge dollop of clear glue came squirting out.

Aerin's eyes rolled wildly. "What are you doing, you idiot!" she cried as she continued to battle. "You'll be sorry you . . ." Aerin Linley's head suddenly stopped straining from side to side.

"My hair!" she screamed. "What's wrong with my hair!"

"Ease off," Theodosia commanded Earl Grey.

Panting heavily, pink tongue lolling out the side of his mouth, Earl Grey gazed at Theodosia, hungry for approval.

She reached down, patted him on the head. "Good dog. *Verrry* good dog."

"What'd you do?" wailed Aerin Linley. "I can't move my head! Help me, oh please, you've got to help me!"

The *whoop whoop* of the police siren was much closer now. It sounded a block away. Now it was directly in front of Drayton's house.

"Help!" Theodosia yelled. She ran to the side fence, boosted herself up as best she could, and waved frantically, trying to capture their attention. "We're in back!" she hollered. "Come quickly!"

❧ 25 ❧

"*Any injuries?*" Detective Burt Tidwell cocked an eye at the paramedic in his navy jumpsuit.

The paramedic, whose name tag read BENTLEY, shook his head, but the corners of his mouth kept twitching upward. It was obvious he was trying to remain professional. In other words, not burst out laughing completely.

"Slight puncture wounds," responded Bentley. "Nothing that requires any *serious* medical treatment, even though your perp is complaining bitterly about what she refers to as *dog bites*."

"The woman does seem quite unhinged," offered Drayton. He had arrived home just minutes after the police cruiser arrived.

The police, at Theodosia's urging, had contacted Detective Tidwell. And Drayton, of course, had immediately phoned Haley, who'd been trying to call Theodosia at home and was frantic to know what was going on. Not one to miss out on excitement, she immediately came dashing over.

Now they were all gathered in a conversational knot on the front walk of Drayton's house, a few steps from where Burt Tidwell's burgundy-colored Crown Victoria was parked at the curb.

"You say she's unhinged," said Tidwell to Drayton. "What a quaint assessment. So very Dr. Watson."

"Hey," piped up Haley as she stroked Earl Grey's head. "Drayton *is* Dr. Watson. To Theodosia's Sherlock, that is. Haven't you figured that out by now?"

Tidwell smiled tolerantly.

"Your suspect's *hair* condition is what's really causing the problem," continued the paramedic, Bentley. His eyes sought out Theodosia's. "I don't know what you squirted on her, lady, but it sure as heck is permanent. My partner and the other two officers are *still* trying to cut her off the pavement."

Drayton's eyes widened. *"Cut* her?"

"Well, her hair, anyway," explained Bentley as he packed a roll of gauze and bottle of antiseptic back into his bag. "Looks like she's gonna get a whole new look. Kind of patchy and choppy. That glue or whatever it was is pretty mean stuff."

This time Drayton threw back his head and howled. "Don't tell me you superglued Aerin Linley's hair to my patio!" he exclaimed.

"How else could I subdue her?" said Theodosia. "She was thrashing around like a crazy woman. I certainly didn't want to see Earl Grey get hurt."

"God forbid," said Tidwell as he rolled his eyes skyward. "And pray tell, while we're on the subject, why exactly *did* you stage this elaborate little charade without benefit of any backup?"

Theodosia threw him a look that was pure innocence. "But I *did* have backup, Detective Tidwell. I had you. I always have you."

"What she means is it's comforting to know we can always count on our law enforcement professionals," said Drayton, jumping into the fray and trying to derail Tidwell's anger. "Thank you so very much, Detective Tidwell."

Tidwell shook his head in bewilderment and gazed down at Earl Grey, who was sitting on his haunches and yawning contently, looking as though he'd just been through a typical, uneventful doggy evening. "I'm afraid the mayor doesn't award certificates of appreciation to canines," said Tidwell. "At least he hasn't up until now. We'll have to find some other way to honor the crime-fighting Earl Grey."

"How about a free cup of Earl Grey tea to all our customers this week," piped up Haley. "And we can put up his photo. With a big *thank-you* banner."

"The dog that helped catch a cat burglar," said Tidwell, and even he couldn't resist a snicker.

"I've got a better idea," said Theodosia. "Let's all go in and have a cup of Earl Grey right now, instead of standing around shivering in the dark."

"When you put it that way," said Tidwell, "it sounds very inviting. The night *is* rather chilly."

"Tea *does* sound nice," said the paramedic, Bentley.

"You have Earl Grey in the house, don't you?" Theodosia asked Drayton. "The tea, I mean, not the dog."

"Of course," said Drayton as he started for the door. "And some nice molasses spice cookies, too." He glanced over at Bentley. "Does your partner drink tea?"

"I guess so," said Bentley. "And we *were* due to go on break," he said, suddenly showing genuine enthusiasm.

"By all means invite him in then," said Drayton. "The other officers, too."

"Hey, aren't they still working on Aerin?" asked Haley.

"She's not going anywhere for a while," said Theodosia with a mischievous twinkle in her eye.

"That's right," chuckled Tidwell. "Let her wait. Let her wait."

RECIPES FROM
The Indigo Tea Shop

Chicken Perloo

1 tsp. olive oil
4–5 pieces of chicken, skin removed
2 slices bacon (cut in ¼" pieces) or 2 oz. diced salt pork
1 large onion, sliced
½ green bell pepper, chopped
1 cup long-grain white rice
1 can chicken broth (1 ¾ cups)
¼ tsp. salt
¼ tsp. pepper
2 Tbsp. minced parsley

HEAT oil over medium-high heat using nonstick 12-inch fry pan. Add chicken and cook about 8 minutes or until golden, turning over once. Transfer chicken to plate. Reduce heat to medium and add bacon or salt pork, cooking for 4 minutes until browned. Remove bacon or salt pork with slotted spoon to small bowl. Discard all but 2 tsp. bacon fat from skillet.

ADD onion and green pepper to same skillet and cook, covered, for 10 minutes, stirring occasionally. Add rice and stir until evenly coated. Stir in bacon, broth, salt, pepper and ½ cup water. Return chicken to skillet; heat to boiling over medium-high heat. Reduce heat to medium-low and cook, covered, 10 to 25 minutes. Sprinkle with parsley and serve. Yields 4 servings.

Tea–Marinated Prawns

2 Tbsp. Lapsang Souchong tea
2 cups water
1 Tbsp. lemon juice
1 lb. shrimp or prawns

STEEP tea in boiling water to desired strength, then strain. Add lemon juice to the tea. Cool tea to room temperature. Marinate shrimp or prawns in tea for at least 30 minutes, then grill or stir-fry as usual.

Tea Smoothie

2 bags of Apple Cinnamon Tea
2 cups vanilla ice cream or frozen yogurt
¼ tsp. cinnamon (optional)

CUT open tea bags and mix tea with ice cream and cinnamon in a blender until fully blended. Pour into a tall glass, garnish with whipped cream. Makes 1 serving.

Hot and Sour Green Tea Soup

3 Tbsp. lite soy sauce
1 ½ Tbsp. rice wine
1 Tbsp. minced fresh ginger
½ tsp. sesame oil
¾ lb. skinless, boneless chicken breasts, cut into thin strips
½ lb. soba noodles
3 cups brewed green tea

¼ lb. snow peas, cut into thin strips
1 medium leek, thinly sliced
2 Tbsp. umeboshi vinegar
2 Tbsp. chopped cilantro

COMBINE soy sauce, rice wine, ginger, and sesame oil in a medium bowl. Add chicken strips, tossing to coat, and let marinate for 10 minutes. Meanwhile, cook noodles in boiling, salted water in a large saucepan for 10 minutes. Drain, transfer to bowl containing chicken mixture and cover. Using the same saucepan, bring the tea to a simmer. Add the chicken mixture, snow peas, and leek and cook over low heat until the chicken is just cooked through, about 3 minutes. Stir in vinegar and cilantro and ladle into bowls. Yields 4 servings.

Pear and Stilton Tea Sandwiches

4 very thin slices honey-oat bread
1 Tbsp. butter
1 ripe pear, halved and thinly sliced
Lemon juice
2 Tbsp. crumbled Stilton cheese (about ½ oz.)

SPREAD each bread slice with softened butter. Sprinkle pear slices with lemon juice. Place ½ of the pear slices in a single layer on one slice of bread. Top with half of the crumbled cheese and the second bread slice. Make a second sandwich the same way. Slice off crusts. Cut each into 4 finger-sized sandwiches. Yields 8 tea sandwiches.

Easy Cream Scones

¼ cup butter
1 cup flour
3 tsp. baking powder
½ tsp. salt
2 Tbsp. sugar
2 beaten eggs
½ cup cream

SIFT flour, then add baking powder and salt and cut butter into dry mixture. Combine eggs and cream and add to dry mixture. Pat to ¾-inch thick. Cut in squares or triangles, sprinkle with sugar and bake at 375 degrees until lightly brown, about 20 minutes. Serve hot with jam or preserves.

Haley's Lemon Curd

3 large lemons
5 eggs
1 cup granulated sugar
8 Tbsp. unsalted butter

GRATE the lemon rind and set aside. Squeeze the juice and put into a blender or food processor. Add remaining ingredients and process until smooth. Pour the mixture into the top half of a double boiler. Stir in the lemon rind and cook over simmering water for about 10 minutes, until thickened. Stir the mixture with a wire whisk if it appears lumpy. Chill the lemon curd before serving (it thickens as it cools). Spread on scones, crumpets, muffins, or toast.

Green Beans with Garlic and Tea

1 lb. fresh green beans, trimmed
2 cloves garlic, minced
1 tsp. canola oil
2 Tbsp. Keemun tea leaves brewed in 2 cups of spring water
Toasted almond slices

STEAM green beans in water. While beans are steaming, sauté minced garlic in canola oil until opaque. Add brewed tea and simmer with garlic for 2 minutes. Remove beans from steamer and put in large bowl. Pour tea marinade over drained beans. Garnish with toasted almond slices, and serve as a side dish.

Stress-Relief Chamomile Tea

1 cup water
1 tsp. dried chamomile flowers
Lemon juice
Honey

BRING water to boil in saucepan. Sprinkle flowers onto water and boil for about 30 seconds with the lid on. Remove from heat and let stand for 1 minute. Serve with honey and lemon juice.

Tub Tea
(For relaxing in the bathtub!)

From your local co-op or herb store, get about 1 cup of each:

Rosemary
Lavender
Chamomile
Peppermint
Rose petals
Calendula petals

MIX together in a large bowl. Sew small squares of muslin or cotton on three sides. Scoop in herb mixture; sew the fourth side closed. Toss a fresh one into your bath each time you want a relaxing soak.

TEATIME ENTERTAINING IDEAS

You don't have to travel to Charleston and the Indigo Tea Shop in order to enjoy a specialty tea. Simply invite a few friends in and be creative.

Choose a "theme" for your tea.

Try a Garden Tea in the out-of-doors when flowers are blooming and breezes wafting. Serve tiny triangles of chicken salad, cucumber sandwiches, deviled eggs, and date nut bread. For dessert don't forget tarts topped with the season's fresh berries. A Darjeeling is ideal, although on hot days, nothing refreshes like iced tea. Invite all your guests to wear floppy straw hats.

A Valentine Tea is a grand excuse to nibble an assortment of chocolate cookies, bars, truffles, and bonbons. To complement the chocolate, serve teas that offer blends of orange, vanilla, and spices. Put a white lace tablecloth over red fabric for extra punch and dress up the table with roses!

Quiche, blinis with sour cream, Eggs Benedict, or fruit compotes make a Brunch Tea extra special. If you have a chafing dish, this is the time to use it. Assam tea, with its rich, refined flavor is a delightful complement.

A Midnight Christmas Tea is perfect at this most special time of the year. Serve brioche, roasted chestnuts, and crepes in front of the fireplace. Cardamom and cinnamon teas warm the heart.

A Mystery Tea can mean a rousing game of Clue, reading tea leaves, or enjoying a mystery book discussion. Break out the candles, douse the lights, and serve steaming cups of Lapsang Souchong, the traditional tea of mystery.

If you have a group of friends who enjoy doing crafts together, why not have a Quilters Tea or Scrapbookers Tea? Don't bother to match teacups with plates; just jumble all your patterns together for a creative look. Jasmine tea or an Indian chai would be lovely.

Turn the page for
new recipes, tea time tips,
and resources
created specially for . . .

TEA FOR THREE

FAVORITE RECIPES FROM
The Indigo Tea Shop

Tropical Chicken Salad Spread

2 cups cooked chicken, diced
½ cup canned crushed pineapple, drained
¼ cup chopped cashews
½ cup celery, diced fine
1 cup mayonnaise
1 Tbsp. orange juice (optional)

MIX all ingredients together in a bowl. Spread on your favorite bread and cut each slice into 4 triangles. May be served as open-faced tea sandwiches—or topped with another triangle of buttered bread.

Charleston Chocolate Chip Scones

2 cups self-rising flour
3 Tbsp. sugar
1 stick butter
1 egg
1 tsp. vanilla
½ cup half-and-half
1 cup semisweet chocolate chips
¼ cup chopped walnuts (optional)

COMBINE flour and sugar in a mixing bowl. Cut in butter until small crumbs are formed. In a separate bowl, use a wire whisk to combine egg, vanilla, and half-and-half. Add egg mixture to dry mixture along with chocolate chips and walnuts. Mix gently until a soft dough forms. Dust hands with flour and carefully knead dough 4 or 5 times on lightly floured surface. Pat dough out into an 8-inch round. Cut dough into 8 wedges and place at least 1 inch apart on a greased cookie sheet. Bake at 425 degrees F for 14 to 16 minutes or until slightly browned. Serve with butter and Devonshire cream.

Drayton's Devonshire Cream

½ cup heavy whipping cream
1 Tbsp. powdered sugar
¾ cup sour cream

WHIP cream until soft peaks form, then add powdered sugar and whip a few seconds more. Add sour cream and continue beating just until mixture gets fluffy. Enjoy as a topping on your scones!

Ham and Apricot Preserve Tea Sandwiches

4 slices raisin bread, sliced very thin
2 Tbsp. apricot preserves
1 Tbsp. Dijon mustard
¼ lb. ham, sliced very thin

SPREAD 2 bread slices with apricot preserves. Spread the remaining 2 slices with mustard, then layer on the ham and top with the bread spread with preserves. Carefully trim crusts and cut each whole sandwich into 4 finger-sized sandwiches.

Charleston Baking Powder Biscuits

2 ¼ cups self-rising flour
¾ cup butter
1 cup milk
1 tsp. baking powder

MIX all ingredients together. Place dough on floured wax paper and gently pat out with your hands, adding a little flour if you need it. Now fold the dough in half and cut out your biscuits with a biscuit cutter. Bake for 20 to 25 minutes at 425 degrees F.

Goat Cheese Tea Sandwiches

4 oz. goat cheese, softened
4 oz. cream cheese, softened
1 Tbsp. cream
½ cup toasted pecans, finely chopped
12 bread slices
⅓ cup red pepper jelly

STIR together goat cheese, cream cheese, cream, and pecans. Spread 6 bread slices with the cheese mixture. Spread the other 6 bread slices with red pepper jelly and place on top of the goat cheese slices. Trim crusts off and cut into triangles or finger sandwiches.

Note: Chutney can be used in place of the red pepper jelly.

Powdered Sugar Cake Cookies

    ½ cup olive oil
    1 ¼ cups quick-rolled oats
    1 pkg. (18 oz.) white cake mix
    2 eggs
    2 tsp. vanilla extract
    ½ cup chopped walnuts
    powdered sugar

COMBINE olive oil and oats, then let stand for 5 minutes. Stir in cake mix, eggs, and vanilla until well combined. Fold in nuts. Form mix into 1-inch balls and place on ungreased cookie sheet. Bake for 8 to 9 minutes at 350 degrees F. Let cool for 1 minute, then roll in powdered sugar.

Cheesy Cheddar Biscuits

    2 cups biscuit baking mix
    1 cup shredded Cheddar cheese
    1 tsp. garlic salt
    ⅔ cup milk
    2 Tbsp. butter, melted
    2 tsp. dried parsley

COMBINE biscuit mix, Cheddar cheese, and garlic salt. Stir in milk. Drop batter onto greased cookie sheet. Bake for 10 minutes at 400 degrees F. Brush biscuits with melted butter, sprinkle with parsley, and bake for 5 more minutes or until lightly browned.

Easiest Ever Pecan Pie

4 eggs
1 cup sugar
1 cup dark corn syrup
4 Tbsp. butter, melted
1 tsp. vanilla extract
2 cups pecans, coarsely chopped
1 9-inch unbaked pie shell

BEAT eggs slightly. Add sugar, corn syrup, melted butter, and vanilla. Beat until well blended. Add pecans and stir thoroughly. Pour into unbaked pie shell. Bake at 375 degrees F for 50 to 60 minutes, or until knife inserted into center comes out clean. Take a peek at the pie about 45 minutes into the baking process to make sure the pecans on top aren't getting too brown. If they are, cover loosely with foil. Cool when done and serve with whipped cream.

Chocolate Zucchini Tea Bread

3 cups all-purpose flour
3 eggs
2 cups sugar
1 cup oil
1 tsp. vanilla extract
1 tsp. cinnamon
1 tsp. baking soda
1 tsp. baking powder
½ cup buttermilk
2 cups shredded zucchini
1 cup semisweet chocolate bits

COMBINE flour, eggs, sugar, oil, vanilla, cinnamon, baking soda, baking powder, and buttermilk in a mixing bowl. Beat at medium speed for 2 minutes. Stir in zucchini and chocolate bits. Pour batter into two well-greased loaf pans and bake at 350 degrees F for 1 hour and 15 minutes. Cool, slice, and serve with cream cheese and orange marmalade.

Peanut Butter Cookies

1 cup butter
1 cup crunchy peanut butter
1 cup white sugar
1 cup brown sugar, packed
2 eggs
2 ½ cups all-purpose flour
1 tsp. baking powder
1 ½ tsp. baking soda
½ tsp. salt

CREAM together butter, peanut butter, and both sugars. Beat in eggs. In separate bowl, sift together flour, baking powder, baking soda, and salt. Stir into batter and refrigerate for 1 hour. Roll dough into 1-inch balls and place on greased baking sheet. Flatten each ball with a fork. Bake for about 9 to 10 minutes at 375 degrees F.

Haley's Apple Bread

3 cups all-purpose flour
1 tsp. baking soda
1 tsp. salt
3 cups apples, peeled and chopped
1 cup vegetable oil

2 cups white sugar

3 eggs, beaten

2 tsp. ground cinnamon

MIX flour, baking soda, salt, and apples in a large bowl. Whisk oil, sugar, eggs, and cinnamon together in a small bowl. Add oil mixture to apple mixture and mix until just moistened. Pour into greased loaf pan and bake for about 80 minutes (until toothpick comes out clean) at 300 degrees F.

Buttermilk Corn Bread

1 cup yellow cornmeal

1 cup flour

½ tsp. baking soda

½ tsp. salt

6 Tbsp. butter

1 cup buttermilk

2 eggs

SIFT together cornmeal, flour, baking soda, and salt, then cut in butter until particles are fine. Beat together buttermilk and eggs, then pour into mixture and blend—but don't overbeat. Pour into buttered 9-inch pan and bake at 400 degrees F for 24 to 28 minutes or until toothpick in center comes out clean.

Southern Cuppa Cuppa Cake

1 cup self-rising flour

1 cup sugar

1 cup fruit cocktail with syrup

1 tsp. baking powder
2 Tbsp. melted butter
Pinch of salt

MIX all ingredients together by hand in an 8-inch square baking pan. Bake at 350 degrees F for 40 to 50 minutes or until brown and bubbly. Serve with vanilla ice cream.

Drayton's Tea Sangria

5 English breakfast tea bags
4 cups boiling water
2 cups sliced fresh fruit
2 Tbsp. sugar
2 cups white grape juice

PLACE tea bags in teapot and add boiling water. Cover and let steep for 5 minutes. Remove tea bags and cool tea. In large pitcher, combine fruit (any combination of apples, peaches, pineapple, oranges, or strawberries) with sugar. Pour brewed tea over fruit and stir in grape juice. Makes 6 servings.

Apple Cinnamon Smoothie

2 tea bags of apple cinnamon tea
2 cups vanilla ice cream or frozen yogurt
¼ tsp. cinnamon (optional)

CUT open tea bags and mix loose tea with ice cream and cinnamon. Scoop mixture into tall glasses and garnish with whipped cream. Makes 2 to 3 servings.

TEA TIME TIPS FROM
Laura Childs

When you're inviting your friends into your home for tea, there are so many wonderful things you can do to make this event memorable.

Make Your Invitations Special

Don't be afraid to think outside the box! A handwritten invitation on the back of a flower seed packet is perfect for a garden tea. Or include a tiny tin of pastilles or a pressed flower in your envelope. You could even roll up an invitation and insert it in a tiny vase. And scrapbook shops carry lots of special papers, lace ribbon, and rubber stamps with teapot images.

Pretty up Your Tea Table

Break out your best linen tablecloth and napkins, set out your fine china, and polish the silver. Handwritten menu cards and vases overflowing with flowers will make your tea feel extra elegant. Go ahead and make a fuss, your guests will adore it!

Pretty napkin rings can even be made from real flowers! Wrap flower stems in flexible wire then follow with a layer of green floral tape. Then simply wind your handiwork around folded or fanned-out napkins.

Staging the Event

Remember, your tea doesn't have to be a sit-down tea. If you have a good-sized group coming, you can do a bountiful buffet on a second table or sideboard. Create a spectacular backdrop with flowers and candles and pull out all the stops by using silver trays, treasured serving pieces, or cake stands. Pick two key colors and try to coordinate everything—flowers, candles, ribbons, even the frosting on your cake!

When it comes to food, keep it simple. Chicken and chutney tea sandwiches, miniature quiches, maraschino cherry scones, and brownie bites.

It's the Little Extras That Impress!

Edible flowers always add color and enhance a tea tray, while music sets a mellow mood. But keep your tunes light and airy—strings, flutes, harp. For favors or a parting gift for your guests, tiny boxes of chocolates or homemade biscotti are lovely.

You Could Even Do a Teacup Exchange

So many people are fast becoming teacup collectors. Why not have all your guests bring a gift bag containing a teacup and saucer, then orchestrate an exchange?

TEA RESOURCES

TEA PUBLICATIONS

Tea Magazine—Quarterly magazine about tea as a beverage and its cultural significance in the arts and society. (teamag.com)

Tea Poetry—Book compiled and published by Pearl Dexter, editor of Tea Magazine. (teamag.com)

TeaTime—Luscious magazine profiling tea and tea lore. Filled with glossy photos and wonderful recipes. (teatimemagazine.com)

Southern Lady—From the publishers of *TeaTime* with a focus on people and places in the South as well as wonderful tea time recipes. (southernladymagazine.com)

The Tea House Times—Go to teahousetimes.com for subscription information and dozens of links to tea shops, purveyors of tea, gift shops, and tea events.

Victoria—Articles and pictorials on homes, home design, gardens, and tea. (victoriamag.com)

The Gilded Lily—Publication from the Ladies Tea Guild. (glily.com)

Tea in Texas—Highlighting Texas tearooms and tea events. (teaintexas.com)

Tea Talk Magazine—Covers tea news and tea shops in Britain. (teatalk-magazine.co.uk)

Fresh Cup Magazine—For tea and coffee professionals. (freshcup.com)

Tea & Coffee—Trade journal for the tea and coffee industry. (teaandcoffee.net)

Bruce Richardson—This author has written several definitive books on tea. (elmwoodinn.com/books)

Jane Pettigrew—This author has written thirteen books on the varied aspects of tea and its history and culture. (janepettigrew.com/books)

A *Tea Reader*—by Katrina Avila Munichiello, an anthology of tea stories and reflections.

AMERICAN TEA PLANTATIONS

Charleston Tea Plantation—The oldest and largest tea plantation in the United States. Order their fine black tea or schedule a visit at bigelowtea.com.

Fairhope Tea Plantation—Tea produced in Fairhope, Alabama, can be purchased though the Church Mouse gift shop. (thechurchmouse.com)

Sakuma Brothers Farm—This tea garden just outside Burlington, Washington, has been growing white and green tea for more than a dozen years. (sakumamarket.com)

Big Island Tea—Organic artisan tea from Hawaii. (bigislandtea.com)

Mauna Kea Tea—Organic green and oolong tea from Hawaii's Big Island. (maunakeatea.com)

Onomea Tea—Nine-acre tea estate near Hilo, Hawaii. (onomeatea.com)

TEA WEBSITES AND INTERESTING BLOGS

Teamap.com—Directory of hundreds of tea shops in the United States and Canada.

GreatTearoomsofAmerica.com—Excellent tea shop guide.

Cookingwithideas.typepad.com—Recipes and book reviews for the bibliochef.

Cuppatea4sheri.blogspot.com—Amazing recipes.

Seedrack.com—Order *camellia* sinensis seeds and grow your own tea!

Friendshiptea.net—Tea shop reviews, recipes, and more.

Jennybakes.com—Fabulous recipes from a real make-it-from-scratch baker.

Teanmystery.com—Tea shop, books, gifts, and gift baskets.

Allteapots.com—Teapots from around the world.

Fireflyvodka.com—South Carolina purveyors of Sweet Tea Vodka, Raspberry Tea Vodka, Peach Tea Vodka, and more. Just visiting this website is a trip in itself!

Teasquared.blogspot.com—Fun, well-written blog about tea, tea shops, and tea musings.

Bernideensteatimeblog.blogspot.com—Tea, baking, decorations, and gardening.

Tealoversroom.com—California tea rooms, Teacasts, links.

Teapages.blogspot.com—All things tea.

Possibili-teas.net—Tea consultants with a terrific monthly newsletter.

Baking.about.com—Carroll Pellegrinelli writes a terrific baking blog complete with recipes and photo instructions.

Teawithfriends.blogspot.com—Lovely blog on tea, friendship, and tea accoutrements.

Sharonsgardenofbookreviews.blogspot—Terrific book reviews by an entertainment journalist.

Teaescapade.wordpress.com—Enjoyable tea blog.

Bellaonline.com/site/tea—Features and forums on tea.

Lattesandlife.com—Witty musings on life.

Napkinfoldingguide.com—Photo illustrations of twenty-seven different (and sometimes elaborate) napkin folds.

World Tea Expo—This premier business-to-business trade show features more than three hundred tea suppliers, vendors, and tea innovators. (worldteaexpo)

Sweetgrassbaskets.net—One of several websites where you can buy sweet-grass baskets direct from the artists.

Goldendelighthoney.com—Carolina honey to sweeten your tea.

FatCatScones.com—Frozen ready-to-bake scones.

KingArthurFlour.com—One of the best flours for baking. This is what many professional pastry chefs use.

Teagw.com—Visit this website and click on Products to find dreamy tea pillows filled with jasmine, rose, lavender, and green tea.

Californiateahouse.com—Order Machu's Blend, a special herbal tea for dogs that promotes healthy skin, lowers stress, and aids digestion.

PURVEYORS OF FINE TEA
Adagio.com

Harney.com

Stashtea.com

Republicoftea.com

Teazaanti.com
Bigelowtea.com
Teasource.com
Celestialseasonings.com
Goldenmoontea.com
Uptontea.com

VISITING CHARLESTON

Charleston.com—Travel and hotel guide.

Charlestoncvb.com—The official Charleston convention and visitor bureau.

Charlestontour.wordpress.com—Private tours of homes and gardens, some including lunch or tea.

Charlestonplace.com—Charleston Place Hotel serves an excellent afternoon tea, Thursday through Saturday, 1 to 3.

Culinarytoursofcharleston.com—Sample specialties from Charleston's local eateries, markets, and bakeries.

Poogansporch.com—This restored Victorian house serves traditional low-country cuisine. Be sure to ask about Poogan!

Preservationsociety.org—Hosts Charleston's annual Fall Candlelight Tour.

Palmettocarriage.com—Horse-drawn carriage rides.

Charlestonharbortours.com—Boat tours and harbor cruises.

Ghostwalk.net—Stroll into Charleston's haunted history. Ask them about the "original" Theodosia!

Charlestontours.net—Tours of Plantations and Historic Homes.

WATCH FOR THE NEXT
TEA SHOP MYSTERY
FROM LAURA CHILDS

STEEPED IN EVIL

A tragedy at a winery, a nasty stepmother, and a knives-in-the-back professional rivalry all add up to murder. The question is, can Theodosia find the killer before she becomes a target, too?